MILLSTONE

L.E. BENNETT

authorHOUSE®

AuthorHouse™
1663 Liberty Drive, Suite 200
Bloomington, IN 47403
www.authorhouse.com
Phone: 1-800-839-8640

First published by AuthorHouse   5/18/2009

ISBN: 978-1-4389-1933-1 (sc)

Library of Congress Control Number: 2009905003

Printed in the United States of America
Bloomington, Indiana

This book is printed on acid-free paper.

To Julie and Eddie, two of my most favorite warm souls.

Until Dust.

— MILLSTONE —

CHAPTER ONE

— FREAKS BANE —

"The more often he feels
without acting, the less he
will be able to act
and in the long run, the
less he will be able to
feel."

C.S. Lewis
—The Screwtape Letters

Alex's boot heels sent a sharp echo through the dense fog draped over the narrow alleyway. He moved with a sense of unhurried malice as he made his way across the damp asphalt. The sound of his steps came to an abrupt halt beneath the metal ladder of a tenement building's fire-escape. Pausing briefly, he took a final pull off the less than half smoked 'Camel Straight'. With his lungs filled, the warm vapor seeping into his satisfaction, he flicked the non-filtered butt into a nearby rain puddle, where it died with a hiss. Reaching into the outer pocket of his trench coat he brought out a pair of brown leather gloves. They were nearly black with usage and stiff with age. These sap gloves were among Alex's most prized possessions.

As Alex exhaled the smoke through his clasped teeth he pulled the gloves snugly on. His stone-faced expression broke slightly, as the faint shadow of a grin tugged modestly at the corners of his mouth. Taking a moment for himself, Alex drew a deep breath of the chilly night air in through his nostrils. Smelling the onset of an early winter in the atmosphere—his eyes closed. For a second he allowed himself to recall how much he used to look forward to this time of year when he was a boy. The night was sweet with the scents of autumn—fallen leaves, wet streets and the not quite odorless smell of cold. The far off sound of a car door being slammed snapped his eyelids open, immediately returning his wandering mind back to the reason why he was there.

After making certain his fedora was on snug, not wishing for it to be blown off, Alex reached up and grasped the dangling chain and pulled the bottom rung into his waiting left hand. He was actually surprised at how little noise the ladder made; he'd expected a bit more than a few whispered creaks and squeaks. Its relatively silent descent ended with a hollow *clunk-click* once the ladder locked into position. Alex afforded himself a brief glance over his shoulders, then after a quick study of the surrounding windows he began his ascent. Wasting no time he made his way up the rusty old ladder, only stopping for a second or two every few rungs to listen for unwanted noises and to peer into the darkness beyond closed windows for the jerky movements of potential witnesses. It didn't take him long at all to reach the seventh story fire escape platform.

The rickety old structure's reaction to the sudden invasion of Alex's two-hundred and fifty-eight pounds was far removed in-comparison to the ladder's much quieter response. The instant he set foot on the slatted metal veranda it shrieked out loudly as if in great physical anguish. Alex stepped swiftly. He knew from past experiences that any attempts to try and control the sudden onslaught of sound with carefully placed, slow steps would be in vain. Best he got it done as fast as possible and took his chances. He moved across the platform, each step sending out a new sharp voice to add to the high-pitched cacophony of grinding iron and shifting rust.

Alex had barely reached the building's cold wall, when suddenly a dog's angry barking interrupted the fading chant of protesting iron. A window directly under him exploded with light. He pressed himself as flat up against the wet brick as possible. After a few long, tense seconds of holding his breath while watching the back and forth movements of a shadow passing before the illuminated rain streaked glass below, the light shut off and the dog fell silent. He remained still a bit longer, keeping himself against the cold wall, intently listening and watching for more surprises. When none came, Alex peeled himself away from the wall with a deep sigh and crept stealthily to the door of the building. Peering around the wooden frame through the door's small window, he carefully studied the long darkened hallway, making certain it was empty. Seeing no one, and glad of it, Alex locked his narrowing vision on the brass number '49' affixed at eye level on the door at the furthest end of the hall.

Again, his deadpan expression relaxed enough to permit a thin lipped smile to tug at his moderately wide slit of a mouth. He took a wallet-sized black leather case from his inside breast pocket, all the while his eyes not straying from their target at the end of the hallway. Alex found himself being reminded of another dark hall, one from long ago. But, he didn't have time for the nightmarish memories of his youth. He shoved the past, struggling to be gazed into, back behind the immediate truth of the here and now; tightening his mental focus.

Opening the small leather case, Alex was about to begin when his attention was abruptly commandeered by the angry sound of a woman's screaming voice. He jerked to one side of the door's window as the disquieted woman went on about some missing cash. Alex got ready to move fast if need be.

The enraged voice was cut short by the violent sound of something being shattered against what Alex had hoped was a table or a wall and not the woman's skull. A baby began wailing, in protest of the sudden assault of noise that had uncouthly interrupted its slumber. The irate woman was back—and with a vengeance.

"GET OUT!" she howled. "Give me the money you took from my purse you bastard and get out of my apartment—NOW!"

Her shrieked command was stifled by the sound of an ear-ringing blow. Alex recognized the fleshy sound as a hand striking unprotected skin. The slap was closely followed by another and yet another. A thin sounding laugh chimed in. It was a man's laughter, or at least, a sort of weak impression of a man's laugh. It seemed to be struggling in its efforts to drown out the woman and her baby's cries.

"Stupid bitch," the voice squeaked. "Fuck you and your nasty little brat! Hell, I was getting sick to death of this reeking dump anyway."

A pause in his speech was filled with a few more blows. "Thanks heaps for the bucks—Peggy!"

"No, no Elvis!" she choked out. "Please, I can't go another month without paying the rent. We'll be thrown out!" her pleas were slapped mute.

"Sorry about your luck," he chuckled.

"Elvis no, how could—"

"Shut your fucking cock-hole of a mouth!" the man ordered. The sound of some solid punches or kicks, Alex wasn't exactly sure which, moved through the darkness. He listened with his back against the damp wall. *We should do something*, he thought as a breeze drifted the spray of a softly falling cold rain across his face.

"This is all your own doing Peg," the man chuckled. "You should have been more understanding to my needs."

"No, please don't take my rent money," she sobbed.

Another blow rang out.

"I'll tell you what I'm willing to do for you Peggy dear," he punched her again. "I'll go ahead and invest a quarter. You should give the land-lord of this shit hole a call and tell him that thing he and I talked about is a done-deal. I'll bet he's knocking at your door first thing in the morning. Hell, Peg, he's got such a stiff one for you, I'll bet if you give that fat slob a good enough toss, he'll give you a years rent."

"Please—no—"

"Shut up, that's the best you get!"

As Alex listened to this woman's tragedy unfold, he dueled with the desire to go help her get her money back. He was beginning to feel a bit uneasy with himself for not doing anything. A jolt of anger surged throughout his skull as he struggled to ignore the event, wishing it would pass so he could get back to work. *Is Five's slot more dire than this poor woman's plight?* He wondered as he stood by and listened.

"Am I the only one hearing this bullshit?" Alex growled as he leaned back away from the wall to see if any of the apartment building's lights had come on during the fight; he saw none.

As Alex panned his vision across the darkened windows, his ears transfixed on the beating, expectantly hoping someone other than him would appear to put an end to her nightmare, he wondered if he should put number five off for now.

Suddenly a blast of light tore through the shroud of darkness cloaking the hallway. The bright flood moved out through the small window on the fire-escape door like a beam of white flame attempting to point out Alex's presence. He ducked beneath it and darted back to his spot against the wall. At first he thought, although with a sense of vain-hope, that it might be a neighbor coming to rescue the woman and her infant. It had been wishful thinking—completely wasted. The increase in the domestic melee's volume apprised Alex to the truth. The light was from the woman's apartment, it had been her door that was flung open. Taking a fool's chance, Alex rubbernecked, peering around the edge of the window sill and saw a tall, thin man sporting stringy red hair and a black leather jacket that appeared to be at least two sizes too small. As he stepped out of the apartment the man swaggered with an awkward walk, apparently caused by the worn-down heels on his blue cowboy boots. They were exactly the sort of foot-wear one would see on a cartoon dog. The snickering coward was moving toward the stairway which happened to be a yard or two from the fire-escape door.

Alex pulled himself away from the window, relying solely on sound to keep track of the man. As he listened to the steady approach of the worn heels, the hallway was returned to its previous darkened state when the woman slammed the door. The once again muffled sound of her sobs paused, or so it seemed; but only briefly, beginning again after the *click* and *thud* of the dead-bolt being locked. *Good girl*, Alex thought.

He listened to the man's steps receding down the stairs. Alex was still mulling over whether or not to save number five until a later date, when the night was less filled with activity and go get the woman's rent money back. While the notion to follow after the red-haired ass-hole was standing toe to toe with Alex's indecision, his ears stayed with the fading sound of the man's steps. Eventually they fell out of ear shot. It wasn't until Alex heard the faint sound of a door being opened and closed, followed soon after by the low echo of dwindling steps melting into the night that he knew for sure Elvis had left the building.

"It just may prove an amusing respite from work," Alex questioned under his breath. "Not to mention we could fetch the poor woman's cash...do a good deed perhaps?" He reached into his coat and gently tapped the rounded butt of Mr. Bane's bone handle with his fingertip.

His meditation was interrupted by a hollow, lifeless voice that resided deep within the inner most depths of Alex's sanguinary mind.

"Don't be idiotic!" The voice in his head said. "You know how dangerously stupid spontaneous dispatching can be. Anyway, although I've complete faith in our ability to handle ourselves, that one may have a gun and we left ours in the van. We can't be every fool's dark shadow. No Alex, this basher of women will have to fall ill to another karmic vehicle." The voice paused a moment then added. "There will be no *Captain Save a Whore* this night Alex my boy."

Alex brought his hand out of his coat empty, "I suppose you're right," he said as he moved quietly out of the limited safety of the shadows.

"Of course I am," the voice faded to silence.

Soon only the soft sound of tiny rain-droplets hitting his hat could be heard, even the controlled sounds of his own breathing melted within the moment. Alex was sure he wouldn't have long to wait, now that Elvis was out of the picture. Soon some of the building's other occupants would come meandering out into the hall. A girlfriend or a kindly old grandmother type perhaps will be out to comfort the Peggy woman and her baby. Alex waited and listened, leaning his back against the wet wall. After he'd stood there for all of ten minutes not a single soul so much as poked a head out of any of the doors. *They could all careless about the woman and her child,* he thought.

"Crying shame," Alex whispered.

"That's right Alex my boy," the metallic voice said softly. "None of them give a damn. Bad for her...yes, but good for us. What do you say we make ourselves known to Number Five?"

It turned out that the fight over rent money was an unexpected test of sorts, in that now Alex knew they would be able to go about their work undisturbed. A bit of knowledge that could afford them a wee bit more slack than usual.

He peered once more into the empty hallway. Opening the little leather case, he took out a playing-card size piece of flat steel. In order to reaffirm what he already knew he checked for any wires or other signs of a fire alarm that might be tripped by opening the door. Satisfied that there were none, he skillfully slid the thin burglar tool between the door and its frame. It took him only a few seconds to force the bolt out of its hole. With just enough pressure on the door to keep it from creaking he eased it open. Alex stepped swiftly and silently over the threshold, closing the self-locking door behind him with not so much as a whisper of sound.

Turning, he focused his sights on the door numbered 49, all the while taking in a brief scrutiny of his interior surroundings. Pleased that all was as he'd hoped it would be, Alex moved with steady, quiet steps across the hard-wood floor toward the other end of the hall. He paid close attention to every sound, only to dismiss them when he sensed no threat in them. Setting most of his concentration on the door he was moving toward and the fiend behind it, he tried to coldly ignore the woman's sobs beyond her apartment door as he passed it. The faint sounds of late night T.V shows seeped into the hallway. A crapper flushed below on the sixth floor, and a door inside one of the apartments behind him clicked closed. With each step toward Five's door Alex's mind grasped tighter and tighter onto the task for which they were there.

Stepping up to his target's door, he barely needed to glance down into the small case in order to select the tools he would need to open it. Alex brought out the number two tension bar. It was a tiny stainless-steel tool no bigger than a cardboard box staple, used for holding lock tumblers in place once found. He also took out only three picks. As Alex slowed to a stop before the door, he removed his fedora and pressed his right ear gently against its cool wooden surface to give a listen. Again, the corners of his mouth were raised into a faint smile as he pulled his head away from the door, placing his hat back on. All he'd heard beyond the weak obstacle were the unmistakable sounds of Five snoring and the drone of a television's steady hiss.

Greatly pleased with this knowledge, the grin lingering on his face a bit longer than usual, he half glanced over his shoulder back down the hallway, then went to work. Although he knew it wasn't wise closing one's eyes in dimly lit spaces where he didn't belong, Alex found that he could pick locks much faster if his eyes were shut, relying completely on touch. Without removing his gloves, he slid the tension bar into the tiny key slot in the center of the doorknob. It was an old building, with old locks to match, so it was an easy task for Alex to unlock this one. Sliding the first pick in, it quickly came upon the first tumbler and forced it down. The second pick found its two tumblers even faster than the first and with almost no effort whatsoever the final pick locked the last tumbler in place. It took Alex no more than six fast seconds to manipulate the cheap lock's tiny mechanism. With the doorknob ready to be turned, he did so slowly. Twisting it left and pulling its bolt out of its latch. He eased the door inward and swiftly slipped into Five's apartment, closing the door and locking it behind him.

He put the picks back in their case and as he drew a deep breath in through his nose his sense of smell was attacked by a variety of rank odors. Alex's guts twisted into tight knots as the stench burned its repugnant way up his nostrils and gagged his throat nearly closed. It was a putrid mixture of rancid food, spoiled beer, foul body odors and moldy piss. Alex was definitely grateful for his ability to tolerate rotten smells. If not for his iron stomach, the stench would have brought the pepperoni pizza he'd had earlier back up and out with projectile force.

Light from a nearby street lamp beamed into the place with barely enough lambent to reveal its state. It found its way in through a dozen or so small holes and rips that riddled a dingy lavender bed-sheet that served as a crude curtain draping the living room's one window. Aside from a narrow pathway beginning at the front door, the floor was almost completely hidden from sight beneath heaps of garbage. The path cut a swath through the middle of the room and split into two separate paths, one forking into a small dark kitchenette. The other one broke off toward the room from where the snoring and hissing T.V was coming from, blocked by an ugly green door which was swung slightly ajar. Pile upon pile of old newspapers and adult magazines were stacked helter-skelter on either side of the pathway. The spears of street light sliced through the chilly darkness like blades cutting their way through blackened fat. They fell on dirty dishes and tossed aside plastic T.V dinner trays, all caked with petrified scraps of unfinished meals. Corpulent adult cockroaches fed voraciously upon their infant young. Filthy clothes, stiff from the hardened residue of countless farts, deeply permeated with the stench of the obese man's sweat and moldy urine were scattered everywhere. Tipped-over bottles of rotted beer, whose slimy spoilage spilled out to soak forever into the grime covered carpet cluttered most every surface.

This was Five's home sweet home. But all of this filth and waste, as well as that of all the disgusting rooms on the entire planet, paled greatly in comparison to the heart wrenching sight of the living room's main feature.

Taped and pinned to the room's longest wall, from corner to corner and nearly covering it from floor to ceiling were an innumerable amount of newspaper clippings. They were the reported accountings of missing children. The clippings were only the beginning of this sad display. In the center of Five's heart-shattering collage were two small shelves, one directly above the other. Sat atop these shelves were seven empty milk-cartons, each of which showing the black and white photographs of more missing kids: four little girls and three small boys, all no older than seven years. These seven empty reminders of the innocence taken seemed to have been placed there as if they were trophies of some sickening sort. But Alex Julius Stone did not see these things as awards, no not at all. What he caught himself staring at were seven little grave-stones.

Tears of sorrow-fed rage trickle down his time chiseled face as he stared at the horrid wall. He reached into his long black coat for 'Freak Bane.' That was the name they'd both decided would best fit the ten inch long, doubled edged 'Roundel Dagger' he wore on his belt. This razor-sharp summoner of screams was far more than a mere knife. More than Alex's staunch comrade in madness; more than even Alex himself had been aware of. It wouldn't be until several long months after Alex's mortal shroud had been stripped away from his very bones that the veil of lies would be parted. Then he would be made to see and hear the truth to both his courage and his insanity. But for now, on this night—a night like so many before it—Freak Bane—Mr. Bane for short, was to be as it had always been; Alex Stone's steadfast confidante and friend.

Turning his back to the wall, he wrapped his fist around the radius bone hand-grip and using his thumb unsnapped the leather strap that locked its brass hilt in place. As Alex slipped the slicing tool out of its self-sharpening sheath, its edges making a fast dragging sound, he set his narrowed steely blue eyes on the ugly green door. "Time to go to work Mr. Bane," he hissed through gnashed teeth.

Quickly and quietly Alex navigated his way over the trash-strewn floor toward the sound of snoring. "As we planned Mr. Bane—cut, watch and leave. No more…no less," he whispered while increasing his grip on the knife.

=≡ ⫟ ≡=

Alex and Mr. Bane had slipped a bit off course with number *Four*— or as the police and newspapers were calling the recipients of Alex and his double edged crime-partner's handiwork; *VICTIMS*.

They'd lost control, or leastwise, Alex had been baited into stepping off the planned path by Mr. Bane. The original design was to simply slice Four's throat then stick around long enough to watch him bleed to death. But Alex had gone and done much, much more than a swift dispatching of a pederast. He'd been only seconds away from lying open Four's skinny, reverent throat when Mr. Bane directed Alex's attention onto the inappropriate expression of defiance staring up at him through the child-molesting priest's eyes. Seeing this and not the amusing look of utter horror that Alex and Mr. Bane had come to expect, as well as demand, he lost control.

The following afternoon, Alex's loss of control was stumbled upon by a homeless teenager girl. She led police to the mangled heap of blood, flesh and exposed bone lying on the concrete floor of a condemned warehouse. The body had been eventually identified as that of Father Louis. Unlike the three so called victims before the priest, his throat hadn't been laid open after a night of beating. Alex and Mr. Bane had painstakingly cut away almost all the skin and meat from Father Louis's face, neck, shoulders and chest. Then, for art's sake, they carefully carved out the rector's eyes and placed one between his teeth and the other was stuffed into the corpse's rectum.

The macabre change in the motive of operation that the cops saw in their latest pattern killer was more than a show of lurid-granting loss of control. It was a clue that told police the killer was one of those "don't give a fuck" types. Maniacs who allowed their rage to slip into a tailspin to such a degree as this eventually made mistakes. Detectives were certain that this new pattern killer would undoubtedly lose it again, and when he did, they'd be waiting.

=≡ ⫟ ≡=

Alex knew full-well that any loss of focus could prove to end badly for both him and Mr. Bane. If they were to succeed in their endeavors they would have to maintain a much sharper edge on self-control. Alex and Mr. Bane agreed to hold their mud, keeping Five's demise as simple as possible.

Alex pressed his spread fingertips against the green door and pushed it inward; sending a high-pitched squeak out through the darkness that seemed to shriek—*WAKE UP!* And, for an instant he was reminded of a similar sound he'd heard during a moment very much like this one when he was a boy.

Stopping just beyond the threshold, he took a brief look around before beginning. Alex's gaze fell on the snoring shape on the bed. *It's only a Five—kill it and go*, he thought. A rushing sort of chill, the type thought to be caused by someone stepping on one's grave shot up Alex's spine into the base of his skull. He glanced over his shoulder at the seven little faces staring deeply into his soul. In and out, he quietly reminded himself. This was Alex's most pleasurable moment throughout the deed—the seconds of stillness and numbing he called it. It was during these seconds that he took a hold of the tethers leashing his inner hounds of rage and sadness, locking them in the closet of his coldness with only a feather barring the door. All the while his heart's desire wanted to make a much deeper, statement out of this sleeping monster. *In and out*, his mind reiterated. Alex pulled his vision away from the children's faces on the milk cartons, sweeping it back around onto Five. For a moment he could have swore he heard seven youthful voices pleading for a more ardent retribution than a simple cut and run. Alex shook their whispers out of his imagination and made a quick study of the pedophile and the surroundings.

Five was as disgusting a creature as the apartment that encased him. He was a short, obese man, sporting a badly shaved head of rust-yellow stubble with several scabby razor nicks around both ears. His fatty husk was the over ripe color of curdled cream. Five's grotesquely derelict carcass lay sleeping in the nude on a filthy, frameless mattress. The room itself was far nastier than the living room in regards to its trashed state. A pink baby blanket hung haphazardly over the room's only window. As with the sheet covering the living room window, several thin shafts of street light found their way in through countless holes and rips. Although, unlike the other room, the beams of light were overpowered and swiftly diminished only a few feet into the bedroom's darkness by the bluish-white glow of the small black and white television set hissing like a dozen pit-vipers on a long wooden coffee table. The table had been placed beside the mattress long-ways, leaving a two foot wide space for walking between them. The TV's luminous glimmer traced a surreal effect across the ceiling, down the dirty walls to eventually end up spilling over the sleeping freak's fleshy mass. The dancing light seemed to move spasmodically over his skin like thousands of black faced maggots wriggling in and out of his fat, gorging ever so happily.

Alex stepped in between the coffee table and the mattress. Stopping directly in front of the T.V screen, he could see his shadow spread out against the wall to his left—an elongated shape with one hand outstretched, slowly rising.

He was a split-second from dropping to one knee and racing Mr. Bane's blade through Five's throat, when a sharp voice rose from within the deepest recesses of Alex's insanity. In an abrupt, almost panicked tone Mr. Bane shouted "—WAIT!"

Alex froze in mid slice "—Wait...what...why?" he asked sharply as he looked around the room for a coming fight.

"Look, look there friend, down there *Pilgrim*. What's that? You see...there, there!" Mr. Bane said in an enraged tone of voice. The voice paused as if to take a closer look at something only the knife could see. Alex was about to ask exactly what in blazes was wrenching his friend's shorts up into his crack, when the knife's metallic voice cut him off.

"Yes...yes there, see Alex...see in its fat fist. Crumpled in foul shame in its fist. There, under its nose." Mr. Bane's voice choked with the sound of tears swelling in a throat. "See it Alex, please—do you see it?"

"Yes," Alex mumbled as he lowered the dagger, and leaned over to get a closer look at the thing causing Mr. Bane to struggle back tears.

"It's what I think it is, is it not pilgrim?" the knife asked.

Alex narrowed his vision, recognizing the pink cloth clutched in Five's sleeping face. Straightening his back, he increased his grip on the knife and in a tone of voice shaking with anger said "—Panties," Alex hissed passed a snarl. "Little girl's panties."

"Oh no, this will not do!" howled Mr. Bane. "No, no-no! Alex old friend this most definitely will not do!"

"Hold on there," Alex interrupted in a tone louder than he intended. "I see where you're going with this and the answer's NO!"

"But Alex, we've an obligation to the little-ones—"

"I said no!" Alex barked, cutting the knife off again. "Are you completely daft? Look around us," Alex held the knife out over the still sleeping freak, moving it slowly around through the air as if to make the blade see for itself. "This ain't the time or the place," Alex whispered through his teeth. Spittle shooting out past his thin lips, glistening in the TV's glow like tiny diamond chips, illustrating his frustration. All the while towering over Five who continued to snore loudly as Alex argued with the knife.

"If you permit this mound of shit to escape with a mere throat slashing," Mr. Bane growled. "With relatively no real pain to speak of. Simply a numb death, void of horror whatsoever." The knife paused, sighed then continued, its tone hollow and cold like someone speaking inside of a great iron bell at the bottom of an icy lake. "If you let that occur Alex my boy then you're no solider. Yes…perhaps I'd been wrong about you after-all."

"How could you think to say such a thing?" Alex rumbled. "After all we've done—together? Don't you understand the fool's chance we'd be taking."

"What's this I'm smelling?" Mr. Bane chuckled. "I believe it's the reek of fear."

"Now you're just being an ass," Alex exclaimed under his breath. "The walls here are paper thin. Someone will hear something."

The debate as to how harsh a punishment should be delivered unto Five fell abruptly silent. For no particular reason Alex's attention had been inadvertently drawn out the open door into the darkened living room. Eventually his wandering gaze drifted to the milk cartons on the shelves. As he attempted to focus through the darkness onto the children's faces he half-assed searched for something more to say. Finally it was his metallic voiced comrade who broke the silence between them.

"Look at it there pilgrim—sleeping all safe and soundly, wrapped snugly in the self-deluding invulnerability of its waning anonymity.

I'll wager its dreaming about the next little one it snatches. How do you suppose it decimates them when it's finished having its filthy way with them? Do you suppose it covers their frightened eyes so that this foul creature's shame is spared their terror. Or perhaps it is their fright, their helplessness and horror that gives the freak's lust the twisted jolt it needs to sleep so soundly and dream of the next little one it takes. For all we know those are the panties of its next victim pressed in its face like some sort of perverse security blanket." Mr. Bane paused to clear its fictitious throat then chuckled softly and paused again; tricking Alex into thinking it was his turn to chime in. Before Alex could offer up some sort of rebuttal the knife cut him off.

"Alex have I ever been wrong about anything?"

"No."

"Then you know that when I tell you no one will hear a thing, that it's the gospel's truth—why do you doubt this? We'll be careful and work as quietly and skillfully as we know how. Anyway—don't you remember the loud beating that the woman was made to suffer? Of course you do. No one, not a single soul so much as peeked out of their holes as she and her baby wept. No one cares. But who on this world knows that as first-hand as you and poor, poor Susan? Alex I fear greatly that this one is far worse than the four before it, perhaps even more wicked than your parents. This one needs a heavier hand; yes…a much sharper touch than an insignificant cutting."

Alex had been staring down at Five, listening closely to every word being spoken into his inner ear. "We'll be mindful of our surroundings?" He asked quickly with a glint in his eyes.

"Yes, it goes without saying," Mr. Bane giggled. "But if it will help…I give my word."

"Then in that case Mr. Bane…I agree, this one is deserving of a heavier hand as you put it. And perhaps a bit extra as well." (So much for self-control.)

Alex took a wide half-step back away from the edge of the mattress, the back of his legs bumping against the coffee table. After placing the knife into its sheath, leaving the hilt strap unsnapped, Alex gave the mattress a good stiff kick with the tip of his steel toe boot and whispered loud enough so that his voice would wake Five. Alex said, "Ashes to ashes and funk to funky we know Major Tom's a junky."

Five's slumber was unaffected. Alex kicked the edge of the mattress a second time. "Come come you fucking freak…wakey—wakey."

Still the sleeping pedophile continued snoring. Alex sent his boot into the mattress a third time—only with a bit more zeal than the first two attempts. "Wake the hell up you sorry sack of shit!" he growled. Still nothing. Alex was rapidly growing tired of this game; already he'd spent more time in the smelly apartment than he'd planned. He was about to send the heel of his boot into the left side of Five's face, when the man's snoring changed to wet sounding air intakes and lip smacking. Five's eyes, deeply sunk within a frame of fat, and the same color as the ugly green door, fluttered open to look unclearly up at Alex. It took his blurred vision and fuzzy mind a moment to claw the cobwebs of sleep away from his muddled awareness. The instant he'd registered the shadowy figure leering over him as a man clad in black, Alex's heel lashed out to make itself known to Five's multiple chins. The numbing blow rocketed the freak head-long into a much deeper degree of unconsciousness than the slumber he'd been brought out of.

Swiftly and with practically no noise, Alex cleared off the coffee table. He sat the television on the mattress, leaving it on to use as a work light. The empty cans of beer and Red Bull he put on the floor out of the way, as well as a thick stack of newspaper advertisements for children's underwear. He slid the table closer to the mattress, and after flopping Five's body on top of it, flipping the freak over onto his back, Alex went in search of something to tie Five down with. He was heading toward the bedroom's adjoining bathroom to flick on its light when he spotted exactly what the Devil ordered. Resting on the seat of a metal folding chair was a fist-size spool of thin steel wire. Not needing the bathroom light after all, he stepped over the trash and clothes, picking up the wire. With a gleeful snicker, an evil glint in his eye and a throaty "—Oh-yes, yes, yes," he made his way back to Five.

The freak was struggling to find his way back to consciousness when Alex stepped next to the table. He noticed Five's eyes were trying to quiver open.

"No you don't," Alex said under his breath. "Not until we're ready." With a solid crack against Five's jaw his gloved fist slammed the pedophile back into a deep state of mental oblivion.

It only took Alex ten minutes to wrap the entire spool of wire around Five and the table, using its wooden pillars to cinch him down with. Despite Alex's efforts not to cause too much of an ill-effect from the wire's stainless steel hold, in some spots it couldn't be helped. Other than unwanted visitors crashing their party the last thing Alex and his talking knife wanted was for the wire to find its way passed Five's skin and fat through to a major artery or vein. Alex positioned the wire over places on Five's fatty frame in the hopes of minimizing the chance of premature bleeding out, although not at the risk of Five getting loose, and especially not to afford the freak an iota of comfort.

For a gag Alex had used the pink panties, rolling them into a tight ball within a crusty sock. With the help of a little force he managed to cram every bit of the make shift gag into Five's mouth. Then to lock it in place Alex employed the use of a thin leather belt he'd found on the floor. After two complete wraps around Five's head and stuffed mouth, Alex could clasp its buckle at the base of his skull and with a hard *clunk* he dropped the head against the table.

Looking the night's entertainment over, and pleased with what appeared to be a good start, Alex patted the side of Five's face with the back of his hand. "Wait here, we'll be right back."

Stepping back into the living room Alex doubled checked the apartment's only intended way in or out, making sure it was locked—it was. Alex was well aware that all it would take to get through that door was a good swift kick or a strong shoulder; he chuckled softly and latched the small chain lock. Turning back toward the bedroom his ear was caught by the refrigerator motor's hum, and figured he'd have himself a look-see for something cold to drink. Tying Five to the table was thirsty work and although he wasn't planning on being there too long, Alex didn't see the harm in helping himself to some sort of refreshment.

Stepping over a pile of dirty clothes he whispered almost soundlessly "—The killer awoke before dawn—" Alex's boot heel snagged on the top of a stack of newspapers and pulled a few to the floor.

"Careful Alex," Mr. Band advised.

"Shhhhhh—" Alex replied, continuing Mr. Morrison's poem quietly to himself. "He put his boots on—then he took the face from the ancient gallery and walked on down the hall—." In the small kitchen, Alex stepped up to the refrigerator, its sick sounding motor's hum shut off with a *click click*—*thunk* the instant his hand touched its door handle. "He went to the room where his sister live—."

Complete with mental images, Alex thought of what sort of nastiness he would find once he opened the door. Pausing, he shot a look around. The kitchen possessed a foul stench and cold darkness all its own. There was a faint scratching noise coming from within the piles of trash on the counter that Alex guessed was either cockroaches or rats. The floor beneath his boots was sticky in some spots and slimy in others. He continued butchering the rock legend's poem "—he paid a visit to his brother then he walked on down the hall. He came to a door—."

The instant Alex pulled open the refrigerator, he was sent back a step by an icy wave of reek that he could actually taste. The thick blast of odor was so horrendous and so abrupt that an acidulous tasting dry-heave rushed up into Alex's throat where it formed a painful lump. He forced most of the bile back down with a hard gulping swallow while clasping his hand firmly over his nose and mouth.

The fridge's dim light bulb hissed and popped with crackling electricity struggling to escape. Seeing nothing but the putrefied remains of fast-food on the top shelf, Alex lowered his search down to the middle rack. His eyes scanned its contents and swiftly locked on the top of an unopened forty-ounce bottle of beer poking up from behind a bucket of fried chicken. He moved the bucket of chicken and a few white cartons of what used to be Chinese take-out aside, along with a big jar of pickled pig's feet and two more jars of the same size filled with sickly discolored boiled eggs. As he was moving these things out of the beer's way, Alex spotted something that cried out to him for closer scrutiny.

It was a baby food jar, still sporting the paper label of a happy infant. It wasn't the dingy little glass vessel itself that picked naggingly at Alex's curiosity, it was the feeling he got deep in his gut the instant his eyes skimmed across it. A sense of misgiving swelled within him the moment his gloved fist took it up. Its lid was on tightly, but not enough to keep Alex out. With a twist and a hollow pop! The jar came open. He looked in but the flicking light bulb wasn't helping much. At first he thought the tiny whitish objects might be nuts of some sort. He emptied some of the jar's holdings out onto the palm of his hand and narrowed his focus. Alex's feelings were once more dead-on. The baby food jar was half filled with human teeth. Not the teeth of adults, no these were the so called baby teeth of children. They were still stained in spots with dried blood and some had bits of hardened meat clinging to them. Three little front teeth were imbedded in a broken piece of lower mandible bone.

Seething rage expanded his heart as he stared down through eyes stinging with emerging tears at the handful of teeth.

Alex said nothing of what he'd found to the razor sharp manifestation of his insanity A.K.A—Mr. Bane. He poured the teeth one by one back into the jar while his silent tears slowly dried down his cheeks. After swallowing the lump of sadness in his throat, Alex placed the lid firmly back on the jar, and grabbed the beer as he stood, dropping the small glass vault of teeth in his coat pocket.

Back in the bedroom, Alex glanced at the still unconscious freak. Taking the folding chair from its place in the corner, he stepped over the mattress, rocking the T.V with each step, causing its blue glow to shift a bit across the walls and ceiling. He sat the chair at the head of the coffee table, less than three feet from Five's pumpkin. Alex took a moment to look the trussed freak over as he took off his coat and hat. After tossing them in a corner, out of the way of any possible splatter or spatter, he then brought out his brass cigarette case and matching lighter from his back pants pocket. Taking out a smoke he tapped one end on the case's closed lid.

Alex's face seemed to darken from somewhere within him, giving his deep set eyes an almost lifeless expression. *Keep the moments to follow from slipping out of your grasp and the rage won't come to rule your actions*, he thought, then replied "—It may be too late," under his breath. Lighting the cigarette, Alex took a long drag as he tossed the case and light on the mattress. With a twisted crack! He took the cap off the big bottle of beer, silently mouthing the words—bottoms up. The bottle cap dropped from his gloved fingers to the floor and with his lungs still filled with warm smoke he took three healthy gulps. The beer had gotten plenty cold sitting at the back of the fridge, colder than Alex's leather clad fist could detect. He would have helped himself to a few more swallows if not for the dull painful onset of brain freeze and the subsequent pulsating that was its hallmark. He shook his head as if doing so could alleviate the mounting throb between his ears. Realizing how silly the notion was, he stopped his lame head-waggling and let the uncomfortable sensation in his skull run its course.

Holding the almost full beer bottle directly over Five's unconscious head Alex tipped it upside down. "One should never drink and murder," he chuckled as the frigid beverage emptied out onto the freak's face. The splashing beer brought Five around quickly. As soon as the last drops of white foam were plopping out onto Five's coming around face, his blood shot eyes struggling to focus past the stinging alcohol, Alex turned the bottle so that its bottom was down and dropped it. Like a glass brick it smacked hard against Five's forehead to bounce off with a sharp sounding *crack* landing on the floor unbroken. An inch long gash materialized over his right eye. Blood, dark and thick trickled down the side of Five's face, mixing with beer and sweat.

Alex dropped to his haunches, leaned over Five's face and gazed closely into his shock and horror. Listening gleefully to the muffled music of the freak's gagged screams for help, Alex took a long draw from his cigarette. Examining its brightly glowing cherry and not yet satisfied with its red-hot size, Alex—still hovering over Five's face, took one more pull off the Camel, its glowing tip mere inches from the tiny red and purple veins spider webbing the freaks bulbous nose. Alex then offered the child-molester an almost friendly smile and in his best mock German voice asked, "Vould you like a zigarette, old man?"

Alex took the cigarette from his lips, power-exhaled a dense column of blue-gray smoke out in Five's already watery eyes, quickly French inhaling some of the discharged vapor back in through his nostrils, only to blow it right back out in Five's face again. Still displaying his toothy grin, Alex—without a word of warning latched a hold of Five's fat incased face, his fingers pressing down painfully hard. He spread the upper and lower lids of Five's right eye, opening it wide with his thumb and forefinger.

"There is a thin, almost nonexistent line drawn between ecstasy and agony," Alex breathed into Five's ear, "On this night you will cross that line." Alex crammed the hot-boxed cigarette's glowing cherry into the killer of little children's eye.

Suddenly a new reeking stink arose into the cold atmosphere. The odors of roasting eyeball, as well as those already thick in the apartment were abruptly overtaken by the pungent aroma of human waste. Five's bowels had dislodged all of their abundant holdings, in other words… the freak had gone and shit himself.

"Well, that's just fucking peachy!" Alex exclaimed with a strong note of disgust. "Now I'll have to work with that stench hovering about. Why can't you fucks!" Alex stood quickly, stepping away from Five's head a pace, "keep from doing that?"

Leaving the crushed, smoldering butt welded so securely to the thin skin of Five's eye that even his pain and fear induced thrashing couldn't dislodge it, Alex turned his back to the freak. He stepped across the mattress, his wide stride tripping over the television and rolling it onto its screen, blocking out the room's primary source of light. There was a stumbling sound in the sudden darkness, along with a barked "sonofabitch!" After another loud thud Alex located the TV set, placing it upright again, giving the room back its dim blue glow.

Speaking to Five, who had slowed his battling against the wire; either because of the pain created by his thrashing or from a realization that he simply couldn't win—Alex asked as he made his way to his coat, "Do you know the meaning of the word…BANE?"

Taking the baby-food jar of children's teeth from out of the pocket, he then folded the heavy coat neatly in half and sat it back on the floor under his fedora. Rattling the teeth in the jar as he stepped back over to stop at the foot of the table, he pulled the knife out of its sheath. The jar in his left hand, Mr. Bane in his right, both in plain view of Five's new one eyed vision, Alex simply stood there and stared down at the freak. It was at this stage of the game that Alex, for whatever reason decided to tell Five, in his own way—WHY. Mostly it was to hear himself talk, but also because he believed doing so would add to the pedophile's suffering.

Like a villain in a 60's B movie going into a long winded monologue, Alex locked his leering gaze onto Five's face, which had twisted into a snarled mask of horror, and began.

"The dictionary that we first looked the word, Bane up in was an old one." He noticed that the freak's Cyclops attention had fixed on the jar and for a brief moment Five's horror had shifted to seething rage, and then quickly back to horror.

"About sixty years old that dictionary was" Alex went on to say "—but it was that book's archaic definition that we liked best." With the jar always in easy sight, every so often giving it a little shake he continued. "It read—Bane, the cause of a catastrophic decline." Alex stopped rattling the teeth and asked off the topic "—You alright? Hell Five, you look like you've seen a ghost."

Half glancing behind him Alex reached back and sat the baby food jar on the dresser, making certain that it was in Five's line of vision.

"Where was I…oh, that's right, his name," Alex shot a fast glance at the knife. "It's a wee bit passé, sure…but you have to admit, it owns the truly definitive ring of finality to it. The cause of a catastrophic decline."

Five's gagged cries for help and muffled pleas for mercy grew weak, fading to almost nonexistent moaning. His kicking and jerking which had only a moment ago started again, slowed to a stop, the wire in spots already eating through skin into fatty meat—mere inches from bone. His eye's attention was snared by the moving of the knife as his late night visitor held it slightly away from his side.

"It's time we draw our time here to a close Alex," Mr. Bane suggested.

"Soon."

"What are you doing Alex, why are you wasting our time speaking to this—this FIVE?" the knife wondered.

"Sometimes it's nice to simply take in as much of the moment as possible." Alex whispered.

"Whatever," the knife barked. "End it and let us leave this place."

"One more thing."

Alex's conversation with the knife strengthened Five's mask of terror, his moaning deepened to a hollow, more consternating pitch. And his eye widened to a green and white bulging blood shot orb that never left the knife's blade.

"What is this—one more thing?" Bane demanded to know.

"Millstone," Alex growled.

"It's not crucial!"

"It is to me." Alex said as he realized by the look of the swiftly fading freak that he best speed things up or Five would die before they killed him. While he bent down to snatch up a white T-shirt from the floor Alex studied Five's steadily waning lifespan. He tossed the shirt down over the freak's limited manhood peaking out from under rolls of bleeding belly fat.

"Why take on this task? You're undoubtedly wondering" Alex said to Five. "We'd first got the idea during the beginning of a ten year prison set. I had begun a ninety day stint in the hole for making a little drinky-drinky. After about the first thirty days of being allowed nothing to read, I finally broke-weak and read the bible."

"This silliness will be the cause of our fall Alex," Mr. Bane warned.

"I'm nearly done," Alex stated, and then went back to telling Five his and the knife's reason for their quest to single-handedly dispatch all child-molesters. "I wish to make something clear to you Five." Alex swung his right leg over the coffee table dressed with a bleeding fat man. Standing over Five straddling his midsection he positioned himself to begin straightaway after his speech—he continued.

"The reasons for reading that ancient book of fiction weren't out of some deep seeded desire to try and gain spiritual sanity. Nor was it because of some lame need for answers. And it sure as hell wasn't an attempt to save my already spoiled soul. No—Five, none of these were why we read that book. We read it simply because we were bored fucking stupid. That—and it was the only book that ass-hole turn key would give us to read."

"This foolishness Alex is a waste of time that we can not afford" the knife rumbled. "Kill it—kill it now Alex!"

"The sooner you stop interrupting me, the sooner we send this one to the worms and go. Anyway—it was you who convinced me to change the plan." Alex was talking directly to the knife now, holding it up in front of his face the same way one holds a hand-held mirror.

"Yes—yes Alex, I saw the need to give this one more than first intended," Mr. Bane acknowledged. "But I never expected that you of all people would spill your guts out to this scoogiatti. Do what you've in mind to do, but for the sake of our lives—do it swiftly," the metallic voice paused then added. "I really like the thing with the cigarette in the eye."

"I figured you might," Alex replied. He lowered his steely blue gaze down onto Five's face in time to catch a glimpse of an expression peering out from his fright and anguish that Alex recognized all too well. It was the same standoffish look he got from people who caught him speaking aloud to Mr. Bane in public. The leering gaze that always called out at him from within the prolonged stares—*you're a goddam lunatic!* Alex shook it off with a grin, not allowing his rage the chance to speak on it, leastwise not yet. Suddenly he saw Five as more than a child-molester to be killed; now he saw the pedophile as all those people who pointed fingers and laughed at him as well.

"We, that is Mr. Bane and myself—we read that book from Genesis to Revelations and out of all those pages we could only come up with one passage that inspired us. It was in the book of Matthew. And from what I could find. also the only place in that book where Christ mentions a crime worthy of death. The passage is in Matthew 18:6, do you know it Five?" Alex leaned over some to see if he still possessed any of Fives' attention. Staring deep into the freak's wandering eye, Alex figured he still had enough of his interest to keep talking. Five was fading fast though and Alex knew he needed to pick up the slack.

Answering his own question, Alex said "No!" then quoted the bible passage. "But who so shall offend one of these little ones," he glanced over his shoulder at the missing kids on the milk cartons. "Which believe in me," panning his vision back around in a wide, fast sweep Alex let it rest on the jar of blood-stained teeth. "It would be better for him," his voice became flat, almost to the point of sounding inhuman. He snapped his eyes onto Five, whose one working eye rolled about in its socket like a stone in a bowl. "It would be better for him that a millstone were hanged about his neck and that he were drowned in the depths of the sea."

Like Alex had done before Mr. Bane directed his attention to the little girl's panties, he readied the blade. Alex could once again see his shadow spread against the wall—an elongated shape with one hand outstretched.

Five's eye stopped spinning round in his skull and locked its fully aware gaze up on the glint of the knife's steel.

"That's right punk! You slimy lump of shit...look at it and see the 'Bane' that will aid in your catastrophic decline."

23

But Five didn't want to look, he most assuredly did not. He clamped both of his eyes shut so tightly that the lids of his right eye finally pinched most of the crushed cigarette butt out of his eye.

"It closes its eyes Alex," Mr. Bane hissed. "No—no, this won't do."

"OPEN YOUR EYES!" Alex barked, a bit louder than he intended.

"It defies us—see, it makes fools of you and I."

"Open your eye!" Alex swung his leg over the freak, and stepped around to stand beside the head of the table. He dropped his knee on the left side of Five's head, locking it in place. The fat man thrashed wildly, but only briefly. His zealous kicking and jerking stopped almost immediately as soon as Alex began cutting.

Talking a hold of his knife by the middle of its blade Alex sliced away all of the skin encompassing Five's left eye, the only movement rising from the freak was that of his flaring nostrils and quivering fat. Alex and Mr. Bane not so delicately removed his eyelids, leaving the skin to hang from clumped strands of fat.

"That's better." Mr. Bane giggled drunkenly as Alex and he retook their place straddling the moaning, trembling freak. Offering no response, Alex's eyes had barely looked down at Five as he swung the long blade up; drawing in a fast intake of Five's fully exposed terror staring up at him. With only the ears of Alex's dark imagination he heard the silent screams rising out from the monster below him while Mr. Bane's blade raced down. Back and forth he sent the sweeping steel through Five's quivering flesh. It began with focused direction and to the eyes watching Alex's performance from Hell's gallery, he must have appeared to move like an artist lost in the rapture of his work. With controlled delivery, he sailed his childhood friend's razor bite swiftly past meat, swiping it over bone. Five's fear of death was suddenly reawoken, and had begun to display a new vigor. Again, as if getting his third wind he fought against the steel wire's tenacious appetite for his blood. But despite Five's hearty efforts all he had accomplished was to add more pain to his flesh and bones by helping the wire feed as it cut into him as cleanly and deeply as Mr. Bane's blade.

Alex's self-deluded firm grip on his self-control was slipping away. The attack went from being executed with graceful precision to blind rage. Soon Alex's ability to maintain some level of mental focus had become so blinded by his own wrath that he was no longer piloting his own vessel. Only his hate reigned the moments supremely. Alex was enmeshed within the snare of his own lust for blood and didn't even realize it. As he hurtled deeper and deeper into the abyss of insanity, with his pal Mr. Bane leading the way, his savagery never missed a stroke. Only now his skillful transaction of the task he'd charged onto himself had reached a degree of brutality unprecedented even for him.

He wind milled the blade wildly in all directions. Blood and bits of flesh fell away from Five's face and much of his upper torso. Pieces were flung off the blade slapping against the walls, floor, and ceiling by Alex's unhinged carving.

It was while Alex was of the mind to remove Five's right ear with a blindingly fast upward swipe that he unintentionally severed the belt holding the gag in the freak's mouth. Still clinging to a faint shadow of life, Five loosed a blood-chillingly loud scream that shot the blood-soaked ball of cloth out of his mouth. The squall for assistance had barely blasted out past Five's yellow teeth when Alex, thinking fast drove all ten inches of Mr. Bane's blade through Five's skull. The dagger's steel pierced the right temporal ridge, impaling sideways through Five's brain to exit out the left temporal ridge, in one fluid stroke.

With as much effort, Alex yanked the sated blade back out of the dead freak's head. The brain and blood streaked murder weapon at his side, Alex stood there utterly motionless, holding his breath; listening. He remained still for several intense minutes, giving his ear's attention to the sounds of his surroundings. No rushing feet or slamming doors filled the hallway outside the apartment, no shouting voices ordering others to *"go, hurry, call the cops, someone's being butchered in apartment 49!"* Alex heard none of these things, only the sounds of his own beating heart over the steady—*Plop Plop Plopping* noise of Five's blood dripping off the edge of the table onto the floor. A thick vermilion pool was spreading out around the coffee table's base and soaking into the bottom of the mattress. Even the soles and heels of Alex's work-boots were engulfed by the dark puddle.

Alex loosed a heavy sigh of hopeful relief, followed by a much needed breath. "No one heard," he whispered the way children might do after dropping something heavy in the middle of the night.

"Luckily for us," Mr. Bane stated sharply. "Finish up so that we may leave this place."

Looking around him, Alex was slightly surprised and greatly amused by what his little loss of control had done to the small room. The place looked as though a large bucket of blood and scraps of raw meat had been flung into a big fan, set on its fastest adjustment. Bits of Five were even splattered up on the baby blanket draped over the small window clear across the room. Lowering his gaze, a chill sped up his spine as he studied the fifth in the series. *Five in as many weeks, not bad for starters,* he thought.

Alex had decided—with Mr. Bane's approval of course, not to include his first two side by side slayings with these five, or any that would follow. The dual slaughtering of those two monsters during his youth was much too special to be bunched in with the likes of these or any others.

As Alex looked down at yet another job well-done, his trance like state of awe was infringed upon by movement out of the corner of his right eye. He looked sharply and was surprised when the four foot tall shadowy figure didn't dart away as usual. This time the robed, hooded vision permitted Alex to get a second's glance at its unfocused appearance. Long enough for him to see its flaming red eyes and hear it say in a child's voice the word—"CHAMPION." In past sightings the odd little apparition had only appeared as a fast blur, but still even in its swift shadowy coming and going Alex always managed to catch sight of its glowing eyes. The first time he'd seen it was eight nights before his acts of patricide at age nine. The sighting had come to Alex in a dream, its appearance as fleeting, then as all the split second showings that would come to follow throughout his life, some of which in dreams like the first and some before his conscious eyes. And always right before or after some act of ferocity executed by Alex's hand.

Although Alex had never been bothered by the ghosty's visits, he still kept their occurrence to himself, believing it best not to mention it to Mr. Bane.

Sensing something had latched onto his student's attention Mr. Bane's metallic voice asked suspiciously—"What is it Alex my boy?"

"A shadow...I think," Alex replied surreptitiously.

"A shadow—you think!" the knife barked, a strong note of irritated intolerance for Alex's lack of explanation. "What's that supposed to mean…a shadow I think? You don't have the luxury of making unclear guesses. So again I ask—what's caught your eye pilgrim?"

"Noting worthy of your backhanded attitude—".

"That response granted me only wasted sound," Bane interrupted. "A third time I ask—what is it?"

"The TV's glow caught my shadow, casting it across the wall in an odd way…fuck! Tighten the hell up," Alex growled.

Mr. Bane loosed a throaty growl that stretched until mellowing out of ear-shot. Alex panned his vision around through the blood smeared darkness to see if his red-eye visitor was peering out at him from some blackened corner. With no signs of the phantom to be seen he sent his full attention back to his work. Alex was swinging his leg over the corpse to step onto the mattress when the knife's razor-sharp voice spoke up again.

"Let me see Alex—don't be so bloody greedy. Show me the freak's face…*pleeease.*"

While wiping the blood off the soles of his boots onto the mattress, Alex saying nothing raised the dagger up away from his side, extending it so the tip was aimed down directly toward Five's glistening wet death mask.

"So…this is what can be accomplished with a little blindly wielded fury," Mr. Bane cackled. "I had expected a tad bit more focused cutting. I suppose it'll have to do."

"I'm fucking thrilled shitless that you approve," Alex said in a low, sarcastic tone.

"All that matters is that this Five's suffering was worthy of his foul deeds. I believe it was. What do you think Alex—was its pain and fear sufficient?"

"I think so," Alex replied as he stared thoughtfully down at their handiwork. "It wasn't as detailed as I'd hoped, but as you'd said—it'll have to do."

"One things for certain Alex."

"Yeah—what's that?"

"This one will never harm another little one again. Not in this dimension or any other," the metallic voice faded once again to silence.

Alex finished smearing his boot soles clean on the mattress, leastwise as clean as they would come without removing them and giving the soles a more scrutinized going over. Looking himself over he realized with a sense of awe what a grisly mess he'd made of himself. It was the knowledge that he knew better that bewildered Alex as he examined the blood soaked state of his clothes. For obvious reasons he usually tried to avoid such messy outcomes. *All I can do is try and clean up some before we leave*, Alex thought while wiping the blade off on the sleeve of his sweat-shirt. One more thing left to do first, his mind quietly mumbled.

Reaching down he snatched up a hunk of severed flesh that had been flung against the glowing screen of the television. *No more time to waste dawdling,* he thought as he took the dripping fistful of meat into the living room. Stopping in the middle of the trash-heap that was the apartment's main room Alex began his search. Placing Mr. Bane into its sheath he scanned the walls. He was looking for a section of wall that would best illustrate their relentless determination. It needed to be some place that would show numbers Six, Seven, Eight, Nine and so on the blood-thirstiness with which the man and knife were willing to inflict their resolve.

While in the process of looking for the perfect spot his attention was drawn onto the clippings and milk cartons. Alex paused his search a moment, and as he gazed into the faces of all those missing little ones he wondered if he should take it all down. A minute, perhaps two had crept past while Alex stood staring through the dark at their eyes; the hunk of freak flesh dripping between his fingers before he decided against it. *Let them see the true level of Five's wicked-ways*, Alex thought.

Turning his back to the wall of sadness, Alex shot his icy sight up onto a section of cracked, dirty wall above the bedroom's ugly green door and grinned.

"That's it," he said under his breath. "What better place than over the entrance-way leading into our latest abattoir." Spotting another child-size folding chair he set it up in front of the doorway.

Whistling the melody to the happy little tune played at the end of Porky Pig cartoons, Alex stepped up; the metal chair creaking beneath his weight as he signed their work. In big red letters, using the hunk of meat as a crude brush he smeared the word: MILLSTONE above the door.

Halfway down, as he dropped the severed flesh on a pile of clothes a noise outside the apartment caught his ear. Stepping as quietly as humanly possible the rest of the way to the floor, Alex locked all of his focus on the door. He was about to dismiss it as a manifestation of nerves and go try and clean some of the blood off in the bathroom when more sounds slipped through the door.

"We've got visitors," Mr. Bane hissed from within the sheath.

Alex's heart leapt into overdrive at the sight of the doorknob being softly jiggled, the lock halting its turn. *Shit house luck,* he thought. "Don't panic Alex old boy," he whispered to himself, "keep your focus tight—tight!"

He was on his way toward the living room window intending on sneaking a peek down at the street when a man's whispering voice just beyond the door stopped Alex cold.

"You had best bring me out pilgrim," Mr. Bane suggested. "It seems I may be needed."

Saying nothing Alex realized the sense in the dagger's assessment and brought the knife back out. But the security the doubled edge weapon usually granted Alex was greatly diminished the instant he heard the unmistakable crackle of a police radio. With almost no required thought to do so, Alex spun about, practically stumbling over a pile of newspapers and the folding chair as he tore into the bedroom. He'd barely managed to close and lock the door when a stingingly loud knock beat against Alex's panic. It was the sort of knock that immediately invoked a sense of trapped fright in those for whom it was meant.

"Mr. Peakor," a man's voice shouted, "Multnomah county sheriffs! You need to come let us in." The cop paused a moment, then added— "We got a call reporting a scream coming from your apartment. Let us come in and see that everything is fine and we'll be on our way."

"Shit house luck!" Alex growled through clinched teeth while staring over at the corpse.

"Talk about getting caught red-handed," Mr. Bane crackled humorlessly.

"Shut up!" Alex snapped.

"Mr. Peakor—we know you're home," the cops tone grew louder, more threatening. "If you don't come and open this door in thirty seconds we'll open it ourselves."

As it turns out, someone had heard Five's death cry after all. Actually most everyone in the building heard it, but only one of the tenants bothered to call the cops. It had been the woman who Alex had overheard being beaten—the woman named *Peggy*.

As with most of the building's tenants, Peggy was aware of the man in apartment 49's status as being a two-time convicted child-molester. And, although she along with the rest of the inhabits in the run-down building had all loudly voiced their strong disapproval over having such a fiend as he living in their apartment building; the *slum-lord* who owned the place still permitted it.

Peggy had thought Five's squall for help sounded like a child's scream and without question called the cops. The sheriff's department was also aware of Five's foul past, and his being registered with State, County and all city law enforcement agencies. Although he'd made it off parole, successfully giving up his number, the cops could still enter his home and search his car at anytime. So, armed with this info, the three county sheriffs at the door had all they needed to make a forced entry.

"Fine, have it your way Peakor!" the cop shouted.

It only took a single kick and the door into the apartment burst open. Once inside the three cops immediately locked their attention up onto Alex and Mr. Bane's calling card smeared over the ugly green door. They realized right-off that what they'd busted into was much more than anticipated. The cops recognized the still dripping message as the same blood clue left at four previous murder scenes spread across the state. The call to look in on a sex-offender had in an instant transformed into a situation they weren't ready for.

The cops didn't dare attempt any sort of forced entry through the green door for fear of one of them possibly getting shot by a cornered killer. They also had no way of knowing if Mr. Peakor was still alive or dead, not that any of them would lose sleep if the pedophile was dead. The eldest of the three told one of his companions to get on the horn and tell dispatch what they'd stumbled into.

Meanwhile, as the three uniformed stooges were trying to figure out what to do next, Alex—who was feeling as trapped as a rat in a blood-splattered little room, paced the floor. He went into the bathroom to see if it might have some type of hatchway in the ceiling that could put him on the roof; no such luck, the tiny room didn't even have a window. Back in the bedroom Alex darted to its window and pulling the baby-blanket aside, peered through the rain streaked pane to see if by chance it could serve as an escape route. The answer was a definitive *No*. Even if his wide shouldered frame could be made to fit through that small square, there was nothing to use to climb down, or even up the wall with; no hand or foot holds. Looking out into the wet darkness, Alex spotted the red and blue flashing lights of police cars reflecting off the windows across the street. He knew that in no time at all the entire city block would be locked up tighter than the iron doors of the State Prison's death chamber. It didn't take Alex long at all to realize he was, in a phrase—*Totally Screwed*.

Stepping over to Five's corpse, half listening to the cop's radios and their whispering chatter in the living room, Alex stood a moment, staring blankly down at his latest masterpiece. The sound of the cop's presence beyond that door had begun to drill straight down into his skull, spinning through his brain with a bit made of dull panic. Alex's mind was being bombarded with the usual would of's, could of's and should of's, while at the same time a flood of unsettling images washed over his mental vision. In a flash of confusion his imagination lead him into a small round room with powder-blue metal walls. An ugly yellow curtain was pulled open to reveal a large window of black glass. There was an oddly shaped wooden table with heavy leather straps and big brass buckles. He saw needles fixed to long clear rubber hoses. Suddenly he was falling through a spinning vortex of gnashing teeth, reaching hands and eyes. Alex was struck with an overwhelming flash of utter darkness only to find himself when it cleared standing in a thickening puddle of blood overlooking a fat dead man tied to a coffee table.

The blood splattered walls pressed down around him as the cop's voices beyond the green door reinforced the heart racing knowledge that he was cornered.

"Need to think my way out of this!" Alex told himself aloud.

"It's too late for that now pilgrim," Mr. Bane hissed in a tone unlike any Alex had ever heard the blade speak in. "May as well go out cutting and stabbing."

"Shut up!" Alex shouted.

"It's a shame we left the pistol in the van. I'll bet you—."

"I said—SHUT THE HELL UP!"

"It's funny that you should mention—Hell Alex," the metallic voice hissed then paused to giggle. The knife went to add something further, but before its thoughts had been transposed into sound and the sound formed into words, Alex stifled it with another pointed "—SHUT THE FUCK UP!"

All the while, as Alex and his disembodied crime-partner were bickering the three deputy-sheriffs in the other room were listening, not sure if he was speaking to Mr. Peakor—an accomplice, or himself.

"I've got to think, there's a-way out of this; I'm just not seeing it," Alex said, stumbling through a minefield of confusion.

"Now the pupil wants to think," Mr. Bane cut in. "Think about what pray-tell? Listen to them out there—it's only a matter of time. Soon...very soon they'll be crashing in through that door—then what? Come, come now big thinker—I'm all on edge, waiting to hear what your up and coming epiphany will grant you. What are you going to do Alex my boy?"

"How can I think if—"Alex tried to reply but the knife's anger wouldn't allow it.

"No Alex! You know what needs to be done. You've always known. You've known ever since I'd first come to you thirty-three years ago in that cold darkness. You remember—yes of course you do. We've a deal you and me. You will keep your word pilgrim—stay the course."

"Shut up!" Alex snapped.

"You need to keep up your end of our bargain."

"Shut up—Shut up!"

"Very well," Mr. Bane's voice almost sounded sad. "Truth be told—you were getting a bit heavy. You're on your own. Go—go on and think. Yes, you should ask Five if he's got any bright ideas. Yes, yes that's it! I'll bet the Devil's eyes that you and he will have yourselves a true meeting of the minds. Farewell Alex."

The moment the metallic voice's final words seeped beyond the reach of Alex's awareness, a wave of remote emptiness, the likes of which he'd not known since he was a boy of nine settled over him. It had been so sudden, this fervent measure of loneliness and loss—so utterly wrenching that Alex vomited on Five's corpse. He actually had to physically steady himself to keep from collapsing to his knees, landing in the sticky red pool under his feet. The dagger slipped from his hand as if it were suddenly made as heavy as the very millstone he likened himself to. It fell in the thickening blood with a lifeless thud when it hid the wood floor. It took a moment, but when the nauseous feeling in Alex's gut subsided enough he bent over, his legs still a bit shaky, and picked up the knife. He could immediately tell from its dead-weight and its empty coldness that Mr. Bane had indeed abandoned him.

"Mr. Bane," he said so softly that almost no sound brushed out over his teeth. "Freak Bane—come on now, quit fucking around." Like a small boy trying to stare the life back into a puppy he'd unintentionally squeezed to death, Alex gazed deeply at the blood-stained inanimate object. Mr. Bane, he mouthed silently. For nearly a full minute he quietly stood staring down at the blade partly responsible for the deaths of seven human-monsters, a small measure of his attention still fixed on the cops in the other room. Finally Alex tightened his grip around the bone handle.

"I was getting fed-up with his endless yammering any-how," Alex glanced at Five's widely exposed eye as he lied.

"You in there—Millstone!?" A cop's voice, tired and heavy with age called through the door. "Is that how I should address you sir? To be honest with you I feel pretty damn silly calling you by that handle. How about you telling me your real name?"

Now it begins, Alex thought as he turned around to look at the door.

"I'm officer—"

"NO NAMES!" Alex barked loudly, interrupting the cop.

"Okay—okay then, we'll keep it strictly business," agreed the cop an obvious placating tone of voice.

"Yeah—whatever," Alex growled almost to himself.

"We don't know what it is you want unless you tell us?"

"I would think that it would be obvious," Alex loosed a forced chuckle.

"What do you mean?"

"Never mind," Alex said as he walloped the corpse solidly up-side its head. "He's not dead …not yet anyway." He clobbered the head again, this time so hard that blood and brain juices jetted out of the knife hole on the left side." But that will change if you give it cause to. Now listen up! You listening?"

"Yes, we're hearing you."

"If I so much as think you jug-heads are about to try something stupid I'll blow this sick-fuck's brain's out. Then I'll shoot the first one of you through that door and keep shootin' until I kill all of you or you kill me. Do you understand me," Alex made himself sound calm and in control. He was gambling on two things. One; that the clowns believed Five was still alive. Two; that they would stay true to form as wise pigly-wiglies by counting on the not-so-certain fact that he had at least one gun. Looking at the now voiceless knife in his fist, Alex couldn't help but wish he hadn't left his revolver under the vans driver-seat. But what really stuck him in the ribs was that when he realized he'd mindlessly forgotten the piece, and he was still in eye-shot of the van, he decided to leave it.

"Would it be okay with you for Mr. Peakor to give us out here some verbal confirmation? You know a shout out to show he's still among the living," the cop asked.

Alex was wondering when they'd be asking to speak to the 'hostage.' Again he punched the corpse.

"No! This piece of shit ain't speakin' to anyone," Alex rumbled at the door, then paused and added. "Hell, I got an idea…you listening?"

"Yes—"

"Why don't you punks grow a pair and bust on in here! Yeah, see if one of you lame fucks can put one between my eyes before I can do likewise to one of you." Alex stepped toward the door. "Do not ask to speak to this child killing bastard again…period!"

"If you have some information concerning a crime or crimes that Mr. Peakor has committed we would be glad to look—."

"Shut up!" Alex cut the cop off. After a long silence the cop asked "—what do you want?"

"What?" Alex mumbled.

"Your demands—do you have any, or are we just here to fuck the dog?" the cop said.

Alex suddenly exploded into laughter. Speaking to the corpse, himself or both, he said "—Deals…they wish to make deals!" He smacked the back of his fist against the left side of Five's face. The blow sending a wet slapping noise out. Alex started to sort of dance around the coffee table, every few paces sweeping the tip of the knife's blade deeply through Five's cold fat.

"What do you have in mind constable?" Alex spun about, facing the door and like an S.S. officer in an old war movie he clicked his boot heels together coming to an abrupt stop.

"What I'd like to see occur is for this to end without you, Mr. Peakor or one of us being injured or killed." The cop's voice drifted noticeably closer to the door. "What do you have in mind sir?" the cop asked.

"It was nice of you to include me in your little wish list," Alex moved closer to the door, his face mere inches from its puke green surface, his tone of voice shifting to as cold and serious as he could invoke.

"My first—demand—as you so colorfully put it is for you and your comrades to back away from the door."

"What door?"

"Don't test me constable. So that I know you're moving back away, I want to hear you counting. Start at one and begin—now."

Without question two of the three deputy-sheriffs did as Alex had said. They'd gotten to four when Alex chuckled coldly and lied, saying "—you must think I'm stupid, yeah that's right, I've my eye on you." Of course Alex hadn't been able to peek in on them. It's just that he was certain he heard at least three or four cops out there, not merely the owners of two voices. "Shall we try this again? Begin counting— now!"

This time all three cops were counting, their voices moving away from the bedroom door. Satisfied that they sounded far enough back Alex said "—That's good." They stopped. "Now constable, I want you to stay there, only you. As for your friends I want you to send them out of the apartment. I'd like it if they'd leave the building but I know that won't happen so out and down the hallway will do for now. Go on constable—send them out and remember, I'm watching."

After a bit of whispered arguing Alex heard the sound of hard-healed boots moving out into the hall. From the sound of it they'd only gone a few short yards and stopped, he'd expected as much.

"I sent them out," the cop said in an unpleased tone.

"Indeed you did constable," Alex replied with a muffled snicker." "Actually it was I who sent them out, you just did as you were told."

"What now?" The cop asked, a note of incensed irritation clinging to his words. He didn't like Alex's cocky attitude one bit. Suddenly Alex could hear the clamor of more cops stomping up the stairs and the cops he'd sent out moving to meet them.

"Stay put constable," Alex said. "I'm counting on you to keep your overzealous pals at bay. I, as well as this load of crap are confident that you're up to the task." Alex paused then asked "—who is it?"

"The Sheriff Department's hostage negotiator, my captain and some tactical brass from the Portland city police department."

"Do not let them through that door!" Alex demanded.

"But this ain't my job," the cop said, "I'm not trained for this type of—"

"It's your fucking job tonight constable," Alex barked. "Can they hear me?" he shouted loudly.

"Yes—we hear you," replied a new voice.

"Then hear me good," Alex growled. "If you ass-holes break the threshold of this apartment I give you my oath—the constable there will die," Alex bluffed. The hollow threat worked, the small army of cops stopped dead in their tracks, remaining in the hallway.

"Constable!"

"Yes?"

"That door looks pretty banged up from here. Will it still close?" Alex had no idea what that front door looked like.

"Not completely," the cop answered.

"Close it as best you can then," Alex ordered.

After a moment of sharp sounding whispers, Alex heard the door squeak horribly as it was forced closed but not latched.

"That's as good as it gets," the cop said.

"That'll be fine," Alex mumbled.

"Well—you got me here, although there's not much I can fucking do. Fuck, I'm just a deputy; I've got practically no juice whatsoever. So what is it, what do you fucking want—sir?"

"I'm going to turn myself in. I'm going to give up." Alex said his voice empty and tired.

"Come again?" the cop said.

"I'm surrendering, but not to you or any of your overeager pals salivating in the hallway."

"Then who?"

"A homicide detective. He's been one of the lead investigators who's been stumbling about trying to find me. His name is Stephen Wolfhart and he lives down in Eugene. Get him here and I'll toss my pistols and knife out this window and unlock that door. Get him here, let me hear his voice speaking to me through that door and all your aspirations concerning no one being harmed or killed will be fulfilled." Alex paused and listened closely as the cops talked among themselves. After hearing steps quickly receding down the hall and a few more low speaking voices, Alex asked, "Well constable—is it a deal or do we go into the next level of violence?"

"Alright, we'll see what we can do—"

"No! Not good enough," Alex snapped. "You won't simply see what you can do! No sir, you'll do it—and you will do it exactly as I've ordered it done. Get Wolfhart here, in that living room or I'll start whittling away on your precious pedophile. I think I've made my point clear enough—have I not?"

"Crystal Clear," replied the tired cop. "It'll take Wolfhart a few hours to drive up from Eugene.

"It's about a hundred and twenty-nine miles from good old Blue-jean up here to Portland on I-5. At seventy-five or eighty miles an hour non stop—I figure it shouldn't take more than an hour and a half, two at the most. And I'll be quite honest with you constable, by the looks of this lump of shit," Alex glanced at Five. "He don't appear to possess

37

the sand to stand too much more of this." He felt his pockets for the cigarette case and lighter. "Now constable, unless the space-monsters from the movie 'Alien' are about to storm the building the only voice I want to hear is detective Wolfhart's."

Not finding his smokes on his person, Alex scanned the dimly lit space. With only the TV's hissing glow to aid his search it took several seconds for his vision to locate the lighter. It was at finding it on the mattress between the back of the television and a wide streak of blood left there by his boot that Alex recalled dropping the lighter and case on the bed. It wasn't until he moved around the foot end of the coffee table that the brass case was found as well. The wallet sized, cigarette holder was lying in the setting puddle of blood. *Oh that's just fucking perfect*, Alex thought as he stepped over to the corner where his coat and hat lay. He remembered stepping over the mattress when he went to fetch the jar of teeth and the darkness that came from the T.V rolling onto its screen. Alex glanced over his shoulder at the baby food jar on the dresser. *I must have knocked it on the floor in the dark*, he figured. The brass case was practically an antique and far from waterproof, much-less blood proof. "Maybe I'll be lucky," he muttered in a low throaty grunt. "Just maybe one or at least part of a cigarette will have escaped untainted?"

Putting on his coat and hat, Alex then stepped over to the head of the coffee table and practically flopped on to the metal folding chair. With a heavy sigh that was more growl than anything else he reached between his boots and lifted the small, flat case up out of the sticky, scarlet crud. He snatched the lighter from the mattress while half-assed wiping the cigarette case off on the lower half of his left pant leg. With another throaty rumble of a sigh Alex pressed the tiny latch, opening the case. All nine of the filterless coffin-nails were inundated with freak blood. They seemed to almost heckle Alex as they swam in their shallow pool, swollen nearly to the point of bursting at the seam. Alex chuckled, sort of tipping the case slightly in order to slowly pour the blood out. He snapped its lid shut, leaving the soggy smokes and quite a bit of the blood inside. "I was planning on giving them up anyhow," he told the top of Five's head as he leaned comfortably back, the chair squeaking and popping beneath his weight.

Alex sat there like that for what seemed like an eternity, clicking the lid of his lighter open and closed, open and closed, open and closed. His vision drifted from Five to the door, back to Five, then the door, again and again all the while his ears locked on the slightest sounds, not only in the other room but throughout the building, as well as outside. He was listening to the soft slapping sound of rain-drops hitting the window, when to his right a hollow tapping noise caught his attention. It was coming from under a pile of clothes against the wall only a few feet to his right. Alex got to his feet and moving toward the sound, went to a knee and carefully pulled the filthy rags away from the wall. The noise was coming up from inside a heating vent on the floor. He leaned his narrowed vision closer and saw in the darkness beyond the small metal grate a tiny telescopic camera lens inching its way up through the vent.

"I'm disappointed in you constable," Alex said barely loud enough for the cop to hear clearly.

"You don't say," the cop replied. "How's that?"

Alex said nothing, he simply watched as the small device inched its intrusive way up toward the grate. He positioned himself so that there'd be no chance of the lens spotting Five's true state.

"How have I disappointed you?" the cops tone sounded a little concerned.

"Not so much you constable," Alex got ready. "It's mainly your overeager friends that are pissing me off." The lens was wriggling up between the thin metal slats Alex grabbed the device, immediately pressing his thumb down over the lens. With a hard yank Alex rose to his feet, pulling the long black video-feed cord up through the vent, cutting it in two with one fast sweep of his knife. The constable's radio as well as those of the cops in the hallway began to squawk with activity. Alex kicked the heating vent's handle with the toe of his boot, shutting it.

"I don't blame you people for not giving a fuck if this freak is killed. As a matter of fact, I'm tickled by it." Alex was checking the room for spots that might aid the fools in furthering their invasion into his private, quiet time.

"Don't do anything brash sir," the cop said, his tone practically pleading. "Detective Wolfhart will be here in less than five minutes."

Two tiny dots of red light dancing searchingly across the window side of the pink baby-blanket caught Alex's eye. At nearly the same time both glowing dots found themselves each a hole in the filthy cloth to stretch into the bedroom's feeble light. Ducking beneath the police sniper's laser-sight beams, Alex stepped around to stand at the head of the table.

"It's about time," he said in response to the news of Wolfharts rapidly approaching arrival. "When I hear his voice I'll send my weapons and rounds out the window—agreed?"

"Agreed sir."

"One more thing constable."

"Yes, what's that?"

"Make sure those snipers don't get too fidgety."

"Their good dogs' sir," the cop said softly.

"How's that?" Alex asked.

"They only bite when their told."

Alex's vision moved over Five's corpse across the floor checking out his fairly clear pathway. "Shit house luck," he said in a lifeless tone of voice he didn't know he possessed.

During Alex Stone's ten years in prison he'd spent most of his yard time on the penitentiary's weight pile jacking heavy iron. It was a practice he had also continued religiously after his release. So even at forty-three years of age and being a heavy smoker, Alex's six-foot four, two hundred and fifty-eight pound frame made him an impressively strong killer.

"Mr. Stone, I'm detective Wolfhart," said the voice Alex recognized from the news. "I'm told you've agreed to surrender—is this so?"

"They found my van" Alex chuckled.

"Yes, quite some time ago I'm told. May I call you Alex?" the detective asked.

"No," Alex answered. "Now that you're here I'm going to toss my things out the window." Alex could hear the cops that he'd earlier ordered to stay in the hallway moving into the living room to take their positions outside the ugly green door. "Constable—you still there?"

"Yes, I wouldn't miss this for the world," the cop's voice was so close to the door that he sounded as though he were shouting directly into Alex's ear. "What do you need sir?"

"Just make sure those snipers don't get trigger happy while I'm at the window throwing my weapons out…that's all."

"Do as you agreed and all will be fine," the cop said.

"Okay—here I go." With a freakishly powerful show of strength, Alex raised the coffee table up on its end and latched a hold of the underside middle of the table's base. Before Five's two-hundred and ninety-six pounds could shift too badly, Alex with a guttural grunt smoothly clean-and-jerked the entire corpse and table up over his head.

"TIMES UP STONE!" Wolfhart shouted.

At the sound of the cops' battering-ram smashing the ugly green door to splinters, Alex, with the coffee table crushing his fedora down on top of his head ran toward the window. As they were rushing in behind him, he let the table fly. It crashed out of the room, taking with it the small window, baby blanket and all, along with a large portion of the wall embracing its frame. Both of the laser-sights cut through the rain, shattered glass, brick and plaster dust to land on Alex's chest. Alex was following the coffee table out into the rainy-night when for no other reason except to simply do so, the snipers fired their model 700.308s. The bullets raced nearly side by side, splitting the speed of sound as they greedily chased their red beams into Alex's body. The first projectile tore through his right lung and punched a fist-size hole out his back. After exiting the bullet sliced through the left shoulder of the cop Alex had renamed consable, and then shattered the jar of teeth on the dresser, ending up in the wall of a bathroom three doors down the hall. The second ball of white hot lead had effortlessly decimated Alex's sternum and narrowly missed his heart to continue on its destructive path out his back, barely missing Wolfhart's head by a hair to blast through a young city cop's right eye.

The bullets ripped through his flesh and bone with such force that by all the rights of physics Alex should have been sent flying backward into the charging cops. But, his momentum forward and the determination with which he invoked that momentum could not be stopped or for that matter, slowed. In a silvery shower of rain, shards of glass and blood, Alex followed the coffee table. His plummet had lasted mere seconds; but to him it seemed to go on forever. As he fell his body managed to twist around, permitting Alex to catch a glimpse up at the stupefied expressions on the cops' faces poking their heads out of the big holes he left in his wake. He flipped back around to face the rapidly approaching pavement. Alex had turned just in time to see the table crash against the sidewalk. As it shattered into a thousand bits and pieces he saw Five's right femur bone, which had apparently snapped on impact tear up-out of the flesh. Alex slammed down on top of the jagged bone, sending it straight through his heart. The leg bone of a freak killed him as easily as he and Mr. Bane had sliced the life out of seven-child-molesting monsters.

Alex Julius Stone's death came to him the same way he had lived his life...swift and violent.

Chapter Two

— VILE —

"We are all prostitutes
We are all for sale
We are all pretty candy
We have all gone to
Hell."

Blake Nelson,
—Girl, a novel

The events of Alex's death and the means by which that end occurred had been set in motion long before his late night visit to apartment 49. And, although the sniper's bullets and the seven-story drop had pretty much sealed his somewhat over the top demise in place, it was the ironic fact of landing on top of the pedophile's femur bone that clinched the deal closed. Not only was Five's corpse the actual cause of Alex's death, it was also the key that unbolted a door into a new level of awareness. It began at the exact instant his mortal veil was stripped away by the long, skinless fingers of Mr. Death, casting his exposed soul head-long into darkness and pain.

The sudden stop that eventually follows all falls, great and small, locked onto Alex's Earthly husk so that it remained on its native plain. In that same instance it permitted his new death induced consciousness to tear past into a dismal realm of existence. In his mind, all the pain and awareness of being which he'd come to know and accept, before, during, and after his death simply dropped miraculously through Five's

43

corpse and kept right on falling into a deep void of black space. Alex thought his body was still with him—and in an odd sort of way it was, or at least all the pain and suffering that usually accompanied flesh and bones was still in attendance. He had no idea that his old sack of bones was in fact shattered on that rain and blood soaked sidewalk above him, with a pedophile's leg bone protruding up out of its back.

In his new, after-death skin, he dropped through the pitch. An unimaginable blackness, wrapped so tightly around him that it felt thick and suffocating. Then there was the cold; it was the sort of icy-cold that tricked one's body and mind into believing it actually burned the skin, not froze it. At break-neck-speed, he plummeted straight down, or so it seemed. The dark, cold fall went on and on with no change for what felt like hours to Alex, but in all actuality lasted less than half of a half a second. Quite suddenly Alex's fast fall changed from a downward sensation to that of being yanked hard right, then left, only to be snapped up and right again. He was being violently jerked and flung in more directions than his confused mind could grasp. It was as if he'd been plucked out of his perpendicular descent and slammed into the seat of a roller-coaster comprised solely of sharp turns, erratic rises and precipices. He was in the middle of a swooping descent when Alex was brought to an abrupt halt that was so jolting he thought for a second his neck might have been snapped.

He was being hovered there in the cold blackness completely motionless, wondering what was next. Without warning, he was rocketed, left, right then dropped. He was falling faster, if that was in fact possible, so fast the "G" force pressing against his face felt like thumbs pushing his eyes into the backs of their sockets. Although Alex had never been one for loud verbal out bursts of panic, he thought this horrifying journey through the void warranted some form of fearful cry. He tried to loose some sort of howl, only to learn that he no longer possessed the power of speech. No matter how conscientiously Alex struggled to utter the verbal validation of his fright, he could not.

It wasn't until he came to another neck shocking stop that he heard and felt sound push out of his mouth. A wordless grunt was forced out, as well as most of the air from his lungs due to the sudden cease in motion. The instant after the inadvertent uttering shot past his teeth; the power of will that had taken command of his being slammed his jaws shut, sealing his mouth tighter than nails through the lid of a casket. It was as if he no longer had a mouth at all.

As with before, Alex's sudden break in movement was brief at best. Again he was latched onto and pulled at the insane rate of speed, only this time he was moving backwards. Shortly after his ride in reverse had started, it was brought to a painful stop. Alex's back was thrown against something as hard as petrified bone. His hands were immediately stretched up over his head and his feet pulled down, locking his legs straight. With his limbs wrenched rigid, Alex's wrists and ankles were overlapped. The power holding him in place ground them down onto one another and pressed them against the surface of whatever it was he'd been slammed onto. It wasn't until he felt the burning, piercing sensation stabbing through them and could hear the metallic bang that he realized what was occurring. *I'm being crucified*, screamed his brain in silent horror.

The instant Alex had been stretched out and nailed securely in place his body was assaulted by more agonizing sensations. Thousands of tiny blade like objects simultaneously raked through his skin. They moved downward, cutting everywhere they touched; beginning at his fingertips to his toes, leaving no spot unopened. A voice as sharp as the razors slicing him to the bone whispered in his left ear, its breath icy as it said, "We've waited so-o-o-o very long for your arrival. Welcome home Alex-s-s-s."

The voice faded away deep into his ear like frozen pus. Suddenly the pitch black emptiness imprisoning him was dispelled by an unexpected flash of blindingly, bright light. When Alex's eyes had eventually readjusted, able to focus well enough through the shimmering brilliance he found himself nailed onto a single beam of wood, overlooking a vast expanse of sun-bleached bones. The icy cold bite of the darkness had also been torn away and replaced by blistering heat to match the stinging white light. Alex forced his attention upward, looking past the spike driven flush into his wrists. As his vision struggled beyond the top of the beam it saw a massive sun-like ball of white fire. Again his sight was temporarily blinded by the light of the insanely bright, giant orb hovering directly above his head. The sun burned down on the sea of bones so relentlessly that escape from the star's light and heat was impossible. Not so much as the faintest of shadows could find a seconds rest from its punishing glare. Gazing around at his new surroundings Alex quickly noticed that all of the bones that made up the landscape were human.

As with everything else that had so far occurred, Alex's mouth was dropped open without warning. A flood of blood and bile exploded out, pulling behind it a loud, crackling laughter. His madness echoed out over the flat ocean of skeletal remains with a boom that steadily faded to a voice—his voice, cracking with pain as he uttered a single word, "Hell."

Far, far away from the ocean of bones where Alex was left to slowly roast, and laugh at himself, a smallish being, no more than four and a half feet tall, made his way up to the wide flat surface atop a monstrously huge monolith. The blood-stone and black iron structure rose out of a dense sheet of black vapor and reached straight up into a sky comprised of a dozen or so different shades of red. The reds churned and twisted into countless shapeless forms like a thousand enraged moods mixing and un-mixing, furiously struggling to become a new, never before known breed of anger. The child-size being made his slow, but steady way up the stairs spiraling around the monolith's outermost wall to the platform. The closer to the top he got, the stronger the wind blew. By the time he'd reached the final few steps, the wind had grown to a violent tempest. The howling windstorm, though powerful enough to send an entire army of heavily armored soldiers flying off the monolith, had no effect on the small being. Even his black and red robes which lay smoothly over his thin frame, were undisturbed by the gale. Moving across the time and wind polished, dark-red stone surface, he came to a stop at its edge, the pointed tips of his shiny black boots a hair beyond the bottomless drop-off. Slowly he turned the wide opening of his hood, first left then right, studying the emptiness of that place, carefully looking at something that only he could see. The darkness cast beneath the visor of his hood was so black and void of shape that the space within appeared to be as empty as a bottomless-pit. Eventually it came to rest, facing straight out at the crimson expanse in front of him.

Speaking with the youthful voice of a small boy, he said, "Caretakers of the Empire's nine great realms…Greetings." His tone hadn't been loud or hushed, it held in its inflection no arousal, nor disappointment. His voice was in a word, lifeless.

He moved his arms slightly away from his sides, sliding two ghostly white hands out of his wide sleeves, palms turned out in a welcoming gesture. No reply had been made in response to his greeting.

"Gate Keepers," he cried out, his tone still flat, "the passing of time has once again brought us all to the end of yet another millennium. It's time to play the game."

Unlike before, a deafening chorus of cheering voices erupted up out of the thick sheet of black smoke that surrounded the monolith base. As the roar of an unseen multitude rose, he reached up and took hold of his hood's rim, sliding the heavy black covering off his head of disheveled red hair. The boy child's face that was revealed was so pale and, devoid of pigment that his skin appeared nearly transparent; a face so pasty that one could see the faint lines of dull-blue veins beneath the surface. Although, at first glance he may look to be a child, there is in fact nothing remotely childish about this creature.

His name is Pike, and he owns the esteemed title of Gate Keeper for the Eighth realm; a land of ceaseless screams, invoked by Agony's hands. Pikes' beloved realm of endless suffering is called B'neem, loosely translated, the word means: Children.

Pike is also one of only a few thousand beings referred to as 'The Original Fallen.' He is as ageless as the Gods themselves and possesses amazing powers. One of these gifts is the power to manipulate the flesh and bones of all creatures that have been cast unto his charge for punishment, particularly humans. It is a skill that Pike takes great pride in and manifests in forms of both rapid healing and tormenting. That is, he can mend and torture a being's body, and he can wield this power with no more than a thought.

A pitch black shadow was drawn heavily over his eyes, covering them completely like a pair of dark lensed sun-glasses. The thin strip of darkness melted away like ink in the rain, streaking down his cheeks to be overpowered by the white of his skin, vanishing out of sight. His closed eyes, now uncovered, glowed red through his lids and swiftly increased in intensity until the eyes were burning so brightly past the thin skin, it almost appeared as though he had no eyelids at all. Pike sprang his eyes open with an abrupt jolt. The red flaming brilliance that gave them their glow was so intense that it appeared as though a raging inferno was alight in his skull. He lowered his ignited gaze down toward the black smog and in a loud, strained voice he cried out over the eulogy, "Gate Keepers."

The unseen throng rapidly quieted the cheer, returning the air to silence. Only the howling wind and Pike's words could be heard, as he said, "What say ye fellow Gate Keepers…have ye made your choices? Are the players being made ready to represent each of Hell's realms?"

Pike's question echoed down to fade with repeated reverberation into the darkness below. As his words lost their strength the sky's multifarious shades of red all grew darker and churned more furiously. The small but omnipotent Pike stepped away from the edge, coming to a stop in the middle of the platform. As he awaited the reply to his enquiry the air around him began glowing with a heavy mist of arterial-red, like a fog of blood had arisen to incase him.

Eight black ribbons of vaporous smoke moved out of the tenebrous cloud encompassing the great structure and crept up its smoothly cut stone sides to the top. It didn't take these dark fingers long to pour over the monolith's edge, slithering like black faceless snakes toward Pike. The moment all eight streams of black vapor were closely surrounding him they stopped before the dark-red mist and rose swiftly up into the sky. As with Pike's robes the wind had no effect on the pillars of smoke whatsoever. When they'd reached their desired height of, about twenty feet, they stopped rising and instantly transformed into solid stone.

The eight giant columns of smooth, black rock, towering ominously over Pike began to shift and twist high up on each apex. As the high-pitched sound of shifting hardened stone cut through the howling wind, faces formed, one on the top of each column.

Pike asked, "What say ye?"

The first to offer up a reply was the stone face of a woman who owned an aristocratic air to her features. In an icy tone of voice she said, "The realm of Zaw'naw has made our choice and will have it ready in time."

That said, the first pillar changed back to black smoke, collapsed and slipped back over the edge. Next to speak was the face of an old man, whose eye-sockets were empty, with deep scars gouged in the stone around the shallow pits. "The realm of Ruakh will be ready when the time to begin is at hand."

As with the first column, the Gate keeper for Ruakh collapsed and receded over the platform's edge. The third to voice their readiness was the rock face of a beautiful young woman. She spoke with a thousand whispering voices all at once that seemed to slightly disturb the outer surface of Pike's crimson mist as she said, "The realm of Chemah is prepared to take our place against all others."

One by one the Gate Keepers for the realms of Awtsal, Awnuke, Hinaw, Rata'ach and Beh'fsah, all announced their readiness to participate in the competition. When the last of the pillars had changed back to black smoke and vanished off the platform, Pike pulled his wide hood up over his head and said softly, "B'neem is ready to play the game."

Several months had passed since Pike's visit to the monolith and Alex's arrival to the bone-yard. The colossal sun that hung directly over his head did not set, nor did it rise. The seemingly angry ball of pure-white-fire never moved at all, not so much as an inch. It hovered in one spot, filling the air with shimmering heat. This being the case, the only way for Alex to judge the slow passage of time was by way of his own steady decay. Alex Stone's body and mind slowly rotted on that beam. Hunger and thirst worked without rest side by side with pain and agony to torment him. It's been said; The subtlest torments are quite often the most torturous.

Nailed onto a beam beneath a hateful sun may not seem so subtle to most. But compared to some of the other forms of suffering Hell had to offer, Alex had it easy...so far.

Alex had finally come to accept the perplexing truth that death wasn't coming to save him from the pain and suffering of his dying. As he watched his body dry and rot, his mind crashed into unanswered question after question, like out-of-control bumper-cars spinning off into darkness. Aside from his confusion and the bleached landscape all he had to occupy his mind were the sights and smells of his flesh falling into ruin. The three holes in his chest, two made by the bullets and the other put there by the leg bone, went from wounds glistening red with freshness to blackened, pus-seeping pits. The reek that rose from his decomposition was foul beyond all description. He'd gone from being a strong man with a somewhat focused mind that was when his brain wasn't being filled with the voice of the talking knife, to one with an insanely rotted mind, trapped inside a withered carcass.

The steady festering of Alex's body and mind was only one aspect of his torment in the bone-yard. Another torturous feature to that place was comprised solely of his own memories. They plagued his mind with vicious relentlessness. Not the pleasant re-accountings of good times gone-by. No, poor Alex wasn't aloud to relive the fond rememberings of him and Mr. Bane slashing the life out of human monsters. Nor was he permitted to mentally revisit past times like, when he'd lost his virginity at the age of thirteen to his seventeen year old foster-sister. Or any of the other clumsy groping and awkward misfiring of teenage back seat endeavors. He couldn't recall the sense of total power he'd come to know when he won his first fist-fight, nor could he remember the shame he felt after the euphoric effects of his first shot of speed had worn off. All of those long ago memories were no more. They'd become shadows to him, faint images drowned out of focus by the evil laughter of his drunken parents and the cries for help of his sister Susan.

Susan Ann Stone was two years younger than Alex, almost to the day. She was also the only living being on Earth that he had ever truly loved.

One memory in particular was made to keep repeating in his mind, more so than the thousands of other heart-crushing recollections housed in Alex's mental cabinets. It was paraded past his mind's eye with the antagonistic tenacity of a 'hobo-spider,' only with a more painful bite.

This toxic remembering always began the same; it ripped intrusively into Alex's awareness with a flash of black light. When the dull shine of its dark veil faded it did so with garbled sounds, some fast while others were slowed. Then with the force of a freight-train, images, shadows mostly, rushed into his consciousness. Suddenly, Alex had been sucked so deep into the past that to his mind, he was no longer rotting on a beam in Hell's waiting-room. In comparison, that sea of bones was far less tragic. Alex was wrapped so tightly in the memory that he was for the time of its mental reenactment a nine year old boy again. He had no knowledge or memories of events that would follow this one he was being forced to re-endure. Not the deaths of his parents, not the foster-homes, or his ten years in prison, not even his own demise, it was as if none of those things had ever taken place. All he knew was the horror, fear, and pain that ruled over his early childhood.

The sights and sounds grew steadily into sharper focus with disturbing familiarity. Dirty walls, a dark ceiling and the thunderous sound of foot steps crashing down fearfully close, moved over him. A girl's cries for help—Susan's—! screamed into his awareness. The stinging pain of his hair being tugged on and the feel of the dirty hard-wood floor sliding beneath his naked skin reminded Alex that he was being dragged. Drunken laughter drowned out the cries of his sister and his own for a moment. The crashing sound of the foot steps moved with him as they grew louder. With a sudden flash of icy realization his vision shot up the arm of the hand clutching his hair to see his half naked father dragging him up the long dark hallway of his childhood home. Alex knew unfortunately, where it was that he was being pulled to, but still he felt the need to try and look. He wrenched his head around, his thick black hair knotted in his old man's large fist. With painful effort he caught sight of the wide open closet. It was the cold darkness within, and the open padlock dangling from its swinging latch that bit the deepest into his fright. With a hard jerk, his father flipped the kicking and screaming boy around onto his back.

As more and more of the curtain into his past was pulled open, other events came into a sharper focus. The sound of Susan's cries for his help came rushing in again.

Less than six feet from the closet, he latched onto his father's ankle as it swung past, thrusting his teeth deep into the man's bare foot.

"You little shit!" howled the drunkard.

The desperate attempt to free himself from the monster's grasp worked. "I'll tear out your teeth!" the man cursed as he kicked the boy loose, flinging his little body hard against a wall. Alex got swiftly to his feet; the cigarette burns on his naked soles from an earlier encounter with his old man were still raw. But Susan's cries overpowered the stinging pain seared into the tender skin.

"Please mommy no, no. I'll be good! Alex! Alex don't let them hurt me! ALEX!" Susan cried.

The lumbering drunk's lurching hands grabbed for the boy, but Alex was too fast for his stumbling efforts. Alex ducked and dodged his father's sloppy attempts, the large hands swooping down, missing their target. Avoiding capture, Alex managed to spin around the man, who had in turn given up the pursuit, stumbling off toward the living room, mumbling something under his breath. At the far end of the hallway he saw Susan. She was being pulled toward the open doorway of their parent's bedroom by their nearly nude mother. The woman shrieked out with a blast of intoxicated laughter intertwined with a slurred, mocked child's voice, saying, "Come, come, come little monkey...come play with mother!"

In one fist the lush clutched the little girl's long black hair, in the other hand an open bottle of beer. As mother struggled to get the child into the room she spilled foamy beer everywhere. Susan had grabbed onto the bedroom's door-jamb with both hands, screaming for dear life. The cackling lush wasn't having it, dead set on the child bending to her will; she raised her naked foot and kicked the desperate little girl's grip loose.

Alex was a few short inches from snatching his sister's reaching hand. Their frightened voices screamed simultaneously as the laughing woman jerked Susan away, tearing her into the darkness of that horrible room. The door slammed shut in Alex's face and his heart, a heart that knew little of joyous things, nearly stopped in mid beat when he heard the hollow click of the lock being latched. A loud slap cracked out through the door, followed by another and another. Susan's terrified tears struggled to choke out words, but her breathless fright and pain would only permit quick, stuttered gasps for air.

"Leave her alone!" Alex yelled through the door, beating his hands against it with all his might. He was so lost in what he was trying to do, and his mind's focus locked solely on the horrid events beyond the door, he'd forgot to watch his own back. Alex never saw the heavy brass belt-buckle whistling down through the darkness toward his head. It caught him with a brain numbing blow behind his left ear. Alex was knocked against the door, and slid down to his knees, quickly pulling himself into a fetal-position in his best attempt to shield his already bruised parts with his bare arms and back. Alex almost couldn't hear the drunk's booming laughter over the pain induced buzzing in his head, much less the sharp whistle of the belts' follow up to its first assault. The strikes were falling faster and harder and the numbness from the first few blows had stepped aside so that Alex could feel the full issue of the beating.

As the onslaught grew more and more intense, each stinging stripe shooting deeper than those before it, Alex surrendered. Without being told to do so by the task-master delivering the punishment, he managed to summon forth enough strength to pull himself over the floor into the closet. Without a word the drunk slammed the door, imprisoning the boy in that dark and cold, cramped space.

The faint cries of his sister were for a moment silenced by his own horror when he heard the almost echoing *click*, of the padlock being snapped shut, sealing him in until one or both of his monster-parents saw fit to let him out...for only God knew what.

Susan's pleas for it to end found their way back into Alex's helplessness again. As did the sounds of his father's foot steps receding back down the hall. There was a hard knocking sound, mixed with that of the drunk's barked order "Let me in Ruth!" The door into the bedroom opened then swiftly closed.

Alex's head was still throbbing, bloody wetness streaming down his neck and back. Everywhere on his body he touched, from his shoulders to his legs he felt the hot rise of swollen welts. As his fingers moved trembling over his raw wounds he silently sobbed. His attention was torn away from his own pain by a long muffled scream. He stumbled up to his feet, his legs weak and shaking as he began beating on the door as furiously as his fists would allow. Yelling at the top of his lungs, he demanded that they leave Susan alone. Alex kept it up for as long as he could, which wasn't very long, before giving up to despair. He collapsed to the floor and pressed himself into a tight ball, pulling his knees up against his chest, and wrapping his arms around them to lock them in place. As he sat in that cold darkness, the copper taste of his blood fresh on his tongue and the strong odor of moldy urine soaked into the wood floor, he rocked slowly side to side and sobbingly whispered a brief prayer, he begged "God, help us please...Amen."

But the ears of the Gods weren't open to hear the heart-melting pleas of terrified children, not that night or any other night in Alex's and Susan's tragic lives. No, this little boy and his sister were on their own.

Alex and Susan's childhood was, to say the least, the stuff of nightmares, and their adult lives weren't all that great either, especially Susan's.

The memory of that night with his parents ended only to begin again and again and again. That's what Alex's time nailed to that beam consisted of; pain, rotting and nightmarish rememberings. That is until things took an abrupt turn.

Alex's mind had only just returned to the bone yard from the closet of his childhood when a voice, a child's voice said, "Hello Mr. Stone."

For the first time in months Alex raised what was left of his head. The slow, jerky movement to look around shot sharp needles of pain up and down his spine that swiftly spread throughout the rest of his body. He had barely enough strength and self-will to hold his head up and glance at the shimmering landscape. Seeing nothing of the youthful voice's owner, he returned his head to its limp angle at the end of his withered neck. For a moment he wondered if Mr. Bane was back, masked in a child's voice for whatever reason. Or maybe his old friend was lost, trapped in that cold, black limbo, fighting to find the way out? No, without the tingle of the dagger's presence kicking about in the lingering residue of Alex's decaying soul, he dismissed the hopeful notion of Bane's return as more of the punishment packages that came with the place. He was being drawn back toward the drunken laughter of his parents, the feelings of childhood despair bleeding into his awareness when the voice pulled him back to the bone-yard. In a soft tone it said, "Yes, you hear me Mr. Stone."

Alex didn't bother with raising his head this time. He was certain that the voice wasn't his old pal Mr. Bane. Alex was sure the voice saying to him, 'Yes, you hear me Mr. Stone' was nothing more than the remaining fragments of his sanity taking the final leap off the razor's edge into madness. Alex choked out what was in his mind a chuckle, but really only sounded like a diseased cat struggling to cough out a fur ball. Then silently mouthed, 'Blah-blah-blah'. His body heaved with searing pain. It raked up his spine and shot into his skull where it thrashed around a bit before racing back down. In the time it takes a wolf's teeth to rip through the tender flesh of a new-born, the pain tore back up into his brain where its throb eventually died away.

"Never mock me," Pike's voice advised.

A section of the bones below Alex had begun to shift and actually melt. A perfectly round portion of the bones transformed into a creamy white, semisolid muck. The thick ooze swiftly changed from white to pink, darkening to a deep red pool. Suddenly all of the maggots dining on Alex's decay, wiggled out of the festering wounds covering his body, to nose diving like thousands of tiny lemmings following one another off a cliff. At first the grubs appeared to be escaping his blackened flesh, but were in fact dropping out to show respect to their master's arrival. Slowly rising up out from the center of the red pool, his robes and hooded outer garment completely dry and clean, was Pike. As he moved up, the maggots, already drying in the sun, lowered their tiny black heads like obedient dogs bowing to a wolf. The moment Pike had fully risen, the pool returned to white bones. Alex looked down at the smallish hooded figure, all the while believing that he'd either fully succumb to the blinding heat and the stench of his own rotting flesh, or the Devil was in fact a munchkin. Too worn-down by pain to be afraid or amazed, he simply watched the small being moved awkwardly over the skulls, ribcages and various other bones toward the beam's base. Facing his hood's opening up at Alex, Pike stopped directly beneath him and in a prideful voice introduced himself, "I am Pike, and this place is Hell. But I've no doubt you've already figured that out. You, Mr. Stone, will do well to do exactly as you're told, and do so without question. I absolutely loath questions and hate being interrupted even more, so there will be none of it."

Pike concluded his short speech with a sharp clap of his hands. A flash of blue light exploded out of his crashing palms, instantaneously transporting Alex, beam and all out of the bone-yard. Before his sight recovered from Pike's explosion of light, Alex loosed a loud cry. It was the first time in months he'd been able to utter anything other than mumbled sounds of madness and pain. His vision first focused out of the fuzzy blindness onto the color red, lots of it. The bone covered ground had been replaced by a floor of dark-red sand. As he painfully looked for the hooded visitor his attention found the sky. It was the same stormy mantel of swirling reds as that over the monolith. Looking back down to gaze out at the desert of crimson sand he saw Pike standing before the beam's base. Although Pike's threat not to speak was still fresh in his mind, Alex figured he'd test the water. In a voice weak and shaky he asked, "So, are you the Devil?"

"Already you prove your foolishness," Pike said.

Alex was barely able to hear Pike's words beyond the pain the Gate Keeper raked into his bones. Blood, black with rot pushed out between his clinched teeth, and oozed out of his eyes, nostrils and ears. The pain was so harsh, that his sight was plunged into darkness. Pike's words were so faint behind the humming sound in Alex's throbbing brain that only a few managed to wriggle through into his awareness.

"That—the—chance—allow. Don't—again!"

Alex felt his wrists and ankles being torn from the spikes nailing him to the beam, followed by his body being flung through the air and dropped unceremoniously in a heap on the warm sand. The pain ended almost as abruptly as it had begun. Alex's vision was swiftly restored with only a few blinks of his eyelids. He slowly pushed up onto his knees and after a moment of unsteadiness, he managed to rise up and straighten his back. Looking up at the red sky and realizing no pain came with the movement, he rolled his head around on his neck, then raising his hands to rub his shoulders; he noticed they were healed. The holes through his wrists, his sliced to the bone fingers, and the blackened rot of decay—were all gone. Not only his hands, but his entire body from his head to his toes was mended. Alex gazed down at himself, his mind filled with a sense of mystified wonder. He ran his hands over his skin, patting at his arms, chest and face in disbelief. Other than his skin color being as white as a bloodless cadaver, all of his prison tattoos completely wiped away, and the fact that not a single hair could be felt anywhere on his body, Alex was as healthy and physically-fit as he'd been the night of his death.

Standing, he looked around, searching for the little fellow to thank him, all the while wondering at what price that make-over would demand.

"Turn around Mr. Stone," Pike instructed.

Alex swiftly did as he was told and standing in front of the wooden beam stood his short, hooded host. Raising his hand Pike motioned toward a neatly folded pile of clothes and said, "Put those garments on, and then walk." Alex stepped hesitantly over to the clothes, and if not for the fact that his rotted carcass had been miraculously made whole and strong again he never would have believed what he was looking at. The clothing at his feet, from his fedora to his work-boots was all the same things he'd worn the night of his death. As he stared down at them, he made the foolish mistake of asking, "Walk where?"

Alex was suddenly nailed back onto the beam, his body returned to its festering state. After a few moments of screaming in great pain beneath the blinding brightness of the torturous sun in the bone-yard, he was brought back to the red desert. Standing on the same spot, looking down at the clothes, he heard Pike say, "You don't listen well. Put on the garments and walk."

Alex, catching his breath, and shaking off the pain and horror of being back in that horrid bone-yard, looked around for Pike, and not seeing the pint-sized tormenter anywhere, he got into his old work clothes still heavily stained with Five's and his blood. Alex quickly checked his pockets and found them all to be empty. No lock pick case, no cigarettes or zippo, nothing. With his boots laced up tight, and his gloves pulled snugly onto his hands, Alex put on his hat, ran his thumbs and forefingers along the brim. Then without taking time to choose a direction Alex did as he was told to do and began walking out into the red desert.

Many thousands of miles away, is the Empire's sixth realm entitled Zaw'naw. The place in damnation where only the lustfully sadistic are sent to eternally scream and bleed. At around the same time Alex began his long hot journey across Hell's Blood-Sand-Desert, a large gold and black skinned lesser angel named Babur was stooping down to pass through a stone doorway into a darkened, throne room. Once inside the great chamber Babur went down onto his hands and knees, as all lesser angels were required to do when entering these double doors. Babur the Merciless, as he was known by his fellow tormenters, was feared by all of those damned who were under his charge to make suffer, and respected by all of the other lesser angels. But now, he crawled across the floor like a frightened human soul, into the throne room of his Queen.

The moment he entered the dimly-lit chamber, he immediately noticed that the temperature had dropped far below freezing. Babur's breath froze to a visible vapor that fell heavily to the frost covered granite floor. The great tormenter had barely managed to crawl six feet, when his great horned head was latched onto by the power of will belonging to the one who'd summoned him. The angel's massive head was yanked up so forcefully that he hardly had time to utter a grunt of surprise. Faster than it had been torn up, his head was slammed face-first against the icy floor. Blood, thick and dark poured freely now from his nostrils and mouth, to becoming frozen red droplets. The silken voice of a woman drifted down through the black air. Even the stone and iron walls put off a sense of imminent doom as her words moved toward the squirming giant.

"You've truly proven your worth to me these past few days... Babur."

Again his head was yanked up and smashed back down. As he was dragged over the sharp stone floor by the power of his Queen's will, he tried to plead for mercy. But before he could loose a single syllable, she willed his tongue out of his throat and transported it down into one of the cut worm pits beyond her palace walls. Dragging him across the floor to an abrupt stop, she raised him straight into the air. Higher and higher he rose, all the while kicking wildly and gagging out choking sounds as if he was being hoisted up by an invisible rope tied around his neck. He was eventually brought to a painful stop no less than a hundred feet above the floor. Babur's hovering body was being steadily turned, as the huge iron doors crashed shut, his rotating slowed and stopped to face the approach of a throne of sorts. It floated toward him with nothing but the mental will of the being that used it as a symbol of her iron fisted rule over the sixth realm. It was a truly morbid sight, this seat of sadistic power, made solely of the contorted bodies of naked men and women. Fourteen bodies in all, every one of them still living helplessly as their arms, legs, chests, and heads twisted and bent through one another in a woven mass of skin and bone. The throne was one of only two things in that chamber which wasn't heavily laden with a layer of ice. The other was regally seated upon it. Her name was Vile, and she is the self-appointed Queen of Hell's sixth realm. Before crowning herself Zaw'naw's ruler, her title was that of Gate Keeper and still acted as such when necessary.

Vile is a lithesome creature, beautiful in a fallen angel sort of way. She wears her long flaming red hair pulled straight back, tightly against her scalp, revealing proudly her high forehead. The thick scarlet strands drop listlessly down her slender back like dark-red liquid moving slowly over white marble. Vile's eyes, as with the eyes of all Gate Keepers, glow red, and the creamy white color of her skin, as well as the black eyeliner which frames them gives her an ancient, statuesque appearance. Her lips are full in shape and also painted black. She has the high cheek bones of a goddess, a small slightly curved nose, and a strong but not too sharply shaped chin. There are no lines or wrinkles which could reveal a clue as to Vile's ageless existence. She preferred to move about her palace nude, though she would sometimes don her battle armor or a long black translucent gown when traveling the sixth realm's city Ebla.

As Vile hovered toward the painfully suspended angel, she willed him closer to meet her approaching throne. She rested comfortably back against her living seat as it came to a steady stop only a few feet from the twitching tormenter. With an empty expression draped over her ghostly-white face, she leaned forward a bit and gazed deeply into the visible depths of his suffering.

"I'm sorry to say that I am unable to pay you the true price of your worth," she whispered, "being that nothing dies in Hell."

Babur's mind was fighting desperately to break free of Vile's mental death-grip, but his body was as useless to his brain's commands as a cadaver would be on a dance floor.

"But, dear Babur, I've a prize for you that's nearly as valuable as a prolonged and painful death. Yes, I'm going to reward you with all those truly wonderfully grim experiences that my realm has to offer one such as yourself. And, the best part is that I myself shall yield all of them up to you. Yes angel, and I will do so again and again and for example...again."

She willed her throne close enough to see her reflection on the moist surface of his glistening black eyes. Gazing past his suffering onto the tiny reflective image of her face, she noticed a bit of askew black face paint on the corner of her mouth. Leaning slightly closer, she tried although with little success to ignore the strong odor of bitter-root emanating from Babur's open mouth. She scraped the tiny black flake away with the sixth finger of her right hand and wiped it off on the end of Babur's pug nose.

"That's what you're worth! A punishment not far removed from that of a damned human soul. Good for only showing others the countless ways Zaw'naw possesses to torture flesh."

Babur's body was suddenly stretched rigid. The sounds of bones popping and skin ripping moved out of his vibrating mass. Vile sent unseen blades racing up and down his spine. She leaned back in her throne, widened her gaze, causing his entire skeleton to grow excruciatingly hot. The layer of ice, already frozen red with his blood, that had formed over his thick hide melted and dripped toward the floor, only to freeze again before landing. Vile loosened her grip enough to allow him some kicking and jerking. Reaching up, he grabbed and clawed at his throat, like someone trying to force their fingers behind a noose. The once proud Babur now resembled someone having second thoughts about killing themselves after already kicking the bucket out from under their feet. Giggling softly to herself, Vile slowly increased her hold on his throat. In a voice devoid of any warmth of life whatsoever she said, "I've grown weary of this game."

In the blink of a harpy's eye, and with the force of a million screams from a billion dark-dreams, Vile's power of will twisted Babur's head sharply to the left snapping his neck with a loud *crack*! The swift snapping sound rang out through the darkened chamber, finding its way past the closed doors to echo down the outer corridor.

Vile willed the twitching body down a bit, closer to her so that she could study the lesser angel's agony, which was still alive, trapped in his paralyzed carcass. She gently stroked the side of his face, and then drove all six of her long fingernails deep into Babur's flesh, smiling secretly as she marveled at his slightly quivering eyelids. Knowing he could hear her, she whispered directly into his ear, "You're going to simply *love* the two escorts I've chosen to show you to your new home. A home by the way, that I've personally invested a lot of my own imagination and time preparing for your arrival."

That said Vile blew him a soft kiss, sending him hurtling backward to slam against the far wall where he slid down its rock surface, dropping to the floor like a wet sack of dung. With a whispered breath, Vile mouthed "Black, Blue…out now."

Leaping out of the shadows that draped the iron pillars on either side of the throne room's great hall were two massive dog-like creatures.

To those who like to employ their services they're referred to as 'Shadow Hounds' and to those who find themselves staring into the beast's gaping jaws, they're Demons. The hairless, toothy hell hounds landed hard at a sliding halt, their long claws crashing onto the frozen stone like blades. The moment they came to a stop the beasts spun about, panning their beady eyed vision swiftly through the darkness, scanning it past Babur's broken heap, then snapping their sight up onto their master. As Black and Blue eagerly awaited Vile's go-ahead sign their reptile like mouths eased open, allowing their gray tongues to flop out. Their nostrils flared wildly as they salivated. The scent of freshly wounded meat was strong in the air and Black and Blue wanted it. Vile gave each a smiling glance, her expression almost like that of a loving mother as she gestured with both hands and softly said, "Feed."

Their razor sharp claws shot hollow clicking noises echoing out with each step. Babur's shattered, paralyzed, very much conscious state of being, with all five of his senses still in perfect working order, could do nothing but lay there and watch. The two beasts gnashed their jaws together with fast air biting snaps as they approached. Their large muscular bodies twitched with every movement, popping and flexing like ebullient unborn serpents, struggling furiously to rip out of a fleshy prison. What circumscribe amount of light managed to find infinitesimal ways into the chamber's darkness, moved spastically against their tight jade-green skin as if the softest touch of incandescence caused them stinging pain. Babur's eyes and ears, trapped open wide, listened and stared as the two monsters made a fast meal of him. They tore into his flesh as if he was the first real nourishment they'd had in centuries. Like two giant crocodiles Black and Blue fought to get a greater issue than the other, snapping at one another between bites. No sooner would they bolt down one large hunk of the angel and they were ripping off the next swallow. Vile clapped her hands softly together, gleefully cheering her pets on, raising her voice louder than her usually controlled whispered tone.

"Yes...yes! Good boys, eat the malingerer. Gobble him all-l-l-l, up!"

Within a few minutes Black and Blue had devoured every bit and scrap of the seventeen foot tall, thirteen-hundred pound angel's flesh and bones. They scraped up the blood that had frozen solid, and quickly gobbled it down like crimson snow-cones. All that was left to show that Babur had ever been in Vile's throne room was a faint tint of frozen blood high up on the wall where she'd dashed him. But the lesser angel's torture wasn't even remotely over, no, not by a long shot. In fact his suffering had only just begun. Alive, but definitely not well, Babur was very much aware, in every sense of the word; aware, that he was being digested in the bellies of the beasts. Not only was he conscious mentally, he could also sort of see, hear and most importantly feel. As Vile had said, 'nothing dies in Hell'.

In a few days Black and Blue would go deep into the inner most bowels of Vile's palace dungeon and defecate the angel's remains out in one of the many pits. Once there Babur's flesh and bones would steadily re-animate, becoming whole again only to be tortured in much more imaginative ways then being eaten alive by Shadow Hounds and shat out into a pit.

The two beasts didn't so much as offer up a grateful glance to their Queen. They sniffed at the cold air, and then briefly checked over the floor. Finding nothing of interest, the two beasts broke into a run and leapt up to vanish in the shadows draped down the wall.

Vile was riding her throne of tangled bodies back up into the frigid darkness, feeling pleased with herself like someone completing a cherished task, satisfied she'd done an adequate job of it. With only the faint music of screams from the damned drifting up out of the vast city below, she settled back. Vile was slipping comfortably back to her day-dreams, when the expedition into her mind's play-grounds were intrusively interrupted by a thick voice.

"I beg a brief moment of your priceless time my Queen," he said.

In a whisper, so softly spoken that Vile herself could barely hear her own words, she asked, "What is it?"

"I've located the female my Queen. I wish to bring it to you."

"So you say? Babur was just here, only his hands were empty," she giggled. "I'll allow you your audience. However, if by some chance it proves disappointing, all of your groveling will not change your fate. Come Warfarin lets see what you think you have."

That said Vile dripped a tiny drop of spittle out, catching it on the pointed tip of her fingernail. The instant the glistening string of spit broke loose from her lips to form a tiny white ball on the nail; she flung it off, sending it flying out into the darkness. It hit the floor, immediately bursting into a tiny white flame that swiftly grew to a swirling vortex of fire. The spinning wheel of flames steadily slowed the pace of its movement, going from white to a darker and darker shade of red in the process. When its turning slowed to a stop and it had grown dark to the point of appearing black, it rose from its horizontal angle coming to rest at an upright position.

"Enter," Vile commanded.

A high, shiny black, renaissance boot stepped out of the blackish pool of fire, pulling with it a tall figure cloaked and hooded in heavy black robes. The moment he was fully through, the portal transformed back into a tiny white ball of frozen spit and fell to the floor as Vile's visitor went to his knees. Seeing that no human female was with him, Vile growled, "I see empty hands."

Warfarin's heart jumped with alarm. His brain commanded, *Quick, say something you fool*! But his mouth wasn't fast enough. The words were racing up his throat only to be crammed back down by the power of Vile's disappointment. Warfarin was yanked up into the air, and as his feet left the floor, his thin bladed sword was torn from its sheath by her mind's reach, and shot into her waiting hand. She snatched it by its grip and half studied it as she moved toward Warfarin. He was brought to an abrupt stop much the same way Babur had been, and dangled before Vile on her throne.

"Speak to me Warfarin, and pray you say the words that will spare you much discomfort."

With a trembling finger and a quivering voice, he pointed down at a small brown, leathery pouch and said, "I transformed her to ash, due to the long journey to you."

Vile's vision followed the direction of his bony finger. She willed Warfarin close enough to reach out and pull the little pouch out of his sash. Needing the use of her other hand as well, she stabbed the long thin blade of Warfarin's sword into the back of one of the bodies that made her throne. "Hold this a bit," she said under her breath. Vile made a fast hand gesture, turning Warfarin's back to her. Still unwilling to release him, she snickered and said, "You're not out of the cold yet. Let's see what you've brought, and whether I'm pleased or I'm not, I'll deal with you...Inquisitor."

She carefully pulled the pouch open, and after a quick peek inside she emptied a small pile of the light-gray ash out onto the open palm of her right hand.

"What is your name?" Vile asked softly.

Tiny sparklers of green, blue, white and yellow light rose slowly up out of the ash. They swirled lazily above and around the slag. The star-like points of colored light drifted steadily back down into the gray powder. Almost as soon as they vanished the pile of ash began to shift into several noticeable shapes in Vile's palm. Like a handful of living dust it struggled to become something specific. One second it formed the tip of a human finger, next a nose, then an eye and a big toe. After transforming into a few more small body parts, the handful of ash finally found its desired shape. A woman's mouth grew out of the dust, lips, gums, teeth, and even a tongue. When it located it's sought after form it answered Vile's question. In a voice filled with deep agony it said, "R-R-Ru-th, Ruth St-St, Stone…Ruth Stone."

Vile showed her own teeth in a wide, wild-eyed grin, something she almost never did. She asked a second question, "Who murdered you?"

The teeth in the mouth of ash gnashed together, clinching tightly as the lips peeled quiveringly back in a display of seething hatred. Vile, not interested in a show of deep loathing, asked her question again, her tone sharply impatient, "Say the name of your killer!"

The reply came behind a low hissing rattle, and was spoken past clenched teeth, "My son."

"His name! Say the name!" Vile demanded.

"Alex Julius Stone," growled the ash.

Satisfied that the search was finally at an end, Vile blew the mouth in her palm a gentle kiss. The mouth crumbled back to a formless mass of gray dust as it whispered the words *"No more pain, mercy, mercy…mercy."*

"Serve me well and your suffering will end," Vile promised under her breath. She carefully poured every single flake back into the pouch and pulled its draw-string tight, closing Ruth Stone's remains inside.

Vile turned Warfarin around to face her, at the same time she pulled his sword out of the fleshy back of her arm-rest and asked, "What is this thing you've brought into my chamber?" She poked the swords tip against his chest as she loosed her hold enough to let him speak.

"It's a sword," he choked out, "it belonged to the human called Niccolo Machiavelli. I'd won it in a game of chance."

Vile giggled girlishly as she examined the rapier's thin blade.

"A sword, you don't say? Not much of a blade, a bit light. This Machiavelli must be a child; why else would he wish to wield a weapon as puny as this."

She poked the blade's tip teasingly into Warfarin's ribs a few times. Then without a word of explanation as to why, she drove the blade straight up into his throat and out the top of his head.

Willing her throne back away from the twitching Grand Inquisitor for her realm, the sword stabbed through his skull, she released her hold on him. Warfarin dropped toward the floor, but before he was to hit, Vile froze him solid through and through. His body shattered into a thousand random shards of icy flesh and frozen bone.

Vile waved her hand casually, sending every last chip and piece of his body, along with his sword far from her realm. Holding the pouch out she gazed almost lovingly at it, cocked her head slightly to the left and whispered, "Warfarin's idea to transform you into human slag was a good one. Yes, Miss Stone. It's given me an idea of my own."

A boy of nine years crept alongside an old sofa. In his small, but steady fist was a long double edged knife. Pulled down over his sun-deprived face was a taut mask of ominous need. He slowly raised his badly bruised, naked self to his feet, standing directly over his sleeping father. The unconscious, child-beating monster's head lay stretched up and across the armrest, leaving his sweaty neck completely exposed. All of the important arteries and veins protruded nicely out against the inside of his skin, like bulging lines openly guiding all who gaze upon them, the best way leading to the man's death. With no further consideration, and without the slightest display of reluctance, the boy raised the knife, holding it firmly in both hands, positioning its blade a centimeter above his father's throat. The instant the cold steel touched the right side of the man's neck his pale, green eyes sprang open in time to see the red stream of his blood jet out to splatter across his son's face.

Taking a few steps back away from his old man, who had immediately clasped his hands over the deep wound, the boy watched intently, a cold expression of wide-eyed interest shadowing his face. Blood escaped easily out from between the man's fingers in the form of thin spurting jets. To the boy's surprise the blade had been sharper than he'd expected. Not only had it sliced through the carotid artery as well as the jugular vein, it had also cleaved cleanly through the esophagus and windpipe. The man stood only to slip on his spilt blood while attempting to take a threatening step toward his son. Falling back to the sofa and after only a few more failed attempts to get back up, he stopped fighting the inevitable inception of his death. A rush of blood cascaded from the five inch long gash the moment he let his hands drop on his blood soaked lap. As all color drained from the man's face, his expression changed from seething rage, framed in a cast of terror, to complete resignation. His head fell limply back on the couch's backrest, his faint breathing through the severed windpipe slowed to a stop. The boy stared in a state of silent accomplishment as he watched his father's eyelids and lower lip quiver a bit, then stop. Wayne Blew Stone was dead.

The boy stood there, quietly studying the man who would never lay another hand, or any other body-part on him or his sister again. The boy was neither pleased nor saddened by what he'd done; he felt no shame or guilt, no joy nor fear. It was nothing more than a chore that needed doing, one not unlike shoveling up dog poop, only a lot easier and with no resentment held for the task.

He set all of his attention out, listening intently to the sounds of the large house, targeting most of his hearing strength toward the downstairs' bathroom. Hearing nothing that would give him cause for alarm, he allowed a crooked grin to tug at the corner of his mouth as he increased his grip on the knife's bone handle.

"The lush heard nothing, she's still out, locked in a drunken-stupor," whispered the metallic voice that had befriended the boy while he wept in the cold darkness of the closet. "Do as we discussed and all will be as it should. The shoes," reminded the voice.

The boy stepped over to the corpse, being careful not to step in the blood. He went to his knees in front of the man's feet. But he would need both hands to remove the black hard leather wing tips from the feet. That meant setting the knife down, something he was unwilling to do. For some reason, he felt certain that if he put his weapon down, even if only for an instant, his new found courage would fall away.

"It's alright my dear boy," hissed the voice, "I'm with you now, and I'll always be with you. We have a deal, and I never break my word...not to my friends. We are friends...arn't we?"

"Yes," whispered the boy.

"Of course we are my boy. Go on put down the dagger so that we may continue. Remove its shoe's."

"Okay...okay."

He laid the knife down next to his right knee, although still a bit hesitantly. It took some careful maneuvering, but he eventually got the shoes off. A wave of pride rushed warmly through him when he saw the deep bite mark he'd left there less than ten hours earlier, still fresh on the sockless foot. With both shoes in his left hand, and the knife in his right, he stood. Only he'd pushed up too quickly and slipped, falling in the blood. So much for staying out of the sticky stuff. With blood smeared all over his back and left leg now, he sensed the onset of panic whispering out of his rapidly beating heart.

"It's nothing," the voice said, "we'll think of something...I promise."

Again he got up, shook the panic out and resumed his task. Leaving a trail of bloody, bare foot-prints in his wake, the boy left the living room into the hallway. Without stopping, he glanced over his shoulder, looking at the pad locked closet. Taking a break from their perverse savagery, the boy's parents decided to take him out of the closet, tossing the girl in for a while.

"One down Susan, and one more to go," the boy said softly.

He set his sights back around, locking all of his senses onto the bathroom's door, or moreover, the fiend beyond it. Stepping up to the slightly ajar baby-blue door, he stopped to set the shoes down on the floor outside the bathroom and listened. The only sounds he heard were that of his mother's passed-out drunk breathing and the rhythmic, muffled thuds of his heart beating. With knife in hand, he peeked in through the thin space between the open door and its jamb. One of her arms was slung limply out of the tub as if she were already dead. A nearly empty bottle of beer was grasped loosely in her slender fingers, ready to slip out and fall to the dirty, white tile floor at any second. The boy quickly pushed the door inward with his right shoulder, sending a long squeak out through the house. For an instant, it almost sounded as if something was warning of trouble on the hoof. There was a sudden splashing of water, followed by the hollow clunk of the beer bottle hitting the floor.

"Damn you Wayne! I told you to—".

The startled, angry words of the woman, whose nap had been shattered, were sharply interrupted the moment she leaned over the rim of the tub to glance at the opening door. She barely managed to get out one short scream, when she saw her naked, blood-splattered son stepping swiftly in, her husbands knife blood smeared and raised in the boy's hands. Throwing herself back, away from the falling blade, her hand slipped off the wet porcelain rim, helping to give the blade its first bite. The boy sent all ten inches of steel into the tender flesh between the right clavicle bone and her neck. No sooner had he tore the blade back out, he was sending it right back down, stabbing it through the skin covering her right cheek bone. She tried grabbing at the knife, but quickly learned how foolish an idea that was. The moment she clasped her right hand around the blade, the boy slashed it loose as easily as pulling it out of water, cutting two fingers off in the process. All she could do was try and avoid the falling blade. She even attempted to raise a foot and kick at the boy, but all she got for her trouble was the blade being thrust through the foot, and her kneecap laid open as the leg retreated. She pressed herself into the rear of the tub against the corner. There was no escaping the back and forth, up and downward assault of the slicing blade. She tried to block her son's feverish attack, vainly trying to protect her more vital body parts, namely her face, throat and chest, shielding herself with her already cut to the bone forearms. All she managed to accomplish was to offer up more snacks for the blade, giving its edge a little something to nibble on before allowing it to dine upon the main-course. With the power of his fury, fueled by years of abuse and his nightmarish memories still fresh in his mind, the boy took complete control of the moment. Within a few seconds, the boy's mother's pleas and sobs for mercy faded away. He stabbed and slashed at her as she slid slowly down the wall, sinking into the scarlet bath-water. After some final twitching movements, Ruth Rose Stone was following her husband on her cold, dark ride to Hell. Her dead husk lay half submerged, her remaining blue-gray eye staring over the wet surface at her killer as he continued stabbing her postmortem. It wasn't until his arms had grown too heavy and fatigued that he finally stopped.

"Well done my boy," verbally stroked the boy's new, perhaps only friend other than his sister. "Yes…well done indeed. Now let us finish up here, my brave, brave lad."

The metallic voice melted away behind the boy's fast, heavy panting, fading eventually to silence. He stared at her a few moments longer, then like a machine, he turned his gaze away from Ruth's wide-eyed death stare and went to the sink. He washed his hands some then stepped around to the toilet and removed its heavy porcelain water-tank lid. The boy was doing his absolute best to follow the plan he and the voice had discussed in the darkness. So far, he'd done everything right to the letter. He dropped the bloody murder weapon into the tank, watching as it sank swiftly to the bottom with a hollow clunk. The plan was to stash it there for safe keeping until he could come back for it on a later date. The boy then replaced the tank lid, and turned to the next step. He picked up the spilt bottle of beer and after dipping it into the red bathwater, filling it full; he took it into the living room and poured the bloody stuff out onto his father's corpse. With that done, he went back to the bathroom and tossed the empty bottle in the tub. He snatched up the shoes outside the door and placed one snugly on each fist. With the wingtips on his hands, he went down onto his knees and pressed the shoes heel to toe into the blood puddles on the floor surrounding the tub. When the soles were adequately covered, he carefully left a bloody trail from the bathroom to the living room sofa. Once he'd put the shoes back on his father's feet, the boy went around to the back of the sofa and brought out the Old Hickory butcher knife that he'd stashed there earlier. He took the kitchen knife into the bathroom and without the slightest disinclination, he started stabbing and slicing on the dead body of his mother. Finished with that phase of the plan, the boy left her corpse without so much as a farewell glance. Back in the living room, the boy carefully turned his father's right hand over, palm up and pressed the butcher knife's wooden hand-grip down hard against the dad man's hand, wrapping the thumb and fingers tightly around it. Locking the closed fist in place, the boy took a hold of the butt of the knife's grip firmly and with a mighty yank, pulled the knife's blade backward out of the corpse's fist. Opening the hand, the boy was pleased to see a deep cut laid across all four fingers. The voice had told the boy that hilt-less knives sometimes leave deep cuts like this due to slipping while stabbing something or someone. His disembodied friend had also made mention of the fact that the police would undoubtedly be looking for such a wound. After resting the phony murder/suicide weapon in his father's lap, the boy got his jeans and headed down into the basement. The reason as to why he'd carried out this duty in the buff was also the voice's idea. It had told the boy that the blood splatter and spatter patterns from an attack have a particular signature all their own, a finger print that's impossible to wipe away or cover up. Such a blood signature would definitely find a home for itself in clothing.

In the basement he took a thorough shower, cleaning all the blood out of his thick black hair, and even out from under his finger and toenails. Drying off, he slipped into his old, unwashed blue-jeans then cleaned any and all signs that he'd been down there that morning. The boy hated to do what had to happen next, especially after such a painstaking shower. But it would be easier than trying to explain the reasons for his bloody bare foot prints back and forth, from the livingroom to the bathroom. Not to mention the obvious proof that someone small had fell on his nine year old butt in the blood.

He went back up into the living room, still bare foot and shirt-less, and purposely slipped in the blood. He did this, once in the living room, and once in the bathroom. The boy didn't need the voice to tell him how hard it would be attempting to explain his foot prints, as well as the signs of his earlier tumble. No, this was easier. It would go something like this; *It was dark, it's always dark, that's how mommy likes it. I heard mommy scream, then she was quiet. I was scared, I went to see what was wrong…mommy's face was bleeding, and she wouldn't answer. I got scared and fell, I fell when I saw daddy too. I'm sorry…I'm afraid…*

The boy went into the hallway, and as he stepped toward the closet he set his vision up on the padlock. The big lock was high out of reach. He wondered if it would be possible to find the key, something he'd never been able to do before. He gave breaking the big lock off some thought. Realizing the strong unlikelihood of both tasks having a favorable outcome, he abandoned the two ideas and pressed his ear against the door. He gently tapped on it with his fingertips.

"Susan...Susan, can you hear me? Susan; it's me, are you awake? Susan, you okay?"

Pausing, he listened closely and could barely hear the little girl's slow, shallow breathing. The boy's heart began to beat faster with worry due to the sound of her weak breathing. He wished his baby sister would offer up some sort of reply, if for no other reason than to show him she was well enough to speak.

"Susan, it's me, please say something...just one little word, only one...please."

"Tears my boy," the voice asked softly, "who do you weep for? Is it for them; the monsters that we've laid to waste, or do you weep for yourself?"

"Neither," whispered the boy, "I have no tears for those two monsters or for myself. I'm afraid to lose her."

"Your sister?"

"She's so little."

"She's in a bad way Alex my boy. I fear that it may be too late for her."

"No!" the boy placed his hands over his ears. "We're safe now, they can't hurt us anymore. She's only resting...she is so little...she is so little."

The boy sat there against that closet door like that for most of the morning. It wasn't until 9:46 am that he got up and set the final phase of their plan into motion. He left the house and went straight over to the front door of a neighbor. Ringing the door-bell, it wasn't long before the old woman who answered the door stood staring in speechless shock at the half dressed blood smeared little boy.

"My daddy hurt my mommy real bad...Susan's locked in the closet...I'm afraid."

Along with Ruth Stone's savagely mutilated corpse marinating in her own juices, and Wayne's lifeless carcass sitting upright on the sofa with his throat flayed nicely open from ear to ear, what the police found in that house went far beyond heart breaking. After the boy told them of his sister locked in the closet, they tore open the door. A few were drawn to tears as they carried the little girls' broken body out of that house. She was barely clinging to her fragile life when they placed her into the ambulance, rushing the girl to the closest hospital. In nearly every room of that dark house of childhood horror, police found signs of just about every form of abuse. It was by far, the most appalling, sad sight any of them had ever seen. It was also the fastest murder investigation that Benton County had ever run, lasting less than thirty-six hours from start to finish. Homicide detectives had written off the boy's handiwork as a murder/suicide. The motivation being that Wayne Stone was caught in the crushing grip of deep guilt and shame over what he and his soul-mate were doing to their two children. So, with the aid of a hell of a lot of booze and the help of a large butcher knife, he slaughtered his wife then immediately killed himself by slashing his own throat, an almost impossible feat to accomplish.

The boy spent the rest of his childhood being shuffled around from foster home to foster home until finally running away at sixteen. The girl on the other hand didn't have it so good. Apparently that last night with mommy and daddy had not only broken her body, it had also shattered both her mind and spirit. She had been beaten into a coma when police handed her over to the paramedics, and although she'd eventually came out of it and her flesh and bones had mended, her mind refused to awaken. That night with her parents had been so severely traumatic, that she'd somehow become trapped in a state of torpidity. With no way to pay for the expensive care she would need to be treated back to the world, the powers that be remanded her to the only place willing to care for her, the State's asylum for the chronically insane. A horrible place for anyone, especially a child. The girl was to suffer more injustices in this Hell on Earth, some of which not at all unlike those she'd suffered at the hands of her parents.

The boy was never to see his sister again for the rest of his life.

Without voicing his arrival, Pike entered into the small rounded observation room. Moving at a hurried pace he crossed the rusty iron floor, his steps making no sound whatsoever as his hard-healed boots landed with solid determination. With private intent, he shot a brief glance onto the small wooden black box atop the white marble table. Pike then shifted his scanning gaze onto Ellzbeth, who was standing at one of the room's four paneless windows with her back to him. She was silently looking out at B'neem's ghastly surroundings; Pike sensing a heavy measure of foreboding rising from her aura. Stepping up to a window of his own, he too took a moment to look out at the realms crimson and black landscape, all the while attempting to not allow Ellzbeth's worried state to affect him. He'd made the long climb to the uppermost chamber of B'neem's Cathedral to collect something of grave importance from her, a task that he hadn't been looking forward to doing. Not because of having to make the eight-hundred stair-steps ascent, nor was it due to ill-feelings toward the realm's Grand Inquisitor. Quite the contrary on both counts. Pike being an archangel, he never grew tired, so it could have been a billion steps and it would have the same effect as but one step. As for ill-feelings for Ellzbeth, not possible. She was his closest comrade and dearest friend and would lay his life down for her without question. Pike's misgivings for this relatively minor remit were brought on by the knowledge that she would undoubtedly attempt to draw him into her paranoid suspicions concerning the sixth realm's Gate Keeper. Ellzbeth's suspicions toward Vile had always been her primary choice of topic for conversation at gatherings, and usually ended up fizzling out once she grudgingly realized no one else was willing to share in her distrusting enthusiasm concerning their fellow archangel, whether they believed any of Ellzbeth's suspicions or not. Pike had dreaded this visit so much that he even considered giving the responsibility of minding their player's implement over to Sader, B'neem's Overseer, in order to avoid Ellzbeth's ravings, but decided not to after all. Such a stripping of duty would be seen by Ellzbeth as a sign of doubt, distrust for her ability to effectively carry out her obligations to the realm, and would be a stinging blow, wounding her self-worth greatly. He recognized it to be worth suffering his friend's paranoid ramblings for a bit if it meant preserving her feelings.

As well as being pains handmaiden, crowned beneath the title of Grand Inquisitor, Ellzbeth was also charged with the responsibility of guardian over the realm's library. A vast labyrinth of darkness and stone deep beneath the Cathedral, wherein was hidden the only known record in Hell of angel kind's entire history. A wealth of knowledge and power that could in the wrong hands imprison all of the Empires caretakers in the chains of eternal servitude. There are few threats that can pierce through an archangel's fear as easily as the promise of slavery. Not even

Vile, arguably the Empire's cruelest of creatures, could bring herself to enslaving one of her own breed of angles.

It was this phase of Ellzbeth's station that made her one of the planet's most powerful beings. Pike had been staring at the back of her hooded head for well over a full minute when he finally decided to say simply, "Greetings Inquisitor."

Ellzbeth turned her head in a mocked half glance and softly replied, "Greetings to you as well Gate Keeper."

She reached up, allowing only the tips of her fingers and thumbs to slip up out from the ends of her sleeves. In an effort to strengthen the almost nonexistent shadow struggling to be cast within her wide, pointed white hood, she took a hold of its stiff rim, and pulled it down tighter around her face. All the while fully aware of the fact that any attempts to shield her worry in the safety of darkness were wasted due to the inescapable brilliance of her golden eyes. Usually Ellzbeth donned a purple porcelain mask beneath her cowl, removing it only when in this, her tower-room, or while she was carving away on the flesh of one of the souls charged unto her. It's not known why she chose to wear the featureless mask, only that her reasoning did not stem from the need to conceal a hideously misshapen face. As with all of Hell's angelic caretakers, Ellzbeth could transform into any fleshly shape she so wished, at will. And as with all of B'neem's custodians, the mocking look she'd chosen was the likeness of a human-girl-child. One with a snow-white oval face, framed in a shroud of raven-black hair.

Even though she knew any efforts to disguise her distress from Pike were in vain, she still tried to limit his ability to gaze clearly upon her cherub features. Not willing to turn the opening of her hood on him completely, she half glanced again as she softly asked.

"I trust it's well on the way?"

Pike was looking out his window, watching the barges filled with more souls for B'neem's touch, move slowly across the black lake that surrounded the Cathedral, replying simply, "Yes."

In a voice filled with anxiety, whispered beneath her breath but still loud enough for Pike to hear she said, "The sixth realm is up to its old tricks I fear."

Pike closed his eyes briefly in a private gesture of personal dread, and thought to himself. *And it begins.*

"Vile is going to surpass all of her past efforts. She won't be stopped so easily this go-around."

Pike made no reply, he stepped back from the window, his attention lingering a moment on the large iron boats before allowing his vision to drift onto his uneasy friend.

"Yes, she is up to something most-foul, mark my word," she warned.

As Pike's ruby-red gaze burned a path past the black veil of emptiness within his hood, trying with little success to peer around Ellzbeth at the box on the table, he said with a harmless chuckle, "So marked."

"Don't mock me!" she snapped, "Not you...please, not you."

"Forgive me old friend," he begged with a humble bow of his head. "Tell me Inquisitor, please...what fills your certainty?"

"I sense the waves of her treachery swelling through the Empire. The reek of her treasonous ambition chokes me greatly."

Pike wanted to ask in a laugh, what's that suppose to mean? But instead said, "Yes, I sense it as well."

"You do?" Ellzbeth said with a heavy sigh of relief.

"Yes, of course I do," he lied, "but it's not unlike that megalomaniac to scheme...after all, she is Vile."

"Pike, she must not win the game," Ellzbeth said in a soft beseeching tone that carried with it a weighty note of consternation as she continued. "I'm certain you're aware of what would become of the Empire if that lunatic were to take the day." She slammed her heel down hard on the floor in an attempt to illustrate what Pike already knew; that she was intent on impressing her beliefs utterly upon him. "Vile would be free to reign as she saw fit," she shrieked, all the while poor Pike trapped helplessly in the tempest of her fears, unable to do anything but listen. "If she wins, the library, our history will be at her mercy. But that's only the beginning; Vile will possess the keys to his chains."

Pike had been doing pretty good up to that point at holding his mud. It wasn't until she made mention of the One's chains that the Gate Keeper loosed a slight chuckle. Actually it was the apparent insinuation that accompanied her statement that invoked his snicker.

"Vile wouldn't dare unleash him," Pike interrupted. "Have you forgotten that it was her army that overpowered his warriors, locking them and him at bay until the rest of us arrived to aid in placing him in chains?"

"You don't understand her as I do," Ellzbeth whispered.

"Nor do I care to," Pike sort of hissed. "Lets say for the sake of argument…"

"Lets not!" she growled.

"Yes, Inquisitor…I insist upon it," Pike demanded. "Let's say Vile's player gets lucky and defeats ours, and she reigns over all of the Empire as she wishes, which would be her right. Yes, and let us say, she for whatever reason, lets that great commander loose from his binds…what could she do with him? He's been bled dry, and his army cast into Second Hell."

Overstepping her authority, and taking a big chance in the process Ellzbeth crashed her boot down again and screamed, "You silly fool! Don't you remember whose idea it was to have him bled out?"

"Mind your tongue Ellzbeth," Pike warned.

"It was Vile's! Can you honestly say you know what became of Satan's blood after we drained it from his body…well Pike, can you?"

He stood silently a moment, shook his head *No*, and then went to voice the same when she cut him off before he could.

"No one does. It mysteriously vanished, not a single drop's whereabouts is known of by any of the Empire's caretakers."

"I suppose you're going to claim Vile is in possession of it?"

"I'm certain she is."

Pike's chuckle had evolved into a full blown belly-laugh at hearing this phase of Ellzbeth's conspiracy theory. He was about to let his friend know how completely daft a notion that was when like a spoilt child she shouted "NO!" Pike had had his fill of all this foolishness. Ellzbeth was in the midst of her howling temper-tantrum when he swept his hand up at chest level, clinching it into a fist. Pike's hand gesture had rendered her suddenly mute, stifling her voice with his power of will. Ellzbeth's eyes instantly grew intensely bright with the seething rage swelling in her heart, that the four beams of golden light that shot out the windows could be seen for miles. In a show of stubborn defiance, she spun around turning her back to Pike.

In a loud, commanding tone of voice he said, "Your paranoia has found strength in your imagination old friend. Let me see if I can lay your unfounded worries to rest once and for all, with this simple truth. You won't have to relinquish your authority to that insane creature, at least not for another thousand years."

Pike had mindlessly neglected to seal his silencing spell. So as he attempted to set her mind at ease Ellzbeth picked the locks of his magic and screamed so loud that when she whipped about to face Pike, the blast of her voice slammed into him with enough fury to knock the omnipotent Gate Keeper backward against the wall. Ellzbeth's reprieve from his will was a brief one. No sooner had Pike hit the floor and he was back up on his feet. She was still screaming when Pike willed her out of her tower-room. In the blink of an eye, he had transported her half way across the Empire, back through the seventh realm into the heart of the sixth. When her split second trek through the veil of time and space came to a stop, Ellzbeth had been rocketed into the icy darkness of Queen Vile's throne room.

Vile was seated as usual in her hovering throne of tangled bodies, less than twenty feet from the spot where Ellzbeth had appeared out of thin air. The little golden eyed Inquisitor's angry howl tore out through the black air, latching onto Vile's attention, ripping the Queen out of her day-dream a split second before Ellzbeth realized where she was, and silenced herself. The two ancient angelic beings locked eyes.

"Ellzbeth..."

"Vile..."

The two hissed at each other. Seeing what Vile recognized as fear in Ellzbeth's eyes, she turned her throne to face her unexpected visitor and was about to will her up into the air for a closer look, when Ellzbeth locked her—best do something fast—focus onto the throne and silently breathed the word, *Va'csm.*

The Queen's ghastly seat immediately unwove, all of the bodies pulling away from one another. The tangled mass of flesh and bone had come undone and was falling to the floor, as was Vile. Stopping herself in mid plummet, she shrieked the summoning command, "Black, Blue...feed!"

At the exact moment the two giant beasts leapt out of the blackness on either side of Ellzbeth, Pike who still had her in his mental grip yanked the golden eyed Inquisitor out of Queen Vile's throne room.

Snapping their jaws at the air as if they were actually tearing their teeth into the tender flesh that had been standing there a split second earlier, the Shadow Hounds, unable to halt their flight in time, slammed head first into one another.

Vile's bare feet slapped gently down on the icy floor with a soft, almost nonexistent patting sound.

"Trespasser—spy—thief—coward," she gnashed. Motioning her pets back to their shadows, she whipped her icy attention around, dropping her crimson vision onto the bodies squirming on the floor. Like a blow meant to kill, she leered at them wriggling about as if they were large maggots at her feet. With no more than a crooked grin, she willed them all back up into the air, and like an old movie being made to be played backward, Vile's horrid seat of power had reassembled.

Back in B'neem's tower-room, Pike was standing at the white marble table looking down at the black box when he brought Ellzbeth home. Her eyes were barely lit, only a dull yellowish glow emanated from them as she gazed at Pike. If he would have bothered with shifting his vision up from the box at her, he would have noticed the hurt, angry expressions on her face. She stepped over to the table opposite him. Although she appeared calm, her stillness was only surface deep. After all, he'd treated her no better than the lowliest of lesser angels. Beneath a layer of self-control, no thicker than an abandoned spider's web, was a storm of rage; begging and howling to be loosed on the smug little Gate Keeper.

She slid the box across the table to him. A gesture that transferred the responsibility for the box and its holding from her to him. Still biting her tongue, wanting so much to let go on him, she took a step back from the table and raised her hands out in front of her. Ellzbeth's eyes brightened some, as she silently mouthed something to herself.

Finally setting his gaze up onto Ellzbeth, Pike watched her as she worked, all the while fully expecting her to attempt some sort of harsh retaliation for the short field-trip to Vile's palace. Resting his hand on the box lid he began tapping it in fast repetitive succession with the tips of his fingers as if to signal his eagerness to get what he'd come for and go. The longer it took Ellzbeth to retrieve the other items the louder his tapping got. *Tap…tap tap tap…tap…tap tap tap…tap…tap tap tap…tap.* And the louder Pike's impatient attempt to annoy Ellzbeth into working faster, the slower she purposely operated. No less than ten painful slow, wordless minutes crawled between the two friends, with only Pike's silly finger tapping and Ellzbeth's hurt, vexed feelings moving through the small rooms' air. When she had her fill of making him wait, she turned her hands over, palms up toward the high vaulted ceiling. Ellzbeth's whispered mumbling stopped, as did Pike's tapping. The moment both were quite a small black leather pouch and a tiny bottle of dark-green glass, corked with a bone stopper, dropped out of the ceiling, one landing in each hand.

Ellzbeth faced Pike who had loosed a heavy sigh as if to say, *it's about time.* She sat the two objects down on the table in front of the box, and without a word stepped over to her window to look out into space, seeing only the wonderfully torturous things she imagined doing to Pike for treating her so horribly.

Pike looked at the back of his friends' hooded head as he picked the pouch and bottle up. "Thank you Inquisitor," he said as he tucked them back behind his waist-sash. Placing the box under his arm as he stepped toward the door, he said in a cold tone of voice, "Sorry Ellzbeth."

She offered no retort, at least not one Pike could hear, or would care to.

Alex had been wandering aimlessly through that terminally flat desert for hours. He figured he'd covered no less than twenty miles all the while seeing no change in the stark scenery. No landmarks such as mountains or tiny pinpoints of far off light to move toward appeared anywhere on that red horizon. Not even a rock bigger than a toenail could be spotted. The vast hollowness of that place was enough to drive any unfocused mind mad. The air was windless and hot, it pressed down on him with the pulsating relentlessness of a dope-sick-fever. His every breath was a searing, laborious intake and exhaling of scorched oxygen, if indeed oxygen was what he was struggling to suck in and out of his lungs. Then there was the sand. It latched onto the soles of his boots with every foot fall like thick red mud, making each step a chore. The only other movement beside his own laborious breathing and arduous walking that he was aware of was the sky high above. It churned in an insane dance of innumerable shades of red.

Alex was wishing his knife, cigarettes and lighter would have been returned to him with his clothes. He was in the middle of telling himself how good a smoke would be right about then, when suddenly his wishful thinking was interrupted by an assaulting invasion of rancid odors. There was no wind in the air that moved the stink down, it just dropped out of the sky on top of him, or rose up out of the sand in his path, he wasn't quite sure, nor did he care. Like an invisible fog he was immersed in the rotting stench of burning flesh, fat and hair. Then as abruptly as it had made its putrid self known to his nostrils, it was gone. Alex was shaking off the effect of the distasteful event and about to continue his directionless hike, when he was sent down to one knee. Not by another onslaught of nasty odors, no this surprise attack was fired at him in a formless explosion of howling screams. One second it was deathly quiet, a split second later he was clasping his hands flat over his ears, trying desperately to block out the shrieks tearing into his skull. Like with the foul smells, the wailing vanished, once again returning the desert to its grave-like silence.

The moment the mind numbing consequence of the screams had mellowed enough for Alex to regain his imperturbability, his sights' strength refocused, pushing past the eye squinting symptom of the buzzing in his head. Alex happened to be looking in the direction of his hands as they moved down from his ears and spotted the small traces of blood. It was glistening in the dark red air with freshness, not dried and crusty like the stained reminders already on his gloves. This new blood was from out of his ears, the screaming had broken something. "Testing...one, two, three," he said loudly in order to check on his hearing. The inescapable familiarity of his own voice seeped in with faint, but steadily growing stronger reverberation. Alex noticed the wave of relief as it wiped away the panic swelling from the possibility of never being allowed the pleasure of music again; as if he'd ever have the chance.

Alex was about to smear the blood off on his jeans, adding a bit more to the collection of vermilion-rust memories gathered there, when what he saw next halted the action. The small wet spots moved, like liquid flat worms, wriggling swiftly off his leather clad palms onto the exposed skin of his wrists where it then sank beneath his flesh out of sight.

"Now that's a bitchin trick," he said to himself aloud as he gawked at the spots where the ear-blood vanished. Removing his right glove, he inserted the tip of his pinky finger in his still slightly tender ear and feeling no wetness took it out, examined it, finding the end of the digit clean. *Shit just keeps getting stranger and stranger by the second doesn't it Mr. Bane*, he thought, not really expecting his friend to reply, although he had allowed himself to hope.

Getting up from his knee, he looked around. *I've most likely been walking in fucking circles*, he thought as he pulled the glove back on. With only his confused and atypical thoughts to occupy his mind, he resumed his aimless march over the red sticky sand. To where, he possessed no clue, nor could his mind formulate the reason or reasons why. All Alex knew for certain was that he'd dropped onto and through Five's corpse. He remembered the leg bone and the subsequent pain in his chest that followed. Alex glanced down at the blood stained hole torn in the center of his sweatshirt, as well as the bullet holes on either side of it. Setting his narrowed vision back up onto the surrounding landscape, he recalled the cold blackness, the hot, stabbing pain through his wrists and ankles as he was nailed to the beam, the bone yard and the white ball of fire that cooked his flesh. He remembered the onslaught of his dreadful memories and the visitor who called himself Pike. *What does that little devil want with me? Why did he give me back my body and clothes…what's the price?* Alex wondered, *I'd seen this Pike somewhere before…but where, when?*

There was one other fact that Alex was most certain of, certain without the slightest doubt; he knew he was wandering across a blood red desert somewhere in Hell.

Aside from all the other unanswered questions trying to strangle his mind with an overload of confusion, what was screwing with Alex's mind the most was that he'd been sent to Hell in the first place. Being the true die-hard narcissist that he liked to think of himself as, Alex couldn't understand, leastwise not yet anyway, why after all the good he and Mr. Bane had done trying to cut the lives of the surface population of Earth's child-molesters down to nil, was he damned to the Bad Place. The only reason that made an iota of sense to him was his not doing anything to help Susan get out of that horrible place. He'd abandoned her, left her to rot in the madhouse. A few, not many, but a few times, he thought about visiting her, he even drove past the long rows of large brick buildings on State street. But whether it was due to seeing all those barred windows or his own fears surrounding the unknown, as to what he'd find his baby sister to be, kept him from following the visit through. Sometimes, during a good drunk he would get all teary eyed, feeling sorry for himself and call the State Hospital. But he wouldn't say a word, just sit there in the dark of his self-pity and listen to the person on the other end of the line get tired of demanding that whoever it was say something, then hang-up.

Alex did believe, and wholeheartedly, that his and Mr. Bane's slaughtering of his parents and the systematic assassinations of the Five, weren't the cause. He saw these killings as the only true good deeds of his entire life. What was pissing him off the most, was that he figured his murderous good deeds/saving dozens if not tens of dozens of little ones from living-nightmares, should have been enough to wipe his slate clean. The self-serving transgressions of his wasted life should have been forgiven him. Alex was positive someone or something had made a grave error, overlooking his good deeds and had accidentally sent him to Tartarus.

The more he dwelled on the apparent mistake made by whoever the shot callers were in this place, the more outwardly his anger grew. Alex's steady walking pace had advanced to a rushed clip, his movements appearing almost machine-like. He was set on finding the one responsible for this blunder and convincing him or it to make it right, by whatever means necessary.

He'd maintained his heated pace for several miles, mumbling to himself like some sort of moronic-boob trying to talk himself into doing something he knew he had no chance of success at accomplishing. Alex was brought to an abrupt stop by a shaking that had risen swiftly up from deep beneath the desert floor. He stood perfectly still, readying himself, for what, he had no idea. After a few seconds the shaking stopped. Deciding to give it a few more seconds before moving, he stood motionless, not so much as a single muscle flexing, and feeling quite lame in the process. Experiencing no after-shocks, he figured it was safe enough to chance a step. In the relatively short space of time between lifting his boot and setting it back down another tremor more jolting than the first shot up through the ground, knocking Alex flat on his ass.

"Now what!" he exclaimed. Again the quake steadily mellowed to a stop. Alex not liking any of this whatsoever, got up onto his haunches. With both hands holding him steady, his fingers spread and half submerged in the warm sand, he waited. Something was about to happen, he could sense it. Glancing up at the sky, he saw that the wild mixture of reds had slowed their frantic dance to an almost unnoticeable peace. The tingling sensation that he sometimes felt in the back of his neck when something unpleasant was about to occur, moved down into his gut. The red sky had stopped completely now, all of its countless formless shapes frozen in time like an impossibly huge snapshot. At least fifteen minutes crept past before Alex once again decided to stand, it wasn't until another five minutes had been spent that he decided to steal a step.

The moment his heel dropped to the sandy surface he was sent back down, not by another ground shaking quake, no this time it was because the entire desert for as far as his eyes could see had begun moving, turning. It started at an already fast pace and was swiftly gathering speed with every counterclockwise spinning revolution. In no time at all his rotating surroundings were moving so fast that it made standing an impossible feat to accomplish. Every attempt to do so ending the same, with Alex being swiftly cast back down. Finally realizing that his efforts to get up and walk were a waste of time and energy, he decided to focus on the easier task of simply sitting. It took a bit of doing but he eventually managed to shove up onto his knees and keep stable enough to maintain an upright, knelt stance. As the desert's spinning persisted, its speed rapidly advancing to an unbelievable rate of momentum, Alex found that his ability to stave off the dizzying affects somewhat taxing. In mere seconds the crimson atmosphere had been transformed into a smeared wall of dark-red air. Soon his pseudo—steady upright pose had shrank, buckling down to a hunched over position, barely able to hold his ground due to the symptoms of vertigo. It was as if Alex had been slammed onto the middle of a colossal turntable stuck on seventy-eight RPM'S. In an effort to maintain his rebellious nature Alex, while struggling against the centrifugal force, raised his head to stare up at the blurred sky and began yelling and laughing at the top of his lungs.

"Is this the best you pussys can come up with?" he shrieked. "Shit, no sense in holding back now. Come on, bring it…PUNKS!"

Alex's raving and insane cackling was suddenly drowned out by a flurry of sound. The blast rose up from all around him in an explosion of wailing voices. It was a thousand times louder than the rush of screams that had made his ears bleed. He tried clasping his hands over his ears, in the vain hope of blocking out the noise, but every time he let go of the ground he was sent rolling due to the swift momentum of the desert's movement. It took some doing but he was eventually able to stop tumbling across the red sand and fight back up onto his knees. After six attempts, he was finally able to cover his ears only to realize it had no affect on the deafening sound's penetrating power. Suddenly the desert stopped, throwing him down again with the unexpected brake in movement. A moment or so following the halt of motion, Alex's head and guts stopped spinning as well, alleviating his temporary bout with vertigo. As soon as Alex was steady enough to stand, he was up on his feet, forcing his sights focus through the blaring pressure of the wailing voices. Looking around he saw that the desert hadn't stopped turning. Only the small island of sand he occupied, a segment no larger than a round, moderately sized kitchen table had ceased. Again he attempted to shield his ears from the painfully loud howls with his hands, only to reaffirm what he'd already learned; that there was nothing he could do to block out the teeth grinding noise. The squalling had grown so piercing; Alex could actually feel the physical weight of it trying to constrain him back to his knees.

It was in realizing his ears were bleeding, feeling the blood move swift and oddly cold down his neck, that the origin of the voices made itself known to Alex. With a single upheaval they erupted out of the spinning sand in an explosion of gnashing teeth, reaching hands and festering flesh. Men and woman of every race and age were caught, helplessly trapped in the swift current of the semisolid ground. They stretched out, surrounding Alex's little island eternally it seemed. The ones closest to the patch of solid sand tried grabbing its bank; Alex was about to kick them away, not willing to share, but quickly learned he wouldn't have to. Every time one would so much as touch Alex's island, they would be immediately torn down beneath the multitude, screaming out of sight. Most of the naked damned were being swept away so fast in the whirlpool that any hope of escape was crushed beneath the weight of the horde that snared them in its swift flux.

Some of the people caught in the warm sand were still wearing all of their skin, completely void of wounds or decay to speak of. They were the ones who seemed to fight and scream the loudest. Then there were those who were horribly rotting away, their bodies showing the deep, clawed scratches and scars that the others had left there as they fought to reach the surface. Finally there were those who'd been reduced to nothing more than living skeletons, held thinly together by only bits of blackened muscle and strands of stringy tendon. Crying out their deafening song of agony, they bobbed up, breaking out of the cresting swells of flesh, only to be yanked back down out of sight by another trying to claw his or her way topside.

While Alex was struggling to concentrate past the pain drilling into his brain he caught sight of someone he never expected to see again, leastwise not in Hell. His heart shrank at first, only to swell with the panicked command, *Don't just stand there…do something.*

Without so much as questioning why she was still seven years old he shouted, "Susan!" Alex hurtled himself off the limited sanctuary of his island. During his summary flight he was mockingly shown his blunder. His eager sight was locked onto Susan's horrified little face when the instant before dropping into the reaching, grabbing hands surrounding her she transformed from that of his frightened sister to the hideously decayed face of an old woman.

Alex was latched onto, and with a neck snapping jolt he was swept away with the fast current and yanked beneath the surface. Once again he was submerged in complete darkness, tightly surrounded by countless wiggling bodies, all fighting one another frantically to get back to the surface. They pressed against him from every angle, their hot, slimy, rotting flesh constricting so heavily that he fully expected to be crushed from the intense weight of it all. The flat desert with its vast emptiness didn't seem so bad now.

The more Alex struggled against being dragged farther and farther downward, the deeper he was pulled. Soon the smashing pressure of decayed, yet still living corpses had squeezed the last bit of air out of his lungs. Foolishly, Alex opened his mouth in the hope of drawing in a breath, only to be fish-hooked by the slime smeared fingers of one of his fellow trapped. The hand grabbed onto Alex's lower jaw and would have torn it off his face, but as it wrenched on it, he clamped down with all his might. Alex's efforts paid off, he'd bit down with such force that his teeth cut through skin and crushed past bone until his upper and lower teeth touched. Alex bit the trespassing digits off the hand and promptly spit them out.

He was being drawn deeper into the bodies, the burning pain in his lungs swelling horribly worse. Alex felt himself being suffocated, and for a moment believed he would finally be delivered over to a second death. He felt a wave of relief over his up and coming demise, when his hopefulness was dashed by a voice that seeped intrusively into his waning awareness, stealing the moment and bringing Alex back, fully aware. It hissed, "You've already gone far beyond the point of smothering to death Alex. Anyway, how can what's already dead be killed?"

The loud moans and groans coming from the suffering souls crushing down around him steadily grew faint eventually fading to muffled grunts. Soon even those died down, being replaced by the sounds of an untold amount of slow heart beats, chattering teeth and skull smacking together.

With the same unexpected suddenness that had plagued him since his death, Alex dropped out of the seemingly unending throng of decay into an empty space. Although he was still falling and still immersed in pitch-blackness, he was glad to be done with that hot, slimy phase of the journey. After what seemed like an eternity, Alex splashed down into icy cold liquid. It was much too thick of a substance to be water and too fluid for it to have been mud. Whatever the muck was, he was being pulled deeper down into it by the same force of will that had dragged him through the mass of bodies above. He tried swimming, to where though he had no clue; his sense of direction was as blind as his sight, still he fought to swim against the power pulling him down. It was beginning to seem like an insane test to him, like someone wanted to peer in at his level of resolve, to check and see how long his spirit would fight before giving in. Like when the prison guards tested his steel, breaking his jaw and six ribs in the process, and still his heart refused to lie down. He would let them beat him to death before allowing himself to lick his nuts, and beg them to stop.

Alex's lungs were on fire again, hungry for a breath of air. He clamped his teeth down tight, while a madman's notion wormed about in his brain, attempting to convince his willpower that it would be safe to open his mouth and take a much needed deep breath. He clinched his jaws down tighter. At some point during this battle of self-wills, Alex allowed himself to believe he was back in control, even though something was pulling him deeper down into the icy muck. Feeling proud of the job he was doing at keeping his mouth locked shut, and confident he could maintain his hold forever, no matter what, he thought pompously, *I'm in control now, understand!*

The voice of a giggling little boy, that he realized to have been his own from his youth, whispered the word "Breathe."

Panic rushed into his heart as his jaws were torn open. As the cold metallic tasting substance filled his lungs a new pain was added to the collection, Alex had unwillingly begun to assemble since the moment of his birth; it was the sensation one comes to know when drowning.

Fighting to shut his mouth, for all the good it would do, he suddenly went rigid. The pain in his lungs seeped out and spread through the rest of his body, even finding its way into the center of his very bones. All he could do was feel himself sink helplessly down deeper through the dark cold abyss.

Then, just as he'd unexpectedly splashed down into the icy muck, he was breaking out of it into a blast of bright light. Alex's sight was quickly returned to him and readjusted to the blinding brilliance of his new surroundings. The first sight his vision locked onto was a vast sea of dark-red liquid. But he wasn't falling toward it, he was moving away from it. As it turns out, Alex had fallen through an upside down ocean of blood. The stormy sea completely mantled the white air, stretching out with no end in all directions like an interminable crimson membrane.

He was plummeting toward an enormous sheet of white cloud-cover. As he dropped further and faster away from the red ceiling, his stiffness subsided, giving Alex back his mobility. The hot air blasting up past him burned all of the red muck off of his skin and clothes, returning Alex's duds to their prior dry, blood stained state. The heat was swiftly taken over by an overpowering rush of clean, crisp air. It would have been a pleasant change if not for the inescapable fact that he was dropping like a stone straight down at an amazing rate of speed. He was falling so fast that his face and neck were assaulted by a stinging pain when he slapped down through the dense clouds, the moisture smacking his skin like tiny needles. It wasn't until he broke out past the clouds into a clear, clean smelling bright blue sky that his destination was made evident to him. The dream-like blue sky stretched out over a beautiful green landscape that generously spread on and on in all directions. From what Alex could make of it with his wind-blown eyes, the green ground racing to make his acquaintance consisted solely of an evenly flat meadow of thick green grass. At about thirteen hundred feet Alex tried to prepare himself for the impact. But in the time it took his mind to wonder, why? he hit the ground.

Alex's body slammed down with such force that he actually smashed a ten inch deep impression in the ground. The unbelievable pain of having all of one's bones shattered and muscles crushed to mush at once, was nothing compared to the agony Alex came to know when all of those broken bones and smashed muscles simultaneously healed themselves immediately after breaking. The pain eventually subsided as the last of the bones fused back together, fading from a teeth-grinding torment to a persistent throb. Alex's fedora drifted gently down to land like an ash squarely on his chest.

"Hello Millstone," he heard Pike say.

The Gate Keeper was standing in the thick grass five feet from where Alex lay flat on his back. He didn't take his eyes off the sky to glance over at Pike; he simply stared in utter disbelief up at the clear blue air.

"Nice landing Mr. Stone. The best I've seen in well…a thousand years."

CHAPTER THREE

— THE FALLEN —

"Here we may reign secure,
And in my choice to reign
Is worth ambition though in
Hell: Better to reign in Hell,
than serve in Heav'n."

John Milton
—Paradise Lost

Queen Vile was in the process of having her portrait painted, this time by an artist who had been relatively unknown during his life. She had been unpleased with the blood and oil painted renderings created of her by those artists damned to her own realm, so she swiped this one from Chemah, the third realm. Stealing souls from another realm without that realm's Gate Keeper's knowledge and blessing was a repeated practice of Vile's. And, although it was in violation of the Empire's doctrine, most of the Gate Keepers could care less. That was all but one; Pike saw Vile's boosting the damned from out of B'neem as nothing short of utter disrespect and had no problem with confronting her about it. So, in order to keep that annoying little pest out of her face, Vile begrudgingly refrained from pinching souls from the eighth realm. She was doing pretty good at it too, that was until she learned the identity of the player for B'neem. For every soul damned to Hell, there were at least half a dozen who had been wronged in someway during their lives by another damned. Evil begets evil and vice versa.

Vile knew all she would have to do was find out who and where in Hell the damned souls wronged by B'neem's player were, and then steal them. It didn't take long for Vile's spies to learn of the nine year old boy's act of parricide, the child that would grow older, die and be damned to Hell only to be chosen for a hellish game. The fact that B'neem's player had murdered his sire and dame, and that both were somewhere in Hell was an incidental occurrence which Vile could not let slip away.

It wasn't until one of her spies came back with the bad news that both parents were damned to B'neem that her hopes sank some. She'd taken the information so poorly, that immediately upon hearing it she turned the messenger's body inside-out right where he knelt. Vile wasn't about to allow this dispiriting verity the power of dashing the golden opportunity befallen her. She knew there would be a wealth of hatred screaming to be loosed from those illegitimated hearts, as well as a lust for revenge that could never be quenched. Six weeks later, Warfarin brought Vile Ruth Stone's ashy remains only to have his deed rewarded with pain and silence. As a matter of fact, Vile had ordered all who knew of the quest for one or both of B'neem's player's parents summoned before her to be silenced as well.

Ellzbeth's unexpected appearance had Vile concerned a bit. She thought her old friend had learned of the theft of B'neem's player's mother, but soon dismissed it as a foolish notion. Vile knew Pike would never allow Ellzbeth to act as a spy, that was a duty reserved solely for lesser angels. Unless Ellzbeth knew something and was acting on her own, there had to be another explanation for her trespassing. Vile was well aware of Ellzbeth's distrustfully sharp words concerning her, as were the rest of the Empire's caretakers. Most viewed Ellzbeth's ravings as the paranoid ramblings of an angle slipping into the deep end of angelic madness, paying Ellzbeth little mind. Still, Vile knew she would have to act with some haste; it was only a matter of time before Pike would receive the news of Ruth Stone's disappearance from her place of suffering, and his attention would fall toward her.

Locked in a cage made of iron bars, and suspended less than a foot above the floor the naked artist worked. He feverishly slung paint on the large canvas of stretched skin. He clung to the knowledge that if his efforts fell short of Vile's expectations, the suffering he'd come to know in the third realm would pale greatly in comparison with what he would know in the sixth.

While Vile posed for her portrait, donning her angelic armor made of polished bronze, her crown of blue iron worn proudly around her head, Vexrile entered Vile's throne room. Vile had summoned Vexrile, the Overseer for Zaw'naw, soon after she'd liberated the pouch of living ash from Warfarin. There was a task for the Overseer, one which Vile believed would guarantee her victory over the other realms, primarily B'neem.

Without breaking her pose, Vile rolled her eyes to Vexrile, watching her as she moved in an acquiescent gesture of obedience to her knees.

"See for me." Vile ordered, "To your feet Vexrile, go look and tell me truthfully if this human's doings are worthy of his brief reprieve from suffering?"

Vexrile rose with a smooth upward motion like a life-size marionette being raised by invisible wires. Keeping her hooded head bowed, she walked to the back of the iron cage and peered over the artist's shoulder as he nervously worked. She'd barely had a glance at the near finished painting when Vile snapped with eager intolerance, "Well! Tell me, what are your thoughts? Has its efforts captured the radiant bloom of my beauty? Is my almighty glow shimmering forth the greatness that is—Me-e-e-e, from this thing's rendering?"

Moving out from behind the cage and going back down to her knees a safe distance from it Vexrile answered, her tone sheepish.

"No creature, not demonic or human, no god nor angelic being could do your image the justice it demands...my Queen. So, in telling this truth which you undoubtedly already know, it is my duty to inform you that this human's efforts are as pathetic as the breed of being with which he is a member."

Vile's deadpan expression cracked as a slight smile pulled at the corners of her mouth, the same dim grin appearing on the painting as well. Without taking the time to look upon the canvas for herself, Vile let fall the scepter and iron orb she'd been modeling with, dropping them both to the floor where they crashed with a loud clanging noise, her rendered image on the canvas doing likewise. The artist dropped his palette and brushes as he scooted back away from the suddenly living painting, trying to put as much space between it and him as the cramped cage would permit. Vile, taking two slow steps toward the cage asked in a soft, almost friendly tone.

"Why do you not plea for mercy, or scream from fright?" Tilting her head slightly to the left, then right as she gazed at him, she continued her enquiry, "Do you not fear me?" she breathed with a whisper.

"Go fuck yourself—", he tried to offer his answer, but was interrupted when Vile's hand swiftly reached out of the painting and ripped the cursing artist's entire face off. The downward sweep of the one dimensional hand tore away not only his fleshy mask but also took with it muscles, bone and the frontal lobe of his brain, pulling it all back into the painting. The other hand of the Queen's image shot out of the wet canvas and like a blade stabbed into the center of his chest, removing his still beating heart. The real Vile, who'd been watching the artist's suffering, a dreamy trance-like expression on her face, turned her back to the squirming display and lightly clapped her hands together once. In so doing, the cage dropped to the floor with a loud echoing bang, then began to bend and shift, getting smaller as its shape changed. High-pitched squeaks of twisting metal cried out through the cold darkness. The iron box closed in on the twitching remains of the mutilated artist, it squeezed down around him, crushing the painter to a bloody, broken mass wrapped within a ball of iron bars.

"Stand Vexrile," commanded the Queen under her breath as she set her crimson gaze onto the kneeling Overseer. "Stand and show me your face, I wish to gaze upon your lovely emerald eyes."

Once again Vexrile rose to her feet. With her head still bowed, she slid her hood back enough to reveal a beautiful, waxen face with bright green eyes, set beneath a mane of snow white hair. Vile stepped toward Vexrile with slow, gracefully planted steps, her bare feet slapping down softly on the frost covered stone floor. As Vile neared the Overseer, her bronze armor melted down into her creamy white skin like a droplet of blood sinking beneath the surface of a pool of milk. The moment the battle-suit had disappeared under her flesh it was replaced by a sheer black gown that magically poured out, running over her shoulders from beneath her hair. The translucent garment draped loosely over Vile's body, the front open, scarcely concealing her breasts, belly and beyond. Her erect nipples beamed through the silken cloth, perky and pink, as if to whisper peek-a-boo. Finally, the gown stretched out behind her forming a long train-like black liquid that was helpless to follow her every step.

"The first of many changes I shall order done once I am the unchallenged Queen and ruler of this entire planet." Vile stopped directly in front of Vexrile... (Her tone of voice, though soft and low was one of assurance)...she continued. "I will command that Satan be taken from his icy cell, brought here to this chamber," she panned her vision around her, through the darkness, bringing it back onto Vexrile. "Where he'll be made to kneel before me."

Vile moved closer to Vexrile, her near naked skin brushing the Overseer's robes. Placing the pointed tip of her middle fingernail under Vexrile's chin, she gently raised her head so that she could look straight into her bright green eyes.

"I will convince that old fool to give me the secret of death over all things...living and dead."

She pressed up against Vexrile, her lips softly brushing the Overseer's as she spoke. "What do you suppose I'll do with him once I've got what I want...go on Overseer, guess?"

"You'll test the power of death on him, you'll slay Satan once and for—"

"No," Vile interrupted with a whisper, "no...not right off. There are plenty for me to test my new gift of killing on...like you, for example."

Softly licking Vexrile's lips with the tip of her tongue, Vile followed with a gentle kiss as she pierced the needle like end of her nail up past the skin covering her chin. Vexrile winced, her lower lip trembling slightly from pain.

"I've a little chore for him first." Vile stepped back, letting Vexrile's chin go. "Then if I think it will please me, I may kill him...but not until after he's watched me eat his heart."

She moved slowly behind Vexrile and slid the Overseer's green hood the rest of the way off her head of white hair. Vile began running her fingernails down through Vexrile's snowy locks, all the while the Overseer seething at Vile's touch as she silently listened to the Queen, wishing this visit would come to a speedy conclusion.

The Queen continued with her to-do-list.

"Next I'll have every last scrap of parchment in that bloody library burned. Every book and scroll, all of it. The written record of all angelic history will be reduced to ash and cast to the wind. Then I shall have it rewritten in the words of my truth." She slid her hands out of Vexrile's hair, resting them on the Overseers narrow shoulders. "While that library of lies is being burned out of existence, that foolish wall will be torn down, thus expanding the new Empire...my Empire so that it will engulf all of creation. My Queendom shall spread out like a great beast devouring all mortal realms; the Gods will even bend their knees before me."

Vile leaned up against Vexrile's back and whispered directly into her right ear. "My Queendom," she squeezed her shoulders, forcing the Overseer back down to her knees, and then began to rub Vexrile's shoulders soothingly, only to clasp down on them again. The throne room grew steadily colder. Vile's icy touch moved down through the thick cloth of Vexrile's robes onto her skin. She could feel her power staving-off Vile's icy will growing weak. Vexrile knew that Vile would soon sense her weakening and that would mean more discomfort.

Vile closed her eyes as she bowed her head to face the top of the Overseer's head; she increased her hand's grip, smiled and said sweetly. "I could never truly express to you in all the moments that time has to offer, how wonderfully cold I feel when the words...*my Queendom* flow over my lips and sing into my own ears." Her hold tightened, painfully clinching around Vexrile's shoulders.

"Yes Overseer, I become as cold as blue steel, my senses as sharp as the razor's touch and as fleet as the deepest of agonies."

Vile's eyes slowly fluttered open, and had changed their color from dark-red to icy-blue. Their piercing gaze locked onto the top of Vexrile's head, Vile was attempting to peer into the Overseers thoughts. But Vexrile had prepared herself for such an event, sealing her mind's real intent behind the mental wall of a concealing spell that would only permit Vile's trespassing to see what she placed there for her to see. The barrier Vexrile had chosen for Vile's hungry mental groping was a dense cloud of unwavering obedience.

Vile asked, "What do you think and feel deep within your pretty bones when you see me in your mind's eye as Hell's sole ruler?," her tone was soft, yet slicing. She tightened her grip, her eyes growing a darker blue as she narrowed their vision deeper into Vexrile's mind.

"Does it get you all quivery and wet with orgasmic arousal, or do you cringe and repel with dread at the thought? Perhaps you could careless, one ruler's as good or bad as the next…isn't that right Overseer?"

Vexrile smothered the rage swelling within her heart and in her usual feelingless tone answered Vile's question. "I'm always eager my Queen, to do whatever is required of me to see you as Empress once and for all."

Vile sensing neither sincerity, falseness, nor betrayal in the Overseer's thoughts and words. She sent all twelve of her fingernails down through Vexrile's robes to swiftly penetrate her skin. The now whimpering Overseer, stiffened with pain, her eyelids and teeth clinched closed as Vile's nails stabbed through to scrape bone. Vile's eyes had become as black as coal.

"How Overseer…how does it make you feel to know that I will soon be Hell's ruler?" Vile asked, her words being spoken so softly that even the ears of Earthly dogs wouldn't have heard them. But Vexrile could, indeed she could, loud and clear. In a voice almost as low as Vile's she replied, her words tripping and trembling through her agony.

"You are my Queen, whether you reign over all Hell or this palace alone…that my Queen, is a truth which shall never change."

Vile finally slid her nails out of the Overseer's shoulders, letting go and allowing her to collapse face first on the cold stone of the floor.

"Well said Vexrile…dear," Vile whispered with a giggle as she stepped over the wincing angel. "If your pathetic efforts to serve pleases me, I may see fit to grant you a world to reign over of your own, once creation is mine. No need to thank me, just lay there like a good piglet and hurt for me."

Vile began moving with slow twirling steps around a few of the large iron columns that served to hold up the great dome ceiling made of dark indigo blue glass. With her arms raised lazily up, swaying her hands gently through the cold, black air she began humming like an insane woman on the upward rise of a mood swing. Her slow pirouetting pace, weaving her through the giant pillars was beginning to gather momentum when she came to a sudden stop.

Glancing over her shoulder, she took a brief inventory of Vexrile's slowly waning pain while moving to the first of several slabs of black stone. They hovered about the throne room, drifting through the vast empty space like rose petals on a black lake. The moment Vile placed the ball of her foot on the slab, the others moved through the air, lining up evenly to build a high flight of stairs that reached her throne of tangled bodies.

Vexrile eventually shook enough of the pain out of her bones to summon the strength to will her wounds healed, all the while fighting to hold her rage at bay.

= ⫶ =

Vexrile had been with Vile since long before Vile took to thinking of herself as Queen of the sixth realm, even before there was a sixth realm. It was during the second Great War, when Queen Vile still went by the name given to her by the principal Gods she was charged to serve, the name Sillona, that Vexrile began following Vile.

As with most of Hell's curators, Sillona was one of the Original Fallen. Before her plummet from the God's good graces, along with the others, she was among those greatest of archangels whose duty it was to create the suns for the worlds.

Vexrile was numbered among the countless lesser angels, her breed being that of Seraphim. Her station in Paradise was no-where as magnificent, or as prime as Sillona's; Vexrile was one of those whose duty it was to give worms their intestines.

During both of the great wars the lesser breeds of angels were employed solely as foot-soldiers. It didn't matter to the so called higher breeds that these grunts owned hearts, fearless, courageous and stout. Or that their unwavering intrepid spirits possessed the unquestionable ability to lay down their very lives for one of their comrades, whether it was for an archangel or the lowliest of houri. Nor did it seem to make a difference whatsoever to any of the greater breeds that if ordered to do so, a lesser angel would charge head-long into a hopeless situation, even if it meant going toe to toe with a God.

Vexrile was one of these fearless lesser angels. It was on the field of battle where the two being's relationship would be changed from that of a high-ranking archangel and a lowly seraphim, to something much more. Sillona was the commander of a great army of fierce battle skilled warriors. Vexrile had been one of these warriors in Sillona's vast army. The lesser angel had looked up to her commander, and had not only admired Sillona's ability to lead an army into battle, but had also revered her skill with the sword and lance against a foe. Sillona had noticed Vexrile as well. Several times she'd caught sight of the lesser creatures while engaged in combat, always out-numbered three or four to her one. Usually Vexrile would be caked from head to toe with the blood of slain enemies. No sooner would she dispatch with the three or four she'd been dancing with and the lesser angel would be on the hunt for another fight. But it wasn't Vexrile's battle style or the fact that she fought with the skill of a war seasoned archangel and not the unschooled tactics of her lesser breed that peaked Sillona's interest. No, it was what she'd seen Vexrile doing after the battle.

The day's fighting had long since ended and only the sounds of birds and wolves squabbling over the dead could be heard moving through the early morning fog. Sillona was out of her tent for a private moment with the fallen warriors that littered the field for miles in every direction. She was taking in the strong metallic scent of spilt blood when a fast movement caught her eye. Drawing her heavy sword Sillona moved into the dense tree line to investigate. With ghost like steps she drifted through the darkness, weaving around the oaks and aspens toward the sound of whispering. Coming to the edge of a small clearing in the woods, she peered around the trunk of a great oak and saw Vexrile hunched over a corpse. The lesser angel had dragged half a dozen enemy bodies into the center of the clearing and was mumbling to either the cadaver she was working on or herself, Sillona wasn't quite sure nor did she care. Sillona thought at first glimpse that the lesser angel she'd seen fighting so valiantly was now helping herself to some necrophilic romance. She was half a moment from interrupting this gruesome romp in the woods when she noticed that Vexrile was rising to her feet, and placing something she'd taken from the corpse in a leather pouch. Sliding her bullock dagger into her boot sheath and slinging the blood drenched pouch around her neck, letting it hang down between her breasts, she darted off into the woods. Sillona allowed Vexrile her personal endeavor, letting the angel go off un-arrested. As soon as Vexrile was well out of ear-shot Sillona stepped into the clearing, she had a fairly good idea what the lesser angel was doing, but still she figured it would be best to be sure. Looking down at the bodies, all of them with their lower jaws cut loose so that the mandible dangled from sliced muscles. Sillona's guess was dead on, Vexrile was collecting battle trophies, tongues to be exact.

Sillona, or Vile as she'd later came to calling herself, had never made mention to Vexrile that she'd seen her that morning in the woods. It was during the tenth battle of the second war that Vexrile's and Sillona's destinies were to become linked together for well over a hundred thousand centuries.

Sillona had been in the thick of the battle, as usual. She was busy hacking the life out of an adversary when an arrow found its mark in her. The barbed shaft slammed into her chest-plate, tearing past iron ring-mail and piercing her right lung. It had hit her with enough force to knock her out of the saddle, sending her off her mount to the blood soaked ground where she smacked her head on a rock, rendering her unconscious.

Vexrile had been less than twenty yards from her wounded commander, having her way with an enemy of her own when she caught sight of Sillona's fall. With an upward sweep of her hilt-less sword she sliced one of the two she'd been playing with in-half at the waistline. Then arching her blade swiftly around and back down she cleaved the other's head in two down the middle. Vexrile was hacking and chopping through the tangled throng of warring angels as quickly as she could, not caring if the bodies she was cutting through were those of her own comrades. She was nearly through to her wounded commander, no more than five or six yards to go, when she saw an eighteen foot tall Daemon, wearing several of her fallen comrade's severed heads on a chain slung over his shoulder, moving through the battle toward Sillona. The giants' massive size, enable him to reach Sillona's unconscious body before Vexrile. Standing over her, knocking a few of the surrounding warriors locked in battle away with some sweeps of his axe, he made himself room to work. Vexrile finally fought her way through the mob in time to see the giant kick Sillona onto her back and remove her helmet with a backhand sweep of his claw. He was raising his axe up to lop off Sillona's head when Vexrile, charging from behind him, swung her sword as hard and fast as her fury would grant. Like a hot blade melting through decayed flesh, she raced her sword's edge through the Achilles tendon behind his right ankle and both hamstrings behind his left leg. The giant fell to his knees snapping his attention around, over his shoulder onto his attacker, all the while his axe-blade still dropped. Vexrile darted between his collapsing legs, sweeping her blade around as she ducked through, opening his femoral artery. She slammed herself into the side of the wide axe blade, veering it off its intended path. The bleeding giant tried to put up a fight, but his rapidly draining efforts were sluggish at best and short lived. For the rest of that battle Vexrile guarded over Sillona, maintaining at least a fifteen foot space, surrounding it with the bodies of those who dared to venture within its ring.

Eventually that battle ended and Vexrile carried Sillona to her camp. Being a lesser angel, Vexrile's powers of healing were limited, so she had to depend mainly on her knowledge of healing roots and old fashion nursing to mend her commander's body. Luckily for Vexrile, more so for Sillona, the archangel had a strong will. It only took Sillona a few days to open her eyes and only a few more to be well enough to summon forth the strength of will to heal herself the rest of the way.

Sillona demanded to know what had happened, why she wasn't back at the main camp, healing in her own tent.

"I don't like it there," Vexrile told her, "I prefer to camp alone," She was using the arrow she'd dug out of Sillona's chest to hold a large rat in the fire, burning off its fur and cooking its meat like roasting a marshmallow.

"Is that the arrow that pierced me?" Sillona asked as she stepped over to her armor neatly placed on a rock. Not seeing her weapon she barked, "My sword! What have you done with it? Don't tell me you left it on the battle field?"

"No, it's there…beside the bed I made for you." Vexrile replied calmly before tearing a bite off the charred rat. With a mouth full of hot meat she added, "I thought it best to keep your weapon close to you. And…yes it is."

"Yes it is what?"

"Yes this is the arrow that nearly laid you cold and stiff."

Picking up her chest-plate, Sillona ran her thumb slowly over the hole made by the arrow, magically closing it as if it had never been there. Setting it back down with the rest of her armor, she stepped over and sat nakedly on the ground across from the lesser angel. As she ran her fingers along the cold surface of her sword's blade, her gaze drifting to the pouch around Vexrile's neck, Sillona asked. "You are of the Seraphim breed...yes?"

Vexrile flung what was left of her meal off the end of the arrow, sending it onto a small mound of rotting half eaten rats. Standing, she drew her sword. Sillona seeing threat in the action swept her blade up, standing as well. But her alarm was false. Vexrile, stabbing the end of her weapon into the ground, bowed her head as she lowered to a knee.

"I am called Vexrile, commander, and I shall forever be your servant...Do with me as you wish."

That night, in the secrecy of Vexrile's camp, Sillona rewarded the lesser angel for saving her life with a single droplet of her superior blood. The gift immediately transformed Vexrile into something much more than a lesser angel. That tiny drop of archangel blood gave her powers far beyond the imagination of her lowly breed. She'd been empowered with the knowledge to magically manipulate all forms of flesh and physical matter, seen and otherwise. All Vexrile had to give for this great reward was her oath that her loyalty to Sillona would never waver. Vexrile had been with Sillona—Vile ever since.

As Vile was making her way up the flight of hovering stairs, her back to Vexrile, she asked in a low voice.

"The pain, Overseer...was it as good for you as it was for me?"

It had been a rhetorical question, intended to antagonize the Overseer. But Vexrile, taking a fool's chance, shot Vile's back a hateful glance and tossed up a mockingly false reply in a blissful tone.

"A-a-a-a-h...it was so good my Queen."

Vile, reaching the top step, her back still to Vexrile, waved her left hand, sending unseen blades of ice up the Overseer's spine.

"Mind your uncivil tongue." Vile said as she turned to take her place atop her fleshy throne.

The brown leathery pouch containing the ashy remains of Alex's mother dropped out of the air to land a few inches from Vexrile's right hand.

"Pick it up piglet and stand."

Vile's transparent black gown melted swiftly into her skin, returning the Queen to her much favored nude state. Seeing that Vexrile wasn't getting to her feet quick enough for her taste, Vile shrieked, "I told you to get up *Bitch*!" She yanked the Overseer upright with an abrupt jolt that snapped Vexrile's jaws shut in the process, causing her to bite the tip of her tongue.

"Now listen carefully Overseer," Vile hissed, "do exactly as I say. Take that pouch to where you've hidden my choice."

Settling comfortably back in her throne, she willed it down through the dark coldness, stopping it slightly above Vexrile. Vile peered over one of the bodies down at her hybrid servant.

"Once you've made my choice's body whole, make a fresh wound someplace, make it deep...I don't care where. Then empty all the ash into the cut, and you best be damn certain you get every last speck of the ash in the wound before you close it."

Leaning back in her seat, she reached her open hand out and willed Vexrile up into the air, catching the Overseer by her throat.

"You shan't disappoint me now...will you piglet?"

Vexrile tried to choke an answer past Vile's fist clenched around her throat, but before the words, *No my Queen,* could squeeze over her teeth, Vile increased her grip. Smiling at Vexrile fondly she drew her closer, gazing deep into the Overseer's emerald green eyes, and said in a tone which held in its lilt both an endearing and threatening note.

"This part is very important Overseer, so do pay close attention. Do I have your utmost attention? Because, my dear Vexrile, if for some reason something goes wrong, I will lay the entire fault upon your pretty little rat eating head."

The pallid color of Vexrile's face had begun to tint from white to a shade of pink due to Vile clasping her windpipe almost completely closed. Her vision was steadily growing darker as the faint sound of Vile's giggling voice bled behind the buzzing that was filling her skull. Letting go of the Overseer, Vile kicked her off the throne, sending the gasping creature to the floor.

"Yes, I do believe I've possession of your full attention. Before my player is sent through the Wall, make certain that you tell him to avoid all the other players...but one. He must seek out the player with the black pouch first. Once he's sent that player out of the game, then and only then can he go after the other players. Do you understand…rat eater?"

Vexrile, pushed up onto her feet and as she tucked the pouch of ash down behind her sash, she answered with a painfully strained voice.

"Perfectly my Queen."

"You had better Vexrile. Remember, if anything goes amiss, your lovely green eyes will adorn my earlobes. Now go…do as I command."

To most, the only good part about being summoned to appear before Queen Vile was when the meeting had reached its conclusion. As with all who were fortunate enough to leave that icy chamber the same way they'd walked in, Vexrile had departed from Vile's company with an apparent spring of effervescence in her step. Zaw'naw's Overseer had wasted no time making her way down through Ebla, Vile's mountain city. Once outside the city walls and across to the other side of the wide canyon moat that surrounded Ebla, Vexrile stopped along-side the city's red-crystal-marker. After a brief moment of complete stillness, only her robes being slightly stimulated to movement by the cold night's breeze, she ran both the palms of her hands across the broken glass-like edge of the marker's corner. The action opened deep cuts in her skin that swelled with blood as she pressed her hands together side by side to fashion them into the shape of a bowl. Softly Vexrile breathed an incantation, she said, "Rise for me within the blood and fire of my condemned soul; worship me alone with sword and spear. Be thou thy gifted blade which bites, gnashes and tramples down mortal spite; be upon them o-warrior…o-shade, and I shall grant unto thee their flesh and bones to feast."

The blood flowing freely from the wounds laid in Vexrile's palms, filled up in her cupped hands, not so much as a single drop escaping out from between her clasped fingers. Only when the small vermilion pool was at the brink of breaching the banks of its fleshy vessel did she separate her hands, sending the thick living liquid down to splatter violently on the cold stone of the ground.

The instant the blood splashed, a pillar of fire rose high into the sky. Straight it reached-like a beacon of dull flame, giving off very little glow or even heat. In an upward corkscrew motion, from the base on, it twisted only to reverse the direction nearly as swiftly as it began. When the lusterless column of flame receded back down from whence it had been invoked, a twenty five foot tall beast, with the upright standing ability of a man and dark-red skin, appeared in the fire's stead. The giant was clad in crude battle dress made of metal plates, ring-mail and petrified bones, all locked tightly against his powerful frame with heavy iron chains and spikes. Its greatly misshapen head appeared out of place in regards to the large body of the beast; particularly its broad shoulders and thick neck due to its head's diminutive size. Two yellowish-white tusks rose up from its protruding lower jaw to a curved stop just below its white beady eyes. Despite this creatures' tiny eyes, it possessed the visual strength of an earthly Peregrine-falcon, and its powers of hearing and olfactory capabilities were equal to that of a wolf.

It was called a Skall, and in no way angelic or demonic. They were first created by higher level angels as servants to perform manual tasks. Skalls had also been later employed as battle mounts during both wars. Unlike demons, which had been created from the resurrected corpses of lesser angels who'd been slain in battle, skalls possessed no will of their own. All that they are instinctively aware of is their unquestionable duty to serve and protect the one who invoked them.

The giant's colorless eyes opened to leer down at Vexrile. Without so much as a grunt, it drew both of its heavy swords and went immediately to one knee, bowing its head and upper body low enough to offer Vexrile the saddle strapped onto its wide shoulders. Using the back of its clawed hand, bent knee, a forearm and its right shoulder-cap as stair-steps, she climbed up and took her place in the seat carved from bone.

The moment the beast felt that she'd settled somewhat comfortably in the hard saddle, he rose and without needing to be turned in the right direction broke into a fast run. For several miles the skall remained on the well traveled road, easily maintaining its swift clip, never once slowing or increasing its pace. Not even when approaching a large throng of damned souls being herded to their places of suffering. Vexrile's red giant would simply raise his blades and like a charging thrasher, slice its way through the chained together men and women, always remaining mindful enough not to fling any scraps of human on his green eyed master.

When the road came to its abrupt end at a drop off which gave way to a wide river of swift moving invisible flame, Vexrile's skall cut a sharp left, heading toward Zaw'naw's vast bad-lands; a perilous expanse of frozen emptiness that was rife with rogue cannibalistic angels and demons. They lay in wait high in the jagged rock and charred remains of once great trees for stray humans who'd somehow escaped their keepers, and travelers that had run out of safer road, but still had further to go. Not Vexrile and her sword wielding mount though. The nomadic flesh bandits had long ago come to know the painful folly of their efforts when they attempted to ambush Vexrile and her skall. The horde of a hundred or so teeth gnashing ghouls had dropped out of their hiding places, surrounding the two travelers. Without so much as slowing their stride or altering their course, Vexrile had shot forth a blinding spell that spread out as an unseen ring of heat that fried the hungry marauder's eyes out of their skulls. Then her red-skinned beast cleaved a wide path through the fools.

It would have taken Vexrile days to cross the sixth realm's icy wastelands on a human drawn land-barge, but astride the powerful shoulders of her skall the journey would last less than half a night. She could have easily called upon her adopted powers of self-transportation, via the magic given to her long ago in Vile's blood, but that would mean missing out on the opportunity of a road trip. Vexrile drew great pleasure from being carried at high rates of speed over these frozen bad-lands. She especially enjoyed it when her mount would sprint through rivers and lakes of boiling mud and fire, or when he would take to the air as he leapt across bottomless pits and wide ravines. She didn't care much for having to pass through the deep pockets of pitch-black void or when they were forced to charge face first into a sudden ice storm, neither of these events were high up on her to-do-list. But it was worth suffering such minor inconveniences for the chance of being taken for a ride on a behemoth. It was always at reaching the far side of the realm's Wailing-woods; with its trees blackened by a long ago battle fire, their petrified trunks bulging with the howling souls of the damned that Vexrile would feel a twinge of sadness wriggling against the outer layer of her calloused heart. It meant Vexrile's journey had come to its end.

The woods opened out onto a narrow road cobblestoned with human skull-caps, crudely locked in place with loose teeth and shattered finger bones crammed down between the rounded domes. After only ten miles this bizarre dirty-white pathway vanished with the abruptness that was commonplace in Hell. The road dropped off at the rocky edge of a cliff. A wide, twenty mile pit-like crevasse encompassed an enormous naturally formed pillar of solid rock. The black granite megalith rose straight up, dead center amidst a dense sheet of dark-gray vapor within the pit. At the pillar's apex was built a solitary iron tower that was dark-red, brown and black with age and rust. No gated wall surrounded it, or door that could offer some clue to an entrance. It reached up into the sky like a great arm of decaying metal, attempting to stab the emptiness above, scraping the heavy red vapor as it swayed slightly back and forth in the windless air. This was Vexrile's castle.

The space between the cliff's edge and her home was much too great for her skall, or any wingless beast to leap across. The giant knelt in order to offer his master an easy dismount. Without a word of thanks for another task well done, she stepped to the ground and moved toward the cliff's edge. The skall transformed to red ash and crumbled to the cold dirt where it would await a wind worthy enough to carry it off.

Vexrile brought her boots to a stop at the edge of the drop off and removed her hood. As she lowered her arms listlessly to her sides, she leaned her head all the way back as if to look straight up into the sky. The moment she opened her eyes a ghostly green mist flowed out of them in two long streams. When the glowing mist had pulled free from her eyes all the green that had filled them was gone, leaving the two orbs as white as dried stones. The streams of emerald gas formed a single cloud that hovered above Vexrile. Opening her mouth, she held it silently slack-jawed for a moment before loosing a loud blood-chilling scream that would have effortlessly put to shame any and all screams uttered in the whole of damnation that night. The shriek that she sent out pulled with it several ribbons of black and gray shadow that lashed forth like whips from her mouth, attacking the glistening cloud of green mist. The dark tentacles of dense air immediately wrapped around the cloud and began squeezing it. Vexrile snapped her mouth shut, cutting the dark strands loose as if her teeth and lips were razor sharp blades. Like thick bands of black rubber they sprang up to aid the rest of it in the attack against the mist, choking the green cloud as if it were an enemy that needed killing. The mist started shifting as though it were struggling against death itself and appeared as though it were losing the fight. Suddenly it drew the dark ribbons in, devouring them into its green cloud. As the ribbons of shadow melted out of sight, the cloud victoriously began to swell and shift, morphing into a larger and larger shape. Soon it had grown three times larger than Vexrile's red-skinned skall, and in the short amount of time it took her to whisper the words, "Ankh-af-na-khonsu," the shapeless mass of green gas had completed its transformation.

The emerald color of Vexrile's eyes and dark shadows of her scream had become a huge winged beast made of a green light. The flying phantom turned its empty eyeless sockets down onto Vexrile and let out a loud cry that sounded exactly like her own scream, blowing her hair and robes back with the wind-like force of its howl. It snapped its huge jaws shut and spun around to tear up into the sky. After a swift pass around Vexrile's castle it climbed like a spear straight up into the frigid air. It had nearly rose far beyond her power of sight, when without slowing its speed swooped back around and shot straight toward Vexrile. She stood her ground, like a willing sacrifice awaiting the bite of the blade. As the great beast drew rapidly near it eased its mouth open and with a loud high pitched shriek swung its head down and as it passed snatched Vexrile up. With the Overseer in the apparition's transparent jaws it spun about and once again climbed high into the night's red sky. With no warning it let itself free-fall listlessly back down, letting itself drop like a rock for several hundred feet before it rolled, once, twice than on the third turning tumble retook control and whipped toward Vexrile's castle. It passed through the solid metal wall of the tower as if the structure were made of smoke and shadow, landing on the iron floor of the castles main chamber. The moment its clear, clawed feet came to a stop, it lowered its massive green head and opened its mouth. Vexrile stood and stepped down off its tongue like a countess stepping out of a carriage. Turning, she faced the ghost and bowed her head in a slow thanks, then blew it a gentle kiss. The translucent beast shifted back down to a small, formless cloud of shimmering mist and streamed back into Vexrile's eyes, giving them their emerald hue once again.

Vexrile allowed herself to relax as she made her way down through her castle's labyrinth of complex corridors, perplexing passageways and sharply rising and descending flights of stairs. She was home, far from Vile's cold throne room, far from that insane creature's probing thoughts. She could rest a bit easier, let her guard down some and draw open the curtain that she'd devised to conceal her innermost thoughts from that maniac who would be Queen. Treacherous thoughts, which would certainly prove unpleasant for Vexrile and her co-conspirator if Vile was to learn of the scheme that was at that very moment unfolding and moving closer to de-throne the red-haired tyrant.

Into total darkness Vexrile moved down through air that grew noticeably warmer the deeper she went. With each sure placing of her boots she made her way steadily into the bowels of her castle tower. Soon the heat was sweltering, almost unbearable, even for Vexrile who loved stifling temperatures. Deeper and deeper she went, heading into the lowest, darkest and hottest chamber of the tower. Passing the point where the huge structure's iron foundation gave way to solid stone she stepped down through a narrow door made of petrified wood into an equally narrow stairwell. The heat this deep into her tower was smothering and dense, but to Vexrile it was still a pleasant change from Vile's icy throne room. The steep descent opened out into her personal dungeon. The moment she passed in through the doorless entrance Vexrile waved her hand, a gesture that magically opened the metal double doors to her single most prized possession. It was an early sixteenth century iron maiden, in better than mint condition. Little more than six hundred earthly years ago, give or take a decade, Vile had caught Vexrile creeping into her vault. The Overseer was sure she'd find some clue that would lead her to Vile's stash of angel's blood and hearts. It was Satan's blood that Vexrile sought. After coming to know first hand what the blood of an archangel could do for a lesser breed such as herself, and aware of the fact that Satan was the first angel that a God breathed life into, she was certain that a single drop of his ancient blood would give her power beyond even her own dreams. The truth was that Vile had possessed Satan's blood, every last drop of it, but was afraid to chance a taste, and was unwilling to test it on someone else, for fear that it might make a guinea-pig too powerful, even for her to control. So Queen Vile had destroyed all but one tiny drop of Satan's blood.

She waited in the shadows for Vexrile to come slithering out like a lowly human thief. When the Overseer had stepped out of the vault, her hands empty, Vile was quick to show Vexrile her anger. Without warning Vile transported her to Earth with only limited magic. She'd sent Vexrile into the body of a mortal infant at the moment of birth. All the while the Overseer for Hell's sixth realm was fully aware of who and what she really was, cursed to live the span of a human life, unable to cut that mortal life-span short with her own hand or actions.

Luckily for Vexrile the late sixteenth century infant that Vile had randomly cast her into was of noble birth and not that of a lowly peasant. Vile had sent her Overseer in to the flesh of a being that would grow up to be one of Europe's most feared rulers of the fifteen hundreds. A countess by the name of Elizabeth Bathory. Vexrile would make the best out of her punishment as she could with what she was left to work with. Locked in her mortal cell of flesh and blood she used the power of the countess to take out her anger and frustration on whoever she pleased until she was stopped by the church and charged with the crimes of murdering six-hundred and fifty young women and girls. It was said that she'd bled them dry so that she could bathe in their blood. Elizabeth...*slash*, Vexrile, the Overseer for Hell's sixth realm was sealed into a bed-chamber at the top of her castle's highest tower the only way in or out bricked shut. Her mortal shell lasted less than five years imprisoned alone in a cell of darkness until Elizabeth's body gave into death, thus setting Vexrile free. That iron maiden was all she brought back to Hell with her. That and the memories of the good times she and the blood countess shared.

It was inside this ancient—by mortal standards—torture device where Vexrile had stashed Vile's hand-picked player for the game. A choice that Vexrile believed to be grievously poor. Stanley Fiction had only just arrived in Hell when Queen Vile ordered Vexrile and Warfarin to gather together those humans who were physically and diabolically suitable to represent the sixth realm in the game. Once the Overseer and Grand Inquisitor had assembled well over a thousand men and women, they healed the possible players and took them to Ebla's coliseum. Vile was informed of the prospects made ready for her inspection and was on her way to choose the man or woman who she saw victory in. Vile was half way to the coliseum when her attention was drawn to a skinny, weak looking man dangling from one of the thousands of 'Waiting Hooks' driven through the back of his neck. The new arrival raised his head to watch Vile's precession passing by when she locked eyes with his leering gaze. Usually such a defiant look from any creature, especially the back-handed stare shot from a human's eyes directly into her's, would be rewarded with immediate pain, the likes never imagined possible by the foolish soul. But Vile saw wickedness deep in Stanley's eyes that told her, her choice was made. This new arrival would lead Zaw'naw to victory, she was sure of it. Compared to even the weakest of Vexrile's and Warfarin's gathered prospects vainly awaiting Vile's scrutiny, Stanley Fiction was a pathetic choice indeed.

After choosing Stanley, Vile told the captain of her Imperial Guard, a female angel of mixed breed by the name of Sumac, to inform the realm's Overseer and Grand Inquisitor that her choice had been made and to have all other prospects imprisoned within the solid stone of the coliseum's walls.

Vile's choice was delivered to Vexrile who was ordered to stash him away. In the relatively short space of time between being handed over to Vexrile and being stuffed into that iron maiden, the Overseer had illustrated to Mr. Fiction all of her frustration concerning her Queen's decision. His stay in Vexrile's dungeon had been filled with every form of flesh-tearing and bone-splitting torture demonically imaginable. For months he'd been her main source of entertainment until Vile had summoned her to the palace. Vexrile placed Mr. Fiction in the iron lady to await her return.

The crimes for which Stanley Fiction was handed over to Hell's sixth realm warranted such measures as eternal desolation. During his last seven years of life on Earth, he had lured eighteen homosexual young men into his car, drugged and kidnapped them. Stanley, who had held the position of Washington State's King county lead district attorney, would take his trapped prey to his home in the Queen Ann district of Seattle and get them ready. He would first go to work on stitching their mouths closed, and then carefully slice off both upper and lower eyelids. All the while methodically cauterizing the cuts in order to keep them from bleeding all over the rest of his work, blocking his view. It took him several failed attempts to master the art of a thousand cuts, but after his fifth victim Stanley had perfected his little pass time.

Hanging his captured queers from two hooks driven into the shoulder-caps, keeping them upright so Stanley could work anywhere on the body that the scrap of paper directed him to; the D.A. would begin. In a small wicker blood stained basket, Stanley would take out one piece of paper, about the size of a fortune-cookies message, where on was written a section of skin that covered a body-part. Some days he would draw half a dozen scraps of paper from the basket, where as others he would only take out one. It all depended on how he felt that day and what the first message read. Like for instance, if he was successful in a case, that is to say, if he sent someone to prison that day he would celebrate by spending most of the night working on his quarry in the basement. Or if the first scrap of paper read; *Remove nail from left big toe*, he would draw from the basket again, but only after he'd cut away the toenail.

There were a thousand scraps of paper in that little basket, and he would go through every one. It usually took him a week, sometimes less, to cut away all the skin on a body, leaving only the face, neck and groin areas untouched. The amazing thing was, in a grisly sort of way, Stanley had learned how to keep his victims alive and somewhat aware through the whole horrendous event. Other than a wood-burning tool that he would use to cauterize the cuts as he worked, all Stanley had to make the cuts with were two straight razors that he lovingly named Slasher and Slicer.

No one that knew good-old Stanley would have ever guessed that he was the one newspapers were calling...*The Skin Stealer*. To date, not a single scrap of any of his victim's removed epidermis has been located, nor was the skin's intended culinary conclusion ever learned of. Stanley had taken his ghastly secret with him to the grave. A grave that was opened by a death that was as uneventful as a turd dropping out from a dog's ass.

The moment the iron maiden's sections swung open and its long metal spikes pulled out of Stanley, his festering husk of a body was yanked out by Vexrile's mental will. She flung him all the way across the huge dungeon and slammed him against the far wall like a broken doll. He slid down the slime covered stone to splash in the foot deep flood that inundated the floor. Vexrile waved her hand again, dragging Stanley's body through the swamp of putrid blood; black and thick with spoilage and decaying flesh. He was moved quickly, face down through the ruin, and brought to a painful stop when his skull smacked against the base of Vexrile's stone platform. Again she waved her hand, and before her fast flick of the wrist was completed Stanley was scraped up, out of the foul ooze and suspended in the air before her. As Vexrile's mental power held him up at eye level she gazed deep into his rotted black eyes and smiled fondly at him.

"I'm truly sorry Mr. Fiction for having to leave you for so long."

Wiping some of the blackened slime away from his eyes with the balls of her thumbs, she positioned the tips of each nail under what was left of his rotted eyelids and explained.

"I'd been called away," she said with a soft smile as she pressed the ends of her thumbnails against his festered skin. Two yellowish-brown drops of pus rose from the tiny punctured holes and trickled like thick tears down his cheeks. "I'm back now and I've some news for you. Whether or not its good news will depend upon your ability to persevere over adversity."

Vexrile positioned her thumbnails under his eyes again, and took a hold of both sides of his head. Pulling him a few inches closer, she added, "Yes, as a matter of fact…Mr. Fiction, if you do well, there'll be no more of this."

With that said, Vexrile pressed her thumbnails into the centers of Stanley's eyes, causing the muscles in his cheeks to twitch with pain. His teeth chattered together as she rammed the nails home, piercing them through the rubbery membrane and thin layers of moist tissue. Thick mud-like bloody mucus bled out passed the sinking thumbs. Stanley let out a low rattling sound, his best attempt at a scream perhaps. Vexrile's invading digits eventually broke past the orbital sockets of his skull. After giving her probing thumbs a bit of a twist, making Stanley jerk and twitch spastically like a rotting meat puppet struggling in its attempt to cheat its way to life, Vexrile yanked her thumbs out of his brain. Giggling girlishly, she wiped most of the grey-matter off on his chest, while marveling at the sight of the fat maggots wriggling beneath the skin sparsely covering his face and neck.

In the few seconds that it took Vexrile to smear the gunk off her thumbs onto his skin, she'd magically willed his body completely healed. She grinned hungrily at him as his new eyes reformed within their sockets. The moment Stanley's sight was strong enough to focus and she was certain all of his visual attention was fixed onto her face, she latched a hold of his head again, drew him near, and contemporaneously leaned closer. She smiled at him, an endearing expression on her cold, stony face before running her long blue tongue slow over his newly formed lips. She was in the process of giving him a passionate kiss, sliding her tongue into his mouth over his, her right hand caressing his torso.

To Stanley the touch of a female, whether they be from Earth or Hell was as excruciating as the most harrowing torment that he'd been made to suffer. During his life he'd gone to great-pains to keep as much distance between them and himself as possible and still appear to maintain a comparatively normal coexistence with those he referred to as Gash Breeders. It was at his second most favorite place on the planet—work, where he ran across his greatest difficulties. Once he'd even had a woman D.A. transferred to another office simply because she pressed one of her breasts against his arm while leaning over him at his desk to look at some documents, claiming sexual-harassment. In criminal cases where the accused was a woman he went after them with all the power and zeal his office had to offer. Although his conviction rate with women was far more impressive than of his male perpetrators, most of his fellow D.A.s could care-less.

Yes, Stanley saw all women, young and old, rich or poor, as disgusting creatures that he was forced to endure. So, this being the case, it wouldn't be a stretch to say having Vexrile's tongue deep down his throat and her hand being slid gently down his body was as torturous for him as when she'd torn his bones, one by one out of his flesh.

A crooked smile pulled secretly onto Vexrile's intentions as her slowly descending hand reached its destination. She broke the kiss, bringing her tongue out of Stanley's mouth and pulling her gaze from his face's horrified expression to look down. She grabbed onto his penis and testicles with a powerful grip, saying as she squeezed, "You won't be needing these."

With an abrupt yank Vexrile tore his puny manhood off and dropped the severed parts toward the black pool of slime covering the floor. The instant before Stanley's family-jewels splashed down into the thick ooze, a fist-size head like that of a sea snake sprang up past the mucky surface and snatched the falling flesh in its toothy jaws.

A drunken gaze sparkled in Vexrile's green eyes, warning Stanley that she was just getting started. Stepping back one pace she healed the gaping wound closed with nothing more than a smooth layer of skin, rendering him a sexless eunuch. Licking her fingers clean of blood, she asked rhetorically, "So lover...how would you rate my kiss against that of one of your stolen queers?"

Stanley had been trying to scream out ever since Vexrile had made her touch known to him, but was unable to utter a sound other than a hiss or chattering teeth. She'd taken his voice. For whatever reason she believed it would make his suffering more enjoyable for her. Perhaps it had something to do with him stitching his victim's mouths shut.

Bringing Warfarin's leather pouch out from behind her waist-sash, she began searching over Stanley's body, looking carefully at his new skin for a suitable place to make the fresh opening Vile had ordered done. Stopping her roaming gaze on a spot, she whispered barely loud enough for him to hear.

"I've got the spot. Hows about right—here."

Before she'd completed the word here, Vexrile sent her left hand straight into his chest and after rooting it around for a few seconds, all the while drinking in his agony, she tore out Stanley's still beating heart. With a forceful pull she ripped it loose from the arteries and veins. Spurts of blood jetted out wildly like several high pressure water lines being cut apart until they snapped back into the hole her fist made in his chest.

Without hesitation, Vexrile raised the dripping organ up to her wide-opening jaws. As the heart drew near, her teeth grew pointed and longer before Stanley's eyes. Her entire top row of teeth had stretched outward a full two inches when she'd brought his heart close enough. The Overseer sank the top row of teeth down into the fleshy blood pump only to bring them directly back out. Stanley had thought for a moment she was going to eat his heart right before his own eyes, but what her true intentions were had turned out to be even more gruesome and perplexing.

She willed Stanley's right hand raised, turning his open palm up. "Hold this a moment please." Placing his heart on his palm and willing his fingers and thumb to grip it, she allowed her teeth to recede back to their normal size and pulled open the pouch. "Thank you," she said softly as she retook possession of the heart, squeezing it in her fist in order to force the incision open she'd made with her teeth. With the gash formed to a gaping hole she emptied Alex's mothers ashy remains into Stanley's heart, every last flake.

Once this strange task was completed as instructed, Vexrile rammed the organ back into its intended place, immediately reattaching all the arteries and veins. The moment her hand had slid out of his chest cavity, she willed the wound closed, healing his chest.

Of course Stanley had no clue as to why Vexrile had used his heart as an ash-tray. Before his confused mind could give the event a moment's thought she wiped its occurrence out of his memory. All she left for him to recall of that event was the pain and horror.

Vexrile stepped back, waving her hand with an almost uninterested gesture sending Stanley flying backward through the sweltering air. He slammed back into the iron maiden, the dagger like spikes stabbing through his mended body with the closing of its doors.

Vexrile was passing through the doorway of her play-room when she stopped and said under her breath, "Silly me, I nearly forgot."

She vanished out of Stanley's line of sight beyond the maiden's eye-holes when the former district attorney loosed a loud scream that blasted out of the hollow statue to echo throughout the chambers and corridors of Vexrile's castle. She'd given Stanley back his voice.

Although the rest of Hell's Empire was engulfed within the grips of a scarlet night, the sky Alex had dropped out of was still that of a mid summer's day. It had been while Vile was ordering Vexrile to check on the artist's work in the cage, that Alex left the impression of his bone crushing landing in the ground.

"Sit up Mr. Stone," Pike said. "You've no time for dawdling about or staring stupidly up into the sky."

Alex shook off the lingering effects of the landing and set his bewildered attention onto the Gate Keeper, his bones and joints popping with the stiffness of rapid healing as he sat up. He saw that Pike was holding a shoe box size black wooden case. Alex locked his leering gaze into the blackness within Pike's wide hood in an effort to see through the shadow and put a face to the child's voice. Alex had a strong feeling that he'd known or at least seen this little fellow somewhere. It wasn't Pike's voice or the being's movements that peaked his sense of familiarity. Alex was certain he'd never heard Pike's voice before, and as for his movements, all Alex had been able to give notice to was a few hand gestures and some slight shifting of his hooded head. The rest of Pike's motion of body was hidden beneath layers of black and red cloth.

Alex, not taking into account the raking pain that so far had always accompanied Pike's appearances, saw the Gate Keeper's arrival as an opportunity to get some answers. He sprang up and lurched toward Pike who in turn stepped to one side faster than Alex's mortal vision could follow. He stumbled past the Gate Keeper, nearly tumbling face first into the grass. Catching himself, he spun about and immediately dropped his sights onto Pike, who was standing less than five paces from him.

"You were simply told to sit up—not stand."

Alex was about to reply with another charge when his eyes burst into flames. Before the scream invoked by the searing pain in his skull could explode out passed his teeth, Alex's eyes had been incinerated out of their sockets.

"My eyes!" He ran his trembling gloved fingers lightly over the scorched meat and bone, carefully groping the small shallow pits that had only a moment ago housed his baby-blues. He dropped to his knees, stumbled back up, only to fall once more and steady himself up onto his feet again.

"What the fuck's up with you? Are you so damned retarded that you don't realize the fact that I don't belong here? Don't you know who I am...you blinded me! Fix it! Fix my eyes you fucking little punk!" Alex demanded as he stumbled toward the sound of Pike's muffled snickering, the Gate Keeper clasping a hand over his mouth in an attempt to stifle his laughter.

Alex staggered toward the faint sound of Pike's enjoyment. With his hands outstretched and swinging back and forth through the empty air, he stumbled clumsily over the thick grass that snagged onto his boots, nearly tripping him with each shuffled step.

The Gate Keeper crept up behind Alex, following him step for step, all the while finding it increasingly more difficult to maintain his silence. His chosen player's awkward hunt for him was proven too much for Pike's self-control to tolerate. Unable to hold his laughter at bay for another second, Pike let fly a belly-laugh that only served to piss Alex off even more. He spun around, sweeping his hands down, missing the still chuckling Pike by mere inches.

"Go ahead, laugh you little freak," Alex barked.

"Blah—blah—blah," Pike replied, "isn't that what you said to me when I came to introduce myself back in the boneyard—blah—blah—blah?"

"When I get my hands on you," Alex was nearly stuttering with rage, "you'll wish you'd taken my arms as well!"

Pike was having too much fun bedeviling Alex to let his insignificant threats wriggle their way under his skin. All was going fine until Alex's boot got caught in the ankle high grass and he tripped, brushing his right elbow acrossed Pile's left shoulder. As touches go it was hardly feather light, but still it was all it took to spoil the giggling Gate Keeper's good fun.

Pike caught Alex's fall in mid tumble with only the power of his mind, locking him between the fabrics of time and space like a flesh and blood statue. Setting the box he'd been carrying down on the grass, he then turned his attention around onto Alex's burned out eye-sockets and calmly said. "You touched me. No being—not of my own breed or that of a lesser creature has so much as considered laying a finger on me in well over a hundred thousand years." Pike declared. It was a lie of course; his fellow caretakers greeted him almost daily with hugs and hand-shakes, not to mention sparring matches with sword and lance against other archangels. There were times, though few, when a damned soul had the unfortunate luck of skimming too closely against his robes. Phenomenons such as those always ended with the clumsy human being immediately fed to something highly unpleasant. Pike had lied to Alex simply to make himself seem even more inauspicious. It was unnecessary over-kill persiflage…nothing more.

Pike released his mental hold on him, allowing Alex to complete the interrupted fall. No sooner had he hit the ground and he was yanked up into the air. Being suddenly raised high up into the sky against one's will is disconcerting on its own. But to a soul trapped in the grips of blindness, whether it be temporary or never-ending, the unsettling occurrence is quantified greatly by the horror of the unknown.

Alex had no idea how high Pike had sent him up. To him in his visually blackened state, the abrupt, almost neck snapping stop may as well have been a mile high or less than ten feet. It was neither, Pike willed Alex to a hovering pause thirty feet above the ground and spoke directly into the inner-most core of Alex's mental consciousness.

"Your insolence stops here and now Mr. Stone," said the Gate Keeper before letting go.

It hadn't been a bone crushing landing, but it was still painful never-the-less, instantly and with solid force knocking all the air out of Alex's lungs. He tried to move as he attempted to refill his lungs with oxygen, each sucking intake a painful gulp, as if every eager breath was filled with molten lead. Shaky with the dull throb of pain and seething rage, Alex forced himself up, or at least was in the process of doing so when hundreds of chains shot up out of the ground surrounding him. Like a moving cage they encircled him. Alex could hear them clanging together and could smell the strong scent of rust and metal.

"What are you waiting for? I can't see, that should make it easy for you!" Alex struggled to shout, the pain in his chest and lungs making his attempt to sound fearsome come off forced and weak. He swung his fist at the chains, missing them by inches as they move out of the way of Alex's leather clad flesh club. "Whats going on? What is it you're doing!" he demanded to know.

Pike offered no answer to Alex's enquiry, he just silently looked out past the darkness of his hood and secretly smiled as small hooks grew up out onto the ends of each dancing chain. Alex kicked at the sound of clanging metal, again missing. He was nearly up on his knees when they all simultaneously reared their hooked ends like snakes about to strike and whipped down. All the air Alex had fought to refill his lungs with was blasted back out with the help of a loud howling scream as the barbed ends of those hooks made themselves known to his flesh. They tore down through his clothes, past his outer skin to drive deep into the meat of his arms, legs, chest and face. Alex was snapped to the ground, locked in place flat on his back and held there with the same unyielding relentlessness of titanium shackles. Still he fought furiously against their flesh piercing, bone scraping embrace. All he earned for his efforts were lessons in misery and futility. The more he thrashed and the harder he struggled to rip himself loose, the deeper and tighter the barbed restraints sank and gripped.

As Alex was beginning to think that things couldn't possibly get any worse, two hooks that had been stabbed into both of his upper inner thighs wriggled back out and re-positioned themselves in his lower jaw bone. With unbelievable power of will the hooks, with the steady aid of their chains forced Alex's mouth open wider than he'd ever thought humanly possible. The snapping and popping sounds of his jaw's objection to this treatment affirmed loudly the painfulness of this unpleasant development.

Pike, who'd been cleaning a bit of dirt out from beneath his fingernails, stepped around Alex to stand over his head. Looking silently down at his chosen player's blind, bleeding face, he watched as Alex's unsurrendering spirit fought a battle it had to know it couldn't possibly win. It pleased Pike, Alex's unwillingness to give in; he knew he'd made an excellent choice in this killer who'd called himself 'Millstone.' Never-the-less, this human still needed to be taught his place, an uncontrollable beast, strong-willed or not is still only that—an uncontrollable beast. No good for anything but screaming and bleeding. Pike lowered to one knee and leaned the opening to his hood down close to Alex's face, the dense shadow within churning an inch from the tip of his nose. "You're going to really want to see this Mr. Stone."

Alex tried to utter an indiscernibly verbal threat but Pike interrupted his gagging grunts with. "If you wish your sight returned to you, you'll hold your vain words at bay."

At learning this Alex even mellowed his struggling against the hook's bite. Pike straightened his back, remaining on one knee as he healed Alex's charred, empty eye-sockets, giving him back his steely blue eyes, all but his eyelids. Rising up off his knee, Pike stayed standing over Alex's head, and said as he waited for his eyes to focus. "Time is short Mr. Stone and though that is an unchangeable truth, I fear you must be made to understand."

Alex's eyesight forced past the bright fuzziness of rebirth to focus on Pike towering over him. The Gate Keeper raised his right hand and snapped his fingers. In a flash of black light he was suddenly clutching in his small fist the biggest damn maggot that Alex had ever seen. At least, it's long slimy legless body resembled a maggot's. Its head on the other hand, or the lack there of, was nothing more than a small, but wide mouth—filled with dozens of sharp looking teeth. They were the sort of arrow-head shaped teeth that would have made a great-white shark proud. Its width and length was about the size of a sixteen once beer can and its color was the same as hardened pus.

"This breed of cutworm is found only on this world, we've given it the name Cha'szkid, loosely translated into your bland language Mr. Stone, its name means Tongue Worm. Guess what it eats?"

Alex didn't need eyelids to illustrate his terror, fed by the realization of Pike's intent for that jaw snapping creature he was positioning directly over his forced open mouth. He was trying to shout *No, don't do that!* As he started thrashing against the chains and hooks, but his plea came out a "Yuoo cunk uo fat!"

As Pike leaned over, lowering the snapping, wiggling maggot closer, he saw that the hooks were bleeding his player out, and though no real harm could come of it, Pike was reminded of something he heard Alex say to someone once. With a slight chuckle Pike quoted the player using Alex's voice. "It would be a damn tragedy if you were to bleed to death before we had a chance to kill you."

That said Pike relaxed his grip allowing the creature to slide from his hand straight into Alex gaping jaws. As it squirmed and worked over half of its slimy girth into his mouth, Pike began his lecture.

"You will do exactly as you're told Mr. Stone—yes you shall or upon my oath, if you continue acting out your suffering will reach epic proportions. It'll go like this—when you're told to walk; you'll walk and when you're told to sit, what will you do?—you'll sit! There will be no more foolishness. From hence forward you will unquestionably follow all orders."

Pike paused a moment to gaze on the worm's progress. There was only about three inches of its fat twitching rear-end protruding out of

Alex's mouth. Alex's jerking and kicking had grown so violent that the hooks were forced to depend on more than skin and meat to hold him, their barbed ends had imbedded into bone. But even with all of his wild thrashing, and through the immense pain of having his flesh torn and his tongue eaten away bite by bite, he never took his leering gaze out of the pitch black emptiness within Pike's hood.

"Now to answer the conundrum that's been strangling your brain ever since you first laid eyes upon the boneyard. No…an error has not been made concerning your being condemned to Damnation. We do not commit false moves, not ever! You're in Hell Mr. Stone because you've earned it."

The worm was making its voracious way down Alex's throat, gagging him without mercy while it ate his tongue clear down to the roots. Pike's eyes drifted onto Alex's crumpled hat lying on the grass half way between the black box and their little party. Pike reached his hand toward the black fedora and as if it were fastened to the end of a long rubber-band it flew straight into his beckoning grip. After pressing it back into its intended shape, he slid his hood back, dragging the heavy shadow with it. It was at this point that Alex, even in this grisly predicament, realized from where he'd seen Pike at before. The Gate Keeper for the eighth realm of Hell was the same red haired phantom that has been appearing to him off and on since he was a boy.

Pike's expression silently told Alex, *that's right Mr. Stone, I've been watching you for a very long time…what are you going to do about it?*

The instant he placed Alex's hat on his head of messy red hair it decreased in size, fitting his child's dome perfectly.

From the moment Pike had dropped the tongue worm down Alex's throat it only took it a few long and pain-filled minutes for it to make a quick meal of his tongue. As soon as it was finished it worked its way backward out of his mouth, releasing an acid-like secretion from two glands in the back of its jaws that cauterized the bleeding wound closed where Alex's tongue had been. Once out it slid down the side of his face, leaving a smeared mix of slime and blood down his cheek. As soon as it vanished into the thick grass with Alex's tongue in its maggot belly Pike waved his hand through the air over Alex, causing the two hooks to tear out of his jaw and swiftly whip back down into the ground. Alex tried shutting his mouth, but the chains had wrenched it open so wide that his jaw bone had been jerked out of joint. Noticing Alex's dilemma, Pike willed his jaw reset and closed. His teeth slammed shut with a great deal of pain, but it wasn't so much his pearly-whites being crashed together that hurt as it was the muscles in his jowls from being so painfully stretched.

"If you agree Mr. Stone to behave yourself and listen to what I've got to say, I'll return to you your tongue."

Pike waved his hand over Alex again, making the nest of hooks rip out of his flesh and bones with a single concerted tearing snap. The scream Alex sent out was as loud—if not louder—than the one he voiced when the hooks had been driven in. Before his pain-filled cry had faded to silence in the clear blue sky, the chains with their hateful hooks had disappeared back into the ground. The deep holes and rips that riddled Alex's body from his face down to his hands and feet healed, and the blood that literally drenched his clothes moved out of the cloth back into the closing wounds. Other than his eyelids and tongue not being returned to their correct places Alex, was completely made whole again. As his torn clothes, gloves and boots mended, Pike stepped leisurely over to where he'd laid the box and stood behind it, turning to face Alex.

"I'm going against my better judgment. I'll relax my mind's grip on you—don't disappoint me Mr. Stone."

Alex felt the crushing weight of thst Gate Keeper's power rise up off him.

"Sit upright Mr. Stone, face me…please."

Moving with slow disinclination Alex did exactly as he was instructed. Although Alex was fairly certain that this Pike fellow was much more than some sort of hellish child, and though during his adult life he'd never so much as considered doing anything to harm a little one, there was nothing he wanted more at that moment than to bend that brat over his knee and give him what-for. He leered spitefully at Pike's face beneath his shrunken fedora, wearing it cocked slightly to the right like a kid mimicking Frank Sinatra. *That's my hat*, Alex caught himself thinking like a child, unwilling to share nicely with the other children…*give it back now! Its mine!*

The human like appearance of Pike's icy-blue eyes was abruptly overpowered by their true crimson hue. His eyes had taken their real color so suddenly that Alex jerked as if he were about to put more space between him and his host, but stopped himself. As he struggled against the phantom sensation of his nonexistent tongue pressing up onto the roof of his mouth, he kept remembering times when during his life he'd catch brief glimpses of Pike peering out of the shadows at him. He remembered Mr. Bane asking him what he'd seen in Five's bedroom that last night of fun and how upset the metallic voice got when he wouldn't give it a straight answer. Suddenly, as he was recalling Pike's shadowy visits, he was struck by an unsettling possibility. *Was all of it meant to happen the way it had,* he wondered, *was it all some sort of deliberate experiment and if so—why?*

Pike interrupted Alex's thoughts, his youthful sounding voice owning a pleasant, friendly tone. "I'll allow you your eyelids back now if you at least make some effort to mellow that vexed gaze you seem so foolishly intent on aiming my way. Nod your head if you agree to try."

Pike's offer had barely begun to fade to silence when Alex's head motioned a single, sharp Yes. His eyelids were back in an instant. He started blinking his eyes immediately in an attempt to moisten them. At first the fast closing and opening of the lids felt as though tiny bits of glass was being dragged over the dry surfaces of the soft orbs. It wasn't until his eyes started to water that the scratchy, burning sensation in them began to cool and sooth some. Alex consciously attempted to control his expression when he looked back at Pike. The Gate Keeper shook his head, smiled and said, "It needs work...but I'll let it slide by for a while." After a long silence, perhaps ten whole minutes of nothing but the two staring at one another, Pike let himself fall listlessly backward. At the same time a rounded white rock rose up out of the grass to catch his descending rear-end. When Pike was settled somewhat comfortably on his stone stool he broke the quiet saying, "It appears as though you're finally willing to pay-attention—good. Crawl over here."

Pike motioned his hand to a spot opposite the box in front of him. Alex went to stand as if to walk over when Pike hissed coldly, "I said crawl." Seeing the possibility of something rakingly painful swelling in Pike's expression, Alex dropped grudgingly to his hands and knees and crawled to where Pike's finger was pointing. Sitting on his knees in front of the box, Alex looked down at it and for the first time since his death caught sight of his face, or at least what he looked like now. It was looking up at him from the reflective surface of the black boxes' polished lid. It wasn't the fact that his skin color or the lack of it was as white as wet cotton or that he had no hair on his head, no eye brows or even lashes that put him off, it was that his mustache was gone. Alex had of course known it wasn't there from the moment he first felt his healed face in the red desert, but he had no idea how silly he thought he would look without it. From the time Alex had been able to grow it; he'd had it, only shaving it off once when he was twenty-two after losing a football bet in the county-jail.

Pike brought Alex out of his reflection back into the here and now, telling Alex to lean a bit closer. He glanced up at the white face beneath his hat and reluctantly inched toward Pike on his rock. "A little closer please." Pike said with a trusting smile like that of a public defender telling his penniless client. "Don't worry; I've got this case in the bag. The D.A.'s office has nothing on you."

As Pike's little ghostly white hand reached out to touch Alex's forehead, Alex jerked back away.

"Don't you ever pull away from me again! Now come here and don't move."

Hearing the strong note of threat in Pike's tone Alex drew near. As Pike's open hand moved, Alex noticed the red glow in the Gate Keeper's eyes was steadily dimming. Like the tiny flames of candles coming to the ends of their diminishing wicks, the lights in Pike's eyes flickered out until they were as black as cobalt stars. The hand was less than an inch from Alex's head when Pike opened his mouth to release a pitch black flood of dense smoke. It poured forth like a thick cloud of ink jetting out of cephalopod into a vast space of crystal clear water. The moment Pike's cold hand laid against Alex's forehead the vaporous darkness emerging out of the Gate Keeper had completely enveloped all light. It was so totally void of any lambent whatsoever that if not for the fact that he could feel Pike's touch, he wouldn't have been able to discern whether or not he was in one place, or being hurtled through the endless black ether of space. Pike's voice began moving through the darkness. Alex couldn't tell if it was whispering toward him from far off or was speaking out from deep within his own awareness. The words moved softly—gently into every fiber of Alex's being, saying, "Now see what only celestial hearts have been made to suffer. Understand what it is to embrace the weight of angelic woe. Ve'zua'vuo La'Qots."

Pike's words faded away behind the faint whisper of a gentle breeze that brushed easily past Alex's face and neck. The darkness cleared and Alex found himself standing upright beside Pike atop the flat roof of a great cathedral's highest tower. The enormous structure was made of the whitest stone that Alex had ever seen. It seemed to have no seams or joints of any sort that might offer some clue as to how it was built, as though cut from a mountain of solid stone. All of the windows, large and small—arched, round and square, were made of stained-glass with beautifully colored images. A magnificent lake, crystal clear and huge surrounded the cathedral's massive rock foundation and beyond this blue body of water stretched a spectacular mountain landscape. Alex saw deep forests rich with a seemingly endless wealth of trees. A vast panoramic labyrinth of clean rivers and streams zigzagged through wooded valleys and canyons. This beautiful sight was mantled beneath a sky so completely quintessence that it would be worth killing millions to preserve.

Looking up at Alex from under the fedora's brim, Pike waved his hand out slowly like a guide motioning one's awestruck gaze onto this sublime kingdom and said, "All of this was our prison—our place of eternal banishment from our home world."

His outstretched hand dropped limply to his side and after a long pause he set his attention back onto the splendor before him and continued, his tone of voice noticeably melancholy.

"The world we were banished from would make this planet and a million—billion like it resemble desolate moons."

Again he paused, but only to clear his throat of the lump of sadness swelling in it, returning his voice back to its usually flat monotone inflection. "Beautiful…isn't it?" He asked as he glanced up at Alex again to see his tongueless reply with a slow nod.

"You've no doubt heard tell of, or perhaps read about a war that was supposed to have taken place long before the stars were set in the heavens around your world. A war of angelic beings, good and bad angels, one army fighting on the side of a God and the opposing army fighting on the side of a rebellious archangel by the name of Satan. Well, Mr. Stone, there was a war, two of them actually. The first of which had occurred almost close to the account you've been told. It had been a struggle against servitude. In other words, we were fighting for our freedom. Only it wasn't a third of us standing head to head against the rest of God's unwavering angels. No Mr. Stone...it was all of us. Every Archangel and Seraphim, all of Daemon and Hourii, even the great-giant Cherubim took up the sword and raised the lance against the Gods. Yes, you heard me correctly, I said gods, as in the plural. Most human tellings of that war tell of only a single God, an almighty creator of all things who reigns creation alone. The truth is—and it is the truth, there are many thousands of deities, more in fact than your moronic imagination could ever hope to envision. As with the vast numbers of the Gods, our count was great as well. I still feel an overwhelming sense of power and find myself slipping headlong into the belief that we were invincible, that we actually stood a chance at victory."

Pike's shiny black eyes closed as he paused a moment, his expression resembling a child's day-dreaming demeanor. "I still see that grand ocean of angelic might spread out before my memory, intoxicating my heart with the notion that we were strong enough to overpower all of those Gods. It had been then—and forever will remain—a fool's dream. The battles were relatively short by immortal standards, the entire war lasting less than thirteen hundred human years. At its conclusion the final body count of my fallen comrades was well over seven-hundred-thousand, leaving only four-hundred and forty-four thousand wounded and war weary angels left in the whole of creation. As for the God's casualties, its number was nil, we barely left them with a black-eye. Now, the Gods being the pompous lot that they are known to be, foresaw their victory long before the war's end and created this world for us. They gave us this planet as a sort of lesson, as in: be careful what you ask for...you just might get it. It had been an angelic duty to name a new world, but after our little would-be rebellion, the Gods thought it best that they should title this one. They called it Bay'soar, translated into man's tongue it means Gehanna or Hell. But to those of us who had the misfortune to have survived the God's wrath over our quest for freedom, we called this green and blue ball of rock and mud, prison."

Again Pike paused, falling silent as if his train of thought was being slowly pulled out of focus by the endless beauty of the surrounding landscape.

Alex immediately recognized the tone in Pike's voice. It was the beaten lilt, though masked in the pride that reverberates in the spoken words of all prisoners. A tone of voice that easily finds its way into the ears that truly know it due to their personal familiarity with the loneliness, loss and silent rage that bleeds out from between the words themselves. Alex knew all too well that it didn't matter what a cage or cell looked like. It could be filled from the bars to the stainless-steel crapper with all the bull-shit amenities that the State dangled in front of the convicts noses in order to pacify them it was still just a cage.

"You're most likely thinking 'not bad for trying to forcefully unseat the Gods', but if you had the slightest idea as to what we were cast out of, the true paradise we'd lost, you would understand what a foolish error in judgment we had made...you would come to know a level of loss so dreadful that it crushes all hope.

"The Gods in their self-awarded infinitely bumptious wisdom, exiled us to this wilderness. Allowing us higher breeds of angels to retain a limited measure of what you perceive as being supernatural powers. We licked our wounds and tried our best to make a home for ourselves here. But despite this planet's grand beauty it could in no way replace the majesty of our parent world. Still we tried, all the while clinging to the hope that someday the Gods might see their way into forgiving us. That is, most of us tried. Satan on the other hand wasn't as willing to settle the matter of our defeat so inoffensively.

Satan and his most devoted followers refused to simply lay down their arms and swallow the bitter elixir of being vanquished and exiled for their efforts. He tried to convince the rest of us into making another go at conquering the Gods, but his cry for a return to war was muted by the all still too fresh memory of how easily we had been subjugated. We, that is those of us who chose to pay Satan's ravings no mind, had grown jaded of battle. All we wanted to do was make the best of our second chance. But he and his followers were so overwrought by our defeat and subsequent expulsion from our true home that they'd rather have been slain in battle than remain sheepishly here on this wilderness planet.

Satan once again took up arms, only this time it was against those of us who refused to stand with him. There were nine of us commanded in all who chose not to follow Satan's folly a second time. It was a fairly safe bet that the Gods wouldn't take being challenged again as kindly as the first time. Each of us commanding our own armies which we promptly made ready. We offered our old friend a chance, urging him to stop his fool hardly quest. With an arrow sent message we warned him that there would be no way we would allow him to wage a second war against the Gods.

Satan's hatred for them had eaten away all of his sense of reason. He had assembled a great gathering of followers, some of which were powerful archangels whom he sent out to raise as many fallen warriors as they could from their graves, thus the creation of this world's demons and monsters. He armed his army of darkness with blades and arrows, empowering them with the knowledge of combative skills which far surpassed all that they had known before their deaths.

We on the other hand still out numbered him, nine armies to his one. It didn't matter; his lust for war blinded his ability to realize the utter futility of his blood-thirsty ambitions.

"I would rather suffer death in battle at the end of my old comrade's blades than lay down my sword and rot on this world," proclaimed Satan.

"So came the second great war," Pike went silent.

Suddenly Alex's attention was drawn around onto several columns of thick black smoke far off on the horizon. They reached up out of the woods completely surrounding the cathedral. The faint sounds of yelling voices and clattering metal pushed swiftly through the once peaceful-quiet that had only a moment earlier owned the air. Within a matter of seconds the far away sounds of battle had grown to a roar of blood-chilling cries and crashing steel. The thunder and smoke of war drew close; soon Alex could see the glow of fire deep within the dense forests as well as the tips of the flames erupting up past the tree tops. They lashed out like dancing tongues, laying the surrounding woods to waste. As for that beautiful sky, it was quickly engulfed by a pitch black veil of smoke. The cool breeze was assassinated by a strangling heat. With the hot wind came the overpowering stench of blood and burning flesh. The sound of clanging metal and death howls had swelled to a deafening chorus. Alex stared intently at the far side of the lake, expectantly watching for the hordes of battling angelic warriors to burst out of the tree line any second. With streams of blood leading the way out of the woods onto the rocky banks of the lake the battle pushed out of the burning forests. The lake's thin strip of drift-wood and stone covered beach was in moments filled with warring angels and nightmarish creatures of all breeds. There were two separate distinguishable groups; one clad heavily in dark-red armor; the other wearing black metal. They fought furiously, wielding every style of bladed weapon ever devised within the deepest depths of a million children's night-terrors. The warring throng hacked, chopped, clawed and bit into each other with the fury of being trapped helplessly in the bone crushing grip of their own blood-lusts. Those who could fight well enough to maintain their space on the lake's bank did so without missing a strike or thrust. Those who couldn't battle their way out of the burning woods were caught within the all consuming flames of the rapidly diminishing forests.

Again Alex's vision was obscured by black smoke. He went to move but was stopped by Pike's voice ordering him to remain still, saying, "Don't move Mr. Stone, lest you fall over the edge thus delivering yourself unto the battle forever."

After a few long minutes the thunderous sound of war thinned away fading completely to silence. The thick smoke cleared soon after the last howl melted off into space. Alex gasped with the shock of a child at the appalling sight that stretched out before him once the black cloud was gone. The Eden-like landscape had vanished; all that remained was the burned bare stone of the mountains. Not a single tree had escaped the flames. Only charred skeletons and blackened stumps spread out in all directions. The once crystal clear lake that surrounded the cathedral was now swollen with horribly mutilated bodies and as thick and black as tar. Monstrously huge leech-like creatures and giant maggots with teeth filled jaws slithered through the lake as they fed greedily on the dead. All of the cathedral's beautiful stained-glass windows had been smashed out of their frames and the corpses of child-sized and fully grown warriors slumped half-way out to be squabbled over by large black birds for their cold flesh. The great structure's seamless white marble walls were now splattered violently with blood and stained with soot. Featherless winged giants and fur barren half dog, half reptile beasts fought furiously for ownership of the carcasses that littered the charred battle field. The black clouds and dense ash that had risen up to blot out the sky steadily cleared to mockingly reveal a new angry empyrean comprised of multiple shades of red like that of the sky Alex had seen above the desert. The paradise world that had been created to serve as a place of angelic punishment had been transformed into a true vision of Hell.

With an uneventful flash of light Alex's sight readjusted to find himself in the exact same spot on his knees in front of Pike. His eyes focused swiftly in time to see the Gate Keepers hand pulling away from his forehead.

"You're the only mortal whose been shown a peek into the history of our beginning here on this world."

Alex noticed that Pike's eyes were still as lifeless and dark as those of a shark's. It wasn't until he took off the fedora, passing it in front of his face that his peepers were returned their usual blood-like crimson hue. With a friendly smile he offered Alex his hat back and said with a forced chuckle:

"If it were ever to be learned of, my sharing with you that ancient knowledge—both of our fates would prove eternally distasteful."

Alex's hat returned to its adult fitting size the instant he took possession of it. He gave the Gate Keeper a thank you nod and after a brief inspection put it on. Pike's toothy grin faded, giving his face back its cold expressionless look.

Alex had more than enough reason to hate Pike, his every appearance being filled with unprecedented agony, like his eyes being scorched out of his skull and his tongue eaten right out of his mouth by a maggot. He caught himself growing curiously fond of the odd little fellow, even somewhat concerned for him due to the risk he claims he'd taken by showing Alex Hell's birth. Despite beginning to like Pike, he did not trust the Gate Keeper, not one bit.

"No doubt Mr. Stone you have a few questions. That is why I brought you to this place. To dispatch some of your minds' confusion, so that your focus is at its sharpest before sending you back through to begin."

If Alex hadn't been confused before—which he was, he was really confused now. *Send me through to begin?* He wondered, *through what… begin what?*

Again Pike's face offered a wide, toothy grin that made Alex nervous. It was as if Pike was inside Alex's head, humorously listening in on his thoughts as they fumbled about blindly for answers. He leered coldly at the smiling Gate Keeper as if to say; *Get out of my mind you little freak!*

"A word of warning Mr. Stone, threating looks will be dealt with harshly, and if I think my time is being wasted on you with lessons, I'll seek out another to take your place—even at this short notice."

Pike hadn't been peeking in on Alex's thoughts. It takes an unbelievable amount of mental power to read one's thoughts, even for an archangel as powerful as Pike. It was far easier to get what one needed from a being's body language. A skill Pike had honed to a fine art.

"I'll give you back your tongue if you give me your oath with a nod that you will only speak when told to do so. Is it a deal Mr. Stone?"

Alex's yes nod was still in motion, when without intending to do so, he blurted out the word "Yes," loud and clear. Forgiving Alex his unintentional out-burst; Pike stopped rocking, leaning toward him and said almost at a whisper.

"Good—but remember to mind your tongue. Don't let your anger get in the way of your well being." Pausing, Pike pretended to be cleaning dirt out from under his fingernails again as he asked Alex, "You don't quite know what to make of me, isn't that so Mr. Stone?"

Alex wasn't sure if it was a rhetorical question or if in fact he was meant to offer some sort of retort. *Of course it's rhetorical, this devil don't give a rat's ass what you think of him,* he thought with some certainty only to be shown his error when Pike barked, "It's a question that you may answer…in fact I demand that you do so."

"Yes, I believe I know exactly what to make of you."

"You don't say? Very well then, let's have it. Yes, and do be honest. Groveling will only get you more misery."

Alex was insulted by the implication, he wanted to snatch Pike by his throat and tell him *I don't grovel or beg…you little prick!* Instead he chose to simply answer Pike's odd question, in his usual truthful fashion.

"You're one to fear at all times. You demand complete respect and you will tolerate nothing less. Despite your child-like appearance you're no doubt very old, if not ageless. For whatever reason you've been stalking me since I was a young boy. You seldom reveal your plans—"

Pike cut Alex off, motioning him silent with a fast hand gesture followed with, "What makes you say that?"

"Say what…what part?"

"That I've been stalking you, as you so crassly put it?"

"I've been seeing you since I was nine."

"Have you now?"

"Yes…peeping out of the shadows at me like some sort of ghostly voyeur."

A pleased expression lit up in Pike's eyes, "Yes, you were a good choice," he said under his breath barely loud enough for Alex to hear.

"Good choice for what! What do you mean were—?"

"You were warned not to speak unless told to," Pike growled.

"I thought it was another question—"

"Liar!" Pike snapped, "I'll allow you this one out-burst. If it occurs again I'll give you more than a tongue eating maggot to worry about Mr. Stone."

Pike began rocking again, and as he went back to studying the backs of his hands, he began humming a tune Alex immediately recognized. It was the same happy little tune he himself had been whistling while smearing his and Mr. Bane's calling card over Five's bedroom door. Pike stopped humming and setting his gaze up onto Alex's face asked, "What is this melody? What is its title?"

"The Merry-Go-Round Is Broken," Alex replied.

Pike's expression suddenly appeared more child-like. It was as if the long-lost answer to a great and ancient riddle had finally been revealed to him.

"It's time to tell you of the game and why I've chosen you as the player for B'neem." Pike pulled his hood up over his head once again concealing his white face within a screen of darkness.

While Pike was in the process of explaining the game to Alex, Vexrile was making her way up the rust incrusted flight of stairs wrapped haphazardly around her tower's outer wall. In her hands cradled lovingly against her cold bosom she held the pouch Warfarin had made especially to deliver Ruth Stone's ashes to Vile in. Reaching the incredibly high structures summit Vexrile glanced up from out of her hood at the iron door and without slowing her pace willed it open. The instant she'd passed beneath the octagon shaped entryway the heavy door closed behind her, its latch swinging down to drop with a loud crash as it locked into position. The closing of the door had returned the round, windowless chamber to its previously darkened state. Moving through the black air, her steps swift and softly placed, echoed off the walls and high iron ceiling like faintly spoken threats, falling to an eventual reverberated silence after she came to a stop. Only the shallow whispery sound of Vexrile's breathing and the gentle movement of her robes could be heard in the crypt-like quiet as she knelt down onto her knees.

"Ar'hou'khuit!" Vexrile's brief incantation set three green flames rising swiftly upward lashing the ceiling. They emanated from the pointed corners of an emerald triangle inlaid on the surface of a bloodstone platform alter. Three large chains stretched down from rings fixed onto the ceiling to hold the heavy round platform exactly three feet above the chamber's iron floor. Kissing the leathery bag she laid it down before her and with silent tears streaming down her face she straightened her back. Vexrile reached up and slid her hood slowly off her head, then unclasped the green crystal and brass clip that held her cowl around her shoulders, letting both fall to the platform's surface. With her outer garment off she took a hold of her inner robe's collar on both sides of her neck and ripped it all the way down to her waistline fully exposing her smooth white skin from her shoulders to her slender waist. Vexrile slipped both halves of her torn robe off her shoulders, pulling her arms out of the sleeves, allowing the cloth to hang loosely from her silken black sash. Without ceremony she used her thumbnail to pierce the skin covering her sternum. Sliding her hand down she opened a deep, six-inch long cut. Blood, dark and red flowed from the self-inflicted wound and moved swiftly down her flat belly. Before too much of the crimson liquid could soak wastefully out into her sash and the lower half of her robe, she leaned over placing her palms flat on the stone so that the dripping wound was directly over the pouch. When the leathery bag of dried archangel skin was sufficiently saturated with her blood, she rose up. Before Vexrile had straightened her back, all of the blood staining her belly and sash moved backward up into the closing cut. Waving her hands slowly back and forth inches above the pouch, she whispered a poem—spell, her voice cracking with deep sadness as the words trembled passed her painted green lips.

"Thrill with ageless delight over the exposed truth of life's self-serving lie. Dance with glad knowledge of flesh's over-do demise. Ah! Thy life shall be cold and dark of heart: who so seethe it shall be given unto the dust of thy will. Thy mocked breath bends to ye Lord over deathless dying and with fallen knees and unguarded eyes I...Vexrile Overseer for Zaw'naw beseech thee, make ready and open thy heart's cell's seal."

With her ripped robe still hanging from her waist, Vexrile rose to her feet and stepped quickly out of the triangle and down off the platform, brushing her right hand through one of the pillars of green flame. She moved almost at a run to the wall and turned around to face the spell. Pressing her back flat up against the cold metal and stone she watched and waited; never once taking her eyes off the blood doused pouch. Time crept by with cruel spiritless effort as she eagerly stared at the dormant spell wishing it would take hold. Slowly one minute stretched out to five, then crawled its way to fifteen and on and on. Whatever she was waiting on didn't seem to be transpiring as rapidly as she was lead to believe it would. Tired of standing there half naked against that cold wall, Vexrile pulled herself away from her chosen vantage point and walked at a vexed clip back into the triangle. Dropping to her knees with no regard whatsoever for the dull pain shooting opportunistically up into her kneecaps, she leaned over to gaze deeply at the already dried blood inundating the pouch. She poked at it with the tip of her middle fingernail, wondering if she'd forgotten some critical detail—*No*, she mouthed silently, then whispered.

"I've done exactly as you instructed, so why won't the spell unravel your binds?" She leaned closer to the pouch and for whatever reason sniffed at it, her nose skimming the still slightly sticky surface as it took the coppery scent of blood. Her long white hair draping down around her face, concealing her tears within the shadow dancing across her confused, sad expression.

"Warfarin—Warfarin can you hear me? I've done as you've instructed, so why do you not come back to me?"

She tore herself up away from the pouch and was about to lay open the skin between her breasts again when several thin wisps of milky white smoke began to rise up from the dried blood.

Vexrile got to her feet for a second time and ran toward her place on the wall. She was on her way out of the triangle when she was knocked back down onto the platform. She had neglected to pass her hand through the flame before attempting to step off the alter. Now Vexrile would have to brush her hand through all three flames, three times each in order to be allowed to pass through the platforms invisible barrier. Glancing frantically over her shoulders as she shoved back up onto her feet, she saw that the thin ribbons of white vapor were rapidly swelling in size. By the time the swinging alter permitted her rushed awkward steps to reach the first flame, she could hear screams rising out of the expanding smoke. She swept her right hand through the green pillar of fire one, two, three times each pass blistering her skin. Losing her footing as she ran toward the second flame, she fell against the altar's unseen barrier, slamming her down hard to the platform. She would have to start over. Getting up, she checked on the smoke's progression and noticed that not only had it grown larger and the screams louder, she could see several shapes struggling to reach out at her. Making it across the rocking alter back to the first flame she swiftly ran her hand through the fire three times and immediately ran to the second flame where she quickly passed her hand through that flame as well. Vexrile's hand was horribly burned to the bone when she'd made it to the third and final flame. As she swiped her cooked hand through the fire she peered over her shoulder and saw faceless jaws of white smoke snapping toward her. With her fee paid the altar's barrier opened allowing Vexrile to fall off of the swinging platform. At a crawling run she scurried to her feet. Although the invisible barrier demanded that Vexrile pay tribute with physical pain, its power wasn't strong enough to imprison the swelling smoke. Vexrile barely managed to make it back to her place against the wall in time. At the exact moment she turned around to face the enlarging spell, the white smoke had reached its limit of permitted growth. It filled the cornerless room from floor to ceiling, leaving little more than a three foot space between the wall and the living smoke's outer-most surface. If Vexrile hadn't escaped in time she would have been consumed by the voracious appetite of the churning vapor.

This angry tempest of waxen-white smoke Vexrile had invoked was the doorway into a dimension so horrendous, so utterly frightening that even the evilest of fiends couldn't imagine the nightmares waiting for fresh souls within its gates. It has been given the nicknames of True Hell, Second Hell and Angel's Hell, but its true title was 'Vault.' It was created by the nine commanders who defeated Satan, thus putting an end to the second war. At first it was intended that the Vault be used as a prison for Satan and all of his followers. But Vile, who was still going by Sillona—the commander for the sixth army; and Pike who led the eighth army, both decided after already condemning all of Satan's warriors to the Vault that Satan be spared such an indignity. Instead it was agreed upon that his punishment be less harsh than that of his misguided comrades at arms. It was Sillona's idea to place Satan in chains, bleed his body dry, and lock him in a cell deep within the planet's frozen core with only his madness to keep him company.

As the smoke spinning around the chamber changed colors from solid white to a darkening shade of red, the screams rising out of it grew louder, painful for Vexrile's ears to endure. Faces of demonic creatures and condemned angels, some Vexrile knew and recognized, others she'd only heard mention of, appeared throughout the scarlet cloud. They howled at her as they swept passed, reaching hungrily for her with claws and gnashing jaws. Vainly the phantoms tried to grab her and though Vexrile knew their greedy efforts were wasted, she still longed for more space between her and them.

The crimson tempest of wailing, biting smoke had barely enveloped the tower's top chamber and it was already diminishing, being drawn backward past the three columns of green flame into the triangle. The phantasms trapped within fought valiantly against the power pulling it back, but no matter how furiously they resisted, their battle was lost. Soon Vexrile could see beyond the thinning smoke into the center of the triangle. Hunched over in a bloody-mass of exposed muscles and bone was what had been left of Warfarin, Machiavelli's rapier driven in through his left shoulder and out his right. Vexrile seeing her beloved in such direstraits tore herself away from the wall and moved swiftly to help him.

"Wait Vexrile!" He shouted his tone filled with more pain than sound. Warfarin's shaky command though weak still owned enough power of will to send Vexrile back, slamming her against the wall where she'd been standing. The skinless face of the sixth realm's Grand Inquisitor struggled to rise in an effort to chance a glance across the large room at Vexrile, picking herself up off the floor.

"The gate has yet to close," Warfarin's labored warning shook with excruciating pain. "Do not move into the entrance way, lest we both be dragged in."

He pushed himself up to his skin barren knees, locked eyes on Vexrile and in a pleading tone cried, "Finish—now!"

Stretching her back so that the skin covering her belly was as tight as a drum, Vexrile then swept her hand up and faster than it raised she sent it back down, stabbing her open hand into her stomach. She kept her scream at bay; Vexrile didn't want to chance spoiling the last phase of the spell with displays of weakness. It only took her a moment to find what she was hunting for. With a guttural grunt she yanked her hand from her gut tearing out her left ovary. In the same exiting motion she flung the angelic sack of eggs out toward the last of the diminishing smoke seconds before it was to vanish, taking Warfarin with it. A low howling shriek rose out to a deafening roar and in a flash of speed, too fast for even angel's eyes to catch, a set of jaws snapped out to intercept the bloody gift. The smoke vanished thus closing the Vault's gate.

Too done-in to heal themselves right-away both Vexrile and Warfarin simply laid there and grinned at each other.

As Vexrile and Warfarin healed one another's wounds, and Queen Vile awaited the news that her player was on his way through the wall to take his place in the game; Pike and Alex took part in a little game of their own. Actually it was Pike who had taken to playing around, mostly with Alex mind.

CHAPTER FOUR
— PHANTOMS —

"A Queen a Rook with the snap of
a hook
A phantom so powerful; one taste
and you're took
Feast on its evil addict of pain, lost
to its pleasure; consumed by its fame
The bringer of misery; a taker of good
The Son of lies and Daughter of
could
Cling to a feeling for you're lost to
the rush
Ashes to ashes and dust to dust."

The Me
—Murder

Pike sat straight back on his rock and gestured with his hands for Alex to scoot back a bit. As he willed the shiny black box up, bringing its hovering rise to a levitated rest at chest height, he brought the black pouch and green bottle that Ellzbeth had given him out from behind his sash.

"The game I've chosen you to participate in," Pike went on to say as he opened the leather pouch, carefully emptying eight teeth out onto the box lid, employing its surface as a makeshift work-bench, "takes place every thousand years, give or take a week or two. It is the means by which we determine who of the Empire's nine realms will reign over all of Hell."

The teeth he'd dumped out were about the size and pointed shape as a large dog's canine teeth and were yellowish brown. Alex watched with the attentive interest of an awe-struck kid watching a magician preparing to perform a card-trick. He wanted to ask, *what do you intend to do with those,* but didn't dare. Instead he chose the simpler, less painful alternative, which of course, was to keep his trap shut and pay attention. So that is exactly what Alex did, watched and listened as Pike worked and talked.

"After Satan was defeated, the Gods who created this world for us saw what we'd done to our gilded-prison during that foolish second war and were not pleased to say the least. Think of the Gods, if you would please as artists, very mighty, omnipotent artists that are insanely protective of their creations. Each group of God's trying like spoiled children to out-do the others. There's only one rule to their celestial art-contest: do not create a planet as beautifully royal as our/their home world. The four Gods who had created this world looked down at it with utter abomination when they'd seen what the second war had reduced it to. They wanted to have all of those who fought alongside Satan, as well as those of us who stood against him, to be decimated as punishment for gutting their master-piece. They would have done exactly that if not for Bellona, one of the four creatures of this spinning ball of mud. She had come up with a much more torturous punishment than merely wiping us from existence. She'd convinced her fellow artisans into curing all of us who had survived the second war as well as the planet. The Goddess willed that this world forever remain in its battle-scarred state. That the sky would always be red with the energy of war and the spilt blood that names it. She raised rivers of fire and lakes of boiling tar. No plant nor tree shall grow from its soil, and vast spaces of pitch black emptiness drift aimlessly over the seas. She trapped this world in an eternal state of dark enchantment that exists more of substance than that of shadow and trickery."

Pike glanced up from his work across at Alex and noticed he was shifting his gaze up from the vast field of grasses to the powder-blue sky. Pulling the tiny bone cork out of the little green bottle neck with a faint *pop*, he said as he slowly tipped the vessel over one of the teeth. "It's an illusion Mr. Stone. I conjured all of this forth so that I may speak to you without having to compete for your attention. You'll understand what I mean soon enough."

With methodical steadiness Pike allowed only a single glistening drop of a thick reddish substance to ooze out of the bottle mouth onto the tooth. When that droplet broke loose to immediately vanish on impact into the solid surface of the tooth he carefully sat the bottle down to place the first tooth back in the pouch. Picking the little bottle up again, he continued with his lecture as he moved to the second tooth.

"Bellona willed that this world be used for all time as the place for eternal damnation for all of creations unworthy souls, with us angels as its sole custodians."

Finishing with the last of the eight teeth and dropping it in the black pouch, he re-capped the bottle and crammed it back into his sash. Pulling the pouches draw-string closed tight, Pike tossed it to Alex who in-turn snatched it out of its flight with a, *I don't want it* expression on his face.

"You'll need to wear that pouch around your neck. It must remain in full view at all times during the game; I'll explain why when I give you the game's rules."

Alex's jaws ground together over his strong disliking for the obvious fact that he was being made ready for something and was being given no fair choice in the matter. He took off his hat, setting it almost ceremoniously on the grass beside him, blatantly taking his time. That was, until Pike sent a slight reminder of his intolerance for insubordination burning through Alex's skeleton. He was immediately doubled over by the searing pain. While it burned his bones Pike took control of Alex's movements and with no show of physical opposition on Alex's part whatsoever, Pike made him hang the pouch by its drawstring around his neck.

"Now, where was I? Ah-h-h yes, I remember," Pike said as he drew the fire from out of Alex's bones, giving him back control of his body.

"Here's the best part," Pike continued. "Bellona took from this world the gift of death. In other words, nothing can be killed or die on this planet, not demonic beasts, not even angelic beings. Mortals who are found worthy of being damned are also stripped out of death's soothing embrace, and cursed back to life as they are pulled through so that they can live within the grip of eternal suffrage, whether that existence be in a state of physical decay or healed as you are now."

Pike paused a moment as if to carefully choose his next words, all the while watching Alex who was still experiencing some of the residual effects of Pike's reminder.

"This would all move so much more smoothly for you Mr. Stone if you would merely show some gratitude. Know this Mr. Stone, there are places and things on this world that could without effort illustrate to you what the true meaning of desolation is. I'm spending this time with you of my own choice. Believe me Alex when I say none of the other Gate Keepers care enough about their players to speak with them as I am with you here and now. This game you've been chosen for owns benefits for the winning player as well as for the realm for which he or she stands. A prize will be given to the victor."

Pike's mentioning of a prize caught Alex's attention. He shot a gaze up past his hairless eyebrows as he straightened his back and put his hat on. *Well why didn't you say there would be a prize,* Alex thought. *Shit, I'm all ears little fella.* The first notion that tugged at Alex's interest when Pike made mention of the prize was that it may lead to a way out of Hell. *What else could Hell have to offer other than a chance at freedom from this place,* he secretly told himself, certain that he was right. Again he gave the Gate Keeper all of his attention, listening more intently than ever as Pike finally began telling of the game and its rules.

"After cursing this world, and making it the prison for the cosmos, Bellona let us keep all of the magic we'd been banished with after the first Great War. We rose up nine cities to replace those that were leveled during the second war. The nine remaining commanders; myself included, decided that it would be best to divide the planet into nine separate principalities; realms if you will. To avoid a power-struggle that could someday lead us into a third war we devised the game. It gives each realm a chance to win in an even-handed contest the right to reign over the entire Empire as they see fit, for a thousand years. The rules that we, the caretakers for the realms must follow are thus: only humans damned may represent a realm as its chosen contestant. All players will be given the same strength and speed as the principle player. The principle player is the one representing the realm that won the game the last time it was played."

An expression of pride suddenly beamed forth from Pike's face. Pike placed his open palm flat against his chest and in a regal tone said, "B'neem, the greatest realm in the whole of the Empire, won the game the last three times it was played." Pike leaned slightly forward on his rock, motioning Alex a bit closer and within a genuine giggle Pike whispered, "That makes you the game's principle player." Setting back on his seat, Pike's expression and tone drifted swiftly back to its usual flatness, all the while still speaking.

"Being the ruling realm, it was my right to choose our player from out of any of the other realms. I chose you Mr. Stone long before placing you in that boneyard for safe keeping. But that's another story all together; one we've no time for."

Being told that he'd been chosen for some game in Hell before his death filled Alex's head with yet more questions. But Pike was right, he didn't have time for questions, he had to hear more about the game, about the prize. Alex shoved the new wonderings to the back of his mind and focused only on what Pike had to tell him concerning the game, listening closely for clues as to the prize's identity.

"I chose you from out of the third realm called Chemah. In turn the Gate Keeper from there was required to make her pick from B'neem, the eighth realm. This is to insure that there is only one player participating in the game from each realm. B'neem also gets to choose the planet and where on that world the game is to take place."

Pike's eyes were already locked onto Alex's which made Alex feel a bit uneasy, a feeling that only increased with the advent of another one of Pike's toothy grins. "Guess where I've chosen for the game's playing field Mr. Stone."

Alex barely needed to give the riddle a seconds thought. With a snide, crooked grin of his own he replied, "On Earth would be my guess, in a small burg in Oregon…a town called Corvallis."

Pike's smile melted away and was replaced by an expression of surprised bewilderment.

"Why there, why'd you guess there?"

"It's the only logical place other than the Oregon State Prison. That is if you were to choose a location that would give me an edge over the others, providing none of them know their way around Corvallis as well as I do."

Pike's smile returned and he nodded his head in a gesture of silent approval for the choice he'd made in Alex.

"Before I go into the does and don'ts of the game that you'll need to follow, I'll allow you to ask two questions Mr. Stone. Keep them brief."

As with the quiz Pike had posed to Alex concerning the location of the game, he didn't even need a second to think about which two out of countless other questions he would ask. Pretending to inspect the seams on his gloves, he clinched his hands into tight fists and asked with a false note of indifference.

"Is my sister…is Susan alive and well?"

Pike's reply was cold and swift. "Yes, she is alive and no she's not well."

Alex's fake lack of empathy for his baby sister's well-being was unmasked by Pike's reply. His brain had suddenly exploded with questions surrounding Susan. Like starving baby birds they rushed up his throat in a race to be the first inquiry put forth. He was about to let the barrage of questions fly when Pike brought his right hand up with a fast snap, palm out like a traffic cop. Without having to employ his powers Alex put the brakes on the flood of words himself. They stumbled into one another crashing up against the inside of his clinched teeth.

"Ask your second question Mr. Stone."

"Where is Susan? Is she—"

"No Mr. Stone." Pike interrupted Alex. "I'm not permitted to answer any further enquires concerning your sibling at this stage of the game. Ask another question."

Alex swallowed the questions surrounding Susan's mental and physical health back down with a spiteful gulp. He was growing increasingly exasperated with being trapped at the mercy of this pint-size tormenter. It was taking most of Alex's tolerant energy to keep himself from verbally unloading on his self-congratulatory host. Alex tried with little success not to leer at Pike as he asked his second question, but the look in his eyes could melt nails.

"Why was I sent here to this place? You'd said earlier that I had earned my place here, how can that be after all we—I mean, I'd done to spare little ones from falling prey to the wicked lust of child-molesters. Why was I sent to Hell?"

Pike's expression was as unforgivingly cold as Alex's and the lilt in his tone even colder. "For the self-serving slaughter of five men. No one may take it upon themselves to murder. Only with the blessing of the Eyeless Goddess may one slay mortal life. You were not in peril of losing your life like you and your sister had been at the hands of your not so loving parents. There were other means by which you could have sought justice, less violent ways to put an end to those you proudly refer to as your 'Five.' You've been damned to this world because of your desire for—".

"They were fiends!" interrupted Alex. "We had to stop them once and for all!—"

"SILENCE!" Pike shouted, the spoken force of his voice blasting into Alex where he knelt and sent him tumbling over the grass backward head over heels. After rolling several yards he managed to stop himself. With his ears still ringing from the deafening volume of Pike's command, Alex sat up to see that the Gate Keeper, his rock seat, the hovering box and even his fedora was gone.

"Behind you Mr. Stone," Pike's voice growled from around his back. Alex snapped his head about so abruptly that the bones in his neck popped painfully. Pike was seated atop his stone stool behind the hovering box. It was as if he'd not been knocked hurtling backward, but only turned around.

"I'm going to permit you that little rant Mr. Stone, do not let it happen again. As for interrupting me whilst I was speaking, that's unforgivable." Pike waved his left hand like brushing away an annoying gnat. The swift flick of his wrist transported Alex out of the fields of grass with its soft breezes and clean smelling clear blue sky, into a stiflingly hot, dark chamber made of stone. Looking around Alex saw no doors or windows that might offer a way out. In the center of the perfectly square space there was a huge stone bowl filled with glowing white-hot rocks which not only served as the chamber's solitary source of light, it was also apparently used to heat the steel of several sharp and blunt looking implements. The moment Alex had stood up off his knees all of his clothing from his gloves down to his socks turned to ash and fell to the floor. An indiscernible amount of bare steel wire, almost exactly like the wire he'd used to tie Five down with, shot out of the floor, walls and ceiling like razor sharp "Crazy String" being sprayed at him from cans. Before Alex could complete a shouted, "WAIT A MIN—!" The wire wrapped excruciatingly tight around his entire body and stitched his lips together.

Stepping into the chamber through the solid stone of the wall was Pike. "You were told! I'd told you when we first met in the boneyard that above all else I hate being interrupted," the Gate Keeper said. "There are some souls here that wish to reacquaint themselves with you Mr. Stone. While that's taking place I'm going to reassess the entire situation where you're concerned."

Pike turned his back to Alex and without another word passed out through the wall. The instant the Gate Keeper disappeared, Alex trapped in the steel snare, heard his work title being unevenly chanted over his muffled cursing.

"Millstone—Mills-to-ne—M-i-llstone," repeated the voices drawing nearer. The wires stretching down from out of the ceiling raised Alex up off his feet several inches above the floor, causing the wires reaching out of the walls to pull tighter and cut into his skin. He began making vain offers in the form of muffled plea agreements, swearing on everything he held dear (which wasn't much). Alex gave his word that he would from this point forward keep his mouth shut and never again interrupt the Gate Keeper, all the while hoping like hell that Pike was listening to his thoughts. It wasn't until the reunion began that he realized how truly grievous an error he'd made by speaking out of place.

They passed through the walls one by one in the order that they'd been killed. The first visitor from Alex's glory-days to move through the stone was Number One. The naked pedophile's hairless, waxen body was healed, all except for the ear to ear slash wound that Alex and Mr. Bane had laid deeply across One's throat.

When Alex and his razor sharp crime-partner had carried out the act of dispatching Number One, they were fairly new to the ageless art of throat cutting. Other than when they'd opened Alex's father's neck, which had been done with far too much zeal than necessary, they hadn't sliced any other throats. Alex, for whatever reason thought that to do the job on One properly it would require a healthy issue of strength when he'd gone to work, and Mr. Bane only made matters worse by telling Alex to put his back into it. Not taking into account the knife's unearthly sharp edges, as well as the lack of knowledge concerning human anatomy, Alex and Mr. Bane had almost cut One's head clean off. The pedophile's head was resting awkwardly on his left shoulder, the elongated gash bloodlessly pink like the bled out, sliced open belly of a catfish. One stepped in toward Alex trapped in the steel web, his horizontal brown eyed gaze shifting from the tools in the fire, back onto Alex's.

"Millstone," One hissed before falling silent while the others made their way in. One's thin lipped mouth pulled into a wide grin revealing the same teeth he'd sported during his life; blackened with the stains of decay.

When One first stepped into the chamber Alex had gone mute as if being caught in a sort of disbelief induced shock. But, realizing that this was really happening, his state of silence was brief. His muffled voice returned as loud and as clearly as his stitched together lips would permit.

Number Two passed through, closely followed by Number Three. Two's throat wound, although not as exaggerated as One's, was still executed with a bit too much enthusiasm. Three's throat wound on the other hand was done perfectly. The why as to Alex suddenly figuring out the proper way to cut Three's throat after doing so poorly on the previous two child-molesters should be accredited to his ability at ease-dropping. A few nights after sending Two on his way to Hell, Alex was sitting at the bar of a strip club in Salem Oregon reading the newspaper about his latest endeavor. It was while peering over the top of the paper onto the mirror behind the bar, at the reflection of a dancer wiggling her ass inches in front of a fat man's pink face, that he over heard three men talking about the two murders. Alex's head swelled as he listened to them verbally applaud his and Mr. Bane's efforts.

"I've got an eight year old son at home," said a tall man wearing a leather jacket. "If some piece of shit was to so much as look at my boy I'd beat him to death with my bare hands."

"Yeah, you'd think the cops would be grateful to this Millstone fellow for ridding the streets of some of the scum," said the shortest of the three into his beer glass. He wiped his lips with the back of his hand

and continued, "But of course they're not. No, if and when they catch up with him they'll want to make an example out of him."

"They'll make a real show out of it to, you'll see," said the third man. "I only hope that he can put a few dozen of those sick fucks in the ground before he's stopped."

"Oh, he'll be stopped and it will happen fairly soon, you can bet on it," chimed in a fourth man not with the others. He was a tall, physically strong looking man sporting a closely cropped head of blond hair. Alex noticed he'd wore a pair of desert combat boots and that the brass lighter he was playing with had the small face of a bull-dog and the letters: U.S. M.C inlaid on its surface.

"What makes you so damn sure?" asked the man in the leather jacket.

The off-duty soldier panned his vision around to face the question, slowing it slightly onto Alex at the far end of the bar only to snap his thousand-mile-stare dead onto the man asking.

"He's a sloppy amateur—a dilettante with no eye for detail. Fools like that always fall flat on their faces."

"What make you so fucking smart?" barked the short man.

"I've been an active Marine for the last fourteen years; it's been my job to know a little something about killing men. Take for instance the sloppy way this clown's been cutting throats." The Marine stood and stepped around behind a red haired dancer who was sitting at the bar counting up her tips. "Pardon me angel but may I use your pretty neck for a moment to school those three misguided gentlemen the proper way to slash a throat?" He asked with a smile. She let out a shy, girlish giggle, shook her long straight hair off her neck and said, "Sure, I'm all yours."

Alex watched almost disbelievingly while the trained killer, using his thumb as a blade explained step by step the right way to open a throat.

"What this Millstone is doing wrong is this." He took a hold of the woman's jaw and pulled her head all the way back, stretching her neck exactly how Alex had been doing. "When the throat is stretched in this manner the sternocleidomastoid muscles pull back and block the carotid artery on the left side of the neck and the jugular vein on the right side. This makes for a lot of unnecessary cutting and sometimes even sawing. The swiftest way to get the job done is also the right and easiest way." He pushed her head forward, placing his open left hand firmly on the top of her head. Pulling her hair out of the way so all could see the right side of her neck; he positioned his extended thumb under her ear and said. "When the head is moved forward and forced down, the only thing covering the veins is skin." He looked past the others straight onto Alex, grinned and slowly slid his thumb down from her ear, across her throat.

This new found knowledge enabled Alex to open Three's throat with expert execution.

Two and Three moved into the luminous glow of the rocks in the large stone bowl. As Three stepped over to stare wild-eyed down at the implements of torture heating up in the fire, Two stepped up closer to Alex and in a painfully strained voice said, "I always knew that my screaming your name wasn't in vain. It pays to be patient." Two sniffed at the blood trickling from the cuts made by the wires wrapped around Alex's face and cackled past a gleeful, "Millstone."

Alex had of course been doing his damnedest to free himself from the thin steel web ensnaring him from the moment the wire lashed out. And as it had done to Five on the coffee table, it wormed its flesh slicing way deeper into his skin. It was when Number Four entered the dimly lit chamber that his vain thrashing abandoned all consideration for the stinging pain of the wire eating into his flesh. With fresh fervor, fueled by the horror of what he saw passing through the wall, he increased his futile attempts at tearing himself out of the trap's embrace. As with the other three that arrived before him, the pederast priest's body was healed of all signs of festering. Only the mark of Alex and Mr. Bane's work had been left untouched. In Four's case that meant almost all of the skin that had once covered his face and upper body was carved away to dangle from meat and bone. Both of Four's eyes were still missing out of their intended places in his skull. Opening his mouth wide, Four's cloudy brown eye rested on his tongue staring out at Alex. In a voice that sounded like someone speaking with their mouth full, Four said. "So my son, do you prefer the brown eye that winks or the eye that stinks?"

Four turned his nude back to Alex and bent all the way over. Reaching behind him he grabbed onto both butt cheeks and spread them apart to show Alex his rectum. With a pushing grunt and a long, high-pitched fart, Four's left eye peeked out of his turd cutter and turned up to leer at Alex. As Four stood straight and turned back around to face Alex with the others Number Five finally entered the chamber to join the party. Alex stopped his thrashing and muffled cursing, watching as Five moved upright toward the glowing hot stone bowl on only one leg. His left was being uselessly dragged behind him, its femur bone snapped in two with the longest half protruding out of a hole in his thigh, the lame foot sort of twitching with each labored hopping step, as if to mock steps of its own. Five's bloodless, cut to shit face was turned toward Alex all the way to the stone bowl. As the other four took out the tool of their choosing, the low hissing sound of burning flesh filling the air the instant their fists latched onto the bare iron, Five drove his hand down into the center of the fire and brought out a small glass baby food jar.

The child molesters set their attention onto Alex and moved toward him with wide grins that silently informed Alex of the pain to come. With Five leading the way he slammed the baby food jar against the right side of Alex's head, shattering the small glass vessel. The tiny shards of glistening glass and blood stained babies' teeth didn't cascade down to the stone floor, but instead froze motionlessly, hovering around Alex's head. As the others surrounded Alex, eagerly awaiting their turn with him, Five plucked the front piece of broken lower mandible bone with the three teeth still embedded in it out of the air and holding it's sharpest looking edge out, said. "It's not a lit cigarette…no its not, but it will do for starters." He latched a hold of Alex's face and spread open the eyelids over his right eye with a thumb and forefinger. The wires locking Alex's mouth shut tore through his upper lip as he screamed, "Pike!"

Alex opened his eyes to find himself kneeling on the grass in front of Pike beneath the blue sky again.

"That is what awaits you if your insubordination persists." Pike looked deeply into Alex's eyes as if he was searching for signs of defiance. Seeing none that might dare challenge his authority again, he continued right where Alex had interrupted him when he was in the process of answering his question as to why he'd been damned. As Pike's eyes dimmed to a shade of red that appeared almost purple he said, "no being owns the right to take it upon themselves to murder one of their own breed. Your horrible childhood did not grant you the authority to continue killing others like your parents Mr. Stone. When you were a boy, I had by chance caught sight and sound of yours and your sister's dreadful plight during one of my passes through your world. When I'd returned to this world I brought with me the news of your tragedy. I told the eyeless Goddess of you and your sister's lives and beseeched her in your behalf to allow me to intervene; she would not give me her blessing. But as it turns out, you helped yourself and rightfully so. The actions you'd taken against your parents was forgivable—barely. It was recognized that you moved on them out of fear for not only your wellbeing, but that of your sister's. It was that selflessness that earned you the eyeless one's tolerance. But, the actions surrounding those you refer to as your Five owned but only a single motive, to kill and leave your mark on the world. What makes your sin even more unforgiving is that you allowed your heart to use the tragedy of your past as an excuse to justify your blood lust."

Pike's explanation as to why Alex was sent to the Bad Place had in that single retort abolished what he believed to be the only good deeds of his miserable life.

"It's time for me to inform you of the game's rules you'll need to follow if you are to carry B'neem into victory. The most consequential rule you'll need to keep in mind is also the game's primary goal. Like yourself, all of the other players are relatively commonplace humans, in that all of you possess no infamously renowned criminal histories. In other words there are no Adolph Hitler's or John Gottis among you. All players are required to hail from the principle player's home world as well as out of the same century. Whatever the weapon was that each of you used to commit the sins that led you to Hell is the weapon you will all be using against one another in the game. But if the principle's weapon was not some sort of firearm, then no firearms will be allowed. Now for the consequential part I'd mentioned. From the instant your feet touch down on your world the game will begin. You'll have all of thirty hours to find and send back the eight other players, not a second more."

Pike raised his hand, causing Alex's anxiety to swell a bit. Alex had grown used to such hand gestures leading to some form of pain. Pike smiled at the alarm he'd invoked in Alex as he pointed at the black pouch hanging around his players neck.

"No doubt Mr. Stone the memory of my helping you hang that pouch around your neck is still fresh in your mind. You do recall the event?"

"Of course," Alex replied trying not to come off sounding even slightly spiteful.

"The reason for my telling you that the pouch needs to be hung about the neck in full view is two fold. The first reason is for your benefit, in that it helps to insure that the pouches contents are easily obtainable. The second reason is sort of vain on my part. Black is the banner color of the realm for which I serve, B'neem. I want that color to be the last thing the other players see while still in the light before you send them back into the darkness—back to Hell. I noticed that you had been paying close attention to me as I prepared the teeth. The substance you saw me drip on each tooth was a powerful mixture of roots and blood. The blood is that of the game's last champion, as well as the blood of various archangels, including that of my own. A note before I tell you what those demon's teeth are for: Do not put the teeth in your mouth, not for any reason. As a matter of fact don't even sniff at them. The whys are not to concern you—simply do not do it. Now, before I tell you what the teeth are for, do you have any questions surrounding what I have mentioned thus far?"

Alex didn't so much as allow his brain to think about asking one of the countless questions pressing up against the inside of his skull.

"No, nothing right off hand," he said so quickly that the words nearly tripped over one another on their blurted way through his clinched teeth.

"Good then," Pike chuckled, not believing Alex for an instant.

"Simply put, those eight teeth are keys to aid you in sending the other players back. It goes like this: once you come upon one of the others, or he or she comes upon you, it doesn't really matter who finds who first. But, as soon as that happens you must make your cut in their flesh, the longer and deeper the cut, the better. The moment you've opened a wound take one tooth out of the pouch and toss it at the opposing player's feet, the tooth will do the rest. I strongly suggest though, that as soon as you let the tooth fly you move away from the player." Pike smiled, cleared his throat and continued. "Now, once you open the players flesh you will need to act fast because the same rapid healing powers that have been afforded to you on this world will also be given to all of you during the game. Wounds heal faster in the game, so get the tooth out and send it down. If the wound has mended before you can release the tooth you will need to make a new cut. One more, no two more facts about the teeth: Once a tooth has been taken out of the pouch with a player in mind, that tooth can only be used by you on that player, it will not work on another. The last thing, do not lose any of the teeth; it would be very bad for you to do so."

Pike went silent and after readjusting his seated pose atop his stone stool his attention drifted from Alex down onto the fedora on the grass. It took a minute but Alex realized that Pike wasn't staring at the hat at all; the Gate Keeper was looking off into space, like a day-dreaming child. Alex was beginning to wonder if Pike was finished, when he snapped his attention back up onto Alex and said:

"Because of yours and your sister's past I believe you should be allowed to know a little something about the realm you've been chosen to represent. I told you its title B'neem, that it's the eighth realm of nine and that I'm its Gate Keeper. Each realm deals with a particular degree of wickedness. B'neem is the designated place in Hell for those who've dared to commit sins against children, hence the eighth realm's name B'neem which means loosely translated: Children. All of the caretakers of B'neem can if we so choose take on the size and all around appearance of human children. The reasons for this childish transformation are really quite simple: what better way to torment someone damned to Hell for harming a little one, than to have those administering the punishment appear as children. Yes that's correct Mr. Stone, both of your parents are being eternally made to scream in my realm, as well as the five, how you say—*freaks* you sent us." Pike leaned slightly forward and asked in a low, cold tone, "So far do you understand all that I've told you?"

Alex locked eyes with the Gate Keeper and in his most definitive voice replied. "Yes, perfectly."

"Does it please you to be the chosen player for damnation's place of suffering set aside for those you loathe more than authority?"

"Yes," Alex answered simply.

Pike's eyes brightened as his sight left Alex's face to fall on the box still hovering between them. It moved down through the air and as it settled gently on the grass in front of Alex, Pike said, "Open the box Mr. Stone, what is inside belongs to you."

Unlatching the tiny gold clasp, Alex felt a rush of excited suspense much like that of a child opening an unexpected gift. He had a fairly good idea what was in the box from the moment Pike made mention of the fact that he would be cutting on people. The thing the Gate Keeper had said about the weapons in the game having to be the same implement of destruction that helped to carve out their places in Hell was a pretty good clue too. Alex raised the lid and scarcely noticed the bed of five beating hearts beneath Mr. Bane.

"Hello Alex my boy, long time no see," spoke the metallic voice of the sheathed dagger. It was speaking so deep within Alex's mind that not even Pike could have heard the voice if he'd been listening.

"Hello Mr. Bane."

The Gate keeper heard Alex's whispered reply, only to dismiss it as a mortal's foolish attachment to an inanimate object. It was what Pike heard woven within Alex's greeting that pleased the Gate Keeper, a sharp note of malice swelled out into the tormenter's awareness from between his player's words, a malice that promised victory.

"We'll speak later Alex, away from that one's burglarizing eyes and ears." Mr. Bane's voice faded. Alex actually had to stop himself from blurting out *No don't go,* gagging the impulse with a quick thinking, "thank you," as he looked briefly up at Pike, then back at the knife.

"You really must stop speaking out of place, even to thank me, but I will let it slide—again. Don't push it though." Pike looked into the box. "Those are the actual hearts of the five fiends you sent to Hell with the aid of that blade. The hearts of your parents were not included in the making of that bed for reasons not worth mentioning at this time. Go on Mr. Stone, take up your weapon, bring it up off its fleshy cushion."

As if it were as fragile as smoke, using both hands Alex lifted the knife off the pulsating hearts. The moment he brought Mr. Bane out of the small coffin the hearts disappeared with five fading shrieks. A grin formed onto Alex's thin lips when he heard the sound of tightly stretching leather as he clasped his gloved fist around the bone handle. Using the end of his thumb he unsnapped the strap securing the hilt. Alex slid all ten inches of the double edged blade out of its sheath. While he gazed coldly at the sheen of its murderous steel, gazing far beyond his own blurred reflective image, Alex thought he spotted seven screaming faces trapped forever in Mr. Bane's grasp. Alex pushed the blade back into its sheath and remaining on his knees slid it onto his belt, positioning the knife behind him in its old spot. Alex was beginning to feel like himself again. A visibly noticeable chill shot up his spine that seemed to help melt the crooked grin on his face, returning his look to its usual inexpressive gaze.

"It's time to send you through." Pike said. There was a faint note of sadness in the Gate Keeper's tone that made Alex feel uneasy in an untrusting sort of way. "On your feet Mr. Stone." Pike said sharply as he himself stood atop his rock. As soon as Alex got to his feet he was forced to step quickly backward, nearly tripping over his own retreating steps due to Pike's rock growing larger. The white stone carried the standing Gate Keeper up into the powder blue sky, coming to an easy stop about thirty feet up. The sod and soil that had been torn up when the rock's base had swelled, liquefied to a green and brown ooze that swiftly hardened the moment it evened out flat. The box was half buried in the green and brown stone that surrounded Pike's rock, its lid and sides broken.

"I nearly forgot a not so minor detail concerning your brief reprieve from Hell." Pike said loudly, "Do not attempt to leave the city-limits, and refusal to participate in the game will be, to say the least Mr. Stone, bad for you." Pike pulled his hood up over his head as he told Alex, "Your hat Mr. Stone." Before he could pan his vision around to see where it had gone to the fedora materialized comfortably atop Alex's head. Pike turned the wide opening of his hood up to face the beautiful blue sky and shouted with a chuckle.

"You're going to absolutely love this." He stretched his arms out, holding them up in the shape of a 'V' and in a thunderously loud voice that didn't sound anything like his child's tone, cried, "Behold the Wall!"

$$\Rightarrow \cdot | | \cdot \Leftarrow$$

The light powder blue sky with its soft caressing breeze and sweet smelling air began to melt away like wax on the floor of a burning house. It was replaced by a sky the color of spoiled blood. Dark gray clouds, alive with strobing flashes of lightning emerged rapidly from out of the empty atmosphere. Soon the entire mantel of blue beauty had been overtaken. While the sky was being shrouded in darkness the endless expanse of lush grasses withered and dried to dust; the remnants carried away by a hot wind. Before the ground had baked to a surface as hard as granite, sharp rocks and large thorny-bushes, black and as dense as razor-wire pushed up out of the soil. The stone pedestal Pike had been standing on had transformed into a huge mound of tangled, half burned bodies. It resembled the black and white photographed images of a holocaust aftermath.

Alex looked up at Pike to see that the opening of his hood was glowing brighter than molten steel. He crashed the palms of his hands together sending out a massive shock wave that carried with it an explosion of light and sound. It knocked Alex backward through the air several yards. His forced flight was brought to an almost back breaking halt when he'd slammed into a throne covered rock that had tore up out of the ground directly in his path. Despite all of his wind being knocked smooth out of his lungs and the numbing pain brought on by his bone jolting stop, Alex still got right back up to his feet and proceeded to shake off the shock-wave's unpleasant effects. The instant his sight fought past the momentary blindness brought on by Pike's loud flash of light, he looked up to see an unbelievable, nightmarish sight. Alex suddenly found himself standing only a few yards from the base of a wall-like structure that was so immense in size that it nearly defies all mortal description.

The Wall as Pike had referred to it, stretched out to Alex's right and left for as far as his eyes could see. It tore straight up out of the stony ground into the living sky of crimson and gray to vanish beyond the strength of his sight. But it wasn't its gargantuan dimensions that boggled Alex's mind; it was the building materials that had been employed to construct the hellish monstrosity. It had been comprised solely from the severed body parts and wholly intact cadavers of human men and women. The entire configuration heaved and shifted slightly with the squirming movements of Hell's oath to its condemned: that no thing shall come to know true death. Its perpetual pulsating gave the Wall's conjoined meaty surface it shimmering wet appearance, sweat, pus and bile, along with clumps of human fat smeared the surface. Its great reeking stench was so thick it was almost visible. It not only stung Alex's eyes and burned up into his nostrils, it attacked his taste-buds with the bitterly foul taste of spoilage, leaving a gritty texture on his teeth. Heat emanated forth from the fleshy structure in waves like the breath of a giant wounded beast.

The only other thing besides the twitching bodies that moved was an army of maggots that fed voraciously on the decaying meat. Some of the cutworms were the size of a human infant's arm, where as others were no bigger than a tear drop. The feeding swarm of grubs wriggled in and out of the tangled mass of rot, dining insatiably on putrefying flesh. When the slime covered larvae had glutted themselves swollen beyond their ability to bolt down another bite, they would push their ugly little heads out of the decay and vomit. Once their unquenchable bellies were emptied they slid back in and continued gorging on the Wall.

Although it was going against his better judgment, Alex drew himself cautiously toward it. The closer he got to the glistening wet, with maggot, puke, and pus nightmare, the louder his intuition's fright cried out from deep within the inner most core of his common-sense. It screamed: *Stay back you damned half-wit!*

The lure pulling Alex closer to the planet-size wall of bodies was like that of the siren song drawing a child into a movie, theater showing a horror film. The boy is fully aware of the night-terrors the movies images will undoubtedly bring later on that night, but still he's compelled to buy a ticket and go inside, via his own unsilencing curiosity.

As Alex reached behind him for Mr. Bane's handle, he glanced up over his shoulder to make sure the Gate keeper didn't disapprove of his bringing the knife out. Looking at the top of the mound of charred bodies where Pike had been only a moment earlier, Alex found the apex abandoned; the Gate Keeper was gone. Pulling Mr. Bane free from its sheath, Alex spun all the way around, panning his vision over his surroundings, seeing no sign of his red-eyed host. Alex wasn't sure if he should be happy or alarmed that the tormenter who had imposed so much pain into his body was finally gone. Alex was well aware of the fact that simply because Pike couldn't be seen, didn't mean he was free of the being's attention.

Alex set his gaze back around onto the Wall and as he made his way toward it for a closer look, Pike let Alex know that his eyes were indeed on him.

"So Mr. Stone, what do you think of the only physical partition keeping this world's nightmares from bleeding out onto all of the other worlds, including yours?" Pike's voice boomed the question from out of no discernable direction.

Alex offered no reply; he simply stared up onto the topic at hand and marveled at the twisted sight, admiring the unadulterated skill and sinister imagination it must have taken to erect the structure. As he moved closer, Mr. Bane clutched securely in his fist ready for the unknown, he noticed that the Wall's entire surface was flat; as smooth as a jewel. Not a single finger or toe, not even a hunk of rotten flesh which had pulled away from the bone sat out further from the surface than that of another. Only the feeding cutworms extended beyond the Wall's face. It was as though a giant pane of thick glass had been dropped down and pressed against it. When he was close enough to reach out and touch it, Alex went to poke at it with Mr. Bane's tip. The end of the blade was less than an inch from pressing down into the pus and fat incrusted cheek of a woman's face, when her milky gray eyes sprang open. Alex leapt back with a jolt of fright. "Son of a bitch!" He barked almost involuntary.

"Why so surprised Mr. Stone?" Pike's disembodied voice chuckled loudly. "I do believe I had made mention of the fact that nothing dies on this planet."

Pike's voice paused a moment so that Alex could take in all of the Wall's gruesome magnificence, allowing his chosen player to fully acknowledge the scope of horror stretching out before him.

"They can sing—do you care to hear a sample?"

Before Alex was given a second's chance to utter an absolute *No!* a deafening chorus of squalling shrieks erupted with a simultaneous blast of sound. It slammed into Alex with physical force, sending him back a few paces before dropping him to his knees. Then as suddenly as it had begun, the Wall's bodies went silent again.

"Remember, you'll have only thirty hours to find the others and send them back."

"What if I don't find them all?" Alex shouted, "What if there are two of us left at the end of that time?"

"You don't want to know." Pike's voice echoed, "Now be a good little killer and go take the day for B'neem as well as for yourself."

Pike went silent, and as the Gate Keeper's words faded out of ear shot into the hot wind, Alex gazed at the Wall of putrefaction, wondering if he should go in search of a gate or doorway of some sort.

"So, what do you think Mr. Bane, do we go left or right?" Asking under his breath.

Several seconds passed before Alex's wait for an answer ended. "Neither Alex," hissed Mr. Bane, "I believe it is the Gate Keeper's wish that we remain here."

The moment the metallic voice had melted to silence, a section of the Wall directly in front of Alex began to move. The bodies and severed parts pulled away from the center of a focal-point in a steady counter-clockwise motion like a slow moving vortex of living flesh. It began with an inward funnel shape that morphed into a rounded tunnel of flesh, bones and total darkness no larger than a Volkswagen Beetle.

Alex had for whatever reason expected something a bit bigger with less darkness and no slime or stink, not this pitch black ass hole like cave of rot. Mr. Bane must have sensed the rapid approach of Alex's swelling desire to voice his strong disapproval over what he was expected to do.

"No, Alex my boy, I beg you mind your tongue. We'll make do, trust me!" Mr. Bane's attempt to talk some sense into Alex was ignored. It was as if Alex had forgotten how intolerant the Gate Keeper could be.

"No fucking way am I g—!"

Alex was violently yanked into the air and slammed flat on his back, once again having the wind knocked out of his lungs. The instant Pike had Alex where and how he wanted him, he tore Mr. Bane from out of his player's grip and swiftly sliced open both sides of Alex's stretched out exposed throat. The Gate Keepers then slapped the knife's bone handle back onto Alex's gloved palm and wrapped his fist tightly around it.

"You are a true fool if there ever was one Mr. Stone." Pike's voice growled. "You have until you bleed out or the passageway through that wall closes, which ever comes first, to get up and into that porthole."

Luckily for Alex, Pike hadn't severed many of the vital arteries or veins, buying him a few extra seconds. Clasping his left hand over his profusely bleeding throat, Alex got quickly to his feet and staggered toward the rapidly closing passageway. It had shrunk to a size no bigger around than a man-hole when Alex was close enough to hurtle himself in. With Alex and Mr. Bane inside the Wall the porthole closed shut and once again Alex was engulfed within complete darkness.

Warfarin's recovery from having his entire epidermis raked off his flesh and bones by the Vault's taskmasters was excruciating but swift. After a brief, intimate reunion with Vexrile, who had also experienced a fast, painful recovery, Warfarin and his green-eyed co-conspirator went to work. First they informed Vile's ridiculous choice of the game's rules, particularly the power-hungry Queen's instruction: to avoid all other players until after confronting the player with the black pouch. Warfarin and Vexrile sent the former district attorney through to play not—so—nicely with the others. Once that was checked off their mental to-do-lists, the two schemers prepared themselves for the final phase of their plot.

Seated high upon her levitating homage to sadism, Queen Vile, in all her nude splendor, fantasized about all of the wonderfully torturous means by which she would order the other realms wiped out of existence. Vile's plans for her up and coming Queendom did not include the other realms. There would only be Zaw'naw's crimson banner over the Empire and no other. Vile was especially looking forward to taking upon herself the task of dispatching B'neem's three caretakers. Her un-surfeiting hatred for the eighth realm's three overlords had nothing at all to do with B'neem's reigning over the planet for the last three millennium. Vile has never recognized the eighth realm's authority, especially when it came to matters concerning Zaw'naw's affairs. Her contempt for the eighth realm's leaders went much deeper than covetous want for power. Vile's spite stemmed from disdain she held in her icy soul for Ellzbeth. Pike and Sader were to be nothing more than mere bonuses. Truth of the matter was that Vile could care-less about B'neem's Gate Keeper and Overseer. Actually, Hell's would-be Queen had always rather admired Pike's unwavering ability to wield his strength with honed brutality. She knew Pike wouldn't simply step aside as she moved toward Ellzbeth, and Sader's allegiance to Pike was as steadfast as her own hate. Pike and Sader would have to be dealt with harshly.

Vile's hate for Ellzbeth, the golden eyed Inquisitor for B'neem began ages before the first war, back when Vile went by Sillona and Ellzbeth by her God given name of Sarah. Long before most of the stars had been given their places in the heavens, the two archangels were the best of friends; both willing to lay down their lives for the other. That friendship was doomed to change when Sarah saw her friend coming out of the God's Library of Wonders. It is in this great library where the secrets to the deities power of creation are stored.

It is unquestionably forbidden for any being other than a God or Goddess to enter that great hall of knowledge. Even they weren't permitted to go into the library without another God present to keep an eye on one another for fear that even a God might be tempted to take all of creation for themselves. Creatures regarded by the deities as lesser beings than themselves were not allowed in their precious library. The reason is really quite simple: total elitism. No self-respecting God, no deity of the high order of creators, would let themselves consider an angelic-being or human-being worthy of gazing upon a single word scribed in one of those great books. The punishment for a non-deity trespassing across the threshold into that library is the same as that of a God or Goddess who dared enter the library alone. All their powers were to be stripped from the transgressor and they are to be banished to one of the moons surrounding an unfinished world; alone for no less than five-hundred years.

Ellzbeth/Sarah caught her friend sneaking out of the God's library; in Sillona's arms were as many books as she could carry out of that celestial body of ageless knowledge. Sarah confronted Sillona, demanding that she immediately put the books back exactly how she'd found them. Sillona huffed and grumbled under her breath as she resentfully did as she had been told. All might have gone undetected, at least for a little while if Sillona, in her haste, hadn't broken the seal barring the library's entryway. The seal was composed of complex webs made solely from stands of gold and blood so thin and fragile that to the unaided eye they were utterly invisible. With vain effort they worked frantically to repair Sillona's misdeed, only to be met with failure. Every time they would attempt to take a hold of the shredded strands, whether it be with their hands or with magic, the lucid webbing would become visible and bleed down between their fingers.

Realizing the hopelessness of her situation, Sillona offered up the best recourse her defiant, panicked mind could devise. To grab as many of the God's books as they could carry, pack up a few of their most prized possessions and flee. Never in the entire history of creation has a being who had blatantly or otherwise defied the Gods in even the slightest of violations, been successful at escaping their wrath. Sillona pleaded with Sarah to try and elude the Gods and their child-like fury. But to Sarah, the idea of leaving their beloved home world never to return was as unthinkable as the notion that they could even consider such an endeavor. She had a better way out of the predicament, or so she thought.

With only her best intentions at heart Sarah mislead her friend into believing that she would escape with her to one of the new worlds, only as long as she agreed not to steal any of the Gods books. It wasn't easy, but Sillona eventually agreed. Sarah told her to go quickly and gather only those possessions she could easily carry on the run. She convinced Sillona that she would hurry to her place and do the same.

"I'll be waiting for you at the Silver-Oak," Sarah said, "but if I'm not there when you arrive, wait for me—be sure and keep your head down. I'll be there soon."

"We should stay together," Sillona argued.

"No, we've not the time!" Sarah replied sharply. "Now go and remember, keep your head down my friend."

Instead of heading to her place to collect a few things like she'd said she would do, Sarah went behind her friend's back to speak with the seven Gods that held charge over her and Sillona. Sarah believed that by coming forward and honestly throwing herself at the mercy of the

Gods that they might see Sarah's willingness to come clean as a worthy trait, deserving of forgiveness for her and Sillona.

As it turned out, the Gods she'd delivered herself unto had shown some leniency, although only where Sarah was concerned. Because of her stepping forward they saw fit to only take her eyes, as well as all of her magic, sparing Sarah a lengthy expulsion.

When Sillona arrived at their agreed meeting place she did so to find her friend eyelessly groping around the base of the Sliver-Oak's trunk on her hands and knees. Sillona barely had enough time to drop to her knees and hear Sarah's mumbled plea, "Forgive me Sillona," when the Gods took her.

The Gods, in an effort to make an example out of Sillona's trespassing, made her inquisition into a spectacle for all of Paradise to witness. Angels by nature are shy creatures, highly uncomfortable with exposing their flesh. So in order to humiliate Sillona, they thought it might be fun to strip off her robes as well as her power. The last sounds she heard beyond her own screams for mercy was her fellow angel's laughing voices as she was cast through space and time to be imprisoned on the moon of an unfinished world. For every second of a thousand years Sillona existed on that cold dark rock, naked and completely alone with only the promise of revenge to keep her company.

When she'd completed her banishment and was brought back to the home world, Sillona had withdrawn deep into herself, keeping all others back and never again allowing herself to trust another being's word, particularly that of an angel. Sillona had seen Sarah going to the Gods behind her back as nothing short of betrayal. The fact that Sarah had offered to take not only her punishment, but Sillona's as well changed nothing, in Sillona's mind Sarah would forever be her foe, never to speak to her again.

It took Sillona a few hundred years, but she eventually earned all of her magic back, and then some. There was a new look in Sillona's crimson gaze, a leering stare that hissed to all who dared lock eyes with her, *I hate you all.*

 ⇒ ⫷ ⇐

Vile was in the middle of smugly imagining how truly wonderful it was going to be once the Empire was her's, when she was ripped up off of her throne. She had allowed herself to become so lost in her day-dreams that she was caught by surprise. As Vile was being hurtled through the chamber's frigid air, Warfarin and Vexrile materialized out of the blackness. They locked their eyes on her at the exact instant she slammed face first against the same spot where Babur's body had been crashed into. With their conjoined wills set sharply onto Vile as she hit the floor they yanked her screaming back up through the air, slamming her into another wall. Again Vile hit the floor, this time barely managing to struggle up onto her feet. No sooner had she caught Vexrile in her sights across the throne room and her feet were knocked out from under her by her attackers. Vile smacked down once again only to be torn up into the air for a third time. They sent the stunned archangel, who would be Queen of all Hell, flying head first toward one of the spiked iron pillars. Vile was less than ten feet from having her skull dashed against the huge support when she whipped herself all the way around. Instead of her head meeting the pillar's surface it was the balls of her feet that slammed against it. She loosed a loud scream, brought on as one of the iron spikes pierced all the way through her left foot. Vile, using the pillar like a spring-board, shoved herself off of it. She spun around, flipping herself about so that her feet were pointed toward the rapidly approaching floor. In the split second following her landing, as she snapped her eyes onto Vexrile, the Overseer shrieked loudly.

"I don't think so—bitch!" With Vexrile's sharp words followed a stream of green gas out of her mouth. The vomited vapor shot through the air to hit Vile the moment the two locked eyes. Vexrile's weapon rushed straight up Vile's nostrils and jetted into her mouth as she choked the command,

"Black and Blue, out now!"

Vexrile's gassy attack made its poisonous way down Vile's long throat and as the two Shadow Hound leapt up out of the stone floor, the nude, red-haired empress of Hell was swiftly transformed into a living statue of emerald glass.

The two large, teethy-beasties hurtled themselves at the invaders. While the one called Blue locked his attack onto Vexrile, Black was rocketing head-long toward Warfarin. With gaping jaws and reaching claws, the giant hairless beast attacked. Seeing the advancing hounds,

Warfarin swung his iron staff around and with amazing speed caught Black squarely on the side of its skull. The blow knocked the five-hundred pound beast backward, flipping it all the way around with an ear piercing *yelp*. As Warfarin spun himself about in a complete three-sixty, whipping his staff out for another strike, he chanced a quick glimpse at Vile to see if the Gate Keeper was still incapacitated…she was. He also took the opportunity to check on Vexrile to see how she was doing against Blue. Pleased to see that she was fairing well, he continued on. Coming full about he raised his staff high, then swept it down fast and hard. A sharp sounding crack rang out with the suddenness of a gun-shot the instant metal smacked against meat and dense bone. This second, more solidly delivered blow slammed the beast down. Black was attempting to scramble back up onto his feet, when Warfarin flipped his staff around in his grip. He'd spun it so that its ball side was up and its rock-hammer like spiked end was aimed down toward his target. Black barely had enough time to snap his beady colorless eyes up on to Warfarin before his weapon's bronze spike was driven into the beast's skull. Yanking it back out, he stepped back away from the twitching hound, noticing right off that the hole he'd left in its head was already beginning to heal shut. Stomping the heel of his boot down against the ice laden floor a thin-hair-line crack raced straight toward the still twitching Hell hound. The swift moving rupture stretched out to vanish beneath the beast and stopped. A flash of red and white light tore up out of the crack and with it came dozens of black, blade like tentacles. They lashed out and sliced the Shadow Hound into countless pieces, then snatched up the hunks of flesh and bone, pulling them down out of sight into the crack. The lights disappeared and the rupture closed.

Warfarin, hearing Vexrile scream, turned swiftly on his heels to face the sound of her distress in time to see Blue standing over her, his huge jaws snapping shut around her head. The beast jerked its massive mouth up, strands of Vexrile's torn flesh dangling from Blue's clinched jaws as the beast set his satiated gaze back over his shoulder onto Warfarin. Blue's lipless, incessant grin broke with the steady opening of his elongated mouth. As he shifted his blood splattered attention from Warfarin to the green statue of Vile, the beast whipped his tongue out and licked Vexrile's blood away from his right eye. Stepping off the

Overseer's twitching, headless corpse his gaze listlessly drifted to the spot where Black had been ripped apart and taken. After a few sniffs in Warfarin's direction Blue let out a long cry that almost sounded human. The beast's expressionless smile returned with the snapping shut of its jaws. Warfarin moved toward the hound at a steady pace, Blue doing likewise to meet the approaching Inquisitor. Then, as if a fire had suddenly been lit beneath the beast's feet, Blue leapt toward Warfarin. A flood of golden light exploded out of the archangel's wide hood. The moment the column of gold flame engulfed the hurtling Shadow Hound, the beast burst into a screaming ball of yellow fire that burned out in an instant, crumbling to white ash while still in flight. The outer corridor beyond the throne rooms' large double doors was suddenly alive with activity. It was the thunderous sound of clattering armor, running boots, and shouting, incoherent voices. Vile's palace guards had finally gathered the courage to investigate. As soon as they broke past the door's threshold Warfarin raised his hand, palm out to face the charging horde. Like cannon balls on fire, a blitz of flaming skulls as black as coal shot out of his hand and crashed at the guards feet. As the line of fire bombs hit the floor a huge wall of black flame erupted in their path. It had risen so quickly that it completely engulfed Vile's approaching guards, trapping them all within the cobalt inferno. The searing heat consumed all the flesh out of their armor, leaving only charred skeletons inside the metal shells. Having all of the soft tissue scorched off their bones wasn't enough to halt the horde's intention. Vile's demonic guards swiftly adapted to being reduced to armor wearing skeletons and burst out of the rescinding wall of flame. Stopping a moment to shake off the residual pain clinging to their smoldering bones, they regained their wit and resumed the attack. They moved simultaneously as if they all followed the command of but a single mind. They set their blackened, empty sockets onto Warfarin and advanced.

As if the approaching guards, bent on hacking and ripping Warfarin to pieces, were nothing to be concerned with, he shot a glance over his shoulder to make sure Vile was still imprisoned within her emerald casing. At the same time he brought his hand up, waving it at them like an annoyed adult shooing children away. Seeing that the Queen was locked in the glass vessel, he set his attention back onto the guards to see that his hand gesture had done exactly as it was intended to do.

The flick off the wrist had immediately re-invoked the dwindling wall of fire behind them, making it a raging inferno once more. Large tongues of black flame lashed out like dark solar flares and snatched up all of Vile's tin soldiers, yanking them back into the burning wall. Warfarin waved his hand again as he turned his attention finally onto Vexrile's body. The wall of flame with its trapped warriors had transformed into a wall of black molten glass that swiftly cooled and hardened. Warfarin went down to one knee beside Vexrile and with his back to the throne room's doors, hearing the sound of more palace guards coming, he willed the doors slammed shut, then sealed them with a solid stone and iron wall.

Vexrile's decapitated body had long since stopped its twitching, all of the blood that had resided within its flesh had poured out to form a frozen puddle that completely surrounded her.

"It's done Vexrile, the sixth realm is ours," he said while leaning over his amputated comrade, scraping up handfuls of her frozen blood, carefully moving the red slush into a pile in front of the large hole in her neck. When the small mound of crimson ice was the size of a head he laid open a deep cut across his right palm with his left thumbnail. The moment Warfarin's moderately warm blood dripped onto the pile of red slush, steam rose up like water being poured on dry-ice.

"Zaw'naws finally ours Vexrile," Warfarin affirmed a second time while glancing over his shoulder at the glass statue. He was in the process of placing his attention back around onto his work when a large hook fixed onto the end of a long chain whipped down through the black air. Warfarin's healing spell had begun to take hold, bone and flesh was starting to form in the steaming slush when the hook raced down behind him and drove into the center of his back, tearing out of his chest. The slack in the chain snapped tight and yanked Warfarin up ten feet above the floor. His kicking, jerking body was turned on its hook to face the statue and in an instant the Grand Inquisitor's elation was overran by utter dismay. From the glass statues hooded head down to the tips of its boots peeking out from its robes, the emerald shell that only a moment earlier owned Vile's likeness now looked exactly like Vexrile.

After Vile had summoned the Shadow Hounds, and a split second before Vexrile's green cloud could overtake her, the Queen switched bodies with the Overseer.

With her healing head not yet fully formed, Vile's nude self got up off the floor and stepped slowly between the would-be King and Queen of her realm. Turning her attention solely onto Vexrile, Vile offered a crooked smile and whispered, "What a shameful waste of effort."

The large hook that swooped out of the darkness toward Vexrile's back shattered the green glass incasing the Overseer as its steel blade-like tip stabbed all the way through the center of her torso. Unlike Warfarin, who was still fighting to rip himself off the hook, Vexrile made no attempts. Her limp body had been snapped up and dangled beside Warfarin's without so much as a shadow of protest.

While Vile took in Vexrile's despair like someone embracing a long awaited orgasm, she willed her throne of tangled flesh down from its hovering perch. Warfarin tried desperately to summon forth enough strength to call upon his powers.

"Don't waste your time Inquisitor; I own you and what pathetic strengths you may possess."

Warfarin pulled a ball of bloody spit up his throat into his mouth, and with as defiant a look as the pain would permit, he launched the projectile of spittle down toward Vile's face. Like a dog snapping at a fly Vile caught Warfarin's bloody spit in her mouth, licked her lips and said as she took her seat, "I've had better." She willed her throne up, bringing it to a levitated stop before the two.

"So, either of you happen to know what will occur if a drop of my blood, angel's blood, is given to a mortal?" Vile asked softly, her tone almost forgiving and friendly. "No, I didn't think so. I do, and it's a lot less disappointing than when an archangel shares her strength with an ungrateful seraphim breed."

Vile's eyes narrowed with an angry leer aimed at Vexrile, causing the Overseers body to go stiff with intense pain.

"You wouldn't dare," Warfarin said with a strained voice through his teeth. "Not even you're that insane. You would never—"

"Enough!" Vile growled, willing his throat closed.

Vexrile, hearing her comrade's claim that Vile wasn't mad enough, invoked an unexpected giggle from the Overseer.

"Do I amuse you Vexrile?" Vile willed Vexrile's head up from its limp position with the question, so that she could look deeply into the Overseer's green eyes.

"Yes, but that's not why I laugh."

"Then why?"

"He said you weren't insane."

"You believe me mad Vexrile?"

"Yes—yes indeed I do, quite mad for sure."

"Perhaps so," Vile said as she positioned herself on her throne so that she was kneeling on her fleshy seat. She leaned close to Vexrile, gently brushing some of the green glass dust off her face, Vile sadly added.

"You were my last attempt at trusting. I was going to make you a Goddess." Cradling Vexrile's head in her palms she kissed her lips and as Vile pulled away, Vexrile whispered, "forgive me Sillona."

Vile drove both of her thumbs into Vexrile's eyes and with a single yank pulled them out of her skull.

"Yes, perhaps I am a bit mad, but it's not me who's dangling from hooks."

Alex landed with a painful thud inside the Wall and had barely managed to pull his legs in before its small entrance closed around his ankles. With the closing of what appeared to be the only way in and quite possibly out, came darkness. But it wasn't the sudden elimination of the light or even that he was surrounded by a mountain of decay that was top on his percent list of concerns. No, it was the lacerations laying his throat open. Alex still hadn't gotten used to the idea that his body's reactions as to physical trauma were no longer bound by the usual laws governing cause and effect. What Alex was accustom to was the first-hand knowledge that when a throat is cut, death usually follows. Unbeknownst to him, the moment he hit the rotten surface of flesh and bone the blood pouring from his neck wounds had begun moving back up into the veins as the cuts mended themselves closed. The second he realized he wasn't going to bleed out, his attention switched onto his next concern. At some point during his crash landing on the soggy ground and his rush to yank his legs in he'd lost his grip on his knife, dropping it inside the black tunnel.

"Mr. Bane," he whispered, "say something, I'll follow your voice… Mr. Bane?"

Like a blind fool frantically groping for a lost cane Alex felt for his weapon. *Shit-house-luck*, he thought as he searched. After mistaking various bones, which had apparently torn out of their rotting vessels, for Mr. Bane's handle, he heard a familiar chuckle.

"Here Alex, I'm between your right hand and knee, lying in a pool of liquefying fat."

Following the metallic voice's instructions, Alex slid his hand over the slime onto Mr. Bane's blade.

"I believe it may be best if I'm put away for the time-being." Suggested the knife. "I don't see that I'll be needed. Not as of yet anyhow."

"It's good to be working with you again old friend." Alex whispered under his breath as he put the knife safely away into its sheath, snapping its hilt down beneath the strap.

"Yes, of course it is Alex," Mr. Bane hissed before fading to silence.

As Alex brought his hand back around he made sure the pouch of teeth was still hanging from his neck; it was.

The stifling heat and the putrid stench that emerged heavily from the untold amount of bodies, crashed into his senses with life smothering force as he struggled to gather his bearings. The constrictingly low mantel and the narrow walls clamped around him so snugly in spots as he crawled that every few feet, or even inches, Alex would have to wiggle himself loose. Then there were the splintered bones that had ripped through their fleshy hosts. More often than not they would snag onto his clothes, forcing Alex to tear himself free. Lastly there was the ceiling. Every time his head brushed up against the low mantel, clumps of icy cold maggots, wet with slime, dropped on his head, sliding into his sweatshirt. They would even find their foul way down past the waist-band into his pants.

Alex put his hat back on, in the hopes that it would be of some help, and buttoned his coat's top button, only to learn of the futility in his efforts. The hat kept getting caught by the low hanging bones and other body parts, forcing Alex to stop and retrieve it. As for his coat collar; it kept twisting around, constricting his breathing. So with an exasperated "...Fuck it!" Alex unbuttoned his collar and took off the fedora, cramming the hat back in his coat for safe keeping. Continuing on through the smelly darkness with ooze and who knows what else raining down on him.

This craps gone way beyond ridiculous, he thought as he crawled. At least he had his gloves. Never before had he been so grateful for having them. He especially appreciated them when his hand would bust down into a chest cavity weakened by rot, or when one of his fingers grope their blind way into the gel-like orb of an eye socket.

After what seemed like hours of belly crawling through the sweltering heat and muck Alex figured he'd covered at least a hundred yards or so. Truth is that he had actually only been traveling for slightly more than forty minutes and had dragged himself a mere sixty feet. He was of the mind to pause for a bit of a breather when all at once Alex's slow, dark journey came to an abrupt end. The narrow passageway of bodies had collapsed on top of him.

Alex was trapped beneath tons of mutilated spoilage again. The Wall pressed down on him so completely that the slightest of movements proved practically impossible. Alex attempted to call out to Pike, for all the good it would do, but all he was able to utter were wet sounding grunts and muffled groans. Alex's face was being smashed down into the soggy surface of the bodies. For all he knew it was being crammed between the slimy crack of a rotting buttocks or the pus seeping flesh of a scrotum. It took Alex all of thirty minutes to wriggle his right hand behind himself and another hour for him to feel Mr. Bane's handle with his fingertips. The plan was that if he could bring the blade out, he could hack his way to freedom. Of course, it was a half baked scheme with about as much likelihood of actually occurring as Alex getting a second chance at life before death, but it was the best he could come up with at the moment. The crushing weight and boiling heat was beginning to take its toll. With a forced surge of die-hard determination Alex had finally inched his fist around Mr. Bane's bone handle. Unsnapping the strap from off its hilt with his thumb he loosed a labored sigh of success as he eased the long blade out of its sheath. *Yes, that's it,* he encouraged with his thoughts, *come out old friend.* There was less than three inches to go when a sudden tremor shook down through the mountain of living carcasses. Alex, feeling the shifting weight pressing down on him paused, holding his breath as the shaking steadily subsided.

When it stopped Alex noticed a heavier change in pressure pushing down on top of him. Alex was still able to move his arm enough to bring the knife out, and continued doing so. There wasn't more than a centimeter of its tip left to come out when a stronger quake tore violently down through the bodies. With this second tremor came a crushing, downshifting slide of weight so sudden that Alex didn't even have time to think the words *shit house luck,* much less say them. With a muted cracking noise all of Alex's bones large enough to be broken were snapped or shattered. His mind screamed, *NO!* as his skull was being slowly crushed. Alex felt the oozing sensation of his icy cold blood trickling out of his ears, eyes, and nose. Moments before the integrity of his skull had no choice but to surrender to the bone compressing weight of the Wall; the increasing pressure stopped. Like the muffled cries of voices being spoken under water Alex heard the steady pounding of countless hearts all around him. Their steady palpitating pressed intrusively down against him as did the bodies.

He was finding it prolifically difficult to inhale breathable oxygen with his face being wedged into a buttocks, ball-sack or whatever it is that blocked his mouth's air intake. As Alex struggled against passing out from excruciating pain and physical fatigue, as if he could only be so lucky, he began mentally mocking himself. *It's all a lie,* his brain laughingly needled. *That's right—a—big—fucking—lie and you bit, hook-line-and-sinker. No wonder you were stopped at only five. Millstone, what a joke. Game? There's no damn game. Hell stupid, the only game being played here is on you, Pike lied. You should change your handle to Suckerstone…Millstone indeed, what a fucking joke.*

It was while Alex's mind grasped at the disbelief that the Gate Keeper might in fact be playing a detailed ruse on him that the heart beats began to dwindle. Suddenly the tons of sweltering bodies were swept away and with it the terror of forever being imprisoned within Hell's Wall. The slime, heat and foul reek had simply vanished; all that was left behind was Alex's crushed body and the darkness.

Still on his belly Alex felt the surface beneath him changing from that of spongy decay to hard damp stone. Its bumpy texture and wet familiar scent was strongly reminiscent of fresh rain on pavement.

Steadily his bones once again healed as every drop of his blood that had been squeezed out of the orifices of his body returned from whence it came. His sight eventually returned as well and in so doing Alex found himself in the blackest veil of space yet. When his bones and strength had mended well enough to follow his mind's commands Alex eased up onto his hands and knees.

His vision immediately locked onto two tiny star-like pinpoints of light far off in the distant void. They appeared to be perfectly parallel with him, maintaining an even pattern with one another. At first notice the tiny lights seemed to be suspended motionlessly in space. Then, as unexpectedly as Alex's heel had been sent into Five's double chins, the lights rocketed forward straight toward Alex. They evenly increased in size, intensity and speed, an ear-piercing whistle rose in volume to a blaring, raspy sounding shriek. The lights and sound were nearly on top of him when Alex realized that they were the high-beams and alarming horn of a rapidly approaching automobile. With his body still in the process of healing, he pushed beyond the pain and shoved himself with a loud grunt up to his feet and leapt out of the way of the oncoming vehicle racing eagerly to be acquainted with his flesh. The car missed Alex by mere inches when he spun about to get a look at the driver. A young woman was seated behind the wheel of a powder-blue 59 Impala. What Alex found odd was that the woman didn't appear to give a damn that she'd nearly run him down. The woman driver simply leaned on her horn and sped past him. He watched as the Impala's taillights suddenly beamed brighter, followed by the sharp sound of rubber tires being brought to an abrupt stop and a subsequent thump. *The dopey dame hit something*, Alex thought.

He was on his way over to see what happened, when the reason as to why she hadn't noticed him was revealed. Alex caught a second pair of head-lights rushing in his direction. With plenty of time to move out of the way, he mindlessly side stepped into the path of a 68 Mustang speeding in the opposite direction. Alex barely had enough time to think the word—*oops!* All he could do was his best to prepare for the impact. But, instead of being sent hurtling through the night by the cars front-end, he was left standing as he watched the car drive straight through his body. It was as if he were comprised of smoke. The visible streams of black and gray mist caught in the car's wake broke loose to pull back and reform the lower half of Alex's body. Alex spun sharply around, his boggled attention fixed on the Mustang's taillights as they receded up the street. He thought, *of course...it would have to be that way.*

"I'm a phantom," he whispered, "a sort of ghosty."

Still standing bewildered in the middle of the street, cars racing past him in both directions, Alex zigged-zagged his way through traffic. Even after the revelation that he was impervious to the body smashing effects delivered by tons of rolling iron, he still hadn't wrapped his mind around it fully. So he figured it best to avoid the cars for now. He spotted an elderly couple out for an evening stroll and deciding to test his new found ability to avoid the eyes of the living on the two pedestrians. Meeting them head on he yelled, "Hey—you, old people. Can you see me?" Stepping up in their weathered old faces, leaning his mouth close to the man's ear and shouted, "You hear me? Hey I'm talking to you!"

The smiling old couple were unaffected by Alex's uncouth efforts, they simply walked right through him hand in hand.

"It's a wee bit chilly out tonight Poppa." The silver haired woman said, shivering her shoulders as they moved through the phantom. Her portly, white haired mate removed his brown overcoat and gently draped it over the woman's narrow shoulders, kissing her on the cheek with a sweet, "How's that Mamma?" Her gray blue eyes sparkled a silent, *thank you* as they continued their night's walk.

Alex let his eyes follow the couple as he stepped backward off the curb right in front of a 1971 black Cadillac. It was much too late to move out of its path. Again his mind automatically prepared his body for the pain that usually comes with being struck by a car, only to catch himself feeling rather stupid when the big car and half a dozen others raced through him.

"It might have been wise to mention this little detail," Alex shouted up into the night. What Pike had failed to make known to his player was that few earthly objects and no mortals still among the living could see, hear or touch Alex. Pike figured that unless it was vital to the game, he'd let Alex find this out on his own. Although, there was one aspect to Alex's inability to be affected by earthly physical matter that the Gate Keeper shouldn't have left up to Alex to learn of on his own.

An aspect that he'll be thrown against with an unexpected introduction soon enough.

Looking himself over he noticed his clothes showed no signs of his slimy journey through the Wall. Only the dried stained reminders of his last night of life caked his things. Alex pulled his fedora out of his coat, checking on Mr. Bane in the process. After resnapping the strap back down over the hilt he pressed the crown of his hat into shape as he put it on, sweeping the thumb and forefinger along the edge of its brim. Studying his surroundings he spotted the powder-blue Impala still stopped up the street. A small throng of witnesses were gathered around the car's front-end gawking. *She'd hit something,* Alex remembered.

The young woman who'd been driving the car was sitting sideways on the driver's side front-seat, the door swung open wide, her nylon clad legs crossed outside the car. A blond haired boy of about ten years of age was standing rigidly only a few feet directly in front of her. The boy quietly watched her, his lower lip pressed stiffly up against his top lip, waiting for her to get off the cell phone she giggled into. Alex also noticed that the boy was clutching what appeared to be a dog-leash. A wave of relief rushed up Alex's spine at the visual confirmation issued by this boy's clue as to what this woman apparently hit. As he stepped between the woman driver and the boy Alex also saw that the kid was fighting back tears. Alex shifted his gaze onto the woman still giggling into the phone and with a leering stare that could have dissolved glass he mumbled, "Stupid woman."

Stepping behind the crowd he paused and reached his right hand up, to make sure he could in fact pass through flesh and bone as easily as it moved through him. But when Alex's hand came up he was surprised to see that Mr. Bane was clinched in his fist.

"Mr. Bane, how'd you get there?" He asked softly.

"I'm not at liberty to divulge that information," replied the metallic voice. "But you may want to keep me handy Alex."

Alex looked around, taking the knife's suggestion as a warning. Seeing no signs of anyone or thing that could prove threatening to him, Alex chuckled, "You're paranoid."

"Don't say you weren't warned."

Alex acted as though he was paying the fading voice no mind as he placed the weapon back into its sheath and went back to what he'd been doing. Focusing his attention onto the back of a tall red-haired man's head, Alex raised his now empty hand and marveled at what he could do. His gloved fingertips disappeared into the man's skull and other than sending a slight chill through the bystander, the presence of the ghostly digits had no harmful affects on him. With a swift downward sweep Alex sliced his hand along the man's spinal-cord, swooping it out of the small of his back.

"Wow! That's some wildly bitchin' shit," Alex declared. With no further hesitation Alex stepped through the bodies of the living, his brief passing caused the four men and two women to shiver suddenly. Stepping out past the wall of warm souls Alex's eyes fell on the big white German Shepard wedged up into the driver's side fender-wall. The tire hadn't only run over the unfortunate quadruped, it had also twisted the beast into a dozen painful to look at positions. Still, the trapped animal managed to cling to life. As Alex knelt down in front of the suffering beast for a closer look the little blond boy with the leash pushed his way through the legs and hips. He was about to step toward his dying friend when a fat, greasy faced man placed his stubby, trembling fingers over both of the boy's shoulders and said, "There's nothing to be done, best let me give you a lift home son. Do you live close by?"

The man's appearance and the sight of his glistening with spittle, quivering lips, not to mention his not knowing the boy or where the child lived, brought Alex up. The eager fat man was gently pulling him back through the crowd when Alex rocketed his fist toward the man's jaw. He stumbled, nearly falling forward with the force that he delivered with the punch as the blow passed harmlessly through the man's head. Alex was reaching for Mr. Bane, sending his left hand out to grab ahold of the boy to pull him out of the man's grasp when the child jerked out from under the stranger's grip.

"Keep your hands off me!" The boy snapped as he stepped toward his dog.

"Well done boy," Alex said under his breath as he watched the greasy man slither out through the crowed. Alex waited until the man was in his car and down the road before dropping back down onto his haunches between the boy and his trapped pet. Fully aware that the boy couldn't see or hear him, Alex still spoke to the kid as if he could.

Gazing into the boy's face Alex said, using his strongest matter-of-fact tone.

"That's right boy…don't trust anyone unless you know them, I mean really know them. It's moments like this, when you're at your weakest, that the freaks creep out and pounce."

Alex let his attention drift back onto the dog and noticed that its pale blue eyes were following his hand's movements. "You can see me," he said, "isn't that right boy?" The dog's left ear twitched as if to issue a silent reply. Alex slowly extended his hand, knowing full well that hurt animals disliked being touched. The wounded beast let Alex's fingers ease close enough so that its last act of disdain toward man wouldn't be in vain. Alex was fairly certain his hand would sail down through the dog's head, whether it could truly see him or not. His fingers were less than an inch from its snout when the beast snapped out and bit through his glove into the meat of his fingers. Jerking his hand back he shouted, "Damn it! Sonofabitch—"

Before Alex could complete the curse and as he was about to stand a thin leather strap was slung over his head and pulled tight around his throat. It was the leash; the boy's dog-leash. Alex was yanked backward off his feet and swiftly dragged out of the crowd by the boy; both him and the now laughing child were exiting through the wall of legs as if they weren't there. On his way out and away from the car Alex caught a glimpse of the dog leering at him. Its pale blue eyes changed to a bright gold, that locked onto Alex's eyes to magically drained all the fight out of him. Raising its bleeding head the dog peeled its lips back in a teeth exposing grin and in a girl's voice scolded saying, "Malingerer—Slacker—Lollygagger."

Alex's mind struggled furiously against the boy's leash, but his body was as limply useless as a dead rat. No sooner had his brief journey been brought to a halt a few yards from the crowd and the boy dropped on Alex's chest. He pressed his sharp bony knees down into his shoulders, grinding against them and giggled. *Get the fuck off me,* Alex tried to say but could only think. The boy's knees dug deeper into Alex's shoulders, driving out a low rumble of voiced agony through his clinched teeth. Leaning down to leer closely into Alex's face the boy stopped his knee grinding. His hazel green eyes had begun to increase in size, bulging out at Alex hungrily as their whites steadily filled with blood.

"You're not here to fucking sight-see—human."

The dark-red blood overpowering the whites of his eyes found its way out of his tear-ducts, trickling down his sickly pale cheeks, dripping onto Alex's face and neck.

"We're always watching," hissed the boy as he nodded his head with a quick twitch toward the crowd. Alex's head was forcefully turned by unseen hands onto his right cheek, making him face the crowd. He was horrified to see that all of the men and women's heads and hands had transformed into horribly misshapen faces, hideous claws and all of which comprised of large red eyes, long sharp teeth and hard, pointed fingernails. Alex looked at the woman who ran over the dog. She was still sitting cross-legged, half out of her car, only the cell phone she was still giggling into was now a big black skinned, leech-like thing with a circular mouth filled with an incalculable amount of tiny sharp teeth. Its doll-sized head swiftly reared back away from the woman's ear, then lunged its teeth deep into her left cheek. As it snapped and wriggled its head from side to side, working its bite away from the bone the woman's wide-eyed, smiling expression never wavered. The big leech in her fist tore off a mouth full of her face, bolted it down with a gulp, and then immediately dug in for seconds.

Alex's attention was set back onto the monsters gathered around the dog. They parted, opening a visual pathway so that the trapped animal was in his line of sight. The dog's golden eyes burned brightly onto Alex, its mouth barely moving as it spoke, its voice still that of a little girl.

"I do not care for you." Its tone of voice filled with proof of the statement. "No, not one bit. But the Gate Keeper believes that you're the worthy choice—the only choice. Do not end this game lacking, for if you do I'll see to it personally that you're given over to your parents. Yes, I'm beyond certain they've missed you greatly."

The girl's voice fell silent and the dog's head dropped limp over the side of the blood stained tire. Its wide eyes evenly dimmed to their pale blue hue. Almost simultaneously the nightmares posted up around the dead dog returned to their human forms. The leech-like thing dining upon the young woman's face transformed to its former cell phone shape, giving the woman back her pretty looks. The child atop Alex's chest however, remained unchanged.

"We're always watching you Mr. Stone," he threatened with a grin that continued to stretch. Opening his mouth wider than humanly possible, the boy's mortally shaped teeth grew pointed and steadily longer. When his mouth was wide enough to fit comfortably over a house-cat's entire head, he dropped down and sank his teeth through Alex's coat and sweatshirt, stabbing them deep into the flesh of his right shoulder.

Alex cried out, a loud scream that was conceived by the joining of excruciating pain and pure unadulterated rage. At first the howl was muted by the blond boy's power over Alex's ability to speak. But when Alex's eyes opened past the pain, they'd done so to the sound of his own screaming voice. He immediately saw that the boy was no longer sitting on top of him and leapt up onto his feet. The boy had left his leash behind; Alex quickly pulled it off from around his throat and tossed it up onto a near by house roof.

"What in the hell was all of that about?" Alex demanded. It was a stupid question, he knew exactly what it was about—it was about getting started. Looking around Alex realized that he was four whole blocks from where the crowd of people were goggling over the dead dog. His attention went from his surroundings down onto his right shoulder. He saw no teeth holes in his coat and aside from the phantom pain stinging out from deep within his shoulder; it appeared to be in perfect working order. Looking at his right hand he saw that the marks left by the dogs' bite were also gone. He'd only taken his eyes off his hand for an instant, but when he went to rub his bare head, wondering where his hat was, he'd nearly stabbed himself in the eye with Mr. Bane.

"What the fuck!" he barked.

"I told you to leave me out, at the ready Alex. But you chose not to," Mr. Bane whispered.

"Fine!" Alex snapped.

"Don't be cross with me Alex my boy. This is just their way of telling you, time is short. So what do you say to us going to work?"

"Yes, of course."

"One more thing Alex my friend."

"Yes?"

"Welcome home."

If a place on earth ever existed that Alex could even half-assed refer to as home, Corvallis, Oregon would have been that place. The last time he'd laid his eyes on the small college town was forty-seven days before sending Number One to Hell. The day Alex had been released from prison the first thing he did was to hop on the first bus going to Corvallis. He had only stayed long enough to keep a childhood promise he'd made twenty-two years earlier. To resurrect Mr. Bane from the ammo-box casket buried in a river side grave. Before that he'd not been to Corvallis since he was nine.

After freeing his friend from the small metal coffin, Alex left that town planning on never stepping foot there again. Not because he thought of that quaint little hamlet as an evil place, but because it held only evil memories, none of which were Corvallis', fault. Here he was though, right back where all of his nightmares were spawned.

The blond boy, demon child or whatever it was had transported Alex onto the corner of Polk and Ninth Street. Deciding that it might be a good idea to keep Mr. Bane out he said in a low, dark sounding tone, "Well old friend, what do you say to joining the dance?" Alex's double edged crime-partner offered no reply. In the past Mr. Bane would have volunteered some sort of concise retort or cheeky come-back, whether it was wanted or not. But with or without an answer, Alex could sense his friends' presence; verbal confirmation of Mr. Bane's existence was seldom necessary.

Alex was about to begin his hunt on Polk Street, but as he was heading around the corner his steps were brought to a halt and his direction changed by something catching his eye. Across Ninth Street, resting on top of a stop sign's pole was Alex's fedora. It wasn't that his hat seemingly appeared out of thin air that Alex found to be odd. It was the location where it had appeared and the means by which it had to have been placed there. Almost from the moment of his arrival out of Hell he'd noticed that the weather had no affect on his body or the clothing he wore over it. A tempest of wind and rain could suddenly rise up and still his skin and clothes would remain bone dry, hanging evenly down over his frame, disturbed only by his movements. Water droplets, whether they be as large as crocodile's tears or as minuscule in size as cloud-mist, it all simply passed through leaving no mark on him. So, this being the case he was left with only one conclusion; since the wind was unable to blow his hat up onto that sign-post it had to have been placed there by someone. *The Gate Keeper*, Alex wondered. *Or maybe it was that blond boy—a player perhaps*, his mind questioned. The stop sign was facing inward toward the exit of a shopping mall's parking-lot. The only reason Alex could come up with as to why his fedora was put there of all places, was that someone or something wanted him on that side of the street.

"Looks as though somebody wants us to do a little shopping Mr. Bane." He growled under his breath while stepping off the curb. Alex reached the other side of Ninth and moved toward his hat resting motionless atop the pole. Holding his weapon down, at the ready but not blatantly-so; he scrutinized the area surrounding the sign as he drew near. It was relatively out in the open, as were most stop-signs, not much for anyone to hide behind. Without slowing his pace Alex reached up and snatched his hat off the pole and after a brief inspection put it on. He decided he would check out the mall.

As soon as he passed through the oak and glass double doors into the busy lobby Alex was assaulted by the chaotic sights, sounds and smells of the overly-lighted, noisy place. An instrumental rendition of Madonna's: Like A Virgin was being trumpeted out over the roar of shoppers. The strong odors of deep-fried food from the mall's food-court, men and women's perfumes, and a variety of other smells mixed together to conjure up a sickly sweet reek. The living moved through Alex like hands waving through smoke, shivering slightly as they continued on their busy way. He tried side-stepping out of their path in hopes of avoiding the unpleasant experience, but only ended up stepping into the way of another warm soul. There seemed to be no escape from the brightly lit space and rushing bodies. Babies wailed, preteens screamed and adolescents giggled mindlessly. Alex's head had begun to throb with the overwhelming jolt of sensory-overload.

It wasn't until he'd spotted the big clown faced clock on the wall of the mall's ice cream shop that his mind settled down. 6:50 was the time and as he shook off the feelings of anxiety and panic he remembered the Gate Keepers verbal heads up.

Gathering his wits, Alex strengthened his hold on Mr. Bane's hand-grip and went in-search of his fellow damned souls. It took Alex all of twenty-five minutes to search the mall's basement, its lower level shops, the mid level shops and the bathrooms. As he was finishing with the main-floor he located the mall's tobacco and pipe shop. Or moreover it found him. The sweet smells of rich tobaccos reached out and gaffed onto Alex's longing. Like a dope sick junky locked in a pharmacy alone after hours, Alex stood staring almost stupefied at all the wonderful cancer causing products. Stepping with a sense of self-entitlement over to the Camel cigarette display rack, he didn't see the harm in helping himself to one of the packs. Remembering a movie he'd seen in the late 80s about a ghost who had to concentrate on an object before he could move it, Alex unsure if his hand could take a hold of the pack, figured he'd give the movie ghost's method a try. Reaching out his gloved hand, he focused all of his want onto the shiny pack of smokes. With a quick tap of his middle fingertip the cigarette pack moved. "Yes!" Alex whispered as he went to snatch his prize off the rack. The instant he took the pack in his fist, Alex, along with his greed, were slammed down onto his knees as a teeth exploding, eyeball popping zap of electricity reached out of the pack into Alex's body. Toothless and blind, he dropped the pack of smokes to the floor and waited for the raking pain racing up and down his spine to mellow. As the pain eventually eased, his eyeballs and teeth healing themselves, Alex could hear the voice of the blond boy.

"We're always watching," he said.

Alex's vision returned to him and was already focused on the floor where the blond boy's face was peering up out at him from the carpet, he echoed, "We're always watching."

The moment the boy's face melted away out of sight and his words faded, Alex was brought up onto his feet by an insanely loud man's voice. It was an enraged voice, owning in its un-tethered tone the unmistakable lilt of madness. It only took Alex a second to pin-point its location. Leaving the tobacco shop on his way up to the malls second floor, he glanced at the faces of the living as he made his way past a few of them. Alex noticed that no one appeared effected by the screaming up-stairs. That could only mean one of two things, either every man, woman and children in that mall was deaf or the angry voice was one of the players.

When he reached the top of the stairs, stepping onto the landing, he immediately realized that the wailing was coming from behind a wall only a few yards in front of him. The wall was beautifully painted with a large mural depicting a battle between a white haired wizard and a black skinned fire breathing dragon.

"Look at me!" Screamed the quivering voice on the other side of the wall.

"Easy, Alex my boy," whispered Mr. Bane. "Take it one step at a time."

"Thanks for the heads up on the smokes by the way." Alex whispered as he eased toward the mural.

"Don't place the fault of your tendency to put want before common sense on my shoulders. Now focus on the task at hand—"

"Shush, I'm trying to think."

"Well, it's about time."

Stopping at the painted wall, Alex listened a moment to the madman's howling while he came up with a plan of attack.

"Whores! Pimps! Why won't any of you diseased pups bleed? Look at me! Scream! Ble-e-ed!"

Pressing the palm of his hand against the wall, Alex secretly grinned at the sight of it vanishing beyond its colorful surface. Wanting to peer through the wall in hopes of getting a look at what he was going to contend with, Alex pushed his face through. At first he pulled right back out, his slight reluctance stemming from the very idea that he was actually moving his face through a solid concrete wall. It was a somewhat disconcerting concept to wrap one's acceptance around, not to mention, it felt odd. With a deep breath and a quiet, "Here goes," Alex pressed his face through the concrete and metal.

The front rim of his hat's brim broke out on the opposite side into a clothing shop, when an instant before his face was to follow, the heavy metal head of an axe swept through the surface of the wall, missing the bridge of Alex's nose by a hair. Alex threw himself back out of the concrete partition with a loud, "Mother fucking sonofabitch!"

Unwittingly, in his haste to escape the head hunting blade, he'd taken one too many retreating steps. Over the edge he went, and as he tumbled head over heels down the flight of thinly carpeted oak stairs, he could see mental images of him being thrown down into the reaching hands of his parents. With Mr. Bane still clutched in his fist he rolled through the living as they trudged up and down the stairs, utterly unaware of his presence other than an unexplained coldness. Alex's ride came to an end with a thud at the exact moment he heard the man's voice shouting down at him.

"Pimp! You're one of those I was sent to chop to bits. Good, finally someone I can kill!"

Alex snapped his attention up to face the loud, wet sounding words, and saw standing at the top of the stairs leering down at him a giant of a man. In his right hand he held an axe, in his left Alex's crumpled fedora. He stood no less than six feet seven inches, with close to four hundred pounds of muscle and fat housed within his frame. As with Alex, he sported no hair anywhere on his waxy, wet looking body and his skin color was a bloodless white, owning only a slight yellow hue. Other than the dark brown leather pouch hanging from around his thick, but still almost nonexistent neck, all he wore was a pair of light-gray overalls. They were horribly stained with dried blood and the ends of the pant legs were tattered, the frayed strips dangling over a pair of big black work boots.

His name is David Baily Fisk and he is the first realm's choice to play in the game. That dark land of suffering is called Awtsal; it is there in Hell where the hopelessly slothful are sent to eternally scream. Fisk was one of those wretchedly slothful damned.

Ten years and four and a half months ago he was sent to Hell's tormenters for the sins of chopping two families to death with an axe. The body count he'd left behind was two men, both of their wives, and nine children in all. They had been Mr. Fisk's closest neighbors; close to his house, not his heart. It seems they, along with the rest of the neighborhood, had grown sick of living next to the filthy squalor that was Fisk's home-sweet-home. So, instead of moving, the neighbors had gotten together a petition and signed it. The piece of paper, which had also been signed by a magistrate and hand delivered by a sheriff, ordered David Fisk to either clean all of the garbage and junk off his property or be forced to sell and move.

Needless to say, Fisk didn't take too kindly to having his good neighbors going behind his rather large back, it simply wasn't neighborly. So, one night he sharpened the blade of his axe and went to work. His sticky, messy, drudgery was brought to an abrupt end almost as soon as it had begun. With two families down and still several more to go, he was stopped by the most unlikely of people; at least as far as he was concerned—his own teenage son. Eddie Fisk was sixteen when, as he was taking a short-cut home through a neighbor's backyard, he'd spotted something odd through one of the windows. Taking it upon himself to have a closer look, he crept alongside the house's exterior wall, hidden in the shadows and peeked through a blood splattered pane of glass to see his dear old dad hacking the six year old little Bobby Fisher to pieces.

Not wishing to be the kid known throughout his high-school as the boy who called the cops on his axe murdering father, Eddie did what he believed to be the right thing. Being the bright lad that he was, Ed ran straight home lickety-split and snatched up his pop's ten-gauge double-barreled shotgun. The boy then went promptly back and without a word of warning blew his father's head off.

Fisk tossed Alex's hat aside, raised the axe above his head, and with a guttural yell hurtled himself from the top of the stairs. Alex barely managed to roll out of the way before the big boots slammed down flat-footed on the spot where he'd been. The axe blade fell with a downward swoop that swiftly curved back up, sending an air slicing whistle past the back of Alex's head. Scrambling at a running crawl back up onto his feet, Alex wheeled around blindly sweeping Mr. Bane's blade out as he faced his attacker. Both players ducked and dodged each others strikes. Fisk almost seemed to be toying with Alex, much the way a prize-fighter sizes up an opponent before setting him up for the good-night-Gracie punch. Where as Alex on the other hand was doing his damnedest to hold his ground against this much larger adversary.

Alex's primary problem wasn't so much Fisk's physical size but the fact that his weapon had a greater reach than Mr. Bane's ten inch blade. Seeing a window of opportunity open as Fisk wildly wind milled the axe around, trying to cleave his head in two, Alex lunged forward in an effort to stab the big man's throat. Fisk, taking sharp notice of the delivery, jerked his upper body hard right dodging the blade's pass while rocketing the hickory axe-handle's butt out, catching Alex in the jaw. The blow was solid, stunning Alex enough to send him stumbling backward a few paces. In a desperate attempt to issue a counter-attack Alex, almost blinded by the strike, crisscrossed his knife, slicing only air until Mr. Bane's edge dragged along the axe handle to unintentionally sever all four of Fisk's fingers and the tip of his thumb off his right hand. The digits dropped to the floor and wiggled spastically like the disembodied tails of Blue belly lizards.

Fisk, forced to wield his weapon one handed, did so with blood thirsty ambition. But his rage obstructed his aim, missing Alex with every swing. Alex raced Mr. Bane down drawing a dark-red shallow line from Fisk's left wrist to his elbow. He swiftly curved the knife blade back up to try and open the arteries in the man's left arm-pit. Fisk quickly snapped back out of Mr. Bane's path, dropping his axe toward the player and missing by a mile. Alex swung his fist into the right side of the large head, following the punch with a solid blow from his elbow, crossing both strikes with the knife blade. Fisk dodged the hungry blade again as it sliced inches past his face and sent the back of his mutilated hand into the left side of Alex's face unforgivingly hard. The blow had him stumbling once more. Before he could fall away, Fisk reached his fingerless hand out between the misdirected swipes and sweeps of Alex's weapon and latched a hold of his wrist.

"Where in the hell do you think you're going?" Fisk barked. With only the use of a palm and little more than half a thumb Fisk tore Alex up into the air and flung him toward a gaggle of giggling teenage girls. The instant he hit the floor Alex got back to his feet and broke out of the now shrieking from the sudden cold teens. Fisk was on one knee; leering at him. The big man was pressing his bloody palm flat on the floor, allowing the severed fingers to squirm like inch-worms back onto his knuckles. Alex charged at the exact instant the fingers were reattaching themselves, although out of the correct order. Stepping toward the advancing player and with the speed of a grizzly bear, Fisk open hand slapped Alex aside, knocking him down once again. Alex went to get up but had only made it onto one knee as Fisk's big boot came up to break three of Alex's ribs. The kick hit him so hard that it actually helped Alex up onto his feet. One of his ribs had pierced his right lung, filling it with blood that was being sent up into his mouth with every exhaled breath. Managing to maintain his upright position,

Alex tried to get his bearings as he struggled to dodge Fisk's axe. The axe-blade arched down past Alex's head grazing his right shoulder cap. Alex tried to move in, sweeping Mr. Bane left, right, up and down, but Fisk's axe wasn't letting him come close enough to open his flesh. That, along with the pain in his lung, left Alex with only one alternative, to withdraw long enough to heal. Alex caught a peripheral glimpse of the wall nearing behind him. Confident that his now ghost-like ability would allow him to further his back-stepping exit, he didn't bother to alter his attention from the madman's flying axe-blade to see where he was going.

It was at this most inopportune time that Alex was to be introduced to that aspect of the game Pike had left up to Alex to learn of on his own. It had to do with a player's face to face dealing with passing through physical matter. Hell's caretakers thought of this rule as one of the game's amusing obstacles. But to those damned souls playing the game it was more of a pain in the ass than anything else. What Pike had intentionally failed to mention, was the rule that the only time while engaged in physical combat that a player can move through solid matter is when he or she is focusing visually on it. That is to say, if Alex wanted to continue his retreat he must turn and face the wall fully. There is only one exception, floors. No player can pass down beneath a floor or the ground, unless the surface being stood on at the time is a roof-top.

Not yet aware of this not so minor detail, Alex with all of his attention locked onto Fisk and the big man's weapon being swung wildly toward his skull, he back-stepped against the wall. Fisk, noticing the expression of grievous surprise that had sprung to life in Alex's eyes, grinned as he sent the axe down to cleave asunder Alex's dome. Alex managed to avoid that strike, attempting to dart around Fisk, who in turn slammed Alex back into the wall with a shove of his palm. "Stay put pimp!"

Alex stabbed and sliced at the man, but he was too busy trying to avoid the axe-blade to get close enough. With little space to maneuver and nearly choking on the blood filling his mouth from his punctured lung, he figured his time to act was now or never. Waiting for the heavy blade to fall he made his move. Gripping Mr. Bane in both fists, he jerked out of the descending weapon's path and spit the mouth full of blood in Fisk's eyes while driving all ten inches of his knife blade straight into the big man's guts. With all the strength Alex could summon, he pulled Mr. Bane across Fisk's midsection while ducking out from under the sweeping axe.

After his sudden, unexpected halt caused by the wall's refusal to let him pass, Alex was fairly convinced that he could no longer move through walls and the like. So, certain of that being the case, he figured the large concrete pillar he'd hurtled himself toward in his haste to get away from the axe wielding lunatic could serve as a sort of berm to spin around against. Nope, he kept right on going, straight through the interior building support as if it wasn't even there. He'd done so with such force that when he crossed out on the other side he kept going, tripping over his own feet. Alex was really confused now, one minute he's passing through walls, the next he's not, then a second later he's moving through a solid concrete pillar. Alex got swiftly up and had spun about at the very moment Fisk was stepping around the pillar. The whole right side of his belly was laid open by Mr. Bane's lacerating bite. A substantial portion of his intestines had poured out and were speckled with clumps of blood smeared, yellow fat. Despite the gaping incision or the fact that he was practically tripping over his own guts, Fisk wasn't slowed. With quickly executed steps, although erratically placed and jerky, he advanced. Alex readied himself, his broken ribs and the hole in his right lung all but completely mended. His breathing was still a bit laborious but nothing he couldn't work with. He watched in a mental state of morbid amazement, coupled with utter revolution, as the blood and fat covered entrails still smelling of yeast and bile slithered back up into Fisk's closing gut wound. Alex had long since grown weary of all this foolishness, he needed an edge over this player's size and longer reach with his weapon; an edge that would bring this bout to a close.

Fisk swung the axe up, held it at a swinging position and grinned, his large teeth freakishly white.

"So—pimp, you just gunna stand there and piss on yourself, or you gunna come get some?"

"Yeah yeah…blah blah." Alex replied as he faked left then darted right, charging toward Fisk. The axe-blade swept down, falling for Alex's staged maneuver then swiftly readjusted and changed course in mid flight. It shot past the right side of Alex's head so fast that the air caught in the heavy hunk of metal's wake stung the rim of Alex's ear. Stepping a sharp left Alex sliced Mr. Bane's blade down with the aimed intent of a pit-bull, sending the entire length of its edge clean through both hamstrings behind the maniac's right leg. Without slowing his progress Alex followed the crippling strike by stabbing the falling player in the left kidney with an upward thrust. Slicing Mr. Bane out of the man's back, Alex was on the verge of closing the deal with a swift spiking of Fisk's skull. In a split second, last-ditch effort to avoid the distasteful experience, the big man threw himself out of the plunging blade's way and rammed the dull, flat side of the axe-blade up into Alex's forehead. The blow knocked him back, sending Alex staggering against the same pillar he'd only moments earlier stumbled through. The iron delivery had been issued so solidly it split open a deep cut across Alex's brow causing blood to pour generously into his eyes, clouding his vision behind a veil of red.

Still on his knees, Fisk seeing that he was successful in laying open a gash on Alex's forehead had also seen it as his chance to end the party. Shaking off some of the throbbing pain and wiping blood from out of his eyes, Alex caught sight of Fisk struggling with his pouch, trying to get it open while the thing was hanging from his neck. It seemed that his right hand, with its wrongly misplaced fingers, was having difficulty with the tightly cinched draw-string. Alex's attention shifted to Mr. Bane lying on the floor about fifteen feet away, then back up onto Fisk or moreover the steadily dwindling blood stains on his overalls. The dark-red stains on the man's back and behind his right leg were getting smaller as the blood was being drawn out of the gray cloth back into the already closing wounds. Fisk was angrily biting at the leather cord, frantically fighting to pull the bag open as Alex felt the gash on his forehead. There was no way Alex would be able to get a tooth out of his own pouch, grab Mr. Bane and open a fresh cut on Fisk before the axe-murderer could beat him to the punch. Alex was forced to do something he'd hoped to avoid—RUN.

Fisk, who was still having no luck opening his pouch, took it off from around his neck and stood. With his axe in his right fist and the bag of teeth in his left he moved toward Alex, who was on his way to Mr. Bane. As he was snatching the knife up he shot a glance over his shoulder in time to see the axe-blade flying at the back of his head.

Dropping to the floor and with a rolling kick Alex swept Fisk's feet out from under him sending the giant down hard. Almost as fast as Alex threw himself down he was back up and running. He tore through the dwindling shoppers, the axe wielding psychopath shouting.

"Come back and take your dismembering like a man! Coward! I won't be denied your screams!" The thunderous sound of his boots pounding out as he chased after B'neem's player.

Alex was still unsure as to whether or not he could pass through walls at will. He was hoping that the fact that he'd passed effortlessly through half a dozen living souls would have been proof that he could. Especially after turning the corner into a dead-end. With Fisk rapidly gaining Alex was certain that the quickest way to end this nonsense was via an ambush and not by continuing the toe to toe contest he had gotten caught up in. Reaching the end of the road he blocked his face with his forearm and charged the concrete wall. Alex was in luck, he moved through the foot thick obstruction as if it weren't there and found himself running into a dimly lit jewelry store. It was a small room, with all the usual jewelry store paraphernalia; glass display cases; moderately well known prints of oil-paintings; a small davenport and two matching chairs all surrounding a small glass coffee table. Samuel Barber's: Adagio for strings was being softly piped in as a white haired man sporting a thick handlebar mustache showed rings to a young couple. There was a single concrete column, like the pillar Alex had tripped through in the center of the small store. *This'll do,* Alex thought as he scanned the room. He could hear Fisk's booming voice quickly drawing near, beyond the same wall he'd passed through. As soon as Alex got into an ambush position behind the pillar he opened his pouch and rolled one of the tiny yellow chompers out onto his left palm clenching his fist around it, Freak Bane in his right, waiting to bite.

Fisk burst through the jewelry store wall at a fast walk, his axe already slicing back and forth as if he were trying to cut a humming-bird in half.

"Come out. Come out wherever you are!" Fisk yelled. "Come face me like a man. If you come out now I'll let you have the first swing." As the big man slowed his pace, still swinging his axe one handed, Alex saw that he was also still in the process of trying to pull his pouch open with the aid of his teeth. *This is going to be as easy as stomping on dead cats*, Alex thought, moving around the pillar and keeping out of Fisk's line-of-sight, while trying to keep him in his.

"If you make me work for this," Fisk added. "I'll make it worth my time—pimp! Yes I will, I'll chop-chop-chop your cowardly carcass to bits." Fisk stopped suddenly only a few paces in front of Alex's hiding place. He swung his axe at the young couples as they laughed at something the store-keeper had said.

"Shut-up! Whore...pimp! Shut your mouths!" He demanded while the axe flew harmlessly through their warm bodies. *What an asshole*, Alex thought. Fisk was swinging the axe wildly left and right, seeming to be lost in his vain efforts. Then completely unexpected, at the exact moment Alex had decided to make his move, Fisk spun around.

"Fooled ya!" Fisk shouted as he swung the axe up, meeting Alex's spring loaded assault. Before the axe had a chance to fall Alex sailed Mr. Bane's blade right opening the left side of Fisk's throat, then instantly reversed the knife's direction, slicing open the right side as well. The strike had severed both the carotid artery and the jugular vein hidden deep within Fisk's fat incased neck. Alex threw himself back away from the falling axe-blade, at the same time tossing the demon tooth down at Fisk's feet. But Alex's retreat hadn't gone off without a hitch. The sweeping axe lashed down and like a surgical laser slashed through his sweat shirt, cutting Alex deeply down his chest and abdomen. He slammed back against this hiding place and quickly stumbled around the huge column. Unwilling to take his eyes off Fisk to even so much as glance down at his wound or see where he was going, Alex tripped backward over the glass coffee table. Despite the floods of blood pouring out from both sides of Fisk's neck he still pulled his lips apart in a wide grin at the sight of Alex's split open torso. In a voice resembling someone attempting to speak under water, the big man sort of chuckled and said, "Close but no cigar. You lose—"

Fisk's victory speech was interrupted the instant his shadow moved over the tooth Alex had cast to the floor, causing the canine to melt out of sight into the plush dark-blue carpet. Actually it wasn't the tooth's disappearance that killed his overzealous monologue; it was the huge widely open set of shark-like jaws that sprang straight up around Fisk. The mammoth toothy orifice was the mouth of a giant maggot. Its yellowish-white body, glistening wet and covered with deep zigzagging scars, shot out of the floor surrounding Fisk. As soon as it was up far enough its jaws slammed shut over him. Faster than it had risen the huge worm-creature tore back down into the floor without as much as a burped 'thanks' for the meal.

Alex sat there on the davenport staring blankly down at the spot where the axe-man had been standing a second ago. Looking at his chest he watched as his sternum, flesh and skin steadily closed; the blood moving into the sealing gash and seeping down into his pores. As his sweat-shirt mended itself he pushed up off the piece of furniture and without so much as an over the shoulder glance at the young couple Alex left the way he'd came in.

Chapter Five

— BACK INTO THE HALLWAY —

"How often the fear of one
evil leads us into a worse"

—Boileau

B'neem's Overseer named Sader had burst in through the Cathedral's huge doors. As with the eighth realm's other esteemed custodians, Pike and Ellzbeth in particular, Sader also possessed the outer appearance of a human child. Only his eyes, as with the eyes of all angelic beings, offered a clue as to his true identity. They were pure silver in color and shined as brightly as a newly minted dime. An amok-design of black face-paint framed them, giving his alabaster face an even whiter look. The large vermilion hood that almost always cloaked his perfectly round, bald head draped down from his narrow shoulders to hang flat over his back.

He stepped sharply into the poorly lit great-hall and shouted, "Pike—Ellzbeth, are you here?"

His enquiry echoed off the high walls and tall reaching iron columns, carrying in its fading reverberation a heavy note of misgiving. Pike's reply came so quick and was so full of excitement that it layered over the Overseer's question, devouring it. "Yes, yes Sader, we're back here—in the theater. Come, come join us and see how effortlessly B'neem's choice kills the lofty aspirations of the other players."

Pike was speaking more to the audience of angelic beings seated around the stage than to the Overseer's question. Before his words melted away Ellzbeth's voice reached out for Sader through the darkened air.

"Yes, watch with us Overseer and witness how once again the eighth realm leaves the other realm's leaders wanting."

Ellzbeth had returned from giving Alex a few encouraging words via the broken husk of a dying dog. The blond boy she'd employed to aid her in getting his attention was actually no boy at all, but an unearthly creature called a 'Hellgrammite'. Like skalls, hellgrammites are neither angelic or demonic; they are in a word, servants, nothing more. Their worth shines in their natural aptitude for brutality and a skill for wielding the powers granted them with savage design and single minded aim. It's permitted to use such methods in order to prod one's own player into getting on with the game.

What is not allowed is leading one's own player in the direction of another, much the same way Ellzbeth ordered the hellgrammite to place the hat on the stop sign. It was a minor violation, one that warrants a small fine. Although, it's not Ellzbeth who will be taxed for her rule breaking, it's Alex who will be made to pay the price. The penalty can only be called by the Gate Keepers whose players are unwittingly involved. In this instance it was up to either Pike or Awtsal's Gate Keeper, which one calls the penalty first is who can decide upon a fine. Luckily for Alex, because of the shallow depth of Ellzbeth's transgression and Pike's claiming possession of the violation first, the fee he'll be docked won't be as grievous.

The black battle armor Sader wore over his red leather, quilted jerkin clattered loudly as he moved with hard, hurried steps toward the sounds of Pike's and Ellzbeth's voices. His long walk across the great hall ended at the chain-mail curtain that draped over the entryway leading into the huge circular theater. With the power of his mind he willed the heavy curtain aside and passed beneath it. The instant he entered the cavernous chamber the air filled with a deafening roar of laughter.

"Why friend do you don your armor," chuckled one of the theater-guards standing his post inside the entryway. Saying nothing to the giant demon towering over him, Sader waved his hand transforming the inquisitive guard into a tiny cockroach, and then promptly ground the fool into the stone floor with the toe of his metal boot.

The theater is a large place, at least thirty times greater in size and magnitude than the ancient coliseums of Rome. Not a single seat was unoccupied. Every angelic being and demonic creature that served the eighth realm was in that vast chamber. They all stared up at the smooth surface of a colossal stone orb that hovered no less than a hundred feet above the floor. In real time they watched the images moving across the Gazing Stone like children lost in a hypnotic-trance, staring at Saturday morning cartoons.

The caretakers and other servants of the nine realms may view the game as it takes place. But only their own player. The only time another realm's tormenters and leaders can see a player for one of the other realms is when he or she is engaged in combat with their player. That being said, it had to have taken Ellzbeth some serious channeling to pin-point Mr. Fisk's whereabouts.

Transforming the sentry into a roach was all the multitude needed to realize Sader wasn't in a mood to be laughed at or for that matter, mocked in any way.

"Here Overseer, I've held you a spot." Ellzbeth offered as she half glanced through the eye holes of her porcelain mask at the houri angel to the left of her and Pike. The threatening leer was all the warning the lesser breed needed to surrender his seat. A few muted snickers and giggles pushed out past clinched lips and clasped hands that tried to stifle them as Sader's armor clanged and squeaked across to the far side of the theater. Without so much as a heated look shot toward the direction of the muffled laughter, Sader made half a dozen seats suddenly available.

"Well, aren't you in a foul mood." Pike chuckled then asked, "Why are you wearing all that hardware?"

Taking the seat Ellzbeth had sort of saved for him, Sader leaned over her and said to Pike, "I need a word with you Gate Keeper."

"Just with him?" Ellzbeth asked.

"No, of course not, the news I bring is for both of you." Sader's tone lowered to an almost painful to hear whisper. "She's been taken from her hiding place," he added.

Pike shifted his full attention from the game to the battle clad Overseer and asked, "Who's been taken?"

Sader's expression went noticeably cold as he raised his silvery gaze up onto Alex moving across the surface of the huge orb. In a tone of voice to match the look of dread in his eyes he replied, "His mother."

Pike rose to his feet and in a thunderous voice yelled. "LEAVE! All of you go back to your charges and stations—Now!"

In an instant the theater was empty except for Sader, Ellzbeth and of course Pike.

"—Are you certain Overseer?" Pike asked while attempting to sound calm and in control. The glint in Sader's eyes grew fainter as Pike's and Ellzbeth's increased in intensity.

"Yes Pike I'm certain. Someone has taken her."

Ellzbeth stood and pushed past her two friends. She was silently storming toward the theater's doorway when she sprung back around and headed straight toward Pike.

"Fool!" she screamed, her golden eyes burning so bright and hot that her porcelain mask exploded from the heat, flying off in a million tiny shards. "I warned you…I warned you all!"

"Mind your tone Inquisitor," Pike growled.

Stopping only a few yards from her angelic comrades she sat on the floor and stared silently at the broken pieces of the shattered mask surrounding her.

Pike, sensing almost no threat in her, relaxed some and set his gaze up onto Alex's image moving through the walls of houses between Eighth and Ninth streets. The red fire blazing behind Pike's eyes dimmed slightly as he whispered the name, "Vile."

"Of course this treachery is that lunatic's doing." Ellzbeth tittered as she pulled her hood up over her head to conceal her now exposed face. "Who else?" she added.

"The game's begun, Vile's choice is a man, so I've been told; it's a bit late for her to change her player now—isn't it?" Sader asked. "Unless her player is not really a man."

"No, Vile's not that obvious. She'll attempt to smuggle Ruth Stone into the game some other way, not as her player," Pike said.

"She'll do more than that." Ellzbeth stated. "Vile will undoubtedly empower the pedophile bitch with an angelic gift of her's or another archangel's blood you know, in order to give her mortal assassin an edge too sharp for even our killer to contend with. It's my guess that she's already smuggled Ruth Stone into the game, inside her player and that the stolen soul waits for the moment when her player and our's stand head to head. Only then will Vile allow her treachery to make its move."

"The game must be stopped!" Sader shrieked.

"You say that as if we actually possess the authority to do so," Pike said calmly. "You know that it's almost impossible to stop the game. Anyway we've no bloody proof. No, we best not speak of this to the other realm's Gate Keepers, at least not as of yet. Yes, best let the game play out. The Magistrate, she'll know what to do."

"Pike pulled his hood up and started toward the metal curtain. With a fast flick of his wrist the heavy drape parted. He was on his way out of the theater when he stopped beneath the entryway and without turning to face his friends said, "You two, both of you, go see the Magistrate. Tell her what we know for sure and what we think we know. She'll want proof. See if she'll grant you the authorization to go into Vile's palace and seek proof without Vile's knowledge. Yes, and Overseer, what do you say to scraping the sentry off the bottom of your boot and restoring him back to his true form?"

"Yes, of course Gate Keeper."

Pike passed beneath the curtain, closing it behind him. As the sound of his heels echoed through the Cathedrals great hall Ellzbeth called out after him, "Where are you going?"

"To play Guardian Angel," Pike replied.

At about the same time Alex was dodging the powder-blue Impala, the former Seattle district attorney Stanley Fiction was shaking off the effects of Hell's wall. Unlike Alex, who had been lucky enough to pass through the mountain of rot into the clean smelling open air, Stanley's trek out of Hell had landed him inside a large walk-in aquarium. The big glass cell was the temporary home of Jenny, the Pey-Less pet shop's nine foot long python. Stanley's appearance out of thin air hadn't only upset the temperamental snake, which was slowly easing toward the addled brained trespasser; his sudden materializing also had the rest of the modest little shop's menagerie strongly voicing their disapproval toward the uninvited visitor. It didn't take long for the high-pitched cries of the parrots and the angry barks of the puppies to morph from an indistinguishable mixture of hums and buzzing noises to the recognizable sounds of their true identities. His vision followed close behind his hearing, going swiftly from total darkness to blinding brilliance. When the brightness mellowed to a visually endurable level, Stanley's sight focused onto Jenny's widely open jaws mere inches from his face. His startled brain screamed the command MOVE! but all Stanley's horror would allow of him was to utter a girlish cry. Within the minuscule amount of time it took for the sound of his fright to reach his own ears, Jenny shot forward. The snake's jaws latched a hold of Stanley's right cheek, digging its bite past skin and into flesh. Her saw-like teeth worked their way greedily through the meat until they scraped only bone.

As with the white dog that snapped out and bit Alex's hand before the golden eyed Inquisitor entered its body, Jenny had also done to Stanley's paranormal plains of existence. It's not understood why earthly beasts are able to see, hear and in some instances effect Hell's mortal visitors, it's only known that they can.

Stanley let out another squealing scream that sounded reminiscently like the ear piercing shrieks of a piglet who's in the process of having his testicles bashed off with a rock. The angry reptile yanked her head quickly from side to side, her needle-sharp teeth bearing down into his face as deep and hard as his skull would allow, grinding against bone with every snap and jerk of her long neck. Stanley struggled frantically to tear Jenny off, but although she could take a hold of him, his efforts to do likewise proved disappointing, to say the least. The only thing the ex-prosecutor's hands could latch onto was air as his flailing appendages swept through the snake's cold blooded body. Jenny ripped her jaws out of the queer-killer's face and bit into his left wrist as it passed intrusively through her head. After a second or two of this she let go and snapped her unsatisfied attention around onto his throat. Not willing to give the snake a third nibble, Stanley flung himself toward the aquarium's viewing-glass. Not to try and smash out of the cage, Stanley didn't have the nerve for stunts such as that. No, this was nothing more than a desperate attempt at putting some distance between the serpent and himself.

As Pike had done with Alex, Warfarin and Vexrile had also left it up to Stanley to learn of his newly granted gift of unwittingly manipulating solids with his flesh and bones. A split second before he was to slam against the thick pane of glass Stanley took his eyes off Jenny as she reared her head back to strike and looked at the window. The fact that he'd only moments earlier witnessed his hands passing through the snake's head and body should have served as a hint, preparing him some for what was to follow. But Stanley never was very good at paying attention to details. He helplessly watched as his face pulled the rest of him through the unbreaking glass. He crashed against the floor with such jolting force that he drove his grossly exaggerated overbite down into his lower lip.

The unusually abstract occurrence was so far from anything he could have expected that it didn't allow the pain of the self-inflicted lip wound to gain a toe-hold. Stanley merely spit the blood filling his mouth out and turned over to face the way he'd fallen. Staring at the unbroken glass and the snake striking at him, its hard snout ramming the inside of the window, he sat up and scanned his surroundings. The recent events, primarily the means by which he'd escaped the pissed off animal's overly lighted lair, shifted his horror from fright to a confused state of astonishment. Standing he ran the tip of his tongue over the wound sliced into his lower lip and could actually feel it closing. Unlike the surprise of his moving through things, he'd been told about his ability to heal swiftly as well as the rest of the game's rules. Stanley reached up and with his long trembling fingers touched his face, which was all but completely healed and whispered, "I'm going to like this, and I'm going to like it very much."

As the shock of where he'd been for the last year and all the pain he had been made to suffer melted away behind the dark miracle of his rebirth onto earth, Stanley felt a change surging through him. Then he remembered what the golden eyed man in black had told him.

"You, as with all the other players will be empowered with the same strength, speed and wind as the lead player. He is a powerfully strong man for a mortal, or so I've been told."

Stanley had always been a physically weak man during his life, having always to rely on his cunning and Machiavellian skill at manipulation to crush his adversaries. But now he possessed an addition to his mental advantage over the others, now he owned strength of body, speed, and the stamina of a bull. Now if he only had a fighting spirit he would be unstoppable. Moving his hands over his bony frame he felt no outward difference; but inside he knew Warfarin's promise had undoubtedly been kept.

Stanley's drug-like rush of physical power was suddenly smothered by the memory of having his man-hood ripped off by Vexrile. As his hands neared the barren spot on his crotch a flood of grief and rage poured over him, drowning his limited tolerance for all living things. He loosed a loud wailing cry of loss that could be heard all the way back down in Vexrile's dungeon. It was also heard by the animals in the shop, causing all of them to become even more put off by his ghostly presence. Their wildly angry shrieks, squawks and barks, as well as the sobering reminder of his missing Johnson had overwhelmingly compelled the fiend who the papers referred to as 'The Skin Stealer' into bringing Slasher and Slicer out.

"I know how to shut you bastards up!" he shouted at the protesting animals. But when he dove his hands down into his windbreaker-jacket's pockets, he found one of them empty. *No!* his mind cried in silent panic. He covered his ears with his hands, attempting to mute the animals' loud voices, Slasher in his right fist, its blade still hidden within its handle. The sharp sound of hard heeled shoes were suddenly drawing near, coupled with a woman's voice, a confused lilt in her tone as she tried in vain to shush up the shop's inventory. Stanley flung the straight-razor's blade out of hiding, locking it in place with his thumb and forefinger. Standing at the ready, he searched the floor feverishly, scanning his vision over the spot where he'd landed. It wasn't until his eye's swept into the aquarium that his search was to end. Lying on the floor of the snake's glass cage, half covered beneath saw dust was Slicer.

If it would have been anything else, even the dark-red pouch of demons teeth, Stanley wouldn't have so much as considered reaching his hand back into that aquarium. But this was Slicer, not some thing to be abandoned. After all, it was Slasher and Slicer who aided good old Stanley in the task of methodically removing the skins off those men so that he could make his favorite snack. Stanley had acquired a taste for pork rinds, but found the deep fried epidermis of humans to be far tastier than that of swine.

The sound of the woman's shoes and the smell of her perfume warned Stanley that she would be rounding the corner any second. Leering at Jenny, he stepped quickly up to the aquarium's glass and going to one knee, without reluctance, not certain if his fist would break the glass or miraculously pass through it, he reached in and with speed he'd never believed himself capable of, Stanley snatched up the razor. The python's gaping jaws lunged toward his fist only to miss her mark by a hair, crashing against the glass in the process. As soon as Stanley had completed the rescue, he flicked the straight-razor's blade out and turned to face the approaching warm soul.

The pet-shop's manager was a full-figured, black haired woman of about thirty-eight years of age named Tara O'neil and she was heading straight toward Stanley and his two friends. Looking in his direction but not at him, Tara asked the large blue macaw behind Stanley.

"What's up your ass Dude?"

Stanley, not yet aware that he can't be seen or heard by the living thought she was talking to him. As it turns out, Dude was the macaw's name.

"Stay back!" he screamed, but she kept right on coming. He swung the razors at her in a threating, warning like gesture.

"I said stay back!" He took a few steps backward, swinging the thin blades at her face and throat, all the while screaming. "Stay away! Get back! I said keep away from me you cunt!—Fine, Fine have it your way."

Stanley stopped retreating and with a high-pitched squall he moved toward the steadily approaching woman and sent Slasher's edge from right to left across her throat. The razor's unforgiving steel sailed through the skin around her neck, actually vanishing for an instant from sight until exiting out of her flesh, leaving no mark in its wake.

Remembering what happened when he tried to grab the snake, as well as the unavoidable fact that he was dead, he sent the blade through her face and throat, this time with a lot less zeal.

"Shit, I can't cut you, can I?" He stopped and watched as she stepped through him to the big blue bird. He laughingly zigzagged both straight-razors back and forth across the back of her skull and spine, she shivered.

"Ooooh, we need a bit more heat back here. No wonder all of you are so pissed." Tara said as she stopped to stroke the parrot's head with one of her fingers.

Taking the pouch of teeth out of his jackets inside pocket, Stanley hung it around his neck and headed out of the pet-shop, slicing his weapons through a few warm souls on his way out. At a devil-may-care pace Vile's player stepped out of the animal-house into the larger portion of the busy department store, and after a brief scanning pause, passed through the glass doors and out into the open air.

"Now, what?" Stanley asked himself as he drew in a deep breath of late October air. While making his way across the parking-lot moving in the direction of Circle Boulevard, his gangly gait as oddly exaggerated as his long nose, big teeth and receding chin, he pondered a question. It was a puzzle that had been needling his mind since Warfarin had mentioned the moniker of the player he was ordered to seek out first.

"Make an effort to avoid all of the other players, lest the one clad in black, with the black pouch. He was called Millstone on your world. Find him first and send him back, then you may do likewise with the others."

Stanley had foolishly tried to ask Warfarin if in fact this Millstone playing in the game and the fellow he remembered during his life were one in the same, but the golden eyed being in black robes answered the question with only pain.

A little more than two months before Stanley had choked to death on his hot-dog lunch, he'd read about a killer one State down who had a strong disliking for child-molesters. What amazed and pissed Stanley off the most about this latest pattern killer was that shortly after his first victim he begun to gather a bit of a fan-base among the sheep. This bothered the DA for two reasons: One, that people could actually let themselves admire some crazy who crapped on top of authority by taking the law into his own hands. And two, Stanley was simply envious of this new lunatic's notoriety and fame. After all, The Skin Stealer had been hard at work, doing his thing long before this Millstone fellow. So how was it that in the short space of five weeks from his first victim to his last and even his own death, how is it that he got better publicity than The Skin Stealer ever got? Not to mention, all the press ever had to say about the other side of Stanley's hidden self was how sick and twisted he was. They'd even had the gall to refer to his doings as hate crimes merely because all eighteen of his victims were homosexuals. Truth was, the reason for all of them being gay was because it was the only way he could be sure the skin he was planning on snacking upon wasn't tainted by a female's body having been rubbed up against it.

Stanley remembered reading that this Millstone had raised a table with a fat corpse tied onto it over his head and that he'd taken two bullets in the chest before throwing it through a brick wall. *If in fact this Millstone that I'm hunting and that one are the same, then no wonder I'm so much more than before*, Stanley thought. *Never have I felt so completely invincible.*

Coming to the middle of the parking-lot Stanley paused a moment to scratch his bald head and asked himself aloud, "Where the fuck am I?"

He was about to choose a direction to begin his search for the player in black when he caught sight of something out of place. Standing on the roof of a semi-truck, less than fifteen yards from where he stood scratching his head was a nude, bald headed woman. All she wore on her slender body, devoid of pigment, was a dark-blue pouch that hung from around her neck and something yellow on her feet. Socks perhaps, he guessed. Clutched firmly in her hands, held in a ready to employ position, was a sledgehammer. *A player*, Stanley thought while darting almost rat-like out of sight behind a parked car.

Stanley's grasp at the blatantly obvious was correct, in that the naked woman was of course a player. Her name is Violet Kat and she's the chosen contestant representing Hell's fifth realm entitled Hinaw. The place of eternal suffering for the wickedly invidious.

In 1973 pretty young Kat crept naked into her roommate's bedroom. And while the younger, prettier woman slept, Kat bashed her skull in with a sledgehammer; killing the woman straight away. When she had finished murdering her girl-friend out of envy for her youth and beauty, Kat made herself a cup of tea and calmly drank it down. Then without disinclination she went to the living room window of her twenty-story high apartment and hurtled her blood splattered naked self down to her death.

While Stanley was hunkered down behind the car, the recent memory of Warfarin's and Vexrile's voices echoed their instructions about in his skull. *Avoid the other players until after confronting the player with the black pouch.* Stanley knew to ignore the two tormenter's orders would be nothing short of toying with Hell-fire itself. Not to mention risking the prize they said would be awarded the game's victor. But the opportunity to invoke the screams of another, no matter how fleeting, or that they would be the frightful cries of a female and not his desired prey, was too great a temptation. The hopeful promise of another's suffering by his hand overpowered the threatening voices bouncing around between his ears. He swung Slicer's thin blade out of its whale-bone and brass handle, leaving Slasher in his pocket. He whispered, "This'll be a one razor job," to himself. Taking a hold of the pouch dangling down behind his thin black neck-tie, he gently caressed its smooth leathery surface with the ball of his thumb. As he felt the shapes of the teeth inside the red bag he hissed under his breath.

"She'll have a bit of an advantage with the reach of her weapon. Best work my way around her, come up from behind. That gash-breeder don't stand a chance."

He eased up, peering over the car's hood to see what the naked woman was up to; only to find the truck's roof vacated. The mental image of the woman's hammer crushing his face flashed before his mind's eye as he rose up a bit more to see if he could locate the revolting nude creature moving through the lot. It was at this point when a shadow cast by one of the parking lot's big lights stretched out over him. Stanley turned to see what had stepped up behind him, although he already had a pretty good idea. His down cast eyes landed on a pair of blood-stained bedroom slippers with little plastic baby-blue smiley faces fixed onto them, one on each. Stanley's entire body had begun shivering uncontrollably as icy waves of panic rushed up and down his spine. His vision made its way up her bare legs which were the color of stale white bread and over her hairless sex, the sight of which made his stomach feel sick and hollow. His eyes continued up over her flat belly and drifted swiftly past her firm, almost perfectly round breasts. Seeing the fleshy orbs filled Stanley with a nauseating sensation that immediately caused him to spew lime-green bile out of his mouth and nose all over her legs and slippers. Most women would have surely kicked Stanley in the teeth and shrieked some profanities down at him after being vomited on, but not Kat. No, she simply took a step back, relaxed her hold on the weapon slightly and said with a chuckle.

"So, you like what you see?"

Stanley, still on his haunches, wiped his face off on his sleeve and trying to ignore the woman's nakedness, raising his attention straight up onto her face to see two wildly staring eyes looking down at him. She shifted her gaze from his horrified expression to the razor shaking in his hand. Bringing the sledge hammer up slowly she grinned at him, letting her weapon's ascent pause a moment, holding it there like a baseball player stepping up to the plate, and said in a friendly, sweet tone of voice.

"You poor thing, you look so fucking scared. It must truly suck to be you right now." She swung the big hammer up over her head and without letting it slow its motion Kat giggled out "Dead bug," as she sent the hunk of metal down. It tore through the chilly air with a faint whispery sound as it arched toward its target. With a mixture of sheer terror and the speed of a soul not his own Stanley barely escaped the full force of the hammer's blow. As it raced squarely for his skull he threw himself down, yanking his head out of its path. The hammer's head scraped across his back and when it had swept past he swung the razor out and opened a shallow cut across Kat's knee cap. She shrieked out a wordless protest and wheeled her weapon all the way around. But before it found its mark, he swung his leg out in a maneuver he never pictured himself capable of, sweeping both her feet out from under her. Kat went down hard, giving Stanley the time he needed to scramble up onto his feet and run. It's one thing to be granted physical strength and speed, but without a fighting heart to go with it, one may as well be as helpless as an infant.

In his eagerness to put as much space between him and the sledgehammer wielding crazy-lady, Stanley had mentally misplaced the recently acquired knowledge that he could pass through solid obstacles. Instead of barreling through the parked and moving vehicles, he weaved around them like a rodent in a maze. Kat on the other hand was completely aware of her newly granted abilities and in total control of all the rules governing them. Stanley executed his stop and go—stop and go escape not once looking back to see where the naked female was. Running with no direction or clue as to what it meant to actually stand toe to toe against an adversary in mortal combat on equal ground and blinded by his own cowardice he couldn't decide on which way to go. Kat was having no trouble with deciding on a plan of attack. Gripping her weapon with bone crushing design she sprinted in a wide circle, her intention being to storm around in front of him, cutting the rabbit off. If he would have broke himself loose from the craven-chains binding his heart and glanced over his right shoulder he would have caught a glimpse of Kat running around him through automobiles. Thus pointing out to him his own stupidity and increasing his chances, although not by much. Instead, he darted around the large metal boxes, his razor still clutched in his fist, and tried desperately to pull open his pouch in the hopes that the little cut he'd laid across her knee wasn't closed yet. Not that he was actually planning on stopping to fight, no, merely because he had no idea what else to do.

Deciding to head back into the department store he cut a sharp right and as he made a beeline toward the plant and garden doors he shot a fast scanning glance over his shoulders. Seeing no sign of the woman and her jiggling parts he eased to a stop and waited for a station-wagon to slowly inch its way past. The pouch pulled open and when he looked up from rolling one of the teeth out onto his palm, he did so to see Kat stepping at a fast pace through the big family wagon toward him, her hammer already raised. Seeing this not only caused his heart to shrink with dread, it had also helped him to realize his error. "Shit!" he voiced aloud as her moving through the car reminded him of his new ability. Feeling quite stupid on top of everything else, Stanley quickly started back-stepping. As she crossed out through the wagons driver's side

side-panel he noticed to his disappointment that the cut on her knee was no-more. "Shit!" he said again as he backed against a van, killing his retreat, "sonofabitch!"

"You don't know all the in's and out's of this silliness do you sweetie?" Kat asked as she eased closer.

"Stay back you!" Stanley shrieked, his words shaking trippingly out at her.

With her sledgehammer above her head she stopped and stood before the trembling D.A sweeping his razor toward her with limp, lame effort and thrusted her hips forward a few times, aiming her pelvis at him. Giving up, Stanley dropped to his knees, "Stop that, please just go away—please," he blubbered.

"You have to be some sort of queer if you want all of this to go away," she replied as she jabbed her crotch toward him three more times. Kat sent the hammer down, straight toward the back of Stanley's bowed head. It was less than a second from caving his skull in, when his left hand shot up and latched hold of the sledgehammer's handle. He came up fast, a wild expression beaming from his eyes as he swung Slicer up toward her belly. His strike swept past, missing her flesh by a fraction of an inch as she pulled her waist back and yanked her weapon out of his grip. "Give that back!" she ordered.

She swung at him with a grunt, but came up empty as he ducked down beneath her swing. Spinning around, Stanley tried again to slice open her stomach only to miss at an even greater distance. He dropped himself to the damp pavement in an attempt to sweep her feet out from under her again, but she was ready for the maneuver and hopped over his passing boot. The instant the balls of her feet hit the asphalt Kat rocketed the business end of the sledgehammer down toward his right hip, but only managed to pinch the cheek of his left buttocks into the pavement. Stanley howled as he shot the riding heel of his cowboy boot straight up into Kat's crotch. The kick knocked her back a few feet, once again opening a window of opportunity for Stanley to escape through.

He crawled quickly to his feet and ran, but not far. When he knew she was chasing after him he slowed his pace. He could hear the whistle of the hammer sweeping back and forth behind his head. Stanley knew if he didn't act swiftly, and get it right on the first try, he would be done for. Taking the tooth out of his jacket pocket he clinched it in his fist and ducked beneath Kat's head-hunting swing. Practically spinning on his heels as he dropped down, facing her belly he came back up quickly and as he did so laid open a long, deep incision up her inner right thigh.

At the very instant the thick stream of blood jetted out of her femoral artery Kat brought her hammer around with a fast underhanded swing and crashed its head dead center into Stanley's weak chin. The unbelievably solid blow exploded the middle lower half of his face raising a dense cloud of crimson mist, shattered teeth, and bone out around his head. Bits of Stanley Fiction's face rained down onto the wet asphalt before his own eyes as he fell like a broken scarecrow backward. The two fractured halves of his lower jaw bone dangled off the torn skin and muscles on both sides of his face, swinging loosely from side to side like the floppy ears of a dog that had been dropped into red paint. Kat, seeing that Stanley was all but defeated, allowed her attention to shift from him down to the blood already moving back up into the steadily closing gash he'd laid across her thigh.

"You tricked me, not bad." She said, looking back at him. "That won't happen again," she added.

With her eyes locked onto his pain she reached up for the pouch hanging down below her breasts and said to herself. "This craps going to be as easy as pissing on flowers."

As she fettled with getting out a tooth for Stanley's ride back to Hell, she noticed that there was an expression in his eyes that in no way resembled the look of terror she so desired. *This is odd*, she thought. The look on Stanley's shattered face was reminiscent of someone eagerly awaiting a trap to be tripped. His jaw bone was also swiftly mending, as was the torn skin and flesh around it. Rapidly growing more and more frustrated with the pouch's refusal to simply open and Stanley's lack of fear, she brought her weapon out from under her left arm where she'd been holding it and went to deliver him a few more bone crushing blows. With nearly all of her blood back up her leg and into the wound which had little less than two inches left to heal shut, Kat raised the hammer and was in mid step toward Stanley when she looked down and spotted the tooth he'd dropped, submerged in a shallow rain-puddle. She glanced up at Stanley, a gentle smile on her lips as she said softly.

"I told you I'd only be tricked the once."

Kat let the hammer fall, splashing in the puddle and crushing the tooth beneath its shimmering surface to bits.

"Yes sir…this is going to be a breeze."

Her sweet smile gave way to a dark expression that Stanley never saw. He was far too interested in the wound on her thigh which had dwindled to a tiny cut less than half an inch long. Stepping over the smashed demon's tooth toward Stanley, three steel javelins like spears shot up out of the asphalt. They pierced all the way through her body, raising her up off her feet, impaling Kat in the frigid air. Two of the shafts stabbed straight up out of both eyes, while the third shot upward out of her mouth, gagging her efforts to scream. The sledgehammer slipped from her failing grip and fell to the ground, vanishing without a sound beneath its black-top surface. As suddenly as the giant metal spikes had appeared they were gone, taking the twitching naked woman with them.

Stanley's teeth, bones and flesh had completed their healing, leaving no signs of the trauma they'd just undergone. Getting to his feet, he picked Slicer up from where he'd dropped it and closing its blade into the handle. He looked around and whispered, "Which way to go?"

Hell's fourth realm is comprised primarily of vast wetlands that expands for thousands of miles. These black bogs and sweltering quagmires are the reserved spaces for homicidal bullies; those souls who were damned because they believed their wealth and station in life gave them the authority to murder. The name of this great swamp is Awnuke and is also the realm for which Buddy Kane Zib plays the game.

A little more than six years before Buddy passed through the Wall to take his place in the contest he was a wealthy member of England's parliament as well as holding a seat in the House of Lords. For fun Buddy liked to frequent east London's seedy gentlemen's clubs; slumming one might say. In mid February 1995, on a cold fog laden night, Buddy and his bloated ego were seated in front of the dance stage of his favorite strip club. His self-congratulated approval of this particular T and A establishment hadn't derived from a secret liking for dark smoky atmospheres, watered down scotch and blaring techno music. No, the crowded place's questionable ambiance aside, it was Lord Buddy's preferred club for only one reason; a twenty-two year old dancer who'd gone by the stage name of Scarlet Dream. She had been given the colorful moniker primarily because of her strawberry blond hair and the unusually bright hue of the dancer's pink nipples.

Buddy had grown bored with staring blankly up at the tits bouncing about before him while awaiting his fiery haired dancer. So, drunk only on his own self-important sense of entitlement he decided to leave the show of sweaty flesh and step back stage to make himself known to Scarlet. Paying the *employees only* sign no mind, he swept the curtain aside and vanished into the darkened corridor. The thin drape seemed to magically muffle the wolf-calls of drunken men and space-music he'd left behind in the bar the moment it swung closed. He moved past the dressing-room doors as if he owned the joint, giving each one an uninterested glance as he made his way through the hall. Buddy was certain Scarlet's top-billing would have earned her a private dressing-room and he was correct in his assumption.

Passing the flight of stairs that lead up to the club owner's office and rounding the long hallways only corner into a much shorter corridor he found what he was looking for. At the other end of the hall a paper star was pinned to a badly painted black door, the name Scarlet written with a red marker on it. The door was cracked open slightly, a thin glow of white light sliced out toward him as he approached it. Despite his certainty that the sweet beyond the door could in no way resist him, his palms still grew damp with cold sweat and his heart pounded like that of an over-eager school-boy about to wet his tool for the first time. Without so much as a respectful rap on her door he swung it inward the rest of the way open and entered the small well lit room. Seated in front of a big round mirror framed with a dozen or so small light-bulbs was the half nude dancer he'd come to see. Scarlet glanced at the reflection of the intruder stepping uninvited into her space. Smiling up at him, still facing her mirror, she slid her hand under the drawer of her vanity and pressed the silent security button as she stood to face the transgressor. Seeing the beguiling expression in her eyes and hungry smile on her lips, Buddy stepped closer.

"I've noticed how you've danced for me alone in a room filled with eyes fixed on only you."

"Of course love, who else?" she replied, all the while struggling against the urge to burst out with laughter. Truth is, Scarlet had no bloody idea who he was, nor did she recall seeing him sitting in front of her stage nearly every night for the last nine weeks. As far as she was concerned, he was nothing more than another face willing to lay his money down for a chance at having her wiggle her ass in his nose.

"It's for me that you danced with unbridled desire upon that—"

Unable to hold her mud, she cut him off in mid sentence. His lustfully bulging eyes, trembling hands and tripping words were too much for her. Beginning with a giggle that swiftly swelled into a full-blown belly-laugh she interrupted his speech. She tried to shove the invading clown back away from her, but he grabbed onto her wrists, squeezing them painfully tight.

"Let loose of me you brute!" she chuckled.

"Stop that," Buddy ordered, but Scarlet's laughter only grew louder and more insulting.

"Stop I say! Quit your damn cackling you little tart!"

He let go of her left wrist and sent his free fist square against the right side of her face. At the exact moment Scarlet slammed backward into the wall three of the club's bouncers charged in through the open dressing-room door. They dragged Lord Buddy Zib out into the alley behind the club and when they'd finished stomping the fish and chips out of him, he in no way resembled someone of noble birth.

Sure, Buddy could have gone to the police and told a convincing lie about how the dancer and the club's bouncers had beaten and robbed him. He could have even paid some unsavory types to stop by the strip club and dish out a little revenge, but he'd had too much pride for either of these choices. Anyway, Buddy's narcissistic nature wouldn't have permitted it. Simply to consider allowing another the privilege of collecting the debt due to him was out of the question.

Four months later, Buddy went back to the red-brick, nearly windowless tity bar beside the Thames and chain-locked the building's three entrances and exits closed. He then lobbed a dozen Molotov cocktails onto the club's flat roof-top, a few of them actually smashing down through the building's sky-light. Buddy stood a moment, listening to the sounds of horror before turning his back to the diminishing screams for help. The petrol bombs burned the club as well as the two adjoining buildings on either side of it to the ground and on its busiest night in weeks. Sixty-nine patrons and all thirteen of the employees had perished in the flames, Scarlet Dream and the three bouncers were among the charred dead.

Less than eighteen hours after his act of retaliation, Lord Buddy Zib was sitting with two detectives in a small lime-green room being shown a street security video. The expression on Buddy's face remained stone-cold as he watched himself burn to death eighty-two people. When the video was shut off and he was asked if he had anything to say, Buddy replied, "Horrible lighting."

After a longer than necessary, highly publicized trial, and a loud out-cry for blood, Lord Buddy Kane Zib was sentenced to life in Newgate prison. The public's screams for more than a simple life sentence would be fulfilled, as it turned out. Newgate's lead physician was also the estranged father of a twenty-two year old dancer with strawberry blond hair who'd gone by the colorful stage name of Scarlet Dream.

Buddy died in the prison's infirmary less than a year after being sentenced.

The fourth realm's player had passed through the Wall to find himself on his knees in a misting rain. Buddy had never been to the States, so passing through onto Corvallis' riverside bicycle path was about as familiar to him as Newgate's crematorium. In his right hand he held all three of the chains he'd used to seal the club's doors. The foot and a half long chains had been linked together at one end with an iron, ring like hand-grip, the three heavy padlocks he is also employed snapped on the chain's other end to make a sort of crude flail. In Buddy's left hand he held a dark-purple leather pouch. He was wearing the same white, one piece jumpsuit with the words Newgate and Prisoner printed on it that he'd worn the day of his death, as well as a pair of dark-blue slip on shoes, no socks.

After finding his way down the dark muddy slope, horribly overgrown with brambles, Buddy crawled over to the Willamette River's rocky bank and stood upright. Like someone heaving fire-bombs into a building he threw his weapon and the pouch of teeth out into the darkness. "I refuse to take part in your bloody gam—"

His speech was terminated the instant the chains and bag of teeth splashed down beneath the surface of the swift moving Willamette. A huge hand made solely of black water shot up out of the river and snatched Buddy off the bank. He was so taken by surprise that he didn't even have enough time to issue a startled peep before being wrenched into the icy water. No sooner had he been yanked under and Buddy was transported all the way back to the forth realm. There was no blinding flash of light; no icy cold wet trek down deeper through blackened fathoms of space and time. One second he was being torn up off his feet and plunged beneath the surface of an earthly river, the next he was being whipped through Hell's hot red air within the grip of a giant claw made of filthy water. The liquid fist flung Buddy down toward the fourth realm's wetlands. It swept him through the stifling atmosphere at speeds so fast that screaming was impossible. Suddenly the claw's direction changed, snapping Buddy straight downward to submerge him beneath a boiling quagmire of thick green muck. The tar-like substance was so hot that the jumpsuit was seared off of him as were the slippers on his feet.

He was whipped back out of the flaming muck and thrown out of the claw's grasp to free fly high into the sky. Buddy was hurtling head first toward the solid rock face of a cliff, when mere seconds before smashing into its unforgiving surface, two white-skinned harpies shot down like arrows and latched onto his ankles, swooping him back up into the sky. They carried him over a high mountain range crowned with sharp black granite, only to fly down the other side where they came to a vast bog of steaming black sludge. When his upside down head was screaming less than a foot above the bog's surface the white she-demons raced him toward its center. Once there they snapped straight up without slowing their speed. Higher and higher they climbed until finally coming to a jolting painful stop amidst the crimson ether. While one of the giggling harpies held Buddy by his ankles, with claws that dug deep into his skin, its companion spun around in front of him, hovering before his upside down face.

The cackling creature face to face with Buddy grabbed his jaw, forcing his mouth open wide, then crammed its withered tit into his mouth making him suckle the bitter tasting pus-like milk from her white breast. He choked on the lumpy gunk, its burning over-flow finding its thick way up and out of his nostrils in the form of yellow bubbles, like luminescent snot. As he was made to feed, the harpy nursing him stabbed its hand through Buddy's skin into his stomach. After rooting around his bowels for a bit she tore part of his entrails loose and yanked them out. It was at this moment that a ten foot long iron beam about fifteen inches in circumference dropped straight down from above and stopped between Buddy's back-side and the harpy holding his ankles. The rounded beam was covered from top to bottom with curved spikes of different sizes, their sharp ends were barbed and pointed. Clutching Buddy's guts in one hand the nursing bogeyed beast using her free hand slammed him, back against the iron pole, its spikes piercing through his skin. The flabby breast slid out of his mouth, its slab-gray elongated nipple erect and swollen, still spiriting a decreasing stream of yellowish milk out like a puppy pissing uncontrollably.

With the fleshy gag out he coughed up a labored cry, pushing out a flood of slow moving vomit. It poured over his teeth and upper lip to ooze down his face, stinging his eyes the instant the foul substance found them. Catching some of the puke dripping off his head in the palm of her empty hand, the harpy sucked it up as if it were honey. She then licked her black lips with an even blacker tongue, and using Buddy's own intestines proceeded to bind him to the beam. Once he was firmly secured the other winged she-devil released his ankles and swooped around to join her comrade, just in time to catch Buddy's second out-pouring of vomit. Like a dog lapping ice-cream off an infants face, the second harpy licked the smelly spew quickly as it flowed generously from his mouth. With Buddy in place the two creatures tore off, giggling like school girls up into the blood colored sky, vanishing out of sight

For little more than a minute Buddy hovered there, twitching and groaning from the punishment, all the while fully aware that the real pain hadn't even begun to rake his flesh. He was wishing he could cry out, but the harpy's breast milk had scalded his throat so horrendously that the only sounds he uttered were squeaks and low groans. His reprieve from the advent of new additions to his suffering came to an abrupt end as he'd expected it would. Like an iron brick with a wounded rat tied to it the beam and Buddy's state of motionlessness broke free and dropped straight down through the hot vaporous air.

He tried to position his head so that he could at least see what he was falling toward, but the spiked headrest locked Buddy's visual attention straight forward. All he was permitted to see was the red sky he fell through. Then the sharp peaks of the far off mountains. Eventually, he saw the out stretching black surface of the steaming bog the harpies had raced him over. As Buddy dropped at an unbelievable speed upside down toward the hot tar, his efforts to utter a cry were rewarded, he was finally able to scream, and scream he did. But not in one voice, not even his own, Buddy's horrified howl was made with eighty-two different voices; they were the terror-filled cries of men and women being burned to death. They pleaded and cried for help. They prayed, choked and cursed. One by one the voices faded and died away to silence and one by one Buddy was made to fully experience their horror and pain. The last voice he heard himself speaking was one he immediately recognized, it was the weeping sound of his own, still blaming the young dancer and her three protectors for all that had happened to him since the night of his beating.

A half a foot from being plunged beneath the surface of the black muck, his downward ride came to a bone jarring halt that drove the beam's spikes deeper into his flesh. When the pain receded enough for his blurred vision to refocus he found himself being suspended motionless again; still tied with his own guts to the beam; still upside down. Staring out over the foul smelling sea of black muck he waited for what was to follow and learned that he didn't have to wait long. Only a few minutes after his neck breaking stop a large head, four times the size of his own, rose slowly up out of the thick crud and eased toward him. The freakishly misshapen head owned a pair of beady eyes that burned bright-red through the ooze streaming over them, their crimson light only going out for an instant as they blinked. Its nostrils flared wildly, sniffing Buddy's meaty scent as it drew slowly near. All the while the great beast's lipless, skinless mouth cracked a perpetual grin as it eased open. Suddenly all Buddy's eyes could focus on were its very long, very sharp looking teeth.

"Chance, chance, ch-ch-ch-ance. Please please just another chance!" he blubbered as the bog demon moved closer, its mouth opening wider and wider. Soon all Buddy could see of its head were its teeth and the wet pink entrance beyond them that led the way down its throat.

Buddy's mumbling was smoothed out by the horrifying image getting closer.

"Please—I'm sorry! I'm a fool; I'll play your game! I'll win! Please—"

The beast cut Buddy's plea for mercy short quite literally by snapping its huge jaws shut, biting off his entire face, muscles, bones and all. That's how Lord Buddy Zib found himself back on the bike path, in the exact same spot where he'd found himself the first time. The bone, brain, muscle and skin swiftly grew back over his head and face. His eyes reformed in time to see his jumpsuit rise up out of his naked skin to cover him. Buddy looked down at the weapon of chains and locks clinched in his fist and when his tongue completed its healing he said.

"Yes, I'll play your bloody game."

Going against Mr. Bane's advice and his own better judgment, Alex decided to take a stroll down Ninth to Jefferson Street and see if his accursed child-hood home was still standing. When he turned the corner and saw that the big old house was still there his heart unexpectedly sank a little. A group of college boys, frat-brats he figured, passed through him as they wrangled over an up and coming football game between the Beavers and Ducks. Moving out of the small throng of young men as they passed, Alex crossed the street. A stiff breeze picked up and blew a pile of wet elm leaves over the asphalt in a low, sort of lazy circular motion. Stepping on the curb he spotted a pair of silvery iridescent eyes peering out at him from beneath the boarded up building's broken steps. As suddenly as they had appeared, they vanished. *A cat* he thought.

"Or a possum perhaps," chuckled Mr. Bane.

Offering no response to the blade's satirical reminder, Alex stepped up onto the rotted front stoop. As he neared the two-by-four sealed door, his feelings of apprehension surrounding this abandoned old house and its memories mellowed some.

"Has it been empty all this time?" Alex asked under his breath.

"All what time? You need to be a wee bit more specific Alex."

"You know what I mean, since we killed them. Has this place been empty all these years?" There was a note of hopefulness whispering out from between his words.

"I've no idea," replied Mr. Bane sharply. "What does it matter anyhow? Let us leave this place; we've no time for such foolishness."

The paper notice stapled over the door brought a faint smile to Alex's bloodless lips. Paying Mr. Bane's eagerness to move-on little attention, he read the old building's death-order at a whisper as if to share the good news with his friend.

"Marked for county destruction on 11-25-02. Looks as though your days are numbered," he said as he stepped back to look the house's neglected façade over.

"Alex," growled Mr. Bane, "I would like it very much if you would take me away from this place."

"Don't you want to have a quick peek inside? You know, a little stroll down memory-lane." Alex chuckled to himself as he swept his hand back and forth through the rotted wood of the door and wall.

"You no doubt remember the last time you stepped foot in that house." Mr. Bane hissed, the metallic tone in the voice vibrating strongly with a note of urgent intensity.

"Yes, yes of course I remember. So what of it?"

"You're being foolish again, Alex my boy, and I refuse to take part in your folly. When you've regained your sense of obligation, and you're ready to devote yourself to more dire matters I'll return. Truly reckless Alex—truly."

"Mr. Bane?" Alex muttered past a forced snicker.

He hadn't really been planning on going into the old house, he'd merely been kidding around with Mr. Bane. Truth is, Alex was as uncomfortable with being on that stoop as the knife was, if not more so. Alex had no intention of going into that large box of rotted wood and bad memories, leastwise not if he could help it. After all, it was a ghost-house, a fact of which he had first hand knowledge of.

The last time he had willingly set foot inside his child-hood home was four nights after he'd decimated his parents. The morning after Alex had shocked the elderly woman next door with tall tales of his daddy's bloody doings, he was sent to a temporary placement home. The county put him there for a few days until the State could find a long-term foster-home, one that dealt with children who'd suffered from abuse issues as damaging as his. On that fourth night in his transient sanctuary he'd overheard the elderly couple who ran the placement home saying that a long-term foster-home had been found and that he would be going there first thing in the morning. He knew that it was only a matter of time before someone would happen upon the real knife that helped butcher his parents. There would be questions, ones that would most certainly prove highly disastrous for him. He'd made plans to eventually retrieve the weapon with the odd voice that had helped him find the courage to slay the two monsters. Alex had figured he would have plenty of time to move it to a safer hiding place, at least a couple of weeks. The sudden learning of his trip out of town being only hours away, and limited time left to deal with the only piece of evidence linking him to the murders, hit young Alex as solidly as his father's fist used to. He had no choice but to finish the last phase of the plan right away.

Once the other kids in the home had drifted off to sleep he crept out of the bedroom and checked on the old couple. After finding them both well on their way to wherever it was that old folks dream about, he helped himself to a flashlight from the kitchen cabinet, then went downstairs to the cellar. Alex had unlocked the trapdoor leading out into the backyard earlier that evening. It was raining heavily that night. A strong wind blew the large icy droplets across the darkness at a seventy-five degree angle that crashed against his face and neck like an endless supply of watery stingers. By the time he'd snuck the two and a half miles through backyards and across empty streets Alex was soaked to the bone. As he trudged through the deluge, he thought about Susan, wondering if she was going to be alright. Susan had been in a bad-way when the police carried her out of the closet. When he asked them about her, the only response the cops or anyone else would give him was; "You're both safe now son. Don't worry yourself about your sister; she's in God's hands now."

In Gods hands, he thought. *God's in heaven, is Susan dead?*

Eventually a woman from Children Services and one of the detectives had spoken with Alex. In the process of asking him the same questions in a dozen discrepant ways they told him that, although his sister had been hurt very badly, she would be okay. When he was told that she would have to remain in the hospital for a few days, and that he couldn't stay with her, Alex had become so upset by the news that he had to be calmed with the help of a sedative. It took two nurses to hold the nine year old boy down for the needle. When Alex awoke from the effects of the doctor's method of calming little boys, his mouth tasted the way he guessed dog shit would taste and his head felt achy. Alex opened his eyes to see an old, thin woman with badly dyed black hair and an even thinner old man with a home-made red and black paisley eye-patch over his left eye. He immediately asked about Susan, but the only information he was able to get out of the old couple was that Susan was still in the hospital, and that she would be fine. On the second day of his stay with the bony, hoary pair of oddities and their half a dozen State owned bed-wetters he demanded to be taken to see Susan. But all he got for his efforts was a glass of milk, a cookie and a hug from the old woman along with an endearing pat on the top of his head from her one-eyed mate.

The wind's strength increased as did the downpour's intensity. By the time the nine year old Alex had reached the backyard gate of his house the howling wind was blowing the rain sideways. He was forced to walk with his head turned down in order to protect his face and eyes from the sting of the drops, exposing the back of his neck to their frigid bite.

The problem young Alex was having aside from the weather was the same reason why he had put off getting the knife until he was forced to; he was scared shitless over the idea of going back into that house. The imaginations of children can be wondrous and magical. But when a little one has known only frightful experiences for his or her daydreams to draw from, the innocence of childish aspiration becomes trapped within the dimensions of shame, confusion, and undue guilt; the child's dreams become terrors. Soon all their tender minds come to know are dark thoughts, cloudy and cluttered with horrifying images few adults could ever come to fathom. Shadows manifest into large hideous creatures and creaky floor boards become fearful sounds and hair-raising howls. All of this, along with the mutilated images of his parent's ghosts waiting inside for their murderer to come home, made Alex's brain spin within a vortex of dread.

Once over the padlocked gate, he stepped quickly through the backyard overgrown grass, each blade weighted heavily with rain adding even more icy water to his already frozen, drenched feet. Coming to the French doors, he brought the big flashlight out of his waistband where he'd tucked it under his jacket like a hidden pistol. With a deep breath Alex clicked it on and sent the bright beam through one of the double door's windows. As his vision reluctantly followed the widening stream of light through the darkness beyond the doors, his heart began pounding a bit faster with the unavoidable knowledge that there was no turning back now. Positioning the flashlight firmly onto the crook of his right arm, he twisted the wire loose with the police crime scene tag off from around the doorknobs. The frozen state of his fingers made the simple task a bit more tedious, but he eventually got the rain weary paper warning to Keep Out off the door and carefully set it on the back stoop. Quickly retrieving the spare key from out of its muddy hiding place beneath a broken sculpture of Augustus, he slid it in the slot and gave it a shivering turn.

These, the only doors at the back of the house, happened to open directly into the one room that Alex and Susan feared more than even the closet; their parent's bedroom. The doors opened inward without a sound, an occurrence which was as disconcerting to the boy as if they had opened with a shrieking squeak. Standing in that open doorway was terrifying in its own right, but it was nothing compared to the atrociously dire feelings that sliced swiftly into his heart and soul the moment he'd stepped beyond its threshold. A flood of memories, not a single one of them pleasant, rushed him. He attempted to push the images back out of his brain, but every time he'd shake one loose another would latch a hold taking its place. A battle had begun between his heart's desire to turn around and run from that place and his mind's need to stay and complete the task.

He shined the light's beam through the darkness and for a brief moment his fearful apprehension was made to de-escalate. The police had transformed his mother's favorite room in the house from its sinisterly immaculate state to a trashed space. They'd torn all of her precious prints of 1920's black and white dominatrix photographs off the walls. Her dressers had been knocked onto their sides, the drawers broken and thrown all over the room. Clothes and pornography covered most of the floor and her cherry-wood vanity and four post canopy bed were both gone. His elation concerning the destruction of his mother's bed chamber was over-powdered by the joy stifling sight of the still upright wooden sea-chest the instant the light's beam passed over it. Its door had been swung open wide, allowing the shine of the light to glint on the hundreds of sixteen penny nails driven from the outside of the trunk in, making the big box a crude sort of iron maiden. Both Alex and his sister were made to spend hours locked within this chest. The nails pointing in on all sides, even the lid, made it impossible to sit, or lean back to rest their small legs.

Stiffening his lower lip and looking away from the horrid reminder, Alex fixed his vision on the closed bedroom door. With every step he took, no matter how softly he placed his sneakers down, the floor boards cried out as if in anguish beneath his hundred and ten pound body. Howling wind found its way through the cracks and breaks in the windows, carrying with it the sharp sound of rain slapping down on the upstairs floor. A strong gust of wet wind blew into the room through the open double door behind him and whipped back around to slam them both shut. Their sudden closing was hard enough to latch them in place but not enough to break or crack the glass. The house's noises and the shutting of his way in only served to increase the boy's desire to get out of there. The hair on the back of Alex's neck was standing at attention, something that only occurred when there was an unknown threat to be worried about somewhere near by. As his belly twisted into knots and his fears churned like flesh eating worms in his brain, goose bumps rose on his arms. Sweat, clammy and cold, emerged on the palms of his hands. Stopping at the door he glanced over his shoulder and gazed longingly at the dark, rainy world outside the windows. A voice rose from deep inside him to speak its piece. It was the voice of reason, sounding somewhat like his own, only in a calm tone he hadn't yet learned to use. It said simply, RUN! His hand, which was on the doorknob, began to slide off. *Yes that's right...run!* his thoughts coaxed. His hand fell away from the door as he turned to face the way back out. *There's a warm bed, dry and comfy waiting for you.* Alex was in mid step toward the doors when another voice spoke up. It was the hollow sounding voice that came to him in the darkness of the closet and spoke with him when he slayed the monsters; it was his new nameless friend.

"Alex my dear boy," it whispered. "Pay no mind to your doubts and fears."

"You're back."

"Of course I am."

"Then you're real?"

"As real as you are my dear dear boy. Do you remember what I told you in the dark?"

"Yes, yes...yes. You said you were my friend."

"No Alex. I told you that I was, and forever will be your's and Susan's only friend. Do you recall the oath I made you in the darkness?"

Alex caught himself staring blankly into the sea-chest again. As the metallic voice moved gently through his awareness, Alex's mind struggled against the possibility that he'd gone crazy. *But I'm just a kid*, he thought over the voice's words. *Kids don't go nuts...do they?*

"We've gone over this twice now my dear boy," the voice said, its tone butting into his questioning thoughts sharply. "Yes, little ones like yourself do go insane, some children actually go stark-raving mad. But not you Alex, no, you've got a strong mind, much too focused for it to succumb to mental-illness. Now, as I was saying. Do you recall the oath I made with you?"

"You said that you would help us...that you would stop them from hurting Susan and me," Alex whispered.

"Yes, and what did I say I would need from you Alex? What is it that you must do for me, for us?"

"My word."

"Your word as to what dear boy?"

"My word to always stand straight and strong, to be brave."

"Yes. Are you being brave now?"

"No." Alex said deep under his breath. A note of shame whispering out, with the words.

"So then, you break your word to me?" the voice's words cracked with the heavy weight of disappointment. "Why dear boy? Why, after showing you what you can do, why do you break the only thing of value that you own, your word?" The voice paused a moment and when it returned it sounded as though it was weeping.

"Why do you do this dear dear boy?"

"I'm afraid," Alex shamefully replied. "They're in there waiting, I can feel them somehow. I know what I said, I'm so sorry…no one will find it," he said hopefully.

"Yes, yes they will I'm afraid, and when they do," it said sadly. "When they do, they'll be angry. They'll come for you and place you in chains. You'll be locked away forever and always. And what of Susan? What will become of poor, poor little Susan? All because you broke your word."

"But I'm afraid—"

"Farewell Alex," the voice wept to silence.

"Wait! Please wait!"

The feelings of complete loneliness he'd known for as far back as he could remember swelled in his heart, intensifying to levels of despair his young awareness had always believed lethal. He felt tears rising to the rims of his eyelids and blinked them away. Then, from deeper than the place in his heart where his mortal-soul resided, a powerful sense of resolve, the likes of which he'd never felt before, poured out. It effortlessly shoved its determined way up past his doubts and fears, binding them with the locks and chains of courage, unwilling to allow the pusillanimous feelings another chance to spread their toxin. Shaking the last of the tears out of his eyes, he stiffened his lower lip again and swallowed the lump in his throat. Alex, armed with his new zeal, turned his back to the double doors and with no further delay opened the way out into the hall.

"I knew I was right about you my boy," whispered the returning voice, a note of pride humming in its metallic tone.

Without a word of response Alex sent the light's beam through the cold darkness as he stepped past the bedroom's threshold and stopped. Something small darted between his feet, causing him to jump slightly. He shot the bright beam down in an attempt to catch a glimpse of it but it vanished within the pitch.

"Rats Alex, pay them no mind, their numbers here are too few to be of concern to us now."

Again Alex offered no reply. He shined the light to the left of the hall, toward the closed bathroom door, and then whipped its beam swiftly to the right. He let its glow rest inside the closet a moment.

The tall, narrow box had been torn open; its solid oak door ripped from its hinges and laid long-ways up against the hallway wall. Seeing the space where he and Susan had been made to spend so much time in destroyed brought as much joy to his heart as the state of ruin the bedroom was in. Lowering the light to the floor, he grinned with a sense of prideful accomplishment when its beam swept over the rust-colored prints of dried blood tracked across the dirty hard-wood surface. It was the ingenious idea to seal his father's guilt in the murder of his wife by leaving the bloody shoe prints that invoked Alex's self-congratulatory smile. The fact that he'd nearly ruined the plan by stepping and slipping in the blood, thus leaving his own bloody feet prints behind as well, didn't even enter into the moment. After giving the stained reminders of a job-well done a moments attention, he aimed the light through the doorless entryway leading from the hall into the living room. From the angle of the bedroom's open door he could follow the light's beam easily to the sofa. As Alex gazed down through the center of the white cone slicing away the darkness, clearing a path for his vision, the image of his father's bled-out corpse projected out from his mind's eye onto the blood-stained couch. Immediately he shook the apparition from his memory and out of his imagination, so that when he looked again it was gone.

"See Alex my boy, it's all in your head," the voice encouraged.

With a deep breath, which he held in his lungs for a bit before letting the cold air back out as a heavy sigh, Alex swung the light back around toward the bathroom. The moment he moved out into the middle of the hallway he was slapped in the face by a rush of rank smelling frigid air. The cold latched onto Alex and wrapped around him like a wet blanket of icy mud, nibbling naggingly into his flesh and bones. The mental imagery of events that had taken place night after night in this hallway flashed through his brain. Alex's heart was beating fast again. He wondered grimly if nine year old boys could be frightened into having heart-attacks.

"Shake it off Alex!" the voice ordered. "It's only your fear trying to steal you away from me. Fight it—fight it off my boy!"

Clenching his teeth he hissed, "Leave me be! Go back to the past and leave me BE!"

Like a television being switched off, the sights and sounds of days and nights gone-by disappeared. The intense cold faded to the slightly lesser degree of cold that had already owned the air.

"Well done Alex."

"I can do this!"

"Of course you can dear boy."

The bathroom was less than twenty feet in front of him, but the moment he took his first step toward it the blue door seemed to move farther back . The hallway actually appeared to be stretching, the door recoiling from either the light's touch or his approach. It wasn't until he spotted the blood stained impression of a perfectly shaped ear print low on the door that the illusion stopped. The bathroom door snapped back to its original place, pulling the floor, walls and ceiling with it at a slightly slower rate of speed. The odd waves of motion, whether they were real or imaginary, sent a cool rippling sensation through Alex's body like feeling the deep dips of the road while riding in the back seat of a car. The instant the unusual event passed, his attention focused on the ear print. Nearing the door he remembered pressing his ear against it, listening to make sure Ruth was passed out. As he studied the crimson reminder of his first-hand participation in his parents timely demise he wondered. *Why didn't the police ask me about this? They had to see it.*

"No one cares for fiends like your sire and dame. Not the authorities or the powers above them. Simply put dear boy, the law did not ask because they did not want to know."

"You can hear my thoughts?" Alex grasped.

"I can do many wonderful things my boy, but only if I've got your help."

"Who are you?" Alex asked for the first time.

"I'm not certain Alex" the voice lied "perhaps we'll find the answer to that question together."

The moment of looking at the clue as to his involvement in the slayings subsided, so did the voice, both of which leaving young Alex with more unanswered pieces of the puzzle than answered. Back to his own thoughts, but not necessarily alone with them, he turned the crystal doorknob. As it had done the last time he'd opened this door, a loud creaking noise stretched out through the darkened house as if to warn all of trouble on the hoof. Alex swung the door all the way inward and as he sent the light's beam into the blood-splattered little bathroom a sharp hissing noise like that of a cat nearly tore Alex out of his P.F. Flyers. Startled, he stumbled backwards and fell flat on his butt. He was intent on getting up and running as fast as his legs could take him all the way back to the warm, dry bed in the placement home when the voice stopped him.

"No need to fear," it said soothingly. "Look—see for yourself."

Reluctantly Alex got to his feet and shinned the light into the bathroom. A more threatening hiss sounded out at him as the flashlight's beam swept across the floor up the wall onto the biggest damn possum Alex had ever seen. It was perched defiantly atop the lid of the toilet's water-tank; the knife's hiding place. The white faced sentinel locked its iridescent eyes beyond the light's brilliance to leer at the boy.

"What do I do now?" Alex asked, his full attention fixed on the animal's needle like teeth.

"Find a tool to help convince the beast into going else where."

The possum hissed again, warning Alex to stay away. In an attempt to appear larger and more menacing it stood on the lid sideways and raised the gray furry hackles on the back of its neck and shoulders.

Alex glanced quickly down at the flashlight in his fist then returned his vision to the animal as he asked, "Will this do?"

"No," the voice replied. "It could prove tragic for the both of us if our only source of light was badly damaged. Best seek out a device to sway the creature that's less crucial to our needs."

Realizing the sense in what the voice had said, Alex looked around for something else to frighten the possum with. Taking a wide step back away from the door, he whipped the light around behind him through the hallway. Seeing nothing at first, he was about to go back into the bedroom, certain he would find something in there. Then, as the light's power of illumination diminished the further its beams reached through the darkness, he saw what he was looking for at the other end of the hallway. The light barely had the strength to stretch out through the black air that reigned relentlessly within the closet. What light did reach managed to cast enough of its lambent for Alex to make out the wooden clothes-hanger dowel high in its intended place. Setting his back to the bathroom and the hissing critter within, he headed toward the cell he'd been dragged into more times than his memory could recall. At first he moved at a fairly steady pace, the remembrance of the last time he'd been whipped and kicked into that place freshly burned in his brain. His father and mother's laughter echoing over Susan's cries and his cursing. The hollow click of the padlock and the cold darkness called out for his attention as he drew nearer. All of these recollections so crisp in his conscious nightmare that they slowed his step to a far less eager rate of speed. The closer he got to the tall narrow box, the more of the flashlight's brilliance filled its space. Still, despite his increasing ability to see in clearly, Alex's belly tightened with the knots of foreboding. Stopping when he reached the closet's torn off door, he helped himself to a deep breath of the chilly air, and with a whispered, "It's been broken, and it can't trap me again."

"Indeed Alex my boy."

Several rats bolted out of the closet, escaping the threat of illumination, causing Alex's heart to jump a bit. They darted past him to cut sharply around the doorless entryway, vanishing into the living room. It seemed as though the house had been inhabited by some of Corvallis' homeless creatures.

Alex knew better than to hesitate, certain that doing so would increase his reluctance, thus strengthening his fear. As if the closet and Alex had never shared a past, he stepped in and set his full attention up onto the dowel. Alex was already well aware of the fact that it was too high for him to simply reach up and grab. Alex had spent hours while locked in that place trying with vain hope to take it down. He was short for his nine years, that along with the fact that he was usually too badly beaten, made getting the wooden pole impossible. The closest he'd ever gotten to being successful was once when his fingertips brushed its rounded surface. "It's too high," he would say sobbingly. He was always left wishing he had something to shove the dowel loose with; a shoe, anything at all. But the monsters always locked him in naked, with no food or water. Looking down at the flashlight he grinned secretly.

"Be careful Alex, if it breaks we'll be as good as blind," the voice warned.

"I know, I'll be careful," he replied softly in a confident tone of voice.

"See that you are my boy."

Standing directly beneath his target, like he'd done countless times before, all of which proving fruitless, he flipped the flashlight around, aiming its beam down. Looking up toward the clothes' hanger pole he was grateful to see that enough of the light hitting the floor rose back up to allow a faint shadow of the dowel to be seen. With the butt end of the light's grip he hopped up, and on the first try knocked the three foot long pole out of its holders to the floor; Alex's heart swelled with a sense of victory he'd seldom known. As he bent over to snatch his prize up in his fist something big shot across the hallway. He barely caught sight of it out the corner of his eye before it disappeared into the bedroom.

"Did you see that?" Alex asked his formless friend.

"No, see what?"

"It went into the bedroom."

"What?"

"I don't know."

"There's nothing there my boy. If there was I'd surely sense its presence. Other than the rodents, a couple of feral cats, and that marsupial in the water-closet we are the only living beings in this house. It's merely your mind playing tricks again."

"Really?"

"Yes."

"Okay, okay then."

"Indeed."

Dismissing whatever he'd thought moved past his peripheral vision as an over active imagination taking advantage of the situation, Alex continued with the rescue. After convincing his heart to slow its intense pounding down to a more natural beating rhythm, the boy left that horrid closet for the last time. With each step he swung the piece of wood swiftly back and forth, *swish—swoosh—swish—swoosh,* as it parted the stale air. Every whistle a threatening promise of pain and misery.

"You best get if you know what's good for you!" Alex warned.

"That's right Alex, show the beast who's boss," chuckled the voice.

The possum stayed put. Its eyes shining with an odd sort of incandescent silvery-green in the light's beam. They locked their mirror cast onto the boy's face, then the weapon and back onto the boy's face again. Twisting his expression into his best mask of fearsome rage, Alex stepped through the bathroom's doorway and stopped. The frightened animal hissed as it faked a leap toward the boy, only to pull back and hiss again. Swinging the dowel down past its head, Alex issued a final warning.

"Last chance, get! Go on, get!" He stomped his foot, and swung the pole at it with a loud wordless shout. But the beast must have figured atop that toilet was simply the best place to make it stand or it was just too damn stupid to realize the futility in its foolhardy choice.

"Fine then!"

With a fast downward swing he sent the solid hickory dowel squarely onto the middle of the animal's spine. The dull sound of wood meeting bone was muffled by fur and its thick hide. The blow was hard, although not enough to move the beast. With a long hiss that stretched out into the small room where only a few mornings past a woman's pleas for mercy had been risen; the possum locked eyes with its attacker.

"AGAIN!" shrieked the voice. "Hit it again Alex. In the head, swing for its head!"

Alex swept the dowel up and over his head and with an air slicing hum sent it right back down twice as fast. A sharp crack rang out the instant the weapon crashed against the base of the animals' skull. The second blow was much more effective than the first, rendering the possum defenselessly limp.

"Looks as though that one may have done the trick. Why don't you whack it a few more times. You know Alex dear boy, just to be certain it's dead."

Saying nothing, Alex did as the voice suggested and hit the suddenly immobile creature again, but only once, and half as hard as the previous assault. It offered up a brief dance of twitching, caused by its confused nervous system struggling to make sense out of what was occurring. After poking at it a few times with the end of the dowel Alex set the club down, leaning it against the wall where it immediately toppled to the floor rolling under the claw foot tub out of sight.

"That was an unwise choice Alex. You best retrieve it straightaway."

"Its okay, the possums dead. I'm sure of it," Alex replied.

"We'll see. Take it off the lid, let us get what we came for and go."

Taking a hold of its thick rat like tail he slid it off the water-tank. Alex found the limp animal to be heavier than he expected, nearly losing his one handed grip on it. Holding the flashlights beam in its face, he gazed deeply at it. Alex was looking closely into its eyes when he noticed the blood in the left ear. With a healthy shake he drew closer to it's upside down head and whispered.

"You had to see if you could stand toe to toe with the big dog. Yeah, well now look at you—"

With an unexpected surge of life the possum swung its head around and nearly bit Alex's left cheek, missing it by less than half an inch. Dropping the pissed off animal Alex kicked at it, only to miss and slip, falling on his butt as the possum made its escape out of the bathroom.

"Your first lesson as to the dangers of assumption. I'm sure you're not too young to have heard the phrase: *Playing Possum*. There's only one way to be certain a thing is dead—one must first kill it." The voice melted away amidst the audible expression in its lilt.

Shoving to his feet, Alex regained his wit and was about to complete the job when his attention was visually snared by the small room's ghastly condition. His frenzied stabbing and hacking away at Ruth's flesh, combined with her vain thrashing had flung blood everywher, creating quite a gruesome sight. Alex remembered that a mess had been made of the place, but not to this untethere degree. Instead of the sight appalling Alex, it raised feelings in him he'd believed existed only in books. For the first time in Alex Julius Stone's young violent life he felt completely tranquil, and quite deeply so. All the fear and anguish had been wiped away as his eyes followed the light's beam slowly over the floor, walls and tub. It was as if he'd stepped into an agreeable nightmare, one where he was the monster.

"Shake it off Alex."

He barely heard the voice speaking to him through the dense waves of power rushing over him.

"Come boy—shake it off!" shouted the voice. "Lest you become lost to yourself, they're coming!"

Alex pulled free from the self-ascendancy fog the moment the warning *they're coming* pierced through to his sense of urgency.

"Who's coming?" he asked.

"You don't want to know."

"Yes I do!"

"You really do not, my dear boy. But if you persist in your efforts to convince yourself that you must know, you'll find all choice in the matter has been torn from your grasp."

Alex was lost at the word "But." Although he didn't need to understand the voice completely to get the gist of what he was being told (which was to stop fooling around, get the knife and beat feet out of there).

Straddling the toilet bowl he set the flashlight down on the sink counter beside him, its bright beam aimed his way casting the huge shadow of a small boy up onto the corner walls. Removing the heavy porcelain lid from off the water tank, he leaned it against the wall to his left. The inside of the tank was too dark for Alex to see down through the water. But with the words *"they're coming"* echoing in his brain he wasn't concerned with whether or not he could see the bottom of that tank. Without rolling his coat sleeve up he stabbed his hand down into the icy cold water. Mindful enough to avoid the knife's two razor edges, he slowed his reach's descent. By the time his fingertips found the bottom of the tank Alex's entire arm all the way up to his armpit was submerged. Carefully he swept his hand over the slimy surface of the tank-bed. It only took him a few seconds to locate the familiar feel of the knife's bone handle. With it clasped firmly in his fist he went to bring the murder weapon up out of its watery vault.

His arm was less than half way out of the water when his feelings of success were halted by the sleeve of his jacket getting snagged on something. After a few tugs he realized his arm wasn't coming out easily. Without bothering to look he swung his free hand around for the flashlight. Only instead of grabbing it as he'd intended, his fumbling reach knocked it on the floor. It crashed with a loud bang that was nearly as unsettling as the stupid action itself. Luckily though for him the light somehow escaped breaking or going out. It hit the floor and rolled slowly into the furthest corner from his reach. Its beam was aimed out the door into the hallway where it caught the dozens of tiny eyes watching him. *Rats*, Alex thought, or hoped. As they gazed in at him from the outer-most limits of the light's luminous glow, the voice said, "Alex my boy, you've some of the worst shit house luck I've ever been party to."

Alex barely heard the disappointed comment over the increasing volume of the earlier warning, *they're coming—they're coming—they're coming*.

Unable to tear his arm loose, he went to take the jacket off, but found its zipper to be stuck.

"Yes boy, shit house luck indeed," whispered the voice as he struggled with the zipper. It was being impossibly stubborn, refusing to give an inch, not half an inch, not even a hair. Grabbing the coat's caller he tried to break the zipper's clasp, but it too wouldn't show Alex any love. With a frustrated "...The hell with it!" Alex went to pull out of the jacket and leave the bloody coat hanging out of the damn tank.

He was in the middle of sliding the soaking wet jacket over his head like a heavy sweater when he heard something behind him. Alex jerked the jacket back down and asked with a shaky whisper.

"Did you hear that?"

"Unfortunately, yes I did my boy."

"What was it?" Alex asked, too afraid to glance over his shoulder.

"You best hurry dear boy, and whatever you do don't look behind you."

"Don't look at what?"

It began as a low, fast clicking noise that steadily smoothed out to the sound of labored breathing. To Alex it sounded the way his imagination had convinced him a death-rattle sounded like. Choking was added, as well as more clicking noises. Something was trying desperately to suck oxygen through thick liquid or mud. For a moment, perhaps less, Alex was frozen with fear.

"No time for that Alex. Quickly, before it's too late."

Alex broke loose from the horror attempting to kill his chances of escape and was back at trying to break free. The gagged breathing sounds grew stronger. Suddenly the unmistakable sounds of hands and feet slapping against and slipping on wet porcelain moved out behind him. Alex, still following the voice's advice refused to look back at whatever it was. He pulled and yanked at his arm, trying harder than ever to rip it out of the tank. Water splashed all over him and on the floor, giving the worn rubber soles of his sneakers less and less grip as he attempted to straddle the toilet. He considered pulling out of the jacket again, but quickly abandoned the idea, unwilling to cover his head for even a second.

"Just don't look!" Alex issued the command louder than he intended. But loudly, or at a whisper, it didn't matter, the sound of labored breathing and the struggling to crawl out of the tub was too much for his terror's curiosity. Overpowered by fear and overwhelmed by his need to see, the order not to look turned out to be a silly notion at best.

With a quick turn of his head, all the while continuing to try and undo the coat's stubborn zipper he looked over his shoulder. The instant his vision caught sight of the thing struggling to stand in the tub he wished he hadn't. Fighting furiously to get out of the tub, slipping in her own putrefied blood and gore was his mutilated mother.

Alex tried to look away but couldn't. Like someone lost in a hypnotic spell, the grisly image before him latched onto his attention and refused to let it go. Ruth's left eyeball was cleaved open across its center. To the aghast Alex the eye resembled a hard-boiled egg, black with decay and seeping some sort of clear muck. Most of Ruth's nose and all of her top lip had been cut away from their original places. Like wet raw-hide the skin hung limply from exposed meat and bone. The skin covering her frame, from her head down to her waist, was slate white with thousands of dark-blue and gray varicose veins racing all over it. Deep stab wounds, ringed with hilt bruising around the holes plagued her flesh. Long slashes, some of which all the way to the bone zigzagged with no rhyme but plenty of reason across her face, neck and pretty much everywhere else on her body.

Ruth stopped struggling at about the same time Alex was snapping out of his shock induced trance. As she was collapsing onto her back, he was shaking off all doubt as to whether or not this was truly happening, the answer being *Yes it was*. Not willing to take his eyes off of her Alex wrenched frantically on the jacket. As he worked to free himself he watched as her head rolled listlessly on to its side to face her murderer. Ruth's teeth began chattering together again with each labored intake of air. At some point she must have realized standing upright was out of the question. Getting her second wind, she pulled herself up over the side of the tub. With a wet thud Ruth flopped out onto the floor. After her head smacked against the tiles it lurched up with a jerky motion to lock her right eye up onto her son. Alex was nearly in tears as he yanked and tugged on his arm. He cried out for help to anyone who cared to hear him. His horror had dragged him well past the point of caring if the police learned of the truth surrounding the slayings. All he gave a damn about at the moment was to be out of this horrifying predicament, even if it meant being locked away forever. He attempted to take his attention off of the ghoulish apparition and devote it solely onto getting his arm and the knife out. The longest he could go before looking back around at Ruth was only a few seconds.

He'd been staring back over his shoulder at her when she let her jaw drop open. To Alex's disgust a flood of rancid blood poured out. Mixed with the rotted liquid was a dozen or so swollen maggots, some of which as big as a shelled Brazil nuts. Lowering her face after the wiggling pile of vomit, she dragged her open mouth over it, scooping the foul stuff up. Jerking her head back as if to stretch her neck, crushed maggots smeared all over her face, she gulped it down while her teeth chattered.

Climbing up onto the toilet seat Alex kicked at her, sending the heel of his sneaker out. "Stay back!" he shouted. She ducked her head beneath the strike, grasping for the flying foot but only catching air. "Stay back!" he echoed as he rocketed his heel at her again only to miss a second time. Alex wrenched on his arm, pulling it back and forth.

"Come out! Why won't you come out?" he grunted.

The icy water had been successful in deadening almost all sense of touch in his fingers. Only cold and a deep pain remained in attendance. In his unfocused struggle to convince the toilet into letting him go he'd bent the metal arm that holds the float, causing the valve to stay open, thus sending a continuous jet of water into the tank. The seat lid Alex had climbed up on was so slick that it made kneeling on it nearly impossible. Doing his best to kept steady and hold his mothers ghost at bay; Alex blindly groped his free hand over the metal fixtures but was unable to feel a reason why his arm couldn't come out. Kicking at Ruth's head as he searched for a potential weapon within his free hands reach, he let go of the knife only to swiftly take hold of it again the instant he learned it wasn't the latch on the trap.

Ruth was trying to speak, but her words were so badly distorted by her severed top lip and swollen tongue that the sounds Alex heard struggling to choke past the chattering teeth came out garbled. What she was fighting to say had been, "Mommy's loving boy has finally come home to play." But what Alex heard was more like, "Nun-niz vu baa gaz pyula hun ue faiz."

Ruth slapped her left hand on the wet toilet seat at the exact moment Alex's hand found the water tank's heavy lid where he'd leaned it against the wall. She was hoisting herself up when, despite his wet grip, Alex wrenched the slab of porcelain up with an under handed swing toward Ruth's head. Missing its mark, the lid slipped out of his fist and crashed against the door-jamb, breaking it in half. Ruth swept her right hand up fast and latched onto Alex's left ankle. She jerked at the boy, trying to pull him down toward her. With a shrieked, "Let me go!" he showed her that he wasn't having any of it. Alex shot the heel of his left foot back, freeing his ankle from her grip as well as smacking the wet sneaker into his mother's face. The soled mule kick snapped Ruth's head back and knocked her away half a pace. She swiftly moved in again, and again Alex rocketed his foot backward. The first two kicks missed but the third and fourth caught the left side of her skull. Ruth reared back some, out of range. She leered up at him with a rattling hiss in an effort to vocalize her deep disapproval of his refusal to submit. Ruth's exposed upper row of teeth and bloodless gums gave her a ghoulish mask, an evilness that allowed its grin to make her intentions known without words or growls.

She drug herself beneath his kicks, avoiding the stomps of his feet and was again slapping her mangled hand on the toilet seat. With a surge of unholy strength her right hand lashed up and grabbed onto the bottom of his shoe while he kicked at her. As if it had never been stuck, the jacket's zipper came down. Alex pulled out of the coat with a speed that would have amazed him if he had the time to notice it. He brought the knife out of the water through the still snagged sleeve.

The instant it was out in the open air Ruth's eye widened in an unintentional illustration of horror at the sight of the instrument that had laid her to waste. Alex was in the process of twisting around to confront his dead mother when she howled, and still in possession of his foot yanked him off balance. He slipped and with a hard *thud* slammed against the wall. She was holding his foot and dragging him out from between the toilet and the wall. When she'd pulled him out far enough, Alex swept the blade right, slicing her wrist with its tip and forcing her to let go of his foot. Without slowing the knife's speed he reversed its direction with a slight upward arch. A full three inches of its blade cut open a deep gash across Ruth's throat. A torrent of foul smelling blood, blackened with rot, poured out. She threw herself back away from the zigzagging blade and was trying to pull her body back up into the tub. Alex got to his feet.

"You know what to do boy," said the metallic voice at a low hiss.

She was nearly up over the tub's rim when he stepped toward her; the knife raised in both hands. With a twisted grin on his face he drove the blade deep into the rotted bone of her skull. In the time it took for her blood-curdling scream to melt away into the walls of the house, his mother's horrid image faded out of sight.

Alex stared down at the spot where she'd been a moment, then unhooked the jacket's sleeve from the chain in the tank. As he was putting the dripping wet coat on, the voice said, "You handled yourself quite well dear boy. You're as natural a knife fighter as there ever were."

Alex said nothing as he placed the two broken halves of the water-tank's lid up on its intended place.

"We best go now Alex."

"Do you have a name?" Alex asked as he headed out of the house the same way he'd come in.

"I don't know. Perhaps when we learn the answer as to what I am, we'll learn the answer to that as well?" Again the voice lied.

With the back double doors closed, locked and the steel wire with its paper police tag twisted around the doorknobs, Alex put the key back in its hiding place beneath the stone head of 'Augustus.' He then walked across the yard to another hiding place. He made his way through the tall weeds and grass to the backyard's furthest most corner. At least the wind and rain had mellowed some. Kneeling down, Alex brought a well hidden army-green metal ammunition box out of a muddy hole covered with old boards and a sheet of black plastic.

"What do we have here?" inquired the voice.

"I have an idea," Alex replied softly.

Opening the heavy ammo box, he removed the top piece of clear plastic that served to keep its contents half-assed dry. He then brought out the thermos with its broken glass insulator that had once been a part of his old Gunsmoke lunch box, but served now merely as a crude storage cylinder. Next the clear heavy-duty plastic bag containing two Bat Man comic-books and an old Oxford dictionary was pulled from the metal box. Alex quickly and without ceremony laid the sheathless knife on the bed of loose marbles and wet plastic at the bottom of the ammunition box. He was about to place the bag of comics in on top of it, when from out of the box spoke the metallic voice.

"A moment if you please Alex my boy."

For the first time since the voice came to Alex in the dark it seemed to speak from all around him, owning no single point of origin, simply words and an odd voice that moved through the air. Staring down into the dark box Alex asked, "Where are you?" his tone puzzled. "Are you in there?"

"Yes."

"I can't see you, where are you? I want to see you."

"Alex my boy, I'm inside the dagger—I'm the blade you just rescued."

"But how? How is it possible?"

"I'm a bit confused dear boy. How is it that you can easily accept the unexplained phenomenon of a voice which owns no form at all speaking to you? But now that I've decided upon a form you struggle with the idea. You're a strange boy Alex, quite strange indeed."

"I'm strange? Shit this whole night's been weird. Up until now I'd just figured the voice…your voice was my own conscience speaking to me. You're confused! Hell man, I'm sitting in the mud talkin' to the knife I killed my—"

"Shhhhhhh—boy," the knife cut him off in mid rant. "At the moment Alex, the hows and whys of things are of little consequence. All that matters is your word dear boy. So, before I allow you to lock me away in this metal vessel please give me your solemn oath that you will not abandon me. Can you do that Alex Stone; will you give me your word?"

The knife fell silent. Several long seconds stretched out between the young killer and his conversing implement of destruction and during that quiet in the rain, young Alex's mind filled with questions.

"You're not real."

"Yes, yes I am. I thought we went over this."

"You're just an old knife. I'm going nuts! I've lost it!"

"No more silliness boy," the knife snapped. "Quickly, your word. I need to hear you say it. Give me your oath boy—or not!"

"But I don't understand."

"You're not meant to yet—now your oath or not boy!"

Alex's head was spinning. Things had gotten much too crazy, way too fast. The slaying of his parents, all the blood, Susan's being taken away. The possum, the rats and Ruth's vomit eating ghost. Now this, the voice he'd hoped was his maturing courage manifesting out through his imagination, and not a symptom of his failing grasp on sanity, was real. And to add to the utter lunacy, the voice that helped him aim his rage was now speaking to him through the tool it directed him to employ.

"I want to see Susan. Why won't they take me to see her? I want it all to stop," Alex sobbed.

"I doubt very much boy that your sister would even know you were there. She's in a sort of deep sleep. Not yet dead, but unable to awaken. Your oath Alex, I need you to give me your word, it's the only way you'll be of help to poor Susan."

"I just want this nightmare to stop!"

"It's too late for that now boy. Your oath Alex, only a promise from your lips can aid me in helping you smooth down the bumps in the road so that your ride is a bit more gratifying. Or is it that you prefer to be alone in the dark again, all alone and for the rest of your life? I told you that I can do amazing things, but only with your help. So, no more of this doubt, enough of your *boohooing reluctance*—your oath!"

"Yes!" Alex barked past tears and rain. "I promise."

"You promise what boy? Say the words."

"I promise not to abandon you."

A sudden crackling of thunder immediately followed by the rippling flash of lighting spread out through the black clouds high above Alex's head.

"Thank you my boy, now you may close me in."

The fading voice was interrupted by another much louder blast of thunder. The almost blinding flash of lightning tore through the clouds like a claw, slicing them open to release a windless shower. The cloudburst dropped straight down like tiny bombs, frozen but not to the point of being considered hail, although still painful to endure. Numb with cold and struggling with all that was occurring, still not sure what to believe, Alex set the comics and thermos in on top of the knife, then closed and latched the ammo boxes lid.

"You've come a long way Alex my boy. I'm truly proud of you," the voice said. "Only that part of me that acts as a means to an end resides deep within that ancient dagger. The part of my consciousness that exists as a symbol of my ageless pursuit now abodes in your desire. Thanks only to your oath dear boy. But don't fret yourself with all that, instead take comfort in the knowledge that unless you break your word, you'll never be alone again. One more thing Alex."

"Yes."

"Turn around, he's coming up behind you."

Alex didn't even have time to stand, much less turn about. As the voice melted away into the sound of the rain, a pair of bloodlessly white bare feet stepped sharply in front of the boy. Immediately he spotted the now festering bite on the right foot. A wound that only served to increase Alex's horror in that it was visual conformation as to the attacker's identity. Alex was still clutching the heavy box as he attempted to simultaneously stand and throw himself back away from the legs. His efforts were crushed swiftly by a pair of blood-stained hands, which were somehow unaffected by the rain. The oddly dry hands grabbed onto Alex beneath his armpits with a horribly painful grip. Yanking him up off his knees, he was raised up past the blood soaked boxer-shorts and tank-top. No sooner had his ride up begun and it was brought to a rattling stop that nearly caused his grip on the ammo box to fail. Alex's abrupt halt showed him what he already knew; that this new apparition was none other than his father come to settle a score.

The dead man's head teetered lackadaisically on his rotten, swollen shoulders like a gruesome bobble-head doll with a stretched neck spring. His eyes were rolled so far back up into their sockets, that only the jaundice colored blood-shot whites could be seen. Wayne Blew Stone's mouth was dropped open wider than merely slack-jawed, appearing all but useful, except to look horribly out of sorts. It was as if he had no further need for the gaping orifice filled with blood smeared yellow teeth. Then, as the hands dug their thick fingertips painfully into Alex's ribs, drawing the boy closer as if to get a better look at his son's fright, Alex saw, and heard why the mouth appeared abandoned. The ear to ear slit he'd so affectively laid across his father's throat spoke in the mouth's stead.

"Give me my birthday present back!" the neck wound demanded. The voice's toothless lilt owned a sticky tone, not quite wet or dry. The edges of the deep gash quivered slightly, moving almost like lips might if they'd been sliced away from the muscles that moved them. The same foul reek that Alex remembered smelling when he popped a dead cat's bloated stomach pushed out of the talking throat into his face with each word.

Wayne had begun shaking Alex as he raved on. Without a word Alex raised the ammo box with both hands over his own head, as the neck was saying, "You're a bad, bad seed boy!"

Alex slammed the bottom edge of the metal box down squarely against the bridge of Wayne's nose. The instant the ammo case made contact with the phantom's face it went the way of his wife, back into Mr. Death's storage-locker. The disappearing ghost dropped Alex to the mud, who had had enough of that house. He got to his feet and with the heavy box in hand, Alex ran as fast as his legs would permit, all the way to the river where he intended to hide his worldly possessions and the murder weapon.

Chapter Six

— COLD AND WET —

...as men, whose reason
long was blind.
from cells of hatred
unconfined, lose whole years
to poisoned mind.

—ibid.

There are more dimensions which make up the fabric of space and time than there are stars in all of the galaxies. Contained within each of these dimensions are more planets than there are grains of sand on all of those worlds combined. Regardless of how primitive or developed a given world may or may not be, they all follow their own measure of order, a rule of law one might say. Granted, some of the laws that govern a few billion or so of these worlds may seem a bit structureless, perhaps even downright savage. Some worlds may appear to possess no order whatsoever. Take the planet Hell for example; all nine of its principalities quite definitely lead most of the damned that are condemned there into believing them as lands devoid of order. A dimension rife with anarchy, owning no chain of rule to link it all together. Only a helter-skelter eternally fueled with the screams uttered by those whose suffering voices illustrate its punitive purpose.

But behind the pitch-black shroud of Hell's perpetual torment machine rests a complex system of rules and laws, some of which can be bent and quite often are; while others are set in stone. One of these laws which is not permitted to be tested, under any circumstance, is more of a creed than a law. It is ordered and understood by all of the Empire's caretakers that the blood of an angelic being is never to be shared with that of a mortal.

Violators of this understanding are to be given over to the Magistrate. It is her task to decide upon and administer the discipline, a punishment which has gone unchanged from its inception before the second war. If the Magistrate finds the accused guilty of coupling their angelic blood with the flesh, blood and bone of a human, she interminably strips the angel of all magical powers and they're to be suspended from the ceiling of her cavernous abode where she will eternally feed upon them.

It was this Magistrate whom Ellzbeth and Sader were waiting to speak with. Their hoods up, they silently stood at the edge of the ruins of what was once a great subterranean city built after the first war by a race of giant cherubim that preferred dark places to lighted ones. For as far as any eye could ever hope to see before the power of sight was devoured by black air, a dense blanket of yellowish-white webs stretched out from around the stone rostrum. More webbing reached up to the ceiling and down, as well as zig-zagging from left to right. The faintly incandescent webs weren't the symmetrically uniform webs of a garden spider; they were more reminiscent of the haphazard webs of a black-widow, a very large one to be sure. This was much more than a giant arachnid cherubim that dwelled in this great cavern, this was Ardnas the Magistrate.

Ellzbeth reached out, and with the tip of her forefinger nail, plucked at one of the webs closest to her. After several slow minutes of quietly waiting a feminine voice drifted down soft and sweetly from above and behind them.

"Visitors, how truly nice. It's been so very long," Ardnas whispered. "To what do I owe this pleasure, Inquisitor and Overseer from the realm of B'neem?"

Turning, Ellzbeth and Sader faced Ardnas. She was clinging to the side of the stone wall over the entranceway with all eight of her clawed feet. Ardnas is without a doubt one of Hell's most abnormal looking creatures. She is the only one of her breed that survived the second war. Little is known about her, but what *is* known is what makes Ardnas one of the most feared and respected being in all of the Empire.

Ardnas possesses the ability to feed on, and drain all the strength and supernatural powers from any and all creatures. No other being in the whole of Hell owns such an all consuming gift. Unfortunately, the only profit she gains by this method of castigation is self-nourishment. Ardnas does not adopt the guilty's powers, for if that was the case her breed of cherubim would not have been all but wiped out of creation. As a matter of truth, it is safe to say; if the great arachnid cherubim had been armed with such an ability as to wield the magical strengths of their *prey*—for lack of a better lemma, hell and all that it is and is not would have most assuredly become a very different world indeed.

Ardnas is the living personification of a flesh and blood nightmare. Her long, thin spider legs and nearly translucent exoskeleton encasing her thorax are fixed to a giant round abdomen. Other than its sickly white color, it is the bloated tear-drop shape of a black-widow's abdomen, complete with a blood-red hourglass design on its underside. Ardnas's spider-like appearance ends where her second likeness begins. Two spindly arms equipped with razor sharp claws appear out of the thorax's shoulders, as does the rest of her upper body. A white cutworm's torso rises up like a fat misshapen penis from out of her center. Resting atop this body glistening with sweat and thick clear slime is the disfigured head and deformed face of a toothless human infant.

As Ardnas moved down to block the only way into and out of her lair with two of her legs, Ellzbeth stepped forward a few paces to meet with the large slowly descending face.

"We believe that Vile, the Gate Keeper—"

"I'm aware of Sillona's designation and which realm she cares for," Ardnas interrupted. "To the point Inquisitor—to the point." It had been several millennium since Ellzbeth heard Vile's God-given name spoken and was half caught within the fog of its unfamiliarity at its mention.

"Yes, of course Magistrate," she said with a slight bow of her head in a gesture of apology.

Ardnas's deep set dark eyes gleamed beneath the heavy shadow cast by her thick brow as she lowered her face down inches from Ellzbeth's mask.

"You've come here to point fingers, I trust you have proof?" She asked while studying the tiny cracks that spread all over the porcelain disguise like an old oil-painting.

"Vile's thieved the mother of our player," Sader barked as he stepped forward. "She'll no doubt arm the mortal with her blood and smuggle the mother into the game. That is if she—"

Ardnas didn't allow Sader to finish. In a show of her distaste for his uninvited advance toward her, she brought one of her legs down in a flash of speed swatting him in mid step. Sader was slammed down flat on his back, then with even more speed Ardnas gently picked him up and set him on his feet. All the while never shifting her attention away from Ellzbeth's golden eyes beaming out of the mask.

"We seek your blessing Magistrate," Ellzbeth said.

"My blessing to do what, or should I be afraid to ask?"

"To go unannounced into Vile's palace and gather proof of her crookedness."

Ardnas loosed an obviously forced chuckle into the opening of Ellzbeth's hood. The false laughter carried in its breath a musty, dry odor, not unlike the sun baked hide of a dead thing stiff and broken in the middle of a desert road.

"I am aware Inquisitor of your distrust concerning Zaw'naw's Gate Keeper, and I'm equally conscious of Sillona's ambitions to reign over the entire Empire. Although, I've no knowledge as to the ways and hows of Sillona's plans to achieve her misguided dream. You come here with this one," Ardnas swung her deformed face onto Sader, pausing briefly until swinging her black eyes back to Ellzbeth who had stepped backward a pace, "and all you have to show me is your paranoia. How could I in good conscience rely on only the suspicions of two? Convince me as to why I should grant B'neem a warrant to go creeping and spying about through Sillona's home—say why?"

Sader went to volunteer the reply, but Ardnas cut him off seconds before his words poured past his lips. "No—Overseer," she raised a clawed foot and pressed the long dagger-like toenail non-threateningly against his thin lips. Shushing Sader, Ardnas looked back into Ellzbeth's golden eyes, grinned widely to expose her toothless black gums and whispered, "You."

"Ruth Stone was in our charge and—"

"Closer Inquisitor," Ardnas interrupted. "I do not wish to miss a word. Yes, and remove your mask if you would please."

Sader jerked his face back, away from the claw pushed over his mouth and was about to issue a sharp protest toward Ardnas's request, when before Ellzbeth could stop Sader, Ardnas snapped her attention onto him. She latched onto his face as it pulled away and yanked him up into the air, drawing him near. The razor edges of her claws cutting down to the skull beneath his face as she dangled him off his feet.

"You're in my house Overseer." She released Sader and let his body drop with a solid smack against the stone platform. "The mask Inquisitor."

Ellzbeth waved her left hand before the opening of her hood, causing the purple clay face-covering to vanish. She continued the face revealing gesture, sweeping the back of her hand past Sader's bleeding face immediately closing the deep wounds.

"As I was saying," Ellzbeth continued, "Ruth Stone is our players' mother, as well as one of his victims. Vile has taken her out of the place of suffering we've made for her. My spies have told me this." Luckily for Ellzbeth, Ardnas hasn't the gift of sight through lies. To strengthen her prevarication she paused to remove her hood while chancing a modest step forward. Sader went to shove up onto his feet, but the clawed foot came down to lie on his chest, pressing him to the ground.

"Please continue—Inquisitor."

"Although my spies did not tell me of Vile's intentions with the mother of our choice, it is our unwavering belief that Vile, for whatever her insane reasoning, is of the credo that B'neem is her only true threat that keeps her from being victorious in the game. Perhaps it is due to B'neem's victory the last three times it was played."

"Yes—congratulations," Ardnas interrupted.

Placing her right hand against her chest Ellzbeth bowed her head and said, "Thank you Magistrate."

"You were saying?"

"You're no doubt aware of the bad-blood between Vile and myself."

"Yes of course, it's an old story."

"It is that past between her and I, compounded with her insane lust to rule all of Hell that powers her madness."

"It's not a crime to be mad," Ardnas chuckled.

"No, it is a crime to share angelic blood with a mortal. And not only her own blood, but the blood of Satan as well.

"Sillona's player is a man, not a woman. You're not the only owner of spies Inquisitor," Ardnas said as she gestured with a glance into the darkness at the red eyes of tiny spiders beaming like small flames out at the visitor, "And Sillona destroyed Satan's blood ages ago."

"Yes, Vile's chosen player is a man, but he only serves her as a vessel to snake her underhandedness into the game. Ruth Rose Stone is no doubt hidden somewhere deep within the player's flesh, and she is fat with angelic blood, seething with vengeful desire. Once the player is face to face with our's, the mother will sense her son's presence and make herself known. The son will not stand a chance against a foe armed with the blood of an angel, and neither will the other remaining players. Vile will have taken the day and it will be too late to stop her from laying-waste to the Empire.

"You say all of this," Ardnas whispered as she raised Sader up and rested him on his feet. "But you've only words, no proof. I need more than accusations before I can have her brought before me. I won't grant you authority to trespass into Sillona's palace—but if one of you were to do so on your own, and proof to what you've told me is found, no mention of your transgressing Sillona's gates will be made against you.

The sound of Ardnas's soft voice invoked one of the bodies bundled within her webs to moan with dread. Thousands of tiny spiders, none of which larger than a child's tear-drop, poured out of the darkness like black smoke moving up the webs. Ardnas pulled herself away from her two guests and moved with swift, fluid motion up toward the prisoner. As if her great girth were as weightless as a strand of silken thread she climbed through the labyrinth of webs and bound bodies. Ardnas moved effortlessly ahead of the black flood of fast legs and tiny fangs. When she was upon her prisoner she reached out and took the twitching package of fright gently into her arms. With the angel pressed lovingly against her wormy torso she shot a blank glance around her at the approaching spiders and silently mouthed the demand, *wait your turns please.* The black swarm halted their vast advances less than ten yards from Ardnas and her prisoner, surrounding her completely. Struggling, or at least offering up a weak effort to resist Ardnas' grasp, the angel tried with vain-hope to cry out for pity. As the faint sounds of sobs and pleas bled out through the hooded veil of webbing, a hidden proboscis slid out of a fleshy sheath from Ardnas's under-belly. It reached up and around the angel she cradled in her arms and worked its hypodermic needle like tip into the back of the prisoner's skull. Ardnas softly stroked the side of its face as if to sooth the helpless angel while she fed. Ardnas's wormy upper body lunged and quivered with each sucking intake as her shiny black eyes rolled back into her misshapen head. Her lower lip trembled as she spoke in a shaky tone.

"Go now, and do what you will. If proof you find, bring it to me and I'll use it. But understand this, both of you, my blessing is with the promise that if you're caught I will deny either of you were ever here. You Overseer, you will be who creeps about Sillona's palace, you and you alone. Now leave me."

That said the Magistrate climbed swiftly up into the darkness, taking her prisoner and the black cloud of tiny spiders with her.

Ellzbeth put her mask back on and pulled her hood up over her head. Looking over at Sader she said calmly, "I understand that it was you Ardnas told could go seek after the proof, but I don't believe it truly matters which one of us finds it. So as long as—"

"I see where you're going with this Ellzbeth," Sader declared with an unsettled tone in his voice that she found surprisingly harsh. "The answer is no, you're not going to that disturbed creature's palace. The Magistrate said that I was to go. You need to find Pike and tell him what Ardnas said."

Sader glanced up over his shoulder at the remains of angelic beings who'd all at one point attempted to empower mortals with their blood.

"Vile's going to look good hanging up there," he said coldly.

Around the corner and one block over from the three story reminder of Alex's childhood tragedy, he noticed a change in how the weather was affecting him. The soft sprinkling of rain and lazy night breeze had steadily increased to a swirling wind and healthy down-pour. Alex suddenly went from not being effected by the weather to feeling its presence fully. It was so unexpected that the wind nearly managed to snatch the fedora off his head. No longer was the frigid bite of the air or the clothes and skin drenching effects of precipitation simply passing through him with no sign or impact. By the time Alex had reached the edge of Corvallis' Central Park his blood-stained rags were soaked. Alex now possessed substance against the living atmosphere of the world's changing climate, but only where he was concerned. For instance, if a dense fog or a thick cloud of smoke were to form around him, there would be no clear bubble shape of his body moving about for the living to see. To warm souls, the wind and rain passed through Alex as effortlessly as their cars and bodies did. Only he was aware of the change—he and the other players he would come to encounter. The reason for this sudden change was the cost for Ellzbeth's slight transgression for guiding Alex to Mr. Fisk, by having his hat placed on the stop-sign in front of the Ninth street mall. For the remainder of the game Alex would experience all of Earth's elements, as if he were one of the living.

Stepping over to one of the park's turn of the century style light posts, Alex swung the back of his clinched fist at the, metal pole. His hand drifted through it without being slowed or deflected. *At least that's the same,* he thought, pleased that he could still move through things. He was about to voice his elation over this knowledge with a sigh of relief when a shadow looming up behind him spun Alex about. With Mr. Bane clutched in his fist with combat ready intent he turned to face down a statue. The high branches of a large elm tree had been blocking some of a street light's phosphorescent lambent. That was, until a rain filled gust of wind blew most of the leafy obstructions aside, allowing the light to cast out over the bronze ballerina statue. The luminous effect shined in such a way that to the corner of Alex's sight the shadow stretching across the wet cobble-stones appeared as a creeper.

"Easy there Alex my boy," Mr. Bane chortled. "A bit on edge—taking on shadows and defenseless park statues, focus Alex."

"Why is the weather suddenly effecting me?"

"I've no clue."

"I figured that since you act as though you know most everything else, that you would have the answer for this crap as well," Alex rumbled.

"It's no act," the knife said sharply. "Perhaps this new cold and wet occurrence is some sort of amusing phase of the game. Or is it simply a form of chastisement for your time-wasting dilly-dally back at the house?"

"Point made Mr. Bane."

"I truly hope so Alex, for both of our sakes." Mr. Bane's voice faded away behind the approaching thunder of a car's stereo speakers blasting out the ear piercing roar of death metal music. A new black Ford Focus fishtailed around the corner off Jefferson onto Eighth Street and sped straight toward Alex. Suddenly a girl clad in soaking wet black clothes, long straight black hair, and a face as pale as a corpse, stepped out of the shadows onto the street. The car's driver seeing the young goth girl, slammed on the brakes and spun the vehicle's rear-end skillfully around in the middle of the street, nearly hitting a parked car and spraying water on the girl. The car's brake-lights flashed on, the death-metal music immediately increasing in volume as the passenger side window rolled down. A wild eyed boy with a sweat shirt's hood pulled up over his head reached a paint-ball gun out the window and shot the girl twice. She tipped backward over her own feet as she tried to dodge the assault.

"Sperm burping, dick jockey!" she screamed at the car as it tore off around the corner, the sound of its loud music receding into the falling rain. Getting to her black boot covered feet, she pulled a red bandanna out of her leather overcoat's inside pocket. Holding it up to catch the rain in the cloth, she stepped over to the curb and took a seat on the cold, wet concrete. It didn't take the shower long to douse the crimson cloth.

"Mother fucking college ass-hole bastards!" she cursed loudly out into the darkness as she tired to scrub the bright yellow paint splatters off of her. The first paintball exploded on her left shoulder, some of it spattering on her hair and cheek. The thick leather of her coat shielded her skin from most of the impact. Her belly wasn't as fortunate. Alex had lowered to a knee and watched as she cursed under her breath while lifting the black t-shirt up. Once she'd wiped away the yellow paint which had bled through the shirt, they both stared angrily at the half dollar size red welt raised dead center on her stomach. *What fucking punks,* Alex thought as he witnessed the teenager's discomfort and rage.

"Fucking ass-holes," she growled while washing most of the yellow paint out of the bandanna in the gutter.

The sound of the death metal music could still be heard a few blocks over, and from about the same distance away in the opposite direction, Alex could also hear the familiar thunder of dual exhaust pipes announcing the arrival of a V-8 flathead. Both sounds were growing louder and moving in their direction. The girl's attention rose toward the howling sound of approaching music. Alex could see the gears spinning in her blue-green eyes as she swiftly considered her two choices. One, to stand her ground and be pelted with more paint-balls, or two, to go so that she may salvage what dignity hadn't been spattered away with yellow paint. As Alex and the girl stood, his attention on the healthy sounding V-8, and her's on the death metal, he said, "They'll be here soon, arm yourself or go."

"She can't hear you Alex," Mr. Bane reminded.

"I'm aware of that."

"Fuck it!" she snapped sharply under her breath as she turned and headed across the darkened park.

"She possesses a foul tongue Alex," Mr. Bane commented. "I doubt very much Susan would ever allow such filth to spew forth from her tips."

"What's my sister got to do with it!" Alex barked. "You didn't even know Susan, so why would you presume to speak of her as if you did?"

"Why so touchy Alex? I know your heart. And in so knowing, I also know Susan. You were thinking, or at least hoping, you could see her in that odd teenager. You are of course aware of the fact that the girl didn't seem to hear the flathead motor coming this way?"

"Yes," Alex answered as he locked his attention onto the healthy sound of power rolling up Monroe Street.

As the black Ford, blasting its death metal tore up Jefferson street, passing Eighth, a lowered burgundy, 1950 Mercury two-door, with black tinted windows rumbled slowly around the corner. Passing Alex on the sidewalk, it sped up a little and turned its long body sideways in the street as if to block it.

"A player?" Alex asked.

"It seems so."

The motor revved loudly as the driver's side window rolled down. Stepping into the middle of the street Alex shouted, "Why didn't I get a bitchin ride?" his tone covetous.

Half a moment after the window was all the way down, a woman's voice replied from out of the black air within the car.

"All you've got is that?" A hand pointing a finger reached out of the darkness to aim at Mr. Bane clutched in Alex's gloved fist. "That pathetic little knife!"

"Pathetic indeed," Mr. Bane growled.

The hand pulled back in as a woman's face, as white as Mr. Death's teeth, pressed out of the veil of pitch. She was as bald as Alex and possessed no eyebrows or even lashes. Her eyes were smeared and streaked with black eyeliner that ran down her cheeks from tears, and her lips sported the darkest shade of red lip-gloss that Alex had ever seen a woman wear. She snickered and said, "Oh, how deliciously easy this will be. Time to run rabbit...run!"

The woman's evil clown face vanished in the darkness much the same way a white rock sinks beneath thick black mud. The smooth sound of the big car being slipped back into gear was drowned out by the throaty cry of the engine being gunned. Its rear wheels sent out a high pitched shriek as they spinned in place. It was an unearthly scream of a sound that could only be heard by Alex and the dead that it had to have awoken. A dense cloud of light-gray smoke spewed out from the spinning wheels filling the night air with a stench that smelled more like burning hair and roasting bone than melting rubber on wet asphalt. When the tires finally latched onto the street, the Merc rocketed forward and drove straight into the two story white house in front of it. It hadn't crashed into it, but drove through its façade as if it weren't there at all. It was out of sight, but not Alex's ear-shot. He listened as the rumbling dual-pipes sped away.

The woman driver's name is Evalyn Love Swagger. She is the chosen player for the Ninth realm called, Rats'ach. The place in Hell for all of those souls who murdered simply because it brings them pleasure. In

Evalyn's case, killing people was the only thing that got her off—(in a matter of speaking). She'd nearly been sent to the sixth realm due to the sexual aspects of her twisted deeds. But for reasons having to do with her underlining motives, and a few of the means by which she executed her wicked acts, she was spared the pleasure of Queen Vile's tormenters and sent to Rats'ach instead.

During Evalyn's short adult life she had single-handedly tortured, raped and butchered ten men and thirteen women, although not necessarily in that order.

It was in mid July, 1967 the so-called summer of love, that Evalyn was finally to be cast into Hell. She'd convinced a young man she met in an uptown San Francisco singles club into stepping out with her to smoke a joint. The moment he settled comfortably back in the front seat of her burgundy dream car she rammed the business end of a hypodermic needle into the side of his neck. The fast acting barbiturate sent the poor horny fool immediately into a mind and body numbing state of oblivion.

When Evalyn eventually awoke him with the aid of some strong smelling salts, they were far from the city parked beneath a large dogwood tree. Rather, Evalyn was parked under that big tree. The young man on the other hand was stretched out naked, and long ways in front of the Mercury. His arms were pulled up over his head, chained at the wrists and wrapped around the tree's trunk; his ankles were also bound with chains and padlocked to the car's front bumper. The old tree was on the top center of a high, fairly steep hill covered with wild clover, inner-rooted with long blades of fescue grass.

"Please do feel free to scream as loudly as you wish," Evalyn encouraged with a soft kiss on his lips. Before pulling her face from his she ran her tongue slowly up his sweaty cheek, a maniacal glint in her bright blue eyes and a sinister smile formed faintly on her mouth.

"My little playmate," she sang. The words wrapped within the lilt of a girlish giggle as she skipped around him. She lightly scratched her fingernails over his stretched body, all the while still singing, "Come out and play with me."

He screamed cursed threats at her in between loud cries for help. She slung her head down in an almost drunken lunge and bit his flaccid penis. Her teeth sunk deep into his flesh, and as he screamed Evalyn placed her right hand on his chest to feel his pain rushing through his thrashing body. Her left hand slid between her legs and as she squeezed and rubbed herself, she jerked her mouth away tearing a bite size hunk of his tool off. Evalyn wiped her lips with her fingers, skipping away singing, "I'll bring my dollies three, and we'll climb up my apple tree...come out and play with me."

With a loving glance over her shoulder at the bleeding, sobbing man, she got behind the wheel of her car, and before slamming the door closed she spit the sucked bloodless hunk of dick out and giggled. Sitting in her seat, she pushed the four-track tape the rest of the way into the player and turned the volume down some. It was between tracks, giving her enough time to take the half smoked joint out of the ash-tray and light it. Janis Joplin's song "Ball and Chain" clicked on at the exact moment her lungs filled with the smoke. Making sure she had a good view of her new lover's suffering, she exhaled most of the warm vapor out through her nostrils and pressed the toe of her white go-go boot down on the brake pedal. Pushing it all the way to the floor-board, she then smoothly released the emergency brake. With her eyes glued to her prey's horror, Evalyn slowly let her foot ease up on the brake pedal. There were no stop and go jerks as the heavy car rolled down the hill. Evalyn had honed this phase of the fiendish act to a fine art. With only the toes of her right foot and a slack grip on the steering-wheel she smoked her joint, listened to Janis sing of heart break and watched through the tinted windshield as the weight of the Merc slowly pulled the man apart. Inch by inch his screams grew louder, awakening the birds to send them out of the surrounding trees. No sooner had his agonizing howls increased in volume and they were already decreasing to the low hissing noise one makes when the anguish is too great to utter other sounds.

As Evalyn watched her modern-day torture device slowly rip his body further and further out of joint, she turned the volume down a little more, in order to let her ears, focus on the sounds of the dying outside. Like someone eagerly awaiting the tingling onset of an L.S.D high, she listened for the faint sounds of flesh and bone being torn and pulled apart. Whether or not Evalyn could truly hear it occurring was of no importance. What did matter was that she believed she could. His tendons and muscles did in fact snap, his bones were audibly torn from their sockets with dull pops, and his skin stretched and ripped with the tearing sound of wet leather. All of this taking place while his fully conscious mind begged for the flesh numbing effects of shock; or the life silencing aftermath of death, which ever came first.

As Evalyn watched number twenty-three's death painfully transpire she felt the warmth rising up her spine from between her legs. Her lower lip quivered as it tucked into her mouth to be bitten on. With a slowly increasing twitch her back eventually went rigid, and no matter how much effort she put into maintaining visual focus, not wishing to miss a second of his agony, her vision still went fuzzy. Evalyn's bosom heaved with faster and faster panting breathes until finally loosing a loudly screamed "Yes!" As she climaxed at the exact moment the car ripped the man's arms off his shoulders. What great timing, and she didn't even have to lay a finger on herself; all it took were the sights and sounds of a living person being torn apart.

The moment she got what she wanted Evalyn tried to reset the emergency brake, but the car wouldn't stop moving. The pitch of the hill was too steep and the freak summer rainstorm a few hours earlier had caused the grassy slope to be too slick for the tires to grab any traction. These factors, along with the car's weight, sent Evalyn sliding uncontrollably backwards fast. And to make matters worse, less than half a football field's length form the tree, was a two hundred foot high cliff, directly in the car's path. Evalyn stayed with her beloved dream car dragging the armless corpse down with it for as long as her courage would hold up, (which was longer than any sane person would have). She stomped furiously on the brake, but nothing. She even considered turning the wheel sharply left or right in hopes that doing so would stop the vehicle, but decided against the idea, certain that at the speed she was sliding all that would end up happening is the car would roll side over side. Eventually her fear got the best of her. She finally did the only thing left to do, Evalyn abandoned her car. Opening her door, she closed her eyes and flung herself out of the moving death trap. But when she wasn't immediately met with the earth speeding passed the car, she opened her eyes. To Evalyn's terrified shock she learned of her error too late; she had waited too long to make her escape. Instead of landing with the solid thud which she had expected, she opened her eyes to see that she had hurtled herself out of the car at the exact instant that it flew over the edge of the cliff. Evalyn's fall ended as all plummets of the wicked conclude; in the waiting arms of Hell's tormenters.

= ⫿⫿ =

Alex listened to the roar of the ghost car's engine as it circled widely around him. An old 1971 green G.M.C van turned the corner onto Eighth and slowed to a curb side stop a little behind Alex. The chosen parking place in a spot where the park's trees blocked out most of the street light. Alex afforded the old step-side van a brief glance while keeping most of his attention on the rumbling sound of the Merc moving around him off in the distance. Seeing the red glow of a cigarette floating about behind the van's windshield as the driver vanished to the rear of the metal box, Alex was fairly certain that he was of the living.

"It's not a player...is it?" he asked.

"I don't believe so Alex."

It was plain to see that the driver had every intention of remaining in his shadowy parking place for the rest of the night. Alex turned his back to the new arrival, setting his complete attention once again on the healthy sounding V-8 flathead. Although he wasn't afraid to go head to head with a ton or so of metal, he wasn't eager to do so either. He was pretty sure that the effects the ghost car would have on him wouldn't be as harmless as the cars of the living.

"At least it stopped fucking raining." Alex pointed out as he took off his hat to shake most of the water out of it. "We will have to be extra cunning Mr. Bane if we're to put this one in her dish."

"You're a clever killer Alex," Mr. Bane reassured. "Yes you are, as long as you maintain your keen focus and willingness to do whatever it takes," the metallic voice paused then added as the sound of the V-8 drew near. "Don't let yourself get impatient with my bite."

Alex took the pouch off from around his neck. He figured it would be a bit faster and easier to get a tooth out if he hung it from his belt instead. Alex was studying his surroundings, searching for a direction to head into if the need arose. Other than the park, only churches, houses, and parked cars encircled him.

"A trap Alex, we'll need to lure this one into a trap."

"Do you have any in mind?"

"No, not right off hand. But I'm confident you'll come up with something. You best make haste though; she'll be on us soon."

"From the sounds of it we've a little time—"

Interrupted, Alex was surprised and even caught off guard to learn how wrong he was. Like a ventriloquist throwing her voice, the engine's groan sounded farther than it was, quite a bit farther. Alex had been tricked. He was turning in place, in mid formulation of a plan of attack, when the moment his sight drifted across the brick wall of the Methodist church the phantom Mercury shot through the building's front doors onto Eighth Street.

With a thunderous sound which could only be heard by those watching in Hell, earthly animals, and players of the game, the large car came down hard on the asphalt. Sparks, unseen by the eyes of the living, exploded on impact the instant metal scraped swiftly across pavement. She whipped her car around toward Alex, its rear-end fishtailing some until the wheels bit. The car screeched past Alex as he threw himself out of its path, barely managing to escape its right front fender. He hit the sidewalk at a hard roll and was stopped by the trunk of a tree, the same tree the homeless man from the G.M.C van was pissing on. Alex was in the midst of shoving away from the golden-shower, getting to his feet, when he heard the sound of the Merc swerving back around. The area around Alex and the tree grew rapidly brighter with ghostly refulgent from the car's fast approaching headlights, a lambent only Alex could see. Like a man dodging a bull half a second before being skewered, Alex leapt out of the way. The roaring box of metal and glass passed swiftly through the tree and the man shaking out his drizzling member.

The Merc spun back around in the middle of the park and she floored it straight toward Alex. He was half way across the narrow street with the ghost car gaining close behind, when the black Ford, blasting the death metal tore around the corner. It passed through Alex and slammed on its brakes. The hooded boy was leaning out the driver's side window this time. He was about to shoot the homeless man with paint-balls, when the rich little bastard was stopped by a sudden wave of freezing cold air rushing through him. It was the ghost car on its way after Alex. It was so icy cold when it swept through the boy and his companion's car, that he dropped the paint-ball gun. When the frigid effects of the car's passing had faded, the boys found themselves staring up at the barrel of their own implement of harassment.

While the homeless man was emptying the gun's paint-ball store into and on the boys and their car Alex was running. He didn't care much for doing so at the on-set of a flight; it looked weak, but there's a time and place for almost anything. Alex quickly realized that taking this madwoman on, on her terms was a fool's game. There were only two ways he would be able to send her back to Hell. He would either have to get the speed demon bitch out of that iron box, or somehow he would need to get himself inside with her. Alex wasn't too keen on the second choice, but knew it had more likelihood of occurring than baiting her out of the safety of her rolling fortress. With the sound of the V-8 moving up behind him, and the beams of its headlights starting to burn past, he tore off between the large Methodist church and an old white three story Victorian style house. As he was breaking out of the narrow walkway the Merc was swerving in behind him. Alex darted sharply left and hurtled himself out of sight into a big blue metal dumpster. Seconds after the sound of the car sped past him in his hiding place, he pressed his face through one of the dumpster's walls far enough to see which direction she was heading. Alex watched the car as it flew across the alley behind the church and disappeared once again into another house. He could see its shadow speed through the darkened residence as it raced past windows with pulled open drapes. Alex rolled out of the big square garbage can the moment he saw the car fly out of the side of the building and tear off down the street. As soon as the coast was clear, Alex ran out of the alley behind the ghost car. Listening, he could hear that it was a block or two away and turning back around. Looking for a good spot to leap out onto the car from, he swiftly found exactly what he was looking for.

"See it Alex?" Mr. Bane hissed.

"Yes."

"Give it a go. Hell, what do we have to loose other than a pain-free existence?" The knife's chuckle faded behind the thunder of the nearing motor.

A large cherry tree that had to be as old as Corvallis itself lived closely beside the intersection of Eighth and Jefferson. Some of its big branches reached out over Jefferson Street low enough for someone to drop out onto the roof of a car passing beneath it. Running to the tree, Alex took his hat off and set it on the road under the over-reaching branches. He barely had time to scale the snarled old tree and hide within its limited leaf cover before the Merc turned off Seventh street.

Alex's plan was to drop onto the car's roof, as she slowed to inspect the hat, smashed out the driver's side windshield and go from there.

He watched as the Merc rumbled around the corner and stopped. Its motor went deathly silent, and the car's headlights slowly faded out. The Merc died. Alex, not willing to take a chance and impulsively abandon his ambush spot, decided to wait awhile, watch and listen as the engine struggled with painfully raspy sounding effort to restart. *Ghost cars ain't supposed to stall,* Alex thought—*are they?*

"This is a window of opportunity Alex," Mr. Bane advised. "Best leap through it before it slams shut."

"It could be a trap?"

"Yes, it could be, but I've a feeling its not."

"I hope your feelings are on time old friend," Alex said as he dropped out of his hidden position onto the street. At a fast clip he walked up the middle of the Jefferson toward the fighting to start car. A light blue, small wheeled scooter carrying two girls zipped past Alex from behind and passed straight through the stalled Merc. He was less than twenty yards from it and could hear the woman's voice cursing at him to stay back and pleading with the engine to restart. Feeling for his pouch of teeth hanging from his belt where he'd earlier moved it to; he slowed his pace and looked down when his hand didn't locate it right off. Alex's heart nearly stopped beating when he found the black pouch to be gone. "Shit!" he barked as he groped his pockets, all the while knowing he hadn't put it in one of them. As he shifted his sight from the car half a block up the street, to look around behind him, he slowed to a stop. With his ears locked onto the raspy sound of the motor trying to start up, he visually back tracked his steps. Carefully his eyes scanned the glistening black surface of the wet asphalt, but he was having no luck.

Alex decided to continue on toward the car and cut the woman's head off. He was hoping that by keeping the head with him until he could locate his pouch she wouldn't be able to heal; he would have been proven wrong by reasons too complicated to mention. Alex was about to move toward the stalled Merc when he spotted the pouch hanging out of the cherry tree by its draw-string from a low branch. He was going to continue with the idea of removing the woman's head, and retrieve his pouch once he had her melon in hand. Alex, sporting a *you lose* expression in his eyes turned to face the car. He'd only taken one full step when the ghost car's engine fired back to life.

Acting fast Alex tore off toward the cherry tree and his leather bag of teeth. He was closer to the tree than the car when it started up, about ten yards closer. Evalyn slammed the Merc into gear and stomped on the gas. Alex didn't dare chance a glance over his shoulder to look at the screaming car as the rear tires spun in place. The pouch was dangling low, easy for him to snatch once he was close enough. The unmistakable sound of wheels sinking their tread into the pavement increased Alex's sprinting pace.

"Run Alex my boy! Run!" Mr. Bane shouted. Images of him being tossed into the horribly decayed arms of his waiting parents flashed in his mind with each foot fall.

"She's gaining Alex!" The beams of the Merc's headlights were growing rapidly brighter and larger. Soon all Alex could hear was the roar of the V-8. Even Mr. Bane's metallic voice had been devoured by the throaty groan of the motor. At the very moment his gloved fist had wrapped around the pouch, a nightmarishly loud shriek caused by rubber sliding swiftly across wet asphalt stretched out into the night. The grisly sound led the way for what was to follow. Alex ripped the bag of teeth out of the tree as Evalyn, using the ton and a half of Detroit steel like a giant ball-bat, power-slid hard left. The maneuver successfully swerved the car's rear, right hand side panel into Alex before he could throw himself to safety. The solid blow knocked him rolling and sliding across the rain soaked pavement a good thirty feet. Not allowing himself the time to consider what just happened, he shoved his torn, road-rashed self up onto his feet. Shaky, with pain Alex first realized that Mr. Bane was no longer clutched in his right fist, although the pouch was in his left. The second he noticed that the ghost car had already turned about and was up the street heading straight for him. Alex swept his vision around in search of his weapon.

"Here Alex, here!" Mr. Bane's voice cried.

Following the sound of his friend's words over the thunderous sound of the engine, little more than a block away and closing, he spotted the knife lying in the middle of the street. A primer gray 84 Dodge pick up truck with only the driver's side headlight turned the corner off Ninth and was heading toward the speeding ghost car. Alex ran as fast as his scraped to shit legs could carry him. The Cyclops Dodge raced through Alex as he was bending to scoop Mr. Bane up. He'd grabbed the knife and was stopped, only for half a second when he saw that he was standing in front of his childhood home again.

"ALEX!" Mr. Bane hollered.

He looked over in time to see the Merc's front end peeling out through the bed of the Dodge. He went to move out of its way, but Evalyn slammed on the brake and cut the steering wheel sharp left, again power sliding the car's rear side panel into Alex's fleeing back. Hitting him quite a bit harder than the first time, the blow sent Alex whipping through the air like a kitten that's sent off the porch with a nine-iron. His flight came to an end with his body slamming against the broken, half knocked over cinder block wall that used to close off the backyard of his old house. Alex's head was buzzing with pain, but still he was able to see the red blurry taillights of the Merc drift out of his line of vision as Evalyn positioned the big car around to drive in after him. As Alex pulled himself off of the broken concrete blocks he could tell that most, if not all of his bones on the right side of his body, were broken or shattered. He tried to make himself stand, but found it to be an impossible feat. At least he hadn't lost his grip on Mr. Bane this time.

"She's coming back to finish us off Alex," Mr. Bane warned, "Quickly, hide. There's still a chance."

"Of course there's a chance. She's not won yet." Alex said through a mouth full of blood and shattered teeth.

The sound of the Merc was already drawing near. With great effort he managed to drag himself into the safety of some overgrown shrubs and tall clumps of crabgrass. Somehow the battle between the woman and him had ended up in the backyard of his old house. He crawled through the soft mud deeper into the shadows within the shrub line and hoped his body's self-healing wouldn't take long. As Alex stared out of the shrubs at the boarded up double doors and windows of the big old house he wondered, *What's the odds of me ending up in this backyard?*

"As to what Alex?"

"Ending up in this backyard."

"No time to lend it any thought." Mr. Bane sounded weary and for the first time—old.

Alex stabbed the blade into the mud and opened the pouch, closing it tightly once he'd rolled a tooth out onto his palm. He slid Mr. Bane back out of the soggy earth and focused his hearing onto the slow growl of the Merc.

"Why hasn't she driven back here?" Alex asked, "She had to have seen where I landed after that second blow."

"Maybe not, or perhaps the witch is waiting for you to step out onto the street." Mr. Bane's reply was so soft and weak sounding that Alex could barely make out the words.

"Are you going to make it?" Alex asked, trying to sound as though he believed his question a silly one, when in fact he was truly concerned.

"Like you some times, I require a moment or two to mend and gather my wits. I'll be back to my exalted state, once you've sent this one back."

Alex could hear the V-8 idling out front, and said with a note of finality. "What do you say to sending this spun bitch and her ride back to Tartarus Mr. Bane?"

"It's about time," the knife replied eagerly.

Alex was feeling his right side, trying to determine how far along his healing had come. He felt most of the bones mending moments ago, while others still had a ways to go. He needed at least four, perhaps five more minutes before he would be completely battle ready. He tried to position himself in the shadows of his soggy hiding place as best as he could without compromising his location. He wanted to be ready to move if need be, even if he couldn't stand easily.

The wind had picked up again and was blowing the bare, branches of a near, dead apple tree in such a way that to Alex it appeared as though it were trying to scratch the sky's eyes out. As the spaces in the dark steel gray clouds closed to block out the indigo night, shutting the view to Polaris and the other stars willing to be seen, the motor revved thunderously. Alex was on the edge of moving out of the shrub line and attempted to kneel behind the apple tree when Mr. Bane snapped, "Wait!"

The car's headlights pushed slowly out through the back of the house. Its long front end, all the way back to the black glass of its windshield, rolled out onto the back-deck, then stopped, most of the car still in the house. After a few tense moments of it just sitting there motionless it revved its engine and out it came. The large car flew the rest of the way out into the backyard, and without slowing drove over the soft mud and overgrown grass, through the apple tree's wide, gnarled trunk, and the dense shrub-line to roll past Alex crouched in his hiding place. As she rumbled by he noticed that the driver's side window was all the way down. Alex could see the side of her head bleeding its white shape out beyond the Hellish darkness within. His right leg and hip were both in the process of mending in several places, so with a silent rush of intense pain tearing frantically throughout his body, Alex sprang up out of the shrubs and shadows. He reached into the passing window, slammed his left boot down on the side-pipe like a narrow running board, and latched a hold of Evalyn's head. Without any thought as to the driver's gender or brief speculation concerning the reasons why she'd been cast into Hell, Alex stabbed Mr. Bane's blade all the way through her throat. In a voice straining to scream she slammed the car into reverse and shrieked, "Get the fuck off my car!"

Dropping her foot on the gas, the car jerked backward, and before Alex could yank his weapon back out of her neck she dug the fingernails of her right hand across his face and opened the door with a hard shove of her shoulder. Alex was knocked off the car and landed on his back hard enough to send all the air out of his lungs. Evalyn pulled Mr. Bane out of her neck, and without offering the dagger a second's consideration, she tossed it over her shoulder onto the back seat.

Alex was able to catch what she'd done with Mr. Bane as she spun the car around to aim its front end at him while still in reverse. *Shit house luck*, he thought as the car jerked to a stop. With his weapon and only friend in the car Alex's only chance was the demon's tooth. But where had it landed? Alex wasn't sure if it fell in the car or in the mud with him. Nothing was happening; no giant maggots were springing up out of the ground to take her to Hell. "Why wasn't the tooth doing its thing?" he asked himself under his breath.

"Alex, you really should try and get me out of this creature's bucket of bolts," Mr. Bane said calmly.

Giving no reply, Alex went to shove himself up onto his feet. It must have been what Evalyn was waiting for, because as soon as he was standing half-assed upright she slammed the car into drive and stomped on the gas pedal, driving the car's nose smack into Alex. Hitting the brakes the instant she'd struck him the car stopped, but Alex did not. He was knocked into the dead apple tree's trunk and broke his back. Alex could hear the driver trying to laugh, but the still healing hole through her throat gave her chuckle a wheezing quality. Lying in the mud on the side of his face, Alex's shattered spine had rendered him physically paralyzed. The only parts of his person that still served him as useful were his eyesight and his hearing. That is of course if being capable of witnessing one's own failure can be perceived as being of use.

Evalyn backed the car slowly to a stop a few yards from where he lay and shifted it back into forward drive. She gave the big car a little gas, and holding it at bay, she revved its engine loudly a couple times like a bull stomping one of its front hooves on the ground before charging. Alex struggled to get himself up, or at least make some effort to crawl, but all of his attempts weren't making it from his mind to the rest of his body. All he could do was silently watch and listen, hoping that whatever was broke would heal, and do so fast. But all hope and wishing aside, Alex at that point was as good as being back in that accured boneyard again.

Evalyn leaned her head far enough out of her window for Alex to see the wound in her neck hadn't yet healed completely. She looked at him and smiled before pulling her head back into the car. Alex could hear Janis Joplin singing the song "Ball and Chain" coming out of the car. It was at that moment, at the very instant that the car rocketed forward, that he spotted the demon's tooth he'd got out for her. It was lying in the mud directly in the Merc's path. The second that it vanished beneath the car passing over it, thousands of iron chains, almost too fast for Alex or Evalyn to see, shot up out from under the vehicle and wrapped around it. They instantly brought the big car to an abrupt halt. Alex could see the faint shapes of Evalyn's hands slapping against the inside of the darkened windshield, and as Janis sang about heartbreak and loneliness the madwoman behind the wheel of her dream car screamed in horror. The chains squeezed down around the middle of the Merc, crushing its roof down as if it were made of soft clay. With the loud sounds of twisting metal, shattering glass, and bursting tires Alex could still hear Evalyn's muffled cries. The car folded up like a big burgundy pocket-knife and was pulled into the ground out of sight; her muted pleas went deathly quiet the instant the large, glowing red hole collapsed closed. The beautiful old Merc was gone, enveloped back to Hell.

In the mud, stabbed in the spot where the car had disappeared, was Mr. Bane. It took Alex's broken back, as well as his other injuries, several long and painful minutes to mend completely. When his body was ready he got up and pulled his weapon out of the mud.

"I thought I might have lost you for real old friend." Alex said. Wiping the blade clean on his pant leg. He looked around for his hat, and then remembered that they'd laid it in the middle of Jefferson as bait.

"We gave each other our words, an oath that we would never abandon one another. Yes Alex, right here in this very yard."

"I remember."

"Yes, of course you do Alex," the voice drifted to silence.

"Let's go get my fedora," Alex said under his breath and without so much as a brief glance up at the house, he left that backyard for what he planned to be the last time. A soft rain began to fall.

Alex and his razor edged team-mate were both feeling a bit done in. The wind had died down some, but not the rain. The gentle sprinkle had in an instant changed to a moderate shower. Alex was sopping wet and didn't care. He'd come so close to being sent back, that nothing else seemed to matter. Only the fact that he and Mr. Bane were still in the game was of importance to him, that and his determination not to come so close to failure again. Alex remembered that the woman's Merc had never appeared wet with rain and was wondering if Mr. Bane was correct in the assumption that his being effected by the changing weather was punishment for wasting-time. If so, and the other players weren't being effected by the weather, he figured there might be a way that he could use it to his advantage.

Alex had placed his pouch out of sight in his coat pocket and was counting on the others mistaking him for one of the living; a warm soul with very pale skin hopefully.

The two killers, Alex and his metallic voice friend went immediately to hunt for the next contestant eager to be sent back to scream beneath that furious red sky. Alex was moving at a fast walk within the shadows beyond the street light's reach, when he spotted a bald man wearing a yellow windbreaker jacket scurrying almost rat like into an alley a block up the street.

"Did you see that?" Alex asked.

"Indeed I did," Mr. Bane's tone sounded strong and vibrant again, "and Alex, he did not appear to be wet."

While Alex was moving fast toward the alley that the bald man had crept into, two of the other players were in the process of getting acquainted. Nancy White and Peter Meadows were nineteen blocks away from Alex and Mr. Bane, inside the brightly lit Laundromat on King's Boulevard, and playing together quite nicely.

Nancy was playing for Ruakb, another one of Hell's unpleasant addresses. A lightless place, watched over by a giant breed of cherubic called 'Scorpbeings.' It is these ancient creatures charge to make those souls suffer who in mortal life were unforgivably vain. Nancy's slot in Ruakb had been given unto her when she slaughtered two people. Her reasons being that she was refused something that she believed herself due.

There'd been an opening for a partnership in the law firm she worked for. Nancy had been with the firm for close to seven years and believed wholeheartedly that it would be her chosen to take the seat around the partner's table. Unfortunately for her the senior partners had someone else in mind. The position was given to an ingenious young man who'd only been with the firm for slightly more than three years. The fact that this brilliant lawyer had been made partner and not her was intolerable. It mattered little to her that he'd won every single case that was dropped on his lap, several of them being some of the firms' biggest money makers. Where as, she'd lost the last four cases she had been charged with (one of which costing the law offices hundreds of thousands of dollars). The only reason why she hadn't been tossed out on her pretty little ass was because she had a talent for administering oral delectation. Not to mention, she was a thing of sexual beauty when bent over the edge of a desk. Skills she wielded generously upon her aging bosses, two of which being women. Nancy had figured that her behind locked-door-duties had earned her the partnership. When the news of the coveted position being given to another seeped into the awareness of her sperm pickled brain, she was incensed.

On the morning after the young lawyer's acceptance party, Nancy put on her sharkskin-gray skirt suit and left her Madison Avenue apartment for what she knew would be the last time. She was the first of the firm's small army of lawyers to arrive in the towering sky-scraper that housed the firm's sixty seventh floor law offices. There was no one else on the floor who gave a damn to question her as to why she had a key-card into the boss's office, or why she was using it. After helping herself to a well-glass of the old man's aged bourbon, she took the Scottish claymore sword down from off the wall behind the desk. The sun was beginning to inch away the morning's dark veil when she pressed herself into the shadows behind the door. She stood there in the diminishing night while the hazy touch of dawn burned in through the large window. An hour had crept passed and before her common sense was able to convince her of the insanity which was smothering what intelligence she still possessed, it was too late.

When the silver-haired venerable lawyer stepped into his office and turned to hang his coat, he barely had enough time to catch sight of the glimmering blade clutched in the disgruntled woman's fists. The first fall of the sword cut down into the top of his skull, getting caught in the bone, forcing her to give it a good tug in order to free it so that she may continue. While Nancy was hacking the old man to bits, she recalled all the times she'd day-dreamed about that moment while she was on her knees gazing hatefully up past this man's swollen belly. Although he was way beyond dead, she stabbed the end of the long blade down into what was left of his mouth and said though clinched teeth, "So, how do you like the taste of my…dick!"

265

When she'd finished *chop-chop-chopping* the old man's life away, Nancy stepped over what she had done and poured herself another deep glass of bourbon. Brushing a few stray strands of her blood speckled blond hair out of her face; she glanced slowly around at the teak-wood walls. She felt a sense of self-approval move through her, and as the full force of the summer morning sun beamed in to shine on her crimson re-decoration, she was truly pleased for the first time in her life with something she'd done. *It seems as though I missed my true calling*, she thought as she tossed the last of the drink down her throat, without so much as a slight grimace. Unbeknownst to Nancy as she was stepping over the body heading toward the door with sword in hand, the entire deed had been seen. In the high-rise building directly across from the firm's top dog's office, a middle aged accountant was hanging up the 911 call. For months the lonely book-keeper had been watching some of the naughty goings-on through a big telephoto-lens. He hadn't really expected to catch anything of X-rated interest that early, but figured— why not? and chanced a peek anyway. Man was he surprised.

The firm's newest partner had barely settled in behind his new desk, his head still feeling a little thick from the party, when he was nearly yanked out of his skin by a blood-chilling scream. Promptly getting up to investigate, he swung open the door to his new office to see what the hubbub was about. The young litigator was in time to see a blood-splattered Nancy White straddling what was left of his new paralegal's body. She was finishing up with chopping the thirty something red-head to death when she raised her gaze up from the carnage between her spiked heels. Nancy's eyes shot up the hall and locked on the ass-hole who had up staged her out of a partnership.

Lost in the sight of the horror unfolding right before his eyes, he was trapped in a motionless state of fright. That was until Nancy gave him a blood smeared wink. Like being awoken from a spell with a kiss he shook out of the trance. Grinning up at the office door being closed, Nancy gave the lifeless carcass one more whack before charging up the hallway to finish the job. She slammed into the smoked glass door with the force of an enraged boar. Her body smashed through it as if it were made of rotten news-print. In a shower of shattered glass she rammed into the foolish lawyer attempting to brace his shoulder against the door. Although he out-weighed her by at least forty pounds, he was no match for the momentum of her rage. He slammed backward into the wall and like a frightened dog slid to the floor. Realizing that he would be going the way of all fleshy things, he began to wail pleas for mercy.

"No! No please I, I don't want to die!"

Nancy cocked her head to the right slightly and with an endearing smile on her lips said, "Yes, I know." She raised the sword, its stained scarlet tip scraping the white panel ceiling. The lawyer, not quite prepared to meet his maker, reached out to block, or perhaps grab the falling blade racing to split his skull. The razor sharp weapon would have done exactly that, arm in its way or not, but in the last second she changed the blade's course, sweeping it fast left, cutting off his hand at the wrist. He was in too much shock to utter some sort of painful cry. Pissing on himself, he clutched the bloody stump and whispered, "Please—no."

"Shhhhh," she offered soothingly.

The friendly smile gave way to a wild eyed leer as she swung the blade back up, and without a word sent it down, this time with no intention of altering its direction. Its edge was less than half, of half of a second from cleaving evenly down through the center of his head, when a shot rang out. The top of Nancy's forehead exploded outward in a thick red mist of blood, brain, and bone. The dense vermilion cloud reached out of her skull to beautifully catch the morning light beaming in through the office's round window. The cop's bullet tore into the back of her head and channeled its destructive path out the front, rocketing Nancy White into Hell.

Nancy was laughing like a drunken loon as she chased Peter around the washers and driers, and through the bodies of a few warm souls out for some late evening clothes washing. She swung the sword back and forth, inches away from the back of his fleeing head and neck.

"Give it up!" she advised. "You don't stand a chance! None of you unworthy slobs can beat me. Give it up!"

Peter was too busy running away from the sword wielding bald woman to offer some sort of cheeky retort. While in close pursuit, a feat she was somehow able to accomplish in a skirt cut tightly above her knees and six inch spiked heels, she executed a fast pirouette, swinging her weapon. It raced around with a downward arch and sliced its tip cleanly through his right Achilles tendon. Nancy's cutting action dropped the running Peter flat on his face. The instant the thin lad slammed to the floor he flipped himself around on his back and was immediately blocking and veering away her long blade with his aluminum bat.

Peter Meadows was the hand-picked player for the seventh realm, a fearsome land made up mainly of red crystal, invisible flames and countless souls howling in agony. The title of Peter's prison is the difficult to pronounce name of Beh'tsah. This is Hell's reserved trap for the incorrigibly greedy.

Six years and four months before Peter was chosen to take part in Hell's game, he'd been living his life of thieving and conniving. That was, until he had decided to follow an old homeless man to a modest camp in a densely wooded area at the edge of an Arkansas town. Impatiently, the twenty-two year old Peter watched and waited from the shadows of the trees for the old man to climb into his sleeping bag and pass out. As soon as he heard the man's snores rise out slow and steady, like a misery-whip hand saw being pulled back and forth through a piece of iron-wood, Peter made his move. He crept ever so greedily into the man's camp, its fire still burning bright enough to see the quietest spots to place his feet. With the slow stealthiness of a rat inching its diseased way toward a clump of moldy limburger cheese smeared on a trap, he moved around the sleeping man. The air existing around the old guy was thick with body odor and the vaporous smells of alcohol and tobacco. They grew stronger with every exhale and noticeably weaker with each snored inhale. Peter didn't so much as allow himself to breath as he slowly eased the man's fat wallet out of the boot.

Earlier that day Peter was in the market picking up a pack of smokes, when he caught sight of the old tramp breaking a hundred dollar bill in the check out line. *How the hell does an old derelict come up with that much cashola?* Peter wondered as he watched the man cram the bills into the cracked black leather wallet. Peter was certain that he could find better use for that money than the old bum. So, he spent the rest of that day following the man.

With the wallet in hand, Peter quickly and quietly headed out of the small clearing back into the trees. He was less than a yard from his chosen exit, when a strong hand grabbed ahold of his shoulder. In a voice scarred from a life time of cigarette smoking and rotgut wine the tramp barked, "I ain't thinkin' so!"

Peter was yanked back into the camp and flung down on his thieving ass. By the time Peter had focused past the surprise, the homeless man had already armed himself with a black aluminum baseball bat. Moving toward Peter sitting in the dirt, the man ordered him, "Toss what's mine there boy." He swung the bat down, pointing it at the spread-out bedroll. "Do it, you stupid little shit-head!"

The dwindling fire cast barely enough light up onto the old man's time marked face, allowing Peter to see the depth of trouble he was in, looking down at him from those deeply set eyes. He was in-store for some real pain, and no amount of lies or pleading would change it, so he didn't even try. The would-be thief would need to think of something, and do so fast. Peter did as he was told and tossed the wallet on the sleeping bag. The man's attention left the trespasser, and the moment his eyes were off him; Peter seized his chance. In the short space of time that the man's eyes followed his wallet and reset back onto the thief, Peter grabbed an empty vodka bottle and lobbed it as hard as his fear could invoke straight at the man's head. It shattered in a glittering display of clear glass shards and tiny chips that sparkled as it rained to the dirt in the light of the full moon. The stunning blow dropped the man to his knees, and before he could regain control of his wit, Peter began laying into the man's head with his own ball-bat. Peter hit the bum with that aluminum skull crusher again, and again, and again, killing him swiftly, only to continue beating on the corpse. When Peter was too worn down to further the bashing, the homeless man's head resembled a blood soaked sack, made of torn skin and filled with busted bone, collapsed eyeballs, loose teeth and mashed brains.

Picking up the dead man's wallet, Peter then left that small camp. He went first to his own camp beneath the La Guelle Bridge and washed most of the man's blood out of his hair and off his body. It took three milk jugs of water to get the job done. Then, once he had that out of the way he dug out a filthy t-shirt and put it on, leaving the blood splattered sweater he'd been wearing on the dirt in plain view. The only pair of jeans Peter possessed were the ones he'd worn during the murder. He had tried, although with practically no success, to scrub some of the dried blood off, but less than ten minutes into the chore Peter had given up. With nothing left to do, sporting a smelly shirt and wet, blood-stained trousers, he eagerly went off to spend his new found wealth. At 7:47 the following morning, Peter's drug overdosed corpse was found by some kids taking a short-cut to school. He was sitting up against a wall between two dumpsters. Rats had already eaten out both of his eyes and half of his upper and lower lips; the needle dangling from his arm and the homeless man's wallet still clutched in his fist.

Nancy swept the blade up and around with the swift grace and ease of a master swords-woman. She halted its progress over her head a moment before sending it down. In a last-ditch-effort to remain in the game, Peter rolled himself to the right. With the same dodging movement he spun himself back left, spinning on his butt beneath the flying blade like a break-dancer on the floor. Peter, clutching the bat in his left fist, swung it as hard as his desperation could afford. The sharp sounding *CRACK* of ankle bone being snapped was immediately drowned out by Nancy's loud teeth grinding shriek, which was mostly an out-cry manifested of rage rather than pain. Peter's strike hadn't only sent Nancy's weapon off course, missing his head by a fraction of an inch, it had also broken her right tibia. Unfortunately for Peter, Nancy's resolve was stronger than the pain shooting up her leg. Peter tried scramble up onto his feet, but his Achilles tendon was still in the middle of mending. He crawled away from the woman hopping after him on one high-heel clad foot. Peter might have had a chance if only he would have tried to fight back, but his craven spirit wouldn't permit it. Teetering one legged over the player, Nancy swung the blade back up over her head at the very moment Peter had chanced a glance over his shoulder. Before he could react, she shot the sword's blade down driving it all the way though the center of his back. With a grunt and a hard twist she yanked it out. The howl Peter released was loud enough to be heard all the way back in Hell, informing the Gate Keeper for the seventh realm of his poorly chosen pick for the game.

She stabbed Peter again, this time through his right shoulder. He voiced his pain with a low hiss that sprayed blood out between clasped teeth. Again, she gave the sword a sadistic twist before tearing it out of bone and flesh, and again she drove it in. Nancy swept her steel out of him, and using the blade as a pry-bar; she slid it under his chest and flipped him over. As Peter set his misshapen mask of failure and pain up onto the woman standing over, she replied with a sweetly formed smile.

Able to put some weight on her healing ankle, she slowly raised the antique sword with both hands and dropped its blade fast. From the crown of his head down the center of his skull, clean to his neck, Nancy's weapon sliced his head in two. Both sides flopped limply over to lay cheeks to shoulders. Peter's eyes rolled blindly around in their sockets, until both eventually turned up to sort of focus through the blood, onto Nancy. Her shin bone was nearly healed through and through allowing her to steady herself better. Humming the melody to 'Mammas little baby loves shortin' bread' she sat her weapon down on a washing machine currently in use, and took a tooth from out of the mulberry-colored pouch hanging about her neck. Peter was struggling to sit upright, but could barely manage to lean up on his left elbow. The right side of his split in half head slid off his shoulder to dangle down his back; the left side slipped down to hang over his chest. In a final act of defiance Peter threw the bat at her with a wide, wild swing that missed Nancy greatly and caused him to lose his balance and his elbow to slip out from under him. He flopped to the floor on his back, lying on the right side of his head. Peter was done, he didn't even try to push up again, he merely laid there in a pool of his icy blood and waited.

Nancy was still humming when she let the tooth fly. It twirled and curved in a downward arc. Bouncing off his hip, it landed in the puddle of blood which was already pulling back into Pete's body. The instant the tooth dissolved in the crimson fluid to a bubbling yellowish ooze, hundreds of long shards of glass tore up and pierced through Peter's body from his already split head to his feet. With flashing speed they zipped about, slicing and dicing their razor sharp way through flesh and bone. They swiftly slashed in every direction, racing in a glistening blur of cutting glass and spastically twitching flesh and muscle. Within a matter of seconds Peter Meadows was transformed into a bloody heap of butchered meat and cut bone. When no part of him resembled the breed of being he was, the shards of dagger like glass slid down through the mound of carnage out of sight. As Peter's remains melted down into the white tile floor, Nancy picked her weapon up off the washer and marveled as the blood smeared on its blade raced off to follow the rest of Peter back to Hell.

Queen Vile summoned forth all of the screams that had ever been uttered in anguish within the walls of her dungeons. The collective sounds of suffering hadn't risen up by degrees with gradual steadiness. They came as an explosion of screams, blasting out with all the horror and pain that had brought each and every one of them into being. The force of their howling, icy cold breath swirled around Vile through the black air of her torture chamber deafeningly fast. They swiftly moved to form a single chain of sound translucently embodied in a frantic mixture of colors, wrapped loosely in the foul reek of icy fright and frozen meat; raw and horribly decayed. The reds, yellows, whites and bluish-grays whipped about the huge space for as long as Vile cared to watch the loud, colorful display. Never once altering its volume, steadily maintaining the same ear bleeding pitch. Some took on the shapes and appearance of faces trapped in eternal anguish before melting away back into the frenzied mass of spinning noise and color.

Slowly raising her outstretched arms up from her nude thighs, Vile silently mouthed the word Frow'lock. The swirling screams immediately stopped a few yards in front of her and froze solid in mid air. They became a broad sheet of rice-paper thin ice. Drawing the open palms of her six fingered hands to her lips, Vile gently kissed each hand, and then blew the kisses out onto the sheet of frozen screams. The instant her visibly cold-blue kiss settled on its surface, a vaporous ring spread out from the center until evenly vanishing within the steadily appearing images of Stanley Fiction playing the game, or at least acting as though he was searching for the player in black.

Vile had been watching the events following her players' arrival, and saw how close he'd come to being removed from the game. The slim fact that it was Mr. Fiction who had dispatched Kat and not the other way around, did not make up for him not following orders. Although, she was rather thrilled to see how Stanley managed to recover from what was almost a swift defeat, even if it was by the yellowish skin of his teeth.

Vile had only moments earlier returned from being pulled away to deal with an important matter. If she hadn't been called away she would have seen how close her plan was to being achieved. Stanley had without knowing it slipped away from Alex, who had spotted him creeping into an alley. The former D.A. and the player in black would be forced to wait a bit longer before they would chance to meet.

As with the other eight realm's caretakers, Vile can only see what her player is confronted with, she hadn't missed anything else. Luckily for Stanley, other than his inadvertent dodging of Alex, he'd also successfully avoided the others as well during Vile's absence. But, now the Queen was back in her beloved dungeon, once again intently watching the game with her two devoted servants.

As Vile gazed out onto the dark rainy streets of Corvallis via her icy screen of frozen screams, she reached her right hand up and delicately took hold of the smooth green orb hanging from her right earlobe. Pressed between her thumb and forefinger, she turned the small cold orb up, aiming its still seeing pupil toward the screen and said, "See Vexrile? See how confident my choice moves through that Earthly night."

Reaching her left hand up, Vile took hold of the matching orb dangling from her left lobe and directed its still intact sight up onto its previous host.

"See yourself; see how silly you look Overseer, hanging upside down by your pretty ankles from my ceiling. How does it feel looking like a slab of unskinned meat?" Vile cooed mockingly. "I agree, it's a boo-hoo crying shame." Vile shot Vexrile a sideways look and added coldly, "Yes—yes poor Vexrile, what a foolish creature she's turned out to be. So very ungrateful, so stupidly impulsive. If it wasn't for the fact that I myself am incapable of making mistakes, I might actually place some of the blame upon my own head for trusting a rat eating lesser breed." Vile paused a moment, as if her attention had been for an instant drawn toward a far off noise she alone could hear.

"I was going to give you a world of your own." Vile continued, "To reign over as you saw fit."

Vile had made such a promise to Vexrile on several occasions and would have most assuredly kept her word. Much the same way she'd honored her oath to Vexrile concerning the Overseer's eyes. Vile let go of the soft orbs, and shifted her gaze off the icy screen, resting her full attention up onto Vexrile's naked, broken body. She swept her fist toward the Overseer's direction, and holding it there, opened her clinched fingers, slowly stretching and spreading them out. Vexrile's mouth quivered steadily open. Icy air poured in past her broken teeth to rush through her windpipe, raising her chest with a deep breath.

"Speak Overseer…what do you have to say for yourself?"

A long succession of choking coughs and hacking sounds pushed a flood of blood out of her throat. In a voice fatigued with pain Vexrile spoke, saying, "Please forgive me my Queen."

"Really, and why should I?"

"It was Warfarin, he bewitched me. My will was not my own," Vexrile sobbed.

Vile's attention was finding it difficult to stay with her interrogation of Vexrile. The Queen's focus kept drifting back to the game, only half listening to the strung up Overseer's pleas. She glanced around at Warfarin, or moreover what she'd allowed to be left of him, and said as she looked back at the screen.

"Look at your all powerful sorcerer now Overseer."

There was more to Vile's mocking gesture than verbal cattiness. Vexriles eyes could still see perfectly and send the images they took into her brain. Taking the right eyeball in her fingertips again, she pointed it around onto Warfarin.

"See him up there—he doesn't appear so menacing now, does he?"

"Forgive me. Please my Queen," Vexrile echoed her plea.

"Forgive you! No, Vexrile my dear, what I've in mind for you and your wizard will in no way resemble absolution," Vile giggled softly. "I've got no idea what you saw in him rat eater, tongue stealer. Look at him, do you still see it? Maybe you were bewitched. No matter…my mind is made up."

Vile released the green orb once more, letting it rest, bouncing against her long neck from the ear where it hung. She watched Stanley moving across the screen, making his way from shadow to shadow. He moved through the wet night at a fast stop and go, go and stop pace; not quite at a run and too swift for a walk. More like a sort of spastic creature creeping closer and closer to the side of a sleeping child's bed. He'd ducked into the black air between two houses, and was making his way through the narrow walkway when he stopped and turned a sharp one-eighty.

"What's this?" Vile said under her breath, hoping he had finally caught sight of the eighth realms' player. Stanley brought both Slasher and Slicer out of his jacket pockets as he slithered along the shadowy side of a house. With a razor in each hand he skillfully ejected both blades out with a fast flick of his wrists. Stepping up to a window with light pushing out past its parted drapes, he leaned forward and peered in.

To Vile's disappointment, Stanley hadn't stopped to spy on the player in black before springing out to pounce, or any player for that matter. What had caught his twistedly sick attention was a half nude boy of about seventeen or eighteen years of age. Or rather, the boy's delicious looking skin. It's been a common practice for most of the realms Gate Keepers to release their player from the deep hunger that's swelled within their bellies since they'd arrived in Hell. But not Vile, she left Stanley with the starving need for food, or in his case, human skin. Vile believed it would help him to be a better opponent; that the desire to eat would make Stanley into a sort of juggernaut. She was wrong. Actually all the lingering hunger did was break his focus and slow him down.

With half of his face pressed into the room through the glass, Stanley longingly watched the teenager getting dressed as if he were studying a choice piece of meat. Licking his lips, or at least trying to do so, he ran his cold, dry tongue across his overbite. Unable to salivate, Stanley's tongue was incapable of gliding smoothly over his large teeth, instead it moved with skin catching stickiness. Moving fully into the room, Stanley stepped invisibly next to the thin youth and sailed both Slicer and Slasher's blades through the boy's tender white skin. Vile's player's vain waste of valuable time began with slow, focused sweeps, as if he truly believed they would cut thin slabs of flesh from the young man's back, chest and thighs. But as Stanley realized what he already knew; that his efforts would only prove bloodlessly fruitless, his aimed assault became a wailing display of total loss of control. Tears streamed profusely down his cheeks as he screamed at the unaffected teenager. With wild thrusts and strikes he arced the thin blades in a blur of frenzied sweeps, all of which mocking Stanley Fiction with his own futile attempts to cut himself a bit of raw meat to snack on. Eventually he gave up and let the blades slip from his grasp like quicksilver from his fingers.

Seeing her player drop his weapons, Vile whispered a displeased "No." Stanley was so discomposed he hadn't even noticed that the youth had finished putting on his clothes and had left the room. It was Vile's single word of protest that shook Stanley out of his blubbering state of vulnerability. The word reached out of Hell with the speed of a cracked whip and yanked Stanley up onto his feet. Its whispered lilt stabbed into his skull and raced down through his body like icy claws. His arms swung to his sides, and the second Stanley's hands-sprang open both razors rose up off the floor and shot into his palms. As Vile spoke the words, "Seek out the player in black," softly into Stanley's brain, ice rose out of his skin, covering him in a thin sheet of glistening frost. With a swift wave of her hand he was flung backward through the air, out of the house and onto the street. Stanley leapt to his feet, and of his own steam went in search of the eighth realm's player, his belly rumbling with hunger.

As she watched her player move once again through the night, Vile shook her head with deep disapproval. Not because of Stanley's voyeuristic window peeping or his longing for the taste of raw flesh. No, these things Vile understood and even sort of admired, regardless of his being human. It wasn't even Stanley's weepy show of mortal frailty that vexed the Queen so. It was his complete disregard for his surroundings. The chance he'd selfishly seized, leaving his back open—unprotected, so that a player could come along and spoil everything before B'neem's chosen and Mr. Fiction could square off, was unsettling to say the least.

"It looks as though I need to come up with a way to expedite Mr. Fiction and Mr. Stone's little get together," Vile said softly.

Shifting her attention back around to Warfarin, she asked with a staged giggle, "So Inquisitor, what do you have to say of these stingingly harsh charges Vexrile has made concerning your conduct? Did you in fact trap her within the webs of your will as she claims, or is Vexrile lying in an effort to save herself from what she knows is to come?"

To look at Warfarin one would have believed it impossible for him to be conscious of anything other than physical pain, but he was. Warfarin was completely aware of every agonizing sensation, especially the icy voice of his tormenter. But, even if he would have wanted to answer Vile's senseless interrogation, he could not. His Queen had stitched his mouth shut, running the steel wire through flesh and even bone. She'd employed so much of the metal thread, that the entire lower half of his face was hidden beneath a steel mask of crisscrossing wire and hooks. Only his skull, spine and the remains of a few broken ribs still remained within his skin; the rest of Warfarin's bones had been pulled from the inner meat of his body. All of Warfarin's muscle tissue, arteries, and veins were scraped cleanly from bone and skin. Vile had laid it all on the frost coated floor in a disorganized heap. His head, spine and emptied epidermis draped down, hanging from several large hooks fixed onto the ends of iron chains, that hung from out of holes in the ceiling. Warfarin's fleshy shell resembled a dripping wet banner. The organs that had once been housed within his now flayed skin surrounded Warfarin, each pulsating with lingering life, impaled separately on its own spear, endlessly echoing his failure to be King of the sixth realm. Beating inches in front of his face, the only organ spared from being stabbed onto the end of a lance, was Warfarin's large angel heart. It hovered in place, starving hungrily for blood and longing for death. Blinded by the pain gnashing upon his awareness, he was barely able to see his surroundings. Warfarin's once precious golden eyes rolled in and out of focus, turning in their sockets, all the while silently howling in pain.

"The planet Hell, the Empire, all of the other worlds...even the God's precious Paradise will be mine to do with as I choose." Vile hissed under her breath as she set her crimson eyed vision back to the game. She watched Stanley as he crept through the shadows of the wet Earthly night.

Vile began to laugh aloud.

It was a little after two in the morning. The only warm bodies meandering about on the streets were a few drunken slobs. Poor souls who had at some point during their courseless lives convinced themselves that it was their obligation in life to be the last alcoholics out of the bars at closing. The wind was blowing again, drifting the rain it caught across the roof-tops of parked cars and onto the colorfully painted canvas awnings over the store fronts of down-town shops. Like the beating rhythm of a fast primordial melody, the tiny droplets played their song for the night. The ringing sound of a bottle being kicked or perhaps blown over the street filled the air with the sharp tone of glass skipping swiftly across asphalt. With an abrupt thunk the sound of the rolling vessel stopped. Every so often Alex would hear, and then see, a police interceptor dart past a far off intersection in search of drunk drivers struggling to find their ways home. Alex's ears were drawn onto the steady hum of the huge street sweeper's vacuum and the noise of its spinning brushes growing louder the moment the lumbering machine turned onto Second Street. The sound of foot steps attempting to move quietly over the gravel parking lot spun Alex around to catch the creeper coming up behind him in his cross-hairs. It was the goth girl who'd been attacked with paint-balls. She stepped past Alex, "Shouldn't you be in a warm bed some place?" Alex said in a stern tone.

"She can't see or hear—"

"I know," Alex interrupted Mr. Bane as he followed behind the teenage night-stalker.

"You're wasting time again Alex."

"No, I'm not."

"Yes you are!"

"Shhhhhh—"

"Fine, but don't say you weren't warned."

Alex watched as the dripping wet child in black moved from car to parked car. *She's a jockey-boxer,* he thought humorously as she peered in through rain streaked windows. Stepping up to the passenger side of a bright red 1995 Mazda RX-7, she peeked in and after a moment of inspection, she breathed the word, "Bing-go."

Alex stepped up beside her and silently watched as she slipped the long piece of flat stainless-steel out of her coat's lining, commonly known by criddlers and car-thieves as a Slim Jim. Within a matter of seconds she'd worked the tool down into the door via the window slot and with the first upward pull unlocked the car.

"You're fast," he said as he leaned over to watch her settle into the passenger seat and finger through the C.D. case. Only finding half a dozen she liked, the girl stuffed them into a big pocket stitched to her coat's lining and brought out a pocket-knife. She slid the thin blade into the glove-box key slot. With no more effort than a quick jiggling of her hand and a twist, the lid opened. Finding nothing of interest in the glove-box, she mumbled something that Alex couldn't make out. He lowered to his haunches and watched as she whipped her wet hair out of her pale-white face and criddled through the car. Reaching under the driver's seat, she stopped mumbling and paused a moment as an odd glint sparkled in her eyes. A grin spread over her wide mouth as she whispered the word "Jackpot!" When her hand came back up into the dim light she was clutching a .357, S and W Bulldog.

Alex nearly fell forward into the car as he leaned toward her. Catching himself on the door-jam, he moved his face next to her's and stared at the gun.

"Put it back girl!" he ordered.

"She can't hear you Al—"

"Shut up!" he cut the metallic voice off. "Put it back! Please."

Alex reached for the pistol only to see his hand pass through it. Her inexperienced hands fumbled with the piece for a few seconds, until her cold fingers figured out the puzzle to open its cylinder. Her blue-green eyes seemed to darken when she saw that all but one of the six chambers housed a round.

"I'll show those bitches now!" she said as she clicked the spinning cylinder closed. "Yeah...I'll show you whores in front of everyone. They'll piss themselves. Tomorrow will be my turn in the sun."

"For God's sake child, put it back!" Alex pleaded as she dropped the heavy killing tool in her coat pocket.

"She's on her own Mr. Stone," said the Shade Ellzbeth had employed in the form of the blond boy. He was still in child form and standing on the other side of the car's open door opposite Alex.

"Do something!" Alex snapped.

"I'm not allowed to interfere," the cherub faced little being said sadly as he gazed at the girl rifling through the back seat of the car.

"Bull-shit!" Alex blasted. "She's going to do something horribly stupid! What do you mean—"

"Mind your tongue human…lest it betrays your ability of careful speaking." With an abrupt turn of his head the Shade warned Alex, cutting him off in a voice that sounded anything but child-like.

"Fuck you!" Alex yelled. "I'm not mindin' shit. Don't you see, didn't you hear her? Do something you little fucking punk!"

"Are you finished Mr. Stone?"

"Hell no I'm not—"

With the speed of a bullet, the Shade shot its hand out like a blade through the car door window and drove his fingers into the side of Alex's neck. With a monotone, "Yes…you are." Ellzbeth's baby faced minion tore the seventh cervical vertebrae out of his throat. Alex, still crouching on his haunches didn't have time to blink. He rolled over with the small fist exiting his neck and like a big toy being shut off fell through the open door onto his face.

"The Inquisitor said you would be a lot of fun," the Shade giggled.

Alex was left only with his sight and hearing, the rest of his body was as useless as tits on a goldfish. He couldn't even grunt, or blink his eyes closed. He caught sight of the Shade's sneakers stepping up out of the corner of his eye and tried to follow them as they moved passed, but the feet vanished from his line of vision. Alex heard other steps behind him, crunching on the gravel, and then he heard the car door click quietly closed. He could barely see the faint shadow of the girl's boots move by his head. The sound of her steps on the small rocks drifted away into the darkness, leaving a deep sense of helplessness to settle over him. Not for his own immobile situation, no—it was for her. Alex was being made to watch this child cast herself head-long into Hell's greedily waiting hands, and knew that nothing may be done to stop her.

Without a word, a child-size blood smeared hand reached down and set the vertebrae on the ground less than a foot in front of Alex's face. The blood splattered bone, packed with severed spinal-cord hanging out of both ends, began to melt and bubble, transforming into a thick ooze. The bloody semisolid white mud moved between the small stones toward his neck. Still bubbling like boiling pus, the dissolved vertebrae vanished from his limited line of sight. If a warm soul would have suffered such a wound and lived through it, he or she would be incapable of feeling anything touching them. They certainly would not have felt the icy cold line that Alex felt stream up the side of his neck. The melted bone poured into the hole left there by the Shade's hand and reformed into a vertebrae, the spinal-cord fusing itself back together.

As quickly as it had been snatched from him the power of movement was returned. Before he'd so much as completed his first breath Alex pushed up onto his feet. Rubbing the side of his neck with his gloved fingers and finding the closed wound still a bit tender, Alex growled, "Little bastard."

The Shade was nowhere to be seen and neither was the goth girl.

"I feel for you Alex my boy," Mr. Bane said. "But it's as that little devil said, she's on her own."

"I don't believe that."

"That's too-bad," Mr. Bane laughed. "Suddenly you care. It's a shame you couldn't feel the same for Susan—"

"Fuck off!" Alex shouted.

"You need to listen Alex. Things are as they are. The plight of the living is of no concern of ours; it can't be. Alex, come, lets win this blasted game."

"Fine," Alex said as he stared into the darkness, wondering which direction the girl went off toward.

"What do you know?" Alex asked. "Bane, what do you know about the prize we're playing for?"

"Much, but I'm not at liberty to say."

"Come now old friend, we've no secrets."

"I've got several secrets boy, all of which you could never come to understand. I doubt you would wish to. Now, stop attempting to prod answers, you will get none."

"Did you ever stop and think that if I was to know a little about what we're playing for, that I just might tighten up my focus and—"

"No! Enough Alex, enough!" snapped the metallic voice.

Stepping into the shadows of trees spread heavily over a near by bike-path, Alex picked up his pace. "Very well Mr. Bane," he said in a flat tone. "I'll stop asking." He paused a moment, his eyes scanning through the blackness for a sign of the girl. "No more foolin' around old friend. From this moment forward I'm strictly work."

The knife gave no reply; still Alex knew it heard him.

Alex's steps fell heavily through the rain-puddles, and still he was unable to cause the slightest splash. He remembered how he used to like taking late night walks in the rain. Winter had always been Alex's favorite season. He enjoyed it so much as a boy that he would risk suffering the wrath of his parents by sneaking out of the house when they'd passed out. All night he would wander the streets, these streets, taking in the smells of the wet nights, and feel the icy bite of the cold, loving every second of it. Sometimes Alex would even manage to sneak Susan out with him, and for a few brief hours the nightmare that was their lives would magically transform into a wonderful world of night and clean rain. A place free of pain and screams, a place where only they existed hand and hand, laughing and stomping through rain-puddles.

Waves of regret began to push down on him; Alex tried to pay them no mind but learned that for whatever reason it was too late. He was wishing he'd done more during his life, taken more late night walks in the rain. But most of all, he regretted not going to see Susan. Stopping at the inside edge of a shadow before stepping beneath a street light's beam cast over the bike-path, he attempted to shake off the guilt of his abandoning Susan. Looking around, he was sweeping his vision up toward the tops of the buildings when he caught sight of someone standing on the edge of the Corvallis Hotel roof. Alex stepped into the center of the light in order for the fellow phantom to get a good look at him. The player atop the ten story building dropped his gaze onto Alex right off.

"So much for the element of surprise," Mr. Bane grunted.

"Fuck it!"

"He's a big one Alex."

"Yeah, so what."

"Doesn't he strike you as familiar? Look sharply Alex."

≡ ⑈ ≡

The man on the roof was more than merely another player; he was also someone straight out of Alex's prison past. His name is Napoleon Albert King, and he was as foul a creature in life as he is in Hell's sleepless death.

While Alex was beginning his sixth year in prison, Mr. King was starting his first day of a life sentence. Napoleon King is what mothers and fathers world-wide refer to as; every parent's worst nightmare. In other words, King is absolutely the most fiendish breed of child killing pedophile that ever wore human skin. King had murdered twenty-seven little boys. Although the authorities could only prove and convict King for seven of the murdered children. The other twenty victims he took with him to his grave.

The press had given King the chilly title of 'Dolly Man' because of his leaving a rubber doll's head with the right side of its face burned and melted on the spot where he'd snatched the last seven little boys. For seven months he terrorized the mothers and fathers of Salem in this way. The significance as to the reasons why he left these horrid calling cards was made clear to police the instant they could look him in the face. Like Alex's childhood, King's had also been rife with torturous forms of sexual, physical and mental abuse, all at the hands of his own father. During one of these little father and son get togethers, the right side of King's seven year old face had been horribly burned with a clothing iron. A passer by had heard the boy's pleading screams for his daddy to stop and called the police. The cops arrived to kick the apartment door down in time to stop the fathers' drunken fun before he could begin with the left side of the boy's face. Unlike Alex's adulthood, King chose to follow his old man's foot steps; become something so vile that he easily surpassed his own childhood tormenter by twenty fold.

From the first time Alex had read about Dolly Man he'd begun crossing his fingers for a chance to meet this monster. He kept up on all of the latest news concerning the child killer, beating a child-molester senseless on the prison yard every time he read about another young boy's body being found. When King's reign of terror had finally been brought to an end via his apprehension, Alex knocked the dog-shit out of another child-molester in celebration of King's over-due arrest. He knew it was only a matter of time and King would be showing up on the prison's Death-row. Alex had long since read the passage in the book of Matthew, and in so doing appointed himself the flesh and blood millstone who, in a manner of speaking, ties himself around the throats of those who dare to harm children. After a brief, long distance conversation with Mr. Bane, Alex and his metallic voiced comrade agreed to make King their number one. This meant Alex would need to figure out a way to get on Death-row, an almost impossible feat to accomplish. When Alex read that King had somehow managed to strike a deal for a life sentence without the possibility of parole in order to slide out from beneath the State's lethal injection, he was delighted. This meant King would be placed on the prison's main-line, thus making Alex's task as simple as crushing a sleeping rat with a brick.

With the aid of two of Alex's yard dogs and a female guard, (who also happened to be a close friend with the mother of King's first Salem victim) Alex would give Napoleon Albert King one hell of a prison welcome party. One that the child-killer would never forget. Alex spoke with the so-called shot callers on the yard before doing anything. Not even the Brothers had a word to say in King's defense. All were in total agreement as to what should be his fate.

As soon as Alex was given the proverbial green-light, he put the first phase of his scheme into action. This part of the plan consisted simply of allowing Mr. King to settle comfortably into his own daily prison routine. No one, not a single convict, was to shoot King so much as a hard glance. This part of the plan was necessary for two reasons. One: to let him feel safe enough to drop his guard, resistance to an attack of any degree may draw unwanted attention. Alex needed the deed to go off smooth and swift, without any fight whatsoever. The second reason was that if the security staffer-who's job it is to be abreast of behaviors and situations which may pose a threat to the tranquility of the facility, believe King's safety is in no way at risk; they'll look away.

Most freaks with King's level of notoriety are somewhat reluctant to show their much publicized faces on the yard right off, (if ever). Usually sex-offenders of most all stripes cower in their cells on a sort of self-imposed protective custody. That is of course providing they have a cell-mate who's not irritated by being locked in an eight by five foot box all night and most of the day with a cell mouse who also happens to be a child molesting piece of shit. Not Mr. King though. At six-foot-four, two hundred and sixty-six pounds of muscle with almost no body fat, Napoleon King was an ominous black man. And his hideously scarred face, with its custard colored right eye, gave him an appearance that was in a word, ugly. This being the case, King's arrival to prison and subsequent assent into its population appeared to go without a hitch. The day he arrived, other than a few head nods, no one other than staff gave him a second glance. He went straight to afternoon yard and walked the track, sat on the benches, used the phone, and even stepped boldly onto the iron pile and worked out. His outward demeanor was calm and cool, as if he were a solid convict, doing time on a righteous beef by criminal's standards. King immediately fell into the dull pattern of incarcerated life, exactly as Alex expected he would.

On the morning of King's one-hundredth day in that cold-gray place of walls, bars, and hate Alex moved in to sort of introduce himself to Number One, or at least his intended beginning. King's morning ritual always began with a few fast laps around the yard's track, followed by a bit more stretching. Then ending with him mercilessly smacking a little blue ball against a section of the thirty-five foot high wall that surrounds the prison. The female guard was in her place, high up in the northeast tower, the only tower that could clearly look over the handball court. Alex's two yard dogs were keeping their watchful eyes out for less understanding staff, as well as possible rats clad in blue jeans and t-shirts. When King was done playing his first round of solitary handball, he broke for some water and to take a piss. After a drink from the water-fountain he stepped into the open-air toilet, his bugger boy in-tow.

Alex, who'd been seated on one of the benches enjoying a cup of coffee in the crisp smelling morning air, got up and followed King and his punk into the doorless restroom. Without slowing his pace, the seven inch long shank, lovingly honed on the concrete floor of his cell, slipped down his sleeve into his waiting palm. King's bugger boy shot a half smile up at the swift stepping assassin as he moved aside, clearing the path to King's back. The child-killer was in the middle of shaking out his trickling tool when he noticed his punk moving away.

"Where in the fuck do you think you're going—bitch?" King barked as he half turned, his manhood still in his hand.

The first bite of the welding rod shank sank like a white hot ice-pick through a lump of unprotected fat, catching King with a hard downward swing in the center of the back of his neck. King's body went rigid, then a split second after, fell limp. That first strike was perfect, in that it rendered King powerless. It pierced between two of the vertebrae in his neck, instantly paralyzing him. As King's bowels vacated their solid waste, Alex continued to stab the monster; as Dolly Man lay on the pigeon crap covered ground. Six more times Alex drove the shiv down into King, seven in all. One for each little boy that Alex was aware of.

After punching all of those holes into King's body and successfully getting away scot-free with what some might perceive as an act of violence, all Alex managed to do was transform King into a fully aware mental vegetable. Napoleon Albert King had once again escaped a death sentence—barely. Dolly Man ended up as a bedridden husk of withering flesh in the prison's infirmary, and lingered for two years and four months. That was, until late one night a pair of female hands had not so gently pulled the pillow out from under his head and pressed it down over his face, smothering to death the killer of her best friend's six year old little boy.

And now, King was a player in Hell's prestigious game. Go figure? He'd been chosen by the third realm from out of the eighth. The Gate Keeper for Chemah truly had no clue as to Alex's identity, nor did she have any idea of the history King and B'neem's player shared. Her's was a one in a billion, honest mistake. Unlike Vile's act of treachery to smuggle Ruth Stone into the game.

King's nubian skin, which had been so dark that some of those who knew him well enough, called him by the nickname of Big Blue, was now the color of gray ash. As with all of the other players, his head and body possessed no hair. King was wearing what he'd worn the night of his death, the vomit-green hospital gown with the word, INMATE stenciled in big orange letters across his chest, nothing else. In his left hand with its drawstring wrapped around his wrist was a white leather pouch. In his right fist was a rather large bowie knife, the same weapon he'd used to murder all twenty-seven children with. One might of thought that after two years of being bedridden, King would appear somewhat atrophied and horribly skeletal; but as with the others, his frame appeared to be completely whole. King was as physically healthy as he had been the morning he stepped into that prison-pisser.

King began pacing slowly back and forth on the roof's edge like a caged beast, all the while keeping his attention locked onto Alex.

"It is you…Stone! Well, fuck me running. Hell boy, what you waitin' for? Get your bitch ass up here!"

King moved back away from the edge of the building's roof, out of Alex's line of vision, yelling as he disappeared, "Come get some Stone! Come get what I gave to all those little white boys."

Alex stepped off the bike path at a fast walk toward the back door of the hotel.

"Easy Alex," Mr. Bane advised. "For years this one has done nothing else since his death but scream your name as he gnashed his teeth in torment at the hands of B'neem's Taskmasters. Alex, he's prayed for nothing more than to have a chance at you."

"Good," Alex chuckled hatefully, increasing his pace to a flat out run. Moving onto the hotel's parking-lot, Alex tore through the cold metal of the parked cars like black smoke streaming passed veils of willowy silk. Not slowing, he moved through the locked glass back door into a darkened hallway, only to pass through another locked door into the hotel's spacious lobby. His boots made the sudden transition from the carpeted floor in the narrow hallway to the polished tile at a slight slide. Without needing to stop or even slow his run, he easily kept his footing under his control, while at the same time panning his vision sharply across the dimly lighted space. A young woman was on the sofa reading a book beneath the soft glow of a lamp. The middle aged man seated in his red, high backed chair behind the check in desk had drifted off to sleep, the small hand held labeler slipping from his fingers onto his lap.

Cutting hard, Alex turned up the wide stairs that narrowed on the second floor landing before being blocked by a closed fire-door. Through the solid oak door into the steep stairwell he made his charged ascent. Alex was fairly confident that King would remain on the roof, choosing it as his place to play. Barely breathing heavy, Alex reached the fire-escapes tenth floor landing.

"Easy Alex," Mr. Bane said softly. "This one's chances are few at best, as long as you maintain a strong grip on your rage."

"He kills children," Alex whispered.

"Yes, I'm aware of this Alex."

"But do you know why?" Alex stopped at the door before passing through.

"I've a few theories, why—what's yours?"

"Because to kill a man is not within his reach, little boys possess no threat…King's afraid."

"It sounds good, but don't hold too closely to it Alex."

Alex moved through the door into the tenth floor hallway. Walking passed the closed doors of rooms on both sides of him, he wondered if he should poke his face into each one, but quickly dismissed the idea as a waste of time. He was looking up at the sky-light window as he stepped beneath it and thought he spotted something moving on the roof past its rain speckled, dirty glass. The elevator bell rang out as he passed its metal doors, catching Alex off guard. The single sharp tone spun him about, Mr. Bane tight in his fist ready to cut as the doors rolled open. The young woman who'd been reading in the lobby stepped out of the elevator and moved up the hall. Alex followed closely behind her and glanced down at the book she clutched in her hand. It was a hard bound copy of Dostoyevsky's; Notes from Underground.

"I read that," he said the way a pseudo intellectual might say in an attempt to come off as brainy.

"Focus Alex!" Mr. Bane snapped.

"Only making a little small talk," Alex stated as he walked with her around the corner onto a section of hall that cut left and right.

"Your foolishness will end badly Alex," Mr. Bane warned, a strong note of threat in the tone.

Saying nothing, Alex's attention turned onto a red door at the end of the hall to the left. As the woman cut right Alex, offering no good-bye, moved toward the red door. Seeing no other way that may lead up onto the roof, Alex figured this padlocked passageway must be it.

"Wait Alex."

"What for? He's up there!"

"Possibly, but if so, why give him the advantage?"

Alex chuckled, "He's up there for sure, and as for giving him some sort of advantage by meeting him face on…well, he'll need it." Alex stepped out of the dim hallway through the red door into darkness nearly as deep as Hell's blackest air.

"Your confidence is impressive Alex."

"Thank you," Alex whispered as he reached out to find himself in a very cramped stairwell. It only took a few tense seconds for his vision to adjust. By the time he'd placed his boot on the first step, he had not only been able to make out the door at the top of the narrow flight of stairs, he also saw that the space was empty. King wasn't hiding in the darkness waiting. Alex wouldn't have admitted it, not even to himself, but he'd been hit by a wave of apprehension that had about sent him swiftly back stepping out of that darkness. If not for King's challenge playing in his head over and over again like some teeth grinding tune repeating itself. *"Come get some Stone! Come get what I gave to all those little white boys,"* he might have backed out of that stairway.

Coming to the top step, Alex reached his gloved fingers out, pressing them through the cold metal of the locked access door to the roof. Pausing a moment he helped himself to a deep breath, then with no further delay stepped swiftly through the door out onto the roof. Between the time he'd ran into the hotel and his moving through that door into the open air, the rain had gone from a misting drizzle to a light shower. The wind had picked up again as well. There was also a needling chill cutting swiftly in the air, it caused the tiny drops of falling water to sting coldly like grains of frozen sand being whipped about. The diminutive missiles of moisture shot into Alex's face and found their irritative way behind his up turned collar, to stream naggingly down his face, neck and even beneath his already soaked sweat-shirt.

The air smelled strongly of wet dust and old tar. The roof was equipped with all the usual hotel roof-top fixtures. Miles of black cable, running in a labyrinth of directions wormed out of sight into metal conduits that in-turn, bent and vanished into the black-ice looking surface. A large satellite dish aimed its proboscis-like receiver up toward the black-iron sky. There were a dozen or so red clay and metal vent pipes protruding up out of the cracked tar. Some television and radio antennas reached out hungrily to catch sound and picture waves, dining on the images and noises greedily like baby birds. A few yards from the red-brick stairwell shack Alex had stepped through was the skylight he'd walked beneath. There was enough light pushing up through its dingy glass for Alex to see his elevated surroundings. Other than the stairwell shack and the satellite dish there was nowhere to hide.

The moment he stepped onto the roof Alex scanned his sight across the shiny black surface. Seeing no sign of King in the open, he spun about; snapping his search up, certain he would find his prey on the shack's small roof preparing to pounce. Empty; the child-killer wasn't there; he didn't appear to be on that roof at all. Stepping scrupulously while maintaining his expeditious pace, Alex moved around the brick structure, shooting swift glances left, right and behind him. He saw no one; that roof appeared to be as empty as the red desert Pike had made him walk through. *I missed the sonofabitch*, he thought as he stepped toward the edge of the roof, looking behind the satellite dish as he passed it.

"No, Alex," Mr. Bane said, "I don't think so."

"What's that?"

"I'm not certain, but I believe our old friend to be close by."

"Still up here?"

"I think...yes, I believe so."

"Where?" Alex asked through clasped teeth as he peered over the edge to see if King was clinging to the side of the building.

"I'm not sure Alex, but step easy."

Walking slowly along the edge, Alex saw only empty air and the dark alley below, King had vanished.

"I fear old friend, that this time you may be wrong," Alex said, his eyes moving across the roof.

"I sense him near Alex."

"Well, I've searched and I'm here to tell you, the freak's not up here. The fucking chicken shit ran away."

"He's here Alex!"

"No he's not—look, see for yourself." Alex raised Mr. Bane up, outstretching his arm and slowly sweeping it around, showing his blade the empty space. Suddenly the shower became a full-out rainstorm. The wind grew stronger and more frigid. It bullied its way into the game, blowing the deluge at an almost perfect sixty-five degree angle. For a few seconds the wind would carry the large droplets left then blow them right, only to follow the erratic shifting water display by sending the storm straight into Alex's face. His fedora was snatched off his head as if by an unruly child. He rocketed his empty hand after it, but the storm must have really liked that old hat, because it was faster than his reach. "Shit house luck!" Alex cursed as he watched his hat get swallowed up by the darkness toward Second street. The storm dropped out of the sky and slammed onto the roof with such fury, that

Alex begun to wonder if it was Hell sent. He attempted to shield his face with his forearm as he headed toward the stairwell.

"There Alex, see it?"

"See what?"

"Over there, on the skylight's windowpane," Mr. Bane trumpeted. "It wasn't there a moment ago."

Alex visored his brow with his left hand, slowing his exit as he looked in the skylight's direction. Something was on the glass. But the screen of rain was too dense for him to see the white object clear enough to make-it out. Deciding to have a closer look-see, he put off leaving the roof and made his way toward whatever had Mr. Bane in an up roar. Alex was less than ten feet from it, when at the exact moment that he realized what the object was Mr. Bane shouted, "Its King's pouch of teeth. Now why do you suppose he would allow himself to relinquish something so utterly necessary?"

Alex, seeing that it was King's pouch swept his vision around the whole of the roof. Seeing nothing that looked even remotely like a trap, Alex figured King must have dropped it on his way down through the skylight.

"Careful Alex," Mr. Bane said. "It reeks of a trap."

"I agree, but from where?" Alex replied as he approached the flat window. Again he panned his sight back across the empty roof. Stopping at the skylight, he looked around once more and seeing nothing but rain, reached down to pick the white bag of teeth up.

"No Alex!" snapped Mr. Bane. "It's not permitted."

Alex straightened his back as he spun his attention around the instant he heard the (No Alex!) part of Mr. Bane's barked warning, thinking that it was a call to arms. Seeing that it wasn't, and catching the (It's not permitted) part of the warning, Alex growled, "Don't do that!" Looking back down at the pouch he asked, "How do you know it's not allowed? Just how long did you and that little red haired weirdo Pike spend together anyway?"

"Truth is Alex my boy, the Gate Keeper called Pike has no knowledge of my existence except as a symptom of your insanity. What I know of this event Pike calls a game, I know from my own experience. What I do not understand is why you insist Alex on questioning what I say?"

There was a noticeable note of disdain clinging to Bane's tone. "Do as I say boy, do not touch that pouch," Mr. Bane hissed.

Alex, not sure if he was being warned or threatened, eased defiantly down to his haunches, resting his forearms on his wet knees.

"This pissing-match between your will and that of my own ends here and now Alex."

Alex said nothing, he looked down at the pouch increasing his grip on his only friend's—bone handle.

"Very well Bane…you call the shots, I'll follow. Is that what you wish to hear?"

"Yes."

"Then you got it—" Alex paused then added, "But understand this. I've got questions, and when this craps over, I will be demanding some answers."

"If we get out of this as champions, I'll answer all of your questions." This time Mr. Bane paused, then in a calm tone of voice said, "Behind you Alex."

King rose swiftly up out of the roof's shiny black surface, less than four feet behind Alex. He'd been beneath the roof's timbers, pipes and wires, listening eagerly to Alex's steps vibrating over head. He also heard Alex talking with Mr. Bane. Of course, King was unaware of the relationship between Alex and the dagger, leaving Dolly Man with but one explanation; the man who had attacked him from behind in that prison pisser was insane.

When Mr. Bane had ever so calmly voiced King's appearance coming up from behind, Alex was still studying the white pouch on the glass. So, at the very instant the metallic voice spoke up, Alex caught King's faint reflection emerging like a weed out of black mud. Alex sprang up from his squatted position, spinning about at the same time and coming face to face with King.

It is up to the Gate Keeper for the realm a chosen player is picked from, what parts of the mortal's body will be mended for the game. If the Gate Keeper wishes that all of their player be healed, then it is done. Truth is it really doesn't matter what state a player's physical condition is in, he or she could be left in a state of skeletal rot and still they would possess the same strength and speed as the lead player. The Gate Keeper for the third realm chose to heal all but King's horribly scarred face. She did however give his yellowish right eye the power of sight, not wishing her chosen to be handicapped with a blind spot.

The moment Alex came about, he saw the large knife racing down toward him. Catching King's wrist in his fist, he stopped the weapon's descent and with a loud grunt that gave voice to his intent. Alex sent Mr. Bane's blade up, thrusting it into King's gut with a throaty chuckle, "Fuck, you're an ugly nigger!" Alex shoved all ten inches into King's stomach, slamming the knife's hilt hard against his cloth covered skin.

"A bit like old times," Alex hissed through his teeth.

"Fuck you!" King growled as he slid his grip off of the hand locking the blade into his guts, and sent it like a brick against the side of Alex's head. It was a solid blow, but not enough to loosen the hold Alex had on his wrist. Alex pulled Mr. Bane's blade back a few inches only to ram it home again, this time adding a bit more twist to the thrust. King punched Alex again, and again it did no good.

"Get back you blue-eyed devil!" King shrieked in a broken voice filled with mucus and blood. Realizing that Alex's skull was too thick to have any effect on him with a clinched fist, King latched onto Alex's throat and tried to squeeze it closed. Alex, keeping the blade in the man's stomach, went to force him back in an attempt to walk King off the roof. But no sooner had he gone to put his plan into action, and King spit in Alex's face as he lurched back. Alex shoved the blade into the retreating midsection as he tried to flex his neck muscles against King's tightening grip.

Then, quite unexpectedly King head-butted Alex hard, and with a guttural yell he threw himself forward into Alex. King's maneuver upset Alex's footing, toppling him backward over the edge of the skylight's low metal sill. Alex, with his weapon still sunk deep in King's abdomen, and still maintaining his hold on the child-killer's knife hand, fell. As they dropped toward the large window, Alex was able to twist his head around, his neck clasped in King's fist, to see where the fall was taking him. The swift shifting of his vision from King's yellow and brown eyes to the skylight paid off. Instead of crashing down through the metal and glass, they were able to drift through it. The two players hit the floor solidly with a loud bang only they and those watching in Hell could hear. Alex was beneath King, who was still squeezing his throat.

Mr. Bane's tip pierced a full two inches out of King's back on impact with the floor, and Alex had managed to still keep his grip on King's wrist. All the air in Alex's lungs was sent rocketing out past the hand crushing his windpipe closed.

He didn't wait for his lungs to try and refill, he immediately began the struggle of fighting King off of him. King's hold on Alex's throat was impressive, to say the least, and was steadily growing stronger, but not as impressive as Alex's grip on King's knife hand. Not having any luck forcing his wrist free, King began trying to force his big knife's blade down into Alex's face. Alex was at a bit of a disadvantage, with King on top and the point of his blade only a few inches away from being pushed into his skull.

"I believe I've done all the damage I can do in here Alex," Mr. Bane said in a muffled voice. "What do you say to bringing me out of this monster's entrails so that I may try my luck somewhere else…say for instance, his throat?"

Alex, too busy to offer up some sort of reply, was considering letting go of Mr. Bane's handle so he had a free hand to begin beating against King's face. The bowie knife was shaking slowly closer to Alex's right eye. King's fist was successfully choking off all of Alex's air now; his head was beginning to feel thick with pins and needles. He could feel his eyes bulging in their sockets. The hollow sound of his heart beating pounded in his skull.

It was King who was snickering through gnashed teeth now as the tip of his weapon inched closer. The blade's point was a frog's hair from scraping the skin of Alex's eye. He didn't dare close his eyelid though, or even attempt to move the soft orb's blurred focus. With his choices few, he let go of Mr. Bane and struggled to pull his right hand out from between them. With the help of a half-assed second wind, Alex was able to shove the lowering blade back up a few inches; he wriggled his fist out and slammed the lead-beads in his sap-glove into the side of King's head. The blow was effective, in opening a deep gash on the scarred half of King's face above his yellow eye.

With rapid succession Alex delivered three more, much harder blows to King's face, the first one busting his nose, the second knocking him back some and the third loosing his grip on Alex's neck. As King's upper body was lifted up by the second punch, Alex swept his hand back down and sliced Mr. Bane out of King's guts. It was actually Mr. Bane's bone handle crashing into the right side of King's jaw that convinced the child-killer into letting go of Alex's throat on that third blow. King's hand was blindly grabbing for the fist before it could land a fourth strike. But it wasn't a punch Alex had in mind. With Mr. Bane's blade back out in the open, Alex sent its steel up between King's wildly swinging block, and with a hard thrust drove it into the right side of his neck. With a howl that was not unlike the ear piercing shriek of a dying pig, King voiced his strong disapproval to being shanked a third time by this man. The high pitched cry had led the way for a flood of lifelessly cold blood. The thick fluid splashed out and landed in Alex's face an instant before he'd thrown King off of him. King scrambled away, getting to his feet while Alex did the same, wiping away the blood obscuring his vision.

Alex cleared the blood from his eyes in time to catch sight of King vanishing through the red door leading back up onto the roof. Alex remembered King's white pouch. As he ran after the child-killer, Alex glanced up and saw that the bag of teeth was still there. Somehow it avoided being pulled through the glass along with the two falling men. Alex flew after him, through the door and up the steps. Like an explosion of black shadows Alex burst through the metal door back into the howling wind and rain on the roof. King was already leaping back down through the skylight, snatching his pouch off the glass on his way down. At a running jump Alex followed after King. His boots slamming down flat-footed in the same spot where he'd landed a moment ago. Alex ran through the old hotel's dimly lit corridors and even a few dozen rooms, but he kept coming up empty. Dolly Man had either found a really good hiding place, or he'd left the building all together.

In a room which had been occupied by the sleeping shapes of a thin little man and a very large woman, Alex stood at the window looking out into the night. As he studied the black silhouette of the tree line, Mr. Bane's voice said, almost at a whisper, "There Alex, down on the bike path."

Alex lowered his gaze, and standing practically on the exact same spot where Alex had been when he'd seen King on the hotel's roof, was a shadowy figure. It was the child-killer.

"Hurry Alex, go after him," Mr. Bane directed.

Alex turned from the window and was on his way out of the darkened room. He was stepping past the bed with the two juxtaposing shapes when the large one blasted out a loud fart, followed by three quieter squeaks from her rotund ass. The little old man beside her rolled over to face Alex's direction as he stepped toward the door, and the expression in the man's eyes was murderous.

Alex left the room.

Chapter Seven

— Spy —

From shadows the
creepers peek, for
secrets to glean and
sneak.
They slither and slide,
stealing that which you
hide.
These creepers, these prowlers,
these sneaks.

The Me
—Back Stabbers

After carrying Sader thousands of miles from B'neem deep into the center of Zaw'naw, the spy's winged mount was directed down, out of the red vaporous sky. It was as soft a landing as a stone sinking to the bottom of a lake after being skipped half way across. Despite their bumpy descent over sharp rocks and icy ground, Sader's beast slowed to a well controlled stop. The place where the Overseer chose to land was safely isolated at the bottom of a steep rise of ice laden black stone. Several mounds of human and angel bones were neatly stacked on either side of a wide well worn road that ran straight up the mountain side. The road had also been lined with the bodies and severed heads of frozen men and woman impaled on iron shafts and spears. Only their eyes moved behind clear sheets of ice, or at least those of them that still possessed eyeballs in their skulls watched as Sader dismounted. Placing his vermilion hood back up over his cold, bald head, he then motioned with a slow wave of his hand for his beast to lower its massive head so that he may speak into its ear-hole.

"You'll wait for my return over there," Sader whispered as he pointed at a large mound of rocks and discarded bones. He continued, "If the petals upon this rose." Sader held out his hand, and a dark red rose materialized pinched between his thumb and forefinger. Again he continued, "If it begins to wither away, its petals fall to dust before your very eyes, go straightaway back to B'neem and seek out Ellzbeth." Sader laid the blood-red flower gently on his beast's waiting palm "…Ellzbeth will know what to do."

He patted his winged beast on its lumpy white head, much the same way a young boy might pat a dog. "Now go…go and keep your head down, your eyes wide and your ears and nose open."

Sader stood watching as his big lumbering beast crawled off without so much as a farewell glance back over its shoulder. Ducking behind the hiding place it was instructed to take, the great beast laid on the frozen ground and locked its bronze colored beady eyes onto the rose and waited.

With no further delay, the little armor clad spy turned and begrudgingly began the steep hike to the top of the mountain. It was an unpleasant, toilsome march over the sharp rocks and slick black ice. What made the climb even more disagreeable was that his freedom to wield his powers of will and magic were greatly limited. With each step up that slope Sader wished he could simply will himself directly into Vile's palace, restrain her and torture the proof he sought out of the scheming creature's screams. But Vile was far too powerful an angelic force for even Sader, the Overseer for B'neem, to challenge on his own. Especially against her while she was wrapped within the icy darkness of her palace. Vile would be expecting B'neem to retaliate against her treachery. She'd be waiting to sense any great deployment of power not of her realm, and she'd loose her Sentinels once she was conscious of his presence. Or worse, Vile would come for him herself. No, stealth was the answer to being successful in this endeavor. And if magic must be employed, it would have to be sparingly and shielded to the best of his ability.

The steep climb ended at the top of an apex made solely of black ice. Atop this frozen rise was an enormous megalith constructed of clear blue crystal. It was one of three marking-stones, one placed like this before each of the city's three entrances. A red stone, a violet stone, and this blue stone before Sader. Other than their contradistinction of color, they were all three the same in size, shape, translucent hue and each incased bodies. Trapped within each megalith were nine women. Like insects engulfed in hardened tree sap they hovered motionless. Their eyelids and lips were sliced off of their faces and a different word had been carved deeply across each of the women's bellies. They were positioned in such a way that the words formed a grisly welcome sign which read when translated to mortal tongue:

Suffering for all, and pain eternal. Hail Queen Vile.

Sader spit on the welcome-stone as he moved past it to duck down behind one of many toppled over red granite pillars. Carefully, he peered around the broken edge of the ancient stone. At the bottom of the mountain was a wide ravine that he knew to be as good as bottomless. On the other side was Ebla, Vile's city. Behind Ebla's six-hundred foot high iron and stone wall surrounding this ancient metropolis raised a great mountain of ice and rock. Littering these steep, jagged slopes were tall and wide buildings made of blackened iron, aged with rust colored ice. Like thick hairs reaching up out of the stone, metal, and glass, millions of impaled and crucified bodies rose from the bridges and roof-tops for winged creatures to nibble on.

Columns of dense smoke as black in color as the emptiness in a murderer's heart billowed up out of giant smokestacks and chimneys. Elba resembled images of London during the birth of its industrial period, vomiting foul blackness into the sky. The smoke pouring out was the embodiment of relentless suffering. Housed within its pitch black vapor were the end results of the agonizing goings-on in Elba's mountain city. The thick stink of roasting flesh and burning bones filled the air with the reek of charred rot and festered meat.

Even at Sader's distance, the sound of the screams streaming out of the black mountain brutally reigned over the atmosphere, filling his ears with their endless song of damnation. It would take no less than a hundred-thousand years of ceaseless wind and rain to cleanse this place of the putrid stench permeating all things within those walls. If the crimson space surrounding Vile's city were to be rendered still, it would require a count of centuries far removed from mortal measure to stifle the reverberating echo to silence. The black pillars of smoke drifted up passed the petrified remains of a colossal warrior cherubim slain during the second war by Vile's own army. Some say it was Vile herself who delivered the killing blow and that she'd been laughing at the time. This fossilized reminder of the planet Hell's beginning lay in the very spot where it had loosed its last breath. And now the stone-like flesh and bones of this fallen soldier served as the foundation for Vile's palace. The Queen's abode reached up out of the mountain's pinnacle like rusted blades of steel, stone and glass to overlook the city below.

Linking Sader's side of the canyon to the other side was a bridge of sorts. It stretched through the cold air without the aid of ropes or cables. No rods nor iron beams held its line straight. Although it wasn't among the Empires prominent sights or wonders it was spoken of quite often in conversation during gatherings as being truly an original concept. What gave Vile's footbridge its notoriety was that she herself had built it and the materials she chose to construct it with were never before used in such a manner. Vile made her bridge solely out of severed human heads, all of which she chopped off her self to methodically hand-place them in a somewhat straight row, hovering on the icy emptiness of thin air. Alive and of course suffering, these bodiless souls were not spared the discoloring effects of decay, all of the heads displayed advanced signs of putrefaction. This single-file row of rot and slime stretched across to the other side, ending at the giant cloven hooves of a gargantuan sentry with deep, indigo blue skin.

Sader knew crossing Vile's so-called bridge unseen without the aid of his powers to be an impossible feat. He considered turning around and going to see if either of the other two ways in would appear less risky, but decided to stay and try here. After a brief moment of contemplation Sader made the decision to chance a relatively minor spell, combined with another spell to try and conceal the first. Concealing spells are only effective when the being an angel is attempting to hide from is of minimal wit. Sader knew this gate-guard to be among that breed, he would have no trouble concealing his magic usage from the big creature. Vile on the other hand was something else to consider. If she was scanning the sixth realm for outside powers within its boundaries while

Sader was wrapped in his spell, She would sense it and be on him before he knew it, but it was a chance the silver-eyed spy was willing to take.

Ducking back behind the fallen stone pillar, Sader chose a spell which would generate a minimal amount of B'neem's energy. He swept his hand once passed the dark opening of his hood. The impenetrable shadow that shrouded beneath its wide visor poured out like a thick liquid to engulf his four foot frame entirely. Once he was hidden in shadow, Sader whispered, "Va'new." The black fog swiftly sank, being drawn into the seams of his metal boots, leaving no visual clue to his presence; Sader had rendered himself invisible.

He waited a bit before heading down the slope, watching the gate-guard as well as glancing up at Vile's palace, although he was dead-certain that if she did sense him, he wouldn't have time to see her coming. *Vile loves the game,* Sader thought. *She's no doubt engrossed in it,* he hoped.

Seeing no change in the gate-guard's demeanor, Sader stepped out from behind the stone and made his way down to the edge of the cliff. After an hour of carefully placing his steps, all the while silently cursing himself for wearing his armor, he reached the foot of the mountain. He'd oiled all of the squeaks out of his battle-wear before leaving B'neem, and other than some slight jingling of his metal chain-mail his attire made no noise. That is all but the sounds his metal boots as they crunched down on ice and stone. It was for this reason that his descent down the mountain took so long. Although, Sader was grateful for the steel cleats fixed to their soles. If not for the tiny spikes he would have found his hike down the slope a slippery one for sure.

At the edge of the cliff, Sader gazed out across the row of ice incrusted heads. There was two and a half, perhaps a three foot gap between each one and barely enough room to place a single foot, much-less two. Raising his overworked attention up onto the gate-guard on the other side, he hoped the blue giant's napping appearance was genuine and deep. Without permitting himself the luxury of reluctance Sader dropped his sights onto the skull-cap and began to cross. Like a small boy hopping from slime covered rock to slime covered rock in order to get across a wide stream, he skipped with fast, wide steps from head to head. The magic Vile had employed to set her bridge in place was as strong as iron cable. The hovering heads didn't move a hair under

Sader's leaping weight, his steel cleats biting down through ice, rot, and bone on impact with each crown as they helplessly watched him cross. There was no room for error in this death-defying hopscotch game. Cleats or no cleats, one off center placement of his boot and he would fall. Falling would leave him no choice but to use more of B'neem's power to catch himself. Vile would certainly pick up his presence. She would most-likely pin-point him as he dropped and pluck him out of the air as easily as pinching a speck of dust off of a sheet of ice.

Sader was little more than half way to the other side when the gate-guard changed his position from lethargically leaning against his iron spear to an abrupt state of readiness. The guard's narrowing eyes followed his nostrils to Sader's cloaked position. Leaning down some he grunted, sniffed the air and leered at the empty bridge. Again the blue monster smelled the cold, squinting his scrutiny over the hovering heads.

Without standing, he swung his spear widely toward the bridge. Sader, who had stopped, was teetering on one foot, balancing as steady as a statue on a frozen skull-cap with most of its skin peeled back. The rusty blade, which was three times Sader's size, swooped down with an air slicing noise straight toward the invisible spy. *I perhaps should have thrown in a scent concealing spell,* he thought as the huge hunk of metal raced his way. Sader leapt up from the head high enough to avoid the spear skimming between his feet and the bridge. Half an instant after the blade tore past he came down with one foot squarely atop the next head. Almost as soon as the steel cleats clasped onto the small frozen surface the spear was on its way back down. Timing was everything. Sader watched as the guard's spear-head whistled straight toward him for another go. Once again he jumped; easily avoiding the rusty blade's desire to cleave whatever the guard thought he smelled in two. It zipped past, pulling with it enough wind caught in its wake, to shift Sader's leap and alter his landing. He came down faster than he'd gone up, his boot missing the following head completely.

With less than a second to react, Sader reached out his hand and latched onto the open jaw-bone of the next head as he dropped past it. Resisting the panic driven impulse to call upon more of the eighth realm's power, and at the exact instant that the jaw-bone tore loose in his grip, he swung to the proceeding mandible hanging slack. Like a child swinging across monkey-bars in a play-ground he went from head to head. The blue skinned giant's spear swept back and forth a few more times, skimming mere inches above the bridge before finally stopping its air cutting search. The gate-guard had come to believe the odor he was smelling was simply some of B'neem's stench caught in the wind. He was in the process of leaning against his great spear again, awaiting his napping sleep to settle over him, when he heard how wrong he'd been.

Sader, coming to the last few heads, flung himself up onto the canyon's other side. Unfortunately his landing was no where near as graceful as his acrobatic maneuver across, and beneath the bridge. With a grunt and a loud crashing made by his armor hitting the hard, frozen ground he touched down, rolling to a noisy stop only a few yards from the guard's right hoof. Hearing Sader's loud landing the giant stood and immediately began stomping his hooves on the spot where he'd heard the racket. Growling angrily he crashed his heavy hooves down, each stomp ending with a loud *bang!* Again and again the guard attempted to squish the unseen spy beneath his large cloven foot, but Sader was too fast for his efforts. He was finding the desire to transform the blue giant into a tiny cockroach difficult to resist as he dodged the crashing hooves. Struggling to remain on his feet, the ground shook violently with each stone shaking stomp. To make the task of getting past the giant even more arduous, the angry gate-guard began stabbing the tip of his spear down. Vigorously he jabbed the large pointed blade onto the hard ground, raising sparks as iron struck stone. Like a blind spear-fisherman trying to impale a tiny gold-fish that was purposefully taunting him, he fought to pierce the unseen spy. Sader ducked, dodged and rolled his way past the thrusting spear and between the huge crashing hooves through the gate-less entryway into the city.

Ebla's busy streets immediately caught Sader by surprise, he'd expected most of Zaw'naw's populous to be watching the game, but learned to be wrong. The streets and walkways were packed. All breed of lesser beings, from demons to houris, were either dragging cages bursting at the seams with damned souls, or leading carts filled with cursed men and women, being drawn by the same. Huge demons staggered drunkenly in and out of buildings, some falling into doorways or onto the street while others fought one another.

Sader had barely made it through the gate and begun searching through the horde for the swiftest and easiest way up the mountain into Vile's palace, when his situation's intensity increased by ten fold. The giant he'd barely managed to slip past blew his horn, sounding the alarm to the presence of an intruder. Suddenly the wave of demonic and angelic beings stopped dead in their tracks. All at once every creature in the city, even the damned souls, began to turn their attention up toward Vile's palace and howl. The enormous blue dome atop the palace steadily started to glow brighter, its icy hue pouring out of its glass and iron to bleed down the mountain. Like an ultramarine flood the light spread through the buildings and streets, filling every pit, and reaching into the thinnest of cracks.

The wailing went silent and the horde broke into a running mob, arming themselves and leaving their damned charges on iron hooks fixed to the walls of every building. The cities' nightmarish populous was on the hunt for the spy. Sader, maintaining his wit as best he could, tried desperately to make some sense out of the maze of crowded streets and towering structures. He'd only been to Ebla twice, both times with Pike, and they could use their powers to help lead the way up the mountain. Sader was completely lost. Stopping briefly in order to catch his breath, he darted out of the way of the rushing mob of armed Sentinels running straight toward him. Ducking into an alley and nearly getting trampled by yet another horde of yelling Sentinels pouring out onto the wider street, he pressed flat against a wall. As he rested, Sader looked up and saw that the blue light moving down the mountain would soon be on him.

Sader hadn't had much of a plan when he'd first set out on this quest. He figured he would simply take things head on, as they came—face the worst and hope for the best. Well, here it was, coming straight toward him in waves of ugly…the worst.

He knew it would only be a matter of time before one of the sixth realm's tormenters, a guard or Sentinel running past him, would be empowered with the ability to see beyond his invisibility spell. Or worse, Vile's glowing blue flood would reach him. Sader shoved away from the wall. He ran out of the alley back into the street, weaving in and out around the legs feverishly, all the while scanning his surroundings for the fastest and safest way up the mountain. He was about to give up and transport himself back to where he'd left his beast when he found what he was looking for. On the other side of a scaffold filled with hundreds of bodies hanging by hooks and ropes was a lightless drainage pipe cut smoothly into the black stone. By the time he'd reached the tunnel's opening and slipped in, the blue light was half way down the mountain. He waited until he'd gone deep enough into the dark space, and was certain no one was following before shedding the invisibility spell. He pulled his scimitar sword out of its sheath hanging over his shoulder and melted deeper into the darkness.

The heavy downpour had mellowed once again to a light, almost nonexistent sprinkle by 3:30 in the morning. A stray dog, mangy looking and appearing desperate in a wolfish sort of way caught Lord Buddy Zib's attention. Slowing its pace to a stop, the drenched beast leered across the parking lot back at Buddy as it attempted to shake some of the water out of what fur still sparsely covered its ash-colored hide. He was sent back by the animal's ill fated expression, deeper into the shadows being cast by the University's football coliseum as if to conceal himself from the creature's hateful look. For a moment Buddy thought the dog might move closer for a better look at the visitor from Hell. He readied himself in-case the homeless mutt decided to illustrate its fanged disapproval over Buddy's presence within the plain of existence reserved primarily for souls still wearing warm flesh. But the skinny beast didn't approach the man watching it from the shadows. Instead, it bared its teeth and growled at him as it vanished into the thick darkness of the tree line on the far side of the parking lot.

From the moment he'd agreed to participate in the game Buddy had been tirelessly searching for the others. He was having no luck at finding so much as a shadow of a player and was beginning to have doubts in his ability to keep his oath; after all—how could he hold true to his word and win if he couldn't find someone to win against? By his sixth hour of hunting and coming up empty, Buddy had taken to move about out in the open. Walking up and down the middle of streets, even shouting out insults and challenges, but the only beings that seemed to see and hear him were the dogs locked in gated backyards, barking and howling out angry replies, and Hell's voyeurs. He'd even gone so far as to climb up onto the flat roof of a five story campus dormitory and openly sit, waiting—hoping to be spotted by one of his playmates. Buddy sat on that roof in the pouring rain; rain that unlike Alex, had no affect on him, for all of two hours and nothing. Passing through the chain-link fence surrounding the huge football stadium, he'd begun wondering if the others had even been sent through yet. *Perhaps they sent me through early,* he thought. *Or maybe the others had already lost to one another. Maybe there's only myself and one other player left?* Panning his vision around before stepping into the darkness of the empty stadium, he smiled privately and said under his breath, "I hope if that's the case, that the player I'm left with is a tasty sweet." He melted out of sight into the lightless, spacious, almost cave-like reception area and after moving in a few yards, paused and listened. Buddy's ears were drifting out beyond the rain run-off dripping with echoed impact onto concrete surfaces, listening for the slightest sound that might, or might not be breathing. Moving toward the exit, the sound of steel being swiftly swept across cold concrete spun his attention around to face the way he'd came. The unmistakable noise made by a woman's steps moving fast in hard-heeled shoes turned him around again.

"If you're a player speak out please," he yelled. There was a long moment of silence, only the steady drip of rain water reaching out through the stillness. Finally the tense quiet was shoved aside by the hollow clicks of slow steps moving away from him.

The pace of the steps slowed even more as the softly spoken words of a woman said, "Fishy fishy in a brook," the voice paused as did the steps. Again he heard the sharp sound of steel being swept swiftly over concrete. "Daddy caught you on a hook."

"How many have you sent packing?" Buddy asked, his tone friendly and eager like someone attempting to strike up a conversation with a stranger in a pub. "I've laid five players to waste," he lied proudly as if he believed the falsehood himself.

"Liar," replied the woman's voice past her own giggling. She continued her odd little rhyme, all the while giggling like a drunken school girl. "Mommy fry you in a pan so that baby may eat you as fast as…I CAN!" Screamed the voice, then added in a calm, soft tone again "—do you want to…plaaay?"

Buddy's answer came in the form of soft but swift steps moving in the direction of the woman's question. He sliced the dark air with his chains and locks, swing his weapon back and forth as he walked. He moved through the doorless opening leading out into the open air of the stadium's bleachers. Stopping on the rain soaked concrete pad between the backless benches, his eyes scanned the seats then swept over the dark playing-field.

The fast sound of something long and sharp being swung down through the air caught his ear and sent him wheeling both himself and the chains back around. He'd come about in time to duck beneath Nancy White's claymore sword blade. It raced past the top of his scalp as the heavy padlocks on the ends of his chains skimmed across Nancy's breast. He'd been successful at dodging the long blade she'd swung in her right hand, but not the six inch spikes of her shoes clutched in her left. The instant Buddy's Hell made flail had swept by she sent her shoe's heels crashing into the right side of his head. Again the old Scottish weapon was on its way toward his neck, but despite the sharp pain caused by the shoes he still managed to avoid the sword's blade. Dodging the sword a second time came at a price.

The fast, hard shifting of his weight, and the wet concrete in combination with the slick rubber soles of his shoes caused Buddy to slip and tumble backward down the stairs. His plummet came to a painful stop on the mid level landing, when his ribs smacked against the metal railing between sections of bleachers. The stabbing pain of two busted ribs and a twisted left ankle made getting back to his feet slow and agonizing, affording Nancy plenty of time to slip her shoes back on before following after Buddy. It was the clicking nose of her Gucci high-heels and girlish giggle that convinced Buddy to shake out of the pain and get up.

Nancy moved amazingly fast in those six inch spikes and was only a few steps above him when he shoved up and turned to face the approaching woman raising her weapon. Nancy's face was twisted into a surreal mask of insane glee shadowed beneath a veil of unwavering self-confidence. The sight of it alone was enough to cram Buddy's balls up into his own ass-hole. With a loudly shrieked, "DIE!" she sent the long blade down. Buddy's focus was a bit shaky from his tumble, but he was still in control of his faculties enough to step out from beneath the falling blade. It was as the sword whistled past his right ear that he realized he was lacking something.

Nancy was bringing the claymore's blade around for another try when he shot his vision up the way he'd fallen. Lying on the steps, half way up was his weapon of chains and locks. Again the blade whizzed passed his head, missing him by mere inches. As he'd ducked beneath Nancy's slicing intent, he slammed his elbow up into her abdomen below her rib-cage. The blow not only knocked most of the air out of her lungs, but had also sent her stumbling backward into the bleachers. Buddy's ribs were still in the process of mending and his ankle was painful to walk on. Moving as best he could Buddy headed back up the stairs.

Nancy's rebound from the blow was fast, he'd only covered five steps and still had seven to go before she was already up and moving. Looking over his shoulder, Buddy threw himself across the remaining four steps, his right hand outstretched. Landing with a solid thud, rebreaking the two not-yet-healed ribs, his hand slapped down on the big iron ring linking the three chains together. Loosing a loud wordless yell he swung his weapon around as he rolled over onto his back to face the wild eyed woman's approach. Buddy was in time to catch sight of the claymore's glistening tip slicing half an inch past the bridge of his nose. His wildly blind swing had barely missed the left side of her face as well, although no where near as closely as her's had his. She swung herself all the way around as if being pulled within the wake of her own weapon. Scrambling to his feet, Buddy came about as well and like two toy soldiers executing a clumsy about-face maneuvers they each stopped abruptly, nearly tripping over the momentum of their own bodies and locked eyes. Lowering her weapon loosely to her right hip, she stretched her lips up into an unattractive grin and giggled hissingly through her teeth, positioning herself in a battle-ready stance.

"What do you say to being a good bird and laying that sword down," Buddy said. "You won't beat me you know."

Bending slightly at the knees and swinging the claymore lazily back and forth almost like a tennis player awaiting the serve, Nancy's insane looking smile mellowed some as she replied simply, "You don't say?"

He took a step toward her and she in turn took one back. "The wise thing for you love, would be to take advantage of your little break from wherever it was in Hell dolls like you come from and allow me to pleasure you," Buddy offered with an inviting raise of his hairless eyebrows. "You may never get the chance again…love."

"Newgate," she pointed her sword at the name stenciled on the front of his jumpsuit. "Isn't that an English prison?" The tone in her enquiry owned a strong note of sarcasm. "It's too faded for me to read, the other word, under Newgate what's it say?"

"So I take it you don't want to meet Willie," Buddy chuckled as he took hold of his crotch and gave his manhood a vigorous shake.

"No thank you," she answered. "I'm not in the mood. Anyway—I don't fuck lowlife ass-hole limeys like yourself."

Nancy's reply must have struck Buddy as demeaning because he suddenly reared his weapon back and charged. Nancy stood her ground. She brought the sword up and around with amazing speed, crashing the flat side of the blade hard into the locks, knocking them off-course. She'd swatted Buddy's weapon away with such strength that he'd nearly been sent off balance and disarmed a second time. As he stumbled around, ducking the blade sailing over his head, Nancy got a better look at the words printed on his jumpsuit and saw that the faded word she'd asked about read; Prisoner. Dodging the locks and chains flying over her, she crashed the heavy brass basket-hilt of her sword into the right side of his neck. After several tripping steps backward he took control of his footing and was again shaking off another head numbing blow.

"You're nothing but a criminal, a pathetic convict. What did you do?" Nancy chuckled. "Wait, don't tell me, I know. You're an animal fucker, pigs I'll bet. What, did someone find out about your disgusting secret? Did you kill them for it…well, did you pig fucker?"

Again Buddy charged. He swung his flail and she the sword. The weight of the fast flying locks pulled the chains around the blade. Buddy yanked back on his weapon trying to rip the claymore out of the foul mouthed woman's possession. But Nancy's two fisted hold on the old swords was as secure as the padlocks on the ends of the chains. She countered with a hard yank of her own, sliding the long blade out of the makeshift flail's iron grip. Both players wheeled their weapons around with the murderous force of determined intent.

The steel and iron clashed, filling the wet darkness cloaked over the huge stadium with sharp echoes. The sound of their desperate struggle rang out through the empty bleachers like the metallic roar of an invisible crowd, cheering them on with each flesh opening attempt. Swing and crash—swing and crash. The two grunted, growled and cursed as they exchanged blow after blow, neither of them letting up for an instant. They'd locked themselves into a tight contest of strength, stamina, and luck; each delivering punches, elbow strikes and jabbing stabs with knees and knuckles between the sweeps and swings of their weapons.

Like two ancient soldiers from days of old, Nancy and Buddy fought and watched for the moment when the other would tire and open a window of opportunity. Again the chains whipped around the blade, taking hold of it. Only this time instead of sliding her weapon out of the iron links, she twisted her wrists down and quickly rammed the brass butt of the hilt up into Buddy's lower jaw.

With solid delivery and blood invoking rapid succession she struck his face three times with the ornately decorated hand shield. Doing his damndest to keep from succumbing to the skull numbing effects given him, Buddy jerked his head to the right, out of the hilts path. The fourth attempt tore past his cheek with intense force that would have most-likely laid him low if its intent could have been successful. As it sped harmlessly out into space, Buddy, his chains still wrapped around the sword's blade, sent his left fist straight into Nancy's pretty little nose. As his knuckles were busting her face, she jetted her right elbow into his left temple, dragging it across his face to shatter his nose as well. Two dark-red ribbons of blood streamed out of the players noses. Both strikes were equally effective dazing one another although only briefly. With both weapons still locked, Nancy, who'd been the first of the two to shake out of the pain induced state went to free her's with a quick snap and pull.

"Let go!" she ordered through gnashed teeth. "Let go you limey pig fucking piece of shit!"

"Fuck off!" he replied with a prolonged grunt and a hard pulling jerk on his own weapon. "Cunt!" he barked as he rammed his forehead against her's, sliding his chains off the blade and flinging her loose. Stumbling backward like a drunken politician, Nancy swiftly shoved her will past the pain and regained her balance of foot before falling into the bleachers. Snapping her attention back around, sharply on to Buddy, she kicked off her shoes, raised her sword and charged as an enraged scream blasted past her lips. Ducking left then dodging right he barely managed to escape the blade's blindingly fast assault.

Nancy was successfull in keeping him from being able to mount a counter attack. She could have opened his flesh at any time during her showering reign of steel, but she was toying with him. She was allowing herself a bit of fun, locking Buddy in a state of complete defense with a razor edge onslaught. It wasn't until she made the tactical error of spinning around in an unnecessary attempt to issue her intended final strike with more force and speed that Buddy swung his chains, crashing the locks into the side of her face as she came about. The sword sliced off a good size portion of Buddy's scalp to expose the clean-white surface of his skull cap. The locks had shattered Nancy's jaw, right cheek bone and the rim of her eye socket. It had been a mind numbing blow, but nowhere near as devastating as what was to follow.

On her way down Buddy swung the chains with all of the speed and strength of the lead player. The locks caught Nancy squarely on the same side of her face as the first blow, crushing it so utterly that she in no way resembled her former self of only a moment earlier. Her right eyeball, most of her teeth along with bits of bone and torn flesh broke loose from her skull in an explosion of blood and spit. Like an antique doll with most of its porcelain face shattered, she slammed into the railing of a metal post, cracking several ribs on impact and collapsed between the bleachers in a puddle of filthy rain water.

Stepping toward her broken heap, Buddy kicked her sword down a few of the steps and grinning widely as he stood over her.

"My name is Buddy Alan Zib—"

In a series of growling undistinguishable words and several different octaves of sucking sounds, Nancy interrupted Buddy's speech before it could gain momentum. What she'd attempted to say was, *what makes you think I give a rat's-ass who the fuck you are?* but her toothless, broken face wouldn't permit it. Buddy, able to read the question in her one eyed expression offered.

"I want you to know whose name you'll be screaming after I send you back...Buddy Alan Zib. Please do try and say it once for me.

She grunted, snorted and blew blood out of her mouth at him, and although it was her best attempt at an unrecognizable—*Go fuck yourself*—Buddy took it as Nancy meeting his request and saying his name.

While he was visually drinking in her fear, agony and defeat he noticed that her blood-stained skirt was pulled half way up her thighs, and with little effort he could see the black panties covering her crotch.

"Well well, what do we have here?" he said hungrily as he pushed the gray skirt up further with the toe of his shoe, exposing a bit more of the treasure hidden between her legs.

Nancy's lower jaw had mended enough for her to voice a toothless, "Pig!" which sounded more like "Peeg!" She tried to close her legs, but Buddy showed his disapproval by hitting them apart with his chains, peeling her right knee-cap back in the process.

"Well love, you know what they say…waste not want not." Buddy said in a voice trembling with sexual eagerness. Dropping to his knees between her's, he sat his flail on the seat of the bleacher to his right and pulled open the snaps of his jumpsuit. Before exposing Willie, he went to move her mulberry colored pouch of teeth from between her breasts so that he could tear open her shirt. The instant Buddy's fingertips touched the leathery bag, he was latched onto by an invisible power and torn up off his knees. He was slammed down across the top of the metal railing, snapping his back with a loud crack, and then released to fall limply on the concrete landing. He struggled vainly to move but other than some spastic muscle twitching his body would not heed the call.

Nancy's right eyeball was almost completely reformed and all of her teeth and busted facial bones were nearly as good as new. Reaching down her leg she laid the torn away knee-cap back over its intended place and pushed upright onto her bare feet. Still a bit drunk with pain she nearly fell over before attempting her first step. She managed to catch herself on the way down against one of the big light posts and leaned there a moment while she sharpened her focus. Nancy's steps were shaky as she limped down the stairs to her sword. Moving past Buddy, who was twitching on the ground only a few feet from her weapon, she half glanced at his face, the blood that had poured out his open mouth already moving back up into him the way it had come.

"I don't believe I'll tell you my name, pig fucker," she said; with each word her voice sounding more like her own. "No, I like the idea of you spending eternity not screaming my name. I want you to cry out...who was she?—who was she?—who was she? Forever and ever—"

Nancy raised her sword high and fast "—and ever!"

She sent the blade down, and with that single sweeping descent lopped Lord Buddy Zib's head off cleanly at the neck. It rolled to an upright stop and immediately turned its eyes up onto Nancy, who was smiling back down at it lovingly like a woman gazing down at a newborn baby. Suddenly Buddy's head began to fade away, it was vanishing slowly right before her eyes. She shifted her attention over onto his still twitching body and saw that the blood that had jetted out of his neck when the head popped off was now pulling back into the gaping hole. A long rope of red nerves reached out and a brain began to steadily form. Two smaller cords of nerve grew out from behind the brain and like blooming flowers eyeballs swelled to life. A skull moved out around the brain and eyes, followed by muscles and veins. Skin was starting to stretch up over it all. Nancy realized she'd best hurry and send the limey sonofabitch back to Hell, or she would have to fight him again. She swept the sword-blade's tip back and forth through the emerging head with no effect on it whatsoever. Holding the sword in the crook of her arm, she opened her pouch and dropped a tooth out into her hand. Buddy's eyelids, nose, and lips were still in the process of regrowth when she tossed the pointed yellow tooth, her mouth smiling while her eyes were locked in a narrow expression of hate.

Buddy's newly formed blue eyes followed the twirling tooth's short flight through the night. And while Buddy watched it move down toward him, the only thought playing in his skull, was *bloody video cameras*. For whatever reason he was remembering the video the Scotland-Yard detectives forced him to watch over and over again. Fuzzy black and white images of him lobbing fire bombs onto the roof of a strip-club.

The tooth hit him squarely on his exposed chest and immediately sank into his skin out of sight. Like an ugly marionette being yanked up into the air by invisible strings, Buddy was pulled upright and dangled in place, the toes of his Newgate prison shoes barely skimming the concrete. A woman's voice, hot and sexy sounding called out his name. "Buddy," cried the voice from beyond the darkness at the top of the bleachers. "I want to dance for you...we all do."

A white hot glow rose up out of the steps above him and within the light was a woman's body, naked and made solely of white flames. She took to the air, flying slowly down to hover only a few short feet from him. Buddy had been relatively silent, barely sobbing until he recognized the flaming body and fiery face of the apparition moving nearer to him. It was Scarlet Dream, or for horror's sake, it was meant to sort of look like her. The moment the familiar likeness was made evident to him, his whispered sobs increased in volume and intensity. In other words Buddy's stiff upper lip, British composure had become the panic filled wailings of a terrified fiend.

Blisters swiftly rose up and swelled over his face, neck and exposed chest as the fiery visitor drew near. Stopping only a few inches in front of him, she raised her hands and slowly stroked his face, burning his cheeks as the flaming fingertips caressed the man's skin. Pulling Buddy's screaming face to her's she kissed his lips, muting his cries with her scorching mouth. The loving embrace seared off the entire lower half of Buddy's face, even his tongue was burned back to Hell ahead of him.

"Your eyes long to see me dance for you," she said seductively slow as she moved back and began to dance. The fiery likeness of Scarlet moved with steady, fluid motion, swaying her body back and forth with hungry desire. With an abrupt stop, she looked up at Buddy, stood with her legs spread in a wide upside down V and said, "We all want to dance for you." Hundreds of glowing hot iron chains with searing steel hooks lashed out of her flaming crotch and tore Buddy's body apart. The second each hook had possession of a hunk of flesh or a bit of broken bone they all whipped back up into the mock Scarlet Dream. When Buddy was gone, the flaming woman cooled to a glowing ash that gently blew apart to be carried off into the night by the wind.

Nancy cheered saying, "bravo...bravo!" as she clapped her hands. After her almost awe-struck show of appreciation for the fiery display, she scanned her vision around in a swift but close inspection of her surroundings. Satisfied she was alone Nancy, holding her sword loosely at her side made her way down the steps toward the playing field. A large raven perched on the goal-post cried out loudly at her.

Nancy offered the black bird a smile and a wink as she passed beneath it on her way south of town.

The bike-path Alex and Mr. Bane had followed King a.k.a Dolly Man, into was a poorly lighted, narrow ribbon of black pavement that bent and curved along the west bank of the Willamette river. Alex couldn't help but remember the riverbank appearing much different than what was stretched out before him now. He recalled that there had been more trees and plants. At first glance Alex had begun to dismiss the river's changes as the damage left behind after a flood. But, looking over at the Willamette's east bank and seeing that it appeared undamaged, he realized that the bank's overzealous thinning had been of man's design. What Alex wasn't unaware of was shortly after his mortal death, Corvallis' city leaders had in their self-appointed wisdom ordered that most of the riverbank's ageless, natural beauty be torn away and stupidly replaced with large, ugly granite boulders, all in the name of visibility. After spending the last two hours hunting for King along the raped banks of the river and not finding his prey, Alex and Mr. Bane decided to move their search off of the bike-path.

As Alex moved up over the muddy slope of the bank onto the paved road for bicyclists and joggers, he noticed that Corvallis was beginning to wake up. The sights and sounds of life had begun to emerge. Warm souls were leaving their homes, climbing into their cars in the still darkness of predawn. The noise of traffic on the highway 34 bridge had rose from an occasional semi roaring overhead to the fast sounds of countless automobile tires slicing across wet asphalt. House and car doors opened and closed, the sound of engines warming and far off dogs barking informing Alex and his metallic voiced friend of the living flood about to befall them. Alex had hoped to find King and at least one other player before daybreak. As far as Alex knew, there was still six players left, not including himself, and only fifteen hours give or take left to find them.

"We still have little more than two full hours of darkness remaining before dawn, and another hour and a half until the streets become cluttered with the all consuming disorder of the living," Mr. Bane said, calmly as Alex panned his vision across what appeared to be an almost treeless park that he didn't remember being there.

"At least it stopped raining," Alex rumbled under his breath as he gazed up at the sky. Stars could be seen peering down from patches of an inky-blue void framed unevenly by black iron and slate-gray colored clouds. Even the whipping wind had stopped, allowing a thin fog to settle a foot or two over the ground and streets. Despite the steadily increasing stir of warm souls, the lucid white blanket stretching out in all directions gave the early morning ambiance a cemetery effect.

Alex was soaked to the bone and his cold blood and body's inability to compose heat caused his teeth to chatter when he relaxed his jaw. The November chill settled down and made camp deep in the center of his bones. The rain water that inundated his clothes clear down to his socks began to freeze, weighting his garments with a thin sheet of ice. The lead beads between the padding of his sap gloves sucked in the cold and made the backs of his hands and knuckles ache, and the steel in the toes of his boots did likewise for his feet. Alex was damn cold, but he wouldn't have admitted it, not even to himself, much-less Mr. Bane.

He was cutting over a patch of waterlogged grass toward Pioneer Street when the clattering rattle of a disheveled man carrying a large, clear plastic garbage bag half filled with empty cans stepped out of an alley. Despite the fact that he appeared to be wearing two heavy coats over what had to have been three changes of clothes, he looked to be colder than Alex. It was apparent to Alex that this fellow had been climbing in and out of dumpsters during most of the night, thus cluing him in on the man's homeless state of being. Spotting the city police car rounding the corner onto Pioneer, the unhoused vagabond swiftly turned a can rattling about face and was trying to dart back into the alley. But he had been too slow and was seen. His efforts to slip into the cold safety of the shadows were in vain.

The interceptor's engine hummed with a brief increase of power, rocketing the car across the alley's entrance before the man could cover a five foot distance. The car lurched to a stop, its bright spot light whipped around to land on the man's back as the driver's side window rolled down.

"Mr. Kennedy," the cop shouted as his door swung open. "Hold on there, I've got to speak with you."

"Why?" the man asked without turning to face the slowly approaching law-man. "About what?"

"You know. When was the last time you were in to see your PO?" the cop stepped widely around in front of the man. "Well...when was it?"

"Friday."

"See, now you're lying to me."

"It was last Thursday, then—shit! I don't know. Why don't you people just leave me be!"

"There's a P.V. warrant on my computer screen with your name on it," the cop said, his eyes staring almost sadly down at the bag of cans.

Alex eased his pace to a slow stop in front of the homeless fellow. For a moment he thought he caught the faint glimpse of a urge to try and make a break for it swelling deep in the man's tired gaze. Shifting his attention around onto the cop's face, Alex recognized that this one wasn't the sort to shoot a running man in the back. In the same instance, Alex could also see that he would do whatever else it would take to stop one. For fun, Alex leaned over and whispered, "Kick this wiggly in the stones. Come on, I'll bet you could take his gun before he could stop you. Yes, yes. Then put two in his skull. You know, one to kill and one for fun."

Incapable of hearing Alex's colorful suggestions and knowing full-well that any attempt to flee would only end up with a pissed-off cop grinding a knee down onto the back of his neck, the homeless man simply stayed put and slowly smoked his hand rolled cigarette, drawing in every drag as if he knew it would be the last smoke for a while.

"Fuck, it's colder than my wife's heart out here," the cop said, his hand sliding off his gun. "How the hell do you sleep in this shit?"

"I gave up sleepin' years ago," the man replied his tone flat and humorless. The expression in his blood-shot gray eyes sank deeper into his awareness. It was the same look Alex remembered seeing in the eyes of old convicts, lifers usually. A sort of thousand mile stare that appeared to see nothing, but in fact saw everything.

"Alex...you gave me your word that you would not dally anymore," Mr. Bane growled.

"Yes I did thank you for the pull up."

"For the what—Alex?"

317

"For bringing it to my attention."

"It should not be necessary."

"Well what can I say…you know me, sometimes my focus drifts a bit off course. Luckily for me I've got you to draw it back in."

Mr. Bane's final reply came in the form of a weary sounding, "Your cheeky tongue is as insincere as your efforts to win this game."

Saying nothing, Alex stepped between the two men, still listening to the cop's words. "It's only a ten day bump Kennedy. It'll be over before you know it. Anyway it will give you a chance to warm up, eat something and gather up your second wind."

Another city police car eased around the corner and was about to slow to a stop along side the first car when the cop in the alley waved his hand in a gesture that illustrated he had it under control. As the second car was backing back onto Second Street, Alex walked slowly across Pioneer, stepping up onto the curb, and after panning his vision around through the shadows he glanced over his shoulder. The homeless man Alex was certain he'd done time with somewhere, was already cuffed and stuffed into the back seat of the car. He watched as the cop placed the man's bag of cans into the trunk and thought, *now that's somethim' I've not seen before.*

Coming to the intersection of Third and Pioneer, Alex stopped to look around before crossing through the early morning traffic. Sweeping his vision onto the roof-top's of businesses, office buildings, gas-stations, and a few homes searching for a player to send back, one in particular—Dolly Man. Alex was in the process of stepping off the curb when, at the exact instant his sight drifted onto it, Mr. Bane asked with an unsurprised chuckle, "Alex…isn't that your hat?"

On the edge of a gas-station lot, pressed into the corner of a phone-booth on the floor was Alex's black fedora. Changing his direction, he made his way to the glass booth.

"Honestly Mr. Bane, I'm of the mind to leave the damn thing there."

"That would be a very bad idea Alex."

"Yeah…why's that?"

"Someone will undoubtedly find it, one of the still living…a child perhaps," the metallic voice grew noticeably colder and intensely serious. "That would indeed prove most tragic."

"But how? I was under the impression that I couldn't be seen, not my flash or my clothing."

"If anything of you which has been dragged into Hell and pulled back out is away from your person or worse, left behind, whether we win or fail, it will eventually materialize. Already that hat's been away from your Hell owned soul for far too long. Alex you've no choice but to fetch it."

"I don't get it," Alex mumbled as he stood before the open door of the phone-booth. He stared down at the hat crumpled in an inch of water, wind blown into the corner, adding. "It's just a fucking old hat what harm could it—"

"Yes, a fucking old hat," Mr. Bane echoed, interrupting Alex's voiced confusion. "An old hat...and yet so much more. Our deeds, all seven of the slayings we shared radiated deep within the fibers. Every scream, every droplet of blood and every second of horror that our acts spawned replay over and over again in the folds and shadows of those things you wear. From that very hat down to your boots, your bones and flesh and all that covers them has been cursed, kissed by the breath of Hell-herself. Even I'm stained deeply with the never resting terror of those events," Mr. Bane paused, a heavy sigh rose softly from the metallic voice and drifted down to settle over Alex like a shadowy shroud. Alex dropped to his haunches and rescued the fedora from its cold, muddy abandonment, listening closely as Mr. Bane continued.

"You may believe it no less than a pleasure of sorts to experience the suffering and fright of your parents and the five at the moments of their dying. And you would be correct in such an assumption if in fact the angle of our deeds was that of my own recollection and perception. But alas...the imagery I'm forced to endure is from their pathetic point of view. And Alex, it never lets up. Even now this very second I'm made to suffer their horror and pain. I feel their gagging as they try to scream and the emptying of their bowels. It requires a great deal of my strength to keep from being drawn in and lost to it forever."

Picking the hat up, Alex stood and attempted to shake most of the water out of it. "I feel for you old friend," Alex said, as he did his best to reform the fedora back into its intended shape. "But I still fail to understand. How leaving this thing behind could harm a child?"

"Our acts, the deeds that hat was witness to, may seep into the unaware, innocent heart of a little one. Causing him or her, or anyone who puts it on to mimic our work. That old hat is now a maker of killers."

"Well shit then…I'd best keep it." Alex said as he placed the dripping wet, cold thing on his already cold and wet head. After checking the coin return slot and finding it empty, Alex went to step out of the overly lighted glass booth. He was passing through on of the glass sides when he nearly leapt clear out of his boots by the unexpected ringing of the phone. The sound was abnormally loud and noticeably growing louder with each raucous blast.

"Now what?" Alex leered at the phone, a dense wave of skepticism rushed through him as he wondered if he should answer it? *No…I don't think so,* he thought as he made his decision. He went to continue out of the booth and leave the annoyingly loud ring behind when he heard Mr. Bane suggest, "Answer the phone, what harm could it do you?"

"What, don't you think it a waste of time?"

"No Alex, not in this instance."

"I do."

"So you won't answer it?"

"I think…no." Alex said softly, adding "I don't believe I feel up to reaching out and touching anyone at the moment. You don't mind do you?" he chuckled.

"As a matter of fact Alex my boy, yes I do."

Alex had passed through the glass wall of the booth only to find himself still somehow standing inside the tall glass box. He went to step out through one of its sides a second time and bashed into it face first. The booth's door closed, slamming shut in his face the instant he turned to head through it. Alex was trapped inside the phone-booth, the ringing at a deafening pitch. It was so loud he could barely hear Mr. Bane shouting.

"Answer the bloody telephone Alex," over and over again.

Giving up on the door's refusal to open, Alex spun about and yanked the receiver off its cradle and with a loudly barked, "WHAT!" he put the ear-piece against his head.

"You'd done well with the first two Mr. Stone, the fat one and the female in the automobile," spoke the same voice Alex had heard speaking out of the white dog hit by the car. It was Ellzbeth on the other end of the line. "But the third player you let escape. A grievous error. Wouldn't you agree?"

"Shit happens!" Alex snapped back into the mouth piece. The fading sound of a childish giggle died with a hollow *click*, followed immediately by the sharp noise of a dial-tone buzzing. Ellzbeth had hung up.

Alex didn't even bother with placing the receiver back on its hook. "No time for bullshit," he muttered as it slipped intentionally out of his grasp to dangle swingingly at the end of its short cord. Behind his back the phone-booth's door pulled itself open. Ignoring it Alex stepped into the glass barrier again, and again he smacked against it. Unable to pass out of the booth phantasmly, Alex turned on his heels, "more damn games!" he grunted while heading through the open door. Alex was a good six feet out of the tall glass box when he was stopped cold by Dolly Man's voice barking out Alex's prison-yard nickname, "Doberman!"

Alex whipped back around, simultaneously bringing Mr. Bane out of its sheath. The instant his gaze swung into the empty phone-booth a funnel shaped column of golden fire lashed out of the receiver's mouth piece and engulfed him. In less than the tenth of a second the horizontal pillar of flame had not only burned to ash every stitch of his clothing away, it had also seared away all of Alex's skin. Only charred muscles, roasted tendons, veins, and blackened bones still remained standing when the flame receded back to Hell. Having his entire epidermis scorched off was only the beginning. The true torment that followed from this new nakedness was in having all of his fully functioning nerve-endings exposed to the elements. The only shield he had against the cold wind and rain was pain. Alex had never been one who was easily forced into loud verbal out-bursts, but this was more than even his self disciplined tolerance was willing to endure. The howl Alex loosed was so loud and pain-filled, dogs for miles joined in and stretched the agonizing clamor of his anguish all the way back up to Hell.

Alex was dropped to his knees by a morning breeze that at any other time wouldn't even have caused him to pay it notice. It began to softly rain, the tiny droplets fell so slowly that it was more like a wet mist than a light sprinkle. But to Alex the drops felt as large as bullets and the breeze that carried them as hard as an icy gale. It was all Alex could do to maintain his grip on Mr. Bane's scorched handle, not to mention trying to keep himself half-assed upright. Along with his ability to still experience physical pain in all of its unforgiving degrees, Alex could also hear. And although his eyeballs were fried out of their meaty orbits; he could still somehow see as if his baby blues hadn't been cooked to the size and appearance of two burned rat turds.

The holes on the sides of his roasted head that had only a moment ago been ears heard the approaching sound of clicking. Something deep in his mind told him he knew the steadily growing closer noise. As he struggled to remember where it was that he'd heard the sharp rhythmic pattern moving toward him, an image began to grow into clear focus before his mind's eye. It was a busted open window in a darkened building. A torn strip of black and red flannel material snagged on a bent nail fluttered beyond the window's frame in the night.

Suddenly Alex remembered from where he'd heard the clicking before. And as it had done when he was a boy of fourteen; the hollow sound caused his heart's beating to increase its pace.

It was while the adolescent Alex and another teenager were burglarizing a sporting-goods warehouse. The two would-be thieves were in the process of gathering together as many shotguns as their skinny arms could carry when they heard the steady approach of clicking. The hollow noise was coming closer from all directions it seemed. The sound sped up then gradually stopped. The other, older boy looked over at Alex and quietly mouthed the word—shit! With several slow stepping *click...click click...click click click...click,* four of the biggest, ill-tempered Doberman Pinschers Alex had ever seen moved into the dim moon light struggling down through the dust covered windows. Dropping their loads, both boys' beat feet toward the small window they'd crawled in through. Alex was the first to reach their intended exit. He was pulling himself through when the other boy grabbed hold of his ankle and tried to yank Alex out of his way. Tearing his flannel shirt on a nail, Alex went to mule kick the boy's hand loose, but his aim slipped and his heel caught his youthful crime-partner squarely in the face. The blow knocked the boy backward onto the concrete floor of the warehouse. Alex hit the dirt at a run, the sounds of the other boy's screams reaching out for his help swiftly died within the snarling, jaw-snapping, flesh tearing sounds of the canine sentinels. Alex never looked back, and never told a soul of that night.

This was the same sound; the same hollow clicking—only somehow heavier. Although Alex knew he was in no shape to go toe to toe with a pack of dogs, especially looking like a big chunk of cooked meat, he still did his best to ready himself for a fight. He tried to say something to Mr. Bane, but the garbled together gathering of sounds could form no recognizable noise that came out remotely sounding like words. But Mr. Bane knew what Alex was attempting to say and interrupted his effort by saying, "You're doing fine Alex my boy. I'm here and together we'll dish out misery."

With intense pain and much effort, Alex stood upright, using the phone-booth to pull himself onto his feet. It was necessary, even imperative for him to at least appear strong, ready and fearless. Twice on his way up Alex was nearly sent back down from the pain screaming through him by the slightest of movements, much-less rising. But still he managed to steady himself. Letting go of the phone-booth, he turned his empty sockets toward the clicking. The moment Alex's uncanny ability of sight without the aid of complete eyes had come to rest on the sound's direction; four very large dog like creatures turned the corner. Coincidentally they swept their glowing red and gold, beady eyes up the street onto Alex who was readying himself. Thin wisps of blackish smoke trained behind their sweeping steps as they approached up the sidewalk. Their large heads, long necks and powerful looking bodies possessed a slight Doberman appearance, while in the same instance owning no earthly qualities. Their muscles pressed out against their black hides with such profound definition, twitching with each step that their coats almost looked to be spray-painted on furless skin. The closer they got the more apparent it was that these beasts were not of this world. Their snouts were longer and more pointed with smaller noses that sniffed the air with wildly flaring nostrils. Soon Alex could see that they owned no jowls or lips, giving the things an evil grin that framed glowing white, pointed teeth.

Alex tried to say to himself, "Shit house luck," but what actually stumbled past his exposed teeth was something like "…Chuk wack duk!"

The hounds spread out, slowly surrounding Alex, all the while their long jaws falling slack, thick strings of saliva dripping out off countless teeth. With steady side to side motions they swayed their heads low to the damp concrete, always their round fiery eyes leering hungrily at him.

In a show of defiance Alex stomped his skinless foot against the pavement, waved his knife and yelled an angry wordless challenge at the nearing monsters. Searing pain tore through his body with every moment, but not so the beasts could detect. All at once the Hell hounds released long, low throaty growls; their beady eyes widened and began to burn steadily brighter. Suddenly they all exploded into a chorus of loud, sharp barking. Like four spring-loaded traps they leapt into the air. As if in some sort of contest to be the first set of teeth to tear out Alex's throat, they flew toward the same bull's-eye. The instant their snapping jaws would have slammed down on him, they simultaneously disappeared. Alex was left standing their wildly swinging and stabbing Mr. Bane's blade. Less than a second after the realization that he wasn't being torn apart he noticed his skin and all of his clothing had been restored to him. Once more Alex had been made instantly whole. He stood there a moment looking himself over.

"What was the fucking point of all that?" Alex snapped sharply under his breath. The phone rang. Clinching his teeth, he glanced over his shoulder.

"You best hear what she's got to say Alex. And please do choose your words carefully."

Stepping swiftly into the booth Alex snatched the receiver up, and slowing his tongue's true intent, calmly spoke into the mouth piece, "Hello."

"I trust you enjoyed my little test," Ellzbeth said rhetorically.

"Little test?" Alex growled.

"Do not speak Mr. Stone. Your permitting Mr. King to slip from your grasp is a bit incensing and your propensity for wasting time which is not yours to waste is vexing…deeply so. What's this, no snappy retort…no back handed response—"

"Give me a moment, I'll come up—"

"Alex shut up!" Mr. Bane advised quietly, cutting off Alex's foolish interruption.

After a few long seconds of cold silence the golden eyed being on the other end of the line cleared her throat, paused for a second longer, then continued her long-distance call from the netherworld.

"Recent events beyond my immediate control have compelled me to test your ability to persevere over unexpected tribulation. I'm not allowed to say much, only that there is one…an archangel who sees herself as a Queen. She also believes you to be her greatest threat. Be ready for a face from the past." There was a hollow *click* followed by a dial-tone.

Stepping out of the phone-booth again, Alex looking around and decided to head in the direction the Hell hounds had come from.

"What do you suppose she was trying to say," Mr. Bane asked. "She was horribly vague."

"To be ready for anything…would be my guess."

"I detect a hint of foreboding in your heart Alex."

"Do you now?"

"Yes."

"I'm fine."

"Really?"

"A bit tired…that's all."

"Alex."

"Yes?"

"I wanted you to know that I'm proud of you."

"Truth is old friend, I never could have done it without your help," Alex turned onto B Street.

"Where are we heading Alex?"

"The Oak," Alex replied softly. "There's something I need to get."

"The child's voice on the phone mentioned to beware of a face from the past," Mr. Bane reminded enquiringly.

"Hell, look around…this entire town is a face from the past," Alex chuckled aloud as he cut across Fourth Street.

A large raven caught Alex's attention as it flew toward south-town.

$$\Rightarrow \ \cdot \| \cdot \ \Leftarrow$$

At about the same time Alex was approaching the railroad tracks at the end of B Street, Stanley Fiction was on highway 99 staring stupidly at the green road sign that read CORVALLIS CITY LIMITS.

Glancing over his shoulder back in the direction of town, Stanley mouthed the words *Fuck this crap* as he took the red pouch of teeth from around his neck. Since Kat, he'd not seen anyone who might resemble another player—especially one clad in black. A large raven swooped past his face crying an ear-piercing *caw* as it circled around to perch atop the road sign, snaring Stanley's attention in its wake. Holding the pouch by its long drawstring, he swung it up at the blackbird which was making a hacking sound that was reminiscent of cackling.

"Shut up!" he shrieked up at it. "I said, shut your cursed beak!"

Stanley's new found resolve to be the last player left standing at the game's conclusion had fallen to the wayside during the long night. It had been replaced by a level of pusillanimity unprecedented even for his own cowardice. And to make matters worse, there was a burning sensation relentlessly tickling deep inside his chest. For the last three hours Stanley had been struggling against Warfarin's and Vexrile's threats not to try and slip out of the game. With each labored step against the oath of nightmarish pain toward the city's limits, the memory of the tormenter's warning screamed with increasing skull splitting fury through Stanley's entire being. But despite wave after wave of Hellish images rushing with almost physical force before his mind's-eye and the forehand knowledge of unearthly agony, his craven spirit won the battle of wills and carried Stanley to this point on highway 99.

Holding the pouch out straight-armed, he was about to let it slip off his fingertips when the raven spread its wings and spoke with a mortal's tongue in a voice that seared like white hot blades into his ears.

"That would be unwise," the bird advised.

"Go to Hell!" Stanley shrieked as the drawstring slid from his fingers. The pouch's fall to the wet gravel roadside was stopped in mid-air less than two feet from its completion. Stanley stepped swiftly back away from it.

"You're truly a fool of fool's," the bird hissed in a woman's icy tone of voice.

Stanley nearly slipped on the gravel under his feet as he spun around to run. Like billions of bright-red webs shooting out of as many spiders spinnerets, countless strands of crimson hair shot out of the blackness within the raven's open wings. The red hair lashed down and pierced through his clothes, flesh and bone yanking him up off his feet to slam him against the back of the sign. The instant the strands pulled free from the bird's wings they latched a hold of the large sign to lock Stanley in place. Like steel wires stitched in and out of his flesh they pulled and tugged tighter and tighter, stretching his skin against the wooden backing.

The bird flew around before him, laughing in its woman's voice as he screamed for mercy. Hovering in front of Stanley, its wings moving too slowly to keep it aloft but still somehow maintaining it's in place flight, the raven began to melt into a black shadow that swiftly grew. It stretched to the ground to form, a woman's face. The countless strands of red hair tearing Stanley slowly apart snapped out of his body like thin bands of rubber and vanished into strings of red smoke. Stanley fell to the roadside, his torn flesh healing faster than ever. The face of black shadow became the pale color of bloodless flesh and sprang open its eyelids to reveal fiery-red eyes. Stanley suddenly remembered seeing the woman's face before; she was seated on a throne of naked men and woman that moved through the streets of a nightmarish city. She was traveling in the lead of a great procession of unholy creatures when she'd stopped to look at him on his hook.

"Go back!" Vile commanded. "Find the player clad in black! Find him or know the meaning of my disappointment." Vile's face faded out of sight and no sooner had it vanished and Stanley was snatching his red pouch from it's frozen in mid-air state and running back toward town.

The tunnel Sader had slipped into turned out to be a segment of the drainage system not only for all of the torture chambers, pits, and abattoirs that littered Vile's mountain city; it was also the sewer for her palace as well. All of the palace's and city's waste poured down through this dark, cold labyrinth of pipes, corridors, and tunnels. They ran throughout the rock and frozen mud like the arteries of an enormous beast. The only aspect concerning this dark maze that was worse than its putrid stench was the unavoidable fact that the closer to Vile's palace he climbed, the colder it got. So far the three things Sader hated above all others he had been made to endure during this journey to glean proof of Vile's treachery. Being limited with the use of his angelic powers was number one. Second was being forced to travel by foot, he unquestionably despised walking great distances and worked diligently throughout his days to avoid doing so. And the third aspect of this expedition that taxed his forbearance was the steadily increasing cold. Sader loathed all things cold. He'd considered briefly invoking a warming spell, just a small one, but abandoned the foolish notion. He may as well wave his hand and transport himself directly into Vile's dungeon and place himself in chains.

He'd been climbing steadily for the better part of an hour up a steep seventy degree rise, struggling manually to hoist his iron clad self up through the darkness without slipping. Finally reaching what felt like a spot wide enough to catch his breath on; he pulled himself up and over the lip of sharp, cold stone to find that he'd actually arrived at the rise's zenith. Sader stood atop the flat surface and saw he'd come upon another section of the mountain's drainage system. The ceiling, walls and smoothly worn-down floor were generously smeared with an incandescent white slime. The foul smelling substance shoved aside enough of the darkness with its dim glow for Sader to see that the tunnel stretched horizontally for a good thirty or forty feet then forked into two tunnels. At the far end of the section that stretched to his right there was a tiny pinpoint of bright yellowish red light. And to his left the second tunnel only offered more darkness. Both directions rose at a steady twenty degree angle.

While Sader was deciding on a direction there was a sudden, drastic change in the atmosphere. An icy gust of wind, foul reeking and bitingly painful blew up over the rise he'd climbed and crashed into him nearly knocking him off his feet. Pushing against it, he stepped toward the edge of the drop off and peered over into the darkness. Along with the rotten stench and stinging cold the transmogrifying climate carried with it an overwhelming sense of deep foreboding.

The icy blast of wind stopped as suddenly as it had begun. Sader narrowed his focus, sharpening his vision into the dark below. Not loosening his state of readiness, he was about to turn back to the task at hand, when an ear-bleeding explosion of screaming voices slammed into him and knocked him backward off his feet. The squall sent him rolling up through the tunnel a few yards before he was able to bring himself to a stop.

Vile, his mind shouted in silent, thought. A powder-blue glow pushed slowly up over the drop-off's edge and poured toward him. It was the blue fog that had moved out of the palace down through the city. Getting to his feet, and with nowhere to hide Sader prepared to do battle. Raising his scimitar sword he silently called upon its flaming magical-power—nothing happened. His sword's steel remained coldly void of magic. The blue glow was beginning to increase in intensity, its screams growing deafeningly louder and its indigo brilliance becoming brighter. Sader attempted to draw upon different magical powers, but nothing. Vile had sent out a spell to stifle all magic not her own, Sader had been rendered completely powerless. Turning he had no other choice but to run. The will of his pursuer had other plans in mind, and chasing after the intruder wasn't among them. The howling shrieks sent forth another blast of icy wind that crashed into his back, slamming Sader flat on his face. He scrambled to his feet only to be blown back down by an even louder, stronger volley of wind and screams.

As he was being slid and rolled through the dark across the frozen slime of the tunnel, he managed to catch sight of the blue glowing fog's source as it pushed up past the drop-off's edge. Peering up over the razor sharp black stone was a giant glowing ball of blinding blue light. Its brilliant surface was littered completely with an incalculable amount of mutilated, howling faces. Whipping widely out from around the great orb's cracks, between the suffering heads, were long tentacle like appendages.

The huge angry sphere of wailing torment came over the edge of the rise and swiftly moved up the tunnel after Sader. Two tentacles lashed down and pierced through the armor covering Sader's shoulders into his flesh and out his back. They yanked him up and bashed his body against the ceiling and walls until every piece of his metal suit was battered off of his helpless frame. Four more tentacles whipped around and like striking Cobras, snapped down to stab through him. They pulled his body closer to the glowing blue surface of howling faces. The center of the orb began to shift and twist, some of the heads melting out of the way, making room for a face ten times larger than those surrounding the sphere's center. As the tentacles drew Sader closer he immediately recognized the huge emerging face as that of Vile's. Her red eyes snapped open wide and locked onto Sader's. He stared with a mixed state of seething rage and deep horror into the crimson mirrors catching an unwanted glimpse of his own horrified reflection. Vile's voice seeped mentally into his brain and whispered.

"I foresaw the possibility of a trespassing provocateur from B'neem. Although I expected that it would have been that little fool Pike."

She opened her mouth wide enough for the tentacles to cram him in past her teeth and down her throat. The instant her lips snapped shut the giant sphere of faces vanished, delivering the tunnels back unto the darkness.

Sader's shattered little body was found cast alongside the boundary-wall of B'neem's outskirts. The eighth realm's silver eyed Overseer had been dumped there like a bloody sack of scrapings from off of a butcher shop floor. Lying on the black sandy ground beside Sader's broken husk was the large severed head of the white skinned, winged beast that had carried the Overseer into the sixth realm. Clinched in-between its jaws was a petalless rose stem. Carved deeply into the skin on Sader's forehead was the word, SPY.

It had been a lesser breed of angel, a yellow skinned seraph named Scipio who'd found Sader. The nine foot tall seraph carried the wounded Overseer at an all-out run every step of the seven-hundred miles to the black lake's port. Scipio caught a ride on the first barge across the lake to B'neem's Cathedral. Once inside the great building he took Sader to Ellzbeth in her tower room and laid her broken friend on the floor at her feet. With his spiked head bowed to her, he told Ellzbeth where he'd found Sader, then asked in an almost pleading tone of voice.

"Please Inquisitor…please allow me, Scipio, B'neem's staunch servant to go forth and find the fiends who have done this horrid deed."

As Ellzbeth knelt she brushed her hood back off her head and removed her mask. Beside her battered friend she silently wept. Without looking up from Sader's eyeless sockets, Ellzbeth asked in a voice so faint Scipio could barely hear her question.

"What would you do to the criminal responsible for this?" she waved her hand slowly over Sader.

Scipio raised his coal-black eyes to do what he would have never of done at any other time, he looked Ellzbeth, a higher breed, squarely in the face and said, "I would show those responsible for this crime…this atrocity, why B'neem's damned scream louder than all of those suffering throughout the whole of the Empire." He stood without being told he may do so and added in an enraged, cold tone. "Give it unto me to seek them out Grand Inquisitor, and I swear to you upon my own eyes their cries for pity will entertain your heart for a thousand years."

Ellzbeth stood and said softly "—strengthen the guard around the far bank as well as the outer walls of the realm."

Scipio turned toward the door and was in mid step to do as he was ordered when she said sharply, "Wait…come back and go to your knees—seraph."

Scipio did as he was told without question. Ellzbeth stepped carefully around Sander's wounded flesh and piercing the middle finger on her right hand with the fingernail of her left, she stood before the yellow angel. A tiny droplet of blood rose on her fingertip like a small chip of red glass. Without a word she held the finger over his head and tipped the drop of blood off. The tiny crimson liquid jewel fell and the instant it touched the dome of Scipio's yellow head its redness swelled down over his entire body. Ellzbeth turned and stepped back around to retake her kneeling position beside her wounded comrade. "Rise Scipio," she said under her breath, sweeping the back of her hand unceremoniously at him. "I've advanced your lowly station from that of a tormenter and wall-mender, void of any magical gifts, to an exalted creature possessing power of great sorcery and strategical knowledge. Now and for all time you, Scipio, will be First Captain of the Cathedral Guard."

"But what of she who holds that title already?" he asked as he stood staring in awe at his new arterial colored hide.

"She is now as yellow as pus," Ellzbeth replied with a forced giggle. She glanced up from Sader's bloody face; her golden eyes flashed brightly, and in so doing a large black-steel key materialized in the air before Scipio's face. "This key unlocks the chamber door to B'neem's armory," Ellzbeth whispered. "There you will find the ancient arsenal employed during both great wars. Arm the entire realm with those weapons. Now…go and leave with my sadness and rage."

Without question the new red-skinned captain walked swiftly out of Ellzbeth's tower room. As she gazed down onto Sader, she wiped blood from his face with her long raven black hair. "I will make you whole dear-dear friend, and when that time has past, soon that it shall, I will stand at your side as you invoke screams for mercy from Vile's lips."

With no signs of warning, Sader's broken hands lashed up and with great speed latched a hold of both sides of Ellzbeth's head. As his eyes turned from empty sockets to swiftly forming dark-red orbs, a voice not his own began to laugh loudly out of his lipless mouth. It was a woman's laugh, possessing within its lilt a strong hint of wicked intent consolidatedly wrapped within the shroud of evil pleasure. It was Vile's laughter booming forth from out of Sader's being.

The sharp snapping sound of bones being cracked and broken popped to lift as Sader's body stretched, shifted and swelled outward like something trapped in a wet rubber sack struggling to tear out. Ellzbeth screamed past the crushing pain of having her head squeezed.

"Guards! Gua-rrr-rds!" she cried out, all the while trying to pry Sader's hands off her head.

Scipio, hearing the Grand Inquisitor's screams, charged up the tower stairs and burst back into the small room. Immediately after tearing past the room's threshold, Vile's power of will snatched him off his running feet and hurtled Scipio up into the iron ceiling. Then crashed him like a doll against the walls before throwing him out the door to roll down the stone stairs. The heavy metal door slammed shut and was transformed instantly to solid stone.

Sader's body began to rip open, tearing apart from the center of his bald head down. Still clutching Ellzbeth's head, larger hands and arms slipped out of his much smaller appendages. Rising fast up from his flesh and bones like an evil, naked Jack-in-the box came Queen Vile. Some of Sader's torn skin and a few bits of broken bone clung to Vile's blood smeared body. Without letting go of Ellzbeth, Vile stood fully upright holding the golden eyed Inquisitor several feet off the floor. Vile stepped slowly out of and over the mutilated remains of Sader.

She dangled Ellzbeth's kicking, screaming body and laughed as she squeezed the sides of her head together. Vile's laughter faded behind her toothy grin and said, "It has been a long-long time, Ellzbeth...too bloody long truth be known." Vile shook her blood drenched hair out with several jerks of her neck. "It would take all of the hours time has to offer for me to express to you Ellzbeth dear how deeply I've dreamed of this moment," Vile hissed coldly as she slid her thumbnails over Ellzbeth's face to ease their blade-like tips into her eyes. As Vile was slowly pressing her nails between the clinched closed eyelids, piercing the soft skin of the golden orbs, Ellzbeth stopped struggling and let go of Vile's wrists. Her blood-red lips stretched into a wide smile as blood from her eyes trickled down her white cheeks like tears. Vile—sensing a trick, drover her thumbnails quickly the rest of the way into the eyes, stabbing them deep into Ellzbeth's skull. At the exact moment they sunk through the sockets Ellzbeth dropped her mouth open so cavernously wide that the head of a human infant could have easily fit inside. Before Vile's stabbing touch had time enough to freeze Ellzbeth's head to ice, thousands, perhaps hundreds of thousands of inch long red and gold hornets poured out of the Inquisitor mouth. The thick swarm attacked Vile, completely covering her upper body from the top of her head to her waistline. Voraciously the hornets bit and stung the would-be Queen of Hell. They climbed into her screaming mouth and crawled down her throat, all the while stinging furiously as they gagged her.

Vile flung Ellzbeth as hard as she could against a far wall before collapsing to her knees. Vile's back pulled straight and her arm and neck went rigid. Her muffled cries were choked, rendering her silent and statue still as the hornets drove the business ends of their stingers all the way home into her flesh.

Ellzbeth blindly felt her way up onto her feet and pressing back against the wall she tried to be faster on the draw than Vile in-regards to stifling Vile's powers before she could do likewise to her. Groping along the wall Ellzbeth attempted to mend her eyes, but something was blocking her ability to heal herself. She was too late; Vile had already robbed Ellzbeth of all her powers.

The Queen's silence ended with a loud blood-chilling laugh. She willed Ellzbeth into the air. Vile rose up off her knees, all of the hornets froze solid and dropped to the floor. With a fairly loud gulp she swallowed those hornets in her mouth and throat then loosed an unladylike belch as she stepped over the pile of frozen insects surrounding her on the floor. The sting-wounds that littered her body swiftly healed and vanished. The stingers which had broken loose from their previous owners to embed deeply into Vile's breasts, shoulders, arms and belly wormed out of her flesh to cascade like pine-tree needles to the floor. Vile waved both her hands uneventfully through the air as she stepped up to the hovering Ellzbeth, healing her golden eyes.

"I want you to see your blood splattering across my smiling face as I work on you. I half expected something a bit more imaginative from you than that silly old hornet trick," Vile giggled.

She could hear B'neem's guards beating on the stone, trying to bust down Vile's walled doorway.

"I believe it's time to take our little reunion back to my place." Vile smiled as she snatched a hold of Ellzbeth's iron throat guard and pulled her close to whisper directly into her ear.

"It took some doing old friend, but after centuries of tireless study I learned how to share with you the maddening loneliness I'd come to know on that moon." Vile softly stroked Ellzbeth's face.

"No matter what's done to me, you still won't win the game Vile."

Vile kissed Ellzbeth gently on the lips, and when she pulled away Ellzbeth's mouth was gone, covered over by smooth skin.

"I've already won the game," Vile said, her smile melting to a blank expression; and in a flash of icy cold blue light Vile and Ellzbeth vanished.

CHAPTER EIGHT
— MOTHER —

What though the field be
lost?
All is not lost; the unconquerable
will, and study of revenge,
immortal hate, and courage never
to submit or yield.

—Paradise Lost
John Milton

Alex watched the steady rising of the sun as it stained the cold-gray clouds with reds, purples, and golds. Seated cross-legged beneath a dying oak-tree that reached out over the Mary's river he lowered his gaze back down to the strip of black and white photo-booth snapshots he held gently in his lap. The photographs were of Alex at eight years of age, and his then six year old sister Susan. As he studied the narrow strip of five photographs Alex remembered when they were taken and how he and Susan had to sneak off together and slip into the booth to get them done. He recalled the feelings of fear mixing wildly in his heart with the childhood knowledge that they were getting away with a forbidden deed. He remembered how they giggled and made goofy faces at the black glass. Turning up the tips of their noses, stretching lips and pulling down lower eyelids with thumbs and fingers. That was in all but one of the photos; the last one on the strip. In that picture their sun-deprived little faces were expressionless, deadpan masks. Only their eyes showed faint shadows of the terror nibbling away at their hearts.

Pike had answered Yes when I asked if Susan was alive, Alex silently reminded himself. He thought about her in that dirty madhouse, he thought about the teenage girl thieving the gun out of the car. "Yeah… I'll show you whores in front of everyone." Alex remembered her saying in a voice that shook with fear.

'She's on her own,' the blond demon-boy had told him moments before tearing the neck-bone out of Alex's throat.

In an attempt to shift his thoughts off the goth girl, Alex looked deeper into the fifth photograph on the strip. "She too is on her own," Alex said softly, his voice hollow and cold in an effort to mask the regret peering out from around the words.

"She needn't be Alex my boy," Mr. Bane said in a tone that came out so gentle that it almost sounded feminine.

"What do you mean?" Alex asked shifting his gaze sharply to the knife stabbed in the mud between his right knee and the metal ammo box.

"I'm not permitted to say," there was distress in Mr. Bane's voice, something Alex had never heard out of the weapon before; it caused him to feel a bit uneasy deep in his gut.

"I can help Susan then," Alex asked anyway. "I can make right my wrong?"

"Our wrong Alex," the knife whispered so faintly Alex barely heard. "Please my boy…do not press. Win this game—take the day and all will be made clear. Now please Alex, press me no further on the matter."

"It was you who brought it up."

"We're wasting time here."

"What do you know about Susan! What do I need to do?"

"Win!"

Slicing the blade out of the soft ground Alex stood quickly, "What are you and that little bastard Pike keeping from me?" he demanded to know.

"NO MORE!" Mr. Bane shrieked so loudly and sharp that the metallic voice stung Alex's ears. "We will leave this place and successfully slice Napoleon Albert King as well as those who may still be left back to the Inferno! Now put those childhood things back in their metal box and let us go…I'm begging you, please Alex!"

Alex went to state his protest when a high pitched metallic ring shot out of the knife in his fist, piercing his ears sharply. He was nearly dropped to his knees. He flung the dagger down, its blade inadvertently stabbed through both of the Bat Man comic-books to stick in the soft earth beneath them.

"I said no more!" Mr. Bane echoed. "This will be my last warning… upon my oath it shall."

With a growl humming deep in his throat and a tight grimaced expression twisted on his face, Alex bit his tongue. Going back down to his haunches he quietly picked up the small zip-lock plastic baggy and after carefully folding the strip of photos he slid them into the bag with the baseball cards and sealed it closed. He gently stuffed the baggy down into the broken Gunsmoke thermos and placed it on a bed of black plastic at the bottom of the ammunition box. Swiping the blade out of the comics he spitefully shoved its mud smeared steel into the sheath and laid the wounded comics in on top of the thermos. After putting the rest of the plastic in on top of these things, he slowly closed and latched the metal lid like someone closing a coffin. Stepping almost solemnly around to the side of the huge oak, Alex slid the ammo-box down into a deep hole surrounded by a dense cluster of black, knotty roots. A sound snapped his attention up toward the bike-path. Seeing that it was only an early morning jogger he went back to what he was doing. Grabbing a heavy flat slab of concrete Alex placed it atop the hole, sealing the makeshift crypt for what he intended to be the last time. Taking his trench coat and hat from the jaggedly broken off branch jutting at eye level out of the wide tree trunk, he put them on and made his way up to the paved-path.

He was in the process of reaching the top of the bramble covered slope when out of nowhere his chin was jarringly introduced to the sharp heel of a man's cowboy boot. Alex was sent back down the slope landing solidly, flat on his back.

Glaring down at him from the edge of the path, clutching a straight razor in each fist, his arms crossed over his chest like the over done pose of a comic-book villain was Stanley Fiction. Peeling his thick gray lips back to expose his large teeth in a grinning leer, he hissed, "You're the one…Oh yes, yes-yes-yes you are."

"Yeah, which one would that be?" Alex growled while rubbing his sore chin and getting to his feet.

"Something's not right, with this one Alex," Mr. Bane suggested. "I sense something wickedly familiar about him."

"You're the one clad in black, the one I was told to find first…the one who called himself Millstone," Stanley replied. "I remember reading about your deep disdain for pedophile types. How many was it before the police sent you to Hell?"

Alex took a few short, slow steps back, stopping in the middle of the small river side clearing. Bringing Mr. Bane out, he held the knife at his side blade down. Taking off his hat Alex tossed it out of the way on a growth of thorny shrubs.

"Five after my release from the Walls, seven in all including my parents…I was nine."

"Your parents?" Stanley snickered. "And as a boy of nine no-less." Stanley began to make his way down the slope. "You were a prodigy then. Let me guess—daddy made you suck his pee-pee, and mommy did nothing to stop him. Is that what caused your act of parricide?"

"Perhaps," Alex answered his tone empty. "—and you…Mr.?" Alex slowly side-stepped around the man.

"The hell with all this chitchat!" Mr. Bane cut in. "Cut him Alex, cut him quickly and send this one back now! I've a horrible feeling about—"

"Fiction…my name is Stanley Fiction."

"Who gives a bloody damn what his fucking name is…cut him Alex!"

"Very-well," Alex hissed. "What were your transgressions Mr. Fiction?"

"Enough of this foolishness Alex! Cut him-cut him!"

Stepping off the slope onto the clearing, Stanley ducked beneath the broken branch Alex had used to hang his coat and hat on only a moment ago.

"Eighteen faggots. You may have read of my doings. I was the one the papers dubbed, the Skin Stealer?"

"Nope, I can't say that I had," Alex lied, of course he'd read about this freak before him, but he figured, why give him the pleasure of emphasis notoriety.

"Fags though," Alex said. "Were you some queer's toy? Did some cross-dressing thing convince you into doing something dirty and you felt guilty...ashamed when you woke up the next morning? Or perhaps your own hidden lust to act as some freak's punk got the attention of your wife and kids."

"No," Stanley laughed. "I simply have a taste for killing, one might say."

"Stop this moronic banter and open his flesh Alex.!"

"Anyway...who are you to pass judgment on anyone else's motives. Your under the assumption that because you murdered child-molesters, that you're better than the rest of us. Your a killer nothing more...you and I Mr. Millstone, we're one in the same; in that we kill because we love doing so."

Stanley began to side-step around Alex who was in turn moving slowly around him. Testing Alex by sweeping his razors left. "This is Slicer," he said through clenched teeth as the thin blade raced by Alex's right cheek, missing it greatly. "And this is Slasher," he added with a fast sweep right with the other blade, also missing Alex's face by more than a foot. Stanley quickly realized that Alex wasn't going to be as easy an opponent as Kat had been.

He sent the razor called Slasher through the air past the front of Alex's throat, this time only missing his flesh by inches. Alex jerked his upper body back as he crossed Stanley's failed strike with his left fist, crashing his gloved knuckles against his right ear. If not for the fact that Stanley had been empowered with Alex's strength and endurance, the blow would have easily dropped the hundred and thirty pound man. Although Alex's punch hadn't sent Stanley flying, it had managed to stagger him back a few paces. Catching his arm-flailing, backward stumble in mid flight, Stanley dug his heels into the mud, swiftly shook off the blow and lunged at Alex. He sent both razors crisscrossing simultaneously in opposite directions with matching threat toward Alex's face and throat.

Dodging the unfocused attack, Alex dropped beneath the flashing steel and for fun's sake punched Stanley in the side, busting his right short-rib with a fast muffled *snap*! Stanley's arm swung back and raced Slicer's thin blade from the middle back of Alex's head across his left ear and exiting through his cheek. Alex threw himself to the ground and swept both of Stanley's long spindly legs out from under him with a hard kick. Stanley slammed to the mud face first, landing with an air ejecting thud. Loosing a loud primal growl Alex turned with a straight-armed roundhouse rolling his body over. Seeing Alex's intention, Stanley rolled away from the plummeting blade giving Mr. Bane only mud to be driven down into. Both men were up at the exact same time. No sooner had they locked eyes and they were charging. Through a slivery blur of clashing steel each man fought furiously to be the first to find an opening. Ear-ringing steel infused with guttural grunts and slurred curses cleared the surrounding trees of birds and other forms of wild-life. Stanley's dual bladed advantage combined with Alex's own speed gave Alex and Mr. Bane quite a contest indeed. If not for Alex's experience and Stanley's lack of, Alex and his double edged comrade might have been concerned.

"Don't fool with this one Alex," Mr. Bane said. "End this dance… NOW!"

With the command Alex brought his blade up beneath one of Stanley's wild strikes, slicing Mr. Bane's edge up through his coat and shirt, cutting easily into the flesh of Stanley's arm-pit, severing all of the arteries and veins. As Alex's weapon swept skyward, pulling a thick ribbon of Stanley's blood up in its wake, Alex shot his left fist out and grabbed Stanley's left wrist. With a single fluid motion Alex spun around and whipped Stanley backward. Turning the wrist loose he flung the former prosecutor toward the oak tree. Stanley's footing struggled comically to maintain some measure of backward stability but failed disastrously. He stumbled backward impaling himself through the back of his neck and out the front of his throat on a pointed, broken tree limb—the same jagged branch Alex had earlier employed as a coat and hat rack.

Without hesitation Alex spun completely around, his right arm extended out straight, Freak Bane locked tightly in his fist. Dropping down bent kneed as he swiftly turned he slashed the blade through Stanley's dangling waistline, nearly slicing him in two. Most of Stanley's entrails spilled out and plopped on the mud.

"Swiftly Alex, send him back!"

"What's the rush?"

"I implore you Alex, send him back now!"

Even with only his spine and a few strands of stringy muscle and skin being all that connected his legs to the rest of him, he still fought furiously to free himself from off the jagged limb. Despite all of his jerking and wiggling, his efforts to inch his way off were in vain. Stanley had swiftly realized the flat-out hopelessness he was being faced with. There was at least a full foot's length of the thick branch sticking straight out of the ex-D.A.'s throat. And although his cut away lower half, as well as all of his body's spilled holdings were already struggling to reattach, he suddenly saw no use and stopped trying. Stanley simply surrendered to the apparent consequence of his failure and let his razors slip from his purposely waning grip.

Deciding he'd seen enough of the Skin Stealer's agony, Alex put his weapon in its sheath and took a tooth out of the black leathery bag. "Something for you to gnash your teeth on while you burn Mr. Fiction. The woman player I'd sent back put up a far better fight than whatever it was that you just tried to do. Even with the gift of my strength your efforts were sadly pathetic."

Stanley attempted to choke out a sharp-tongued response past the hunk of wood blocking his wind pipe. But all he could manage to utter were a few broken squeaks and some spit mixed with foamy blood. His chattering overbite hissed as his eyes narrowed hatefully.

"Pathetic!" Alex barked as he flipped the demon's tooth off the tip of his thumb like a nickel. The instant it landed on the glistening pile of quivering guts it sank out of sight within the meaty heap. Some of the birds had returned to their places in the surrounding trees and while they filled the clean crisp morning air with their songs two wiry black tree roots wormed up out of the mud. They snaked about blindly, groping across the mound of wet fleshy innards to move up and between the droplets of blood rising to refill Stanley's twitching veins. Almost simultaneously, as if they possessed eyes of some sort, they lashed down and wrapped around Stanley's straight-razors. After sweeping them up to dance their edges wildly through his decimated flesh for a bit, the roots pulled the matching blades down into the blood soaked earth.

Several seconds lapsed after the thin roots vanished with Slicer and Slasher. Stanley's spilled bowels were beginning to reach upward and slither back into his hollow frame. Alex was starting to wonder what was taking so long when hundreds of roots tore up out of the muddy ground beneath Stanley and commenced to pull him apart. They greedily ripped his body off the limb, tearing his shoulders loose from his neck and head which teetered for a moment on the branch. Stanley's eyes leered at Alex as the head rolled over and fell to the waiting roots below. Like snakes fighting over the same rat they lashed onto the head and tore it to pieces. Even the skull was easily broken into bits by the voracious greed of the roots. In less than half a minute the human monster who'd been given the title of Skin Stealer had been completely dismantled and taken back to the sixth realm. Or so Alex thought. When the red cloud drifted down to settle and sink into the mud Stanley's still beating heart was left behind, embedded in the mud.

"No Alex! Don't go near it." Mr. Bane advised ominously as Alex brought the dagger back out, stepping toward the gruesome sight, and stuffing the pouch of teeth down into his hip pocket. "Calm down," Alex suggested, his tone amused. Easing to his haunches he moved closer for a better look.

"This is unwise Alex. Please listen to me, you gave me your word… you said you would pay heed to my advice."

"Crap! What's wrong now?"

"I sense something horribly out of sorts."

"No shit!" Alex snapped. "What makes you think so?"

"This is no time for your cockiness. I'm not sure what it is I'm sensing, only that it's emanating from that hunk of palpitating meat and that it means the both of us great harm," the metallic voice paused. "Remember what the youthful voice over the phone said? Be ready for a face from the past."

"Yeah…I remember. So what," Alex said as he poked at it with the tip of the knife like a wicked child stabbing at a wounded toad for the fun of watching it squirm. With an almost unexpected jab he thrust the blade through both right and left ventricles. Standing upright, he picked the heart up on the knife in order to examine it more closely.

"See old friend, there's nothing to fear."

"I believe that's where you're wrong Alex."

"The only thing wrong here Mr. Bane is what's going on with you... yeah you're beginning to sound like a frightened little bitch. Maybe I should paint your sheath hot-pink?"

"Cast it into the river Alex and let us leave this place."

"Alright—alright, settle down," Alex said, mixed with a muffled chuckle. "I don't recall ever hearing you so freaked out about—"

A milky-blue eye, human in appearance pushed out past the beating heart's surface. "Sonofabitch!" Alex yelled, interrupting himself. The eye peered through a thin layer of clear, glistening mucous, rolling its attention around onto Alex's dumbstruck expression. The pinkish meat surrounding the eye narrowed much in the same way eyelids might do when attempting to sharpen visual-focus. Before the thought to do so had completed forming between his ears, Alex flung the bizarre thing off his knife, sending it toward the swift moving river. It flew from the blade, but only went a few yards. The heart's journey suddenly stopped in mid flight as if it had smacked against a pane of glass. It fell to the dirt with a soggy sounding *plop*, landing on top of the eye.

"Send it into the water with your boot Alex," advised Mr. Bane.

Alex was about to take the advise when the cloudy eye popped up out of a new spot on the heart to immediately turn its single orbed vision up at Alex. It looked for a moment into Alex's face, then lowered lazily down to Mr. Bane clutched in his fist, only to return its attention back up onto his awestruck expression. As unexpectedly as it had appeared the eye vanished, sinking out of sight back down into the heart. It began beating faster.

"Run Alex, its may not be too late!"

Alex took a few steps backward then stopped and growled. "I'm not going anywhere."

"Your being foolish Alex my boy," Mr. Bane warned. "Look...times up."

The heart's violent throbbing began to rapidly increase to a faster pulsating palpitation. Ribbons of black vaporous smoke rose in a spiraling climb to form a dense cloud that streamed out of the spastically beating blood-pump.

"It may not be too late Alex," Mr. Bane whispered almost fearfully. "I won't think any less of you."

"I'm staying put!" Alex snapped. "Now, if you're not going to be of help…shut up!" he added through clinched teeth as he watched the black cloud hovering only a few yards before him. Readying himself for the possibility of a fight, Alex stepped back a few paces. The cloud hovered in place at eye level. Holding the knife tightly at his side, he bent his knee slightly, prepared to charge if need-be. As the cloud swelled and shrank with the beats, the heart itself began to dissolve. Flashes and sparks appeared throughout the dark smoke Blues and reds danced with no set pattern or rhythm. Steadily the heart melted into a small bubbling puddle of red and white goo. All the while the black cloud growing denser, heavier. It drew into itself and out as if it were breathing. Something was forming beyond its blackened veil, something that stood upright at about five and a half feet tall.

"All is lost…all is truly lost," Mr. Bane voiced, a strong note of dread moving through the words. Alex could make out the dark shape of a bowed head, narrow shoulders and arms. Whatever the appearing figure was, it seemed human. As more and more of its shape could be seen behind the flashes of colored lights within the smoke Alex strengthened his grip on the knife. Soon he could easily see the slender contours of a woman stirring inside the vaporous veil's core. The moment her darkened outline became visually clear to Alex a wave of dread rose up into his heart from out of his passesd. The black cloud shrouding her began to drift heavily down and melt like fog into the earth, leaving a blackened stain in the mud.

"Stop this foolishness Alex…leave this place. I beg of you… please!"

At first she was only vaguely familiar beyond the thinning black mist and sinking flashes of light. But once the last of the dark screen had dwindled, her identity was made horrifyingly clear to Alex. Standing before him in all of her selfish beauty, completely nude and totally healed, wrapped proudly in her smooth twenty-seven year old frame was Ruth Rose Stone, Alex's mother, as well as his second murder victim.

Shaking loose from the paralyzing affects of shock and terror, Alex raised Mr. Bane and with a throaty roar charged the flesh and blood apparition. He was less than six feet from being close enough to sweep the blade through her throat, when in mid stride both of his feet sank into the ground. The instant his boots were submerged up to both ankles the suddenly liquefied mud hardened to stone, sealing Alex's feet in place. *Be ready for a face from the past,* echoed the child's voice deep in his brain with an almost *I told you so* incongruity clinging mockingly to its recollection.

Immediately, Alex struggled to free his power of mobility, stabbing and beating the blade and his knuckles down against the unexpected prison incasing his feet. And as he shouted curses and grunts, Ruth slowly raised her head. Parting her long, black hair evenly through the middle with graceful, slender fingers. She pulled the listless black strands over her milky-white shoulders to send then cascading down her back. Eyes so pale-blue that they scarcely appeared living trembled open. Ruth's dispassionate gaze swung immediately onto Alex's face, looking blankly onto his eyes. Pausing his frantic struggle to escape the trap clasping painful and tight around his ankles like iron shackles, he raised his narrowed brow from the task before him to leer hatefully up at Ruth smiling down at him. He growled past slightly parted teeth, a cold sweat smearing his stone-faced expression with a shimmering glint that gave his cadaver-like skin color an almost ghostly glow. Ruth sighed the way a new mother might sigh at the first sight of her baby, and although her smile was loving, the dull expression in her eyes was as empty as the blackest space between dying stars.

"Cunt!" Alex rumbled. "It's really you…how nice; I get to open your foul flesh once again. Lucky me!" He swung Mr. Bane's blade back and forth, trying to reach her with its tip from his stuck position. "Damn you! Come closer!" he ordered. "Its okay, I'll only make it hurt a lot! Step over here…just a little closer." He grunted and growled like a wild beast on a short chain. "COME HERE BITCH!" Alex screamed at the top of his lungs, his voice cracking with rage. He swung the knife down to his side holding it out slightly, straightening his back as best he could, despite the awkward position of his wide strided stance.

"Does it look familiar?" Alex hissed.

Ruth lowered her death-eyed stare from Alex's angry face to the blade shaking in his fist—not from fear, but from the all consuming fury rushing like dope throughout his body. She smiled again as she looked back up into his eyes.

"Here…perhaps this will help kick start your memory, cunt!" Alex raised the knife up over his head, clasping its handle with both hands then brought it down. Again and again, he stabbed at the air as if he were stabbing a naked woman in a bath-tub. "Well bitch…does that help?"

In the same phony southern drawl Ruth used to try and mock when Alex was a child, she replied, "I see you still have the dagger I gave to your father on his thirty-third birthday. I certainly do hope you put it to good uses." Her pale-blue gaze shimmered. "What do you know about that knife…sweetie?"

"It's none of your fucking business bitch, what I do or don't know! GO fuck yourself cun—t—"

With a swift wave of her left hand she took Alex's voice from him. "Shhhh…sweetie, mommy don't care for being called the C word." She looked down at the knife. "That old dagger has been with my mother's side of the family for well over five and a half centuries. When I was a little girl my grandmamma shared a timeworn tale about that blade and a curse."

As if an invisible wire had been lashed out from her will and hooked onto the knife, it tore easily out of Alex's strong fist and shot up through the air. When the fast spinning blade was less than a foot from driving into the center of Ruth's face, she snapped her hand up; palm turned out and stopped the blade by simply allowing it to pierce to the hilt through her hand.

"My grandmamma loved telling her dark tales, almost as much as she loved the horror they rose in our childish night-terrors," Ruth said fondly. "And the favorite of her tales to share was the one surrounding this lovely old dagger." She slid the long blade slowly out of her hand. The whispery sound of sharpened steel being pulled from tender skin and bone found Alex's ears. If bringing Mr. Bane out of her hand was in anyway physically painful to Ruth, Alex couldn't tell from the blank eyed leer and unwavering smile on her face.

"Don't you wish to hear about this blade son?" She paused briefly to watch humorously as Alex, struggling to speak more then muffled grunts, beat his fists against the concrete like ground imprisoning his feet. "Of course you want to know," she continued "—about this, your means to so many ends…this weapon…this, your stunted Excalibur." She cackled with a witches' lilt in her tone. The darkened rain-cloud drifting searchingly over the small river-side clearing stopped above their heads casting an uncomfortable shadow. Ruth ran the bleeding palm over her bleached white skin, smearing dark-red stains on her left breast, across her lower ribs and down to her left hip.

"Don't listen to her Alex! She lied...she—"

Bringing her hand's slow journey to a stop, Ruth pinched together a few inches of the skin covering her hip-bone. Stretching it out some, she interrupted Mr. Bane's whispered warning, silencing the metallic voice by stabbing the blade down through her own flesh, making a sort of grisly sheath.

"Alex sweetie...you've placed so much prized value on this old knife that I believe it to be only right...son," she paused to cackle. "That the truth concerning it be made known to you," her false southern drawl dropped off in mid word. Ruth was speaking in her native south Los Angeles bland tongue now. The sudden change in her verbal inflection drew Alex's attention up from his work, but only briefly. After a quick, hateful gaze he set his focus back down to the task at hand (which was to somehow bust loose and rip Ruth apart with his bare hands if need be). Blood from his battered knuckles was seeping abundantly onto the black, hardened ground out through the seams in his gloves. Alex could tell by the throbbing mixture of sharp and dull pain shooting up his arms from both fists that he busted some if not most of the bones in his hands. And still he did not stop or even cool his efforts, leastwise not of his own capitulation.

Ruth's desire to be heard commanded all of Alex's attention. Dropping her arms lifelessly to her sides she tipped her head slightly forward in his ground beating direction and screamed the word "—STOP!" Alex was instantly yanked straight in a rigid upright position. His hands were stretched flat, fingers out and clasped tightly together, his arms were slapped flatly against his sides and his bowed head was forced up and painfully turned to face Ruth.

"Please do pay attention." Ruth paused to watch a couple of joggers pass by beyond the tree line up on the path. Her pale-blue eyes became coal-black and as dull as lightless air. Alex could only see Ruth, the two joggers being behind his line of sight. The instant her eyes grew dark both unaware runners immediately froze in place and turned to white ash. Ruth opened her mouth wider than humanly possible. Alex saw no teeth or tongue, or even the opening of a throat beyond her stretched thinly lips, only empty darkness. She threw her head back with a neck snapping jerk and in so doing the two bone-colored statues of ash on the path flecked apart and were drawn into Ruth's mouth. Her belly swelled as every white flecks funneled into her. When she'd finished ingesting the warm souls she shut her mouth and swung her head up, facing Alex again.

Ruth's eyes had returned to their pale-blue hue. She pulled her lips apart forming a toothy grin. The teeth that had reappeared in her mouth were blood smeared and looked to be slightly larger. Ruth rubbed her fingertip across her swollen belly and with a gentle push a tight sounding fart squeezed past her cheeks. With the puff of white dust that rose out behind her, Ruth's belly flattened. She giggled shyly, "Now where were we?" she asked softly. "Ah…I remember, grandmamma's story. When I was a little girl she'd told me of a young Italian nobleman that lived with a hand full of gypsy servants in an ancient Roman stronghold deep in the Tuscany Mountains." Ruth began walking around Alex, smearing the tips of her blood stained fingers over his tightly clinched lips, across his right cheek, his ear, the back of his head his left ear, cheek and finally back to his lips. Stopping directly in front of him again she reached down and taking hold of his belt buckle, pulled the waistline of his jeans out and peered down into his pants.

"Well well, looky there," she giggled. "Alex you're as bald as a baby…but my, have you grown."

Alex's brain screamed back at him, *why don't you break her neck? Move…do something, stupid! Why in the hell are you not ripping this foul bitch to bits?*

Releasing his waist band she whispered softly with a privet chuckle, "I prefer the sweet, smooth taste of little boys." There was a lustful dreaminess clinging to her need that filled Alex with the unexpected terror; known only in the hearts of children. "But we will have plenty of time for that later. First I should perhaps finish the history lesson concerning the knife."

"The young Italian noble had learned of a dark spell, one which promised the power of demonic flight as well as eternal life with the oath never to age. And all the spell asked for in trade were the hearts of two children—one boy and one girl. It was an insignificant price to pay for such a grand gift. During the full moon of a mid winter night the noble sent his gypsy servants down the mountain into the village below. From out of their beds the servants snatch a brother and sister. As instructed by the ritual the young noble methodically cut out the boy's heart and forced his little sister to eat it. Then once she finished every last bite of her horrid meal the noble cut out her heart and while its beat slowed to nothing, fed on it.

"To make an already long story shorter—the spell of course didn't work. Four nights after the disappearance of the brother and sister, while the noble was making plans to attempt the spell again, the villagers stormed his ancient home. After finding the mutilated bodies of the two children hidden in a crypt the villagers using only their bare hands and teeth tore the young noble apart. As the noble's screams took flight, his gypsy witch, who'd managed to escape the mob's attention by hiding in the shadows, pulled his dark soul out of his cries. The witch then cast her evil lords mortal spirit into the blade of a bone handled, brass hilted 'rondel dagger.' The same dagger he'd used to cut the hearts out of those two little ones. The same dagger you employed to murder me."

Something moving through the shadows of the trees to Ruth's left turned her eyes black again. Without looking toward the direction of the movement, she swept her left hand up, its palm turned to face the motionless black clouds above. Pulling her fingers into a fist, the blond-haired demon boy Ellzbeth had sent to keep Alex focused, rose into the air.

"What do we have here," Ruth asked.

With his little hands scratching at his own throat, like someone trying to loosen something else's deathly grip, the Shade said in a strained tone of voice.

"Release me whore! Release m—e—"

Ruth slapped her fist down against her own thigh. The Shade's entire body began to glow bright red from the inside out. It screamed in horrible pain as its body started to vibrate violently. The red glow burning within the Shade's skin grew steadily more intense until its little body's shape was nothing more than a bright yellowish white outline in the core of a beaming red ball. Then like the explosion of a sun, the Shade that had tormented Alex throughout the game was gone.

Ruth's eyes were blue once more. "I've no time for interfering bullshit," she said as she took a step back away from Alex. "So sweetie, how does it feel to know the truth about your weapon of choice?"

Thousands of questions, all of which surrounding Mr. Bane screamed in a deafening chorus of indiscernible enquiries. Then suddenly from out of the confusing cluster—fuck of noises and blurry images struggled forth a single word. It emerged both visually before his mind's-eye and verbally, spoken softly into his inner ear. Mr. Bane's metallic voice rose up from deep in Alex's dark soul saying "—ABSOLUTION." And in that single word Alex heard all he needed to understand, at least, so he thought.

"From the moment of my untimely arrival in Hell", Ruth said, her seemingly perpetual smile melted away casting the rest of her expression into the lifeless shadow invoked by her eyes. "I prayed to the foul creatures raking my flesh for one second with you…I prayed for this very moment. Never did I or could I have dreamed it would be this fucking good."

Ruth raised her arms, elbows out, crossing the left forearm over the right. Then mimicking the beautiful blond genie from the sixties television sitcom she blinked her eyes with a sharp nod of her head. There was no flash of colored light or loud crashing roar of thunder. He felt no pain throughout his frame, it had simply taken place. In the time it takes one second to leap to the next, Alex had been physically transformed into the body of his nine year old self, and his feet were no longer imbedded in the ground.

"Now that's much much better," Ruth said coldly as she stepped over and lowered down to her knees. Sliding the dagger free from its makeshift sheath, she gazed deeply into his new youthful face. "Remember all the wonderful times we shared sweetie? Remember how easily I could make you scream? Such good times."

All Alex could do was watch in silent horror as she drew the blade up toward his face. His mind cried in privet panic for Mr. Bane's help, praying that there was still help for him somewhere within its blade. If there was, Alex had no clue whatsoever in what form his crime-partner's aid might occur. As he watched the blade's tip inch up toward his throat Alex hoped that somehow his old friend would find the strength of will to resist Ruth's intent. But nothing was happening, her aim hadn't slowed, there were no signs of strain or the hand shaking struggle of wills as Mr. Bane's attempted to fight against hers.

Using the knife's tip Ruth flipped Alex's now oversized coat aside so that it hung out of her way loosely from his little boy shoulders. His sweat-shirt dropped over his small body like a blood-stained dark-gray dress, hanging clear down to his knees. His jeans and boxer-shorts had both slipped off his skinny waist, past his stick like legs and bony knees to drape over his boots.

"I've always loved the shade of blue in your eyes. Yes indeed I have. Perhaps because they're so much like my own. It's a crying shame that behind them resides a very bad little boy. A boy who needs a harsh bit of reprimanding," she paused to gaze disapprovingly at the hateful look of defiance smeared across Alex's youthful face. "I see you've forgotten how much mommy dislikes it when you refuse her your tears. Are you going to try and deprive me of the absolute joy of your suffering? Hmmm, are you sweetie?"

Ruth sliced the blade down through the middle of Alex's shirt, cutting it open so that it hung from his skinny shoulders to expose his thin naked front. She leaned back to get a good look at Alex the way she remembered him and said softly to herself, "Now this is more like it."

All Alex could do was beam hatred up at her via his eyes. It was a murderous glare that provoked a stinging slap with the back of the same hand clutching the knife. The stigmata like piercing through her palm and out its back healed closed. Whether it was of Ruth's intentional design or not the backhanded strike shook him out of his motionless state. Alex immediately attacked her. Like a cat being smacked back into consciousness, he shot his hands out and latching onto her throat and upper right arm lunging his teeth into her shoulder. In her caught off guard unexpectedness she let Mr. Bane fall from her grasp in order to grab him with both hands. Alex caught sight of the dropping knife in his peripheral vision. Ruth stood with an upright jerk and flung Alex's to the mud. He hit hard and locked his eyes on Mr. Bane stabbed in the soft dirt. With a desperate grunt he scrambled toward it at a running crawl. Alex's fingertip had barely brushed the knife's bone handle when he was taken a hold of physically by Ruth's high-pitch, wordless scream. As he was being torn into the air and suspended at eye level with her, the knife flew out of the mud into Ruth's hand, this time handle first.

"Your father always said you were a bad seed," Ruth hissed as she willed his dangling in place body around to face her. Despite his doomed predicament an expression of deep pride and self-satisfaction swelled in his enraged eyes as he looked at the bite wound he'd driven into her shoulder. Following his gaze as she approached him, Ruth looked down at the deep teeth marks torn into her flesh. "Bad seed indeed," she chuckled. Pressing the tip of her forefinger against the side of her nose closing the left nostril, she blew a dozen or so tiny maggots out of the open side of her nose onto the bite. They wriggled their little selves into Alex's gnashed reminder of his disdain and swiftly melted, sealing the wound with new skin. Coming to a stop, she swung the back of her fist solidly against the side of his face. Blood trickled out of both sides of his nose.

"Take that expression from your eyes!" she struck him again, this time busting open his lower lip. "How dare you look at your mother in that tone."

He dropped to the ground, his leg bent and his knees slapped to the mud. Ruth followed her son, going down to her own knees before him. Grabbing the back of his head by his hair, she wrenched his head back as far as his skinny neck would permit and pressed the tip of the knife's blade against his throat.

"Before I see what a little boy looks like without any skin," Ruth's pale-blue eyes were steadily growing dark, even the whites were being overpowered by an inky black emptiness. She leaned her face nose to nose close as she hissed. "I'm going to *suck*...both of your beautiful blue eyes out of your wicked little skull and eat them up." She gnashed her teeth snappingly together a few times then smacked her lips twice.

The knife's tip sunk slowly into Alex's neck. His brain screamed at him to reach out and drive his thumbs into those shiny black eyes of her's. But his arms wouldn't respond to his mind's commands. They just dangled uselessly at his sides as he felt his blood, which was somehow warm again, trickle down his chest and belly.

"And when I've finished with you," Ruth took the blade's tip from his throat. "I'll go pay that horrid sister of yours a visit."

Ruth positioned her opening mouth over Alex's left eye. She ran her tongue across his pinched shut eyelids then cupped her parted lips over it and started sucking. It didn't take long at all. Like a red pimento being sucked out of a green olive, Alex's eyeball was painfully drawn from its socket into Ruth's mouth. After biting the salty, soft orb free from its optic-nerve cord she pulled her head back, chewed it up then swallowed.

"Ahhhhh—yummy" she declared smacking her lips and wiping a trickle of glistening juice from her chin with a pinky-finger.

Alex's forty-three year old brain howled with terror and pain, trapped in his nine year old skull. All he could do was watch as Ruth ate him blind.

She was moving her gaping mouth back down, positioning it over his right eye. Alex could see bits of chewed eyeball caught between her teeth as she neared. The icy touch of her lips pressed around his eye. He felt the sucking pull begin. She stopped and jerked up, straightening her back. Something in the air had suddenly reached out and snatched her attention, pulling her away before she could finish her meal. Remaining on her knees, Ruth let go of Alex's hair and panned her vision around her, looking deeply through the surrounding growth of briers, blackberry bushes and trees. Seeing nothing, she swung her coal-black gaze back onto Alex "—No he belongs to me!" she screamed.

"Ruuuthy—Ruuuthy. Its time to come back home," several childish voices called out to Ruth from the shadows.

"No, no no no! Fuck no!" she interrupted. "He's mine. I was told, I was told that he was mine...she promised!"

The children's voices began giggling at her. "We've all missed you so Ruthy, our playtime hasn't been the same without...you-u-u-u."

"No! I'm not going back! I'm never going back! I was promised!" Looking down at Alex still writhing in her spell, Ruth swung Mr. Bane up over her head and yelled, "He's mine!" She thrust the blade at his head, but inches before it was to sink into the top of his skull Ruth was yanked up off her knees. She was torn kicking and screaming into the air. Her body went silently rigid, dangling ten feet off the ground in the center of the clearing. Mr. Bane slipped from her fingertips to fall and stab down into the mud...again.

Still sorely locked in a state of torpidity—a flesh, blood and bone statue trapped in a boy's body with an adult killer's awareness, Alex watched. The childish snickering steadily mellowed to faint whispers, like rat's feet on broken glass.

"Be calm Mr. Stone, all shall be as it should," Pike's voice said from behind Alex.

Four small black robed figures moved out of the shadows of the trees in front of Alex. Their bone-white faces were child-like, their heads bald and hidden beneath wide black hoods. The small beings surrounded Ruth's hovering body. Simultaneously they turned their shiny black eyes toward Alex. All at once, as if in a single voice speaking through four they said, "Take much comfort in the knowledge that this one will suffer relentlessly."

They set their attention sharply back up onto Ruth and began to giggle again. As Ruth faded so did they, taking her back to Hell…back to B'neem.

As soon as Ruth Rose Stone and the echoing giggle of the four cherubs was gone Pike stepped out from the thicket of shrubs and moved around to stand in front of Alex.

"I rather prefer you in this child's frame over that larger one," Pike said with a half chuckle. "If I believed it would help you win the game I would most assuredly leave you this way." Pike shot a glance down at the river, then shifted his scanning gaze around through the trees. With a wave of his hand the dark clouds that Ruth had trapped in a state of aerial motionlessness over the clearing were turned loose. Finally Pike looked back into Alex's one eyed little boy's face and smiled, Alex's missing eye reformed, growing outward in the pink, empty socket. His broken nose and busted lower lip reset and healed. The shallow stab wound in his throat mended itself closed. Alex's forced state of immobility was wiped away as Pike motioned his hand toward Alex's clothes and said, "You may get dressed if you wish."

Still locked in his nine year old frame he was about to make reference to it when he was uneventfully returned to his forty-three year old self. As Alex stepped to his things he took a chance and asked, "What the hell was that about?" referring to Ruth's appearance. At first it seemed as though Pike was going to ignore the question, but with a mumbled "—Very well," Pike gave Alex a brief explanation as to what had occurred.

"The one who stoled your mother from us thought that by using her against you first, then the remaining other players once you were out of the way, would ensure her a victory."

With his jeans on, Alex picked his sliced open shirt up from out of the mud and examined it with a *what in blazes am I supposed to do with this?* expression on his exhausted face. He shook it free of mud and held it out with the thumbs and index-fingers of both hands like clothes-pins on a line. *Someone will undoubtedly find it; one of the still living…a child perhaps*, Alex remembered Mr. Bane saying about his hat when he considered leaving it on the floor of that phone-booth.

"Is there a problem Mr. Stone?" Pike asked snidely as he stepped over to the side of the oak's trunk. Before Alex could offer an equally sardonic response Pike, without so much as the slightest hand gesture mended the sweat-shirt…even cleaning and drying it, only Five's and Alex's own blood stains remaining.

"It seems that we have been faced with an unexpected dilemma Mr. Stone." Looking down at the slab of concrete stomped down over the ammo boxes hiding place. Pike raised his arm, stretching an extended middle finger out, pointing it behind him at Mr. Bane stabbed in the mud. Alex was in the middle of lacing up his boots, when at the instant he looked up, a black chain shot out of Pike's sleeve. It swept through the air, then lashed down and reached into Mr. Bane's blade. Pike's fist wrapped tightly around the chain and with a hard yank he pulled a woman out of the dagger's steel. The chain, which was leashed tightly around her throat, flung her body through the air like a cat in the jaws of a rather large dog, then slammed her solidly onto the ground. Pike's chain slid from her neck to snap out of sight back into his sleeve.

Alex's knees popped with a loud cracking noise as he shoved himself upright fast, the laces of his left boot still hanging loosely down both sides. Taking a step toward her, then quickly changing his mind for whatever reason, he decided no, maybe not and retook three steps backward. Her long, straight hair appeared to be a golden-brown, that is what he could see of it. From the top of her head down to the soles of her feet she was covered with a dark-red sticky substance that to Alex resembled blood. It was blood, although not a drop of it was her own. She raised her head with shaky effort and opened her eyes, eyes that were a piercing dark-brown. In them Alex could see deep horror. And as with the blood that shrouded her slender frame the horrors that reflected in those beautiful eyes were not her own. In a quivering weak voice she spoke saying, "Alex my dear boy—help me." Her head collapsed in the mud.

Alex was for the first time in both of his existences—without words. Speechlessly he stared bewildered down at this sobbing, nude woman; or whatever she was. Alex looked over at Pike in the hope that the Gate Keeper would volunteer an explanation. But as he was waiting for the fiery eyed little angel to speak up, the pained voice of the woman struggled to reach Alex's ears.

"I know that I should have told you," she spoke with a recognizably European accent, Romanian or Italian Alex guessed. "Forgive me—Mi scusi Alessandro—"

"Silence!" Pike swung the opening of his hood from the ammo boxes grave at the base of the tree around onto her. She'd begun pulling herself over the mud toward Alex who was in-turn stepping back away from her.

"You were alone—afraid—in need of help," her voice cracked and shook with great pain. "I heard you crying, both yours and her's—Susan's crying. No one else cared to hear—"

"I said silence," Pike echoed calmly.

Her right arm was yanked straight up, her hand raised to the sky. Off the ground she went as if a line hooked to her hand was pulling her into the air. The back of her wrist slapped flat against one of the thick, high over-hanging branches of the oak tree. "Alessandro!" She screamed as the dagger Alex knew as Freak Bane tore up out of the ground and shot like an arrow through her wrist. Nailed to the limb, her body several feet above the earthen bed she'd been yanked from, she cried in what Alex figured was Italian. "Mis scusi—Alessandro, Mi scusi mi per ingannare Tui. Lo la soltanto via—la soltanto via per mi guadagnane absolute e liberare il mio anima. Mi scusi—Mi scusi—"

"Are you going to tell me what the fuck's going on or not?" Alex barked, looking from the dangling woman over at Pike.

"No," Pike replied, his tone stern. "No—I'm not."

"Well, why the hell not?"

"Because quite frankly Mr. Stone I'm as perplexed as you are. Perhaps she can clear it up for us. Should I ask her?"

"Yes…by all means do…please," Alex choked back the growl swelling in his throat.

Pike removed his hood as he stepped between Alex and the woman. His back to her, looking into Alex's weary face, Pike asked simply "—what is your name?"

"Bianca Delisio," she answered almost immediately.

"How is it that you came to reside within the blade?"

"I had no choice," she sobbed.

"What the fuck have you done with Freaks Bane?" Alex demanded to know.

"No Mr. Stone," Pike cut in. "This acquisitioning is mine to pull forth. Do please mind your tongue." Pike set his back to Alex and continued.

"Explain yourself…what do you mean you had no choice?"

"My master Don Barbetti had learned of a spell that promised endless life and eternal youth. It was I who told him of the spell and what it asked for—"

"Why?"

"Gold."

"Who are you that you should know of such things to trade for gold?"

"I am Bianca, the gypsy witch of Catania," she announced in a tone confused with both pride and shame.

"Tell me of this spell witch, and for what it asks?"

"It is a dark charm that demands a great price."

"What is this cast? For what does it demand?"

"The mortal veils of two small children to be torn from their being and cast into the darkness."

"Explain?"

"The heart of a boy must be cut from its place and fed to a girl child—"

"Was this done?" Pike interrupted, his tone sharply hissed as he glanced over his shoulder up at Alex who was watching the interrogation.

"Yes," she answered with a whisper. "It was."

"And you were a willing part of this horrid act?"

"Yes."

"Continue!"

She set her shame filled gaze across onto Alex, who was leering back up at her with confused hatred.

"Continue!" Pike ordered. "What of the little girl?"

"I took her heart from its place and served it to Don Barbetti, who fed upon it as its beats slowed to a stop," her gaze fell disgracefully away from Alex.

"And the spell...did it take?" Pike's voice was coldly curious.

"It may have, that is if not for the mob."

"What mob?" Pike chuckled as he said to Alex. "There's always a mob."

"Men from the town. They broke down Don Barbetti's palazzo doors. After finding the two children's remains they burned all of the servants alive, then gave my master over to their hounds. I believe Don Barbetti's dark soul fled his flesh while the beasts tore it apart; I saw it riding on the wake of his screams then move into the body of a young man."

"Why do you think this?"

"Because, from my hiding place in the shadows I witnessed a darkness settle over one of the town's men. An evil expression swelled in his eyes that hadn't been there a second earlier."

"And the dagger?" Pike turned and faced Alex. "How is it that you happened to be hidden within its blade?"

"To escape the mob's fury I sliced my own throat." With great pains Bianca raised her head, exposing her neck to show them the almost ear to ear gash laid across her throat. "I spoke the words to an ancient charm as I bled my gypsy soul into the blade. Not my master's soul, mine."

Alex looked down at Pike who in turn gave Alex a slight nod. Pike stepped aside clearing the path for Alex to step by. "You've been deceiving me," Alex said calmly, or at least as calmly as his rage would permit.

"Would you have cared to hear me if you knew I'd once been what you...we hate the most," Bianca asked, her words, despite the accent and female lilt sounding a bit like Mr. Bane. "Even as a child, would you have heard me Alex if I'd told you I was a monster not unlike your parents?"

"You mislead me, even with your voice—"

"What voice is this?" Pike inquired.

"When I was locked in the closet—"

"No, not you Mr. Stone" Pike interrupted, turning his fiery gaze back up onto the dangling witch. "I wish to hear it from her lips."

"From my self-imprisonment in the dagger's blade I moved through the centuries, silently waiting, watching for the key that would unlock the spell to my own curse. The blade always being used for its intended purpose; to open mortal flesh and bleed away life. Every drop of the blood spilled on the blade washed over my trapped soul, staining me with its crimson touch. Then I heard Alex and Susan Stone's cries, and in their suffering I found a chance for redemption. I would right my wrongs through the boy weeping in the darkness and finally find some absolution."

Pike let loose a thunderously loud belly-laugh and said, "I'd always believed you a madman who talked to himself," he paused to blast out more roaring laughter. "When in fact you were a madman speaking not too, but with a bewitched dagger. In any case, the witch belongs to B'neem. She shall avoid her place in Hell no more. And as for you Mr. Stone—you've a game to win if I'm not mistaken."

Pike's ruby colored eyes began to lose their fiery brilliance, dulling to a flat, dark almost spoiled-blood like hue. As his thin lipped grin widened, Bianca's body started to twitch spastically as if being hit with the business end of a live-wire. Her weeping sobs and whispered pleas morphed into full-blown shrieks and screams. Wisps of light-gray smoke drifted lazily up out of her head, hands, feet and crotch. Blisters rose on her skin as hundreds of crack-like tears appeared all over her body. The hair-line thin breaks in her flesh raced in every direction all at once and glowed bright yellow and red from the inferno raging within her.

Taking a fool's chance Alex stepped sharply between Pike and his fun. "Please Gate Keeper...stop," Alex asked calmly, yet still loud enough to be heard over her screams.

"The answer is...No, Mr. Stone," Pike said, foreseeing Alex's request.

"But she's a part of my weapon!" Alex shouted over her howls. "Players must use the weapon employed in their crime, their sin. She was part of my knife when I killed the Five...my crime...my sin!"

Pike stopped, and without a word he sent Bianca the gypsy witch back into Alex's knife.

"Very well Mr. Stone. For now she resides in the blade, wouldn't want you to loose some of your winning streak's cutting edge. But only for now, after the game she takes her place on B'neem's blade." Pike went down to one knee and drew something in the soft earth with his finger. "Good hunting Mr. Stone." The Gate Keeper stood and disappeared back to Hell and the nightmare that awaited him beneath B'neem's angry red sky. Pike's performance as Alex's guardian angle had drawn to a close.

Alex stood motionless for a bit, staring at the spot where Pike had been before vanishing into thin air. Saying nothing, not to himself or to the child killing gypsy sealed in the blade. Looking up he gazed blankly at the bone-handled cutting tool that he had for so long called friend. Suddenly it was simply nothing more than another knife. *I suppose I'd best climb up and get it down*, he thought. Alex was dog-fucking-tired and angry to the point of not giving a damn.

In a low metallic voice, heavily over toned with a note of shame, so self-loathing that if it could be perceived with the human eye it would appear so ugly that the sight of it would cause the strongest of men to sob uncontrollably. In this rattled tongue Bianca said, "Thank you Ale—"

"Don't," Alex said, paused then added. "I need to think…I need to think. Please, just a little time. I need to think." He shook his head hard as if he were mad at it; as if doing so would jimmy loose the fatigue gnashing on his perseverance. He dropped to his right knee and finished tying his left boot lace. Glancing again up at the knife high in the tree Alex mouthed, *shit house luck*, as he pictured himself trying to shimmy out onto that limb. Suddenly he caught himself laughing and couldn't for the life of himself—or moreover—the death of himself see what was so damn funny. It took some doing but he eventually managed to kill his sudden inadvertent out-burst. With that out of the way Alex picked his mud-stomped trench coat up out of the dirt and tossed it onto the thorny shrubs close to his hat.

Stepping grudgingly up to the old tree, he helped himself to a deep sigh while visually negotiating its sizeable width, vertical rise, and height. Spotting a few conveniently placed knot-holes and limbs that had long-since been snapped off and time-worn down to stumps, he felt a smidgen of relief in that the first phase of the resented rescue would be a breeze. With a flatly voiced, "up-up and away," to himself, Alex began his ascent.

As he figured it would be, the climb to the top of the wide trunk was swift and easily executed. He was about eighteen or twenty feet up, he estimated. Alex pulled up onto the trunk's hub, the tree's focal point whereon all the large and small branches reached for space and bowed toward the earth. In a frenzied design with no rhyme nor reason the oak's arms and countless knotting fingers spread out to surround Alex. From where he sat Alex could peer over and see the smooth, rounded butt of the dagger's bone-handle. It was about fifteen feet out. At the point where the branch grew out of the trunk it was no less than two feet around. It reached slightly upward at about a thirty degree angle and sharply narrowed so that where Pike had left the knife was no more than seven or eight inches in diameter. Alex knew this because the knife's blade was ten inches long and he could see at least one full inch of its tip sticking out of the other side. Add in the small amount of space between the knife's hilt and the limb, that had been filled with the witches wrist and you have seven or eight inches.

Alex swung the side of his boot against the branch, striking at it a few times in order to get some idea as to its density and strength. After crashing his heel down hard on it as well, he felt satisfied in that the limb seemed solid enough to support his weight.

The chilly morning air smelled crisp and clean. Alex closed his eyes and straightening his back, drew a deep breath in through his nostrils. The strong scent of wet moss, fallen leaves and damp tree-bark caressed his memory. Susan's face; as he remembered her, as a child...a sweet child with bright, big green eyes, raven black, straight hair and a glowing smile. He suddenly felt as weightless as the gentle image he was looking at. The sound of laughter, evil and lifeless filled the darkness cradling Susan's image. It was a woman's laughter, not Ruth's; it was new laughter, immeasurably vile. It whipped through Alex's skull, clawing across his mind's-eye. The black in Susan's hair bled away becoming an arterial shade of red. What little color had dwelled beneath her pale skin drained from her chubby cheeks giving her complexion a waxen, corpse like hue. Her face grew larger, aging, changing. Black lines were appearing evenly around her eyes and as her lips became full in shape and black in color Alex heard an icy voice say, "There's always your baby sister, Millstone."

The sound of a fish slapping against the surface of the muddy Mary's river snapped open Alex's eyes. His body, clear down into his bones ached with a coldness so icy that it felt as though his bones could shatter.

"Her name is Vile, Alex," Bianca's metallic voice whispered. "And she means you harm."

Alex steadied himself in the tree as he shook out some of the cold left in the events wake. "Yeah...what makes you so mother fucking knowledgeable?" Alex asked past chattering teeth.

"Before the one called Pike carried me to you in the box of hearts, I was with another. A girl I believe. It may have been the voice who spoke to you through the white dog and phone—"

"To the point!" Alex snapped.

"I'd over heard her and Pike quarreling over one who calls herself Queen Vile. It seems she has big plans for Hell. I believe Alex, that she is the one Pike spoke of in his vague explanation as to why Ruth had showed up to eat your eyes. If I'm correct, then this Vile creature will be a tad-bit upset...Susan is apparently on her mind."

"I've got to go to her!" Alex said under his breath.

"You can't leave the city limits Alex."

"But Susan...she's alone, helpless. I've got no choice. I won't abandon her again!"

"If you attempt to leave the game Alex, it'll be bad for you," Bianca reminded. "I've an idea."

"Why should I listen to you?" Alex growled.

"Because Alex, whether you want to believe it or not, other than yourself...I'm all you've got." There was a long pause. Alex panned his sight around as if another choice might be seen hovering in space waiting, hoping to be employed.

"I'm listening," Alex grudgingly hissed.

"Win the game, Pike seems to like you. By winning for him you'll fall deeper into his favor. He may be willing to grant you a wish," the voice paused. "It's your choice Alex."

"We finish the game," Alex replied coldly.

Alex leaned forward on the branch and began pulling himself toward the weapon formally known as Mr. Bane. The narrowing limb rocked against his weight, bobbing up and down as he shimmied along its length. Half way to the target Alex could lean over and see all of the knife's hand-grip. Sliding a bit further and he could see its hilt as well as the inch and a half section of blade between the hilt and the limb. He'd dragged himself close enough to be able to reach out with his left hand and grab its handle.

Simply being able to wrap his fist around it wouldn't be enough. Pike had chosen a branch with no rot or weakness of even the slightest degree. Solid oak, it was through and through, down the whole of its length. Alex would need to be practically on top of the dagger in order to have the leverage it required to pull the bulk of the blade out. It took some careful balance and a few more seconds, but Alex finally positioned himself on the precariously narrow limb over the knife. With both legs and his right arm wrapped around the branch he struggled to work the blade loose. At first its stubbornness put up a good fight, still it was no match for Alex's determination. It was slowly inching out when something caught Alex's eye. He narrowed his tired sight down to the ground and drawn in the soft earth directly beneath him were the letters C.H.S and beneath them 12:10 P.M. It was what Pike had been drawing in the earth before he disappeared. *What's it mean?* he thought questionably. *C.H.S—C.H...S—C.H.S? 12:10. C—humm—Corvallis House.* Corvallis Corvallis.

"Corvallis High School!" Alex announced. In the same instant there was an unpleasant cracking noise and before Alex's realization grasped a hold of the sound's inevitable outcome, the limb snapped free from the tree. One second he was above the ground, the next he'd slammed down against it. Like had happened so many times since his death, the bout with gravity and subsequent landing knocked all the wind from his lungs on impact.

"Ki—King!" he struggled to say with a breathless grunt. It was the only logical explanation Alex's fumbling through pain and darkness brain could, or would grab onto. *Its where and when I'll find him or some other player,* he thought while flat on his back staring beyond the tree he'd dropped out of at a clear-blue morning sky, framed in green leaves and dark-gray clouds. Shoving out from under the broken branch Alex stood and locking it in place with his boot he took hold of the knife. With a single yank he freed the blade and without a word to its true occupant slid it into the sheath and snapped its strap over the hilt.

Alex Stone put on his coat and hat and left the secret place of his childhood forever.

Chapter Nine

— The Baby's Got a Gun! —

Weapons are the tools of fear;
a decent man will avoid them
except in the direst necessity,
and, if compelled, will use
them only with the utmost
restraint.

—Lau Tzu
Tao Te Ching

B'neem was in a state of enraged clatter when Pike returned from the game's playing-field on Earth. Not since the second great war had there been unrest to such an inflamed degree. All breed of angelic beings and demonic beasts were clad in battle dress and armed with the ancient weaponry of Hell's last skirmish, most of which still stained with the blood of long-ago slain foes. The damned souls that hadn't been cast into the eighth realm's molten core for safe keeping were being hitched by the tens of thousands to giant implements of war. Like two legged furless oxen and mules the vast bulk of the realm's mortal charges were being whipped and chained to great stone battering rams, mammothly huge catapults and various other colossal siege weapons. It was truly an amazing sight to behold, the speed and proficiency with which a military force of such an incalculable size in number could be made battle-ready.

365

Pike was led to the top of Ellzbeth's tower to be shown the wall of solid rock where the door had been. Before Pike's return, some of the realm's most powerful sorcerer-archangels had been summoned to try and tear ascender Vile's spell shrouding the stone barrier. For hours during the Gate Keeper's absence they hit the walled doorway with every counter-spell and charm they could invoke, with no sign of success.

"Go! All of you…get out of my sight!" Pike shouted as soon as he turned the corner of the tower stairs. As they moved swiftly down past him he shot his gaze up onto Scipio the lesser angel who Ellzbeth had impowed with red skin. "Not you," Pike said. "Take a place behind me," he added under his breath.

Pike stood before the walled doorway barring the entrance into Ellzbeth's small chamber. Without words or ceremony he swept the thumbnail of his left hand across the black stone. At the exact same time that he'd laid a long, deep scratch in the stone; thousands of miles away, while she was seated on her throng of tangled bodies, a similar scratch was magically drawn across Vile's bosom. As blood dark and heavily frosted with tiny ruby like ice crystals trickled down the black stone, it also streamed down Queen Vile's white skin.

The bleeding wall began sending out sharp hissing noises that rapidly increased in volume, filling the narrow stairway with an ear raking, high-pitched squall. From the base of the wall to the ceiling, Vile's stone barrier started glowing with intense heat. As the now beaming rock shimmered with white-hot energy Pike, without glancing back over his shoulder, waved his hand as if he were swatting at a fly. The step Scipio was standing on rose up above the other steps a few feet. As the red-skinned angel steadied himself on the rising slab he heard Pike say, "Once the flow has cooled follow me."

The shrieking, glowing wall liquefied to molten rock. It shifted and moved like fat beneath a dragon's breath and slid from the entryway to flow with the demeanor of lava down the spiraling stairs. A hole steadily pulled open above Pike's head and segued down, stretching larger. The shallow river of molten slag caught the hemline of the Gate Keeper's robes on fire which he promptly extinguished with a mere thought. It flowed past his boots, melting the soles and heels as he stepped through the glowing, dripping hot doorway, entering Ellzbeth's place of solitude.

The yellowish glow emanating from the melted stone behind Pike was enough light to see the bloody aftermath of Vile's visit. But as the rock cooled so did the lambent. Before leaving the small round chamber with her prisoner, Vile had also sealed the room's four windows, covering them with stone as she'd done with the door. Pike stomped the bottom of his melted boot down with a loud crash against the iron floor. An action that caused the black stone blocking the windows to be transformed into ash and fall away. The planet's enraged sky of battling reds poured in through the windows, brightly casting the room in an abbattireous crimson bath of light. Pike stepped over and knelt beside the bulk of Sader's mutilated remains, still twitching and pulsating with the awareness of immortal life. Lying broken on the floor next to what used to be Sader's head was Ellzbeth's purple clay mask; a large bloody, bare foot print smeared over its shattered pieces.

Scipio went immediately down to his knees as soon as he stepped into the room. Bowing his face all the way to the floor he wailed, "It was I who found the Overseer's wounded body Gate Keeper...it was I who brought him here. I Scipio delivered the trap that did this. I should—nay; I must be dealt with harshly my Lord." Resting his forehead on the blood splattered floor, Scipio swung his arms around and crossed his wrists over the small of his back. "Do with me as your rage demands."

"Ellzbeth," Pike paused. "The Grand Inquisitor advanced your station...yes?"

"Yes my Lord."

"And she granted you a higher breed's authority to draw upon B'neem's magic and power, as well as the knowledge and wisdom to know when to wield such an honor. Is this not true?"

"Yes my Lord, the realm's Grand Inquisitor had," Scipio answered, his spiked head still pressed flat against the floor awaiting Pike's fury to lash out. "A gift my Lord Gate Keeper, far removed from the worth of the carcass which houses my consciousness," he added.

"Up," Pike half mumbled as he glanced over onto piles of still frozen hornets heaped here and there on the floor. "Up—off your knees.

What was your breed before Ellzbeth elevated your station seraph or houri?"

Scipio stood, "seraph my Lord."

"Now when you're asked from which breed you hail, your answer will be archangel. Now go, and order B'neem's scribe to collect his pen and parchment. Tell him to wait for me outside my chamber. Afterward, have seven of B'neem's fastest messengers ready. Now go."

A few slow sliding seconds had stretched out toward the completion of a minute between the time that Scipio left the room and when Pike finally stood. He panned his cool, raging gaze around him. Looking at his friend's chamber, Pike found himself remembering the last time he'd been in Ellzbeth's tower hideaway. A deep sense of regret latched onto his heart as he recalled how upset he'd made her by transporting her into Vile's throne room in an effort to shock Ellzbeth into silence. His sight swept sharply around to drop on Ellzbeth's mask. His brow narrowed and his upper lip peeled back like that of a mad-dog intentionally showing-off its top row of teeth. The mask's shattered sections snapped together, adding more cracks to those already drawn across its purple surface. It flew from the gruesome floor into Pike's reaching hand. He pulled his hood off his head of wildly tangled red hair and placed Ellzbeth's clay veil over his face. Blood, Sader's blood, which was caked thick and sticky on its inner surface stuck to the skin of his face, carrying in it the strong scent of his friend, and a coppery taste. The silent heat in Pike's gaze burned as hot as the hearts of two nightmare-stars, and beamed furiously out through the eye-holes.

Pike clapped his hands twice and stomped his left boot once. Before the thunderously loud echo of the heel's crash had completely faded away into the quiet of his rage, a crimson mist like a fog of fresh blood rose up and filled the chamber. He knelt beside Sader's fragmented body again and laid the palms of both hands flat on the cold iron floor. Sader's torn body parts vibrated with even more zeal. The bones and ripped flesh started to slide over the bloody floor with purpose toward the larger pieces, which in turn slithered over to conjoin with even larger segments of mangled flesh. The streams, smears and puddles of blood swiftly followed suit with the gathering hunks of meat and bone. The red liquid moved up into the ripped veins and arteries as the little flayed body of the Overseer coalesced into a single pile.

Sader's shattered head had begun to swiftly reassemble, snapping back together with wet sounding *claps and pops*, while his brain rose from its squashed state to slither back into the rebuilding brainpan. Muscles along with countless veins reached greedily up over soggy bone. Meat which had begun to dry because of the asphyxiating heat in that chamber was now becoming moist again, and the blood that had started hardening to a blackened, sticky gunk suddenly liquefied.

Skin stretched over the newly forming muscles to cover the Overseer's meaty, eyeless face. Within mere seconds the four pieces of his ripped apart, yet still somehow beating heart moved over the floor to meet and grow back together. It slid with inch-worm like movements into his ripped open chest cavity where it nuzzled comfortably between the two exploded lungs. While Sader's mutilated lungs healed, going from corpse-gray to blueish-pink, rising and falling with steady breathes of hot oxygen, his entrails moved into their intended place. Simultaneously bones and muscles reset and stretched throughout his being. The rib-cage reattached to his spine and promptly wrapped around the organs for which it was meant to defend. The rest of his torn skin pulled together, covering his chest, arms, and legs.

Pike's eyes, closed behind Ellzbeth's mask and were opened by the weak sound of a shaky voice.

"Sh-e-eee's g-gu-gone," Sader said. "Pu-P-Pike –it—it was Va-Vi-Vile!" The empty sockets of the Overseer's eyes filled with blood that churned round to form two perfect orbs which went swiftly from red to black, then to bright eyes of liquid silver. Closed eyelids appeared over the shiny spheres to immediately stutter open. With much effort Sader focused his new gaze up, allowing his vision to drift lazily over the purple mask. For an instant, his fuzzy sight was fooled into thinking Ellzbeth was who knelt over him. But his eye's strength sharpened and as he took notice of the mane of fiery red hair wildly framing the mask, his heart shrank with the realization of events. Shamefully riding his gaze onto the inferno roaring beyond the eye-holes he whispered, "Vile—Vile took Ellzbeth. I failed you both…I failed B'ne—"

"Shhhhh old friend," Pike said softly as he rested his palm on Sader's blood smeared waxen shoulder. "Save your strength, you'll be needing it whilst you stand at my side in battle." Pike shifted his attention around to look out Ellzbeth's window in the direction of Zaw'naw. "We'll bring our Inquisitor back home," Pike's tone of voice was agelessly definitive and unforgivingly cold. "I swear upon my very heart, Vile and all who are foolish enough to stand with her will fall and it will be B'neem's claws that shall be waiting to catch them."

Pike's eyes went white-hot.

Vile's anger at seeing her player fall so effortlessly, not to mention witnessing Alex's nick of time rescue from Ruth's long awaited chance for revenge was unexpectedly quite calm. Even the deep slash wound Pike had laid across her perfectly shaped breasts, from thousands of miles away wasn't sufficient in pulling out the tempest she was so famous for. But her mellow demeanor was but a thin veil. Behind her eyes and deep within the icy core of her evil heart screamed a storm of unprecedented fury. She settled comfortably back in her throne of twisted flesh and bones and gazed smugly into the golden eyes of her prize.

In a small round iron cage, at least fifty feet above Queen Vile's icy throne room floor was Ellzbeth. All that held the sphere of iron bars aloft was a single hair from Vile's own head. The almost invisibly thin strand was tied at one end to the cage, while the other end stretched straight up into the darkness, tied to nothing but cold, empty air and Vile's will.

Seated awkwardly in the cramped cage, Ellzbeth shifted her attention from her captor to the two severed heads hovering lazily around the cage. Despite the male's lower half of his face being torn away, she recognized him as Warfarin, the sixth realm's Grand Inquisitor. The other head, with its eyeless sockets and chattering teeth was so badly disfigured that Ellzbeth could barely determine its gender as female Ellzbeth had never met Vexrile face to face until now, with a private guess she figured this poor creature to be Vile's Overseer.

"They made a bad choice," Vile half giggled as she rode her throne closer to the cage. "I trust you're comfortable?" The throne eased to a stop only a few feet from the cage. "I've a gift for you Ellzbeth, I've learned of your fondness for the wearing of masks, so I took it upon myself to fashion one for you. Yes, with my own two hands—I do hope you like it?"

With her magic lost within Vile's grasp, Ellzbeth's body was powerless to the mad-queen's will. With only the vain efforts of physical resistance she struggled against it. The battle was brief. With the swift ease of a sword's edge slicing down through aged silk, Vile slid passed Ellzbeth's manual contrariety. She latched onto the golden-eyed reminder of a past long gone to dust with the icy power of her will and pulled Ellzbeth toward the edge of the cage. The throne inched closer and Vile leaned forward on her fleshy seat as she forced her prize's head out from between the bars.

"Release me!" Ellzbeth screamed into Vile's face. "Your realm will be crushed to rubble when Pike comes!" Vile sat for a moment, her elbows resting on her knees, listening to Ellzbeth make her threats, all the while her teeth baring grin never fading, Ellzbeth screamed, "Its over! You've been beaten once more! Your player was weak as you are weak! Give yourself over to the magistrate so that you may avoid Pike's wrath and spare the sixth realm from total annihilation—"

"You convinced me long ago to do what you said was our only chance, my only chance. And with my arms cradling some of the God's most powerful of secrets, I listened," Vile's smile melted. "I listened because you were my friend—or so I'd believed. Have you ever asked yourself Sarah," Vile addressing Ellzbeth now by her old name, "how events may have turned out if I wouldn't have listened to you—if I would have kept those books of power?" Vile paused as she slowly turned her open palms up, a foot or so beneath Ellzbeth's chin. "Well, have you, my trusted friend?"

"No Sillona, what would be the point?" Ellzbeth replied, her tone almost sad.

"Why—regret, of course." An iron mask appeared in Vile's hands. It possessed no eye-holes or a slit for a mouth. It had been made to warp around and cover one's entire head. Metal hinges, positioned along the front center of the mask allowed it to open evenly down the middle. Vile flipped open the hooked clasps locking it closed with her thumbnail.

"Its best feature hides within," Vile said softly as she eased it open. A sharp sounding squeak stretched out into the black air around them as the two sections parted.

"Pike will piss on your bones when this is over," Ellzbeth hissed as her vision reached into the darkness of the opening iron shell to fall on dozens of inch long steel spikes. They were pointed and double edged reaching up from the inside surface like the fangs of vipers.

Holding the mask fully open beneath Ellzbeth's face, all she could do was scream over Vile's voice as she laughed saying, "This will never be over." Vile willed Ellzbeth's head down fast and hard, slamming B'neem's golden-eyed Inquisitor's face into the mask. She crashed it around her head and shoved Ellzbeth backward into the cage. Vile waved her hand as she settled back in her throne. While Ellzbeth loosed metallically muffled cries; the seam that ran evenly up over the mask vanished, fusing the iron shell around her head. Blood streamed down Ellzbeth's neck, staining her white robes and freezing to her skin.

"Just in-case, I placed a charm into the steel of those spikes, spikes by the way which were forged from the blade of Satan's sword. I doubt that even that fool Pike will be able to undo their spell. If by some chance you're found and brought back to this world, and if that mask is unlocked and removed, the marks left in the spike's wake will never heal. No matter what form you choose to adopt, your face will forever show to all who gaze upon it the depths of my disdain for you," Vile paused to laugh "—you say its over—you tell me, I've lost. Well Sarah old friend, you've never been more wrong about anything in your entire life than you are about that."

Vile shot a fast glance at Warfarin's hovering head, his golden eyes rolling in his skull as beetles fed upon his brain.

"And as for you! You truly believed I could be overthrown. King of the sixth realm. How bloody absurd. Ruler of fools is more your calling." She caught sight of Vexrile's head floating past her peripheral vision. Without looking Vile swept her right hand out and plucked the eyeless head out of the darkness. Cradling it in her left arm, she stroked Vexrile's practically skinless face, gazing endearingly down into the red, meaty holes of her empty sockets.

"Poor—poor stupid rat eater so easily lead astray, and to think—I actually called you daughter." Vile mimicked Vexrile's chattering teeth by chattering her own, then cast the head aside like a spoiled child bored to death with a new toy.

She willed her throne away from the cage, slightly deeper into the black air of her throne room. Bringing it to a hovering stop she clapped her hands together once. Two fully armored guards stepped just beyond the doorway and saying nothing stopped.

"Summon Sumac," she whispered.

As the guards went in search of their commander as ordered, Vile gazed across the high darkness into the cage, resting her blank expression onto the almost motionless form of her long ago best and closest comrade. An odd sensation wriggled out from deep within her frozen soul. It swelled up in her throat. She fought to shove it back down, but it was even more powerful than her will. It moved into her mouth and like an unstoppable hiccup, it flew out to echo off the walls.

Queen Vile was sobbing.

While Pike and his commanders were drafting a plan of attack against Zaw'naw; the would be Queen and Madam Sumac—Vile's field marshal for the Imperial Guard—were composing a counter assault in response to the impending onslaught soon to befall the sixth realm. And as the two hellish supper-powers prepared to unleash their worst upon one another, Alex and the bewitched dagger—formally known as Freak Bane were unwittingly heading away from another power-struggle.

A quarter mile behind Alex, out of ear-shot from the sound of clashing blades, Nancy White and Dolly Man/Napoleon King were bull-locked in a little skirmish of their own.

They were at least fifty perhaps sixty yards away from one another, Nancy and King. Simultaneously the two cold-blooded killers swept their eager vision around through the dense growth of pines in the middle of Corvallis' Avery Park to lock eyes. The bald-headed, female litigator in her blood-stained skirt suit, in her right hand the old sword, in her left her spiked high heel shoes. She grinned across at the large, half dressed man and charged. The ash-gray black man, sporting his prison-hospital-gown with his corpse colored ass hanging out of the slit; peeled his thick lips back in an apoplectic expression and did likewise—raised his big knife and charged.

Shafts of morning light sliced through the tall trees like spears slicing away at dying shadows. The bright, beams strobed past their wiled-eyed faces as they ran head-long at each other shadow to light—shadow to light—shadow to light. It traced almost magically across the raising blades with star-like glint that skipped in a sort of scorching metal dance over the starved for cold blood steel. Dolly Man's primal cry was muted and practically gagged out of existence by Ms. White's insane cackling. Even at the rapidly dwindling distance, in the uneven shadows of the wooded mound, King could see no signs of fear in her, as the crazy white woman advanced. Nancy on the other hand believed she spotted a bit of doubt and traces of fear in the large player's movements.

If Nancy's thinness in comparison to King's six-foot four, two hundred and sixty-six pound frame seemed a bit of a disadvantage to those watching from Hell's cinemas, it didn't show up in her unbound eagerness. Nancy greatly made up for her petite dimensions with a display of resolve that was not unlike the salivating tenacity of a rabid wolverine. This along with the self-confidence and uncanny skill with which she swept the sword's blade around and around above her laughing head balanced things out nicely.

The apprehension King was experiencing wasn't so much stemming from the possibility that this crazy white lady could actually beat him—not at all. The shadow of terror she'd seen peering out from behind his seared face came from his childhood fear of crazy people, especially fearless, insane, cracker bitches. In the same way some people carry the fear of clowns with them for their entire lifetimes, Dolly Man sported this frightfulness for the mad. It didn't make him any less dangerous though—quite the contrary. After all, a grizzly-bear is at its absolute deadliest when threatened to the point of fearfulness.

Both players zigzagged toward each other around the trees. When they were ten or so yards apart each slowed their pace to a skipping jog, studying one another for the most effective window of attack to leap through. Darting right around a wide tree, Nancy looked at King's knife then gazed lazily along the blade of her own weapon.

"Mine's bigger than yours—na—na—naaaa," she baited. "Goddamn, you're ugly. What the fuck happened to your face boy?"

"Bring your nasty little ass over here and if you work it good enough for my liking, I just may tell you a story," Dolly Man offered as he side-stepped to the right.

"Where's your clothes?" She asked. But before he could issue a reply Nancy dropped one of her shoes, faked forward, stopped, then with a swift cut to the right then left in a sort of bobbing advance she made the first move. King swung his knife back and forth in her approaching direction. His blade whistled above and past her ducking head. The instant it shot impotently over her, Nancy sprang up giggling through a sharkish grin. Nancy's in his face appearance was so unexpected that it caught him off balance for a split second, allotting her the time she needed to ram the spiked heel of her shoe into his right eye.

King howled as he wildly thrust and swung his knife after her. He grabbed at her as she fell away. Nancy was struggling to keep from laughing, wanting to maintain a firmer grip on her focus. She dropped behind him, the shoe still driven into his eye. Turning herself as she fell Nancy swung her blade in a big *S* motion. While following through in her designed fall the tip of the claymore sliced past his O.S.P gown to lay a deep cut across the small of King's back. With a giggling thud she hit the soggy ground, landing flat on her back to bring the sword's tip around and down, cleaving King's right Achilles tendon in two. The big man's deep sounding howl stretched out to form a scream not unlike that of an old woman. Dolly Man jerked himself around as he toppled to his knees.

Nancy, still lying on her back, having the time of her after life, raised the sword blade in an effort to intercept the falling man while at the same time trying to roll out from under him. With his knife he swatted her waiting weapon out of his path, so much so that the force of the strike nearly disarmed her. King tried to grab the woman, but Nancy kept knocking his hand back with the brass basket-hilt of her weapon while also blocking his blade's stabs and sweeps. Kicking herself out from under him, she managed to scoot back far enough to crawl up onto her feet. He grabbed the back of her ankle and stabbed, but his grip was feeble and the strike too slow.

With a determined sounding grunt and a two fisted delivery, Nancy swung her sword. Dolly Man ducked beneath it. Like a slab of rotten lunch-meat her sword sliced a thin piece of his scalp off of the back of his skull. She'd employed a bit too much zeal in her effort to remove King's head. The momentum with which Nancy had sent her blade spun her around, nearly causing her to tumble. She swiftly retook control of her balance and reset her footing, but still her back had been turned to King for a tenth of a second too long. He glanced up from beneath her passing weapon and with an upward lunge, thrust a full six inches of his bowie knife in Nancy's lower back.

Without so much as a grunt, groan or any voiced response which might illustrate her disapproval over having been stabbed, she pulled off the blade before he could further his assault. While escaping King's eviscerating intentions, Nancy had a parting gift. At the exact moment she slid free from the tip of his weapon, Nancy mule kicked the shoe still embedded in his mustard colored right eye. With the slamming force of a ten-gauge shotgun's recoil she sent the spiked heel the rest of the way into his skull.

Dolly Man's response to Nancy's reply was in no way as reserved as her's. A high-pitched scream exploded out of his melted, disfigured face. While in the process of reaching for the shoe nailed to his skull, King's hand caught her withdrawing ankle. In an instant Dolly Man yanked her back, flipping her around and with a straight-armed round-house brought his knife about. She veered his blade off its intended course with her hilt, then swept the three foot long blade back toward his throat. King jerked out of the swords path, it hissed down past his Adam's-apple, the air caught in its wake stinging his skin. Still clutching the sword wielding attorney's ankle, and seeing that her weapon was on its way down to change that fact by chopping off his hand, he flung her loose. With the use of only the one arm , and his anger, Dolly Man launched her hundred and ten pound body into a tree trunk. Nancy slammed against it like a dead snake, the whole while maintaining her grip on her weapon.

In the same instant that her body landed in the mud, King tore the shoe out of his eye and threw it back at her. "Fucking ho!—" he rumbled while struggling to stand. Despite the deep stab wound in her back, and most of the bones that made up the right side of her skull being shattered during her abrupt introduction with Mr. Tree, Nancy wasted no time getting to her feet. King on the other hand, even though the slice across his lower back and the wound cut into his ankle were nearly all but completely healed, moved quite a bit slower. Nancy was paying him little attention as he shoved himself fully upright. Panning her swollen faced vision over the ground she looked for the shoe she'd dropped before engaging the off-colored black man, finding instead the one she'd rammed into his skull.

Nancy giggled as she watched the blood ooze off her heel and slither toward King. Standing with the one shoe, she looked at her sword then locked her searching gaze on him.

He peeled his cicatrix face into a misshapen grin and slowly slid the middle finger of his right hand into his wounded eye. Like a little girl oddly enthralled by the grisly performance of a carnival freak, Nancy slowed her back stepping withdrawal to watch almost hypnotically. Dolly Man brought the glistening digit out of his skull and after sniffing it as if the thing were a fine cigar, he placed it in his mouth and clasping his thick lips close around it then suck the finger clean as he slowly pulled it out.

King began moving slowly around to her right. Nancy was still sort of half searching for her other shoe, while watching King attempting to creep around her. She said nothing in response to this morbid display, she simply giggled and readied her grip on the sword.

King lifted his gown and exposed himself to her. "I'll give you all of this if you promise to try and sound like a screaming child while I cut out your spine."

Nancy's insane chuckling was silenced by this gesture and the words that accompanied his request. She narrowed her expression in a revolted scowl. "I truly believe I'm going to love chopping you into as many tiny bits as possible before sending you back to whatever foul pit owns you." Nancy picked up her pace as she added, "and as for your offering to give me that," she pointed at his crotch with the heel of her shoe. "I refuse to taint my integrity by fucking out of my race." Nancy squeaked out a brief giggle, concluding her little speech, "hell, I may as well let a dog screw me."

King loosed a loud yell and charged. Nancy was full-out laughing when she faked left then cut sharply to the right. King spun about, nearly tripping over his own feet in his enraged haste to stay with her. With an unexpected leap into the air, she threw her body almost completely sideways, pushing off of a tree to aim herself. Before her feet touched the ground, Nancy stabbed a full foot's length of her blade down through the back of King's trapezius muscle, slicing it in a downward slant through the top of his spine. Her feet hit the dirt as his knees did likewise. Nancy's laughter was sounding more like an insane woman's uncontrollable screaming as she tore her sword out of King's back. As she flung the weapon up to begin chopping, Dolly Man swept the bowie knife back with a fast, wide swing, racing most of its blade through Nancy's belly. She threw herself back away from his knife as it attempted to come back around for a second taste. King collapsed forward, twitching spastically with his face in the mud.

Nancy shoved up onto shaky legs only to watch her innards spill out onto the dirt. Stabbing her sword into the earth and hanging the shoe from the brass butt of its hand-grip, she stared speechlessly at her guts. "Now there's something I never thought I'd see," she chuckled while squatting down in order to gather up the pile of viscera stringing out of her, and stuff it all back in.

Even in her gutted condition, with one hand holding her entrails in, she could have put a final close to her play time with Dolly Man. Nancy strolled over to King's side. She stabbed at his temporarily paralyzed body, bedeviling his skin with shallow, puncturing jabs of her sword's tip. All she would have to do was toss down a tooth and be done with this heap of shit. There was even plenty of time to keep her promise and chop him into countless little pieces. All she needed was one hand to swing the sword down; the blade's perpetually sharp edge and weight would do the rest. But no, for whatever reason Nancy decided to allow their bout to move on into the next round.

King's spine was beginning to mend, she watched a moment as his jerks and twitches advanced to controlled muscle-flexing. Soon he would be right-as-rain. Nancy's wounds were also mending themselves. The shattered bones in her face were nothing more than a slight ache as was the stab wound in her lower back. King's dark-brown eye rolled up her legs, but could see no further. Nancy lowered her gaze to peer straight into the unburned side of his face.

"I've not finished with you yet Toby," she stood and rested the sword's tip on the back of his head. "When your body is done fixing itself, follow the line drawn in the ground," she shoved the blade down hard all the way through his melon, Nancy then stepped on his head to hold it in place and yanked her blade back out of his skull.

Napoleon Albert King was in a foul mood to say the least when his body had finally permitted him to get up. Aside from the insane bitch getting the better of him during the first round of the blade dance, she'd also cut him deeply with her racist tongue. The fact that she believed, and rather strongly by the look of hate in her eyes when she'd said it, that allowing herself to be screwed by a black man was as bad as being bent over by a dog, was harsh. Her *white* high and mighty attitude was as stinging to his pride as a stiff kick in the nuts. King snatched a hold of his knife as he pushed up onto his knees. *Yeah,* his mind chuckled, *we'll see who laughs this time.*

"Yeah bitch!" Dolly Man yelled into the trees. A chorus of crows cawed down out of the surrounding branches. "I'm going to take my motherfuckin' time cutting your spine out. And guess what my honry dog'll be doin' as I'm cuttin'," his voice had risen to a booming roar. Dogs could be heard barking far off. "Diggin' deep up in your white guts! Before I'm done poundin' against your ass bitch, I'll have you sounding just like a child! Yeah I will!"

The line Nancy had drawn in the earth with her sword was easy for King to find and nearly as easy for him to follow. It cut through the blanket of pine-needles, moss and dirt leading straight through the heavily wooded rise toward a clearing beyond the trees. King's eager vision located Nancy right off with no real effort.

She was waiting for Dolly Man atop an old steam locomotive. The huge antique black and white pin-stripped iron-horse had long ago been retired from the tracks and transformed into a very big object for kids to play on. Its permanently motionless station was parked on two short lengths of track and ties surrounded by nicely cut grass in one of the park's four play areas.

At a fevered pace Dolly Man marched out of the trees, down the modest slope straight toward the snickering crazy woman pacing like a caged beast back and forth on top of the old engine.

"Bring your skinny little ass down here—ho!" King shouted, his voice squeaking with fury. "I got something for ya!" he took a hold of his crotch and with a firm squeeze gave it a shake.

"I was under the impression that I'd made myself clear earlier," Nancy said, her tone shifting its lilt from humorous to disgustedly hateful and cold. "I don't fuck out of my race."

"You ain't got no damn choice—bitch!"

"Sure I do. Climb on up here and I'll show you again, stupid."

King threw the bowie knife down, sticking its blade to the hilt in the grass. "Twenty-seven," he said with a toothy grin. "Twenty-seven small white boys screamed for me with the help of that knife—twenty-seven. What do you think of that?"

Nancy stopped pacing and lowered to a squatting position and leered at King as he continued his sick boast.

"But all of their screams combined will be nothing more than whispers compared to the sounds I'll cut out of you."

She silently watched as he unwrapped the drawstring of his pouch from around his wrist, and although he knew all of her wounds were healed closed by this time, King still rolled a tooth out onto his palm. King pulled the pouch closed tight and tossed it on the grass while reaching down to pick up the knife.

"My-my, you are a stupid one aren't you?"

"Come down here and we'll talk about it."

"What's wrong big fellah, afraid of heights?"

"Come down here bitch!"

"Nope, I don't believe I will. But I'll tell you what I'm willing to do in order to help bring our time together to an end." She stood from her haunches and began pacing again, only slower this time. "I'll move to the nose of this old thing and wait there until after you've climbed up here to share one last dance with me." Nancy stepped to the front of the engine and rested her butt against the smoke-stack.

"How do I know you'll keep your word?" King asked.

"You don't, of course. But think about it a moment, ask yourself—why didn't I chop you to bits when I had the chance to do so in the trees?"

"Because you're a crazy bitch, that's why!"

"Yeah, well I'm still just as nuts," Nancy laughed. "So why don't you climb your lazy black ass up here and try your luck."

King stood there a moment staring stupidly up at Nancy's grinning face. "Fucking white ho—" he cursed spitefully through gnashed teeth as he climbed the metal steps onto the engineer's platform.

"That's right," Nancy needled. "Yes, come up and get what you got coming—Toby."

"Keep runnin' your fucking neck, bitch!" King replied at a whisper which carried in its lilt a promise of pain more threatening than if he would have screamed it. Like a pirate climbing up a ship's rigging, King clasped the bowie knife between his teeth. With no pockets in the gown to put the demon tooth into, he was forced to pinch it between his thumb and index finger. Only his ears to rely on, he listened sharply for the sound of approaching steps running toward him from above. As quickly as he could King hoisted himself up and swung his legs around onto the small iron awning that served as a roof over the engineer's platform. With the demon's tooth safely clutched in his fist, he swept the knife from his teeth as he shoved upright to immediately assume a battle-ready stance.

The air slicing whistle of Nancy's murder weapon as she swung its blade lazily back and forth was accompanied by the softly landing sound of her bare feet slapping down against the cold iron as she drew near. King's hideous face tugged into an ugly grin that sent a shiver up Nancy's spine. Stopping her easy paced advance fifteen feet from King, she looked him up and down. As she studied the self-proclaimed kid-killer, she attempted to whistle the show down melody from the spaghetti western 'The Good, the Bad and the Ugly' but was interrupted by her own uncontrollable girlish giggling.

"I'm going to hurt you bitch—really bad," Dolly Man threatened. "I'm going to crush that skinny neck of yours in my fist. Yeah—that's right. And as I cut you from cunt to gut," King paused to show Nancy the yellowish-brown demon's tooth, holding it out between his thumb and finger. He continued, "As I open you up I'm going to spit this down your motherfuckin' throat—bitch!" King popped the tooth in his mouth as if it were a piece of candy-corn.

Nancy's eyes widened with awestruck surprise at seeing this. She remembered the Gate Keeper from the realm that had sent her into the game saying "—Do not put any of the teeth in your mouth! Not for any reason." King's Gate Keeper had issued the same warning, but Dolly Man had apparently forgotten. Nancy's laughter had faded with her melting grin and shocked expression. She started to slowly back away from King, not knowing what to expect.

"Yeah—that's right bitch! You've lost, its over and you fucking know it." Dolly Man announced while holding the tooth in his cheek. "Why ain't you laughin' now—well, why not. What's wrong?—Cat got your—"

King suddenly began choking. The bowie knife slipped from his fingers. It hit the roof of the train with a loud, heavy bang, falling to the grass below. His left hand grabbed his throat as he crammed the fingers of his right into his mouth. His gaze looked across the top of the train at Nancy who was still back stepping away from him. The expression on his scarred face appeared to be pleading for help of some sort. Realizing this Nancy let blast a brief bark of laughter. She caught sight of a small lump working its way down his throat. King had crammed practically his entire fist into his mouth after the tooth. The lump wriggled swiftly passed the hand clasped around his own neck and was gone. King dropped to his knees and was doing his damndest to vomit the tooth back out. Nancy's retreat stopped after moving beyond the train's smoke-stack. She didn't dare charge the gagging black man for fear of whatever was occurring lashing out and drawing her into the consequence of his foolish error. All that was left for her to do was leap off the train. But her curiosity would not permit it. Nancy was trapped in a state of astonished shock, eagerly waiting to see what was to befall the fool.

Tearing off his ugly hospital-gown, King flopped about on the roof of the train like a bottom fish out of water. He scratched and clawed at his stomach all the while screaming, "Cut it out! Cut it out of me!"

King flung himself off the train, hitting the ground so hard that Nancy could actually hear all of the air blast out of his lungs on impact over her own giggling. She leapt to the ground and followed King at a safe distance as he squirmed and crawled around to the other side of the train toward his knife. *The idiot wants to try and fight*, she thought while attempting to make some sense out of his high-pitched caterwauling. He was only a few feet from his blade stabbed deeply into the grass when his reaching fist was yanked back by a surge of intense pain that doubled Dolly Man up in a screaming fetal position.

"CUT IT OUT!" he howled, his voice trembling.

Tearing his hand from his belly, he swung it out wide, rolling over onto his back and stretching his body out as flat as the pain would permit. King's fist found the knife and raising it in an awkward grip, he drove its blade clear to the hilt into his own stomach. Grabbing his weapon's handle with his left hand as well, he pushed it downward and sliced himself open from the bottom of his sternum to just below his bellybutton.

Just when you've thought you've seen it all, something cool unfolds, Nancy thought as she took a seat on the wet grass cross-legged to watch the show.

"Some hot buttered popcorn would be nice—thank you," she yelled up at those watching in Hell.

Dolly Man had pulled most of his bowels out and in a pool of his own blood and bile he chopped them open, feverishly searching through the cold heap of guts for the tooth. With a loud, "I GOT IT! I GOT IT!" King held the tooth up in his blood soaked fist.

That's it, Nancy thought. *That's all? No shards of glass shooting up out of the ground—no flaming naked woman?* "Last time I come to this theater," Nancy said as she pushed up onto her feet.

King was so consumed by finding the tooth and putting an end to the Hellish pain that he didn't even notice Nancy's shadow looming up over him from behind. Without a word she swung her sword up over her head and at the exact instant that Dolly Man decided to turn his gaze around to see where the crazy white woman had gone to, the blade came down. With the single swipe of a one handed swing Nancy had sliced through flesh, bone and brain to remove a third of King's head. That was only the beginning. The quiet morning air that owned space throughout the park was overthrown by the flesh chopping sounds of a very large body being hacked to bits and the untethered laughter of a madwoman. Twenty-seven times she shot the blade down, once for each of the children he'd boasted about murdering. Peter Meadows and Buddy Zib were both simply chores which needed dealt with, players to put down-so to say. But this one was more than that—more than just another obstacle in the game. This one with its scarred face and yellow eye was a honor—a privilege for Nancy to dispatch.

When she'd finish keeping her word to Dolly Man by chopping him into a pile of mangled meat she stood blood-splattered and winded in the middle of the carnage and felt genuinely good about herself. She tossed her weapon down a few feet outside of the ring of ruin and began pulling her pouch open. She went to step over the dismantled carcass when she felt something slice open the bottom of her foot. Nancy glanced down to see that she'd swept the side of her foot across the upturned edge of Dolly Man's knife. That wasn't the worst of it. The bad part was, that lying between her bare feet was King's severed left hand. And resting in the center of its open palm was the demon's tooth he'd cut out of his own guts.

In an instant Nancy had gone from victor to vanquished. *Shit—I never saw that coming*, she thought with a humorless chuckle. Nancy didn't try to escape her fate by moving away from it. No, she simply fumbled with her pouch. "Not alone!" she demanded. "I'm not going back without a prize! You're fucking coming with me…NIGG—"

Nancy White was shocked to silence the instant she saw the giant scorpion moving swiftly out of the trees. The huge arachnid moved down and around to stop less than twenty feet in front of her standing in her blood-splatter splendor. It was of a whitish color with red tiger-stripes and as big as a 1955 Buick Road Master. But it wasn't its great size, speed of movement, or colors that took complete possession of her attention—it was the human face that peered out of its head. Wearing what looked to be a British baluster's wig was Mr. Dovar, the venerable head partner of the law-firm she'd given so much of herself to. The same white haired litigator she'd hacked to death with his great-grandfather's Scottish sword.

Its right claw shot out as the thing darted closer and stopped again. The huge red and white claw snatched the pouch of teeth from her fumbling fingers.

"Thissss…hasss…n-not…be-be-e-been…en-tered…in—into ev-evid-ence," the old lawyer said, his voice strained and his lips hardly moving. His eyes rolled stutteringly over Dolly Man's already struggling to reassemble body. His attention drifted onto his grandfather's sword. "Thisss…hasss…be-eeen…en-t-tered." The claw swept down and picked up the old weapon. Its long tail began whipping back and forth through the air, a black tar-like substance flinging out of its long red, slightly curved stinger.

"What the fuck are you waiting for?" Nancy screamed.

"Ve-very we-ll co-u coun-seler," a tight, thin lipped grin stretched on to Mr. Dovar's waxen face. "Th-e...c-co-u-cour-t...fi-n-nes-ss...y-o you-u-u...gu-ilty."

Nancy didn't make a sound as the tail lashed down, not a giggle nor a scream. It shot down toward her head with lightening speed. But within the split second that it was to pierce through the center of her face she ducked beneath its strike and latched onto it. With Nancy's arms and legs wrapped around it the tail whipped widely about, trying to fling her off. It slammed her to the ground once, twice, a third time and still she hung onto the thrashing appendage for the ride of her after life. Finally it swung her down within reach of both claws. Letting loose of the pouch and sword, they tore her off the end of its tail and ripped Nancy's body in two. She was still sort of laughing as she watched Mr. Dovar eat her lower half. In mere seconds he devoured her hips, legs and feet, right down to her toes. Starting with her laughing, screaming head the giant scorpion with the old man's face finished its meal. After doing its best to lick its claws clean of Nancy's blood the creature transformed into red and white smoke and melted heavily down into the grass, being followed back to Hell by her weapon and pouch of teeth.

It was almost a full twenty minutes after Nancy White was eaten that King's chopped to shit body had finished pulling back together. Shaking off some of the pain and shock of being reduced to a quivering pile of indistinguishable meat, and after coming terrifyingly close to being sent back as a big-fat-loser, his own self, he, his knife, and pouch of teeth then went looking for his ugly, prison, hospital gown.

Dolly Man was still in the game—barely.

$$\Longrightarrow \cdot \text{\textbardbl} \cdot \Longleftarrow$$

The last time Alex could remember experiencing anything remotely close to real sleep was the dreamless state of unconsciousness he'd had the night before his visit to apartment 49. By 8:30 the morning of the game, Alex was feeling both mentally and physically the same way he used to feel toward the overdo end of a methamphetamine marathon run. By 9:00, his visual focus was beginning to demonstrate symptoms of deep fatigue. When 10:30 crawled up into his face—paranoia had begun to wriggle its infectious way through his mind, needling his enervated attention toward the silly dodging and sometimes chasing of shadows. To make matters even more trying—the streets, sidewalks and shops were swarming with traffic and busy warm souls. Several times Alex had actually mistaken the shadows and the swift approach of peripheral movement as his old pal King creeping up on him. Once Alex had even swept the blade of his knife across the throat of a light-skinned black man sporting a shaved head. Exhaustion was kicking Alex's ass, or at least giving him a black-eye and a fat lip.

What Alex didn't know was that the heavy wave of fatigue settling over him was the price for Pike's cryptic clue in the mud. Much the same way Alex was made to pay for Ellzbeth's leading him into the Mall by experiencing the cold and wet elements of rain and wind, the fee for Pike's direction came in the form of exhaustion. A costly price indeed, perhaps.

Cutting across Van Burien through the thick one-way traffic, Alex didn't quicken or slow his pace to avoid the cars. He simply marched right through the river of colored metal and shiny steel. He was heading to the small, Mom and Pop's Market located on the other side of the busy street in order to check on the time while taking a short-cut through the corner building. He moved across the small parking lot, through the yellow cinder block wall and immediately spotted the large back-lit plastic faced clock to his left up in the corner-front of the store. 10:51 it read. *Plenty of time to get to the school and lay a trap*, Alex thought, an exhausted rush of sinister glee sluggishly struggled up his spine. "If I'm lucky it'll be that punk-ass piece of shit King," he muttered under his breath.

"How many players do you suppose are left?" Bianca chanced to ask, her gypsy voice muffled by the steel screen of her bladed prison.

Alex, not wanting to be drawn into a distraction that might dim his focus by responding toward any questions the witch may pose with an angry comeback, he replied simply "—I don't know." It was a cold, matter of fact response intended to illustrate in few words that he wasn't in the mood for questions—particularly from Bianca. As far as Alex was concerned—the child murdering gypsy witch had been working him, playing him like a chump, an easy-mark. And had been doing so since he was a boy, all the while shrouded under the veil of comradeship. Why he'd stepped between Pike, risking great pain to stop the red-eyed little devil from dragging her to Hell—where she undoubtedly belonged he had no clue. Perhaps Alex was afraid—afraid to finish the game alone, or simply afraid to be alone.

Bianca caught the obvious meaning between the words of his short, icy answer. Still she continued with her not so subtle attempt to chip away at the ice forming between her and Alex. Only this time she tried by employing the voice she'd invented for Mr. Bane.

"Do you know how to locate the schoo—"

"Don't!" Alex snapped. "Do not use that voice! If I hear it again, even so much as a whisper of it, I'll toss you into the pit myself." He was on his way toward the back of the store. "Yes," he hissed through clenched teeth. "I know the way to the high-school."

Moving between two check-out counters, Alex's attention was snagged onto by the front page heading of Corvallis' local newspaper. He paused and read: Los Angeles Police Captain arrested after investigation leads homicide detectives to missing children's remains in his home basement.

Alex couldn't help shaking his head with abhorrence as he continued on toward the back of the store. Allowing himself a brief moment's daydream while passing through the beer coolers and subsequent back-wall out onto Eleventh street; a thin grin tugged conservatively up at the right-side corner of his mouth as he fantasized about the wonderfully savage time he and Mr. Bane would show the LA police captain to; if given half a chance. Then Alex remembered that Mr. Bane had been murdered this morning. The dreamy grin fell away, giving his face back its corpse-white expression.

It only took Alex ten minutes to walk the five blocks and arrive in front of the school. Panning his fatigued vision evenly over the terrain he steadily increased his already swift pace toward the school's main entrance.

"Go easy Alex," Bianca advise in her own voice. "No need for blind-minded impulsiveness."

"If you want to be of help—witch," Alex growled as he swept his vision carefully across his surroundings. "You may silently watch my back…in-other-words, I only want to hear your voice if you spot someone or thing. Do you understand?"

"Yes, I understand Alex," Bianca's voice fell sadly silent.

Climbing the concrete steps, he was moments from moving with his ghostly ability through the high-school's double-doored entryway when a thunderously loud gun-shot boomed from within the school. The nerve jolting noise was immediately succeeded by an explosion of screams. Within seconds a fire-alarm bell was sounded and the main corridor beyond the double doors had filled with panic-stricken teenagers. If at anytime there'd been a sense of order in these children, it had abandoned them to hide beneath their own fright. With their young faces twisted into misshapen masks of confusion and wide-eyed horror they charged straight through Alex standing just outside the school. Larger, faster kids trampled over smaller, slowed by panic kids. The shrieking flood of teens and teachers swept through Alex like a hat wind. At first he allowed himself to be caught by its fleshy current, but only for a few withdrawing steps. He stopped and held his ground atop the concrete steps. As the wave of howling kids thinned down to the last few dozen, Alex caught sight of students leaping and being handed out of the old building's windows. His ears were snared by the high-pitched screams of a girl's voice crying, "No! no no no!" Alex swept his eyes up, and low-and-behold, a chubby girl was being shoved out a window and dangled by her wrist directly over Alex's head. He stepped back, moving out from under her. He was surprised when he saw that the person doing all of the holding was a woman who appeared too old and too small of body to be strong enough for what she was doing. *Horror is a powerful motivator,* Alex thought as he shook his head in disbelief.

"I'm going to let you go now!" the white-haired teacher yelled.

"Nooooooo!" howled the fat girl as her wrists were let loose. The girl hit the concrete slab flat-footed. Alex heard a sharp snap, as her right and left tibia-bones broke on impact. Two boys at the back of the heap grabbed a hold of the wailing fat girl's arms and without slowing their escape dragged her to safety. The elderly woman who sent the girl falling was positioning herself on the window so that she could lower herself out and drop. She swung her legs out and was about to turn around on the sill when with a loud 'KA BANG!' her face exploded outward in an almost mystical vermilion cloud of blood. Her instantly lifeless husk lurched forward and like an over-done movie prop fell to the concrete below. A roar of horrified screams rose from out of the students, teachers and anyone else who witnessed the slaying.

In an apparent response to the deafening outcry a fist wrapped tightly around a rather large caliber, short barreled revolver reached out of the same window on the second floor and fired. 'KA BANG! KA BANG! KA BANG!' voiced the gun's strong disapproval to the crowd's wordless wailings. The three shots echoed cracklingly through the wave of abominating cries, muting for an instant the blaring ring of the fire-alarm's bell. The pistol's much louder roar, rippled through the trees and stretched out over the roof-tops of the surrounding neighborhoods. As for the three balls of white-hot lead that had been rocketed out of the noise and flame spitting muzzle, they could care-less about the verbalized horror of the frightened souls. The only things that concerned the three tiny assassins were their new found freedom to fly and the chance to feed. Two of the three would-be killers, found their meals—one in the back of a running boy's right leg, dropping him like a roped calf. The other lucky shot tore greedily into the small of a girl's back, decimating her lower lumbar vertebrae. They weren't killing strikes, true—but they both faired better then their comrade who'd ended up in a tree-trunk.

As the teens and teachers ran about like blind mice trying to escape the crushing falls of a hammer wielding child; the shooter moved before the window into Alex's line of sight. Although his heart sank some when he saw her, he wasn't shocked by it—not really. Still wearing the same black on black gothic getup she'd been wearing during the previous night was the girl Alex had watched being assaulted by paint-balls and stealing from cars.

Swinging one leg out of the window and dangling it lazily off of the edge, she sat sort of sidesaddle on the sill. And while humming the melody to a tune Alex didn't know, she emptied the spent shell-casings into her palm and stood them in a neat row on the wooden ledge before reloading the gun. She leaned comfortably back against the window frame and without looking stretched her arm out, pointing the piece in the direction of the noise and squeezed one off into the crowd. The slug zipped harmlessly past several people scrambling frantically to dart out of the way of a thing they could not see coming. That was until it drilled a fingertip-size hole into a man's cheek, just beneath his right eye. After punching a fist-size exit wound out through the back of his skull, spraying those closest with blood, brains and bits of bone, the bullet tore sideways through a boy's chest, piercing both lungs. It hit a rib on its way out of the lad, veering its continued direction sharply to the left. The supersonic projectile ended its busy trek by embedding its sociopathic little self into the vice-principal's fat incrusted heart. The boys death came slow, he drowned on his own blood as it poured into his lungs. The man who'd suffered the face shot was killed outright as was the vice-principal. It was truly the sort of lucky shot nightmares are made of.

The goth girl smiled as she raised the short barrel to her lips and blew the lingering smoke away with a gentle kiss and a wink of an eye. She slid out of the window, melting slowly back into the school. There seemed to be a lost look in her gaze. Not scared or even worried, simply lost. Her expression confused Alex in an uneasy sort of way. With a sweep of her hand she brushed the empty shells off the sill. The six silver dead soldiers seemed to fall in a sort of hypnotic slow-motion that held Alex's attention for several seconds after they'd landed.

As he watched them bounce and roll into the dead teacher's pool of blood, Alex remembered that when she'd found the gun under the car-seat, she'd left with only those rounds already in its cylinder. *So where did she get more bullets?* he wondered. Moving up the concrete stairs Alex stepped over the old woman's corpse. "She must have went back to the car after I'd left the parking lot," Alex mumbled, answering his own question as he passed through the double doors into the corridor. He stopped to listen, standing just inside. Alex heard the muffled sobs and frightened whispers of those kids who'd been too caught off guard, afraid, and too confused to flee with the school's mass exodus. Alex stepped over and peered into the first class-room. It was empty; he walked over to the next flung open door. As with the first classroom chairs and even a few desks were toppled over. There was a boy of about fifteen years of age hiding under the teacher's black-oak desk. He'd pissed himself and was sobbing girlishly into his hands while rocking swiftly back and forth. The all too familiar sound of police and other emergency sirens were approaching from what sounded like every direction.

"Cowboy the fuck up lad," Alex said as he turned his back to the boy cowering under the desk. "The Calvary's on the way. It's only a matter of time now." He added as he stepped back out into the corridor. Trying to ignore the heart choking sounds of other hiding cry-babies, and doing so with easy success, Alex was making his way toward the wide doorless entry to the stairs when movement out of the lower corner of his right eye spun him full-about. With his knife ready to open some arteries, he was immediately made to realize how foolishly on edge he must appear. Sitting on the floor, pressing themselves into the corner of the wall and a large glass trophy case were two horrified girls. They were hugging each other so tightly that at first glance the two embracing shapes resembled a trembling nightmare of cloth, hair, skin and noiseless color. The blaring ring of the fire-alarm stammered then died to silence. It's about time, Alex thought gratefully. "Damn bell was beginning to get a bit annoying," he said, speaking to the scared girls as if they could actually hear him.

With the alarm shut off Alex could hear the weeping of frightened kids much more clearly. Especially the boohoos of several youthful voices moving down through the corridor ceiling. He could make out the softly placed steps of hard heeled foot-wear moving over head toward the sobbing pleas. The steps stopped and 'KA BANG!' The joltingly abrupt noise was followed straightaway by the heavy thud of dead-weight hitting the floor directly above Alex's head. Screams from upstairs stretched out. Alex looked over at the two girls and saw that they were hugging one another impossibly tighter.

"All of you shut up!" commanded the goth girl, her voice muffled by distance. The crying steadily gagged itself to silence, only the steps of the girl with the gun and a few fast intakes of air, like hiccups bled down to be heard.

"You two need to get it together and go," Alex suggested.

"They don't hear you Al—"

"I know that!" Alex interrupted.

"Then why do you insist on speaking to the living," Bianca's tone was worried. "You're wasting time Alex."

"Don't fucking worry about it!" Alex snapped.

"You're allowing your edge to slip from your grasp—"

"Bullshit!" he barked with a humorless laugh. "You're only concern is for yourself—witch. Its all clear to me now. You figured on using me as your get out of Hell free card. Well I've a plan of my own."

"You've never been more wrong Alex," Bianca's voice was weighted heavily with disappointment.

"I'm getting sick to death of your damn yammering."

"If you stifle your anger a moment Alex, I'll tell you a bit of what I know. What I know concerning you and your sister."

"You don't know shit!"

"But I do Alex, I know a great deal. I know that you and Susan will come face to face, and that the out come of that reunion will determine the fate of worlds. Your winning this foolish contest is simply a catalyst. But you must win. Now do what you will Alex, I've nothing further," Bianca went silent.

Alex stood there a moment wondering if anything the witch had said was true. *Why would I so much as consider believing a word of what she had to say,* Alex thought. *She's a child killer; she's been lying to me from the start.* Alex glanced across the hallway at a clock on the wall of a classroom. "11:35," he breathed at a hissing whisper. "35 minutes to go until show-time." He glanced over his shoulder down at the quivering ball of girl flesh pressed against the glass case and said with a smile, "Well girls, its been a real hoot, but I've got to find me a good ambush spot. Its seems worlds are countin' on me. Good luck to ya."

Looking up and down the corridor to choose which way to head off into, he couldn't help but be reminded of a similar sight. The discarded books, pee-chee folders, homework papers and other cast aside school paraphernalia reminded Alex of D-block after the prison guards got done tossing the cells of all five tiers on both low and high sides, in search of a ring of keys misplaced by the security manager. His misguided stroll down memory-lane was torn out from under his feet by another loud KA BANG! followed by the unmistakable thud of a body slamming to the floor. The pleading squeaks of a girl's voice upstairs bled stutteringly into Alex's ears until it was silenced by yet another booming roar of the .357 Bulldog. Thud, dropped another. The girls holding one another next to the glass case broke their horrified oath of silence and began screaming uncontrollably. For a split second Alex thought they'd come to their senses and would be hopping up onto their over-priced sneakers to beat-feet out of there. Or so he'd hoped. Sadly there fright had successfully imprisoned the two girls in a state of inaction, only their ear-piercing cries would rise to the occasion.

Just as Alex was beginning to envision no hope for the little scared birds, three boys wearing blue and white varsity jackets, a large letter T stitched over the right side of their chest, appeared. They ran as quickly and quietly up from the far end of the corridor, each clutching a baseball bat. The three ran straight to the girls, who'd spotted the bats and began screaming even louder. Crouching around the girls, the three young men immediately began arguing. Alex heard the larger of the three bark "—GO!" After a moment of silently looking at the floor the three friends stood the girls up and then the two smaller boys pulled the panic-stricken girls out of the building. The third boy stayed behind.

Alex, as well as the boy heard what sounded like steps moving quickly over head. Still across the hallway from one another, Alex beside the entryway to the stairs, the boy next to the trophy case, they watched as the two boys and two girls ran toward the street. 'KA BANG!' the shot missed the four escaping students. Before she could squeeze off a couple more attempts to drop one or two of the runners, two of her prisoners grew a pair of nuts and charged the shooter. Alex and the boy listened blindly as two pair of running feet moved over head and 'KA BANG! KA BANG!'—two more bodies hit the floor. The metallic tinkling like silver coins falling—crashing to the floor moved through the air as she emptied the shell casings out of the gun. Alex and the boys eyes followed the sound of her foot steps. There was a hollow click, then 'KA BANG!' a slug blasted down through the ceiling, hitting the hard-wood floor between Alex and the boy. Alex had a fairly good idea as to what had occurred. But it wasn't until the sight of blood oozed down through the bullet hole that the boy figured it out. One of the two would-be heroes hadn't been killed by the round that dropped him. So she stopped over the kid and closed the deal with a second issue, this one between his eyes at point-blank range.

Arming himself with one of the bats his pals left behind, giving the lad two clubs to fight with, the boy drew in a deep breath and stepped toward the stairs. Alex glanced over his shoulder at the clock in the class room. 11:47, it warned with slow, whispered—tick—tick—ticks.

Times slip-slip-slippin' away, Alex thought. *Should probably go hide before the player shows up.* It was good self-advice, damn good actually, but like a kid utterly lost in the cinematic goings on of a horror-movie, Alex figured he would watch this drama a bit longer. And if a player showed up—so be it. *Take it as it comes,* Alex thought.

He stepped beside the boy, walking with him as he slid along the wall to the stairway's entrance.

"Sorry to tell you this boy," Alex said as they moved. "I've just got no choice but to place my pay-check on the girl. But hell—good goddamn luck to ya any way." Alex went to give the boy a pat on the shoulder, his gloved hand sweeping down through it, giving the lad a slight shiver instead. "If by some off the wall chance you do catch her slipp'n', please do try not to hurt her. She's just a little mixed-up…that's all."

Creeping around the rounded corner, the boy and Alex stepped side by side up the wide flight of stairs. No matter how gently the young man seemed to place his steps the wooden stairs squeaked and popped beneath his weight. Alex glanced down at the creaking steps and said with a cold-blooded chuckle "—I know the feeling. It sucks, doesn't it." Leaning his thin mouth close to the kid's ear, wishfully wanting his words to somehow seep in and convince this fool to stop, turn around and go from this bad situation. Alex whispered, "Ok kid you got a pair, now get the hell ghost before you get blasted into being one. Go on kid, let the pigs deal with this crap."

'KA BANG!' another body hit the floor.

The boy on the stairs jerked with the nerve jolting noise.

"She's fucking killing people up there boy, come now, you really don't want to get your head blown off. Well do ya? Get out of here stupid! Let the cops end this in their usual assassinating way."

Four steps from the top of the stairs the boy stopped. Leaning his back against the stairwell wall he quietly sighed. It was a rattling, long exhale, illustrating his fear as easily as the beads of sweat were doing as they swelled out over his face and neck. He mouthed the words *fuck this shit*, as he turned to move back down the stairs. The boy was in mid-step when the little goth girl stepped out from around the corner at the head of the stairs. Arm straight, she swept the gun up, stopping its muzzle at the back of the boy's head of wavy brown hair. The boy froze, not knowing what to do other than doing nothing at all. Alex sadly aware that he was helpless to stop her, looked into her large green eyes and whispered a single word "—Why?"

'KA BANG!'

Down the stairs the boy tumbled, his right eye and a substantial portion of his brain had been blasted out into space. Simply because she could, she fired the last two rounds into the corpse the moment that what was left of his head slapped against the floor below. She emptied the spent shells out onto the stairs where they rolled and bounced all the way down to where the dead football player now lay. The young killer stared down at the boy's half face as she brought exactly six, hollow point rounds out of her leather coat pocket and reloaded her new friend.

Her pale white face was badly blood-spattered, like hundreds of tiny dark-red freckles. The black streaks of eye-liner drawn down both cheeks gave her an evil doll like mask of a face. Several thin strands of her straight jet-black hair were clinging in spider-web fashion to some of the glistening red dots peppering her milky skin. The girl's icy expression was that of a true to the bone 'Goth'—lifelessly hollow. She moved with a purpose, in complete control of herself and her surroundings. It was as if her steps were not her own but those of an ageless creature, empowered by the wrath-fed need of her own will. It was apparent to Alex and the last of her still living captives, a red-haired girl standing with her face in a corner that the girl with the gun was totally at ease. At ease with the destruction she would eternally be responsible for, and equally comfortable with the inescapable definitiveness of her soon to follow lifeless fate.

Alex wondered if she would have chosen this path of no return if she would have known what it was awaiting her arrival at its dead-end? *No, I suppose not*, he thought with some first-hand certainty. Alex stepped beside her and swept a glance toward the big clock on the wall. With a half grin he mouthed silently *12, straight-up*. Alex panned his tired vision out through the window. On a roof-top across the street he spotted a shadowy figure kneeling behind a wide, red-brick chimney. The shiny reflective glint of what Alex guessed was the lens to a scope fixed astride a high-powered rifle. Alex wondered if this sniper knew, or was friends with either of the rifle-men pig-bastards that shot him?

He glanced at the goth girl. "Don't worry Doll, you probably won't feel a thing…that is of course providing that Ass-wipe knows what he's doing."

Alex paused to look around at all the bodies she'd collected.

"We need to get ready Alex," Bianca suggested, a note of frustration humming out from between her words. "Time will soon—very soon be our enemy!"

"I've got it handled," Alex backed as he followed the girl.

"But Alex, the tim—"

"I said I've got it under control! Now shut the hell up…witch!"

The goth girl stepped over the corpulent corpse of a woman that Alex figured had been a teacher. Facing the red-haired girl sobbing in the corner, she made a seat for herself on the fat dead teacher's shoulder. Following suit, Alex also sat on the corpse, choosing himself a bit of fleshy hip as his seat.

"Your time out is over," she said softly, a second before shooting the girl in the corner through the right foot. "Sit down."

Loosing an impossibly loud shriek of stinging anguish the red-haired girl fell to the floor and with trembling hands took hold of her mangled foot.

"You're off the hook," Alex said with a shake of his head. He was referring to the savagery with which his little goth friend wielded her viciousness. "They're going to burn you down girl."

The red-haired girl turned from her bleeding foot and started dragging herself over the blood drenched floor, shoving the body of a dead boy half out of her way. In a difficult to understand voice, shaking with pain and fear, she began pleading for her life. The only words which Alex could make out were '—Please—want—die and anything.'

But what she was actually trying to say was, "—Please, please no more! I'm bleeding, I need help. Don't kill me, I don't want to die! I'll be your friend. Yes, yes—that's it, I'll say I did this. I'll do anything you ask. Please…I don't want to die."

An evil grin—toothy and bright pulled slowly over the blood spattered face of the goth girl. She stretched her right leg out, sticking the blood caked boot in the girl's face.

"Lick it clean...go on, STUCK UP, suck your SNOBBY friend's blood off my boot...Do it and I'll let you live," she offered, her tone mellow—soothingly contrast with the choice of words it carried.

The expression on the red-haired girl's face shifted from simple fright to a look of appalled shock, framed in doom. Her lower lip's quivering moved up her cheeks to her tear soaked lower eyelids, while the rest of her fear whitened face clinched into an inhuman-like grimace. She tried to speak as her eyes went from the bloody boot extended out before her to the killer's green-eyes. But the only noises that could squeeze out past her stumbling lips were strained between fast, spastic intakes of air.

"Do it!" the goth girl snapped. "Run your tongue and those fake fucking fat injected lips over my Doc's—bitch!" She stomped the boot down, its sole and heel splashing in the pool of teacher's blood gathered around the corpse. Alex glanced at the clock, 12:04. He swung his sight around to the head of the stairs, then looked out the window at the sniper. The goth girl stood and so did Alex. Not the red-haired girl—she stayed on her belly. Aside from being hobbled by having a ball of lead blasted through her foot, the utter shock of her keeper's request had locked her in an almost questioning belief that all of this wasn't really happening. That it was all nothing more than a horrid night-terror, and any second now she would be waking up to the smells of bacon and eggs, and the sounds of her mother singing along to the soft rock playing on the kitchen's clock radio.

"You had your chance," the goth girl said with a grin. She latched a hold of a fist full of red-hair and wrenched the girl's head back, forcing her to face her killer.

"It's only a bad dream," she mumbled. "Only a dream—only a dream."

"Yeah, sure it is." Pulling the hammer back with her thumb, the girl jockey boxer turned murderess raised the muzzle of the gun and pressed it against the girl's right eye.

"Mommy," was all the red-haired girl could say when the shot rang out.

The sniper's steel-jacketed projectile burned cleanly into the left side of the little goth girl's skull to tear not so cleanly out the right. The intense force of the head shot's impact whipped the hundred and ten pound girl around in a complete three-sixty. Her widely open green eyes swept swiftly through her darkening surroundings as her spinning body turned. Before the icy blackness reached up to claim her damned soul she saw the hate scarred, bloodless face of a man with steely-blue eyes watching her die.

The muscles in her right hand clinched, pulling the trigger; the hammer fell and the hollow point slug that had been meant to shower the red-haired girl's brain's out of the back of her head was now flying wild. It zinged through Alex's right shoulder to ricochet off the second floor steam-heater's brass radiator. At the exact instant the goth girl's head smacked the floor, the bullet crashed through the clock, killing the time-keeper the second its minute hand centered the 2.

All at once the school was hit with barrage of loud, command—response sounds. Running boots and yelling voices, intended to invoke yet more confusion in an already confusing situation, flooded the first floor and were swiftly storming up toward the second. They charged up the stairs, their radios screeching in a hollow sounding chorus of indiscernible voices struggling to be heard over the dominating clatter. Like a surreal scene in an Anthony Burgess novel, the cops poured up over the top of the stairs fully armed and heavily covered in modern-day body-armor to find that the second-floor hallway had been transformed into a slaughtering station. With guns drawn and voices booming they swiftly took control. Without blinking an eye the first cop up spotted the gun still clutched in the girl's fist and kicked it out of her lifeless death-grip, all the while aiming a shotgun at the bloody mass of exposed bone and hair that had a moment ago been the back of her head. As that was taking place four other cops swarmed the red-haired girl and in their usual, stomp now ask questions later fashion, they piled on top of the terror-stricken girl, cuffed her and dragged her back down the stairs.

Alex had seen enough. He was on his way through the over-kill, kevlar clad horde, moving toward the stairs to leave the blood smeared debacle behind. As if Alex had known King was standing among the crowd across the street, he swept his gaze from the goth girl, whose carcass was rapidly growing cold up out the window, bringing his steely-eyed consideration to rest on Dolly Man.

The child-killer drifted through the warm souls with the rigidness of a fun house prop on a slow moving conveyer belt. He appeared to be shadowing a blond boy who looked much younger than his first year of high-school age might suggest. Even at this youths mid pubescent state of being, he was still far older than the ghostly pederast's preferred prey—yet still the freak followed the lad. Every so-often King would chance to tear his yellow-eyed gaze up from the torturous taunt of tender white flesh in order to make sure he wasn't being moved upon by another player.

A wave of rage mixed with the spine rushing chill of foreseen triumph swept suddenly over Alex. The fatigue which had been pressing against his mental and physical being was now snatched from the equation that is Millstone. Stepping in amidst a cluster of cops between himself and the window, he concealed his prescience behind the warm-flesh for a moment's chance to watch the monster before taking action.

"You've caught sight of something," Bianca whispered hopefully. "Is it a player?"

"Yes," Alex replied within a throaty grunt.

"Is it the one…the one called Dolly Man?"

"It is."

"I wish to see Alex. Please show—"

"Shhhhhh," Alex hissed as he raised the tip of the blade up over the cop's heads like a submarine's periscope.

"Go Alex—go cut him, spill his entrails at your feet so that you may send this one back to Hell where—"

"Shhhhh," Alex hushed the voice again. "I'm thinking."

Without argument Bianca fell silent. Alex was deciding whether to leap through the wall and charge straight at the player, or take a stealthier stab at sending Dolly Man back to the world of howling and gnashing of teeth. He was about to make his move, via the quieter approach, when quite unexpectedly King shifted his scarred faced attention up toward Alex. Like a wild beast catching the scent of wild-dogs creeping up through the tall elephant-grass, King swung around and ran from the predator.

"Sonofabitch!" Alex barked.

"What's wrong?"

"It seems I've been spotted."

"By King?"

"Yes!" Alex snapped as he tore through the cold-blooded, warm flesh of the cops. Leaping through the wall he landed hard at a flat-footed run.

King, for whatever reason wasn't prepared to go toe to toe with his old prison pal. He broke out of the crowd and ran openly through the police cars parked awkwardly in the middle of the street. For a moment King seemed confused, stopping, not knowing which way he should go. He spun around frantically looking left and right. Alex was approaching fast, his fedora clutched in his left fist, the knife in his right, and an icy expression in the cold-steel blue slits that were his eyes. Alex was nearly at the street when King finally snapped out of his state of immobility. King ran out of the street up a slightly sloping front-yard then stopped again. After sweeping his vision over the lawn as if he were searching for something, he glanced over his shoulder at Alex rapidly approaching and flipped him the bird before vanishing through the outer wall of a two story brown house.

Alex saw King swiftly pass the pulled open drapes of the large picture window only to disappear through a wall toward the back of the building. Intending to cut King off, Alex darted up the driveway and turned sharply through a red-cedar fence into the backyard—nothing. There was no way in hell King could have beat him to the back-yard. Alex tore through the back of the house and again—nothing—no sign of King. He listened for foot steps as he moved at a swift pace through the home, but all he could hear were the sounds of the humming refrigerator and the bubbling of the fish aquarium's water filter. The house was empty; King had doubled back on him. Hurling himself out through the front of the house Alex again hit the ground at a run. He ran up Eleventh street, his eyes panning swiftly in every direction and no sign of King. *Why didn't he stand and fight?* Alex wondered as he searched. "Because he's a fucking pussy! That's why," answering his own question. Alex was about to slow his pace and consider the idea that Dolly Man had slipped away, when as he was mid-way across a small bridge he spotted King running along Dixon creek toward down-town. Alex swung himself over the railing dropping into the middle of the creek to give chase. King vanished around the bend of the creek, behind its steep sloping bank. After only a few yards Alex had King back in his line of sight; actually it was even better.

Thinking that he'd put enough distance between him and Alex, King slowed his escape some, mindlessly allowing his pursuer to gain ground.

Hearing what sounded disturbingly like heavy breathing, King glanced over his shoulder to see Alex, who was literally hot on his heels. *Where the fuck did he come from?* screamed his brain as he scrambled up the muddy slope in an effort to gain some quick advantage by reaching higher ground.

"Where you going?" Alex growled as he leapt out of the water. With a downward swing he drove all ten inches of his dagger down through the back of King's leg.

"Eeeeeeeeha!" King howled his reply, adding a blindly executed backward sweep with the bowie knife to his retort. King's strike was lucky in that it not only caught Alex unexpectedly, although it shouldn't have, it also opened a long gash across Alex's throat. With a hard yank Alex tore his knife out of King's leg and barely managed to throw himself back in time to avoid King's second strike. Alex slammed back against a flat rock in the middle of the creek, blood jetting out of his neck like a Roman fountain. He wiped the screen of his blood out of his eyes in time to see King up and lurching toward him. The bowie knife was already racing down in an effort to open Alex's chest cavity, and would have done just that if not for Alex sending the steel-toe of his boot into Dolly Man's stones. Again the kid-killer howled, his wind milled strike sweeping bloodlessly past Alex as he rolled off the side of the rock into the icy water.

Alex crawled to his feet and quickly stumbled across the shallow, narrow creek to the opposite side. He expected to turn around and see King, who'd struggled through the dull pain of having his balls kicked up into his guts standing over him. Alex knew the slice laid across his throat would in no way heal before King could drop a tooth out of his pouch—Dolly Man had won.

Alex flopped over onto his back, swinging his knife wildly back and forth as he came about. But instead of seeing King's scarred face grinning down at him, a demon's tooth flying toward him, he saw King's ass peeking out of the slit of his gown as he vanished over the top of the slope. *What the fuck?* Alex wondered. *He'd won—why didn't he finish me off?* With his mud caked, gloved fist clutching his throat,

Alex listened to the sound of King's steps and labored breathing fade behind the noises of the city above.

Alex sat in the mud, wondering why King ran off. He watched as his blood slowly moved up between his fingers to find its way back into the veins and arteries of the closing neck wound that should have been his undoing. He thought about the stupid goth girl and herself dispatching statement, wondering what it was that pissed her off so. He thought about what Bianca had said concerning him and Susan, and their reunion determining the fates of worlds—*yeah right*, he mouthed. And he thought about Dolly Man.

King's regrettable reason for not sending Alex back to Hell was simply because he'd lost his white bag of teeth somewhere between Ninth and Eleventh streets. He'd been in the process of hunting for his pouch of teeth when he was distracted by the blond boy. It was spotting the star-like glint off the tip of Alex's bewitched knife, when he'd raised it above the cop's heads to let Bianca see, that clued King to the player's presence in the school.

Back on Eleventh street Dolly Man had resumed his search close to the corner where he'd been forced to take his leave. The debacle created by the girl's disgruntled showing of her over the top disdain for her school chums had swelled to a full-blown carnival of tragedy. Between the short space of time that King had left and his return, the block in front and halfway around the school was packed with twice as much activity than before his departure. Horrified kids sat sobbing on every inch of street-curb while their irate parents screamed into the faces of cops, teachers and whoever else they could snare within the net of fear induced rage.

Ribbons of yellow and black crime tape wrapped around tree-trunks and telephone poles stretching out to create a make-believe impassable barricade. Uniformed cops braced angry mothers back as they held the line, while other uniformed officers drew chalk circles around blood splatter. Armies of medical people, both physical and mental moved through clusters of shock-stricken kids, targeting those who appeared the most shaken by the event.

Eager to glean some answers while memories of the tragedy were still fresh and seeping, detectives pounced on those kids whose parents hadn't arrived yet. Half a dozen television news vans with big white satellite dishes mounted on their roofs were parked unevenly up and down the small section of street. Newshounds crammed microphones, video cameras and questions in the tear streaked faces of anyone they could catch off guard—young or old.

King caught sight of several cops leading the way out of the school building, being followed by men and even a few woman carefully carrying filled body-bags. He'd counted ten bodies in all being grimly paraded out of the building and loaded into the backs of dark-blue vans; one of which being the goth girl. The three she'd killed with the single lucky shot fired blindly out the window had already been taken away, as was the elderly teacher whose face she'd blown off.

"Looks like one of these little pieces of sweet white meat decided to take a healthy dump on this here school," King giggled gleefully "—tisk tisk tisk, what a shame." He watched as a cop wearing camouflage, a scoped rifle slung over his right shoulder stepped over to talk with a detective in a dark-brown suit. The detective showed the rifleman a clear plastic bag containing a revolver.

"Big-Little-Gun—ooowh," King whispered covetously. "Man-oh man I'd surely like havin' that piece. Yeah, I'd cram it up Millstone's white fucking ass-hole and blow his shit out of the top of his skull. Yes I would."

King crept closer to the detective to have a better look at the gun.

"The shooter's mother is in my car," the detective said. King caught the detective's eyes glance over at a white 88 Ford Thunderbird with small police car hubcaps. In its back seat sat a good-looking, full figured, black haired woman of about thirty eight years. Along with the sickly-white complexion of shock and utter heart break, she wore a Pay-Less pet-shop uniform. The employee name-tag pinned to her red and gray uniform read Tess O'neil.

"Does she have any answers as to why her kid did this?" King heard the sniper ask.

"So far all I can get from her is, 'she's a good girl', over and over. It's all she'll say," replied the detective.

"What was the girl's name?"

"Lucia—Lucia O'neil. She was 16."

"Mr. King," spoke the icy voice of a woman deep within the recesses of Dolly Man's foul brain. "Mr. King…you do hear me—yes?"

King spun around not sure at first where the voice was coming from; then not wanting to believe it once he realized it was speaking from inside his skull.

"No need for alarm Mr. King. I'm going to help you send Millstone back to Hell," the voice whispered. "You would like that—yes?"

King ducked behind a tree, his head snapping sharply left and right—left and right as he looked around.

"Listen closely Mr. King. I can grant you your wish concerning that—how you say—firearm you so lustfully voiced your desire for. I've the power to grant you a great many things. I can also empower the remaining four—booullits—I believe they're called with the ability to effect your old friend Mr. Stone—effect him greatly. You interested?"

King said nothing his mind was throbbing painfully with confusion. His pale brown left eye and the pus colored right eye bulged out of his skull as they strained to see someone—anyone who may be the cause of this speaking voice between his ears.

"There's only you and Stone left Mr. King, and he's several blocks away. Now—do you want my help? Do you wish to win the game?"

"Where are you?" King demanded to know.

"You know where I am. Now I need an answer Mr. King—I need to hear you say—yessss."

"I ain't sayin' nothing until I know where you are and who you are!"

"Very well Mr. King," giggled the icy voice.

A spinning column of blue flame that only King, the one who raised it, and those caretakers of the third realm watching could see, shot up into the earthly gray sky engulfing King. When the pillar of fire had receded back down, out of demonic sight, King was gone.

The flame fell from his vision and he found himself standing on the ice covered stone floor of Queen Vile's throne room. She rode her throne of tangled human flesh down through the black air, bringing it to a slow hovering stop directly before King. Dolly Man went to speak—to give Vile the yes answer she so desired. But it was too late for that now. Vile didn't have time to hear this fool's pleas, or even screams for that matter. Half a second before King's terrified yammering could vomit forth into Vile's ears, she willed his voice mute.

"To your knees," she said almost soothingly. The stone floor beneath his feet cracked like thin ice on a deep lake, and down he went. His fast sinking stopped with an abrupt snap as the floor became stone hard again, sealing him upright an inch above the knees.

"I am Vile, queen of the sixth realm and soon to be ruler of all creation," her tone was matter of fact. "And you Mr. King, you're nothing more than a tool—a sort of weapon, the means by which I will keep B'neem from victory. If you serve me well I'll reward you greatly. If you do not, I will see that you're delivered unto him."

An iron cage moved over the floor out of the darkness, sending a deafeningly loud scraping noise out into the frigid air. Steadily King could see a dark figure standing within its bars. Seconds before it had moved far enough into the dim light for King to make out who it was a voice, scarred with pain growled "—Hello boy." King recognized who it was immediately upon hearing it. It was his father. The man who had beaten and raped King when he was a boy, and the father who burned King's face with an iron when he was seven years of age, forcing him to wear a monster's scar forever.

Vile waved her hand and the cage disappeared into the darkness— silently.

"Time is short Mr. King," Vile's throne hovered around King's head. "Will you say yes?"

King replied immediately by nodding his head up and down.

"Wise decision," Vile's throne carried her up, back into the deepest, darkest and coldest space of her great chamber. "You may take possession of the weapon—the firearm, once the constable places it in the vehicle's boot." Vile sensed King's confusion at the mention of the word *boot* and clarified by adding "—the storage space at the rear of the vehicle."

It's called a trunk; King attempted to correct her in thought, and was hit with an icy pain a thousand times more agonizing than the hottest of Hell's flames for his trouble. The coldness raking throughout his bones fled as swiftly as it had been sent at the sound of Vile's voice.

"Now—go and serve me," she ordered her words moving further into the dark. "Succeed and I'll grant you wonders far more satisfying than simply vengeance over your foe. Fail and you'll be handed over to your father for him to do with you as he wishes for all eternity.

In a flash of icy-cold blue flames Dolly Man was returned to the exact spot from where he'd been taken. King's painfully frozen flesh and bones dropped him to his knees.

"The weapon Mr. King," Vile's voice spoke "—the vehicle is about to depart—HURRY! HURRY!" Vile's voice was desperate and angry.

King swung his vision around, the thin layer of ice which had formed over his face and neck cracked and crumbled with the aching turn of his head. Eventually King's eyes moved through the crowd to find the detective standing over the open trunk of his car. He placed the clear plastic evidence bag with the .357 Mag inside and slammed the lid.

King was trying to crawl up onto his feet, moving painfully slow through the warm souls. He shoved himself up, but no sooner was he standing and down he went. Again and again his efforts ended with his collapsing. Even the images of that naked, red-haired white woman giving him to his father weren't strong enough to terrify King into action.

Sliding behind the wheel of his car the detective glanced briefly over his shoulder to say something King couldn't make out over Vile's shrieking voice "—MOVE YOU FOOL!"

King shoved up off his face again to take a rushed step and down he went.

The detective pulled his door closed, buckled up, said something into the mouth piece of his C.B. radio then put the car in gear.

"GET UP YOU WEAK MORONIC MAGGOT!" Vile screamed.

The car began to roll slowly forward, inching its way through the crowd.

"GET UP! GET UP!" Vile's rage sounded almost as if it were mixed with a pleading lilt in its tone.

With a strained grunt and painfully laborious effort King once again crawled to his feet and hurtled himself in through the trunk's lid—Dolly Man was riding in the police car's boot.

It had required a great-deal of Vile's will power to keep King from simply passing all the way through onto the street. It took even more of her magic to enable him with the ability to take possession of the gun and carry it out with him. But the true test of Queen Vile's powers, a test which had taxed her stores of demonic energy greatly, was instilling the revolver with the ability to effect Alex's physical frame of Hell-cursed flesh and bones long enough for King to use his bowie knife.

The instant King's fumbling hands found the bag with the loaded gun he grabbed it and flung himself out of the moving trunk onto the street. When his body stopped rolling and sliding over the asphalt, he sat up in the middle of the road and looked disbelievingly at the .357 revolver in his fist.

"It worked!" King screamed. "It really worked."

"Of course it worked," Vile said, her voice weary sounding. "Now go back and collect your knife, it's where you dropped it when you leapt. You'll still need to open Stone's flesh with your intended weapon after you've shot him. As for your pouch of teeth, I believe you'll find it on the road called, Alley. Now go—serve me and reward yourself." Vile's voice faded to silence, melting into King's brain like icy claws raking down through his spine.

Dolly Man gazed at his edge and grinned.

Chapter Ten

— DOLLY MAN —

And there before me was
Lucifer, the absolute ruler of
that whole world of grief
and suffering, halfway buried
in the ice himself.

—Dante's Inferno

As Alex Stone made his way through the, streets and alleyways of his childhood home town he found that it was becoming somewhat of a personal battle keeping his mind fixed solely on the job laid out before him. The task of finding and sending back the others before any of them could do likewise to him was becoming steadily muddled by all of it. Images of faces—screaming, terrified faces cascaded so heavily down before his memories sight that to hang onto and control the direction of his own thoughts had become a mentally strenuous task. Every past event from the moment he'd picked the lock of apartment 49's door to him witnessing the stupid goth girl's head being blasted open kept tearing into his brain. The closer game-time crept toward the sounding of the Game Over buzzer, the more intense the invasion of strong-fisted memories got. Alex concentration was slowly slipping from his grasp. And to make matters more disconcerting was that the rapidly becoming arduous remit of maintaining his focus was being compounded by confusion, doubt and yes—even fear. Alex was finally reaching that level of madness found primarily in those who's insane minds had lost the ability to rationalize the unreasonable. In simpler terms, Alex could no-longer brush it all to the back of his brain—there just wasn't anymore room.

At least the thick ampoule of adrenaline, shot from the syringe of hate straight into his heart when he'd first spotted Dolly Man out through the school's window, was still pumping through his veins. That second-wind had been and still was gale-force strong, successfully blowing away the fee of exhaustion he'd been made to pay for Pike's little hint. Now if he could only get a deeper hold on the strands of mental integrity fighting to secure its reign over his mind, he might have a chance.

Desperate to regain his hold on the moments at hand, Alex decided to break the wall of silence he'd erected between himself and Bianca. His intention—or hope—was to wipe some, if not all of the howling images out of his mind with some small-talk. Alex figured that by keeping the topic on the game it might serve to re-sharpen his mental-edge.

"Witch—" he called, practically without the aid of sound to power his voice. There was no answer for a long moment. Alex could still sense the witch's presence with him, so he knew she'd not left like she'd done when she was the voice of Mr. Bane in Five's apartment. Actually, Mr. Bane/Bianca the gypsy witch had never really left Alex when the cops had him cornered in the blood-splattered bedroom of apartment 49, not really. The metallic voice had simply slipped back so deeply into the blade she'd cursed herself into, that Alex's awareness had lost the connection. It was as if Bianca had simply hung up the phone while still remaining in the same house.

Alex was about to call out to the gypsy again, when she said, "Yes Alex." Bianca's tone was low, filled deeply with a sense of melancholy.

"I was wondering if you had any idea how many players were left?" Alex asked.

"Sorry Alex, but no...I do not."

"That's too bad."

"Yes, yes indeed it is too bad."

"I wonder why that punk King ran off?"

"The few brief glimpses I'd managed to get of the player while we were engaging him—"

"We?" Alex interrupted, a note of sharp-fisted indignity clinging to his abeyance.

"Yes Alex—we," Bianca replied. "Whether you like it or not Alex, you wield the blade and I its edge, opens the flesh. Remember—you are the Millstone and I am the Bane. Without your fist to race me through the meat I am no better than a forgotten butter-knife. And without me—your nothing more than a lunatic." Bianca paused in anticipation of a vexed riposte. Alex said nothing, he forced the anger that the child murdering witch had obviously intentionally attempted to call forth, back down. A moderate silence stretched out between them until Bianca gave in and broke her anticipating pause to continue where Alex had interrupted her. "When we were engaging the player I'd noticed he appeared to be looking for something. If so, what do you suppose it may have been? What would be so grievous a lose to make him blind to the advantage he held over you?"

Alex ran Dolly Man's disgusting image through his memory, struggling it past the quagmire of shrieking remembrance choking his brain stupid. Then, like an eager child who'd figured out the answer to a billion dollar question, butting into a riddle meant for another Bianca asked "—What color was his pouch?" not quite handing Alex the answer, merely leading him to it.

"WHITE!" Alex barked "—He'd lost his pouch."

The image of his own black bag of teeth dangling by its drawstring from the branches of the cherry tree on Jefferson street flashed in his mind. "That's why King ran off; he went to find his pouch."

"Yes Alex, I believe it's the only reason which makes since."

Another long silence pulled out to settle between Alex and the witch trapped within his dagger. It wasn't one of those awkward quiets, like one of those—*now what to say?* hushes. No—not at all. Truth is, both Alex and Bianca had plenty to discuss. It was the subjects wriggling naggingly in their skulls and the dire reluctance to spew forth, which created the silence. A silence not unlike pus hardening over the surface of a corpse's eyes. No, they both realized that this was not the time for heated debates as to the whys and hows of things. That time would have to wait until after the game's conclusion—that was providing of course Pike permitted it.

⇒ ⊪ ⇐

Queen Vile was feeling so utterly drained and hollowed out that at times she believed her outer-self was going to collapse inward, like the ever-changing shapelessness of a Solar Brown Dwarf. Casting her will out into the taxing expense of arming Dolly Man with a weapon not yet gifted to Tartarus was a costly choice indeed. Zaw'naw's chance of victory as the game's winner died the instant Alex sent Stanley Fiction back to Hell. And as for Vile's scheme to use Alex's mother as not only his assassin, but also as a tool to crush the other realm's players; that plan had also blown up in Vile's face. Now all she cared about was keeping B'neem from victory. As long as the eighth realm's long reign could be brought to an end, she believed the rest of the Empire could be forced to bend to her rule. As for Pike's ensuing invasion, Vile had no doubt that her armies would easily smash his efforts. *Let them come,* Vile thought. *I'll destroy the eighth realm in the old way.*

She knew Pike would wait until the game had reached its end and the victor was named before beginning his march on Zaw'naw. She also knew that time was mere hours away—sooner if Mr. King acted fast with his new toy. Vile was completely confident in her warrior's ability to crush B'neem's soldiers once they breeched her realm's borders. But, in the unlikely occurrence that Pike managed to push as far as the city walls which would take him no less than three, perhaps four weeks of endless fighting, she would need to prepare herself to face him. As it stood at the moment Vile was in no shape to rip Pike apart in a one on one private battle, an event she was so looking forward to. She'd used too much of her powers in a short space of time, Vile was drained, left with only enough strength to be feared by those who served her. Normally it would require months of rest in a cold and dark place, feeding almost endlessly on the beating hearts of lesser angels to restore her strength. But she didn't have that kind of time. She considered feeding on her old friend Ellzbeth's heart and flesh, but still, even Ellzbeth's archangel blood wouldn't be fast-acting enough. Vile was left with only a single option.

Clad in a confused combination, half battle-armor and half black flowing gown, her albino skin showing in spots the grayish-blue hue of decay, she stormed down through the corridors and passageways of her palace. Thin sheets of black-ice stretched swiftly out over the ceilings, walls and floors before her, almost as if leading the way. Vile's once regal expression showed to all the cost of her treachery. Her face and body now hung off her bones like softening wax. The Queen's lower eyelids drooped heavily like those of an old basset hound. Vile's ears sagged horribly from the weight of Vexrile's festering green eyes still dangling from her lobes. Her nostrils stretched out from beneath her melting nose and her bottom lip flopped limply down over her chin, exposing most of her lower row of teeth. Her right breast swung out past her gown like a long white gym-sock containing in its toe a hand full of wet sand. The skin draping down over her back and buttocks appeared so empty that the skeletal forms of her bone showed sharply beneath.

There was only one whose blood would be strong enough to restore Vile her power in an expeditious order, or at least it could in theory. It was the blood of creation's first archangel: Satan's blood. Vile had thieved it after he'd been bled-dry and hidden it all away, telling no one of its continued existence, except for Vexrile. Fearing the blood, or moreover fearing its unknown qualities, Vile destroyed all but a single drop of that great leader of the rebellion's blood. For thousands upon thousands of years she'd kept that frozen ruby colored, tear-droplet of glistening blood hovering above a wide, bottomless pit in the center of her vault. The vault itself was located deep within the petrified bowels of the slain mammoth cherubim foundation upon which her palace rests.

Vile had long ago after Vexrile's attempted thievery from out of the vault, ordered a ten foot tall creature know as a Sareck Beast to guard the vault's doorless threshold. Sarecks were first created by the gods as a work-force for the angels to employ after their imprisonment on this world. Sareck's powerfully strong bodies and fast problem solving skills made these gentle giants superior architects and builders of everything from bridges to sky-scraping castles. In that long ago beginning Sareck's numbers were in the tens of thousands, but at the end of the second war they'd been reduced to one of Hell's rarest of breeds. Only those few who'd given in-to the calls uttered by the hounds of war survived. Those who insisted on holding true to their pacifist beliefs had simply lain down and allowed themselves to be slaughtered. The Sarecks which had decided to give war a go took to the battle field as easily as a sea-snake takes to water. Few beings who were unfortunate enough to stand opposite the sword or lance of the Sareck, whether they be archangel or that of a battle skilled lesser breed, survived to speak of the encounter.

It was for that reason Vile had chosen this rare, coveted creature as the guardian of her most prized possession. Vile had ordered the Sareck to hack anyone who dared approach the vault to bits then cast every bloody scrap down the vault's pit—including herself. Vile knew that if a time came when she would need to take Satan's blood, mixing it with her own, she would need to prove strong enough to withstand its overwhelming gift of power. She also knew that if that time arrived, that if she'd found reason to commit to such a self-altering engagement, it was because she'd drained herself practically dry. Vile decided long ago that if that time came and she was unable to take what was her's in a test of physical combat without the aid of angelic magic, then she wasn't worthy. If she was not strong enough to defeat this flesh and blood test of steel and pain, she wouldn't be strong enough to survive the blood mingling.

Vile armed herself with a lance like weapon that she'd taken from one of her palace guards on her way to the vault. It wasn't her preferred choice of weapon, that would have been her two fisted broadsword she'd wielded during both great wars. But for this task she decided upon something with a greater reach. The lance she chose resembled a sort of partizon spear, only with a longer, wider blade at one end of its iron shaft and a solid steel ball fixed to its opposite end as a skull crushing counterweight.

Vile, even in her power drained state, moved confidently down through the steep darkened passageway that spiraled deep into the petrified belly of her palace. No sooner had she reached the ice and rock base of the stairs and a deep voice called out from the far end of the vast chamber. It was coming from behind a small fire, speaking out of the shadows beyond the modest flames power of candescence.

"What is it you seek...my Queen?" the voice asked. Two blades pulled down in a slow sweeping motion, crossing one another in the flames. "Is it for speaking that you venture," an arm raised, strapped between the elbow and wrist was a small heart-shaped shield made of blue iron. A hand possessing seven clawed fingers pointed one of the talons at Vile's lance, adding, "or is it to fight?"

413

"I've come to collect that which belongs to me," Vile announced, her words reverberating, even in her low tone off the ceiling and walls of the cavern.

"Then the time of talking is over," the guardian of the vault said in a feelingless tone of voice as he moved into the dim light.

Sareck Beasts come in many sizes and no two are built the same. This one owned deep set purple eyes, no nose or even nostrils, yet he still somehow possessed a powerful sense of smell. His ears were two tiny holes located behind his wide lower jaw. Several rows of tiny sharp teeth filled a lipless mouth. His dark-gray skin resembled the thick hide of a rhinoceros. His short, wide neck, rested upon huge shoulders. Two man-like red arms, their color fading away above the elbows to an off-white, reached out over two-more, slightly shorter arms. Clutched in the upper arm's fists were two four foot long, inward curving-bladed swords called 'falcatas'. The lower right fist held a large black-iron gaff-hook, and a heart shaped shield fixed to the left forearm. Six powerfully strong legs supported this impressive torso. As a rule Sarecks don't take names, believing such personal designation as vain wastes of mental expenses, but this Sareck decide to make an exception, calling himself 'Crab'.

Vile moved closer, stepping further into the limited power of the small fire. Her haggardly transformed frame lumbering to a weaving stop like a body who's skeleton was made of rubber. With a fast rake of her weapon's blade she slashed a long line in front of her across the stone ground. Her crimson eyes caught the white flames of the fire in their reflective glint, causing them to glow intensely like volcanic magma.

Without a word Crab accepted Vile's challenge by charging headlong straight at her. Standing her ground for the arrival of the right moment, Vile remained totally motionless. When he was less than fifteen feet from slicing through her like a thrashing device through a single stock of wheat she made her move. Using her lance, Vile pole-vaulted herself in a display of gravitational defiance over the advancing creature. Directly above his head she raced the balled end of her weapon hard-around. A split second before the flying queen could crack the steel sphere against the back of his skull, he caught Vile through her right upper thigh on his hook and slammed her down hard flat on her back. The sharp sounds of snapping bones muffled by thin flesh lashed out to be expeditiously smothered by the grunted expulsion of all her lung's holdings.

Not surrendering to the effects of dull and sharp pain whipping simultaneously about within her frame, Vile swung the spear's blade around in a breathless attempt to open Crab's throat. Too swift for her limited efforts, he jerked his upper body backward out of its razor-edged path. With a backhanded swipe of his shield he knocked her weapon to the ground. Before Vile could bring her lance's blade back up, reversing its direction, Crab dropped one of his feet down on her wrist, locking it and her weapon to the frozen, stony floor. Crab stomped another foot onto her chest, crushing a few of the brass bars that made up her armor, piercing their pointed tips into her breasts. With Vile pinned to the ground beneath the weight of Crab's foot, he crisscrossed his sword blades under her chin, holding the edge of each against both sides of her neck. Taking the gaff-hook out of her leg, Crab repositioned its tip up between her thighs, pressing it unpiercingly against her flesh.

"Concede my Queen," Crab advised.

"Take that thing from between my legs!" Vile's voice rattled with seething rage.

"Concede."

"LOOSE ME NOW!"

"You must first concede my queen," Crab said while pressing the hook's tip slowly into Vile's angelic vagina. Blood oozed with a sudden steadiness the instant the edges of Crab's blades cut into the surface layer of Vile's neck. She struggled motionlessly to summon forth her power of will, but she could find none to draw from—Queen Vile had drained herself helpless. The hook was a full six or seven inches inside Vile, and was pushing up against the inside of her pubic bone. Crab's swords were also moving beyond her skin through muscles.

"You must concede my queen," Crab's voice was as cold and flat as the spiritless expression on his face. Vile knew any efforts to be heard by her palace guard this deep below her palace would be impossible, yet still she screamed. It was a desperate cry, not at all queenly—Vile was for the second time in her ageless existence—afraid. Her long, high-pitched shriek was gagged by the blades cutting through and blocking her windpipe. The hook stabbed up through her lower belly as Crab began to repeat "—concede—"

His request was cut short by an iron shafted arrow suddenly appearing quietly out of his forehead. Two more arrows popped out of his face and a third shot out through his chest. With a loud howl of enraged pain Crab spun about, sweeping both of his swords blindly out of Vile's throat, nearly cutting her head completely off. Two more arrows rocketed out of the darkness from the same direction. Leaving his gaff-hook in the queen, Crab swatted the arrows to the ground with the face of his shield and charged. Vile's lance tore through the small of his back, its speared tip stabbing out his belly. With a fast, slightly concerned glance over his shoulder, Crab saw that Vile herself had thrown it. She was up on her knees, his hook still between her legs, its tip pierced out below her naval. Almost all the skin and muscles which had once created Vile's slender neck was now hanging down like a blood soaked stocking; only an exposed spine supported her teetering head.

Without turning his attention away from her he snatched an arrow meant for his throat out of flight, and threw it like a solid iron dart into the center of Vile's chest. Crab then turned in time to spot Sumac moving out of the darkness astride the massive shoulders of her many colored battle-mount. In its right claw it clutched a large scimitar bladed sword revved to its wrist with a long iron chain. Sumac herself stood nine feet tall, atop her battle-beast towering over Crabs seven and a half foot tall hieghth.

Casting her bow and empty quiver to the ground, she swung her long handled battle-ax up out of its boot and advanced the already charging guardian of the vault. Reaching behind his head, Crab yanked one of the arrows out of his skull, arming the fist that was accustomed to wielding the hook. The instant Crab was within cleaving distance Sumac's mount swung its blade. Crab ducked beneath the sweeping steel, darting himself around to the beast's right side. He stabbed the arrow clear to it's fletching into the beast's flank. Crab then blocked Sumac's falling ax with his shield, grabbing her weapon's iron handle with the hand of his shield arm. As he tore her weapon from her fists Crab raced the blade of his right sword across the mount's throat, opening it deeply. In a shower of arterial blood the guardian of the vault drove his left sword's blade all the way to the hilt into Sumac's ribs.

Crab yanked her up out of the saddle while on his sword and flung her to the ground, when the sharp sound of something slicing air spun him about. He looked up in time to catch sight of the huge scimitar dropping. Crab didn't even have enough time for coherent thought, panicked or otherwise. The giant blade cleaved him in two, evenly through the middle from head to ass-hole. Both halves of his body fell away from one another with a wet-sounding slap on the ground. Crab's halves grabbed and clawed at each other, struggling frantically to pull themselves back together, while at the same time trying in vain to keep his organs from spilling out. And yet still he made an effort, although pathetic, to keep Sumac and her advancing beast at bay. Picking her battle-ax up Sumac stomped Crab's left half over to fall before her mount to deal with while she worked on the right half.

Not long after Crab had thrown the arrow he'd snatched out of the air into Vile's chest, she'd begun the laborious task of dragging herself toward the vault. She had barely managed to pull her wounded self across the frozen floor of rock and bone a few yards. Sumac, forcing herself to break away from her duty, covered from head to heel in Crab's blood and guts, stepped over to help her injured queen.

"Allow me my queen," Sumac offered as she lifted Vile into her arms. "Forgive me my queen for interfering. But if I may in my defense—I'd given unto you long ago my oath to defend you even at the cost of your wrath." Sumac laid Vile as comfortably as possible on a somewhat flat bed of icy stone. She removed the arrow and hook from her queen's flesh as she spoke.

"Your power has faded greatly. Again, forgive me my queen for delving into your affair but I must if I'm to hold true to my oath."

Vile attempted to speak, but her weakened state had greatly slowed her body's ability to mend itself swiftly. The only sounds Vile could utter were the blood suckings and blowings made by her severed throat and wind-pipe. She was trying to order Sumac to the vault, to the vessel of blood. Sumac's mind was strong in that she'd always been gifted with the ability to read the silent meanings that speak from the expressions of ones eyes.

"There is something here, in this place that will restore you?" Sumac asked. Vile's eyes looked up into Sumac's, giving her an assenting gaze. She set her crimson vision into the direction of the vault hidden within a veil of blackness beyond the small fire. Sumac's gaze followed, she asked, "What you seek, is it there?"

Vile replied with a painfully forced, "Yes."

"Shall I fetch this thing for you?"

"Yesssss," Vile hissed.

Sumac bowed her head in an acknowledgement of her unwavering obedience.

In a strained voice Vile ordered "—G G G O O O O !"

Sumac stood and glanced through the darkened space at her mount gorging itself on Crab's still aware flesh. The gaping slash wound across its neck hadn't completely closed yet, allowing a few scraps of meat to escape through it before being fully swallowed. As it fed on the already chewed Crab meat dropping out of its throat, Sumac spoke sharply "—DEFEND!" immediately the feeding beast abandoned its meal and lumbered over to stand guard over Vile.

"My Queen," Sumac offered a final bow of her head then turned and walked toward the small fire.

As with the Sareck beast she'd defeated, Madam Sumac was also a rare breed of being. During the first war some angelic creatures who'd been laid-waste by the gods were risen out of their deathly state by Commander Archangels—thus the creation of demons and devils. These resurrected angels, whether they had been powerful archangels during their former lives or less powerful, breeds; almost all of them had crossed the bridge from death back to life magicless. Most of these new creatures had crossed back over as dim-witted brutes, difficult to control. There were a few rare exceptions, Sumac is one of these. Although her mind is, as with all demons, locked in a never-resting state of war, she still possesses the ability to reason and formulate. Sumac is in short, a –Soldier Hybrid. She possesses no magical gifts except to heal her own wounded flesh. All of Sumac's power rests comfortably in her mind's all knowing knowledge of all things concerning warfare. If not for the fact that she'd been in the middle of fasting, going on several months without food or even drink, she would have crushed Crab easily.

Sumac fashioned a crude torch from what appeared to be a discarded leg bone and some tearings off of a large piece of heavy cloth she found on the ground. Taking the large portion of the cloth with her as well, she lit her makeshift torch and made her way toward the huge doorless entryway. At first glance the doorway appeared featureless, a simple oval shaped hole cut smoothly into stone and ice. But as she drew near,

Sumac realized it was a large mouth. Raising her torch higher, holding it out above her head she immediately recognized the face cut into the high wall; it was the face of Satan himself. It peered down at her with deep-set eyes of blackened stone through a thick shroud of ice. Sumac always found herself feeling odd every time she came upon something that reminded her of the great leader who she'd helped to defeat. It was a sensation of closeness, closer even than deep love or hate, it was a feeling which seemed to own no beginning or end—it simply swept over her like warm breath, then slowly faded.

Sumac shook it off, glanced over her shoulder at Vile and her beast, then continued. There wasn't enough cloth on the leg bone to keep lighting her way, so she caught the larger portion of cloth aflame and draped it over the bone. By the time she'd navigated over the sharp stones and black-ice the rest of the way to the large gaping doorway most of the cloth had burned away as well. With what flame was left she'd not only seen the large stone bowl filled to the rim with liquefied human fat at the inside right of the doorway; she'd also spotted the tiny glass vessel containing what appeared to be blood. It hovered at eye-level, motionless above a very dark pit.

With the rapidly dwindling flame barely burning at the end of the leg bone she lit the bowl of fat. It immediately burst to a large ball of fire, filling the vast space with more than enough light. The vault itself was a rounded, cornerless chamber with an endless wall made of solid ice. Trapped within the wall, for as deep as her eyes could penetrate was an army of demons and angelic warriors. As she stepped around the edge of the pit, gazing with a commander's eye at the imprisoned force surrounding her, she thought with a sense of wonder, *I could rule all with such an army.* Their eyes followed her, she could see in their frozen gaze their lust for war.

Suddenly she pulled herself free from the treasonous thoughts attempting to worm their way between her love for war and her acquiescence to her queen. Without a shred of reluctance Sumac ran and leapt across the pit, carefully snatching the tiny glass bottle out of its hovering safe. She landed on the other side squarely flat-footed less than an inch from the edge. The second her feet slapped down on the stone floor the unmistakable sound of fast grinding stone and ice rushed down toward her. Sumac didn't even bother to chance a glance up to see what was coming. She ran as fast as her long, powerful legs would permit around the pit. With a throaty grunt she hurtled herself out through the doorway. At that exact instant a thunderously loud crash behind Sumac belched a thick cloud of dust, bits of ice, and rock out after her.

Sumac hit the ground hard and tumbled head long over the ice and stones coming to a scraping stop. She immediately sat upright and saw through the cloud that the vault, with its imprisoned army was no more. Even the giant face of Satan had collapsed in on itself. Looking down at her clenched fist she slowly rolled her fingers up off of her palm—the small glass vessel of blood was unbroken. As the dust and ice continued to drift steadily, down Sumac got up onto her feet and swung her vision around to where she'd left Vile. Amazingly the small, seemingly negligible fire had somehow survived the enormous blast. Its surprisingly staunch glow caused the falling bits of ice and rock to be cast in a shimmering twinkle which Sumac paid little notice of. She gazed through the glistening debris and saw that her battle-beast was hunched over her queen, shielding Vile with its wide back against the cloud that had been vomited out of the vault. The beast straightened itself, pulling into an upright position, the thick layer of dust and tiny rocks which had settled over its hide falling to the ground as it moved away from Vile.

Sumac stepped before her queen and going to one knee, she bowed her head and said in a proud voice, "I exist only to serve you my Queen," she reached out her hand.

Vile's eyes burned bright, a thin smile stretched across her trembling lips and saying nothing she took the vessel of blood up from Sumac's palm.

Less than an hour from the moment that Dolly Man had taken possession of the loaded .357 Bulldog, the effects of the naked white woman's help had begun to manifest itself in a highly unpleasant manner. It had started with a sickly feeling in his guts, a rumbling in his bowels that sent an almost endless stream of foul smelling explosions out his ass. Nasty tasting burps pushed up King's throat into his mouth. An odd tickling sensation had begun wriggling about beneath his skin. King's eyeballs and tongue itched furiously, and the insides of his nostrils felt as though they were on fire clear up in to the center of his skull. This was only the beginning of Dolly Man's fee for Vile's gun arming assistance.

King's stinging vision fell immediately onto his pouch the moment he turned the corner of a brick wall into a narrow, gravel alleyway. It was beneath the snapping jaws of two little dogs who's barking made them sound far meaner then they appeared. Something about the unearthly bag of teeth had transfixed the mutts directly over the pouch, gripping them in a spell bound state of snarling, barking and slobbering. The larger dog of the two, although not by much, was as black as Dolly Man's soul and badly infected with manage that ran along the center of its back. The smaller dog was as white as the sun-bleached sea of bones Alex had been made to gaze our over from his wooden beam. Both of the pissed off dogs were mongrel mutts, apparently homeless.

At first the dogs paid King's painfully strained curses and shouting no mind whatsoever, they merely kept right on blasting their barrage of angry sounds down at the pouch, drenching it with doggy drool. It wasn't until his advance moved him within snapping distance that two truths were made shockingly clear to The Dolly Man. He was still unaware of the fact that earthly beasts of all species can not only see and hear Hell's game contestants, they can also bite the players as well.

With the gun in his right fist he locked the knife blade in his teeth in order to free his left hand. At as fast a pace his bare feet would permit on the tiny, pointed gravel stones, King moved on the dogs. He unwittingly lunged his empty hand down between the sets of gnashing teeth with no worries. In the unbelievably swift space of time between the black dog's fangs piercing his skin, the subsequent torment of teeth scraping across bone, and the scream that dropped his knife to the ground, King thought, *I'm not going to like this!* The dog tore a considerable portion of the skin wrapped around his forearm off when King knocked the beast loose by cracking it upside the head with the gun. The flesh had torn from King's wrist as easily as boiled meat pulls free from a chicken bone.

The second truth made apparent to Dolly Man was that the end result of his cost for Vile's aid was that he was suddenly forced to suffer physical decay. In short, King's body was rotting. It wouldn't have been so bad if not for the new fact that his body's ability to heal itself had also been greatly retarded. His flesh and bones could still mend themselves but only at a very slow rate of speed.

The immediate air took on a sudden foul reek the instant the dog's teeth broke King's skin. The reason for the endless tickle tormenting him from within his flesh was revealed as a flood of tiny yellow maggots poured out of the arm wound instead of blood. The white dog, seeing its comrade being smacked with the gun drove its teeth deep into King's right ankle, while its pal got to its paws and wolfed down the festering scrap of meat. King kicked the white dog off, its teeth taking with it a mouthful of flesh. King swung the gun up, aiming it at the mutt he'd kicked loose, as the white dog landed against the base of a telephone-pole with a sharp *yelp*! King pulled the hammer back and at the exact instant the revolver exploded with a deafening *boom*! a black blur flew past Kings vision. The black dog had leapt up and clasped its jaws around King's right wrist. The shot had either missed or the bullets were useless against these beast, whichever the case, it was a wasted shot.

As King was fighting to yank the black dog off the end of his arm, the white dog was up again and wasting no time, chose its target and charged. King had barely managed to tear the black dog off his arm when its white friend lunged it's fangs into Dolly Man's scrotum. King shrieked as he cracked the butt of the gun's handgrip against the snarling beast's skull. Once, twice he hammered the heavy piece down on the mutts head. It was the solid third clubbing that convinced the white dog to let go of King's balls. The dog fell to the gravel motionless, bright-red blood staining its white fur around its left eye and ear. King stomped the heel of his right foot down to make sure it was dead. With gun-shot speed the white bitch swung her jaws up and caught the middle bottom of King's foot in its teeth. He jerked his foot free and before his now pus seeping foot could kick her she had scrambled to her paws and darted out of striking range. King aimed the gun at the dog and fired, another round was wasted.

At the exact second the pistol was made to roar King was made to send forth another pain filled howl. The cause of this out-burst was the set of teeth which were driven deeply into King's right buttocks. He reached back, and latching a hold of a fist full of hide and wiry-fur, he ripped the black dog from his ass, tearing most of the right cheek off as well. Catching sight of the white dog charging out of the corner of his yellow eye, King threw the howling black dog at it. The dogs slammed into each other hard enough to stop the bitch's advance. They swiftly rolled up onto their paws about to attack again, then stopped. They leered up at King, their snouts peeled back to expose snarling fangs. Then, as if being drawn away by a demonic dog-whistle the two beasts vanished out of sight back to the third realm.

"Yeah! That right! Run bitches!" King strained to shout. "Got your fucking asses stomped! Yeah, yeah, yeah—run bitches!" His voice was steadily growing mute with decay as maggots and blood blackened by rot choked up into his throat, filling his mouth. With an unexpected jolt, King's entire body lurched violently, he dropped to his knees, the gravel tearing on impact up into his tender with rot skin and launched forth a flood of putrefied flesh and blood. *WHATS WRONG?* his mind shrieked, *WHATS FUCKIN' HAPPENED TO ME?*

The seemingly endless river of rotten puke eventually thinned to a stringy trickle of thick, sticky, smelly black slobber. He wiped his mouth with the back of his mauled right wrist, the revolver still gripped in his fist. Rolling off of his knees onto his bitten butt, King sat upright beside his pouch of teeth. *Why don't I heal?* He wondered dreadfully. *What's wrong with me. Why ain't my body fixin' itself like before? Why—why?*

After several long confusion filled, painful minutes of sitting, staring stupidly down at his mangled balls. Sobbing almost uncontrollably like a little girl attending the back-yard funeral of her beloved pet cat; King decided it was time to get it together. Hanging his dog-drool soaked pouch around his neck, he pick up his knife and shoved up onto his shaky legs. With the bones in both his ankles and wrists exposed his butt cheek ripped almost completely off, and his mauled crotch, Dolly Man limped out of the alley.

Dark-gray clouds drifted over Corvallis. The wind picked up some, making the air hum with an unsettling whistle as it blew through the branches of leafless trees and power-lines. The dark mantle over head smothered the waning light of day, darkening the evening to an early night. As a light rain began to fall, King set his direction toward the down-town area. He'd wasted two bullets, although both of which had hit their mark, causing the white dog no ill-affect. The rounds were only meant for the flesh and bones of one, they could only draw the blood of Millstone.

≡ ◃╟▹ ≡

Soon after Pike helped Sader's torn body mend itself, and once the whole of B'neem's military force was fully assembled and made battle-ready, he sent forth seven messengers. They were armed with letters for the Gate Keepers of all realms but the sixth. These letter-carriers appeared without warning by magical transport in the chambers, throne rooms and great halls of those seven realms with news of B'neem's plans to march on Zaw'naw.

The seven delivered epistles were identically penned declarations in simple language, they read thusly:

I Pike, the proud Gate Keeper for the eighth realm wishes to communicate my intentions to all of you, my fellow Gate Keepers. Immediately after the game's end and a victor has been named I intend to lead B'neem's legions of war into battle against Zaw'naw. My purpose for this is not conquest or imperialistic subjugation over the sixth realm. My purpose is justice. My purpose is to place Vile, the sixth realm's Gate Keeper in chains so that she may be taken before the magistrate and made to answer for her foul deeds of late. Vile is in violation of the Empire's strictest of laws—specifically those creeds which govern over all treacherous acts perpetrated against any of Hell's custodians of higher breeds. Shrouded beneath the cover of our great game, Vile crept into B'neem and snatched away our Grand Inquisitor—Ellzbeth. Vile had also attempted to abolish B'neem's equal chance for victory in the game by smuggling our player's mother/murder victim into the game within the flesh of Zaw'naw's player. I myself was witness to this phase of Vile's underhanded scheme.

B'neem is not seeking the blessings of the other realms; this is not why I've delivered unto you, my fellow angels, these declarations. Vile will be made to stand in judgment whether any of you approve or not. In chains she will be taken. In chains she will answer for her greedy, foul acts against the eighth realm—against the Empire, and most of all my friends—against all of you.

As I close with this—I wish that all of you understand exhaustively. B'neem is not asking that any of you stand with swords drawn at our side.

Quite the contrary. This is our affair—B'neem's and Zaw'naw's affair alone. I ask that you all respect that.

Until Dust—Pike

Pike knew with complete certainty that his fellow Gate Keepers, despite their love or hate for either Vile or himself, would honor his request for privacy in this matter. The other realms would all settle back and wait for the dust of war to clear. Then and only then would they decide what to do next, depending upon of course which one of Hell's two super-powers were left victorious and which defeated. If B'neem took the day, then the other realms would band together and help set the sixth realm back in order, first by appointing it a new Gate Keeper to replace Vile. If Zaw'naw defeated the invading army, the Empire would have much to worry about. Sides would be taken and the planet Hell would be plunged into a world-war, the third great war would come.

But for now this conflict would be bound to only these two nightmarish superpowers. It would for the time being remain a private duel, watched closely—although at a somewhat safe distance—like the game.

≈ ❯❯ ≈

Because of a nation-wide energy shortage the city of Corvallis' Overlords, more commonly referred to as 'The city fathers', had decided that all holiday lighting decorations, both public and residential be greatly restricted. Homes may only display a single window decorated with a modest string of colored lights. A tree may also be displayed in the same window, although it may not be adorned with lighting. Violations of this ordinance are punishable by a costly fine of upwards to one-thousand dollars. As for public-spaces, such as the streets and shops of down-town, their holiday glimmer and glow is grossly bleak, and that's putting it lightly. Downtown Corvallis' holiday zeal was restricted to a single, dimly lit star, a tiny star at that, no bigger than a child's severed fist, placed atop a tree in front of the Benton County Courthouse.

The previous night Alex had thought something about the town appeared out-of-sorts for the time of year. It wasn't until he'd spotted that pathetic star crammed on top of the courthouse evergreen that he realized what was missing.

"The Grinch came to town early this year it seems," Alex chuckled.

"I don't understand Alex." Bianca whispered.

"Its nothin…just talking to myself, that's all."

"Are you going to be alright Alex? You sound a bit shaky."

"I'm fine," Alex growled. "Just make sure you do your part and—"

Alex was interrupted by the loud *bong* of the courthouse clock-bell. He stepped around the wide tree with its sad little star to look up at the big clock face as another loud *bong!* echoed out over the town. It was 7:00 straight up. *Bong—bong—bong.* Alex was walking across the courthouse's soggy lawn around to the front of the large old, stone building. A big black bird swooped down out of the sky and perched on the head of the Lady Justice statue beneath the front face of the clock. *BONG!* The bell's cries actually sounded as though they were growing louder with each strike. The bird paid the noise no attention it merely loosed a few long loud, cries of its own, then leaned over and began pecking at Lady Justice's unblindfolded stone eyes. *BONG!—KA BANG!* The gun-shot not only owned a very familiar cracking sound, the slug that always accompanies such a sound blasted the fedora off Alex's head, drawing a bone deep crease through the middle of his scalp.

"SONOFABITCH!" Alex threw himself to the ground and quickly rolled behind the trunk of a not quite wide enough tree. Blood trickled like icy fingernails from the bullet's crease. He wiped it off his forehead with the back of his glove before it could ooze into his eyes, and then peered around the tree up at the courthouse. Alex was in time to see a shadowy figure dart back out of a window on the second floor. He could feel cold streams of blood moving back up his neck and head into the closing wound. Alex saw no further signs of the sniper. Deciding that it was as good a time as any, he swiftly crawled to his feet and ran through the granite archway leading to the courthouse basement front entrance. The instant Alex passed through the locked door into the dimly lighted basement corridor he made a swift study of his new surroundings. His eyes located the black and white sign with the word STAIRWAY and bolted up the steep narrow stairs.

"Easy Alex," Bianca warned. "This one has a gun! You will need to use a deeper level of cunning to put this one in—how'd you say it? Put this one, in its dish."

"I thought that little prick Pike said there would be no guns!" Alex hissed through clinched teeth as he swept his vision over the empty main floor. The main floor's lay out was closely similar to that of the basement, a long corridor which gave-way to offices, an elevator to his right and a flight of stairs to his immediate left.

"Step easy—step easy," Bianca urged softly as Alex eased his attention onto the stairs. "We'll need to be clever Alex, more sly than the oath of a gun's bite—"

"Shhhhash!" Alex demanded. "I'm trying to listen." The shot came from the second floor." Alex whispered as he swept his left hand backward over his head. "It came damn close to opening my skull."

"The gun owned a familiar roar...did it not?"

"Yes," Alex answered. "It was a heavy caliber, a revolver like the girl's at the school. I think—"

A sharp *tap-tap-tapping* noise coming from upstairs interrupted Alex. *Tap-tap-tap—tap—tap-tap-tap—CLANG! BANG!—tap-tap-tap.* The sniper was trying to lure Alex up to the second floor.

"It's a trap Alex!" Bianca warned. "Find another way up—one that the player won't see."

Tap-tap—CLANG! CLANG!—tap—tap—BANG!

Alex was panning his eyes around, searching for an unexpected way up when his hunt stopped on the metal elevator door. Stepping swiftly, he crossed the darkened lobby to the elevator and passed his head through the closed sliding door for a peek inside. The lift itself was below him, stopped for the night on the basement floor. Moving the rest of the way into the dark elevator shaft, Alex had to step down a couple feet for his boots to reach the elevator's small roof. His first thought was to use the lift's steel cables and shimmy up the short distance of only four or five yards to the second floor. But the thick cables were too slathered with grease for Alex, even with his gloves he wouldn't be able to get a good enough grip.

BANG! BANG! Tap—tap—clang—clang—CLANG!—tap, the foolish racket continued.

Alex's vision had gotten good at quickly readjusting to changes in light or the sudden lack there of. He locked the knife between his teeth, gripping its blade tight in his bite and using the four by fours and beams as a makeshift ladder he climbed up the shaft. It only took Alex a few gruntless seconds to reach his desired destination. Putting his ear to the cold surface of the metal sliding door, he listened to the sound of labored breathing and movement not far from the other side. The noise his knife's blade whispered as he swept it carefully, yet swiftly from his clasped teeth sounded like he'd pulled the weapon out of its metal sheath, and sent a slight shiver up his spine. Clutching the dagger in a commando fighting fashion—its blade held along his forearm, tip pointed toward his elbow, Alex took a deep, quiet breath and slowly pushed his face through the door. The memory of Fisk's axe sweeping less than an inch past the bridge of his nose in the Mall when he went to peek through a wall flashed in his brain.

"Easy Alex."

Shut the fuck up! Alex ordered in thought. His face passed through the door's surface on the other side and to his suddenly delighted surprise Alex saw King, or at least what was left of him. Alex's sense of smell was instantly assaulted by a mixture of decaying flesh and reekingly foul farts. King's rotting back was to the elevator. He was striking the blunt side of his bowie knife's blade against a brass feed pipe for the floor's steam-heater while aiming a short barreled pistol at the head of the stairs. Alex immediately recognized the .357 Mag as the very same revolver the goth girl had. *How in the name of shit did that child killing fucker get a hold of that piece?* Alex wondered as he pulled most of his face back into the elevator door, keeping just enough out so his left eye was watching King. Alex was waiting for King to start beating the knife against the pipe again in the hope that the racket would mask any noise made by his surprise attack.

CLANG! BANG! BANG! CLANG! Tap-tap-tap-tap.

Alex drifted through the door, the swift flash of the memory of King's wide back to him in an open air 'pisser' clicked like an old black and white snapshot before his mind's eye. Alex had only managed to advance three maybe four feet when King swung the gun around pointing it at Alex's head. The horribly rotted sight of Dolly Man's grinning expression was instantly overtaken by the blinding explosion of a muzzle flash and pain tearing through the right side of Alex's face. The hollow-point slug decimated skin, muscle and the bone of his cheek, transforming it all to mush and dust on its way to destroy most of the base of his skull. It missed all of Alex's brain-stem, tearing only a small portion of his cerebellum off as it blasted out.

The dense crimson fog raised from Alex's head hadn't even begun to settle as the bullet's body stopping force whipped Alex completely around dead in his tracks to face him the way he'd come; sending Alex stumbling back through the elevator door. His body passed into darkness to be slammed against the lift's cables and once more Alex Stone was dropping. The differences between this fall and those he'd been made to experience in Hell were One, he had a fairly good idea where and on what this fall would end, and Two—its ending came fast. Past the ringing in his ear caused by the pistol blast Alex heard the sharp *snap!* of his right upper arm breaking upon impact with the elevator's metal roof.

"Alex! Alex! You've lost your hold on me!" Bianca shrieked. Alex pulled his hand into a fist and indeed he had lost the knife. The only experience his mind owned to compare with the pain tearing through his body at that moment was the teeth grinding, sight blinding trauma delivered to him by Pike.

"Alex!—Alex can you still hear me?" Bianca howled, her voice muffled and distant.

"Yes" Alex replied through half a face. "Can you see where you are?"

"No—no Alex, its much too dark. I feel as though I'm wedge tightly between two hard surfaces, one metal, the other stone and both cold." The metallic voice was coming up from beneath Alex, to his left. He immediately discerned that Bianca's panic—stricken voice was emanating from between the wall of the shaft and the elevator itself.

"Try to keep talking, I'll follow the sound of your voice," Alex said, his words wrapped in a quivering inflection of agony. He was already feeling the tingle of his face and the back of his skull beginning the process of mending. Beyond the buzzing, what sounded like strained laughter came booming down the elevator-shaft from the second floor.

"Hurry please Alex, I believe I can hear the accursed laughing of that egg-plant." Bianca was trying to sound calm and unworried, but Alex could hear the distress in her tone. It screamed out from between her softly spoken words like the last-ditch efforts of a waning alarm siren. For a fleeting moment Alex caught a glint of Mr. Bane's voice bleeding through. It was cut short by the forced hollering of a rattling wet voice, struggling to come off sounding as though it were in control—as if it had already won.

"Hey Stone!" King gagged out down the elevator shaft. "Nice shot, yeah—nice fucking shot! It looked like it hurt you really good. It was my last bullet too." King paused briefly then added through choked laughter. "Hey Stone—I wonder what this here button does?"

Alex had been in the process of rolling himself down through the elevator's roof, when the big motor fired to life. After a split-second of it spitting out some thin blue sparks the huge iron wheel and gears that pulled the cables up and down turned, and with an abrupt jolt the large box was moving.

"Get your white ass up her Stone!"

Alex let himself drop through the roof. He hit the elevator floor hard, landing on his right arm and hissed intensely through gnashed teeth as the already broken bone snapped the rest of the way in two too tearing out of his flesh. With little time to appreciate the pain Alex, hearing Bianca's screams through the wall and the teeth sound of steel scraping hard against stone, slapped the elevator's pause button on the control-panel. The large metal box came to a sudden halt and Alex heard the unmistakable sound of his knife sliding down the elevator's outer wall to clang on the concrete floor below. The elevator broke free from its forced arrest and was once again on its way up. Alex drove his entire upper body down through the floor, his vision immediately locating the knife. He swung his left arm down and barely managed to scoop his weapon up before the steadily increasing distance would not countenance its happening.

Alex pulled back up into the moving box and punched the pause button again. It jerked to a stop. Alex shot a glance up at the indicator and saw that its pointer-arm was stopped between the first and second floors. He felt the right side of his face, the thumb size hole through his cheek was alive with self-healing activity. He could feel the blood and bits of brains moving with the aid of Hellish will up his neck into the base of his skull.

'It was my last bullet too,' Alex remembered King's words and attempted a grin, only the left side corner of his bloodless mouth would lift with a tug. The snapped in two humerus bone was no longer protruding out through the skin of his upper right arm and was actually nearly all but completely mended. Again the elevator jolted upward. With his left fist gripped tightly around the knife's bone handle and his eyes on the door Alex awaited the familiar tone of the bell that tells riders they've reached their floor.

DING!—The doors slid open and King tossed the tooth into an empty elevator. "Oh—really, games! Is that it!" King was yelling at the empty box, black blood, chewed up maggots and hunks of broken loose wind-pipe flew out of his mouth. "Well I've got a few tricks of my own you CRACKER!"

"Hey Dolly Man," Alex was standing right behind King yelling stupidly into the elevator. King swung around, the empty gun in his right hand and his bowie knife held half ready in his left. The instant King turned full-about Alex rocketed the lead beads in his left sap-glove hard against his jaw. King shot backward into the elevator, the doors slid closed and Alex punched the down button.

"Alex, why didn't you end it?" Bianca asked, her voiced weary.

"I'm not done with him yet," Alex growled as he gave chase. He leapt through the closed door into the shaft once again and landed flat-footed on the descending metal roof. Stopping in the basement, Alex heard the DING! of the opening elevator door bell. He grabbed onto a wooden beam and swung himself through the brick and mortar of a solid wall, coming out in the basement only a few feet behind the already running Dolly Man. Alex hit the carpet on one knee and a boot to immediately spring himself after his fleeing prey. With a reaching hand he latched a hold of King's left wrist, the same wrist sporting the fist holding the bowie knife. As soon as Alex had a hold of him, he whipped King around catching the child-killer on the full length of his dagger. The blade formally known as Mr. Bane slammed into the right side of King's chest with such intense force of impact that Alex's entire fist busted through Dolly Man's decaying rib-cavity.

Still in possession of the almost useless .357 Mag, clutched like a blued rock in his right fist; King swung the pistol, cracking it hard against the right side of Alex's head. It was a solid blow, and by all rights should have instantly laid Alex low—but though it had opened skin and cracked bone, it still wasn't enough to loosen the rage-fed resolve of his hate for this foul creature.

Alex tore his knife out of King's rib-cage and round-housed its blade toward his festering head. Alex was far too caught up in the single-minded focus of his intent to notice the black goo and maggots flinging from his falling knife hand. All Alex saw, or could see beyond the screen of rage swelling in his heart was the spot on his target's head—the place he'd chosen to drive his weapon's blade.

King saw Alex's intention as well. He was about to dash Millstone upside his skull again with the pistol, but instead King flailed his right arm out, hooking it around Alex's arm to lock the invading appendage up against his rotting arm-pit. He then quickly pulled up a mouthful of thick liquid rot from deep within his bowels and spit the foul reeking bile squarely in Alex's face. Dolly Man followed that revolting act by ramming his flesh barren, pus incrusted forehead against the bridge of Alex's nose. It was a staggering blow, harder even than the wallop with the gun. The head butt had not only wobbled Alex, temporarily stunning his senses; it also shattered his nose, sending a flood of blood out to mix with the stream already reversing its flow back up into the closing gash he suffered from the earlier pistol-whipping.

The rotted condition of the skin surrounding King's wrist was making Alex's task of holding the child-killer's bowie knife at bay an arduous chore. He caught sight of King setting up for another head butt, and with a hard rightward sweep of his own head he cracked the left side of Dolly Man's skull. Alex quickly reversed his head's swing, smacking the right side of King's meaty coconut as well.

"How do you like it!" Alex inquired sharply before pulling up his own ball of snot and blood, launching hard into King's cloudy brown eye. Alex jerked his right arm free, simultaneously slicing a bone deep slash up across King's arm-pit.

At the very instant that Alex's newly freed knife-hand was crashing its leather and lead clad knuckles against the right side of Dolly Man's neck, the kid-killer tore his own knife-hand loose from the vice like grip clutching it. With a wet sounding, throaty grunt he swung the bowie knife wide. King aimed his effort up toward Alex's neck with every intention of decapitating Millstone. Alex, catching the faint glint of the approaching blade jerked out of its path and wind milled his own weapon around, bringing its blade down with an ear ringing crash against the bowie knife. The moment he'd successfully veered King's intent into oblivion, Alex whipped the edge of his knife up with a fast arcing sweep and sheared a substantial portion of the left side of Dolly Man's face off. The thin slab of meat and skin flung off Alex's blade to slap wetly against the elevator door.

King stumbled backward in a herky-jerky retreat from Alex's crisscrossing onslaught. Tripping backward, over his own feet, King dropped solidly to his ass, landing against a wall beneath the dim refulgent of a small green light. As King pushed himself back up the wall, Alex slowed his attack to a stop. Not in order to allow Dolly Man a fighting chance by giving the piece of shit time to get to his feet—hell no. What stopped Alex was the hideous sight sliding up before him, being revealed by the faint lighting. Dolly Man's entire body appeared to be alive with thousands of tiny yellow worms. They clung to the pus seeping cuts and slices made by Alex's blade. Some lost their handless grip and fell in clumps to the floor. Thick black and green gunk oozed out of Dolly Man's ear-holes. It seeped from the sagging corners of his eyes and poured from his nostrils, blowing out of his nose like snot bubbles with each labored out-going of breath. Clinging to the glistening moisture covering his upper body, Dolly Man's prison infirmary gown stuck to his skin the way a wet t-shirt clings to a coed's breasts. The difference being the moisture smearing his skin wasn't beer or sweat; it was pus and the guts of smashed maggots.

"Goddamn—you just keep getting uglier and uglier!" Alex chuckled as he slowly side stepped toward his prey. With a foul smelling yell that reached out and blasted all the way across into Stone's face, Dolly Man lobbed the revolver at him. It was a fast, hard and lucky throw. Before Alex could duck out of its path, the thing caught the top right side of his head. It managed to slice open a deep line through his scalp with the edge of the hammer's thumb grip. Seeing the gash on Stone's crown, Dolly Man tossed the tooth he'd retrieved from up off the floor of the elevator before it stopped in the basement. It hit Alex's chest then dropped between his boots. Stone, trapped in an abrupt state of *Oh Shit!* Stared down at the demon tooth while quickly moving back away from it. He wiped his glove across the top of his head and seeing blood on his fingers he growled. The two players stared at one another, Dolly Man's festering face pulling into a wide grin.

"Alex—I believe it only works if he makes his cut with his blade," Bianca said softly. Alex looked back down at the uneventful tooth.

"Fuck it then," Alex said under his breath. "Lets find out?" Gripping his weapon, ready to slice the freak if he so much as looked like he was thinking about trying to make a move, Stone stepped directly over the tooth. As he tapped at it with the toe of his boot he smiled coldly and hissed loud enough for Dolly Man to hear him, "Must be a dud."

All at once the expression of victory beaming out of Dolly Man's maggot squirming face melted away. As the expression of vengeful satisfaction sank to the waste-side a voice filled his memory. It was the recollected voice of the naked woman who'd given him the gun, reminding him '—*You'll still need to open Stone's flesh with your intended weapon after you've shot him—*'

Dolly Man raised the bowie knife over his head clutching it in both fists and loosed a yell that blasted forth more evidence of his decomposing innards than sound. He charged.

Alex darted hard left, easily avoiding Dolly Man's clumsy attack. Moving fast he came around behind the freak and swatted the demon tooth with the tip of his knife down the corridor. Dolly Man's blade chased after Stone, sweeping and missing, sweeping and missing, again and again. Despite his wormy, decaying state of being Dolly Man still possessed the same speed and strength as the lead player; Alex.

Alex dropped himself beneath the bowie knife's efforts and swung his right boot out. The maneuver paid off, sweeping Dolly Man's legs out from under him. The freak slammed face first to the floor allowing Alex an entire back to slice open as he rolled up onto his boots. Shoving himself up against the blade crisscrossing through the meat and bone covering his back, Dolly Man rolled over and finding an opening between the blade's strikes, kicked the ball of his rotted foot straight up into Millstone's family—jewels. The freak's foot found its mark with enough strength to pick Stone up off his feet and drop him stumbling backward in pain.

Dolly Man hopped up, his wide back sliced open in a dozen different directions, worms sprinkling out of the wounds like cheese through a grater onto the carpet to land in pools of pus. The freak swung a leering expression onto Alex gripping his junk and attacked. With a two fisted grip and all the muscles in his frame he sent the bowie knife out like a fiend on a mission. The wide blade raced with an upward swing across Alex's upper chest, only cutting through his sweat-shirt, not even tickling the skin within. Growling through the torment of having his balls slammed up into his throat, Alex seeing the bowie knife's return, blocked it with his own knife then sent his blade around and upward, slicing it completely through Dolly Man's right wrist. The severed hand which had been still clutching the brass and wood handle of the knife beside its fisted comrade loosened its grip and flung through the air to slap against the stairwell door.

With his weapon in only his left fist, Dolly Man bellowed as he came about and slammed the bloodless stump backward up into Alex's jaw. The bowie knife, close behind sailed swiftly past the right side of Alex's face, missing by less than a hair it seemed. Shaking out the stars placed in his skull by the stump's blow, Alex barely avoided Dolly Man's blade, ducking beneath its flight path to escape its head-hunting aim. At a sort of stumbling dart he moved around the freak, racing the bewitched blade through the kid-killer's thigh. Tripping to a somewhat safer distance, Alex spun around to put an end to his clumsy dance and saw that Dolly Man was making a run for it. Scooping his severed hand up, the freak vanished through the stairwell door.

"GO ALEX!" Bianca shrieked.

Alex practically flew after the fleeing freak. Dolly Man was half way up the narrow flight of stairs when Alex passed through the door. *Damn—that fucker's fast,* he thought as he tore up after him. With a throaty, guttural grunt Alex shot his reaching hand out like a noose while at the same time throwing himself upward across the stairs. His fist locked around the decaying ankle still sporting the fanged bites of the dog. Alex jerked his catch to a sudden stop, but as Dolly Man's body fell he flipped himself around and stomped the heel of his naked foot dead-center into Alex's face, busting his nose a second time. The blow not only freed his ankle, it also sent Alex rolling head over heels back down the stairs.

Alex was back to his feet in time to see Dolly Man slip through the door at the top of the stairs. As Alex bolted after him he could hear the freak's steps receding throughout the huge building. Almost to the top of the steps, Alex threw himself shoulder first through the wall. The instant he came out on the first floor he caught the sound of Dolly Man's running steps and spun about to follow. He was barely in time to see the rotting freak disappear up another steep flight of stairs. Again Alex heard the heavy pounding of feet falling quickly over head, and again he gave chase.

Once on the second floor landing all Alex needed to do in order to know which direction his prey had went was follow the trail of tiny worms. They'd fallen to the dark-red carpet in a somewhat straight line that lead to and vanished under a black oak door. The wooden plaque fixed to the wall at eye level read—DISTRICT COURTROOM #1. Alex, wasting no time, followed the trail of cutworms swiftly through the door to see Dolly Man moving toward the judge's private door behind the witness box.

"That's right ass-hole run!" Alex laughed. "It's exactly what they all expect from a child murdering punk like you."

Dolly Man made an effort to offer some sort of chicken-shit retort as he shot a glance over his shoulder, but all he could utter were gagged, choking sounds.

"We'll just have to finish this back in Hell," Alex added. Dolly Man stopped a few feet in front of the door. His back was to Alex, standing behind the defendant side of a long table. Dropping his severed hand to the floor Dolly Man spun around and began walking toward Alex. He stepped at a fast, reluctance—free pace at first, until with no warning the freak stopped in the middle of the courtroom's theater, only six or seven feet from Stone. Like an uninterested Outfielder, waiting for the crack of the bat on a cloudy day, Dolly Man stood there. Sluggishly he raised the bowie knife away from his side, gripping it in a weak, challenging gesture.

"Yeah, whatever. Fuck you, you pile of shit!" Alex rumbled as he flipped the dagger's blade around in his hand and using all of his strength and speed threw it. The spinning shiv slammed point fist into the center of Dolly Man's face. It drove through to the hilt with such force that it not only jolted most of the maggots out of his festering head, it also knocked the freak on his ass. Dolly Man shoved to an upright sitting position and immediately began wrenching and yanking on the bone handle protruding out of his face.

As Alex humorously watched the one handed freak's vain wrestling against the blade's desire to stay where it was, he stepped up on the long table. Taking the demon tooth from the black leathery bag hanging around his neck he noticed that Dolly Man had stopped trying to pull the knife out of his head. He moved onto his knees and stared up past the handle at the tooth pinched between Alex's thumb and finger.

"You were meant to be Number One," Alex said. "As it turns out though—you're Six." He tossed the tooth into the air and as its twirling rise arched and fell toward its target, Dolly Man closed his eyes and let his head fall limply down.

The second the tooth hit the floor, landing between his knees, dozens of thin, shiny steel wires shot up out of the floor and wrapped around Dolly Man's entire body. He offered no resistance against the flesh slicing wires as they pulled him to the floor flat on his back and gripped his body down with enough force to lock him in place.

Alex, still atop the table, lowered to his haunches, resting his forearm on his knees intent on watching the show. A single wire lashed out and whipped onto the severed hand, flinging it widely through the air inches from Alex's nose before slapping it back onto the stump. A few eventless seconds crept through the big room, Dolly Man was beginning to mumble or sob, Alex wasn't quite sure which—then they came. Dozens, perhaps tens of dozens of naked, foot-tall headless rubber dolls wriggled and climbed up out of the carpeted floor all around him.

Dolly Man's tearing, horrified eyes looked up at Alex, and without a sound his expression pled for death. Even if Alex had possessed the knowledge needed to successfully slash all of the after life awareness out of Dolly Man's cold soul, he wouldn't have. Why should he want to?

The moment the last of the decapitated dolls was up on its feet and they had all waddled around the trussed out freak, forming a large ring of rubber around him, they moved in. Millstone noticed that as they drew closer their little dolly hands began changing shape, transforming into razor sharp, three inch long, bladed spoons.

They shuffled toward him with spastic, jerky movements and all came to a sudden stop when the first row was less than two feet from

Dolly Man. The ten or fifteen seconds of waiting for it to begin must have seemed like a nightmarishly long space of time to the quivering freak. Dolly Man's silent tears erupted into a loud wordless blubbering of spit and sound. The dolls exploded into the air, leaping on top of him.

They sliced and ripped—ripped and sliced off tiny hunks of skin and flesh, every bit of it filled with feeding worms. They swiftly dropped the scraps of meat down their gaping neck holes, filling their hollow dolly bodies with chunks of Dolly Man. The dolls worked on the freak with such blinding speed, all Alex could see beyond the heavy cloud of rotted blood and maggot-mist was fast, brief flashes of slicing flesh and flying little blades.

When the dolls had finished, their smeared with rot little bodies bulged with every last scrap of Dolly Man's shredded flesh. All that remained of the foul monster who had savagely raped and murdered twenty-seven little boys were picked clean bones. The fat dolls climbed down and out of the skeleton, some lost their footing and slipped off, falling to the floor and spilling some of their meaty holding out on the carpet. Forced to gather it all back up, they stuffed it down their necks and continued on. A few helped to pull the skeleton apart while three of the dolls beat furiously against the skull-cap in order to retrieve Dolly Man's brains. Finally, after several minutes of determination and a little help from a few of their fellow dolls, the skull cracked open. Like a rotten egg its disgusting wealth of worms and spoilage spilled out at their tiny rubber feet. With no time to waste they scooped it all up and finished breaking the skull to smaller, more manageable pieces. The dagger that was nailed down through the skull's face fell to the floor and the dolls paid it no mind, they simply worked around it.

Once they'd cleaned even the smallest sign of what had occurred in that courtroom out of earthly existence the grisly procession of swollen headless toys sank down into the floor, Dolly Man was on his way back to Hell.

Alex stepped off the table and made his way over to where his knife lay.

"Witch," he called down to it. Suddenly a wave of utter loneliness, icy and thick swept through him. The abrupt sensation was more vast and frightening than the feeling that poured through him when Mr.

Bane had abandoned him the night of his death. More alarming even still than all of the times Ruth and Wayne had locked him in the closet at the end of the hallway. The dagger was empty. Then, as if it had never been a part of him, the deep feelings of loneliness and dread were swept away; the knife was simply that, a knife. And the gypsy witch who he'd named 'Freak Bane' was now nothing more than a memory. Alex Stone was truly alone, and he didn't care.

He reached down to lift the ancient implement of pain and death up off the floor. As soon as he closed his fist around it, the dimly lit courtroom went pitch-black. It was as if all light had never existed, it was as if Alex was being made to peer deeply into Millstone's soul. With no warning, none whatsoever; the lightless shroud plunged over Alex was being sliced into by blades of blurred color and light.

Like countless reflections dancing across razor sharp steel the indiscernible shapes whipped inhumanly fast all around him. A few—actually quite a bit more than a few of the blurred images seemed familiar, but it was all moving far too swiftly for Alex to rightly call them to his recollection.

Suddenly one of the blurs snapped to a normal rate of speed as it moved past him, allowing Stone to see what it was clearly before tearing off into the pitch again. The slowed image was a sort of trapped strip of time, a small piece of Alex's past being made to play over and over again. It was a reenactment of Stone and Dolly Man when they were locked in battle down in the basement. The memory was there before him, then in a flash was torn off in the swift current of colors and lights. Another shadow of the past hit its brakes for a split-second. It was of Alex looking up at the dimly lit star atop the tree in front of the courthouse. Several more blurs of color stopped briefly then went. He saw himself walking through alleys and buildings, crossing streets and moving through warm souls. He thought he looked insane, his eyes wide as they scanned his surroundings and his thin lips moving, talking to the voice in the knife.

Alex saw himself drive the blade down through the back of King's leg on the creek bank. He watched himself watching helplessly as the goth girl's skull was blasted open by the sniper's bullet. The blurs of imprisoned time came and went, sometimes in twos and threes. They shot wildly around him like out of reach, badgering phantoms, needling him, mocking him before being caught up in the wake of the whipping tempest of memories.

Two stopped at once, the one to his left was of him as a boy of nine, Ruth in the process of sucking out his eyeball. The image to his right was of him simply walking with a daydreaming expression on his face as he made his way over the bike path. The two moving images were swept away. Stone saw the goth girl again, this time it was as he was watching her thieve the gun from under the car seat then she was gone—gone not from his mortal memory, only out of his immediate sight. A brief portion of the moment when he was ducking and dodging the '50 Merc slowed, then was gone. The piece of past when he was being dragged out of the crowd of bystanders by the end of the blond-boy, demon-thing's dog-leash flashed to an abrupt brake before being zipped off into 'Nothing Nothing Land.'

In no time at all he saw himself staring dumbfoundedly up at Hell's giant wall of living, rotting bodies. The event of Pike giving Alex back Mr. Bane, the murder weapon resting on its bed of beating hearts in a box, stopped and was gone. Soon he was looking at himself as he marched across the red-desert, then he saw himself nailed to the beam overlooking the boneyard. For a few odd seconds the colors and lights of trapped events vanished—but not the memory. It was the remembering of the icy, dark ride he'd been made to take before being put in the sea of sun-bleached bones.

Suddenly, as if it hadn't stopped the colors and lights were back in full, blindingly fast force. Alex watched as his body dropped on Five, he saw the leg bone rip up out through his back. Next he was picking the lock to apartment 49's door, and before he knew it Alex was watching himself pull a last drag of the cigarette. He paid close attention to it as the less than half smoked butt he'd flicked from his fingers twirled through the damp air to land in a rain puddle. The instant its tiny red glow was put out with a fast hiss, Alex wasn't simply seeing the alley he was standing in it.

"I believe congratulations are in order," Pike's voice spoke out from behind him. "You've done well Mr. Stone. Of course, I never once doubted that you would." The Gate Keeper stepped into view.

Too deeply entranced in watching his before death self climbing the fire-escape ladder, Alex barely noticed that Pike wasn't donning the black and red robes he was used to seeing the Gate Keeper wearing. Clad from head to toe in black and red battle armor, Pike stepped in front of Stone and handed him his fedora.

"I believe this belongs to you," Pike said.

"You took the child-killing witch out of the knife?" Alex asked, although it was more statement then guess or question. He took his hat and after a brief examination of the bullet holes through the front and back of its crown he put it on with a mumbled "Thanks."

"She was B'neem's possession Mr. Stone—as you yourself are B'neem's possession. Yes I took her from the dagger's blade, the witches' torments are a long time coming," Pike paused to watch with Stone as his former self slipped through the seventh floor fire-escape door. "But beings since you represented B'neem with such zeal…such passion for the art of winning, I've taken it upon myself to award you with an unprecedented bonus in addition to your principal prize. I'll get to that later. First thing's first, if I'm not mistaken I said I'd let you have two more questions of your choosing—or was it only one?" Pike paused, scratching his chin poking out from beneath the bottom of his metal helmet thoughtfully with his gloved finger. "Two, it was two. If you wish to ask me something now is the time…but as before, keep it brief and to the point.

Alex let his gaze drift from Pike's flaming eyes beaming out past narrow slits cut across his helmet's face. He let his vision come to rest on a cat darting out of the alley.

"I would like it if you would—"

"I said you may ask two questions," Pike cut Stone off. "Not make requests! I've no time for your mutinously foolish needs or wants." He took half a step toward Alex, "Ask your questions or decline—it makes no difference to me."

Alex wanted more than ever to reach out and strangle the little bastard. Instead he reformed his request quickly so that it came out more like a question.

"This prize you say I've won," Alex began.

"The bonus I mentioned or the principal prize?" Pike asked.

"Both."

"Continue then."

"Would it be at all possible for you to allow me to trade it?"

441

"You're pushing it Stone," Pike paused. "But go on, I'll hear this… continue."

"Could you use your healing powers to mend my sister's mind and body instead of awarding me this, these prizes you speak of?" Alex lowered his eyes to the ground and in a faint, slightly shaky voice added "—Please."

Pike hearing the guilt and indismissable selflessness in Alex's tone did something unexpected and completely out of character for the red-eyed being, Pike stepped forward and placed his gauntlet clad hand on Stone's forearm.

"My powers of mending the flesh and minds of human-beings are restricted to the the damned," Pike said softly. "Only a God or Goddess possesses the power to do what you ask…I do not." As his iron glove fell away from Alex's arm he looked up into his eyes and told him "—I'm truly sorry…Alex."

Alex's fists clinched into tight ball of rage. His furiously needful expression narrowed down onto the Gate Keeper as the omnipotent yet diminutive archangel took three modestly distanced steps backward. Removing his Corinthian style helmet but not the purple clay mask, Pike allowed Alex his ranting.

"What the fuck man," Alex rumbled. "Why won't you cut me some goddamn slack? You could convince that eyeless goddess you mentioned to cut some sort of deal. Hell, you could tell her that my suffering will be great. Tell her that I've given my flesh over to you—"

"Enough Mr. Stone," Pike interrupted his tone soft.

"Help Susan!"

"Mr. Stone—"

"I had a vision. I saw Susan's face, it transformed into a red-haired woman's face with black lips and eyes like yours. She treatened to do—"

"The one you say you saw…this vision, she is being dealt with. Your Susan will be safe—on this you have my—"

"BULLSHIT!" Alex took a step toward Pike. "You're taking me to see my sister—NOW!" Lowering the knife to his side he took another threatening step toward Pike. The Gate Keeper's eyes behind the mask went black as he set his gaze on Alex's falling step. The moment the heel of his work-boot touched down, the damp asphalt beneath Stone's feet went from solid black-top to black liquid. Alex's body sank swiftly and just before his face was to go under the asphalt hardened back to its intended state. With only Alex's left nostril, eye and ear protruding above the black pavement Alex watched and listened while the Gate Keeper gave him yet another scolding.

"I understand your desire to help Susan, truly I do. I even understand your 'I want what I want and I want it NOW!' attitude." Pike went to one metal clad knee to the left of Alex's half submerged head. "What I continually fail to grasp is your untethered, tenacious hankering to stand face to face against blatantly unbeatable odds. Although your foolhardy courage is amusing at times, it grows wearisome when it's set on your betters. It stops—" Pike leaned the mask's eye-holes close to Alex's one exposed, widely staring steely blue eye. The Gate Keeper's peepers were still as shiny black as the round eyes of a shark, "NOW!" he hissed, the sound of it so sharply uttered that it sliced painfully deep into Alex's brain.

Standing, Pike went straight into the description of the principal prize Alex had won.

"Your suffering in Hell is for now at rest. You will instead be left here on this; your home world where you will eternally serve as a creature we refer to as a Grim. Your sole task is to be the last thing those you're sent to dispatch will ever see on Earth."

Pike turned his back to Alex and as he walked toward a steadily appearing fog he added with a humorless chuckle," At least you won't be alone—I've given you an apprentice to give you a hand—"

Pike stepped into the fog and was gone.

Chapter Eleven

— FRAY —

As I sit upon my self wrought
throne of loathing and disdain,
I look at the world brimming
with grief and turmoil and war.
I question aloud:
"At what price, what cost before
we finally see the folly of our
actions? How many must die, how
many must suffer before man
finally learns?"
Myself suddenly turns to me,
indignation apparent on my face.
And who the hell are you to judge
with your heart filled with hate
and rage and murder?
You cannot even stomach
to look at another without the
vicious bile of disdain spewing
forth. Who the fuck are you?
Who am I indeed.

—John A. McCann

What would have required months of quiet concealment in utter darkness to convalesce on the blood of a hundred archangels, as well as gorging on their beating hearts, only took three days and four nights with that one drop of blood. Vile was back to her ageless-self and then some. Although her rapid reconditioning hadn't completely fulfilled her expectations, the re-empowerment of her control over the flesh of others and the one additional gift to her original abilities would be enough. It would be all she would need to illustrate her seething contempt for the one responsible for dashing her ambitions against the stones of failure.

Vile had always been of the belief that the secret of death over all flesh, both that of cold souls damned to her world and immortal beings cursed by the gods, was locked away deep in Satan's heart. As it turns out, that belief was in error. Vile felt foolish when she learned she had been in possession of the secret of death all along in her own vault—it was locked within the droplet of blood. She wouldn't need to eat Satan's heart after all.

The droplet demanded rules, requirements to the wielding of this ancient toy named murder. It must be executed by its new master in the old way—without the aid of magic. Vile can kill only by using blade, arrow, or any other hand held weapons. She may crush skulls with rocks or even tear out a target's heart with her bare hands and teeth if she so chooses, to accomplish the deed. She could even use limited magic to set it up, but not in the final act itself.

There was another addition to the Queen, poured over her by the drop of blood. This final change to Vile's make-up was solely cosmetic. Her flaming eyes and hair were changed from their molten hue of red to a sort of dark violet. Two purple horns, a foot high and slightly curved at their pointed tips now rose from out of the top of Vile's high forehead. The black face-paint around her eyes and over her lips had somehow baked into her alabaster white skin, permanently tattooing into her face. And her long stiletto like fingernails were pushed out of her six fingered hands, dropping useless to the floor only to be replaced with twelve curved, much shorter, sharper nails. As for Vile's strength of will and the prowess by which she was legend throughout the Empire, that aspect of her abilities had only been restored to their former reach.

The self-seen queen over all creation was ready to face the one responsible for getting in her way.

"I'll let him come to me," Vile told Sumac, her tone eager yet soft. "He will be made to pay for his nuisance by being forced to watch his beloved realm fall under the fury of my wrath. And once he's seen the other leaders of the Empire die by my hand, I'll kill him as well…though not until after he's seen me feed upon his heart."

"What would you have me do my Queen?" Sumac asked.

"Without it being too easy for him, allow his armies to reach the city walls. I'll let him come to me."

Pike knew it would not be an easy task removing Vile from her throne. Her armies' were well equipped with sharpened steel and ancient powers. Her warriors had through the ages been schooled in all levels of warfare, masters one and all in virtually every aspect of the bloody craft. Vile herself was a legend in her own right as a military leader. After all, it was her armies' who defeated Satan's.

The sixth realm's vast landscape of rock, fire and ice was reduced to flat seas of blood soaked mud and crimson slush. The march through Zaw'naw's territories had been less costly than what Pike and his commanders had anticipated. Left in the wakes of battles behind him as their advance drew steadily closer to Vile's city were the shattered armaments, weaponry, and the mutilated but still living remains of fallen angels, demons and even the human damned. The battles were moving much too fast for any of the archangels on either side to stop long enough and heal their fallen comrades. Their battered, chopped to bits bodies were simply left behind to scream as Hell's birds and other wild creatures filled their bellies on the war's leavings.

Pike's armies alone had suffered the loss of over a quarter of his combat strength during the three weeks it took to cross Vile's realm and reach the wide canyon that encircled her mountain city's walls. Vile's losses were far greater. Nearly half of her fighting force lay in helpless torment on the battlefields behind Pike's shadow, or so it seemed to appear to the invading armies. Truth is that well over half of the fallen on Zaw'naw's side of the battlefield weren't all true soldiers. Most of Vile's losses were lesser breed angels wearing commander colors. Demons were made to serve as cavalry leaders, while summoned forth shades as well as human souls were ordered and forced to stand as front-line fighters. So far Sumac's ruse appeared to be working. Pike was marching face first into a trap.

On the second day of Pike's arrival into the icy heart of the sixth realm the rest of his regiments had crossed over the ring of mountains to take position around Vile's city. Other than the impaled bodies of human men and women that heavily adorned the top of the city's walls and a few hundred archers, Zaw'naw's mountain megalopolis appeared all but completely abandoned. The long day of his warriors and all of the battle-machines taking their places was drifting closer and closer to night. As soon as all the great catapults were set up and loaded, Pike ordered them to begin firing. They sent a barrage of fire-bombs and large stones raining down from all directions surrounding the city.

Pike ordered his commanders to send forth the Bridge Ants and to ready the Lancers for crossing the canyon. Bridge Ants are exactly what their title describes them as—giants ants. Their amazing speed and strength, coupled with their solid brass exoskeleton and large powerful mandible pinchers make them necessary siege weapons. Although, it's not so much in their destructive qualities that make Bridge Ants so needed in battle, it's the skill and speed with which they fulfill their intended purpose that proves their worth. Using their legs, claws, and pinchers they link their long, sectioned bodies together to form a long, wide bridge that can stretch across some of Hell's broadest canyons. There has never been a wind powerful enough to blow these monster ants, from their remit, and no army has ever been too great or heavy in numbers for their backs to support.

Vile's wall archers were sending their arrows so poorly that few were finding their mark. The Bridge Ants were half way across the canyon, Pike's warriors eagerly chomping at the bit, waiting for their commander's sign to storm across the living bridges. Simply for fun Pike ordered his own arches to rain their steel shafted fury down on the city in addition to the fiery barrage of molten stone.

A violent quake shook the frozen rock beneath Pike's invading armies feet. The loud cracking sound of splitting stone and the high-pitch of ripping iron erupted in front as well as behind Pike's forces. Suddenly the enormous walls surrounding Vile's city collapsed, falling forward over the canyon like a massive iron drawbridge, slapping on top of Pike's ants. The falling force of the crashing walls and the quake blasted, Pike's entire front line surrounding the canyon to the ground. As the dust and ice was settling, and while Pike's lead striking force got swiftly to their upright positions, the lower slopes of the mountain encompassing Pike's flanks came to life. Thousands upon thousands of Vile's soldiers moved out of the ice and black stone. The cloud risen up by the collapsing walls cleared to reveal a vast horde known throughout the Empire as Vile's Imperial Guard, Madam Sumac standing beside her battle-mount several yards in front of them.

The quake mellowed to a slow stop; soon the only noises that moved through the air were the grunts and growls of the beasts and the endless loading and firing of Pike's catapults. The mountain city behind Sumac and her horde was rapidly being reduced to an inferno of rubble and flesh. Only Vile's palace and a handful of structures below it were beyond the falling reach of the flaming stones.

Sumac mounted her beast, the army behind her crashing the iron hilts of their broadswords once against their chest plates. The soldiers at the foot of the mountain at Pike's flank followed suit. It was a deafening set of sounds that told Pike and all of his warriors they were completely surrounded. Taking his place in the saddle, he tapped the toe of his armored boot against the wide platform chained to his giant mount's shoulders. The great beast swept its war-hammer up into the darkening air then slammed it down against the solid rock ground. A single crack raced through the ground stretching out evenly from both the left and right sides of the hammer's head; Pike had drawn his line in the sand.

Sumac raised her arms and the instant both of her fists crashed against one another, the air was filled with battle-howls and charging metal. Pike's armies were slammed into; both front and rear practically simultaneously. The sound wave was so forceful from the clashing steel on both sides that Pike actually felt it rush over him. Within seconds Pike was inundated by the deafening noises of war.

Atop his beast, Pike almost effortlessly cut a wide swath through the ocean of flailing scimitars and pole-axes of his warriors and the broadswords and battle-axes of the enemy. As the big iron hammer chained to his beast's wrist swung and smashed Vile's, and sometimes even a few of his own soldiers out of his way, he looked for Sumac in the blur of blood and steel. Pike had always respected and revered Madam Sumac for her sharp wit fast thinking and combat skills. He even admired her steadfast loyalty—although greatly misguided, of late.

Several times during the second war Pike and Sumac had shared bread and wine between battles. Once during one of these meetings an argument arose concerning which arrow it had been that found the killing mark. Pike demanded that it was his arrow which drove deep into the giant's brain that laid it to waste. Sumac voiced sharply that it was her's which had made itself known to the great beast's skull. Neither of them unwilling to concede, they rose from their places and leapt over the camp-fire to cross swords.

Pike put up a good fight, but in the end he was no match for the nine foot tall warrior, not while on foot anyway. After toying with him for a bit, allowing Pike to get just close enough to raise a glint of hope in his soul, she knocked his weapon out of his grip with an upward sweep of her axe. Before his sword could fly harmlessly past her head, she snatched its hand-grip in her fist and tripped his feet out from under him with the long handle of her own weapon. Then at the exact instant Pike's back hit the ground, both the blades, his own sword and her axe were crossed at his throat.

"Who's arrow laid the beast low?" Sumac asked.

"It was my arrow!" Pike replied without the slightest shadow of aversion.

Sumac's eyes dulled to an almost black indigo blue, then in an instant softened to their usual lighter hue. She tossed Pike's sword in the large camp-fire, and without a word vanished into the darkness. Pike and Sumac hadn't spoken to one another since.

Determined to finally settle the argument as to whose arrow it was that had slain Satan's red giant, Pike searched over the battle wielding around him for Vile's field commander. He was about to turn and bash his way through in another direction when the glowing blue dome at the top of Vile's palace tower exploded, sending a storm of thick shards of glass raining down on the battle. Before any of the razor-sharp spears could chance to slice through the armor and flesh of his soldiers, Pike raised his palm out, immediately transforming Vile's shattered dome into arrows of black steel. They tore down out of the blackening red sky and aimed their barbed heads onto Vile's warriors alone. As the arrows darted around Pike's soldiers to find their marks in the heads and hearts of Vile's hordes, Pike was once again sending his beast's hammer down through the warring bodies below, trying, although with little luck, to avoid his own soldiers, while still smashing Vile's.

He was back to looking for Sumac, also having no luck, when suddenly almost as if they'd magically appeared out of the crimson haze he spotted them. Sader, astride his white-skinned beast was going head on with Sumac. Pike had attempted to convince Sader to remain in B'neem, but the silver-eyed Overseer wouldn't hear of it. Sader carried his weight well throughout the campaign, fighting with the zeal of ten angels. And with every arrow he flew and each swing of his sword he secretly blamed himself for Ellzbeth being taken.

Sader and Sumac's affray was taking place a good hundred yards from where Pike was, and from his vantage point he could see that Sumac was playing with Sader. Pike spun his hammer wielding beast toward his friend and began mashing a path. He was halfway there when a deafening squall erupted out of Vile's palace. The ear piercing shriek was immediately followed by a frigid blast of air that rushed down the mountain, freezing the flames that were burning the city out of existence.

The petrified archangel that formed the foundation of Vile's palace rose, crumbling the iron and stone structure on its back and shoulders to dust. The resurrected giant stood atop Vile's mountain, and as it panned its eyeless sockets down over the battle spreading out around it, Pike caught sight of Vile. She was fully armored, standing on the fleshy seat of her throne hovering in the empty hollows of the giant's petrified belly.

The stone and bone behemoth leapt high into the air and in that single jump landed with ground shaking accuracy squarely in the heart of the battle. Towering over the warriors, the giant kicked and stomped on them like a child killing roaches. It latched onto the ankles of a much smaller gargantuan, the largest creature in Pike's army, and using it like club, bashed itself a path to Pike. It swung Pike's large comrade about as if the being were a half-dead fish, Vile's stone monster intentionally cleared a wide, round space. When it was done, only itself, Pike and his beast stood at opposite ends of its center.

Pike attempted to summon forth a stone-crumbling spell, but nothing; *The icy blast of wind that she'd sent down the mountain,* Pike recalled. *Vile's blocked my power!*

Another icy wind, this one howling out from the giant's opened belly, whipped out and swept around the edge of the cleared space. The instant it brushed its frigid touch across the fighting soldiers surrounding Pike and the giant, the battling warriors, at least thirty bodies deep, froze solid. Vile, in her desire for privacy created a wall of frozen flesh and bone for her and Pike's meeting.

Pike, realizing what Vile was intending, and with only his somewhat rusty knowledge of magicless combat to fight with, charged his beast toward Vile's monster. He was hoping to get his beast's hammer close enough to shatter her creature's stone ankle and bring it down. Its eyeless stony face leaned over to peer down at the charging Gate Keeper. As if Pike were a ball of dust riding on the shoulders of a hairless rat, the giant swept the back of its open hand down and sent him out of the saddle. While Pike was rolling quickly over the frozen ground slamming to a stop against the wall of icy bodies, the giant snatched up his beast and tossed it over its shoulder like an old shoe. Pike's hammer wielding mount sailed through the air to land somewhere in the thick of the continuing battle.

The dazed Gate Keeper shoved swiftly up onto his feet, turning about in time to see the stone giant lowering to its bone exposed knees. Vile's great behemoth was turning to dust. As its head, shoulders and chest were latched onto and carried away by a gust of cold wind Vile, still standing on her throne of tangled bodies floated steadily out of the cavernous hole in its belly. In the short space of time that it took for her throne to carry her to the ground, only a few yards from Pike, every last flake of the petrified monster was gone.

Sliding her broadsword's four foot long blade out of the backs, chests and even a head or two of her throne, she turned and locked her new violet colored eyes down onto Pike, then stepped to the ground.

"Before we share a dance, I wish to extend an offer," she said as her throne drifted high up into the darkness. "Join me Pike, Gate Keeper of the eighth realm. Join me and together we will slay the gods, loose the great ships and expand Hell's empire throughout all creation."

"Ellzbeth, what have you done with her?" Pike demanded.

"That little golden-eyed bitch and I have a history. One that goes well beyond your concern for her." Vile replied.

"She was right about you all along. Ellzbeth, she truly knew the color of your greed, I should have—"

"Ellzbeth, Ellzbeth, Ellzbeth," Vile chuckled. "Of course she was right about me. Truth is Pike, she knows me better than I know myself. You should have listened to her a long time ago. So, my offer—what will it be? Join me, or fall before me?"

Pike swept the tip of his scimitar's blade across the ground in front of him, leaving a deep line cut in the stone.

"Pity," Vile said with a toothy smile. "I can't help but wonder what your answer will be once you've seen a modest demonstration of my newly acquired gift." She paused to stroke the back of her hand across her right cheek. "By the way...what do you think of my new look?" Vile winked.

Without taking her gaze from Pike she swept her empty hand out, reaching it into the air to her right. One of her own Imperial Guards was yanked up out of the battle by the power of her will and flew over the wall of frozen bodies. His throat slapped into her waiting fist, and as she held him straight armed above the ground Vile, without hesitation stabbed her sword into the ground, then drove her now empty left hand through his armor breast plate. Clear to the middle of her forearm she reached into his flesh, and silently mouthing the words, *there you are,* she smiled and ripped out his heart. Casting the warrior's heavy husk aside, Vile held the dripping heart out so Pike could see the stopping of its beats. She tossed it toward him and the motionless thing rolled to a slow stop at his feet.

"It's been awhile since you've seen one of those...hasn't it Pike." Vile freed her sword from the cold stone of the ground, her hand smeared dark red. "Death, Gate Keeper, see it?" she said, her tone colder than ever. "It's a thing of beauty...is it not?" Vile half glanced at the heartless angles' corpse behind her.

"How can this be?" Pike mumbled. "Your eyes and hair, the horns, and this?" he looked up from the lifeless thing laying at his feet into Vile's insane face and found himself consciously stopping his back stepping withdraw.

"How much did you mix with your own?" he asked.

"All that I possessed," she replied with an endearing smile.

Pike remembered standing atop the large rocks, watching as they bled Satan's body dry, filling two generously sized wooden casks with that great angel's blood. He imagined Vile bathing in the dark-red pool, pouring cupped handfuls into her waiting mouth, growing unfathomably more powerful with every greedy gulp. Pike would have never guessed that she actually destroyed all but one tiny drop.

Vile narrowed her violet gaze as she slowly began to side-step around to Pike's left, him countering by moving to her right.

"Is that Ellzbeth's sad little mask behind your helmet's face shield?" Vile's sword made air slicing noises as she swung its blade in circles. Pike said nothing; he locked his focus solely on her sword and feet. Even the thunderous roar of the battle surrounding them was muted, only the sounds made between them found Pike's ears. Their steps crunching over the frozen blood, the whispers of their blades sailing, sweeping, and the sound of Vile's voice as she tried to shake his focus loose.

"I've given poor Ellzbeth a new mask to hide her backstabbing face within," Vile stopped moving, she slowed her weapon's controlled flight. "You think you're so much, better than me, you and that pathetic little realm of your's. You sicken me!" Vile glanced briefly up at Pike's sword, tearing it from his gasp. It flew passed Vile's head and landed at the far end of the cleared circle.

"Return to me my powers or face me without yours," Pike demanded. "Or is it that you're afraid of me?"

"Afraid…of you," Vile loose a roaring belly laugh that fell silent as abruptly as it was voiced. "No, you fool—I simply fail to see the point." She swept out her hand and in the time it took for Pike to be yanked up off his feet and his neck to be locked within her fist, all of his body armor melted away. Only Ellzbeth's mask and his leather under padding was left.

Pike tried to kick at her, but his body was unable to follow through. From her straight-armed grip he was dangled above the ground, his body as uselessly limp as an empty skin. *So this is fear,* he thought. *I don't care for it.*

"Don't worry Gate Keeper, I'm not ready to kill you yet…soon, but not yet." Vile threw him to the ground and kicked him over onto his back. "First I want you to watch as I rip!" She snatched the purple mask off his face. "And tear the lives out of the other realms' leaders."

She straddled over Pike driving the end of her weapon's blade into his right shoulder. Pike hissed in pain through clenched teeth.

Vile's eyes brightened, she took the blade from his shoulder and sliced its tip straight across his chest. "I wonder how many bites I can take out of your heart before it stops beating," she pierced the sword into his left shoulder. "I believe I'd like very much to learn the answer to this and many more questions…later though, first things first. She brought the sword out of his flesh and with blinding speed cut off Pike's left hand at the wrist. He choked the howl swelling up through his throat back down, refusing to allow her the pleasure of hearing his cries. The blade flew up again; Pike's eyes were burning so intensely that he caught sight of their flaming glint shimmering across the surface of her grinning teeth. *It's over, she's won,* he thought as the blade fell.

It was at the exact instant Vile's sword sliced off his right hand that a large, dark shape suddenly appeared behind her. Pike watched, his vision blurred from pain as a huge iron hammer swept down. One second she was standing over him, a second later, with a scream and a bone snapping crash she was gone. Pike's eyes quickly focused to see his hammer wielding beast standing over him, Sader in the saddle and Sumac's still living severed head hanging off the saddle horn.

Vile's now shattered body was knocked across the circled clearing and slammed to an abrupt halt as she crashed into her ice wall of frozen soldiers. Before she had a second's chance to respond, Sader and the beast with its hammer were on her. She tried to focus her will past the pain, but the hammer was too fast. Again her body was skipped across the frozen ground, and again she slammed to a painful stop against the wall of bodies. The beast's shadow was over her once more, and as its hammer rose in preparation for a final falling Vile leered across the ground at Pike and speaking directly into his pain raped mind, she said "—This is not over."

The hammer whistled down; Vile spit on the ground beneath her head, and in so doing, a black vortex, spinning with deafening screams opened. Vile dropped through it a hundredth of a second before the beast's hammer could crush her as flat as the ground beneath her. The vortex closed as quickly as it had opened, Vile had escaped.

=≡ ⸱ǀⵏ ≡=

Four nights and three days after the would-be queen's disappearing act, B'neem's warriors had overcome seemingly unbeatable odds and defeated Zaw'naw's armies. On the dawn of the fourth morning the last of the Imperial Guard were cut to pieces, ending the fray. Pike as well as all the higher breed angels of B'neem had their gifts of magic restored almost immediately after Vile's vanishing. All fallen warriors on both sides of the battlefield were healed of their wounds. The sixth realm soldiers once mended were placed in chains until it was decided that they were simply soldiers following orders. Madam Sumac's head was returned to her body, and while still in chains lead by Pike and Sader into what was left of Vile's city. Aside from the demons who somehow managed to avoid the fighting all together, and the damned souls still in their cages and hanging from hooks the city was empty. Only large hell-rats and shade-ravens moved through the shadows and fallen buildings.

Sumac begrudgingly lead Pike and Sader up the mountain to the ruin that had been Zaw'naw's ancient palace. After some rather pointed convincing from Sader, Sumac was eventually able to locate the place among the rubble where Vile's dungeons had been. But despite the days and nights they dedicated to their tireless search, all they could find of their friend amidst the tons of shattered rock and twisted metal was a strip of her blood stained white robe. Ellzbeth was gone.

In the months to follow Pike and Sader would learn that Vile had banished the golden eyed Inquisitor to the moon of an unfinished, long ago forgotten world. The problem was that there were thousands of such moons circling as many unfinished worlds, in twice as many solar systems, and Ellzbeth could be one any one of those. It was a stroke of luck, although a very small stroke when they learned that the moon Vile had cast Ellzbeth to was possibly the same moon Vile herself had been imprisoned on for trespassing into the god's library. What this meant to Pike and Sader was that if they could learn the identity of the god or gods that jailed Vile on that moon they might convince the god or gods to tell them its location. The difficulty with this was that gods are extremely self-absorbed creatures, most-likely the most "I" minded beings in all of creation. This being the truth of the matter, it would be beyond difficult to get any of them interested enough to want to get involved.

As for Queen Vile—she was also in a place far from Hell. It seems the vortex she'd escaped through had lead to Hell's Great Wall of Rot. The very wall she hated and planned on tearing down. Vile opened another doorway, furthering her getaway. She could have chosen any number of worlds to hide on, but she wasn't intending on doing much hiding. Vile had a promise to keep, one that she'd made to a man in a tree.

=≡ ╢╟ ≡=

Locked in a protective custody cell deep within the bowels of the Los Angeles county jail a former member of the L.A.P.D wept bitterly. The pasty-faced ex-police captain was trying to survey the damaged he'd suffered earlier that day at the hands and heels of his fellow inmates. Struggling to look at himself in the scratched surface of the cell's stainless-steel mirror past the swollen flesh that framed his eyes, he mouthed—*They'll all be sorry.* It was a vain threat.

Luckily for the fallen cop a few of the jail's turn-keys were close by to rescue him from the pounding some of the other prisoners were gleefully dishing out. Beside the overly publicized fact that he was once one of L.A.'s so called—Finest—the other inmates were also highly unpleased with his reasons for incarceration.

"Why—why didn't you listen to me," he whispered to his battered reflection. "When I strongly—strong, strong, strongly suggested that we plant the little bastards someplace—anyplace other than under our own fucking house?"

Turning away from his black and blue reflection, he had barely sat on the edge of the cell's bunk when he heard a girl's voice giggling. A pair of blood splattered black work boots dropped on the bunk's mattress on either side of the child-killing cop. Before he could utter some sort of frightful wail a gloved fist crashed against the side of his head, then clasped firmly over his mouth. Another hand latched onto his throat and yanked him up into the air, slamming him against the wall and into the corner over the bunk.

As the large bald visitor in the blood stained clothes and long black trench coat pinned the ex-cop into the corner, another visitor appeared in the darkened cell. She was seated at the foot of the bunk, a teenage girl with black clothes and deathly white skin. She wore a black fedora with a blood-red band which was too big to fit her bald head correctly. Without a word she stood from the bunk, stepping over to the stainless steel sink/toilet, and picked up the clear plastic shaving razor. The big fellow holding the freak against the corner never once took his steely blue gaze off the man's face to check on his student. The man in black did offer up a faint grin though when he heard the sharp *snap* of busting plastic made by his student's boot-heel stomping on the razor. Stepping up on the bunk with her instructor and the soon to be Number Three-hundred and two, she reached into her teacher's long coat and after an unsnapping sound, brought out the bone handled knife. The two smiled at each other the way a big brother smiles at his little sister and likewise as the man in black nodded and quickly pulled his hand off the freak's neck.

The instant her teacher's hand was clear she sliced the knife's blade with a single sweep across the ex-cop's throat. After quietly watching him bleed out, Alex let the body drop to the bunk while its soul continued on to B'neem. His little goth student tossed the un-used razor blade on the blood soaked mattress and watched as her teacher finished up while whistling a happy little tune.

— Epilogue —

Homicide Detective Stephen Wolfhart had been trying like hell to make himself sleep. For hours he tossed and turned, struggling desperately to convince his unwilling brain into permitting his exhausted body some much needed rest. It was 3:21 in the morning when suddenly, just as he was about to give up and get up, it finally happened—Wolfhart drifted into a half sleep. It was 3:41 when his dreamless state of mental numbness was yanked joltingly back into full consciousness by the ringing of his night-stand phone. Like an over worked zombie his blood-shot eyes sprang open and he rose to sit up on the edge of his bed. Seated there, his bare feet on the cold dusty, hard wood floor, his eyes stumbled through the dark clutter as the phone screamed to be answered. With his sight locked on the small black-leather case in the already open-wide night-stand drawer, his hand snatched the receiver off its cradle.

"What?" he barked while reaching into the drawer, and without removing it from its place snapped open the leather case. Wolfhart's eyes caught the glass on glass glint of the small clear cylinder resting on its bed of cotton balls and tiny plastic rinse baggies.

"Detective Wolfhart?" A woman's voice he didn't know inquired hopefully.

"Yeah."

"Sir, I apologize"

"Hang on a minute," he told her. "Still there?"

"Yes."

"Hang on I got to untangle the phone cord." He took the syringe pre-loaded with meth out of the drawer, and using the receiver's cord, he tied off his upper arm. The veins bulged and without checking for air-bubbles in the thick yellowish mix of bottled water and poison, he chose a vein. There was no longer any guilt or shame in him over this abomination he'd given himself to, all of that had been smothered to death by the rush. Even the self-disgust and loathing had drifted out of reach into the abyss of addiction.

After a couple chemical induced coughs and deep inhaling and exhaling of stale bedroom air he laid the out-fit back in its case, licked the blood off his forearm and put the receiver to his ear.

"Still there?" he asked while clearing his throat.

"Yes—"

"It figures," he rumbled into the mouth piece, his head and heart still rolling within the fading grip of the dope's call. Scratching his fingers through his thick premature silver hair, he asked, "—Who in the name of weeping-Jesus are you? And what is so damned urgent that it couldn't wait just a few more hours?"

With a soft clearing of her own throat the voice introduced herself.

"My name is Alice Jabbers. I'm a homicide detective with the Los Angeles police department. I'm truly sorry if I woke you detective—"

"Do not call me detective," he cut her off. "I'm retired."

"Your friends in the Eugene Police Department told me that if I wanted to reach you that this was the best time."

"They're not my friends! Shit...friends wouldn't be handing out my number so goddamned freely."

"And they sounded so sincere too," she said.

"Shit bricks lady—could you just please tell me what it is you want?"

"Fine—I'd like to—"

"Goddamnit!" he snapped. "I said what do you want! I don't give a dead rat's ass about what you'd like. Now for the last time PLEASE— what do you want?"

Several long seconds of dead air crept through the phone line, then as Wolfhart was about to pull the receiver from the side of his head the L.A. detective sighed swiftly and spoke.

"I WANT! to ask you a few questions concerning your last case detecti—I mean Mr. Wolfhart." She was attempting to not come off sounding needy. But even through the anger he'd risen in her with his ass-hole attitude he could hear the whisper of desperation she so vainly tried to mask behind her soft lilt.

"How long have you been with L.A. homicide?" he asked.

"Almost six months, but I don't see what—"

"It's got everything to do with it" he interrupted. "Now what's happened that's got you knuckle-heads down there runnin' into walls? Wait, let me guess—your boss just dropped a cold-case in your lap and you figure to file it under A, for Alex. Is that it girly—you got something with no right answers, so to get it out of your ass you've decided to write it off as Stone's handy work?"

"No, that's not it at all."

"Then you've got yourselves down there in the city of dope-sick angels a copy cat killer. Am I getting warmer?"

"No, not exactly. At least not yet anyway," she said.

"Really, then why don't you tell me?" Holding the receiver against his ear with his shoulder, Wolfhart opened a fresh pack of cigarettes. "What do you want to know about Alex Stone?"

"Was Mr. Stone's body intact when he was buried?"

"What?" he said with a laugh.

"Stone's right thumb, was he buried with the rest of him?"

"First off, Alex Stone was cremated, and yes he still had both his thumbs when they rolled him into the Easy Bake Oven."

"Are you sure?"

"Of course I'm sure!"

"But are you really?"

"Look lady, I was there, I was the only one there when they cooked him to dust. So yes, I'm sure. Now what's this crap all about?"

There was a deep sigh on the other end of the line. It wasn't one of those—*that's good…its over sighs*, no this was a—*it's about to get real strange*, sighs.

"Are you going to just sit there and breathe heavy into my ear or are you going to answer the question?" Wolfhart asked sharply.

"A suspect in the murders of several young boys was found dead in an L.A. county jail P.C. cell two weeks ago. At first it appeared as though he'd done the right thing by slicing his own throat with the blade of a safety razor. The case was about to be signed off as closed when three days ago I got a call from one of our evidence labs. It turns out that a bloody thumb print was found smeared in a pocket size bible taken from the dead suspect's cell. Here's where it gets strange. The print was run through our system and it came up blank. The print's owner had never been arrested in California. So then we ran it through the N.C.I.C system and almost immediately we got a hit, the print was that of Alex Julius Stone."

"Yeah, fuck you…so which one of those lame-dicks put you up to it? I'll bet my balls it was that sonofabitch Jake Lee. Well, I must say you had me for a second or two—laugh's on me. Have a wonderful life—"

"No! Wait detective Wolfhart, please this isn't a damn joke!" At first she wasn't sure if he was still there, the phone-line hadn't gone dead "—Detective Wolfhart?" she called into the mouth piece.

"Are you fucking for real lady? You are, aren't you?"

"Very much so," she replied. "There's more, if you care to hear it?"

"There always is, go on lady…I'm all ears."

"We ran the print again—and again, believing something must be on the frizz with the system, but it kept coming back as Stone's print. So just for shits and grins I had the razor-blade our suspect had used to cut his throat with checked for prints as well as the broken bits of the plastic shaving handle. Nothing clear enough was found on the plastic, but the blade was a different story. As you know blood sets prints, locking them into a surface, that's what had occurred with the razor-blade. The thick pool of blood that it had fallen in sealed a thumb print on one side and an index finger on the other."

"Stone's?" Wolfhart asked.

"No, the prints on the razor-blade belonged to one Lucia O'neil. Does the name ring any bells?"

"It sounds somewhat familiar, can't put a face to it though."

"She was the sixteen year old girl who shot to death fourteen fellow students before she was stopped by a police sniper."

"I remember now, it only just happened a month or so ago. Yeah, the Corvallis High School shooting," there was a brief pause, then Wolfhart forced a chuckle and said, "Lady you just blew my mind…this ain't makin' any sense. Stone's long dead and so is the O'neil girl, someone's playin' some games on the big city L.A.P.D. Well happy huntin'," he paused again then asked sharply "So what do you want from me?"

"I would like—I mean want to fly up there and meet with you."

"Nope, I'm retired."

"I thought that if I let you see what we got, that maybe you could help me shine some light on this confusing mess"

"Have a nice life."

The phone line went dead, Wolfhart had hung up on her.

LaVergne, TN USA
14 October 2009
160863LV00003B/9/P